ALSO BY PHILIPP MEYER

American Rust

THE
SON

... *continued from flap*

Intertwined with Eli's story are those of his son, Peter, a man who bears the emotional cost of his father's drive for power, and Jeannie, Eli's great-granddaughter, a woman who must fight hardened rivals to succeed in a man's world.

Love, honour and children are sacrificed in the name of ambition, as the family becomes one of the richest powers in Texas, a ranching-and-oil dynasty of unsurpassed wealth and privilege. Yet, like all empires, the McCulloughs must eventually face the consequences of their choices.

Harrowing, panoramic and vividly drawn, *The Son* is a masterful achievement from a sublime young talent.

THE SON

PHILIPP MEYER

**SIMON &
SCHUSTER**

London · New York · Sydney · Toronto · New Delhi

A CBS COMPANY

For my family

First published in Great Britain by Simon & Schuster UK Ltd, 2013
A CBS COMPANY

Copyright © by Philipp Meyer 2013

1 3 5 7 9 10 8 6 4 2

Simon & Schuster UK Ltd
1st Floor
222 Gray's Inn Road
London WC1X 8HB

Simon & Schuster Australia, Sydney
Simon & Schuster India, New Delhi

A CIP catalogue record for this book is available from the British Library

ISBN hbk: 978-0-85720-942-9
ISBN tpbk: 978-0-85720-943-6
ISBN ebook: 978-0-85720-945-0

Printed and bound by CPI Group (UK) Ltd, Croydon, CR0 4YY

ACKNOWLEDGMENTS

T hanks to my publisher, Dan Halpern, a fellow artist who gets it. Also Suzanne Baboneau. My agents, Eric Simonoff and Peter Straus. Libby Edelson and Lee Boudreaux.

I am grateful to the following organizations for their generous support: the Dobie Paisano Fellowship Program, Guggenheim Foundation, Ucross Foundation, Lannan Foundation, and the Noah and Alexis Foundation.

While any and all errors are the fault of the author, the following people were invaluable for their knowledge: Don Graham, Michael Adams, Tracy Yett, Jim Magnuson, Tyson Midkiff, Tom and Karen Reynolds (and Debbie Dewees), Raymond Plank, Roger Plank, Patricia Dean Boswell McCall, Mary Ralph Lowe, Richard Butler, Kinley Coyan, "Diego" McGreevy and Lee Shipman, Wes Phillips, Sarah and Hugh Fitzsimons, Tink Pinkard, Bill Marple, Heather and Martin Kohout, Tom and Marsha Caven, Andy Wilkinson, everyone at the James A. Michener Center for Writers, André Bernard, for his sympathetic ear, Ralph Grossman, Kyle Defoor, Alexandra Seifert, Jay Seifert, Whitney Seifert, and Melinda Seifert. Additionally, I am grateful to Jimmy Arterberry of the Comanche Nation Historic Preservation

Office, Juanita Pahdopony and Gene Pekah of Comanche Nation College, Willie Pekah, Harry Mithlo, and the Comanche Language and Cultural Preservation Committee, though this in no way implies their endorsement of this material. It is estimated that the Comanche people suffered a 98 percent population loss during the middle period of the nineteenth century.

RIP Dan McCall.

In the second century of the Christian era, the Empire of Rome comprehended the fairest part of the earth, and the most civilised portion of mankind . . .

. . . its genius was humbled in the dust; and armies of unknown Barbarians, issuing from the frozen regions of the North, had established their victorious reign over the fairest provinces of Europe and Africa.

. . . the vicissitudes of fortune, which spares neither man nor the proudest of his works . . . buries empires and cities in a common grave.

— EDWARD GIBBON

THE MCCULLOUGHS

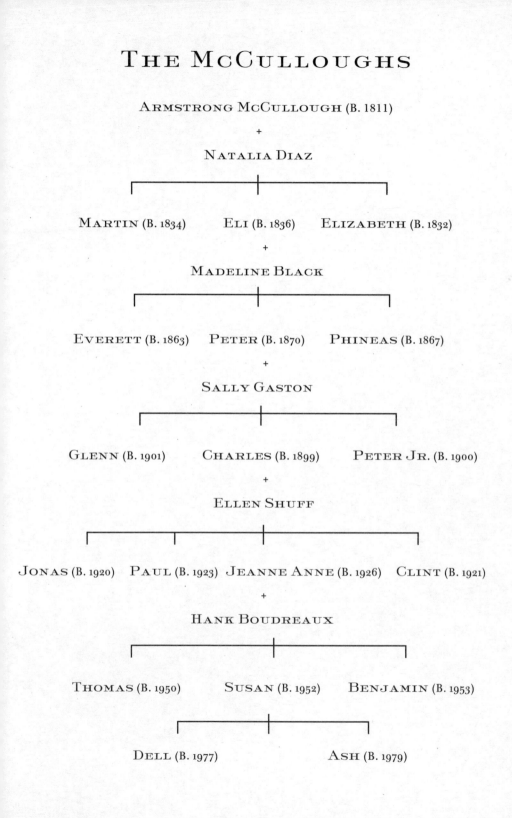

ARMSTRONG MCCULLOUGH (B. 1811)

+

NATALIA DIAZ

MARTIN (B. 1834)   ELI (B. 1836)   ELIZABETH (B. 1832)

+

MADELINE BLACK

EVERETT (B. 1863)   PETER (B. 1870)   PHINEAS (B. 1867)

+

SALLY GASTON

GLENN (B. 1901)   CHARLES (B. 1899)   PETER JR. (B. 1900)

+

ELLEN SHUFF

JONAS (B. 1920)   PAUL (B. 1923)   JEANNE ANNE (B. 1926)   CLINT (B. 1921)

+

HANK BOUDREAUX

THOMAS (B. 1950)   SUSAN (B. 1952)   BENJAMIN (B. 1953)

DELL (B. 1977)   ASH (B. 1979)

THE SON

CHAPTER ONE

COLONEL ELI McCULLOUGH

Taken from a 1936 WPA Recording

It was prophesied I would live to see one hundred and having achieved that age I see no reason to doubt it. I am not dying a Christian though my scalp is intact and if there is an eternal hunting ground, that is where I am headed. That or the river Styx. My opinion at this moment is my life has been far too short: the good I could do if given another year on my feet. Instead I am strapped to this bed, fouling myself like an infant.

Should the Creator see fit to give me strength I will make my way to the waters that run through the pasture. The Nueces River at its eastern bend. I have always preferred the Devil's. In my dreams I have reached it three times and it is known that Alexander the Great, on his last night of mortal life, crawled from his palace and tried to slip into the Euphrates, knowing that if his body disappeared, his people would assume he had ascended to heaven as a god. His wife stopped him at the water's edge. She dragged him home to die mortal. And people ask why I did not remarry.

Should my son appear, I would prefer not to suffer his smile of victory. Seed of my destruction. I know what he did and I suspect he has long graced the banks of the river Jordan, as Quanah Parker, last chief of the Comanches, gave the boy scant chance to reach fifty. In return for this information I gave to Quanah and his warriors a young bull buffalo, a prime animal to be slain the old way with lances, on my pastures that had once been their hunting grounds. One of Quanah's companions was a venerable Arapahoe chief and as we sat partaking of the bull's warm liver in the ancient manner, dipped in the animal's own bile, he gave me a silver band he had personally removed from the finger of George Armstrong Custer. The ring is marked "7th Cav." It bears a deep scar from a lance, and, having no suitable heir, I will take it to the river with me.

Most will be familiar with the date of my birth. The Declaration of Independence that bore the Republic of Texas out of Mexican tyranny was ratified March 2, 1836, in a humble shack at the edge of the Brazos. Half the signatories were malarial; the other half had come to Texas to escape a hangman's noose. I was the first male child of this new republic.

The Spanish had been in Texas hundreds of years but nothing had come of it. Since Columbus they had been conquering all the natives that stood in their way and while I have never met an Aztec, they must have been a pack of mincing choirboys. The Lipan Apaches stopped the old conquistadores in their tracks. Then came the Comanche. The earth had seen nothing like them since the Mongols; they drove the Apaches into the sea, destroyed the Spanish Army, turned Mexico into a slave market. I once saw Comanches herding villagers along the Pecos, hundreds at a time, no different from the way you'd drive cattle.

Having been trounced by the aboriginals, the Mexican government devised a desperate plan to settle Texas. Any man, of any nation, willing to move west of the Sabine River would receive four thousand acres of free land. The fine print was written in blood. The Comanche philosophy toward outsiders was nearly papal in its thoroughness: torture and kill the men, rape and kill the women, take the children for slaves or adoption. Few from the ancient countries of Europe took the Mexicans up on their offer. In fact, no one came at all. Except the Americans. They flooded in. They had women and children to spare and to him that overcometh, I giveth to eat of the tree of life.

IN 1832 MY father arrived in Matagorda, common in those days if you viewed the risk of death by firing squad or a scalping by the Comanches as God's way of telling you there were great rewards to be had. By then the Mexican government, nervous about the growing Anglo horde within its borders, had banned American immigration into Texas.

And still it was better than the Old States, where unless you were son of a plantation owner, there was nothing to be had but the gleanings. Let the records show that the better classes, the Austins and Houstons, were all content to remain citizens of Mexico so long as they could keep their land. Their descendants have waged wars of propaganda to clear their names and have them declared Founders of Texas. In truth it was only the men like my father, who had nothing, who pushed Texas into war.

Like every able-bodied Scotsman, he did his part in the rout at San Jacinto and after the war worked as a blacksmith, gunsmith, and surveyor. He was tall and easy to talk to. He had a straight back and hard hands and people felt safe around him, which proved, for most of them, to be an illusion.

MY FATHER WAS not religious and I attribute my heathen ways to him. Still, he was the sort of man who felt the breath of the pale rider close on his neck. He did not believe in time to waste. We first lived at Bastrop, raising corn, sorghum, and hogs, clearing land until the new settlers came in, those who waited until the Indian dangers had passed, then arrived with their lawyers to challenge the deeds and titles of those who had civilized the country and vanquished the red man. These first Texans had purchased their holdings with the original human currency and most could neither read nor write. By the age

of ten I had dug four graves. The faintest sound of galloping hooves
would wake the entire family, and by the time the news arrived—some
neighbor cut up like a Thanksgiving shoat—my father had checked his
loads and then he and the messenger would disappear into the night.
The brave die young: that is the Comanche saying, but it was true of
the first Anglos as well.

During the ten years Texas stood alone as a nation, the government
was desperate for settlers, especially those with money. And through
some invisible telegraph the message went back to the Old States—this
area is safe now. In 1844 the first stranger arrived at our gate: a barber-
shop shingle, store-bought clothes, a lady-broke sorrel. He asked for
grain as his horse would founder on grass. A horse that could not eat
grass—I had never heard of such a thing.

Two months later, the Smithwicks' title was challenged and then the
Hornsbys and MacLeods were bought out at a pittance. By then there
were more lawyers in Texas, per capita, than any other place on the
continent and within a few years all the original settlers had lost their
land and been driven west again, back into Indian country. The gentler
classes who had stolen the land were already plotting a war to protect
their blacks; the South would be cursed but Texas, a child of the West,
would emerge unscathed.

In the meantime a campaign was launched against my mother, a
Castilian of the old line, dark skinned but finely featured, it was claimed
by the new settlers that she was octoroon. The plantation gentleman
took pride in his eye for such things.

By 1846 we had moved past the line of settlement, to my father's
headright on the Pedernales. It was Comanche hunting grounds. The
trees had never heard an ax, and the land and all the animals who lived
upon it were fat and slick. Grass up to the chest, the soil deep and black
in the bottoms, and even the steepest hillsides overrun with wildflowers. It was not the dry rocky place it is today.

Wild Spanish cattle were easily acquired with a rope—within a
year we had a hundred head. Hogs and mustang horses were also for

the taking. There were deer, turkey, bear, squirrel, the occasional buffalo, turtles and fish from the river, ducks, plums and mustang grapes, bee trees and persimmons—the country was rich with life the way it is rotten with people today. The only problem was keeping your scalp attached.

CHAPTER TWO

JEANNE ANNE McCULLOUGH

March 3, 2012

There were murmurs and quiet voices, not enough light. She was in a large room that she first mistook for a church or courthouse and though she was awake, she couldn't feel anything. It was like floating in a warm bath. There were dim chandeliers, logs smoking in a fireplace, Jacobean chairs and tables and busts of old Greeks. There was a rug that had been a gift from the Shah. She wondered who would find her.

It was a big white house in the Spanish style; nineteen bedrooms, a library, a great room and ballroom. She and her brothers had all been born here but now it was nothing more than a weekend house, a place for family reunions. The maids wouldn't be back until morning. Her mind was perfectly awake but the rest of her seemed to have been left unplugged and she was fairly certain that someone else was responsible for her condition. She was eighty-six years old, but even if she liked telling others that she couldn't wait to cross over to the Land of Mañana, it was not exactly true.

The most important thing is a man who does what I tell him. She had said that to a reporter from *Time* magazine and they'd put her on the cover, forty-one and still sultry, standing on her Cadillac in front of a field of pumpjacks. She was a small, slender woman, though people forgot this soon after meeting her. Her voice carried and her eyes were gray like an old pistol or blue norther; she was striking, though not exactly beautiful. Which the Yankee photographer must have noticed. He had her open her blouse another notch and did her hair like she'd stepped out of an open car. It was not the height of her power—that had come decades later—but it was an important moment. They had begun to take her seriously. Now the man who'd taken the photograph was dead. *No one is going to find you,* she thought.

Of course it was going to happen this way; even as a child she'd been mostly alone. Her family had owned the town. People made no sense to her. Men, with whom she had everything in common, did not want her around. Women, with whom she had nothing in common, smiled too much, laughed too loud, and mostly reminded her of small dogs, their lives lost in interior decorating and other peoples' outfits. There had never been a place for a person like her.

SHE WAS YOUNG, eight or ten, sitting on the porch. It was a cool day in spring and the green hills went on as far as she could see, McCullough land, as far as she could see. But something was wrong: there was her Cadillac, parked in the grass, and the old stables, which her brother had not yet burned, were already gone. *I am going to wake up now,* she thought. But then the Colonel—her great-grandfather— was speaking. Her father was there as well. She'd once had a grand- father, Peter McCullough, but he had disappeared and no one had anything good to say about him and she knew she would not have liked him either.

"I was thinking you might make a showing at the church this Sun- day," her father said.

The Colonel thought those things were best left to the Negroes and Mexicans. He was a hundred years old and did not mind telling people they were wrong. His arms were like gunsticks and his face was splotchy as an old rawhide and they said the next time he fell, it would be right into his own grave.

"The thing about preachers," he was saying, "is if they ain't spar-kin' your daughters, or eatin' all the fried chicken and pie in your ice-box, they're cheatin' your sons on horses."

Her father was twice the size of the Colonel, but, as the Colonel was always pointing out, he had a strong back and a weak mind. Her brother Clint had bought a horse and saddle off that pastor and there had been a setfast under the blanket nearly the size of a griddle cake.

HER FATHER MADE her go to church anyway, waking up early to make the trip to Carrizo, where they had a Sunday school. She was hungry and could barely keep her eyes open. When she asked the teacher what would happen to the Colonel, who was sitting home that very minute, likely drinking a julep, the teacher said he was going to hell, where he would be tortured by Satan himself. *In that case, I am going with him,* Jeannie said. She was a disgraceful little scamp. She would have been whipped if she were Mexican.

On the ride home, she could not understand why her father sided with the teacher, who had a beak like an eagle and smelled like some-thing inside her had died. The woman was ugly as a tar bucket. *During the war,* her father was saying, *I promised God that if I survived, I would go to church every Sunday. But just before you were born, I stopped going because I was busy. And do you know what happened?* She did—she had always known. But he reminded her anyway: *Your mother died.*

Jonas, her oldest brother, said something about not scaring her. Her father told Jonas to be quiet and Clint pinched her arm and whis-pered, *When you go to hell, the first thing they do is shove a pitchfork up your ass.*

She opened her eyes. Clint had been dead sixty years. Nothing in the dim room had moved. *The papers,* she thought. She had saved them from the fire once and had not gotten around to destroying them. Now they would be found.

CHAPTER THREE

DIARIES OF PETER McCULLOUGH

AUGUST 10, 1915

My birthday. Today, without the help of any whiskey, I have reached the conclusion: I am no one. Looking back on my forty-five years I see nothing worthwhile—what I had mistaken for a soul appears more like a black abyss—I have allowed others to shape me as they pleased. To ask the Colonel I am the worst son he has ever had—he has always preferred Phineas and even poor Everett.

This journal will be the only true record of this family. In Austin they are planning a celebration for the Colonel's eightieth birthday, and what will be honestly said about a man who is lionized in capitols, I don't know. Meanwhile, our bloody summer continues. The telephone lines to Brownsville cannot be kept open—every time they are repaired, the insurgents blow them up. The King Ranch was attacked by forty *sediciosos* last night, there was a three-hour gun battle at Los Tulitos, and the president of the Cameron Law and Order League was shot to death, though whether the latter is a gain or loss, I can't say.

As for the Mexicans, to see the number of them shot in bar ditches or hung from trees, you would think them as ill a scourge as the panther or wolf. The *San Antonio Express* no longer mentions their deaths—it would take up too much paper—and so the Tejano die unrecorded and are buried, if at all, in shallow graves, or roped and dragged off where they will not bother anyone.

After Longino and Estaban Morales were killed last month (by whom we don't know, though I suspect Niles Gilbert) the Colonel devised a note for all our vaqueros: *This man is a good Mexican. Please leave him alone. When I am done with him I will kill him myself.* Our men display these notes like badges of honor; they worship the Colonel (along with everyone else), *nuestro patrón.*

Unfortunately for the Tejanos, the area cattlemen continue to lose stock. In the west pastures last week Sullivan and I found a section where the wire was cut and by nightfall we'd found only 263 cows and calves, versus the 478 counted during the spring roundup. A twenty-thousand-dollar loss and all evidence, circumstantially at least, pointing to our neighbors, the Garcias. I myself would rather lose the kingdom than lay blood libel against the wrong person. But that is a rare sentiment.

I HAVE ALWAYS thought I ought to have been born in the Old States, where, though their soil is even more blood soaked than ours, they no longer need their guns. But of course it is against my disposition. Even Austin I find overwhelming, as if each of its sixty thousand inhabitants were shouting at me at once. I have always found it difficult to clear my head—images and sounds linger with me for years—and so here I remain, in the one place that is truly mine, whether it wants me or not.

As we examined the cut fences, Sullivan pointed out, quite unnecessarily, that the tracks led right into the Garcia lands, which border the river, which, as it has been so dry, can be crossed nearly anywhere.

"I do not mind old Pedro," he said, "but his sons-in-law are as vile a pack of niggers as I have ever seen."

"You've been spending too much time with the Colonel," I told him.

"He does *sabe* his Mexicans."

"I have found just the opposite."

"In that case, boss, I am hoping you will learn me the various honest explanations for a cut fence leading to Pedro Garcia's pastures while we are short two hundred head. Time was we would cross and take them back but that is a bit above our bend these days."

"Old Pedro can't watch every inch of his land any more than we can watch every inch of ours."

"You're a big man," he said, "and I don't see why you act like such a small one."

After that he had no further comment. He considers it a personal affront that a Mexican might own so much land in our day and age. Of course the vaqueros do not help: because of his weight and high voice they call him Don Castrado behind his back.

As for Pedro Garcia, trouble seems to follow him like a lonely dog. Two of his sons-in-law are being pursued by the Mexican authorities for cattle theft, a notable accomplishment given that country's views on such matters. I attempted to visit him last week, only to be turned back by José and Chico. *Don Pedro no feel good,* they told me, and pretended not to understand my Spanish. I have known Pedro my entire life, knew he would accept me as a visitor, but of course I turned my horse around and said nothing.

Pedro has been shorthanded so long that the brush is overrunning his land, and for the past two years he has only managed to brand half his calves. Each year he makes less money, each year he cannot hire as many men, and thus each year his income decreases yet again.

Still he has retained his good nature. I have always preferred his household to our own. We both enjoyed the old days, when it was a gentler land, with white caliche roads and adobe villages, not a thornbush to be seen and the grass up to your stirrups. Now the brush is relentless and the old stone villages are abandoned. The only houses built are crooked wood-frame monstrosities that grow like mushrooms but begin rotting just as quickly.

In many ways Pedro has been a truer father to me than the Colonel; if he has ever had a harsh word for me, I have not heard it. He had always hoped I might take an interest in one of his daughters, and for a time I was quite infatuated with María, the eldest, but I could sense the Colonel was strongly against it, and, like a coward, I allowed the feeling to pass. María went to Mexico City to pursue her studies; her sisters married Mexicans, all of whom have their eyes on Pedro's land.

My greatest fear is that Sullivan is right and that Pedro's sons-in-law are involved with the theft of our stock; they may not understand what the consequences will be; they may not understand that Don Pedro cannot protect them.

AUGUST 11, 1915

Sally and Dr. Pilkington are driving Glenn, our youngest, to San Antonio. He was shot tonight when we came across some riders in the dark. The wound is high in the shoulder and is certainly not life threatening and had it not been for the Colonel I would have gone to San Antonio with my son.

The Colonel has decided that the shooters were our neighbors. When I protested that it was too dark for any of us to have seen the guilty parties, it was implied that I was a traitor.

"If you'd learned anything I taught you," he said. "That was Chico and José on those horses."

"Well, you must have eyes like a catamount to be able to see in the dark past a furlong."

"As you well know," he told me, "my vision has always carried farther than that of other men."

About a quarter of the town (the white quarter) is downstairs. Along with the Rangers, all of our vaqueros, and the Midkiff vaqueros as well. In a few minutes we will ride on the Garcias.

CHAPTER FOUR

ELI McCULLOUGH

pring 1849, the last full moon. We'd been two years on our Pedernales acreocracy, not far from Fredericksburg, when our neighbor had two horses stolen in broad daylight. Syphilis Poe, as my father called him, had come down from the Appalachian Mountains, imagining Texas a lazy man's paradise where the firewood split itself, the persimmons fell into your lap, and your pipe was always stuffed with jimsonweed. He was the commonest type on the frontier, though there were plenty like my father—intent on getting rich if they could stay alive long enough—and there were the Germans.

Before the Germans came, it was thought impossible to make butter in a southern climate. It was also thought impossible to grow wheat. A slave economy does that to the human mind, but the Germans, who had not been told otherwise, arrived and began churning first-rate butter and raising heavy crops of the noble cereal, which they sold to their dumbfounded neighbors at a high profit.

Your German had no allergy to work, which was conspicuous when you looked at his possessions. If, upon passing some field, you noticed the soil was level and the rows straight, the land belonged to a German. If the field was full of rocks, if the rows appeared to have been laid by a blind Indian, if it was December and the cotton had not been picked, you knew the land was owned by one of the local whites, who had drifted over from Tennessee and hoped that the bounties of Dame Nature would, by some witchery, yield him up a slave.

But I am ahead of myself. The problem facing my father that morning was the theft of two scrawny horses and a conspicuous trail of unshod pony tracks leading into the hills. Common sense suggested the perpetrators might still be about—no self-respecting horse thief would have been satisfied with Poe's mangy swaybacked mares—but the law of the frontier demanded pursuit, and so my father and the other men rode off, leaving my brother and me with a rifle apiece and two silver-mounted pistols taken off a general at San Jacinto. This was considered plenty to defend a sturdy house, as the army had come to the frontier and the big Indian raids of the early '40s were thought to be over.

The men rode out just before noon, and my brother and I, both between hay and grass but feeling full grown, were not worried. We had no fear of the aborigine; there were dozens of Tonkawas and other strays living nearby, waiting for the government to open a reservation. They might rob lost Yankees, but they knew better than to molest the locals: we all wanted an Indian pelt and would have collected one at the slightest excuse.

BY THE TIME I was twelve, I had killed the biggest panther ever seen in Blanco County. I could trail a deer across hard ground and my sense of direction was as good as our father's. Even my brother, though he had a weakness for books and poetry, could outshoot any man from the Old States.

As for my brother, I was embarrassed for him. I would point out tracks he could not see, telling him which way the buck's head had been turned and whether its belly had been full or empty and what had made it nervous. I saw farther, ran faster, heard things he thought I imagined.

But my brother did not mind. He thought himself superior for reasons I could not fathom. Whereas I hated every fresh wagon track, every sign of a new settler, my brother had always known that he would head east. He talked incessantly about the superiority of cities and it would not be long until he got his wish—our crops were heavy, our herds increasing—our parents would be able to hire a man to replace him.

Thanks to the Germans in Fredericksburg, where more books were stockpiled than in the rest of Texas combined, people like my brother were considered normal. He understood German because our neighbors spoke it, French because it was superior, and Spanish because you could not live in Texas without it. He had finished *The Sorrows of Young Werther* in the original language and claimed to be working on his own superior version, though he would not let anyone read it.

Outside of Goethe and Byron, my sister was the object of most of my brother's thoughts. She was a beautiful girl who played the piano nearly as well as my brother read and wrote, and it was widely considered a shame that they were related. For my part, I had a bit of a hatchet face. The Germans thought I looked French.

As for my brother and sister, if there was anything improper I never knew it, though when she spoke to him her words were made of cotton, or a sweet that dissolves on your tongue, whereas I was addressed as a cur dog. My brother was always writing plays for her to act in, the two of them playing a doomed couple while I was cast as the Indian or badman who caused their ruination. My father pretended interest while shooting me knowing looks. So far as he was concerned, my brother was only acceptable because I'd turned out so close to perfect. But my mother was proud. She had high hopes for my siblings.

THE CABIN WAS two rooms linked by a covered dogtrot. It sat on a bluff where a spring came out of the rock and flowed over a ledge to the Pedernales. The woods were thick as first creation and my father said if we ever got to where the trees didn't rub the house, we would move. Of course my mother felt different.

We fenced and gated a yard and stock pen, built a smokehouse, a corncrib, and a stable where my father did blacksmithing. We had a wood floor and glass windows with shutters and a German-built stove that would burn all night on just a few sticks. The furniture had the look of store-bought; it was whitewashed and turned by the Mormons at Burnet.

In the main room my mother and father kept a canopy bed to themselves and my sister had a cot; my brother and I shared a bed in the unheated room on the other side of the dogtrot, though I often slept outside in a rawhide I'd slung thirty feet or so in the air, in the branches of an old oak. My brother often lit a candle to read (a luxury my mother indulged), which disturbed my sleep.

The centerpiece of the main room was a Spanish square piano, my mother's sole inheritance. It was a rarity, and the Germans came over on Sundays to sing and visit and be subjected to my brother's plays. My mother was formulating plans to move into Fredericksburg, which would allow my brother and sister to resume their schooling. Me she considered a lost cause and had she not witnessed my issuance she would have denied responsibility in my creation. As soon as I was old enough I planned to join a Ranging company and ride against the Indians, Mexicans, or whomever else I could.

THINKING BACK, IT is plain my mother knew what would happen. The human mind was open in those days, we felt every disturbance and ripple; even those like my brother were in tune with the natural laws. Man today lives in a coffin of flesh. Hearing and seeing nothing. The Land and Law are perverted. The Good Book says I will gather you to Jerusalem to the furnace of my wrath. It says thou art the land that is not cleansed. I concur. We need a great fire that will sweep from ocean to ocean and I offer my oath that I will soak myself in kerosene if promised the fire would be allowed to burn.

But I digress. That afternoon I was making myself useful, as children did in those days, carving an ox yoke out of dogwood. My sister came out of the house and said, "Eli, go out to the springhouse and bring Mother all the butter and grape preserves."

At first I did not reply, for in no way did I find her superior, and as for her supposed charms, they had long since worn off. Though I will admit I was often murderous jealous of my brother, the way they sat together smiling about private matters. I was not exactly on her good side, either, having recently stolen the horse of her preferred suitor, an Alsatian named Hiebert. Despite the fact that I had returned the horse better than I found it, having taught it the pleasures of a good rider, Hiebert had not returned to call on her.

"Eli!" She had a voice like a hog caller. I decided I was sorry for whatever unfortunate wretch got roped to her.

"We're near out of butter," I shouted back. "And Daddy will be mad if he comes home and finds it gone." I went back to my whittling. It was nice in the shade with nothing but the green hills and a forty-mile view. Right below me the river made a series of little waterfalls.

In addition to the yoke, I had a new handle to make for my felling ax. It was a bo'dark sapling I had found in my travels. The handle would be springier than what my father liked, with a doe foot on the end for slippage.

"Get up," said my sister. She was standing over me. "Get the butter, Eli. I mean it."

I looked up at her standing there in her best blue homespun and made note of a fresh boil that she was attempting to hide with paint. When I finally brought the butter and preserves, my mother had stoked the stove and opened all the windows to keep the house cool.

"Eli," my mother said, "go down and catch us a few fish, will you? And maybe a pheasant if you see one."

"What about the Indians?" I said.

"Well, if you catch one, don't bring him back. There's no sense kissing the Devil till you've met him."

"Where's Saint Martin?"

"He's out fetching blackberries."

I picked my way down the limestone bluff to the river, taking my fishing pole, war bag, and my father's Jaegerbuchse. The Jaegerbuchse fired a one-ounce ball, had double-set triggers, and was one of the best rifles on the frontier, but my father found it cumbersome to reload from horseback. My brother had first claim on it, but he found its kick too ferocious for his poetical constitution. It got meat on both ends but I did not mind that. It would drive its ball through even the oldermost of the tribe of Ephraim, or, if you preferred, bark a squirrel at nearly any distance. I was happy to carry it.

The Pedernales was narrow and cut deep into the rock, and there was not much water most times, maybe a hundred yards across and a few feet deep. Along the banks were old cypresses and sycamores, and the river itself was full of swimming holes and waterfalls and shaded pools brimming with eels. Like most Texas rivers it was useless to boatmen, though I considered this an advantage, as it kept the boatmen out.

I dug some grubs from the bank, collected a few oak galls for floats, and found a shady pool under a cypress. Just above me on the hill was an enormous mulberry, so heavy with fruit that even the ringtails had not been able to eat it all. I took off my shirt and picked as many as I could, intending to bring them to my mother.

I began to fish, though it was hard relaxing because I couldn't see the house, it being high above me on the bluff. The Indians liked to travel in the riverbeds and my father had taken the only repeating firearms. But that was not bad in its way because it made me watch everything, the water glassing over the stone, skunk tracks in the mud, a heron in a far pool. There was a bobcat ghosting through the willows, thinking no one saw him.

Farther up the bank was a stand of pecans where a cat squirrel was taking bites of green nuts and dropping them to the ground to rot. I wondered why they did that: a squirrel will waste half the nuts on a tree before they are ripe. I thought about teaching him a lesson. Squirrel liver is top bait; if the Creator was a fisherman it is all he would use. But it was hard to reckon a one-ounce ball against a bushytail. I wished I'd brought my brother's .36 Kentucky. I began to graze on the mulberries and soon they were all gone. Mother preferred blackberries anyway. She viewed mulberries the same as sassafras tea, low class.

After another hour of fishing I saw a flock of turkeys on the oppo-site bank and shot one of the poults. It was seventy yards but the head came clean off. I was allowed to aim at the head, my brother was not—the poult flapped its wings crazily, trying to fly while the blood foun-tained up. A shot for the record books.

I braced my fishing pole under a rock, swabbed the barrel clean, measured out a careful charge, seated a ball and capped the nipple. Then I waded across the river to retrieve my prize.

Near where the poult lay in a fan of blood there was a purple spear point sticking out of the sand. It was four inches long and I sat examin-ing it for a long time; it had two flutes at the base that modern man has yet to figure how to replicate. The local flint was all cream to brown, which told me something else about that spear point: it had traveled a long way.

When I got back to my fishing pole it was floating downriver and I saw a big catfish had stuck itself on my bait, another one-in-a-million chance. I set the hook, thinking I'd lose the fish, but it pulled out of the water with no trouble. I decided to think about it. While I was sit-ting there I saw something in the sky and when I looked through my fist I realized it was Venus, that I was seeing it during the daytime. A bad sign if there ever was one. I took the turkey and catfish and my mulberry-stained shirt and hightailed it back to the house.

"That was quick," said my mother. "Only one fish?"

I held up the turkey.

"We were worried when we heard the shot," said my sister.

"I don't think it's good being so far from the house."

"The Indians won't bother you," my mother said. "The army is everywhere."

"I'm worried about you and Lizzie, not me," I said.

"Oh, Eli," said my mother. "My little hero." She appeared not to notice my ruined shirt and she smelled of the brandy that we saved for important guests. My sister smelled of brandy as well. It had gone to her head and she pinched my cheek sweetly. I was annoyed at her. I considered reminding her that Miles Wallace had been kidnapped not a month earlier. But unlike the Wallace boy, who had been taken by the Comanches only to be scalped a few miles later, I was not a walleyed cripple. I knew I would probably enjoy being kidnapped, as all they did was ride and shoot.

After double-checking our supply of patch and ball I went outside and climbed the tree into my rawhide hammock, where I could see out over the riverbed, the road, and the surrounding country. I hung the Jaegerbuchse from a nail. I had been meaning to shoot something while swinging in the hammock—that would be proper living—but had not yet been successful. Through the dogwoods near the spring I could see my brother gathering blackberries. The wind was calm and it was pleasant lying there with the smell of my mother's cooking. My brother had his rifle with him but wandered far from it, a sloppy habit. My father was strict about those things—if a gun is worth carrying it is worth keeping within arm's reach.

But that afternoon my brother was in luck, as we saw no Indians. Near sundown I spotted something moving in the rocks above the flood line, sneaking in and out of the cedar, which turned out to be a wolf. It was so far away it might have been a coyote, but wolves run with their tails straight and proud while coyotes tuck them under like scolded dogs. The tail was straight on this one and he was a pale gray, nearly white. The branches were in my way so I climbed down out of the tree, snuck to the edge of the bluff, and got into a good brace with the sights high over the wolf's back. He had stopped with his nose in the air, picking up the smell of our dinner. I set the first trigger, which made the second trigger only a twelve-ounce pull, then squeezed off the shot. The wolf jumped straight up and fell over dead. My father had us patch our bullets with greased buckskin, and our balls carried farther and straighter than if we'd used cotton patches, like most everyone else on the frontier.

"Eli, was that you shooting?" It was my sister.

"It was just a wolf," I shouted back. I thought about going down to get the skin—a white wolf, I had never seen one of those before—but decided against it, as it was getting dark.

Because of all the food being made, we did not sit down for supper until late. Seven or eight tallow candles were lit around the house, another luxury. My mother and sister had been cooking all day and they brought out dish after dish. We all knew it was to punish my father for leaving us alone, for being guilted into a wild-goose chase, but no one said anything.

My brother and I drank cool buttermilk, my mother and sister drank a bottle of white wine we had gotten from the Germans. My father had been saving the wine for a special occasion. Supper began with wheat bread and butter and the last of the cherry preserves, then ham, sweet potatoes, roast turkey, fish stuffed with wild garlic and fried in tallow, steaks rubbed with salt and chili pepper and cooked directly on the coals, the last of the spring morels, also cooked in butter, and a warm salad of pigweed and Indian spinach, cooked in more butter and with garlic. I had never eaten so much butter in my life. For dessert we had two pies: blackberry and plum, fruit my brother had picked that day. There was nothing left in the larder but hardtack and salt pork. If he wants to run with Syphilis Poe, my mother said, then he can eat like Syphilis Poe.

I felt guilty but that did not stop me from eating my share. My mother did not feel guilty at all. She wished for more wine. Everyone was falling asleep.

I carried the ham bone out to the springhouse, then sat watching the stars. I had my own names for them—the buck, the rattler, the running man—but my brother convinced me to use Ptolemy's, which did not make any sense. Draco looks like a snake, not a dragon. Ursa Major looks like a man running; there is not a bear anywhere in it. But my brother could not abide anything so tainted with common sense and thus my effort to name the heavens was aborted.

I put the horses in the stable, barred the door from the inside, and climbed out through the gap in the eaves. It would take any Indians a while to get at them. The horses seemed calm, which was a good sign, as they could smell Indians better than the dogs.

By the time I got back inside, my mother and sister had retired to my parents' canopy bed and my brother was lying in my sister's cot. Usually my brother and I slept in the room across the dogtrot, but I let him be. After gathering my rifle, war bag, and boots to the foot of the bed, I spit into the last candle and climbed under the covers with my brother.

AROUND MIDNIGHT I heard our dogs rucking up a chorus. I had not been sleeping well anyway so I got up to check the porthole, worried my mother or sister would see what was sticking up under my nightshirt.

Which I forgot about. There were a dozen men near our fence and more in the shadows near the road and still more in our side yard. I heard a dog yelp and then our smallest, a fyce named Perdida, went running off into the brush. She was hunched like a gut shot deer.

"Everyone get the hell up," I said. "Get up, Momma. Get everyone up."

The moon was high and it might as well have been daylight. The Indians led our three horses out of the yard and down the hill. I wondered how they'd figured their way into the stable. Our bulldog was following a tall brave around like they were best friends.

"Move over," said my brother.

He and my mother and sister had gotten out of bed and were both standing behind me.

"There's a lot of Indians."

"It's probably Rooster Joe and the other Tonks," said my brother.

I let him push me out of the way, then went to the fire and poked it so we would have light. Since statehood we'd had good Indian years; most of the U.S. Army had been stationed in Texas to watch the frontier. I wondered where they were. I knew I should load all the guns, then remembered I had already done it. A rhyme came into my head, *buffalo grip, barlow blade, best damn knife that was ever made.* I knew what would happen—the Indians would knock on the door, we would not let them in, and they would try to break in until they got bored. Then they would set fire to the house and shoot us as we came out.

"Martin?" said my mother.

"He's right. There are at least two dozen."

"Then it's whites," said my sister. "It's some gang of horse thieves."

"No, it's definitely Indians."

I got my rifle and sat down in a corner facing the door. It was shadows and dim red light. I wondered if I would go to hell. My brother was pacing and my mother and sister had sat down on their bed. My mother was brushing my sister's hair saying, *Shush now, Lizzie, everything will be fine.* In the dimness their eyes were empty sockets like the buzzards had already found them. I looked the other way.

"Your rifle has a nipple on it," I told my brother, "and so do the pistols."

He shook his head.

"If we put up a fight, they might just be happy with the horses."

I could tell he didn't agree but he went to the corner and took up his squirrel gun, feeling the nipple for a percussion cap.

"I already capped it," I repeated.

"Maybe they'll think we're not home," said my sister. She looked to my brother but he said, "They can see we have a fire going, Lizzie."

We could hear the Indians clanging things around in my father's metal shop, talking in low voices. My mother got up and put a chair in front of the door and stood on it. There was another gun port up high and she removed the board and put her face to it: "I only see seven."

"There are at least thirty," I told her.

"Daddy will be following them," said my sister. "He'll know they're here."

"Maybe when he sees the flames," said my brother.

"They're coming."

"Get down from there, Mammy."

"Not so loud," said my sister.

Someone kicked the door and my mother nearly fell off her perch. *Salir, salir.* There was pounding. Spanish was the language most of the wild tribes spoke, if they spoke anything but Indian. I thought the door might stop a few shots at best and I motioned again for my mother to get down.

Tenemos hambre. Nos dan los alimentos.

"That is ridiculous," said my brother. "Who would believe that?"

There was a long quiet time and then Mother looked at us and said, in her schoolteacher voice: "Eli and Martin, please put your guns on the floor." She began to remove the bar from the door and I realized that everything they ever said about women was true—they had no common sense and you could not trust them.

"Do not open that door, Momma.

"Grab her," I told Martin. But he didn't move. I saw the bar lift and propped the rifle on my knee. The moonlight was coming through the cracks like a white fire but my mother didn't notice; she set the bar aside like she was welcoming an old friend, like she'd been expecting this from the day we were born.

It was said in the newspapers that mothers on the frontier saved their last bullets for their own children, so they would not be taken by the heathens, but you did not hear of anyone doing it. In fact it was the opposite. We all knew I was of prime age—the Indians would want me alive. My brother and sister might have been slightly old, but my sister was pretty and my brother looked younger than he really was. Meanwhile my mother was almost forty. She knew exactly what they would do to her.

The door flung open and two men tackled her. A third man stood behind them in the doorway, squinting into the darkness of the house.

When my shot hit, he windmilled an arm and fell backward. The other Indians sprinted out and I yelled for my brother to shut the door but he didn't move. I ran over to shut it myself but the dead Indian was lying across the sill. I was grabbing for his feet, intending to pull him in and clear the doorway, when he kicked me under the jaw.

When I came to there were trees waving in the moonlight and one loud noise after another. Indians were standing on either side of the doorway, leaning to shoot into the room, then ducking back around the corner. My sister said, *Martin, I think they've shot me.* My brother was just sitting there. I thought he'd taken a ball. The Indians took a break for the powder smoke to thin so I jerked the rifle from his hand, checked that the hammer was cocked, and was swinging it toward the Indians when my mother stopped me.

Then I was on my stomach; at first I thought the house had fallen, but it was a man. I grabbed at his neck but my head kept chunking against the floor. Then I was outside under the trees.

I tried to stand but was kicked and tried again and was kicked again. Now a man's feet, now the ground next to them. Now a pair of legs, covered in buckskin. I bit his foot and was kicked a third time and then my hair was being pulled like it would come out at the roots. I waited for the cutting.

When I opened my eyes there was a big red face; he smelled like onions and a dirty outhouse and he showed me with the knife that I would behave or he would cut my head off. Then he lashed my hands with a piggin string.

When he walked away, he did not look like any Indian I'd ever seen. The aborigines living among the whites were thin, light bodied, and hard wintered. This one was tall and stocky, with a square head and fat nose; he looked more like a Negro than a lathy starving Indian and he walked with his chest out, as if taking everything we owned was his natural right.

There were fifteen or twenty horses outside the gate and as many Indians against our fence, laughing and making jokes. There was no sign of my mother or brother or sister. The Indians were stripped to the waist and covered with paint and designs like they'd escaped from a traveling show; one had painted his face like a skull, another had the same design on his chest.

Some of the Indians were rummaging the house and others rummaging the stables or outbuildings but most were leaning on the fence watching their friends work. All the white men I'd ever seen after a fight were nervous for hours, pacing and talking so fast you couldn't understand them, but the Indians were bored and yawning like they'd just come back from an evening constitutional, except for the man I'd shot, who was sitting against the house. There was blood on his chest and his mouth was frothing. Maybe he'd jumped sideways when the cap popped—they said the aboriginals had reflexes like deer. His friends saw me staring and one came over and said *taibo nɯ wɯkupatɯ?i*, then knocked me in the head.

I had a long dream where I was brought before a man to judge me for my sins. It was Saint Peter, only in the form of the teacher of our school in Bastrop, who had disliked me over all the other students, and I knew I was going to hell.

Then most of the Indians were standing looking at something on the ground. There was a white leg crooked in the air and a man's bare ass and buckskin leggings on top. I realized it was my mother and by the way the man was moving and the bells on his legs were jingling I knew what he was doing to her. After a while he stood up and retied his breechcloth. Another jumped right into place. I had just gotten to my feet when my ears started ringing and the ground came up and I thought I was dead for certain.

A while later I heard noises again. I could see the second group of Indians a little farther down the fence but now I could hear my sister's voice whimpering. The Indians were doing the same to her as my mother.

FINALLY I REALIZED I was in bed. I was having a dream. It was nice until I woke up all the way and heard war whoops and saw I was still in the yard. My mother was naked and crawling away from the Indians; she had reached the porch and was trying to make it to the door. Inside the house, someone was pounding on the piano and there was something waving out from my mother's back that I realized was an arrow.

The Indians must have decided they did not want her in the house because they began shooting more arrows into her. She kept crawling. Finally one of them walked up to her, put his foot between her shoulders and pressed her to the ground. He gathered up her long hair as if he was fixing to wash it, then pulled it tight with one hand and drew his butcher knife. My mother had not made a sound since I woke up, even with the arrows sticking out of her, but she began to scream then, and I saw another Indian walking up to her with my father's broadax.

I had been puddling and moaning but that is when I dried up for good. I did not look at my mother and I might have heard a sound or I might not have. I tried to find Martin and Lizzie. Where Lizzie had been I made out a small white patch and then another and I realized it was her and that she was lying where they had left her. Later, when they led us out, I saw a body with its breasts cut off and its bowels draped around. I knew it was my sister but she no longer looked like herself.

I was dragged over to the fence next to my brother. He was crying and going quiet and crying again. Meanwhile nothing was coming out of me. I gathered myself up to look over at my mother; she was on her belly with the arrows sticking out of her. The Indians were going in and out of the house. My brother was sitting there looking at things. I began to choke and air my paunch and when I was done he said: "I thought you were dead. I was watching you for a long time."

It felt like a wedge had been stuck between my eyes.

"I was thinking Daddy might come home, but now I think we'll be miles away before anyone knows what happened."

A young Indian saw us talking and threatened us with his knife to shut up, but after he walked off Martin said: "Lizzie was hit in the stomach."

I knew what he was getting at and I thought about how he'd sat there while our mother unbarred the door, sat there when I tried to get the Indian out of the doorway, sat with a loaded rifle while Indians were shooting into the house. But my head hurt too much to say any of it. I saw spots again.

"Did you see what they did to her and Momma?"

"A little," I said.

The Comanches went in and out of the house, taking what they wanted and throwing the rest into a pile in the yard. Someone was attacking our piano with an ax. I was hoping the Indians would kill us or that I would pass out again. My brother was staring at my sister. The Indians were carrying out stacks of books that I thought were meant for the fire but instead they put them into their bolsas. Later they would use the pages to stuff their shields, which were two layers of buffalo neckhide. When stuffed with paper the shields would stop almost any bullet.

The mattresses were dragged out and cut open and the wind caught the feathers and spread them over the yard like snow. My mother was in the way. The feathers were falling over her. The ants had found us but we barely noticed; my brother kept staring at my sister.

"You shouldn't look at her anymore."

"I want to," he said.

WHEN I WOKE up it was hot. The pile of everything the Indians didn't want, mostly smashed furniture, had been lit. An agarito was cutting into me. The fire got bigger and I could see into the shadows where our dogs were lying dead and I wondered if the Indians meant to throw us into the fire. They were known for strapping people to wagon wheels and lighting them. Then I was looking down on myself as you would a lead soldier. Interested in what I might do but not really caring.

"I can already shimmy my hands," I told my brother.

"For what?" he said.

"We should stay ready."

He was quiet. We watched the fire.

"Are you thirsty?"

"Of course I'm thirsty," he said.

The fire was getting bigger and the moss in the branches above us was flaring and smoke was coming off the bark. The embers of our own burned things were singeing our faces and hair; I watched the sparks climb up. When I looked over at my brother he was covered in ash like a person who had been dead a long time and I thought of how my mother and sister had looked when they sat together on the bed.

The Indians brought all my father's tools to be examined by fire-light and I decided to remember everything they were taking: horse-shoes, hammers, nails, barrel hoops, the bucksaw, the broadax and felling ax, the barking iron, an adze and froe; all the bits, bridles, saddles and stirrups, other tack; my brother's Kentucky rifle. My Jaeger-buchse they decided was too heavy and smashed against the side of the house. They took our knives, files, picks and awls, bits for drilling, lead bullets, bullet molds, powder kegs, percussion caps, a horsehair rope hanging in the dogtrot. Our three milch cows heard the commotion and wandered up to the house for a feed. The Indians shot them with arrows. They were in high spirits. Burning logs were pulled from the fire and carried inside the house; people were tying their bundles, checking their cinches, making ready to leave. Smoke was coming from the doors and windows and then someone untied my hands and stood me up.

Our clothes were thrown into the fire along with everything else and we were walked naked out of our gate, across the road, and into our field. A big remuda had been driven up, Cayuse ponies mixed with larger American horses. The Indians were ignoring us and talking among themselves, *ums* and *ughs*, grunts, no language at all, though they had words that sounded Spanish, and one word, *taibo*, they said to us often, *taibo* this and *taibo* that. We were barefoot and it was dark and I tried not to kick a prickly pear or be tromped on by the horses stamping and pacing. I felt better that at least something was happening, then I reminded myself that made no sense.

We were lifted up and our legs tied to the animals' bare backs with our hands tied in front of us. It could have been worse as sometimes they just tied you over the horse like a sack of flour. My pony was skittering; he didn't like the way I smelled.

The other horses were stamping and snorting and the Indians were calling back and forth across our field and my brother began to cry and I was mad at him for crying in front of the Indians. Then I began to blubber as well. We trotted out through our lower pasture, three months of grubbing stumps; we passed a stand of walnut I had picked for board trees. I thought about the men who had pushed us out of Bastrop, calling my mother a nigger and suing for our title. Once I had killed all the Indians I would go back and kill all the new settlers; I would burn the town to the bedrock. I wondered where my father was and I hoped he would come and then I felt guilty for hoping that.

Then we were going at a lope with the bluestem whipping our legs. We stretched into a column and I watched as the Indians disappeared into the woods ahead and then my horse passed into the darkness as well.

WE CROSSED GRAPE Creek at the only spot you didn't have to jump, took a path through the bogs I had not known was there, came out at a gallop at the base of Cedar Mountain. Our cattle were white spots on the hillside. We were making ground in a long flat bottom with the hills all around, into the trees and out again, darkness to moonlight and back to darkness, the Indians trusting the horses to see, driving every animal in the forest in front of us. I looked for my brother. Behind me the riders were suddening out of the trees as if they'd been called out of the blackness itself.

Despite the dark and the uneven ground my horse hadn't slipped and had plenty of wind. We were coming to the base of Packsaddle Mountain. It was the last piece of land I knew well. I could turn the horse into the woods, but I doubted I would make it and my brother had no chance alone. Farther up the white hillside, I caught sight of the mustang pack I had intended to rope and break. They stood watching as we passed.

TWO HOURS LATER we changed horses. My legs and backside were already raw and I'd been whipped by branches across the face and chest and arms. My brother was cut even worse; his entire body was caked with blood and dirt. We remounted and took up the same hard tempo. Later we came on a river that had to be the Llano. It didn't seem possible we'd made it that far.

"Is this what I think?" said my brother.

I nodded.

We waited for the horses to cross in the dark.

"We are fucked," he said. "This is a whole day's ride."

Sometime later we hit another river, probably the Colorado, after which we stopped to change horses again. I could smell that my brother had shat himself. When they stood me on the ground I squatted with my hands tied in front of me and the water dripping off and the horses pacing all around. My legs were cramped and I could barely hold a squat. Someone kicked me but I did not want to be riding in my own mess so I finished shitting and they stood me up by the hair. I doubted there was any skin left anywhere below my waist. I was put on another pony. The Comanches didn't trust the horses raised by whites.

SOMETIME AFTER FIRST light we stopped to change horses a third time, but instead of remounting we stood around at the edge of a river. We were in a deep canyon, I guessed it was still the Colorado but not even the army ever went this far up. The sun hadn't risen but it was bright enough to see color, and the Indians were standing around waiting for something. They were drinking from the river or leaning and stretching their backs, packing and repacking their saddlebags. It was the first time I'd seen them in the light.

They carried bows and quivers and lances, short-barreled muskets and war axes and butcher knives, their faces were painted with arrows and blooming suns and their skin was completely smooth, their eyebrows and beards all plucked. They all wore their hair as a Dutch girl might, two long braids on either side, but these Indians had woven in bits of copper and silver and colored beads.

"I can tell what you're thinking," said my brother.

"They look like a pack of mollies," I said, though I didn't really believe it.

"They look more like actors on a stage." Then he added: "Don't get us in any more trouble."

Then a stocky brave walked over and pushed us apart with his lance. There was a dried bloody handprint on his back and a long dark smear down the front of his leggings. What I had thought were pieces of calfskin on his waist turned out to be scalps. I looked up the river.

Ahead of us was a high overlook and behind us the Indians were rotating the horses in and out of the grass along the banks. There was a discussion and then most of the Comanches made their way on foot toward the overlook. One of them was leading a horse and tied to the horse was the body of the man I'd shot. I hadn't known he'd died and I got a cold feeling. My brother waded out into the river. The two Indians guarding us drew their bows but when I opened my eyes my brother was still in one piece, standing splashing himself—he was covered in his own waste. The Indians watched him, shriveled and pale and shivering, his chest caved from reading too many books.

When he was clean he came back and sat next to me.

"I hope it was worth getting shot just to wipe your ass," I said.

He patted my leg. "I want you to know what happened last night."

I didn't want to know any more than I already did but I couldn't tell him that so I stayed quiet.

"Momma wasn't going to make it but I don't think they meant to kill Lizzie. When they saw she was wounded they took off her shirt and looked over her gunshot pretty carefully; they even rigged up a sort of torch so this old Indian could give his opinion. They must have decided it was bad because they all went and talked for a while and then they came back and pulled off the rest of her clothes and raped her." He looked upriver where the Indians were climbing up the canyon. "Lizzie Lizzie Lizzie."

"She's in a better place."

He shrugged. "She's in no place."

"There is still Daddy," I said.

He snorted. "When Daddy finds out he will likely ride straight for that woman he keeps in Austin."

"That is low. Even for you."

"People don't go around saying a thing unless it's true, Eli. That's another thing you ought to know."

The guards looked back. I wanted them to stop our talking but now they didn't care.

"Momma knew she could save you," he said. He shrugged. "Lizzie and I . . . I dunno. But you're a different story."

I pretended not to understand him and looked around. The canyon walls went up a few hundred feet and there was bear grass and agarito spilling out of the cracks. A gnarled old cedar stuck out of the face; it looked like a stovepipe and there was an eagle's nest in it. Upriver were big cypresses with knock-kneed roots. Five hundred years was nothing for them.

When the sun hit the upper walls of the canyon a wailing and chanting went up. There was a shot and the burial party began to file back down to the river and when they reached us they knocked us down and kicked us until my brother shat himself again.

"I can't help it," he said.

"Don't worry."

"I'm worried," he said.

Several of the Indians thought we ought to be marched to the burial site and killed along with the dead man's horse but the one who was in charge of the war party, the one who'd dragged me out of the house, was against it. *Nabituku tekwaniwapi Toshaway*, they would say. My

brother was already starting to pick up bits of Comanche; Toshaway
was the chief's name. There were charges and offers and counteroffers,
but Toshaway would not give in. He caught me watching him but gave
no more account than if I were a dog.

My brother got a philosophical look and I got nervous.

"You know," he said, "the whole time, I was hoping that when the
sun came up they would see us and realize they had made some terrible
mistake, that we were people just like them, or at least just people, but
now I am hoping the opposite."

I didn't say anything.

"What I am getting at is that the very kinship I had hoped might
save us might be the reason they kill us. Because of course we are completely powerless over our fates, but in the end they are as well and
maybe that is why they will kill us. To erase, at least temporarily, their
own reflections."

"Stop it," I said. "Stop talking."

"They don't care," he said. "They don't care about a word we say."

I knew he was right but just then the debate ended and the Indians
who had been for killing us came over and began to stomp and kick us.

When they finished my brother lay in a puddle of water among the
stones, his head at an angle, looking up at the sky. There was blood running into my throat and I threw up into the river. The rocks were floating
all around me. I decided as long as they killed us together it would be
fine. I caught a wolf watching me from a high ledge but when I blinked
he was gone. I thought about the white one I'd shot and how it was bad
luck, then I thought about my mother and sister and wondered if the
animals had found them. I got to blubbering and was cuffed in the head.

Martin looked like he'd lost twenty pounds; his knees and elbows
and chin were bleeding and there was dirt and sand stuck everywhere.
The Indians were changing their saddles onto fresh horses. I was hungry and before they could put me on another horse I sucked water from
the river until my stomach was full.

"You should drink," I told him.

He shook his head. He lay there with his hands cupping his privates. The Indians jerked us up.

"Next time," I said.

"I was thinking how nice it was that I didn't have to get up again. Then I realized they hadn't killed me. Now I'm annoyed."

"It wouldn't be any better."

He shrugged.

WE CONTINUED TO ride at a good pace and if the Indians were tired they didn't show it and if they were hungry they didn't show it, either. They were alert but not nervous. Every now and then I'd get a glimpse of the entire remuda trailing behind us in the canyon. My brother would not stop talking.

"You know I was watching Mother and Lizzie," he said. "I had always thought about where the soul might be, near to the heart or maybe along the bones, I'd always figured you'd have to cut for it. But there was a lot of cutting and I didn't see anything come out. I'm certain I would have seen it."

I ignored him.

A while later he said: "Can you imagine any white man, even a thousand white men, riding this easy in Indian country?"

"No."

"It's funny because everyone calls them heathens and red devils, but now that we've seen them, I think it's the opposite. They act like the gods were supposed to act. Though I guess I mean heroes or demigods because as you have certainly helped demonstrate, though not without a certain cost, these Indians are indeed mortal."

"Please stop."

"It does make you wonder about the Negro problem, doesn't it?"

AT MIDDAY WE climbed out of the canyon. We were on a rolling grassland thick with asters and primrose, ironweed and red poppy. Some bobwhites scuttled into the brush. The prairie went on forever;

there were herds of antelope and deer and a few stray buffalo in the distance. The Indians checked their pace to look around and then we were off.

There was nothing to protect us from the sun and by afternoon I could smell my own burning skin and was going in and out of sleep. We continued through the high grass, over limestone breaks, briefly into the shade along streams—though never stopping to drink—and then back into the sun.

Then the Comanches all reined up and after some chatter my brother and I were led back to a stream we'd just crossed. We were pulled roughly off the horses and tied to each other back to back and put in the shade. A teenager was left to guard us.

"Rangers?"

"This one doesn't look too nervous," said my brother.

We were facing opposite directions and it was strange not seeing his face.

"Maybe it's Daddy and the others."

"I think they would be behind us," he said.

After a while I decided he was right. I called the young Indian over. There were grapes hanging all along the stream.

He shook his head. *Itsa aitn*. Then he added *itsa keta kwasnpn* and when he still wasn't satisfied I understood, he said in Spanish, *no en sazón*.

"He's saying they're not ripe."

"I know that."

I wanted them anyway and I was so hungry I didn't care. The Indian cut a section of vine and dropped it into my lap. Then he rinsed his hands in the stream. The grapes were so bitter I nearly aired my paunch. I thought they would help my fever. My lips were itching.

"They're good," I said.

"For tanning hides, maybe."

"You should eat."

"You are not making any sense," he told me.

I ate more of the grapes. It felt like I'd swallowed boiling water.

I said, "Scoot over to that stream and lean over it," and we did. My brother let his head rest in the water, as sunburned as I was, but I could tell he wasn't drinking. Something about this made me want to puddle up but I kept drinking instead. The young Indian stood on a rock and watched. We sat up again. It seemed like my fever was going down and I could stretch my legs.

"What's your name," I said to our guard. *"Cómo te llamas?"*

He didn't answer for a long time. Then he said: "Nuukaru." He looked around nervously and then walked off as if he'd given away some secret and when I saw him again he was upstream, lying on his belly, sucking up water. It was the first time I'd seen any of the Indians eat or drink much of anything, except for a few swallows. When he stood up he arranged his braids and checked his paint.

"I wonder if they're cockchafers," my brother said.

"Somehow I doubt it."

"You know the Spartans were."

"Who are the Spartans?" I said.

He was about to say something else when there was a rattling of shots far off. There was a scattered return volley and finally the slow knocking of a single repeating pistol. Then it got quiet and I knew it was just the Indians using their bows. I wondered whose bad luck it had been.

Another young Indian came bounding down the rocks and then we were tied back on the horses and led out of the streambed. My fever had gone down and I didn't mind the sun. After crossing a stony plateau we descended to a prairie that seemed to be mostly larkspur and wine-cup. A red dirt wagon road went up the middle and it was a pleasant sight with the blue sky and a few bright clouds and wildflowers everywhere.

The Indians were milling around a pair of ox-drawn freight wagons. A third wagon was far ahead in the grass, turned on its side, a mule team standing dumbly in front of it. Someone was screaming.

"I don't want to see this," said Martin.

There was something white at the edge of the road; a small tow-headed boy in a boiled shirt. An arrow shaft had stuck through his eye and a big red-headed woodpecker was tapping a branch over his head.

Farther up the road blood was dripping from the wagons as if someone had splashed a bucket. There were four or five Texans sprawled in the red dirt and another curled up like a baby in the back of the wagon. Off in the grass and larkspur the Indians were doing something to the last teamster and he was shrieking in a high voice and they were imitating him.

With the exception of the two dealing with the remaining teamster, no one was wasting any time. The mule team was cut loose but they didn't move; they stood with their heads down as if they had done something wrong. A spotted pony was dead in the ditch, his neck covered with blood, the owner trying to free his saddle. Another Indian pony, a handsome strawberry roan, was standing blowing pink froth out of a hole in its chest. His owner removed his saddle, blanket, and bridle and set them carefully in the road. Then, while hugging and kissing the roan's neck, he shot it behind the ear.

Everything was pulled from the wagons, including two more bodies we hadn't noticed. It was hot and the red dust was settling over the flowers. The dead men's pockets were searched, those who hadn't been scalped were scalped; the last teamster had gone quiet. One of the Indians had a poultice applied, a pear pad split and tied with cloth; most of the hide shields had fresh lead streaks and a tall brave with Karankawa blood was cleaning his lance with grass. Others were going through the cargo, mostly flour sacks, which were cut and dumped in the road. A keg of whiskey was tomahawked and smaller kegs of gunpowder were strapped to horses along with several small crates, which from their weight must have been lead. Knives and blankets were taken, plugs of tobacco, bullet molds, a pair of axes and a handsaw, some calico fabric, a few repeating pistols. The locks and mainsprings on the rest of the guns were checked and the ones still good were taken. There was a brief debate over a scalp. Two plum pies were discovered and divvied up with the bloody knives.

The younger Comanches were combing the grass for stray arrows, the mules were put into the horse pack, a few quick circles were made to be sure nothing and no one had been missed, a piece of interesting fabric recovered, then all the guns were recharged and the quivers repacked, straps and hitches tightened, mouths rinsed. The oxen bellowed their final protest as someone cut their throats; by then the rest of the blood in the road had turned black and the bodies covered over with dust. They looked like they'd always been there.

The Indians split into three groups and left a wide set of tracks leading toward civilization, opposite the direction we were actually headed. Everyone was in a good mood. One of the braves rode up and slapped a fresh scalp on my head, the stringy gray hair hanging down. A man's bloody hat was crushed down on top of it, which the Indians found hilarious. We continued northwest, the grass tall with scattered thick motts of oak and the mesquites with their flickering leaves and the yuccas in bloom with their white flowers.

After a few hours the brave decided he didn't want to soil his trophy any further and took it off my head, tying it to his belt and throwing the dead man's hat into the bushes. The scalp and hat had been keeping the sun off and I asked for the hat back but we rode on. By then the other groups had rejoined us.

At the next change of horses, the Indians passed around some jerky they'd taken off the teamsters. My brother and I were offered a few bites. It was still hot but the Indians didn't care about drinking water, and when one of them offered me tobacco I was so thirsty I couldn't take it. My brother was not offered tobacco. He stood with his legs in a straddle and looked miserable.

When the sun finally went down my mouth was so dry I thought I would choke. I reminded myself to pick up a pebble to suck but then I was thinking about the spring near our house, of sitting and letting the water rush over as I looked out past the river. I began to feel better.

It was dark and at some point we stopped at a muddy hole and the horses were held back while the Indians tore up grass and piled it on the mud and took about two swallows each. My brother and I stuck our whole faces in and drank our fill. It tasted like frogs and smelled like animals had been wallowing but we didn't care. After he'd swallowed enough my brother started to cry, and then the Indians were kicking him in the belly and giving him the knife at the throat. *Wɯyupaʔnitɯ,* quiet down. *Nihpɯʔaitɯ,* stop talking.

They were planning something. They changed their mounts but we were kept back with the horse herd.

"I think we've come a hundred miles. We must be right below the San Saba."

"Do you think they'll let me drink again?"

"Sure," I said.

He put his face back in the muddy water. I tried again but now I couldn't stand the smell. My brother drank and drank. It hurt even just to sit in the dirt now. I wondered how long it would take to heal; weeks maybe. We huddled together as best as possible. There was a bad odor and I realized my brother had shat himself.

"I can't stop."

"It's all right."

"There's no point," he said.

"All we have to do is keep going," I told him. "It is not that much when you think about it."

"And then what? What happens when we get where they're taking us?"

I was quiet.

"I don't want to find out," he said.

"There was John Tanner," I said, "Charles Johnston, you yourself have read those books."

"I am not the type to live on bark and gooseberries."

"You'll be a legend," I said. "I'll visit you in Boston and tell your friend Emerson that you're a real man and not just some cockchafing poet."

He didn't say anything.

"You could try a little harder," I told him. "You're risking our hair every time you piss them off."

"I'm doing the best I can."

"That is not true at all."

"Well, I'm glad you know."

He started to cry again. Then he was snoring. I was mad because he was just being lazy. We were not being fed any less, or driven any harder, than the Indians were driving themselves; we'd both had a lot more water than they had and who knew how long they'd been going like this? There was a logic but my brother couldn't see it. If a man has done it, so can you: that is what our father used to tell us.

Then we were slapped awake. It was still dark and they tied us to the horses and there was a bright light in the distance that I knew was a burning homestead. I hadn't thought there were whites this far out, but the land was rich and I could see why they had risked it. A few braves came up and I could tell they were pleased with the youngsters for getting us mounted.

In the darkness we saw another dozen or so horses driven into the remuda. There were two new captives; by their crying we knew they were women and by their language we knew they were German, or Dutch as we called them back then.

By sunrise we'd gone another fifty miles, changing horses twice. The Germans didn't stop crying the entire night. When it was light enough we climbed a mesa, winding around the far side before coming up to watch our backtrail. The land had opened up; there were mesas, buttes, distant views.

The Germans were as naked as we were. One was seventeen or eighteen and the other a little older, and while they were both covered in blood and filth it was obvious they were at the peak of their female charms. The more I looked at them, the more I began to hate them and I hoped the Indians would degrade them some more and I would be able to watch.

My brother said, "I hate those Dutch women and I hope the Indians give them a good fucking."

"Me too."

"You seem to be holding up, though."

"Because I don't keep falling off my horse." We had stopped twice that night so they could lash my brother on tighter.

"I've been trying to catch a hoof in the head, but I haven't been so lucky."

"I'm sure Momma would be happy to hear that."

"You'll make a good little Indian, Eli. I'm sorry I won't be there to see it."

I didn't say anything.

"You know the reason I didn't shoot is because I didn't want them to hurt Mother or Lizzie."

"You froze up."

"They would have killed Mother anyway, that's obvious, but they would have taken Lizzie with us. It was only because she'd been shot that . . ."

"Shut up," I said.

"You didn't have to see what they did to her."

I was looking at him. He looked the same as always with his squinty eyes and thin lips but he seemed like someone I'd known a long time ago.

A little later he told me he was sorry.

The Indians passed around a few pieces of jerked meat from the teamsters. One of the Germans asked me where I thought we were going. I pretended not to understand her. She knew better than to talk to Martin.

THE NEXT DAY the views got longer. We were in a canyon ten miles wide, the walls going up a thousand feet above us, all red rock. There were cottonwoods and hackberries but not many other trees and we passed a magenta spear point in the sand, twin to the one I'd seen below our house. There were stone creatures in every rock and stream bank: a nautilus big as a wagon wheel, the horns and bones of animals larger than anything still alive on the earth.

Toshaway told me in Spanish that by fall the canyon would be full of buffalo. He was appreciating the scene. There were long tufts of black hair streaming from the cedar and mesquite; the buffalo had been using this place a long time.

The Indians showed no sign of tiring or of wanting a proper feed, but the pace had slowed. My mouth was watering; any number of fish could have been speared as we passed: the water was full of yellow cats, eels, buffalo fish, and gar. I lost count of the whitetail and antelope. A cinnamon grizzly, the largest I'd ever seen, was sunning himself on a ledge. Springs flowing down cliff faces, pools underneath.

That night we made our first real camp and I fell asleep in the rocks holding my brother. Someone put a buffalo robe over us and when I looked up, Toshaway was squatting next to me. His smell was becoming familiar. "Tomorrow we'll make a fire," he said.

The next morning we rode past sandstone mesas with figures scratched into the rock: shamans, men in combat, lances and shields and tipis.

"You know they're going to separate us," Martin said.

I looked at him.

"These guys are from two different bands."

"How would you even know?" I said.

"The one who owns you is Kotsoteka," he said. "The one who owns me is Yamparika."

"The one who owns me is Toshaway."

"That's his name. He's from the Kotsoteka band. The one who owns me is Urwat. They've been saying that Urwat has a long way to go, but the guy who owns you is not that far from home."

"They don't own us," I said.

"You're right. Why they might have that impression is completely beyond me."

We continued to ride.

"What about the Penatekas?"

"The Penatekas are sick right now, or something else bad is happening to them. I can't tell except that none of these are Penatekas."

DESPITE TOSHAWAY'S PROMISE, we made another cold camp that night. In the morning we climbed out of the big canyon and onto the plains. There was no timber, no trail, no lines of brush to mark a stream, it was nothing but grass and sky and my stomach felt wobbly just looking at it. I knew where we were: the Llano Estacado. A blank space on the map.

After riding an hour nothing had changed and I was dizzy again. We might have gone ten inches or ten miles and by the end of the day I thought something had come loose in my head. My brother fell asleep and rolled all the way under his horse and the Indians stopped, beat him, and tied him back on.

We made camp at a stream cut so deep into the plain you could not see it until you were on top of it. It was our first fire and because there were no trees to reflect the light, it could not be seen from any distance. A pair of antelopes were thrown on, skin and all, and Toshaway brought us a pile of steaming half-cooked venison. My brother didn't have the energy to eat. I chewed the meat into small pieces and fed it to him.

Then I climbed out of the streambed to have a look. The stars came down to the earth on all sides and the Comanches had pickets looking for other campfires. They ignored me. I went back to our pallet.

A catamount screamed at us for nearly an hour, and wolf calls were echoing from one side of the plain to the other. My brother began to cry out in his sleep; I started to shake him, then stopped. There wasn't any dream he could be having that would be as bad as waking up.

THE NEXT MORNING they didn't bother to tie us. There was nowhere to go.

My brother, despite having eaten real food and slept six hours, was not any better. Meanwhile the Indians were laughing and cutting capers, riding their horses backward or standing up, calling back and forth with jokes. I fell asleep and woke up in the grass. We stopped and I was tied on again, slapped a few times but not beaten. Toshaway came over and gave me a long drink of water, then chewed up some tobacco and rubbed the juice into my eyes. Still I spent the rest of the day not knowing if I was asleep or awake. I had the feeling that somewhere ahead of us was the edge of the earth and if we reached it we would never stop falling.

That afternoon a small herd of buffalo were spotted and run down and after a discussion my brother and I were taken off our horses and led to one of the calves. It was cut open and its innards pulled out. Toshaway cut into the stomach and offered me a handful of curdled milk but I did not want any part of it. Another Indian forced my brother's head into the stomach but he shut his eyes and mouth. I was given the same treatment. I tried to swallow the milk but instead I aired my paunch.

This was done two or three times, with my brother not swallowing at all, me trying and throwing up, until the Indians gave up trying and scooped out all the curdled milk for themselves. When the stomach was empty the liver was cut out. My brother refused to touch it and I saw the way they looked at him so I forced myself to keep it down. The blood turned in my gizzard. I had always thought blood tasted like metal but that is only if you drink a small amount. What it actually tastes like is musk and salt. I reached for more liver and the Indians were happy to see it and I continued to eat until they slapped me away and ate the rest of the liver themselves, squeezing the gallbladder over it as a sauce.

When the organs were gone the calf was skinned out and a piece of meat held up to the sun in an offering and then the rest distributed to everyone, about five pounds apiece. The Indians finished their allotment within a few minutes and I was worried they would take mine so I ate quickly as well.

It was the first time I'd had a full belly in nearly a week and I felt tired and peaceful but my brother just sat there, sunburned and filthy and covered in his own vomit.

"You need to eat."

He was smiling. "You know, I never thought a place like this could exist. I'll bet our tracks will be gone with the first wind."

"They're going to kill you if you don't eat."

"They're going to kill me anyway, Eli."

"Eat," I said. "Daddy ate raw meat all the time."

"I'm quite aware that as a Ranger, Daddy did everything. But I am not him. Sorry," he said. He touched my leg. "I started a new poem about Lizzie. Would you like to hear it?"

"All right."

"'Your virgin blood, spilled by savages, you are whole again in heaven.' Which of course is shit. But it's the best I can do under the circumstances."

The Indians were looking at us. Toshaway brought another chunk of buffalo and indicated I ought to give it to my brother. My brother pushed it away.

"I was sure I would go to Harvard," he said. "And then Rome. I have actually been there in my mind, you know, because when I read, I actually see things; I physically see them in front of me. Did you know that?" He seemed to cheer up. "Even these people can't ruin this place for me." He shook his head. "I've written about ten letters to Emerson but I haven't sent them. I think he would take them seriously, though."

Any letters he'd written had been burned in the fire but I didn't mention this. I told him he needed to eat.

"They're not going to turn me into some fucking filthy Indian, Eli. I'd rather be dead."

I must have gotten a look because then he said, "It wasn't your fault. I go back and forth between thinking we shouldn't have been living out there in the first place, and then I think what else could a man like Daddy do? He had no choice, really. It was fate."

"I'm going to make you a pile of food."

He ignored me. He was staring at something on the ground and then he reached over and pulled up one of the blanketflowers—we were sitting in a big patch. He held it up for all the Indians to see.

"Note the Indian blanket," he said, "or Indian sunburst."

They ignored him.

He continued in a louder voice. "It is worth noting that small, stunted, or useless plants—such as Mexican plum, Mexican walnut, or Mexican apple—are named after the Mexicans, who will doubtless endure among us for centuries, while colorful or beautiful plants are often named after Indians, as they will soon be vanquished from the earth." He looked around at them. "It's a great compliment to your race. Though if your vanquishing had come a bit earlier, I wouldn't have complained."

No one was paying attention.

"It's the fate of a man like myself to be misunderstood. That's Goethe, in case you were wondering."

Toshaway tried a few more times to give him meat, but my brother wouldn't touch it. Within half an hour there was nothing left but bone and hide. The hides were rolled up and put on the back of someone's horse and the Indians began to mount.

Then my brother was looking at someone behind me.

"Don't try to help."

Toshaway pinned me to the grass. He and another Indian sat on me and tied my wrists and ankles as quick as my father might have tied a calf. I was dragged a good distance. When I looked over, Martin hadn't moved. He was sitting there taking things in; I could barely see his face above the flowers. Three Indians had mounted their horses, including Urwat, my brother's owner. They were riding in circles around him, whooping and hollering. He stood and they slapped him with the flats of their lances, giving him an opening and encouraging him to run, but he stayed where he was, up to his knees in the red-and-yellow flowers, looking small against the sky behind him.

Finally Urwat got tired and, instead of using the flat of his lance, lowered the point and ran it through my brother's back. My brother stayed on his feet. Toshaway and the other Indians were holding me. Urwat charged again and my brother was knocked down into the flowers.

Then Toshaway got my head down. I knew I ought to be getting up but Toshaway wouldn't let me, I knew I should get up but I didn't want to. *That is fine,* I thought, *but now I'll get up.* I strained against Toshaway but he wouldn't let go.

My brother was standing again. How many times he'd been knocked down and gotten back up I didn't know. Urwat had discarded his lance and now rode toward him with his ax but my brother didn't flinch and after he fell the last time the Indians rushed forward and made a circle.

Toshaway later explained that my brother, who had acted like such a coward the entire time, was obviously not a coward at all, but a *kɯ?tseena,* a coyote or trickster, a mystical creature who had been sent to test them. It was very bad medicine to kill him—the coyote was so important that Comanches were not allowed to even scratch one. My brother could not be scalped. Urwat was cursed.

There was a good deal of milling and confusion and three of the Indian kids held me while the adults talked. I was telling myself I would kill Urwat. I looked around for a friendly eye, but the German women wouldn't look at me.

The shoulder bones of the dead buffalo were cut loose and several of the braves began to dig. When there was a passable grave my brother was wrapped in calico taken from the freight wagon and lowered into the hole. Urwat left his tomahawk, someone else gave a knife; there was buffalo meat left as well. There was discussion about killing a horse, but it was voted down.

Then we rode off. I watched the grave disappear from sight, as if the blanketflower had already grown over, as if the place would not stand for any record of human life, or death; it would continue as my brother had said it would, our tracks disappearing in the first wind.

CHAPTER FIVE

J. A. McCULLOUGH

If she were a better person she would not leave her family a dime; a few million, maybe, something to pay for college or if they got sick. She had grown up knowing that if a drought went on another year, or the ticks got worse, or the flies, if any single thing went wrong, the family would not eat. Of course they had oil by then, it was an illusion. But her father had acted as if it were true, and she had believed it, and so it was.

When she was a child, her father often gave her orphaned calves to look after, and, every so often, she would fold the grown ones in with the steers when they were shipped off to Fort Worth. She made enough money off her dogies to make investments in stocks, and that, she told people, is what taught her the value of a dollar. *More like the value of a thousand dollars,* some reporter once said. He was not entirely masculine. He was from the North.

The Colonel, though he drank whiskey the entire ten years she'd known him, never slept past sunrise. When she was eight, and he ninety-eight, he had led her slowly across a dry pasture, following a track across the caliche she could not see, around clusters of prickly pear and yellow-flowered huisache, following a track she was certain her great-grandfather was imagining, until finally they arrived at a particular clump of soapbrush and he had reached into it and pulled out a baby rabbit. Its heart was pounding and she cradled it against the skin under her shirt.

"Are there more?" She could not have been more excited. She wanted all of them.

"We'll leave the rest with their dam," he said. His face was brown, cracked and furrowed like a dry riverbed, and his eyes were always running. His hands smelled of cottonwood buds, the sap that was like sugar and cinnamon and some flower she couldn't name; he was always stopping among the cottonwoods to rub the bud sap onto his fingers, a habit she adopted as well. Even at the end of her life she would stop at an old tree and scrape the orange sap onto a thumbnail, that she might smell it the rest of the day, and think of her great-grandfather. Balm of Gilead, someone once told her, that's what the sap was called, though it didn't need a name.

She had taken the kit home and given it milk but the next day the dogs got it. She knew she could go back to the brush for more, but the dogs would get them all eventually, so she decided to leave the remaining rabbits where they were, a decision she knew to be very grown-up and merciful. And yet she could not stop thinking about the kit's fur against her belly, a nearly liquid softness, her great-grandfather's hand on her shoulder, leaning on her for support.

SHE WAS A small, thin girl with light hair and a snub nose and skin that went brown in the sun, though she imagined that when she grew up, she would have dark hair and pale skin and a long straight nose like her mother. Her father snorted at this. *Your mother didn't look like that at all,* he said. *She was a towhead, like you.* But that was not how Jeannie thought of her. Her mother died young, giving birth to her at twenty-six. There were only a handful of pictures, none of them close up, or good, though there were plenty of pictures of her father's horses. But in the pictures of her mother, her hair *did* look dark and long, and her nose *was* straight, and after thinking on it, she decided that her father was simply wrong, that he had no eye for she-stuff, unless it were cattle or horses. She knew that if she had ever seen her mother alive she would have noticed a thousand things that her father had not.

What her father noticed was if an old cow had been left in the brush during roundup, or if another cow was open a second year, or if a new man, who claimed to be a top hand, missed his throws, or didn't charge into the brush with proper enthusiasm. Her father noticed if a *ladino* bull, living wild as an old buck, was mixing with his heifers, and what the Mexicans said about rain, and how much work his sons did, and whether she, Jeannie, was getting in the way. Despite her grandmother's discouragement, Jeannie rode out every morning with her brothers, so long as it was not a school day. During roundup she rode drag, though she knew she was simply extra; her father did not figure her into the head count, and at the branding fire, while her brothers did their best to rope, learned throwing from the *tumbadors* or branding from the *marcadores,* she was only allowed to carry the bucket of lime paste to dab on the fresh brands. Sometimes she would help make the calf fries, scooping them from an overflowing bucket to roast on a bed of coals specially raked out for that purpose. They were sweet and so tender they nearly burst in your mouth, and she would eat them by the handful, ignoring her brothers' snide comments, which she only half understood, about her enthusiasm for that particular delicacy.

Calf fries were one thing—if she even stood near the *tumbadors,* her father would be on her immediately. She had taught herself anyway. By the time she was twelve, she could flank and mug as well as her brothers, she could forefoot anything that moved, but it didn't matter. Her father didn't want her working among the men and her grandmother found it embarrassing. The Colonel, had he been alive, would have supported her; he had always seen in her what no one else did, her unshakable sense of her own perfectibility, her certainty that if she set her mind to something, she would master it. When the Colonel told her, as he often did, that one day she would do something important, she barely took any notice. It was as if he'd pointed out the grass was green, or her eyes large as a deer's, or that she was a pretty girl, if a bit small, that men and women alike enjoyed her presence.

So while the cattle drives struck her as boredom incarnate, a slow trudge behind an endless dusty line of steers, her rope flicking at their feet, walking at the slowest of walks toward the holding pens at the rail station—despite all that—she went on every drive she could. Despite the heat and thirst of the branding fire—best done in August, when it was too hot even for blowflies—she went out anyway, throwing calves when her father wasn't paying attention, her hands covered in their slobber, running the iron if the *marcador* let her, light pressure if the metal was hot, heavy pressure as the iron cooled; she did not allow herself to make mistakes. The vaqueros found her amusing. They knew what she was doing and while they would never have let their own daughters come to a branding fire, they were happy to let her take their place so they could rest in the shade and escape the heat. As long as she didn't make mistakes. And so she didn't.

THERE HAD BEEN a time when this was not unusual. A time when the wealthy were exemplars. When you held yourself to a higher standard, when you lived as an example to others. When you did not parade your inheritance in front of a camera; when you did not accept the spotlight unless you'd *done* something. But that obligation had been lost. The rich were as anxious for attention as any scullery maid.

Perhaps she was no different. She'd hired a historian to compile a history of the ranch, a history of the family, but in ten years he'd done nothing but notate every letter, receipt, and slip of paper the Colonel had ever touched, scanning them into his little computer, going to Austin to look at microfiche. He was, she saw, incapable of writing the book he'd promised. *You can make any story of this you want,* he told her. *Well, pick the best one,* she said. *That would be lying,* he replied.

He was a pudgy, infuriating little man and she could not remember why she'd ever thought the process should be so mysterious. She'd opened her checkbook and the fund-raisers had picked up the scent, a check here, a mention there, another check, another mention; the Colonel's name had spread like roots from a mesquite. The next year he'd be appearing in the new state history books, the ones all the liberals had fought against.

IF YOU DID not work, you did not eat. If you did not wake up in the dark, be it ten degrees or a hundred, if you did not spend all day in the dust and thorns, you would not survive, the family would not survive, you had received God's blessings and been profligate.

Later, when she was old enough to look at the books, she realized the family had been safe all along. But it was too late. She could not sit still without thinking of the coyotes watching her calves, windmills that needed their gearboxes greased or sucker rods checked, fences flattened by weather or animals or careless humans. Later, when she stopped worrying about cattle, it was oil. Which wells were producing more or less than she'd hoped (less, she thought, it was always less), what new fields might be in play and what old plays the majors were giving up on. Which drillers might be hired, who was out of credit, what could be bought on the cheap. All wells went dry—the moment you stopped looking for new ones was the moment your fortunes began to decline.

Why am I on this floor, she thought. She looked around her. There was a haze in the room. She wondered if there was a problem with the flue. And the throbbing in her head; it was not the pain of a stroke. There had been someone in the room with her, she was sure of it.

THE THING THAT had gone wrong in her children . . . she had always assumed some weakness from Hank's side, though it might also have been the city, the schools they attended, the friends they had made, their liberal teachers. There were things children did in the city, but work was not one of them, and spending weekends riding with the vaqueros was just another form of entertainment, like dressage or skiing. Making it worse, in order to get to the ranch and back in time for school on Monday, it was necessary to fly there. Her children were not stupid. They knew that real vaqueros did not take private planes to work.

Meanwhile they had no constitution. Working them during the summer was out of the question. July and August were the hottest of hot months, hot as the plains of Africa, a branding fire you could never escape. Clothes soaked through in minutes, a filthy paste over every inch of skin, and while she'd grown up thinking this was normal, unpleasant but normal, her children could not stand it even for an hour. Susan had passed out and fallen off her horse.

J.A. was embarrassed by this, though no one else was. She had begun to doubt herself. It was only later, when the children were grown, that she knew she had been right, that once people grew used to free money, to laboring only when the mood struck them, they began to think there was something low about work. They became desperate to excuse their own laziness. They came to believe that their family property was something inherent to life itself, like water or air or clean sheets.

You ought to give all this money away right now, she thought. But it was too late. She had ruined her daughter; perhaps her son as well. She thought about this and felt sick . . . the money was not the only thing; she knew what she had done to her children. She could not figure out if leaving them more money was penance or some strange form of additional punishment. *You are a bad Christian,* she thought.

When her father died she had immediately stopped going to church. If prayer could not even keep your family alive, she did not see what good it was. But after she and Hank moved to Houston, she had started going again. You were marked if you didn't. She did not really think about whether she believed, though in the past decade, her faith had come back, and they said that was all that mattered. Being old, you had no real choice—salvation or eternal nothingness—and it was no wonder who you saw in church, it was not young people with hangovers and their entire lives ahead of them.

She remembered a sermon in which the minister named some of the interesting people you would meet in heaven: Martin Luther King Jr. (for the blacks), Mahatma Gandhi, Ronald Reagan. Except the minister would not have mentioned Gandhi. John Wayne, maybe. You wondered: all the interesting people in heaven, everyone would want to talk to them. It didn't take much thinking to realize that there would have to be a separate heaven for famous people, just like on earth, a place they would not be bothered, a private community. She wondered if she would go there. But in heaven there was no such thing as money, so perhaps people would stop caring about her. Trump, Walton, Gates, herself; they would be no more interesting than the garbagemen.

Of course it would be nice to be reunited with Hank, with her boys Tom and Ben, her brothers as well, but what about Ted, who had been her lover for twenty years after Hank? Someone would be jealous. And Thomas—that small detail—would he be there?

If you listened to what they said about heaven, it was a massive city with twelve gates. No eating, bowel movements, or sex; you lay around in a trance listening to harp music. Like a hospice you could never leave. She would sleep with every nice-looking man she met. Which of course meant she would be sent to hell.

Do not let me die, she thought. She opened her eyes. She was still on the floor of her living room, lying on the burgundy rug. The fire was still burning. Was the light growing? She couldn't tell. She willed her head to move, then her legs, but there was nothing.

CHAPTER SIX

DIARIES OF PETER McCULLOUGH

AUGUST 12, 1915

The newspapers are already running their version, straight from the mouth of the Colonel. The following will stand as the only true record:

Yesterday our segundo Ramirez was riding in one of the west pastures when he saw men driving whiteface cattle toward the river. As the Garcias still run mostly unimproved stock, it was obvious to whom the cattle belonged.

It was just after sundown when we caught them at the water. Most of the stock had already been crossed and the range was extreme, nearly three hundred yards, but everyone—Glenn, Charles, myself, the Colonel, Ramirez, our caporal Rafael Garza, and a handful of our other vaqueros—began shooting anyway, hoping to scare the thieves into abandoning the herd. Unfortunately they were old hands and instead of leaving the cattle, a few of them dismounted to shoot back while the others continued to drive the beefs into the *brasada* on the Mexican side. Glenn was hit in the shoulder, a Hail Mary shot from across the water.

Back at the house two Rangers were waiting along with Dr. Pilkington, whom Sally had called when she heard the shooting. The bullet had missed the artery but Glenn would need surgery and Pilkington thought it best to take him to the hospital in San Antonio. While he and Sally patched up Glenn, I spoke to the Ranger sergeant, a hard-faced little blond boy who looks like he escaped from a penitentiary. He is perhaps twenty but the other Ranger is conspicuously afraid of him. Beware the small man in Texas; he must be ten times meaner to survive in this land of giants.

A gang of Mexicans does not just shoot a white teenager without retaliation and I had wanted as many lawmen around as possible, but one look and I knew these Rangers were not going to help things. Still it was better than Niles Gilbert and his friends from the Law and Order League.

"How many more of you are coming?" I asked the sergeant.

"None. You are lucky we are even here. We are supposed to be in Hidalgo County." He went to spit on the rug but then stopped himself.

Of course the King Ranch has an entire company permanently stationed, but it was not worth mentioning.

We loaded Glenn into the back of Pilkington's car. Sally climbed in after him. Glenn looked pitiful and I wanted to ride with him but I knew I was the only voice of reason within twenty miles; if I left I did not want to imagine the scene I might return to.

Sally leaned out of the window and whispered: "You need to go kill every one of those bastards."

I did not say anything. Around here, talk like that turns quickly to action.

"You're the Colonel's son, Pete. Tonight you need to act like it."

"I think it was José and Chico," Glenn called out. "The way they sat their horses."

"It was pretty dark, buddy. And we were all pretty worked up."

"Well, I'm sure of it, Daddy."

Another kind of man would not be doubting his own son as he lay pale in the back of a car. But of course it was not him I was doubting at all; it was my father.

"All right," I told him. "You're a brave man."

They drove off. I doubted that Glenn really thought that he'd seen José and Chico until he'd heard the Colonel say it. My father can put ideas into other men's heads without them realizing.

✴ ✴ ✴

THE MOOD WAS to ride on the Garcias immediately, before they had time to barricade their casa mayor. All the vaqueros had gathered and were waiting outside, smoking cigarettes or chewing tobacco, ready to spill blood for their patrón.

A dozen or so white men had arrived as well: Sheriff Graham from Carrizo, two deputies, another Ranger, the new game warden. Additionally: Niles Gilbert, his two sons, and two members of the Law and Order League visiting from El Paso. Gilbert brought a case of Krag rifles and several thousand rounds of ammunition from his store, as he'd heard that others were coming as well.

"Coming for what?" I said.

"To help you all run them copper-bellies out."

"The copper-bellies in question are across the river," I said.

He gave me a look. I nearly pointed out that I have four years of college to his four years of grammar school. But he is one who believes that power is best used for the humiliation of other men. I might as well have explained myself to a donkey.

I have always possessed a near-perfect recall, of which both Charles and my father are quite aware, but neither supported me when I pointed this out to the others. It had been less than three hours, but the facts were already changing—men who had appeared as apparitions, their white shirts barely visible in the dusk, were now seen clearly. I reminded everyone that it had been too dark to identify any man—so dark, in fact, that the flashes from our guns left us blind—but it no longer mattered. In the light of memory, it was bright enough to see faces, and the faces belonged to the Garcias.

I suggested we might wait for more Rangers or the army—I was anxious to delay until daylight, when men become harder to lynch—but Charles, who spoke for most in the room, said firstly we could not let them get away with shooting Glenn, and secondly that the army would not be coming at all, as General Funston had made clear that he would only interfere if his soldiers were directly fired upon. He would not put his men to chasing common cattle thieves. Unless of course the cattle are King Ranch Brahmas.

At this I got even more depressed. The soldiers are the only government agents in South Texas who have no marked tendency to shoot Mexicans. As for the Rangers, they are both the best and the worst. The sergeant pointed out that there were only thirty-nine of them in the entire state of Texas; the fact we had three in the same room (a third had arrived from Carrizo) was a miracle.

A miracle for whom, I thought. The room had the atmosphere of a cattle association, old friends politely discussing grazing rights and which politicians we ought to be supporting and how we were going to keep our stock competitive in the northern markets. The Colonel chimed in from the peanut gallery and laid out a long argument in support of Charles, in what I have now begun to consider their usual unholy alliance. He claimed that Glenn's wounding was his responsibility, as he'd had a chance fifty years ago to push the Garcias off this land forever, and had not taken it, and damned if he was going to let the same thing happen twice in a single lifetime.

I pointed out that due to various events on our land our family tree had already shed quite a few leaves. My father pretended to ignore me.

"I have lost my mother here and a son and a brother," I said. "And now another son is on his way to the hospital. I would prefer to wait until daylight."

All agreed that our family had suffered great tragedies, but the best thing was to take Pedro as soon as possible. This was the community's problem now—not just ours—no telling who the Garcias' next victim might be.

I laid out another argument, namely that Pedro Garcia was as proud as any other man, and if pressed by a mob, he would certainly not give up his *yerno,* or any other member of his family, but if asked by the law, in the light of day, it would be a different story.

"We *are* the law," said the Ranger sergeant.

The others agreed. Not one of them would have considered surrendering to an armed mob in the middle of the night, but they did not see why the Garcias ought not to. I considered mentioning this but instead I said: "With due respect it might be better to wait until the sun comes up. Pedro will give up the guilty parties if they have anything to do with his family."

Not only was this suggestion dismissed, but now there was rumbling that I might retreat to the kitchen and sit it out with the other women. We would hold a little longer for reinforcements, which were certainly coming, as by now the word was out all over the four counties.

A SHOAT WAS killed and set roasting; a loin of beef set out with tortillas and beans, the good linen, the fireplace lit and coffee served. Men lounged in the great room, talking or flipping through old issues of *Confederate Veteran,* boots up, rifles askew in the palatial dark room with its drawings of Florentine ruins, its busts and statues, idly thumbing the engraving on the chairs and tables, resisting the urge to whittle with their pocketknives, everything around them bought wholesale from a dead Philadelphian, the contents of the entire house including the Tiffany windows bought and shipped, the house built to contain them. Not a single man asked about the marbles; they stopped to admire the picture of *Lee and His Generals,* a dime-store print they have in their own homes, then moved on for another serving of beef or coffee.

Around three A.M., fifteen more men arrived; an hour later another dozen drove up in two Ford trucks. Until then I'd been hopeful the plan would be scotched, as we had less than forty men, versus the Garcias' twenty or so, and them holding a virtual fortress. Now we had over sixty, all with repeating rifles, a few with Remington and Winchester automatics. The Colonel could not contain his satisfaction.

"One of your grandsons has been shot," I told him, "and the other is about to go to war. What you might be happy about I cannot fathom."

He gave me a look that said, for the thousandth time, how sorry he was that I had abandoned my studies to return to the ranch. I reminded myself that he is from another era. He cannot help it. Of course there is the third grandson I did not mention, my namesake, buried now next to my mother and brother.

I went upstairs to my office, lay in the dark among my books—the only comforting thing I have. An exile in my own house, my own family, maybe in my own country. Outside the coyotes were yipping in the distance; on the gallery the vaqueros were talking in quiet Spanish. Someone told a joke. If they were nervous or had second thoughts about attacking their own countrymen, I could not hear it. I knew things would get worse.

I must have fallen asleep because I heard someone shouting my name. At first I thought it was my mother calling me down for supper; we were back in the old house in Austin with its green fields and woods and streams running all night. My mother and her soft hands, the scent of roses lingering everywhere she walked. I thought about those things and allowed myself to forget where I was, and for a few moments I was certain I was young again, that we had not yet moved out to this monstrous country where all our misfortunes began. How the Colonel can love the place that has claimed so many members of our family, and may yet claim a few more, I don't know.

IT WAS NEARLY five in the morning when we rode out. Nearly seventy men. Everyone had been up all night but was as somber and awake as if we were riding to Yorktown or Concord. The Colonel wore the buckskin vest that is famous in town, everyone believing that it is made from Apache scalps. Even the Rangers were deferring to him, as if they were in the presence of a general, rather than an old man who was not even a real colonel, but a brevet colonel, and had fought for the cause of human slavery.

The vaqueros formed a flying squad around him; the Colonel has no great respect for the Mexicans and yet they are all willing to die for him. I, on the other hand, consider myself their ally—no patrón has ever been more generous—and they despise me.

✴　✴　✴

AN HOUR BEFORE sunrise we hobbled the horses and made our way on foot toward the Garcias' house, which overlooks the surrounding country with its watchtower and high stone walls and parapets. A hundred years ago it was a bastion of civilization in a desert, a stronghold against a wilderness of Indians, but now, in the minds of the men marching toward it, it had come to be something else: the guardian of an old, less civilized order, standing against progress and all that was good on the earth.

I slipped off into the brush. I noticed the Colonel squatting nearby. He looked at me and grinned and I couldn't tell if he was smiling because he was looking forward to the gunplay or because he was proud of me for coming out for the old family ritual.

As for our neighbors from town, they all considered themselves great heroes but not a single one had lived here during the old days; they had kept their distance until it was safe. I wondered how I had ended up on the same side as men like that. For that reason alone I thought I ought to be making my stand with the Garcias.

Shortly thereafter I came across Charles. He was very nervous and I asked him to come home with me, to wash his hands of whatever was about to happen, but it was out of the question. He thought he was about to take part in an important ritual; he was about to become a man. I had always worried he might be bitten by a snake or kicked by a horse or gored or trampled, but he had survived all those things and somehow I had still failed him. Here he was, sweating despite the cool night, gripping his rifle, ready to make war on men who had attended his christening.

The Garcia casa mayor overlooked what was left of their old village, a few small buildings and an old *visitas,* all built of adobe or caliche blocks, several acres of *corrales de leña.* A stone wall surrounded the yard—a leftover from the days when you fenced cows out, rather than in—and that was where we made our line, the house surrounded on three sides, at a distance of fifty or sixty yards. The somber mood had not changed. This was no mere lynching; it was an overturning of the ancient order, the remaking of things for a new world.

Then Pedro was standing there. His thick gray hair was combed neatly back; he was wearing a clean white shirt and his pants were tucked into clean boots. He looked surprised as he searched the crowd, noting his many neighbors, men whose families he knew, whose wives and children he knew. With the stiff shuffle of a man mounting the scaffold, he walked out onto the gallery, to the edge of the stairs. He began to speak but had to clear his throat.

"My sons-in-law are not here. I don't know where they are but I would like to see them hanged the same as the rest of you. Unfortunately they are not here."

He gave an embarrassed shrug. If there is a worse sight than a proud man brought to terror, I have not seen it.

"Perhaps some of you might come inside and we can discuss how to find them."

I set down my rifle and stepped over the wall and walked until I was standing in the middle of Pedro's yard, between our men and his. Everyone on our side looked nervous, but they quickly got angry, as they saw I intended to rob them of their fun.

"I am going to talk to Pedro," I told them. "If the sergeant and his men would care to come inside with me, we can figure this all out."

I looked at the sergeant. He shook his head. Maybe he worried it was a trap; maybe he worried it *wasn't* a trap—it was hard to tell.

"Most of you know that Glenn is my son," I continued. "And the cattle lost were mine as well. This is no one's fight but my own. And I do not want it."

Everyone stopped looking at me. Glenn and our cattle no longer had anything to do with this. They settled on their knees and haunches, as if, without a single word exchanged, they had all decided that I did not exist, the way a flock of birds changes direction without any individual appearing to lead. There was a shot somewhere to my right, and then, all at once, a rolling volley from our line. I heard and felt the bullets crack past my head and I fell to the grass.

Pedro fell as well. He lay on the porch clutching his stomach but two men rushed out and pulled him inside as the bullets splintered the doorframe around them.

Over the top of the low rock wall I could see all our neighbors, their heads and gun barrels showing, the smoke puffing out and the shiny brass casings levering through the air, the spray of dust and stone as bullets slapped into the wall. I couldn't move without being shot by one side or the other so I lay there with the grass underneath me and the bullets over top. I felt strangely safe, then wondered if I'd already been shot; there was a feeling of drifting, as if I were in a river, or in the air, looking down from a great height, it was all pointless, we might as well have never crawled from the swamps, we were no more able to understand our own ignorance than a fish, staring up from a pool, can fathom its own.

The bullets continued to snap overhead. I was looking at Bill Hollis when a pale cloud appeared and his eyes went wide as if he'd had some realization. His rifle clattered over the wall and he lay down his head as if taking a nap. I had a vision of him playing the fiddle in our parlor while his brother sang.

Meanwhile the house was being shot to pieces. The heavy oak door, three hundred years old and brought from a family estate in Spain, was nothing but splinters. The parapets were disintegrating, the top of the stone tower as well. The caliche *sillares* were remnants from another era, suitable for stopping arrow and ball but not jacketed bullets, there was a thick cloud of dust rising from the house, the dust of its own bones.

Finally there was no return fire. Sometime during the fight the sun had risen and the beams of light were shining through the old gunports. Every door and window hung from splinters; except for the fresh dust the house might have been abandoned a century ago. I began to inch toward the wall.

"Reload," someone shouted. "Everyone reload."

I reached the wall and crawled over it. The young Ranger sergeant was talking to the men gathered: " ... I go through the door, you follow me, get out of the doorway as soon as you can but don't move faster than you can shoot. The Mexicans will be in the corners. Do not pass a corner, do not turn your back to a corner, unless you or someone else is shooting into it."

He raised his head so everyone could see him.

"When I stand up," he called out, "I want you to empty your guns at the building. But as soon you see me clear this wall, you stop firing. You hear?"

I did not trust that anyone had heard. Between the ringing ears and the spectacle of destruction before us, everyone was in his own world. But somehow most agreed and those who did not had the instructions shouted into their ears.

When the sergeant stood up, there was a long volley that did not stop until finally he waved his hands and shouted for a long time and then he and a dozen other men, including Charles, rushed for the gallery. I called for Charles to come back, but he didn't hear me, or pretended not to, and then I noticed that fat old Niles Gilbert had not gone, nor had either of his two sons.

The front door was so shattered they just walked right through it. The shooting began again, the tempo increasing as each man entered the house until it was nearly continuous. We couldn't see any of what was happening inside, dark shapes passing behind the doors or windows, a few bullets leaking out and kicking up dirt in the yard. Then it got quiet and then there was a sudden *pop pop pop*. Then it got quiet and then there were more orphaned shots. After that I couldn't bear to look. In the distance I could see the Nueces and the green river flats all around, the sun continuing to rise, catching in the pall of dust, the air around the casa mayor turning a brilliant orange as if some miracle were about to occur, a descent of angels, or perhaps the opposite, a kind of eruption, the ascent of some ancient fire that would wipe us all from the earth.

I looked for some sense in it. It was the best piece of land for miles—high, well-watered ground—we had not been the first to fight here. If we were to scratch the earth we would find the bones of crushed legs, ribs gashed from spears.

Then someone was waving his hat. It was Charles. His shirt was in tatters and his arm was bleeding. He shouted for us to put down our guns, but no one moved so I stood and stepped over the wall again, waving my arms and walking up and down the line so the others would lower their rifles.

I ATTEMPTED TO tend to Charles's arm but he pushed me away. It appeared to be birdshot.

"Let me look at it," I said.

"It doesn't even hurt yet." Then, as if I had some disease, he would not allow me any closer.

Inside the house, it looked as if workmen had been called to perform a demolition. Or vandals let into a museum. Antique furniture shot to pieces, upholstery shredded and the stuffing spilled as if the house had been invaded by a swarm of birds, ancient dark paintings of matriarchs and patriarchs, a Byzantine portrait of Christ, antique quilts, sketches, weapons, crosses, all punctured or smashed or knocked onto the floor. An illuminated Bible, the pride of Pedro's family, fallen from its place in the *altarcito* and splayed open in the plaster.

In the living room I counted five dead men and one dead woman, shot so many times that every drop of blood had leaked from their bodies and mixed with the splinters and dust and gutted upholstery. One looked old enough to be Pedro but when I turned him over it was Cesár, a vaquero, a man who had helped us on roundups since I was a boy. In kneeling to turn him my pants soaked through and when I stood up the fabric stuck darkly to my legs.

Underneath one of the sofas something caught my eye: a young girl in a blue dress. Next to her a boy of six or eight, dead as well. By then a barricade had gone up between my eyes and mind; I saw them with scientific interest; here was the blood, there were the holes. Smaller details: standing pools of bright crimson, handprints and bootprints and long smears where the wounded had been dragged, bloody spray over the walls indicating some final moment, some story which would never be told. A young man with the white of his spine, another stretched out as if drunk; his brains had been spooned out onto his shirt. I saw others looking with the same cool interest; when blood does not belong to your kin it might as well be wine or water.

In the kitchen, six dead; three of Pedro's vaqueros—Romaldo, Gregorio, and Martín—along with Pedro's middle daughter, Carmen. Two men staring at each other over the crumpled bodies of Pedro's twin granddaughters, the same white dresses and pigtails. The room smelled like an abattoir; blood and the musky smell of opened bellies, waste from the bodies, but there was something sweet as well—roses— which I suspected my mind had invented from a swamp of confused sensations.

I went to Pedro's office. It was surprisingly untouched and I felt tired; I sat down in the chair opposite his desk as I had done many times. I resolved I would let the others make the necessary discoveries. Though of course that would be worse. There was no absolution. I got up and followed the scent of rosewater toward one of the bedrooms, where the door was perforated with two large holes from a shotgun, plaster dust grinding under my feet.

At the far end of the room, in the middle of his canopy bed, Pedro lay on his back as if taking a nap. The scent of rosewater was so strong I nearly retched. A small price. When I got closer I saw his face, the pillow and bedclothes stained. Something—a pair of teeth— had been knocked from his mouth. A few white feathers had settled on his face.

There had been a fight here—the back wall was pocked by bullets, the dressers and wardrobes splintered, jewelry scattered. I thought I heard Pedro speaking, but it was just a trick of my ringing ears. Near the foot of the bed lay Aná, Pedro's youngest daughter, her church dress soaked to the waist, her back and neck arched as if she had gathered her energy to shout something. There was an old Colt Army.

Lourdes Garcia was on the other side of the bed, still gripping a Spanish fowling piece.

Just then the game warden came into the room, surveyed the damage, and told me not to touch the bodies.

"If you do not get the hell out of here," I told him, "you will be looking for another job tomorrow."

I straightened Aná's skirts and placed her and Lourdes in the bed with Pedro. It was a pointless gesture. They would soon be carried outside. I left the room.

In one of the closets in another bedroom we found a woman in her thirties. She was alive. *¿Estás herida?* I guessed it was María, the unmarried daughter, but her face was so filthy and bloody and her eyes so wild I couldn't be sure. She looked at me. She submitted as I ran my fingers over her scalp and through her hair to check for wounds, then opened her shirt quickly to check front and back for the same, then closed it again, then lifted her skirts to check her hip and waist area. She was not injured. She sat dumbly as I straightened her clothes.

I led her outside and turned her over to Ike Reynolds and his sons, whom I know to be respectable. A minute later they rode off. What family she has left I don't know; the Garcias have been in this country far longer than any of the white families. They were once proper hidalgos, having been granted this land by the king of Spain himself. Pedro never spoke of any family in Mexico; he did not think of himself as Mexican.

Outside the sun was all the way up. Charles and one of the Rangers had both been hit by birdshot, but the pellets had not gone deep. I thought of the shotgun lying next to Lourdes. I wondered if Charles had killed her, or if he had killed Pedro, or maybe Aná.

Niles Gilbert's friend from El Paso, who had been so anxious to "naturalize" some Mexicans, had been shot through the mouth. A brief sense of satisfaction rose within me, then slipped away; he would go down a martyr. The small blond Ranger sergeant had been hit in the hand and forearm and the stock of his carbine split by a bullet.

Wounded or not, the twelve living assaulters sat dumbly on the porch, some lying on their backs, others dangling their legs over the edge, staring at the roof or into the sky. Sullivan was lifting their shirts to check them for injuries, shouting instructions into their ears. I wondered again if Charles had been the one to shoot Pedro and Lourdes, but pushed away the question a second time.

Meanwhile, the men at the wall had begun to come forward. Bill Hollis had been laid out in the shade. His brother Dutch was sitting next to him. Four others were carried over. I could tell that one was a vaquero of ours, though I did not have the heart to get up and see who it was.

A FEW HOURS later the photographer showed up. The Rangers posed with the bodies of the male Garcias, the faces shot off most of the dead men, a detail that would be lost in the printing. They would look blurred, overdirty, as the faces of all dead men do.

No one commented on the absence of Pedro's sons-in-law. It was just as he had told us—they were not in the house. The bodies of the women and children were placed in the shade, away from their men, perhaps out of some old-fashioned impulse, perhaps so they would not show in the pictures.

Watching the photographer take pictures of townspeople posing with the Garcias—a loose queue had formed—I began to feel even more tired. I knew what anyone looking at the pictures would think, or rather not think, of the Garcias, whose remains were so matted with dust and dried blood that they were barely distinguishable from the caliche. The audience would notice only the living men, who had done a brave thing, while the dead would not even register as men. They were props—like a panther or dead buck—they had lived their entire lives in order to die for just this moment.

People from town continued to arrive, women and children now. Our vaqueros disappeared, taking the body of their fallen comrade, while the vigilantes and their wives went through the cupboards. The furniture inside the casa mayor was all quite valuable; most had come from the old country: old Spanish weapons and armor, a good deal of silver. The Garcias had once been quite wealthy and I knew when I returned I would find the house completely plundered.

As for myself, I have always known I will leave nothing behind me in this place, no sign I ever passed, but for the Garcias it was different, because they had hoped, and believed, that they would.

CHAPTER SEVEN

ELI McCULLOUGH

Two days after my brother died I was still in a fever. The Indians kept me tied to my horse. I was still in a fever and we were still on the Llano, and on the morning of the third day I saw something shining in the distance, which I took to be a city, and as we got closer I saw it was floating in the air, a shining city on a hill, and I knew my mother had been right, that the heat or my fever or some hilarious Indian had killed me and I would soon be joining the rest of my family. I knew I ought to be happy but I felt sadder than I'd ever been.

When we got closer I saw it wasn't a city at all. It was a box canyon and it was still floating miles above us, as if a range of mountains had been carved out of the earth; there was a long shining river and drifting herds of deer and my mother had not been right at all. I was being taken by the Indians to their happy hunting ground, where I would remain their prisoner even in death.

I had a dauncy spell but no one heard me over the wind. Soon after, we reached the thing itself. It was a proper canyon cut into the earth but some mirage in the sky was reflecting it. It was even larger than the mirage made it look—a dozen miles across and a thousand feet deep, with fins and towers and hoodoos like observation posts, mesas and minor buttes, springs flowing brightly in the red rock. There were cottonwoods and hackberries, and the valley floor was thick with grass and wildflowers.

We took an hour dropping into it, then made an early camp next to a clear stream. There was a skull with an enormous tusk all turned to stone and sticking out of the bank. I wondered what my brother would have made of it. The Indians were relaxed. For my own protection I was kept tied to a tree, though the Germans were allowed to wander and by her yellow hair I could see one sitting on a far butte. The Indians were not worried; there were wolf and grizzly and panther tracks everywhere and it was no place to be playing a lone hand.

A few deer were killed and a yearling buffalo. Wild potatoes and turnips and sweet onions were dug up, braided, and roasted in the fire. The animals were carefully skinned, the meat filleted from the bones, coals raked out and the big roasts placed on them. The bones were put in the fire and when everything was ready they were cracked and the marrow spread on the potatoes. There were handfuls of chokecherries for dessert and a lemonade made from sumac. Everyone was full as a tick but finally the hump of the buffalo was dug out of the coals; it was dripping with fat and came apart in our fingers. It was the best I'd eaten since I'd left home and at the thought of that I got dauncy again and Nuukaru came over and slapped me.

By sundown the walls of the canyon looked to be on fire and the clouds coming off the prairie were glowing like smoke in the light, as if this place were His forge and the Creator himself were still fashioning the earth.

"Urwat leaves tomorrow," Toshaway said. When the others turned in I was tied down for sleep as I'd been since my brother died—my arms and legs roped to separate stakes in the ground. Toshaway put his buffalo robe over me. The stars were too bright to sleep, the Dipper, Pegasus, the serpent and dragon, Hercules; I watched them turn while meteors left smoking trails that stretched across the canyon.

A few of the Indians had their way with the Germans. This time I tried not to listen.

✷ ✷ ✷

THE NEXT MORNING the spoils of the raid—weapons, tools, equipment, horses, anything valuable including the German girls and me—were set out and divided. The older girl went with Urwat's group; the younger girl and I with Toshaway's. The younger girl was crying as Urwat's group rode away with her cousin, and there was a patch of long dark hair, my mother's, tied to the saddle of a horse in Urwat's band. Nuukaru came over and slapped me. I knew he was doing me a favor.

After climbing back onto the Llano we didn't see water all day. A few hours before sundown we camped at a small playa lake sunk beneath the level of the grass. It was invisible from more than a hundred yards distance and how the Indians had navigated to it, I had no idea, as the plain was so flat and empty you could see the curve of the earth.

Toshaway and Nuukaru led the blond girl and me to the far end of the lake and after we washed ourselves we lay on our bellies while they lanced all the boils and blisters from riding and cleaned our other wounds as well. Our legs and backsides were rinsed with a bark tea and covered with a poultice made from pear pad innards and coneflower root. Despite the sunburn and saddle sores on her legs and rear end, now that she was cleaned up, the German girl was quite beautiful. I looked at her and hoped we might connubiate but she ignored me. I guessed she'd been a haughty one like my sister. Then I couldn't look at her.

Mostly they treated her like an expensive horse, taking care with her feed and water but hitting or throwing sticks if she did anything that got their ire up. I was given plenty of lather myself but never without an explanation; Toshaway and Nuukaru spoke to me constantly, pointing things out, and I was picking up the language already: *paa,* water; *tuhuya,* horse; *tehcaró,* eat. *Tunetsuka*—keep going.

A few days later we came to a big river that I guessed was the Canadian. The country improved. By then, neither I nor the girl were tied up at all. We'd been riding at an easy pace, eating and drinking and nursing our wounds, and even the horses were putting on flesh.

Two buffalo calves were killed and for a change the liver was put on the coals along with all the heavy bones, the warm marrow spread on the liver like butter. Toshaway kept passing me more meat and there was more curdled calves' milk, which got sweeter each time I tried it.

The next morning I woke up thinking about my father and how even with a group of willing men he never would have been able to catch us. Even a young Indian like Nuukaru would have lost them. The Comanches left conflicting trails at every patch of soft ground, changed direction at every stretch of rock or hardpan, took note of the natural line of travel across a landscape and rode a different way. A detour that cost them a few minutes would confuse a pursuer for hours. I had never felt so alone in my life.

I got up to find the Indians. I could hear voices at the river and found all the warriors bathing themselves, scrubbing off the dirt and old war paint. Some were sitting naked in the sun, looking into tiny hand mirrors or small pieces of cracked glass, and, with steel tweezers they must have gotten from the whites, they were plucking all the hair from their faces. When that was done they took small pouches of vermilion and other dyes from their possibles, which they ground with spit to form a paste, then put on their paint, color by color. Each man parted his hair down the middle and rewove his braids and dyed the part red or yellow. *Puha nabisaru,* said Toshaway. He was working on his braids as well. Everyone was feeling grandacious, as if getting dressed for a night of beauing.

I was put to scrubbing down the horses with grass. Each warrior repainted his pony with stripes and handprints. Two of the younger Indians rode away over the hills and didn't return.

The captured scalps were washed and brushed and attached to the tops of lances. I knew my mother's was gone and I couldn't see my sister's, either. I decided it had been Urwat's men who'd killed her.

The girl and I were tied to the horses for the first time in days. To our left the southern bank of the Canadian was a sheer cliff and to the north it was shallow breaks and hills and buttes. We followed a small stream up into the trees and came on a procession of Indians, hundreds of them, all in their best bib and tucker, painted leggings and buckskin dresses, copper bracelets and earrings sparkling and jouncing. The younger boys were naked and they came shouting and dodging among the horses. We kept going and reached the main body; it was like the parade they had when my father returned from the war. Women were calling to men and neighbors calling to neighbors and a somber old grandmother was carrying a pole with scalps attached. Some of the braves tied their scalps to the pole. The children avoided me but the adults all pinched or slapped me as I rode past.

Then we reached the village. The tipis went on out of sight, swirling designs of warriors and horses, soldiers stuck with arrows, soldiers without heads, mountains and rising suns. The air smelled like green hides and drying flesh; there were racks standing everywhere with the flayed meat hanging in the sun like old clothes.

A group of angry-looking Indians pushed through the others. The women were wailing and keening and the men were thumping their lances in the dirt. They beat my legs and tried to pull me off my horse. Toshaway let this go on until one of the old women came at me with a knife. No one paid any attention to the German girl.

There was a long negotiation over my future, with the group of wailing women believing it should be settled with a knife or something worse. Toshaway was defending his property. I was sure it was the family of the man I'd shot, though Toshaway was the only person who could have known I was the culprit.

Nuukaru later explained that the dead man's family was expecting spoils from the raid, but what they got instead was news that their man had taken a ball in the chest. They asked for a white scalp only to hear that my mother's and sister's scalps had gone north with the Yap-Eaters, that my brother had not been scalped as he had died too bravely, and that I was innocent (a lie) and more important I was Tosha-way's property and he would not allow them to give me a haircut. They asked after the three scalps on his belt, but those had been taken from soldiers during such legendary combat that he could not be expected to part with them. He could offer them two rifles. An insult. A horse, then. Five horses would be an insult. In that case he could offer them nothing. They knew the risks and they would be well taken care of by the tribe. Fine. They would take a horse.

Meanwhile, as it was a big haul of guns, ponies, and other supplies, the village was preparing a party. Of the seventy-odd horses captured, Toshaway gave most away to the men who had gone on the raid, one to the family of the dead man, and a few to some poor families who had come to him directly. You could not refuse to give a gift if someone asked for it. He was left with two new horses and me. Stingier war chiefs might keep the entire haul for themselves, but Toshaway's status was greatly improved.

After Toshaway settled with the dead man's family, he and I and Nuukaru rode to all the tipis. I stayed tied to the horse. At each place an old squaw would come over and pinch my leg to bruise it. There was frantic talking and laughing. After several hours I was hot and bored, stiff from being tied up; I could tell there were stories being told about me. Finally we arrived in Toshaway's neighborhood. Everyone was standing waiting. There was a good-looking teenage boy and girl, who I gathered were Toshaway's children, a woman in her late twenties, his wife, and a woman in her late thirties, his other wife.

When everyone finished catching up, three old men came over and untied me and told me to follow them. We were off just like that, between the tipis, around cookfires and staked-out hides, racks of dry-ing meat, tools and weapons scattered everywhere. An old squaw came out of nowhere and slapped me between my legs. I was already sick from nervousness and the rotting meat and the flies swarming. Then a young brave came out of nowhere and hit me in the jaw. I turtled up as he kicked but then he stopped and had a talk with the old men. He had blue eyes and I knew he was white and after a few minutes he walked away as if nothing had happened.

The three old men found a place to sit near someone's tipi. It was late in the afternoon and nice in the sun, the land was open and rolling, the forest was behind us, there were horse herds grazing in the distance, several thousand animals at least. I sat listening to the creek. I'd dozed off when two of them pinned my arms back and rolled me over. The oldermost squatted at my head, I could smell his reeking breechcloth; I was sure I would air my paunch, which bothered me more than the idea of dying, and then Nuukaru came over and I relaxed.

The oldermost was doing something in the fire. When he came back he knelt next to me with a hot awl that he stuck through my ears a few times. Nuukaru was sitting on top of me so I had no air to protest. They threaded strings of greased buckskin through the holes in my ears and let me up.

Then I was given some sumac lemonade and some meat was skewered on sticks that were poked into the ground over the fire. As we sat waiting, a young fat squaw came up and hugged me, slapped me, pushed me into the grass, and climbed on top of me, wrestling the way you might with a dog. I let her drag me around and sit on me and stick my face into a mud puddle that smelled like feet. She held my nose so I'd have to open my mouth to breathe in the mud. After a while she got bored. I went back to the fire. Someone passed me a gourd of water to wash up. Someone else was heating up a kind of sauce in a small metal pan, honey and lard, stirring it with the rib bone from a deer. Everything was smelling finer than cream gravy, but just when we began to eat, Toshaway's son came over and said something. The old men clucked and shook their heads. I saw the family of the dead man making their way toward us and I knew they'd decided to dig up the hatchet.

Nuukaru clapped me on the back for support, then everyone followed as I was led by the neck to an open area in the middle of the village. A big post had been driven into the ground. I was tied to it.

From looking at the people gathered it was clear Judge Lynch was holding court and then three teenage Indians were pacing around me, pointing pistols at my head.

Their sap was up and I expected them to shoot but they were waiting for more people. Finally most of the village was there; children running in and out of the crowd, putting pieces of wood and brush around my legs until there was a pile to my waist.

The young Indians cocked their pistols and pressed them to my temple, into my mouth. My guts went loose. An old squaw came over with a skinning knife and I nearly released my innards, thinking I was about to be unshucked whole, but all she did was give me a few bleeders. Then I had to let some air out, which everyone found hilarious because they knew I was scared. *Pakatsi tsa kuya?atʉ. Pakatsi tsa tʉ?ʉyatʉ!*

Nʉʉkaru was standing at the front of the crowd, watching things; he was the same awkward age as my brother, tall and gangly, he would not be much help. The old woman walked away and one of the boys aimed his pistol and pulled the trigger. It pocked my face and singed my eyebrows but he hadn't loaded a ball. The other two did the same. Then a kid ran up with a torch and feigned at lighting the pile of brush. I nodded at where I thought he ought to start the fire. I encouraged him and finally he lit the brush. The hair between my thighs began to sizzle and I was about to give up when Toshaway walked over and kicked away the burning sticks.

Toshaway made a speech to the villagers, the gist of which was I hadn't minded the idea of being burned or shot to death. The Indians highly approved of that outlook and a few of them slapped me on the back as I returned to Toshaway's tipi. His wives poured tea over my cuts and burns and cleaned my face and dressed me in a new breechcloth. But before all that I went and squatted in the brush till I'd got the evil out of me.

☆   ☆   ☆

THE PARTY BEGAN at suppertime. Later Nuukaru told me this wouldn't normally have been done because a man had been lost on the raid, but in this case no one liked the family and it was hoped they would move on.

There was venison, elk, and buffalo, quail and prairie dog, bones roasted so the marrow could be spread on meat or mixed with mesquite beans and honey for dessert. There were potatoes and onions, corn bread and squash they'd gotten from the New Mexicans. The Comanches traded with the New Mexicans for nearly everything, and also the people at Bent's Fort on the Arkansas River. For corn, squash, and pumpkins, white and brown sugar, tortillas and hard breads, guns, powder, bar lead, and bullet molds. Ornaments for horses, percussion caps and steel knives, hatchets, axes and blankets, ribbons, linens and shrouds, gartering and gun screws, lance- and arrowheads, barrel hoops, bridles, steel wire, copper wire, gold wire, bells of all sizes, saddlebags, iron stirrups, iron pots, brass pots, mirrors and scissors, indigo and vermilion, glass beads and wampum, tobacco and tinder boxes, tweezers, combs, and dried fruit. The Comanches were the wealthiest of all the Indian tribes and spent half of what they made on baubles and cheap jewelry, though they did not, as some have written, care much for the white man's clothing, for top hats or stockings or wedding veils.

After everyone had eaten his fill the oldermost of the tribe began the dance and a warrior was called out and handed a long slender pole with scalps attached. The warrior told a story of bravery and called another warrior, who took the scalp pole and told a story and called up someone else. To tell a lie would bring a curse on the entire tribe and finally a brave was called who didn't have any story better than the ones already told, and instead of talking he took up the scalp pole and began to dance. The people followed him in a big milling circle. I was standing watching. I had been scrubbed clean and painted and was wearing my breechcloth. The three old men had plucked out my eyebrows and the few scraggling hairs off my chin and upper lip. The drums beat and the Indians stepped in time; I was put into the circle and the scalp pole was handed to me and I was pushed to the front. After a few minutes I tried to hand it to the man behind me but he shoved me forward. The drums went faster, the air was red from the setting sun, I saw the wives of the man I'd killed and the next time I saw them they hadn't moved and I knew the scalp pole was protecting me. They would not touch me as long as I held it. Several hours later the moon was up and I could barely stay awake, my feet hurt from stamping and my shoulders burned, but the Indians kept me at the front; there was grunting and whooping, the calls of bear and buffalo, panthers, deer, and elk.

WHEN I WOKE up everything was black. I was under a robe. A small disk of dark sky over my head, a dying fire off to one side, the sound of someone breathing. It was peaceful. I was in a tipi on a soft bed of skins; I'd been washed again and rubbed with oil and my wounds dressed; I was clean and warm and rolled in a soft blanket. There was something about the person breathing, I got to feeling dauncy and it was like the Bible-thumpers say when you're dunked: you think the world is one way and then you come up and find you've been wrong about everything.

I got up from my pallet and went outside. There were stars and as far as I could see there were tipis glowing from their nightfires, around the bonfire people were still awake, talking softly. Women leaning on their men, children asleep against their parents. From some of the tipis there was snoring and in others there was giggling and in others there were women moaning, which went on for a long time and I got excited and then I thought of times I had heard my mother and father doing that, not to mention the few times I had imagined doing it to my sister, which of course I was ashamed of, more now than I'd been before.

I heard someone rustle in their sleep, either Nuukaru or Tosha-way's son Escuté. I decided I would find Urwat and the rest of the Yap-Eaters and I would take from them a collection of scalps so long it would trail behind my horse ten miles.

As for Toshaway and his family, he had saved me and he had tried to save my brother. He might have saved my mother and sister if he had known better. But the Indians had their rules same as we had ours. My father and I had once shot at a pair of runaway slaves collecting pecans from under our trees. My gun snapped and misfired and my father's shot went yards high. I couldn't understand as the niggers were barely at eighty paces and my father the best rifle shot in the county. Then they were dark streaks running through the forest. I said we ought to get Rufe Perry and his nigger dogs but my father said it was likely to rain and we had rows yet to hoe. I asked where the slaves were headed and he said Mexico, most likely, or to live out with the Indians, who would take in Negroes and other types as long as they lived according to their laws. I said how can they take in niggers to live among them? He said plenty of people do. I could not think of anything except I was sorry my gun had snapped and he told me one day I would be thankful for small mercies.

I could hear Nuukaru and Escuté breathing deeply. I listened as long as I could before I fell asleep myself.

CHAPTER EIGHT

J. A. McCULLOUGH

S he was young again, riding an old wooden roller coaster, but
something was going wrong—the cars were running faster and
faster until finally at the very top, the whole train of them leaped
from the tracks. She was flying and then she was not, she was watching
the ground, everything was taking a long time, *This is very serious,* she
thought, and then all the cars came down on top of her.

Then she was in the desert. The biggest frac job of her life, the
engineer directing tankers like the conductor of a symphony; the lines
were charged, twelve thousand PSI, and then a coupler broke. A solid
iron pipe whipped like a snake. Her eyes were stinging, she was looking right into the sun, there was a Life Flight on the way, but it wouldn't
do any good. *Yes,* she thought. *That is what happened.*

She opened her eyes again. Except there had been a man, she was
certain of it. She wondered if he'd gone for help. She watched the logs
and embers in the fireplace. The burgundy rug spread beneath her,
its birds and flowers and curlicues, the busts of old Romans. She was
dreaming.

She wondered how people would remember her. She had not
made enough to spread her wealth around like Carnegie, to erase any
sins that had attached to her name, she had failed, she had not reached
the golden bough. The liberals would cheer her death. They would

light marijuana cigarettes and drive to their sushi restaurants and eat fresh food that had traveled eight thousand miles. They would spend all of supper complaining about people like her, and when they got home their houses would be cold and they'd press a button on a wall to get warm. The whole time complaining about big oil.

People thought Henry Ford had ushered in the automobile age. False. Cart before the horse. It was Spindletop that had begun the automobile age and Howard Hughes, with his miraculous drill bit, who had completed it. Modern life was born at the Lucas gusher, when people suddenly realized how much oil there might be on earth. Before that, gasoline was nothing more than a cheap solvent—used to clean gears and bicycle chains—and all the oil that made John Rockefeller a millionaire was burned in lamps, a replacement for whale oil. It was Spindletop and the Hughes bit that had opened the way for the car, the truck, and the airplane, which all depended on cheap oil the way a church depended on God.

She had done right. Made something out of nothing. The human life span had doubled, you did not get to the hospital without oil, the medicines you took could not be made, the food you ate did not reach the store, the tractor did not leave the farmer's barn. She took something useless under the ground and brought it to the surface, into the light, where it meant something. It was creation. Her entire life.

Once, she had not been unique in this. The industrialists built the country, the oilmen made it run. Now it was just the oilmen. The industrialists, or whatever they called themselves these days, led lives based on destruction, closing down factories and moving them abroad. She did not expect to be loved but there were bastards and there were bastards; those men had taken apart the country brick by brick and if there was anything she hated more than unions, it was people who couldn't work.

Other memories came back in a rush. Visiting the houses of the Mexican hands with her father, the women out of another century, pregnant and carrying water buckets from distant wells, irons over a wood fire, bluing to steaming washpots, wringing the boiling clothes. Canning fruits and vegetables in the worst of the summer heat—hotter in the jacals than it was outside. The men in the shade, braiding lariats from horsehair. *Why don't they buy their ropes from the store?* she asked, but her father didn't answer.

Walking through the pasture hours before sunup, crouching low to find the horses against the dark sky. All around her, the hands roping their mounts. Blowing of horses, clicking of cinches, voices soothing in Spanish. Some of the ponies gave in to the rope, others bucked and kicked, not wanting to spend the day running in the sun and thorns. Many of them were nothing but scar tissue from wither to hoof; the brush took all the hair off.

A never-ending creak of windmills, kneeling with the Colonel to study the wet ground at the stock tanks, the night's fresh tracks. Cattle, deer, foxes, javelina, rabbits, paisano, hares, mice, raccoons, snakes, turkey, bobcats. The appearance of a panther track brought her father and brothers, an old Mexican with his dogs. At some point, she did not remember when, the Colonel began to put his hand over every panther track he saw, obliterating it completely. *Don't tell anyone.* The adult world ran on secrets. The derision of her father and brothers when she said she wanted to see a wolf or bear. They are better in zoos, said her father. They are better gone forever.

And what had she learned? She had lost half her family before their time. The land was hard on its sons, harder yet on the sons of other lands. Her grandmother had once proposed a bounty for each pair of Mexican ears—*treat them the same as coyotes.* She thought of her brothers killed by the Germans, her uncle Glenn blown to bits in a trench.

She had tried to retire twelve years ago. She had been a child kneeling by the stock tank and then her own children were middle-aged; she had not been perfect, she wanted to patch things, she wanted to know her grandchildren. There had been a window. But oil had been low, cheaper than water, they said, and the bids she got for her leases were a fraction of what they should have been. She knew it was her last chance to make things right with the family. But to sell at such a bottom—the thought made her physically ill.

Then the Arabs hit New York. She began hiring drillers. Her children had their own lives, they did not need her, oil began to climb. To see a well come in where there had just been desert, to see flow after a good frac job, from a hole everyone had given up on—that was what she lived for. Something out of nothing. Act of creation. There would always be time for family.

CHAPTER NINE

DIARIES OF PETER McCULLOUGH

AUGUST 13, 1915

Memory is a curse. When I close my eyes I see Pedro's shot-off face and the weeping hole in Lourdes's cheek, a clear fluid issuing forth like a tear. Aná's blood-soaked dress. When I sleep I am back in their room. Pedro is sitting up in bed, pointing at me, speaking in some ancient language, and as I get closer I realize the sound is not coming from his mouth, but from the hole in his temple. Upon waking I lie still a long time and hope for my heart to stop beating, as if death might absolve me from my place in this.

What happened at the Garcias' was only the beginning. In town, there are at least a hundred armed men that no one knows, carrying rifles and shotguns as if it were half a century ago, as if there were no town at all. Amado Batista was murdered sometime in the night, his store looted, an attempt made to burn the building though the fire did not catch.

The Garcias are described in all the papers as Mexican radicals; in truth they were the most conservative landowners in Webb and Dimmit Counties. The picture of their bodies is reprinted in every corner of the state and in Mexico, where, despite the fact that old landowners are not quite in favor, they will doubtless go down as martyrs.

Glenn remains in San Antonio, recovering at the hospital. Neither he nor Sally reacted to the news of the Garcias' annihilation. I wonder if I am going crazy or if I do not love my family enough, or if it is the opposite, if I love them too much. If I am the only sane person I know.

Meanwhile, the rooming houses are full of the worst sorts the Rio Grande Valley has to offer and the Rangers are having trouble keeping order. I suggested to Sergeant Campbell (Was he the one to shoot Pedro and Lourdes? Was it my own son?) that he send for the rest of his company, but they are occupied up and down the border, guarding other ranches.

Campbell, despite his mean looks, is troubled that half the dead were women and children. I refuse to talk to him about it. People like him think you can apologize things away, that you can confess over and over until you are free to repeat your crime.

OUR HOUSE WAS busy all day with well-wishers; at one point I drove into town to escape them, whereupon I came on two trucks with a dozen men each, well armed and hoping to make battle with Mexican insurgents. I told them everyone was dead. They looked disappointed but after some discussion they decided to go into town anyway: no point giving up hope just yet.

Returned to find Judge Poole eating our beef and drinking our whiskey and taking statements from all present. I gave him my story—*just the facts*—he corrected me several times—*not your interpretation.* Finally he asked me to step outside, away from the others.

"This is just a formality, Pete. Don't let anyone think I'll side with a wetback over a white man."

Nearly pointed out that *we* are the wetbacks, having swum our horses across the Nueces a century after the Garcias first settled here. But of course I said nothing. He clapped me on the back—his butcher's hands—and went in to eat more free beef.

People continued to arrive at the house, bringing cakes, roasts, and regrets that they had not been able to reach us in time to help—how brave we were to assault the Mexicans with such a small force. By that they mean seventy-three against ten. Fifteen if you count the women. Nineteen if you count the children.

AUGUST 14, 1915

Sally asked why I had not yet come to see Glenn at the hospital. I explained my reasons:

Three houses were burned last night and eight townspeople killed, all Mexican except Llewellyn Pierce, who had a Mexican wife.

Sergeant Campbell shot at least three looters, though two escaped into the brush. The dead man is from Eagle Pass. The three were in the process of setting fire to the home of Custodio and Adriana Morales. The Moraleses were already dead. I thought of Custodio and how he loved our fine horses; he always charged too little to repair the tack and other goods I brought him. I had been meaning to invite him over to ride for twenty years now.

Campbell confided that one of his men refused to shoot at white looters. Also a sheriff's deputy was found dead, but no one knew any details.

Campbell has cabled again for the rest of his company but was told that they were busy with bigger problems farther south.

"We need to do something about these Mexicans," he told me. "They're not going to be safe here."

He had not seemed very concerned about the safety of the Garcias. I did not say this but he must have read my face.

"Our job is to enforce the peace against anyone who disturbs it," he said. "I don't care what color they are."

SEVERAL TEJANO FAMILIES — the Alberto Gonzaleses, the Claudio Lopezes, the Janeros, Sapinosos, and the Urracas—left town this afternoon with all their belongings.

Campbell thinks tonight will be worse than last. His men are outnumbered fifty to one. "They've been talking about buying us machine guns," he said. "They should have done it already." Then he asked: "What do you think about this Sheriff Graham?"

"I think he will be sad if he misses out on all this looting."

"That's what I thought."

It was quiet. We sat there on the porch looking out over the country.

"What is it like to have all this?" he said.

"I don't know, really."

He nodded as if he'd expected this answer.

"Would you like some supper to bring with you for later?" I said.

He didn't reply. We looked toward the town but you cannot see it from the porch.

"Your old man is something, I'll say that."

"He's something all right."

"My daddy is dead," he said.

Something made me wonder if he were responsible for this condition. Still, I liked him. He could not have been over five foot five in boots and every man in town was afraid of him.

"What are you planning to do about tonight?"

"Shoot a lot of people, I guess."

"That does not sound like much of a plan."

"Well, that's what we got."

"Have you done much work like this?"

"I shot two guys in Beaumont. But this is like turkey season compared to that."

It was quiet.

"How do you do it?"

"You use your sights," he said.

AUGUST 15, 1915

The light of several fires visible from my window last night; gunfire sporadic but constant.

By morning another dozen Mexican families were gone; they appear to have left under their own power. Fourteen more dead, six of them white. On the phone, Campbell admitted that he was the one who shot the deputy the other evening. The deputy was wearing his badge and looting a house.

Charles and I drove into town and came on a Tejano man hanging from a live oak.

"That's Fulgencio Ypina," Charles said.

We stopped and Charles climbed the tree and cut him down. We lifted and deposited him as gently as possible in the back of the truck. Fulgencio had cleared brush for us for years. His body was already beginning to swell.

"Who is going to bury these people?" said Charles.

"I don't know."

"Is the army coming?"

"I don't know that, either."

"We should call Uncle Phineas."

"He is on a fishing trip."

"Well, you need to do something."

"Like what?"

"I don't know. But you need to."

THE STREETS WERE empty. There were handwritten signs posted everywhere:

ANYONE FOUND ON THESE STREETS AFTER DARK (INCLUDING WHITES) WILL BE SHOT. ORDER OF THE TEXAS RANGERS.

When we found Sergeant Campbell, he had been shot again, this time through the upper part of his calf. He was sitting in a chair in the back of the feed store with his boots off and his pants down.

"At least people seem to aim for your extremities," I joked. The leg did not look bad—the bullet had missed the bone and the artery.

Campbell was watching the doctor. "You get hit in the hands because your hands are in front of your chest when you aim a gun. And I got hit in the leg because when I shot the guy last night, he discharged his weapon when he fell over." He looked at me as if our ages were reversed.

"You can tell every Mexican family in town that they can come to my ranch," I said.

"That will make things easier on me." He did not seem to consider it a big favor. He continued to watch Guillermo Chavez, who at twenty-five is the town veterinarian, having taken over from his father. Chavez unbandaged his hand and arm.

"Who did these dressings?"

"I did. Are you a real doctor?"

"Mostly with animals."

"Licensed?"

"Look at me and take a guess."

Campbell shook his head: "This is a goatfuck."

"I am happy you are here," said Guillermo. "Which is something I never thought I would say to a *Rinche*."

Campbell ignored the insult. "What's gonna happen if those bones knit like that?"

"You'll have trouble with your hand." He shrugged. "But the fore-arm is the real trouble, because there is a lot of bruising and that will need to be cut out."

"Or I lose the arm?" His voice cracked and for an instant I saw Campbell for what he was, a scared twenty-year-old; but the mask quickly returned.

"Just keep packing this powder into it. When it begins to ooze and get sticky, add more. Always keep dry powder in the wound."

"That looks like yellow sugar."

"Sugar and sulfa."

"Table sugar."

"It's a reliable remedy. The sugar alone would be enough."

"This is fuckin' stupid."

"Use it or not, I don't care. Your colleagues in Starr County mur-dered my cousin, your colleagues in Brownsville murdered my uncle and his son, and here I am, fixing you up."

"There's rotten ones in every barrel," said Campbell.

"Tell that to Alfredo Cerda or Gregorio Cortez or Pedro Garcia. Or their wives and children, who are also dead. Your colleagues arrive and stir things up and the army comes and settles them down. But this is obvious. It is not even a matter for serious discussion."

Campbell was flexing his fingers to see if he could still grip his gun. "Do you have morphine?" he said to Guillermo. To me he said: "We can't pay you for the use of the ranch."

"When is the army getting here?"

"Never," he said.

"Well . . . One riot, one Ranger."

"Sure. Unless you're the one Ranger."

SALLY WAS FURIOUS that I'd invited all the Mexicans in the town to our house and immediately demanded I put Consuela on the phone. I could hear her ordering Consuela to have the other maids hide the silver and take up the expensive rugs. Consuela handed the phone back.

"What is wrong with you, Peter?"

"These people are going to die if they don't come here."

She didn't say anything.

"Glenn is going to be fine," I told her.

"You can't say that," she said. "You can't say that when you're not even here with him."

I HOPED THE Mexicans would make the move quietly, but by dark, half the Tejano residents of the town, nearly a hundred people, had walked, driven, or ridden up to the ranch, carrying, pushing, or pulling their valuables in donkey carts or handcarts or on their backs.

Midkiff and Reynolds, without being prompted, both sent men to help protect the Mexicans. *They are protecting our ranch,* the Colonel corrected me, *don't be an idiot.*

Campbell came to check in in person, deputized the eight men (though he had no legal power to do so), and returned to town, limping badly, his right arm in a sling. Somewhere he acquired a .351 Winchester, which can be operated with one hand. I did not ask how he got it. We have chained and locked the gates to the ranch and Charles and the vaqueros have dug themselves in by the road.

CHAPTER TEN

ELI / TIEHTETI

1849

The Kotsoteka Comanche lived mostly along the Canadian River, where the Llano ended and the dry plains turned into grassy canyonlands. Historically they'd ranged down to the outskirts of Austin; Toshaway knew my family's headright better than I did. The Texans had signed a treaty saying that there would be no more settlements west of town, but in the end they were a certain breed, and when an agreement became troublesome, they did not mind breaking it.

"One day a few houses appeared," said Toshaway. "Someone had been cutting the trees. Of course we did not mind, in the same way you would not mind if someone came into your family home, disposed of your belongings, and moved in their own family. But perhaps, I don't know. Perhaps white people are different. Perhaps a Texan, if someone stole his house, he would say: 'Oh, I have made a mistake, I have built this house, but I guess you like it also so you may have it, along with all this good land that feeds my family. I am but a *kahúu*, little mouse. Please allow me to tell you where my ancestors lie, so you may dig them up and plunder their graves.' Do you think that is what he would say, Tiehteti-taibo?"

That was my name. I shook my head.

"That's right," said Toshaway. "He would kill the men who had stolen his house. He would tell them, '*Itsa nɯ kahni*. Now I will cut out your heart.'"

We were lying in a grove of cottonwoods, looking out over the valley of the Canadian. The grass was thick around us, grama and bluestem, more than could ever be eaten. The sun was going down and the crickets were sawing away and the birds were making a slaughter. On our side of the river the cane was glowing like it would spark at any minute but across the water, toward the south and the white settlements, the cliffs had already gone dusky. I was thinking of all the times I'd been mad at my brother for keeping a candle lit and I'd gone to sleep by myself outside.

Toshaway was still talking: "Of course we are not stupid, the land did not always belong to the Comanche, many years ago it was Tonkawa land, but we liked it, so we killed the Tonkawa and took it from them . . . and now they are *tawohho* and try to kill us whenever they see us. But the whites do not think this way—they prefer to forget that everything they want already belongs to someone else. They think, *Oh, I am white, this must be mine*. And they really believe it, Tiehteti. I have never seen a white person who did not look surprised when you killed them." He shrugged. "Me, when I steal something, I expect the person will try to kill me, and I know the song I will sing when I die."

I nodded.

"Am I crazy to think this?"

"*No sé nada.*"

He shook his head. "I am not even slightly crazy. The white people are crazy. They all want to be rich, same as we do, but they do not admit to themselves that you only get rich by taking things from other people. They think that if you do not see the people you are stealing from, or if you do not know them, or if they do not look like you, it is not really stealing."

A bear came down to the water and flights of teal and wigeon were settling in the far pools. Toshaway continued to braid his lariat.

"*Moowi,*" he said.

"*Moowi*," I repeated.

"I have watched you many times, Tiehteti. Your father has seen me twice, but allowed himself to believe he had seen nothing. I have watched your mother feed the disgraced starving Indians who come to her door, I have watched you lying on your belly studying deer tracks, and I have watched when you killed the big *tumakupa* that night." He sighed. "But the Yap-Eaters smelled the smoke from your evening meal, and when I lied and told them I knew the family that lived there, that you were very poor, *nabukuwaatu*, they insisted that for a poor family, you seemed to be eating very well, and then Urwat decided to check for himself."

I looked out past the hills and saw my mother on the porch and my sister in the grass and my brother in a shallow pit. I wondered if my brother and sister had done something and that was what brought the Indians on us. Then I wondered if my sister had been winking in and out the way I was. My mother would not have let herself. But my sister . . . She would have let herself wink out, I decided. She had not been awake for most of it.

Then I was thinking about my father. I pushed him out of my mind. There was nothing but shame between us.

"*Moowi*," I said to Toshaway.

"*Moowi*," he said.

TOSHAWAY HAD NO idea how old he was, though he looked around forty. Like the other Comanche purebloods he had a big forehead, a fat nose, and a heavy square melon. He looked like a field hand, and on the ground he was slow as an old cowboy, but put him on a horse and the natural laws did not apply. The Comanches all rode like this, though they did not all look like Toshaway: they were darker or lighter, they were lathy as Karankawas and fat as bankers, they had faces like hatchets or Spanish kings, it was a democratic-looking mix. They all had a few captives somewhere in the bloodline—from other Indian tribes or the Spanish, or more recently, the Anglos and Germans.

★   ★   ★

UNLESS I WANTED a hiding, I was up before the stars set, walking through the wet grass, filling the water jugs in the cold stream and getting the fire going. The rest of the day I did whatever the women didn't feel like doing. Pounding corn for Toshaway's wife, cleaning and flaying game the men brought in, getting more water or firewood. Most Comanches used a flint and steel, same as the whites, but they made me learn the hand drill, which was a yucca stalk you spun between your palms while leaning it into a cedar board. You spun and leaned with all your strength until a coal formed or your hands began to bleed. The coal was the size of a pinhead. Usually it broke up before you could get it into the bundle of cattail down or punk or whatever you'd collected for tinder.

Meanwhile, when they weren't hunting, Escuté and Nuukaru spent their days sleeping, smoking, or gambling, and if I tried to talk to them when others could see, I would be ignored or beaten, though it was nothing compared to the beatings the women gave me.

When everything else was done I was set to making *ta?siwoo uhu*—buffalo robes—which was like printing money on a slow press. Each robe took a week. It would then be traded for a handful of glass beads and end up in the coat of a soldier who was out fighting other Indians or perhaps on a sofa in Boston or New York, where, having wiped out their own aboriginals, they held a great affinity for anything Native.

But all that was women's work. If Toshaway called me over everything else stopped. Sometimes to catch and saddle his horse, sometimes to light his pipe or paint him for his evenings out. When he got back from a raid or trip I would spend a few hours picking lice, lancing his boils, cooking his dinner, plucking any beard hairs that had come in, and then his paint. He spent more time getting himself up than my sister ever had, going through slews of makeup and spending hours raking his hair with a porcupine brush, greasing and rebraiding it with slivers of copper and fur until it looked just like when he'd started.

Depending on what was in season, I was also put to gathering. Fruit from the *wokwéesi* (prickly pear), *tɹahpi* (wild plum), and *tuna-séka* (persimmon), beans from the *wohi?huu* (mesquite), *kʊʊka* (wild onion), *paapasi* (wild potato), or *mutsi natsamukwe* (mustang grapes). I was not allowed to carry a knife or gun or bow, just a digging stick, and there were wolf and bear and panther tracks everywhere.

No white person, even an Irishman, would have spent an hour digging a handful of runty potatoes, but I knew I had gotten off easy. I had not taken the big jump. I still got the feeling of a full stomach, a hot fire against a cold night, the sound of other people sleeping close. I knew what it would look like with the grass waving over me; the road to heaven would be slick with my own blood.

IT WOULD BE nice to expound upon the kinship I discovered between myself and the black Africans my countrymen kept in bondage, but, unfortunately, I made no such discovery. I thought only of my own troubles. I was an empty bucket that needing filling with whatever food or favors the Indians would allow, crippling my way through each day, hoping for extra food or praise or a few easy minutes to myself.

As for escaping, there were eight hundred miles of dry wilderness between the ranchería and civilization. The first time I was caught by the other children. The second time I was caught by Toshaway, who turned me over to his wives. They and their mothers beat me hollow, cut up the soles of my feet, and had a long discussion about blinding me in one eye, and I knew the next time I bucked would be the end of me.

TO PREPARE A hide, you stretched out the skin in the grass, hair side down, staking the corners. Then you knelt on the bloody surface, pushing and scraping off the fat and sinew with a piece of blunt bone or metal. If the tool was too sharp or you weren't careful you would push through to the other side, ruining the hide, for which you would be beaten.

Between scrapings I spread a layer of wood ash so the lye would soften the fat; while that was happening I was sent for more water or wood, or I would skin, bone, and flay out a deer one of the men or boys had dragged in. The only thing I didn't do was repair or make clothing, though the women would have taught me if they could have—they were always months behind what the men needed: a new pair of moccasins or leggings (one hide), a bearskin robe (two hides), a wolf robe (four hides). The hides had to be cut so the shape of the animal matched the shape of the wearer, and, as it took all day to finish even a single deer or wolf hide, mistakes could not be made.

In addition to making all the tools the band needed—axes, awls, needles, digging sticks, scrapers, knives and utensils—the women also made all the thread, rope, and twine. The band went through miles of it—for tipis and clothing, for saddles and bridles and hobbles, for every tool or weapon they made—everything in their lives was held together by string, which had to be twisted inch by inch. The leaves of a yucca or agave would be soaked or pounded, or the fibers separated from grasses or cedar bark. Once the fibers were loose they were braided. Animal sinews were also saved—tendons from a deer's ankles were chewed until they split. The sinews along the spine were longer and very easy to work with, but these were in short supply and saved to make weapons, and the women were not allowed to use them.

If you were in a tight spot, cordage could be made from rawhide, but there were better uses for it and it stretched when wet. A hide would be laid flat and a spiral cut into it an inch or two wide, starting from the outside and cutting inward until the entire hide was one long strand. A single lariat required six different strands, though mostly the men made their own lariats, unless a woman was seen sitting with nothing to do.

The Comanches had no patience for the ignorance of their white captives when they themselves had been raised knowing that whether it took a minute or an hour to build a fire or make a weapon or track a man or animal might, at some point, be the difference between living and dying. When there was nothing to do, no one could match them in laziness; otherwise they were careful as goldsmiths. When they looked at a forest they saw each individual plant and knew its name and the seasons they could eat or use it as medicine; they saw the tracks of every living thing that had passed through. Any of them might have been dropped naked upon the earth and within a few days would be living comfortably.

By comparison we were dumb as steers. They could not understand why they had not defeated us. Toshaway always said that white women laid crops of eggs like ducks, which hatched every night, so it didn't matter how many you killed.

AS FOR ME, I dreamed about scraping hides and woke up with the feel of the scraper in my hands. Once a hide was scraped and dried, we took a rawhide bowl and mashed in whatever brains were around, tallow, soap water from yucca (which I had dug up, cut up, carried back to the camp, then pounded and boiled), and maybe some old liver. Bear tallow was used most of the time, and this was the main reason bears were killed. My father and the other frontiersmen considered bear meat and honey the king's supper, but the Indians would only eat bear if there was no hoofed creature to be found.

As for the hides, if the hair was left on, you tanned one side; if the hair was off, you tanned both sides. Then it was the worst part of the process—two days of kneading and twisting to get the hide broken. The final step with buckskin was to smoke it to make it waterproof, though not if it was for trade.

ONE DAY IN August, Nuukaru caught up to me as I was fetching water. I was happy to see him as he'd been gone most of the summer, and even though we shared a tipi, we hardly got the chance to augur, because the women kept me working from can't see to can't see.

He'd come back from his last raid with a scalp, so even though he still looked like a boy, with bony arms and legs, the women now wanted his approval and the men invited him to their gambling. The Comanches had no ceremony for ending boyhood—no vision quests or hooks through the nipples—when you felt like it you started going on raids, watching the horses until gradually you were allowed into the fight.

"It's women's work," he said, by way of greeting me.

I was carrying water up the hill. After I delivered it, I would go dig for potatoes in the mud. "They make me do it," I said.

"So tell them you won't."

"Toshaway will beat me."

"Definitely not."

"Then his wives and mother and the neighbor woman will."

"So what?"

We kept walking.

"What do I say to them?"

"Just stop doing it," he said. "The rest is just details."

We continued to climb the hill. The afternoon was cool and the women had not been asking so much of me. I saw no reason to stir the kettle. Nʉʉkaru must have sensed this, because he turned and punched me suddenly in the groin. I went to my knees.

"For your own good you will give me your full attention now."

I nodded. It occurred to me that in the old days I would have wanted to kill him; now I just hoped he wouldn't hit me again.

"Everyone in the world wants to be Nʉmʉnʉʉ and here it is being given to you, but you are not taking it. When the Indians starve on their reservations, for instance the Chickasaw, Cherokee, Wichita, Shawnee, Seminole, Quapaw, Delaware"—he paused—"even the Apaches and Osages and plenty of Mexicans, they all want to join our band. They leave their reservations, they risk ooibehkarʉ, half of them die just trying to find us. And why do you think that is?"

"I don't know."

"Because we are free. They speak Comanche before they get here, Tiehteti. They speak their own language and they also speak Comanche. Do you know why?"

I looked after my water jug.

"Because Comanches don't act like women."

"I have to get the water," I said.

"Whatever you want. But soon it'll be too late and no one will think of you as anything but a *na?raiboo*."

THE NEXT MORNING Toshaway's wives and mother and the neighbor woman were straightening up camp. The men were sitting around the fire, smoking or eating breakfast.

"Get me some water, Tiehteti-taibo." That was my full name. It meant Pathetic Little White Man. It was not bad as Comanche names went, and I went for the water carrier without thinking about it. Then I felt Nɯɯkaru's eyes on me.

"Go on," said Toshaway's daughter. She gave Nɯɯkaru a look; she must have known what was happening. The work that wore me out had equally worn out her mother and grandmother, and if I quit, it would fall to them again.

"I'm not getting any more water," I said. "*Okwéetuku nɯ miarɯ.*"

The neighbor woman, who had a voice like a burro and outweighed me by six or eight stone, picked up a hatchet in one hand and grabbed for my wrist with the other. I lit a shuck between the tipis, dodging around pots and equipment. The men were hooting and finally she threw the hatchet at my head, which, in my best stroke of luck in months, hit handle first. My bell was ringing but she stopped chasing me. She was trying to catch her breath. I slowed to a walk.

"I will kill you, Tiehteti."

"*Nasiinɯ*," I told her. Piss on yourself.

The men looked in the other direction and began to talk in loud voices about a hunting trip they were planning.

"I'm going to the river," I repeated. "But I am not getting any more water."

"In that case fetch some wood," called Toshaway's mother. "You don't have to get water anymore."

"No," I said. "I'm done with those things."

I followed the stream down to the Canadian and sat in the sun. There were elk on the opposite side and Indians a couple of furlongs downstream. I fell asleep awhile and woke up feeling narrow at the equator—I'd left camp before eating breakfast—but I had no knife and all I was wearing was a breechcloth. There were plenty of old mesquite beans, but I wanted meat, so I went into the cane and spent half an hour catching a turtle. Fish were taboo but turtles weren't. I had nothing to kill him with so I carried him around until I found a good piece of rainbow flint, then stepped on his shell till his head stuck out and cut through his neck with my flint. I sucked down a bit of the blood and it was fishy but not too bad so I drank some more of it and then turned the turtle upside down and sucked him dry.

Then I thought my mother wouldn't be happy if she saw me drinking turtle blood like a wild Indian. I figured I'd been with the Comanches six months, but I'd had no time to think, just work and sleep, and I wondered if my mind had been rubbed clean. When I thought of my mother I saw a pretty woman's face, but part of me was not sure it was really her. I forgot about the turtle and sat down. I watched the other Indians downriver. They had a new captive with them, a red Mexican. I waved and they waved back. That made me feel better.

Meanwhile the turtle was still leaking blood. I wondered if Nuukaru was right or if he had played me for a gump. If the women were allowed to cut me up again—the only fun they ever got to have—it would be better to carry water.

I saw another turtle sunning himself and decided to catch him, then saw two more. After I cut their heads off I had nothing to make a fire. That was fine; I found some dead cedar and shaved off the bark. I found another flint to dig the notch for a fireboard and a short straight stick for the drill. My hands were hard and I got a coal in a few minutes and the tinder caught easily.

When Toshaway's father rode up I was dozing in the grass with my belly full of turtle. He looked at the empty shells.

"You leave any for me, fat boy?"

"I didn't know you were coming."

He sat there on his horse, looking out over the river and thinking about things. "Get on behind me," he finally said. "You don't have to worry about the women anymore."

THE NEXT MORNING I slept the latest I had in months, waking up to the sound of Nuukaru and Escuté chattering.

"The white one becomes a man," said Nuukaru as I emerged from the tipi. I could not believe how long I'd slept.

"Actually," said Escuté, "he has become a boy." They offered me some meat they'd been roasting, and some sumac lemonade, a couple of small potatoes. We sat and smoked.

"What are we doing today?"

"*We* are doing nothing," said Escuté. "*You* are going out with the other children."

I looked at them but they were not joking. Being retarded in all things they found important, the men had decided that I was best matched with the eight- and nine-year-olds.

BY THE AGE of ten, shooting a rough bow he made himself, a Comanche child could kill anything smaller than a buffalo. At the Council House Fight in San Antonio, when the great chiefs came in for peace talks and the whites massacred them, an eight-year-old Comanche boy, hearing the news that his people were betrayed, picked up his toy bow and shot the nearest white man through the heart. He was trying to retrieve his arrow when the mob of whites killed him.

The children I was sent to play with were smaller than they would have been if they had grown up among the Anglos, but they'd spent every minute of their short lives riding, shooting, and hunting. They could sit a horse that would have thrown any white man, they could hit each other with blunt arrows at a dead run. There had never been any church or lessons; in fact, nothing had ever been asked of them, except to do what came naturally, which was to be out hunting and tracking, playing at making war. By the time their short hairs came in they would be going on raids to watch the horses, until the practice for making war and the making of war itself had become the same thing.

They were also encouraged to steal, though only if the owner of the item were present, and only if the item were returned. Toshaway's butcher knife was taken from his sheath as he ate lunch, his pistol was stolen from under his robe. The whites knew that an Indian could steal your horse while you were sleeping, even if you'd tied the reins around your wrist, and for a Comanche to say "that man is the best horse thief in our tribe" was nearly the highest compliment that could be paid, a way of saying that a person could walk into the heart of an enemy camp without being seen and, horses being common currency among both whites and Indians, was likely to become rich. The Comanches were just as happy to steal all the horses of a group of Rangers or settlers as they were to actually kill them, knowing that the buffalo wolves, mountain lions, or sparse water would eventually do them in.

AFTER A FEW weeks of instruction I was considered ready to go hunting with the bow, and so three other boys and I went down to the canebrakes near the river and sat waiting a long time. There was nothing moving and one of the boys took a section of reed and put it in his mouth, which, when he blew through it, made a sound like a fawn in distress. Within a few moments we heard stamping, then nothing, and then more stamping. Then I saw a doe walking slowly through the tall grass and blowdown. She pricked her ears and looked straight at me and I knew I couldn't draw the bow without her seeing me. Not to mention arrows wouldn't cut through the frontal bones, only the ribs.

The ten-year-old made a noise with his mouth that seemed to come from the other side of the thicket. The doe turned her head, but her body was still facing us.

"Now would be a good time to shoot," he whispered.

"But the chest . . ."

"Shoot her in the neck."

"Remember to aim low so she ducks into it."

I drew the bow and began to feel better about everything—the deer still hadn't moved—but at the sound of the string she crouched and took a leap. By a miracle the arrow went into her, but it only cut muscle. Then she was running at full speed with her flag up.

The youngest one shook his head. "*Yee,*" he said, "*Tiehteti tsa? awinu.*"

"What do you think?" I said.

"*Aitu,*" said the oldest. "Very poor. We will be tracking her all day."

The others sighed.

We snuck down to the river and looked for turtles to catch, made a few snares, and when the boys decided the doe had calmed down and likely begun to stiffen from her wound, we followed her through featureless tall grass to where she was bedded a half mile away, using four spots of blood and a scuffed patch of moss on a log. She took off running but was hit with three more arrows. We sat awhile longer and when we found her again she was dead.

I said: "That seemed like cheating, using the call to bring her in."

"So next time get closer and use a lance."

"Or a knife."

"Or go after a bear."

"I was only saying about the fawn call."

The oldest one waved his hand impatiently. "We were told to bring a deer back, Tiehteti, and they'd be mad if we didn't get one. And next time you might try to break the neck so we don't have to track the deer all day."

"It would also be fine to hit one of the big arteries."

"You're rolling your fingers," said the eight-year-old. He drew an imaginary bow. "You have to pop them away from the string."

"Like we showed you," said the oldest.

I didn't say anything.

"If you roll your string, you will never shoot straight."

"Toshaway will tell you I'm a good shot with a gun."

"So go find us a sapling, Mr. Good Shot."

THE BOYS MADE their own bows and arrows, but the people who made the real weapons were the old men, retired warriors who had become too blind or too slow to go on raids, or maybe their wind had given out, or maybe, unbelievably to us, they had grown tired of killing and wanted to spend their last years making items of an artistic nature.

Osage was preferred for the bows—though ash, mulberry, or hickory could substitute—and dogwood for the arrows. We carried the big *ohapuupi* seeds with us, planting them anywhere they might grow, and as this had been done by the various tribes for hundreds or maybe thousands of years, bois d'arc trees were found all along the plains. Equally important was the *parua,* or dogwood. When we found a grove of them we would prune back the trunks almost to the ground. The next spring each trunk would send out dozens of thin new shoots, which grew very straight and were easy to make into good arrows. The location of these arrow groves was kept track of, and they were harvested carefully, making sure that the trees would survive.

A regular bow—better than any factory could make today—was worth one horse. The upper and lower limbs had to release with even pressure while pulling a specific weight at a specific distance from the grip. A fancy or unusually good bow was worth two or three horses. They were all about a yard in length (short compared to the eastern tribes', as, unlike them, we fought from horseback) and backed with the spine sinews from a deer or buffalo. If times were bad, the bowyers would turn out bows very quickly; if times were good—if our warriors were not being killed and their equipment not being lost on raids—the bowyers would take their time and their bows would be the stuff of legend.

Arrows were no different. It could take half a day to make one just right: straight, the proper length and stiffness, the feathers all in alignment—though in a single minute of fighting you might need two dozen. The shafts were felt and squeezed and held up to the light and straightened in the teeth. A crooked arrow was no different from a bent rifle barrel. The Comanches expected their bows to reach fifty yards when they were shooting quickly, hundreds of yards if they were taking their time. On a calm day I saw Toshaway kill an antelope at a full furlong, the first shot going over the animal's back (though falling so quietly it was not noticed) the second falling just short, also in silence, and the third finally telling between the ribs.

The strings were commonly sinew, which when dry shot arrows the fastest but could not be depended on when wet. Some preferred horsehair, which shot slower but was reliable in all conditions, and still others preferred bear gut.

The best feathers for fletching were turkey feathers, but owl or buzzard feathers were also fine. Hawk or eagle feathers were never used as they were damaged by blood. The best shafts were grooved along their length. We used two grooves and the Lipan used four. This prevented the arrow from stanching the wound it had just cut, but it also kept the shaft from warping.

The blades of hunting arrows were fixed vertically, as the ribs of game animals are vertical to the earth. The blades of war arrows were fixed parallel to the earth, the same as human ribs. Hunting points were made without barbs and tied tightly to the shaft so they could be pulled from an animal and reused. War arrows had barbs and the blades were tied loosely, so that if the arrow was pulled, the head would remain lodged in the enemy's body. If you were shot with a war arrow, it had to be pushed through the other side to be removed. By then all the white people knew that, though they did not know that we used different arrows for hunting.

All the plains tribes used arrows with three feathers, though some of the eastern bands used only two, which we looked down on, as they were not accurate. Of course the eastern Indians did not care much, as they lived on a weekly meat allowance from the white man and were drunk most of the time anyway, wishing they had died with their ancestors.

OCCASIONALLY, THROUGHOUT THE fall and winter, I would see the German girl who'd been taken captive with me. Most families had at least one slave or captive, often a young Mexican boy or girl, as Mexico was where they did most of their raiding and horse stealing—the Comanches' toll on that country was on another scale, entire villages wiped out in a single night—Texans had nothing to complain about.

Of course there were numerous white captives as well, from settlements near Dallas, Austin, and San Antonio; there was a boy who had been snatched in far East Texas; there were captives from other tribes. But as I was considered to have a great future, I avoided talking to them.

The only one I broke this rule for was the German girl, whose name was *Suhi?ohapitʉ,* Yellow Hair Between the Legs, but who was mostly referred to as Yellow Hair. Whatever she had been to her family, to the Comanches she was invisible, a nonperson. She spent all her time scraping skins, hauling wood and water, digging *tutupipʉ,* everything I had done my first six months. But for her, there would be no end.

In spring, I ran into her in one of the pastures, looking after the horses. She looked well fed, though her muscles were ropy for a white woman and she didn't have much fat. She appeared to have grown water shy. I could smell her from a good distance and her back was dotted with *mohto?a* as if she had not bathed in months.

"It's you," she said in English. "The chosen one."

I could tell she was sulking.

"I see they're treating you well."

It threw me off to hear English. I told her—in Comanche—that she might consider washing herself. Which was not fair, but I was mad at her for saying I ought to be read out as some kind of deserter.

"Why should I?" she said. "I hoped it would make them stop touching me, but it hasn't."

"They aren't supposed to do that anymore. They could get in big trouble."

"Well, they are."

"Well, they're not supposed to."

"That's very useful of you to say."

"Is it like before?"

"It's one or two in particular," she said. "Though why that makes a difference I don't know."

"How are the horses?" I said. "That one with the sore foot, I could get some wet rawhide."

"Do you think about what we are?" she said. "Me, if I speak to them, they pretend not to hear me. They've given me a new name, because of this." She pointed between her legs. "That's all I am."

I didn't say anything.

"The only thing that makes me happy is the thought that if I die I'll cost them money, because they'll get fewer hides finished." She looked at me. "And you, Tiehteti"—she used my Indian name—"can you see yourself?"

"Sure," I said.

"You're too young. They were smart when they got you."

This annoyed me as well. "You know I can help you if you just ask," I said, though I was not sure what I meant by that.

"Then kill me. Or take me out of here. I don't care which one."

She went back to scraping her hide. I looked around for Ekanaki, the red-eared pinto Toshaway had given me. The sun was getting low and it was cold and there was horseshit everywhere.

"I need to fetch my pony," I said.

"That's what I thought."

I would have been happy to never speak another word to her in my life.

"Tiehteti," she called after me, "if I know it's you I won't fight back." She pointed to the side of her neck, where you'd put a knife in. "I promise. I just can't bring myself to do it."

CHAPTER ELEVEN

J . A . McCULLOUGH

The house had been dead a long time; she was the last of its children. She willed herself to get up. The chandeliers hung quietly above her, indifferent to her suffering. *Get up,* she thought. But nothing happened.

DURING HER CHILDHOOD it been a gay, chattering place, not a moment of silence or privacy; the idea that she might one day be lying alone, the house silent as a graveyard . . . When she came home from school there was always someone talking in the great room or on the gallery or she would wander around and there would be the Colonel, a cluster of his friends talking and drinking or shooting clay pigeons. There were serious-looking young men who came to take notes, ancient plainsmen living out their last days in rented rooms, and there were others who, like the Colonel, were millionaires.

There were reporters and politicians and Indians who came in great bunches, six or eight to a car. The Colonel was different around the Indians; he did not hold court as he did among the whites but rather sat and nodded and listened. She did not like to see it. The Indians did not dress the way they should have—they might as well have been grangers or Mexicans—and they smelled strongly and did not pay her any attention. She would find them stalking around the house and her father thought they stole. But the Colonel did not seem to mind, and the Indians got along fine with the waddies; many mornings she came into the great room to discover a dozen old men asleep among their former enemies, spilled beer and whiskey, a beef quarter half-eaten in the fireplace.

It was the Colonel's house, there was no mistaking it, though he mostly slept in a jacal down the hill. Her father complained about the noise and grandstanding and endless strangers and houseguests, about the food bills and the size of the domestic staff. The Colonel did not care for him, either; he found her father's interest in cattle quite taxing. "We have not made a dime off the dumb brutes in twenty years" or "That man can't take a shit without asking the county agent."

The Colonel was in favor of oil, in favor of Jonas going to Princeton, and as for Clint and Paul, they would make damn fine hands. But you, he would say, tapping her on the shoulder, you are going to do something. She had not known how fragile that all was. Now, looking across the dim room from her place on the floor, she saw the house as it would soon be: a haven for bats and owls, for mice and coyotes, the deer leaving footprints in the dust. The roof would give way and brush would begin to grow inside the house until there was nothing left but stone walls in a desert.

ASIDE FROM THE Colonel, her grandmother was the only one who paid her any mind. On hot days they would sit in the library while her grandmother sorted, for the thousandth time, the contents of various boxes, pictures and tintypes, here was her first husband, who had died before they had children, here were her two sisters, dead of typhoid, here was Uncle Glenn in his army uniform. There were more pictures of Glendale—who had been shot by the Mexicans but had died fighting the Huns—than there were of Jeannie's mother. If her grandmother knew a single thing about the woman who'd brought Jeannie into this world, she didn't share it. *Here is your great-grandfather Cornellius, the most famous lawyer in Dallas, your great-great-grandfather Silas Burns, who owned the biggest plantation in Texas before the Yankees ran the niggers off.* Jeannie did not know much about niggers, except for the few she'd seen working on the trains. They said East Texas was full of them. But she did know something about the old men in the tin-types, their ridiculous collars and mustaches, coats buttoned to their necks, looking like they had sat on a splinter. She did not care what her grandmother said; she was not related to them and never would be.

Invitations to parties, calling cards, gaudy pins. Cheap jewelry only a child would wear. The engagement ring from her first husband, who had died before she met Peter McCullough. Jeannie's grandfather. The Great Disgrace.

Her grandmother occasionally took her riding; a hand would prepare her horse and sidesaddle, the only one in Dimmit County. She was a fair horsewoman, even on the awkward device. She scolded Jeannie for going bareback and for climbing fences. *You will do things to yourself you will be sorry about later.* What those things were, she wouldn't say, and sometimes, if Jeannie fell asleep during the stories of her grandmother's dull girlhood, she would awake to a firm pinch.

Her grandmother and the other grown-ups did not mind being boring; they often went on until Jeannie wished *she* were the dead one, instead of the person in the story, who was always more clever, or handsome, with more style and grace and wit than anyone Jeannie had ever met. If the Colonel had any boring stories, he must have forgotten them. He never said the same thing twice. Here was where to find a hawk's nest or a pair of bucks who had died with their antlers locked, here was a leaf fossil or old bone or piece of purple flint. They kept a box of things they had found together, the skulls of little mice, squirrels, raccoons, and other animals.

When there were no visitors the Colonel would sit on the gallery making arrowheads or whittling cedar. Once, after whittling a piece into shavings, he told her: "If I wasn't so old we'd get into the airplane business. We could build 'em here and sell 'em to the government and they would fly 'em at that field near Sanderson."

He had tried to teach her to make arrowheads, but it had not taken. She had gashed her palm on a piece of sharp flint, at first surprised that a simple rock could cut her so deeply, then fascinated by the free flow of her own blood, then nauseated. The Colonel had come out of his trance and they had hobbled into the kitchen, where he bandaged her up and brought her back to the porch.

"I guess you're off drinks duty," he said, and winked. He went to the cart and made her a julep without the whiskey, and, against her father's rules, let her sip straight from the cold silver shaker, the two of them conspiring against all that was right and good. She sat happily, forgetting the pain in her hand.

"It's a foolish activity," he said, taking up the arrowhead she'd begun. "Though if you make a knife, you can do anything. One day I will take all the arrowheads I've made and scatter them around the ranch and then maybe in a thousand years, some historian will find them and make up stories that aren't true." Then he looked up. "There is a thrush in that granjeno."

She looked out over the pasture, but she didn't see anything. The sun was bright but it was early in the year; the grass was still green and the live oaks beginning their springtime shed.

"They have told me there is a German named Hertz," he said, "who has given his name to, among other things, the way flint breaks when you strike it. It is always the same way." He held up a chip. "Though of course Hertz did not discover this. In fact the man who did discover it has been dead two million years. Which is how long people have been knocking rocks together to make tools." He took another flake. "Remember that," he said. "None of it's worth a shit until you put your name on it."

CHAPTER TWELVE

DIARIES OF PETER McCULLOUGH

AUGUST 16, 1915

The shooting could be heard as soon as it got dark. Near midnight about fifty men came to the gate, carrying torches, shouting for us to turn over the Mexicans.

They hesitated there in the road—fifty men or not, it is no small thing to trespass on McCullough land—but after a long period of milling around, one of them put his foot on the bar and began to climb over. At which point we opened fire over their heads. Charles put his automatic Remington to good use, unleashing all fifteen rounds as the crowd broke and fled down the road. We spent a good deal of time afterward stomping out the fires that started when they dropped their torches.

Later Niles Gilbert and two others from the Law and Order League drove up and pleaded with me to kick the Mexicans out, lest the town be burned.

Charles shouted: "So go shoot the assholes who are burning your town. It ain't like you don't have enough guns."

"How many men do you have, Peter?"

"I've got enough. And I've armed all the Mexicans as well." Which was not true.

"This isn't going to turn out well for you," he said.

*   *   *

CONSUELA AND SULLIVAN had been cooking all night so there was plenty of beef and cabrito. By morning half the families had asked permission to stay at the ranch until the town was safe. The other half loaded up with food and water and began to walk or ride across our pastures, toward the river and Mexico. They are going into a war zone but apparently it is preferable to this.

Naturally they all believe the Colonel is responsible for their salvation—who else could it be but Don Eli? This rankles greatly but I did not bother to correct them. How they will ever get democracy I don't know—they are very comfortable with the idea that powerful men rule their lives. Or perhaps they are simply more honest about it than we allow ourselves to be.

My father was well behaved, entertaining all the children on the gallery with his Indian stories, showing them how to start a fire with two sticks, giving archery demonstrations as well (he can still draw his old Indian bow, which I can barely pull back myself). He was happy and at ease and laughed a lot—I do not remember seeing him like this since before my mother died. Perhaps he was meant to be a schoolteacher. As we watched the refugees walking and riding toward the river, their belongings piled on mules and carts, he said: "That'll be the last time we see any of 'em moving south, I'd imagine."

And yet they love him. They go back to their jacals at night, which are hot in the summer and cold in the winter, while he goes back to our house, a sprawling white monstrosity, a thousand years' salary for them, or a thousand thousand. Meanwhile their children are stillborn and they bury them near the corrals. *Who are you to say they ain't happy?* That is what a white man will tell you, looking you straight in the eye as he says it.

*   *   *

AFTER THE LARGEST group of Mexicans left, a group of us went door-to-door in town and gave everyone we didn't recognize five minutes to be on their way. Campbell put up new signs: ANYONE CARRYING A FIREARM WILL BE SHOT AND/OR ARRESTED.

By six o'clock the streets were deserted. Fourteen houses have been burned. Sergeant Campbell is leaving tomorrow to get medical attention for his wounds. Apparently he has gotten quite a hiding for not going south to protect the big ranches: two hundred sections is considered middling. But, thanks to Guillermo's sugar remedy, his arm does not appear to be getting any worse.

To help me relax I read the newspapers for the first time in a week. A storm hit Galveston yesterday, killing three hundred. A great victory as the last one killed ten thousand, ending Galveston's reign as our state's queen city.

SALLY CALLED AT FIVE A.M. Glenn's fever appears to have broken.

AUGUST 18, 1915

Today at the meeting of all the remaining townspeople, I suggested that the train station be named after Bill Hollis (killed at the Garcias'), a motion seconded and carried. Feel extremely poorly for Marjorie Hollis. While Glenn was repeatedly mentioned by name in all the newspaper articles as having been wounded, and Charles singled out for leading the charge on the Garcia compound (each time mentioning he is the grandson of the famous Indian fighter Eli McCullough)—Bill Hollis was only mentioned once, in the local paper.

Afterward I wondered why I did not suggest the station be named after one of the many dead Mexicans.

AUGUST 20, 1915

Storm giving us a good soaking. Everyone in high spirits. Except me. Can't sleep—faces of the Garcias have returned—spent most of the morning in a nervous daze, searching for things to do, as if I did not find something to occupy my mind . . . I avoid looking into the shadows, as I know what I'll find there.

Visited with the Reynolds family, inquired about the surviving girl, who we all now know was María Garcia. Apparently she locked herself in their spare bedroom and then disappeared during the night, stealing an old pair of boots, as she had no shoes.

Ike motioned for me to follow him out to the gallery, where the others couldn't hear us.

"Pete, don't take this the wrong way, but if I were that girl, I might believe I was the only living witness to a murder." He held up his hands. "Not that I'm saying she is, but from her point of view . . ."

"I was against it from the start."

"I know that." He scuffed his boot. "Sometimes I wish there was another way to live here."

CHAPTER THIRTEEN

ELI / TIEHTETI

1850

By the time I'd been with them a year, I was treated the same as any other Comanche, though they kept a bright eye on me, like some derelict uncle who'd taken the pledge. Dame Nature had made my eyes and hair naturally dark and in winter I kept my skin brown by lying out in the sun on a robe. Most nights I slept as gentle as a dead calf and had no thoughts of going off with the whites. There was nothing back there but shame and if my father had come looking for me, I hadn't heard about it.

Escuté and Nuukaru still ignored me so I spent my time with the younger boys; we'd graduated to breaking the band's horses and soon we would go to hold the remuda during the raids. A steady trickle of unbroken ponies came off the plains: whenever a herd was spotted, the fastest braves would ride out and rope them and the animals whose necks didn't break would be brought back to camp. Then their nostrils were held shut until they sagged to the ground. They were tied that way and left for us to handle.

There is something in the white man that loves a sorrel but the Indians had no use for them; there were only five horses we cared about: red paints, black paints, Appaloosas, red medicine hats, and black medicine hats. The medicine hats had dark bands around their heads and dark ears and a blaze in the shape of a medieval shield on their chests. There was one type—the *pia tso?nika* or war bonnet—that had black eye patches as well and from a distance looked like a skull or death's head. Centuries of hard living had made them as frothy as panthers; they had as much in common with a domestic horse as a wolf has with a lapdog and they would stave in your ribs if you gave them half a chance. We loved them.

I SLEPT WHEN I wanted and ate when I wanted and did nothing all day that I didn't feel like doing. The white in me expected any minute that I would be ordered to do chores or some other form of slave labor but it never happened. We rode and hunted and wrestled and made arrows. We slayed every living thing we laid eyes on—prairie chickens and prairie dogs, plovers and pheasants, blacktail deer and antelope; we launched arrows at panther and elk and bears of every size, dumping our kills in camp for the women to clean, then walking off with our chests out like men. Along the river we dug up the bones from giant bison and enormous shells turned to stone and almost too heavy to lift; we found crayfish and shards of pottery and carried it all to the tops of cliffs and smashed it on the rocks below. We arrowed bobcats at night while they stalked ducks in the cane and the weather was warming and the flowers coming out, the yucca had shot their stalks and big white flowers hung ten feet in the air; there were patches of bluebonnet or blanketflower or greenthread that went on for miles, now it was green, now it was blue, now it was red and orange as far as the eye would carry. The snow was gone and fat high clouds hung everywhere, and the sun blinked on and off as they moved across the wind, heading south toward Mexico, where they would burn away forever.

It was considered a sure thing that a few of us would be asked to go raiding. I was the oldest, the only one whose short hair had come in, but I was also deficient; I shot fine from the ground but the other kids could hit pheasants and rabbits from a gallop. Still, when Toshaway came out to the pasture one morning carrying his pistol and a new buffalo-hide shield, it was me he picked out of the crowd. The others made comments but I ignored them.

We walked a good distance and set the shield against a runty cottonwood and he handed me the gun.

"Go ahead."

"Just like that?"

"Sure."

I shot and the shield fell over. It was smeared with lead but not dented. He grinned and set it up again and I shot it until the gun was empty.

"Okay," he said. "A shield will stop a ball. But if a ball ever hits a stationary shield, you are an idiot." He put the straps over his arm and moved it in quick circles. "Always it's moving. Of course the feathers hide you, but more important is that a stationary shield will only stop a pistol ball. A rifle ball will go through it, the same as if you jump from a high tree and land on flat ground, you will break your legs, but if you land on a steep hill, you will be fine. A moving shield will stop a rifle ball. *Nahkusuabern?*"

I nodded.

"Good," he said. "Now we come to the fun part."

We walked a few more minutes to the middle of an old pasture at the edge of camp. Whatever was going to happen, everyone would see it. A dozen or so braves were sitting in the sun playing *tnkii* but when they saw me they got up and retrieved some equipment. Each man was carrying his bow and a basket of arrows.

"Okay," said Toshaway. "This will be very easy. You will remain standing here and these men will shoot you. I would prefer if you used the shield as much as possible."

"Where are you going?"

"I don't want to be shot!" He grinned and patted me on the head.

The braves formed a skirmish line a hundred yards away and when everything was arranged Toshaway shouted at me and waved an arrow. "*Ke matʉʉ mutsipʉ!* They are blunt!" The warriors found this humorous. "They have no spikes!" he repeated.

People were trickling out from their tipis to watch and I wondered if Toshaway had actually checked each arrow, as by certain lights it would be a very funny joke if there were a few spikes mixed in with the blunt ones. I was only worth a horse or two and plenty of people in the village still had no use for me.

"*Tiehteti tsa maka?mukitʉ-tʉ!*"

I nodded.

"Keep the shield moving!"

I made myself small. Arrows take a few seconds to go a hundred yards, which seems like forever unless they're coming toward you. Most thumped off the shield; one or two missed entirely; others hit me in the thigh and shin and then again in the same shin.

This was thought hilarious and several of the warriors began to imitate me, hopping around on one foot and calling out *anáa anáa anáa* until Toshaway made them go back to their places.

"You have to move!" he shouted. "It is too small to hide you!"

The hilarious Indians opened fire and my legs took another pounding. One arrow grazed my forehead where I had looked over the shield.

"You don't have to block the ones that will miss you," someone shouted. I was in a crouch, trying to make myself as small as possible; it was the funniest thing the Indians had ever seen and it went on until they were out of ammunition.

I started to limp back to the village, but there was an uproar from the audience so instead the braves and I switched sides so they could collect their arrows.

"It is for your own benefit," someone yelled, but now the sun was in my face. I squinted at one particular arrow that seemed to not be moving at all.

Sometime later I woke up. Toshaway was standing over me, murmuring like a pulpiteer.

"What?" I said.

"Are you awake now?"

"Haa." I felt my breechcloth. It was dry.

"Good. Now if you can listen for a moment I will tell you something my father once told me. The difference between a brave man and a coward is very simple. It is a problem of love. A coward loves only himself . . ."

I got very dizzy and I could feel the cold ground. I wondered if my skull was cracked. You could shoot a blunt arrow through a deer if it was close enough.

" . . . a coward cares only for his own body," Toshaway said, "and he loves it above all other things. The brave man loves other men first and himself last. *Nahkusuaberu?*"

I nodded.

"This"—he tapped me—"must mean nothing to you." Then he tapped me again, on my face, my chest, my belly, my hands and feet. "All of this means nothing."

"Haa," I said.

"Good. You're a brave little Indian. But everyone is bored. Get up and let them shoot you."

A short while later I was down again. The warriors went back to the shade and gambled while Toshaway gave me cool water and wrapped my head with a blanket scrap. Only my eyes were exposed. This caused more hilarious laughter but it worked like a helmet and I stopped being afraid. By the end of the day they had cut the distance in half and the shooters were working hard to get their hits. After a week they couldn't hit me at all.

As a graduation ceremony I held the shield while a big fat buck named Pizon, who made no secret that he thought I ought to be a *na?raiboo* rather than a member of the tribe, aimed at me with Toshaway's pistol. All the slack went out of my rope but I blocked each shot and kept the shield moving the whole time. Pizon gave me a look that said he would have liked if I had gotten my lamp blown out, but I got to keep the shield. Being a sacred item, it was kept in a protective case far from camp. If a menstruating woman ever touched it, it would have to be destroyed.

THE HUNTING THAT spring was the worst anyone could remember. Toshaway had grown up with herds of buffalo blackening the prairie for weeks, but none of the younger Indians had seen anything like it. There had been a drought in parts of the plains, but mostly it was because of the eastern tribes, whose numbers were growing by the month in the Territories. They all took liberties in our hunting grounds and we spent as much time killing them as we did the whites. It was considered a good way to break in the youth without having to ride too far.

When the yucca were done blooming Toshaway and I and a few dozen others rode out to patrol for buffalo or trespassing Indians. After a few days we came on a small herd moving west, toward New Mexico and the drier part of the plains, which meant something was disturbing them. The scouts rode east while the rest of us killed buffalo and then it came back that a group of Tonks had been seen. Some of the fort Indians were treated with caution, but the Tonkawa had a great taste for firewater and it was not considered much to kill one. A decade later they would be wiped out completely.

Nuukaru, who had been coaching me on the skinning, put his knife into his sheath and was into his saddle in three long steps. I had misplaced my bow and by the time I got mounted the entire party was riding to haul hell out of its shuck.

The prairie is not as flat as it looks, it is more like the swells of an ocean, there are peaks and troughs, and, being in less of a hurry to kill a Tonk, it wasn't long till I lost sight of the others. It was a nice day, the grass going down and standing up in waves, in all directions, the sky very clear and blue with a few clouds lingering. The sun was nice on my back. The idea of running down a Tonk could not have seemed less appealing. I was not allowed to carry a firearm and even with both feet on the ground I was only average with the bow; unless the target was standing still, directly in front of me, shooting from a moving horse was impossible.

The horse knew something was wrong and he kept trying to catch the others. He had a good smooth lope so I held him there. I made a note of the sun and it occurred to me that I might just turn southeast, toward the Llano breaks; I could hunt easily enough with the bow and it was maybe a two-week ride to the frontier if I wasn't caught. There were patches of small red flowers, *puha natsu*. I thought about the English name but I didn't know it. I thought about my father. Then I gave the horse his head and we were running.

A few minutes later I could hear shots and hollering and then there were riders and horses. Toshaway and Pizon and a few others were standing around a man on the ground. He was lying in a patch of blanketflower with several arrows sticking out of him. He had lost enough blood to paint a house and it was bright in the greenery around him.

"Tiehteti-taibo, very nice of you to come."

The Comanches were breathing easy and their sweat was dry and their horses were off grazing. Except for Nuukaru, who was holding his lance in case the Tonk got his sap back, not one of them had a weapon in hand. They might have been judging the quality of a deer or elk they'd brought down. As for the Tonkawa, he was chanting and wheezing, his torso smeared and his chin dripping with blood as if he had been feeding on human bodies.

Toshaway and Pizon had a word and then Pizon took an old single-shot pistol from his sash and handed it over butt-first. It was a .69 caliber, a cannon as handguns went.

"Go ahead, Tiehteti."

Pizon added: "If it were him, he would be slicing off your breast and eating it in front of you."

The man looked up and recognized me, then stared out over the prairie. His chanting got more insistent and there was no point lingering so I squeezed the trigger. The gun snapped into my wrist and the man leaned farther against the rock. His music stopped and his legs began to twitch like a dog in sleep.

He was a good-looking brave with long beautiful hair and Pizon took the entire scalp beneath the ears. The ball must have loosened something because when Pizon ripped off his hair, the man's head fell open as if it were hinged at the bottom, his face going forward and the back of his head going the other direction. No one had ever seen a pistol ball do that. It was good medicine.

The others got distracted but I continued to stare, the man's face looking down at his own chest, all his secrets open to the wind.

"You're acting very strange, Tiehteti-taibo."

"*Haa,*" I said. "*Tsaa manusukaru.*"

Nʉʉkaru and I were sent to retrieve the dead man's weapons and anything else he had dropped and there was something about him lying there with the blanketflowers all around stained with blood and I rode after Nʉʉkaru as quickly as I could. After an hour we found the Tonk's rifle. It was a fire-new Springfield musket and Nʉʉkaru couldn't believe it—the Tonks were poor and their equipment was usually poor as well. "This thing must have come from the whites," he said. "And his horse also."

I didn't care. I was bored looking for the man's valuables—I doubted he owned much and didn't intend on spending the rest of the day looking for a filthy war bag. I wondered if I was the only one who knew how many rifles and horses the whites had.

The rest of the group was out of sight; it was waist-high grass in every direction, then sky. My horse was eating flowers; bluebonnets were hanging from his mouth. I wondered if they would let me keep the Tonk's scalp.

One of the Tonks had gotten away, but as he was afoot in unfamiliar territory, and being a reservation Indian probably only a few notches above a white man, he was almost certain to die eventually, so we didn't bother chasing him. Not to mention that with the confusion of the fight over, he would easily spot us before we spotted him, making it likely he would be able to shoot at least one of us. Unlike the whites, whose noble leaders were willing to sacrifice any number of followers to kill a single Indian, the Comanches did not believe in trading any of their own for the enemy. It was another unfortunate character trait, as far as fighting the Anglos was concerned.

So instead of following the lone Tonk, we prepared for a cel-ebration, taking their scalps and horses and brand-new rifles, whose newness, though no one said it, was another sign of a storm coming. Nuukaru found the Tonk's war bag, which contained dozens of paper cartridges, another luxury from the whites.

"Look at this shit," he said.

No one paid any attention. We made our way back to the buffalo we'd killed, having a big feast of the liver and bile and then building a fire of mesquite and buffalo chips and roasting the meat and mar-row. The Tonk's scalp belonged to Pizon. My shooting him was just a formality.

THE NEXT MORNING the wind had shifted and there was a faint rotten smell. I could barely pick it up and of course things were always dying on the prairie, but the other Comanches thought it noteworthy, and after we packed the buffalo's meat back into their skins and tied the bundles onto the spare horses, we began to ride. A few hours later we came to a small canyon, the grass tall and a creek running down the middle, and as we rode into it the smell became worse, and then the horses refused to go farther.

There was no sound except the wind and the running of the stream and the flapping of tent skins. There were several hundred tipis, with thousands of black vultures tottering among them, as if they had decided to give up their wild ways and become civilized.

I leaned over and retched and someone behind me did the same.

It was decided that I would go in alone and make an inspection while the others stayed back.

"Are you joking?" I said.

"There are no living people in this drainage except us," said Toshaway. He gave me a cloth to tie over my mouth and nose.

"Then give me your pistol."

"You won't need it."

"Let me have it anyway."

He shrugged and handed over the revolver, then leaned to help me tie the cloth over my face. "Remember to lift it if you have to vomit. Otherwise you will be very sorry."

A few of the buzzards flew off, others stepped aside to let me through, and the flies took off and landed in great black waves. The ground was covered with human bodies, whether hundreds or thousands I couldn't tell; they were all pulled apart and rotted, partially eaten, blackened and contorted and uncountable. My horse stepped gingerly at first, but soon saw it was hopeless and began to tread directly on what was left of the people.

There were heads and sections of spine, feet and hands, rib cages, the muscle black and the bones very white, lumps of fat stuck to rocks, arms and legs wedged in the branches of cottonwoods where they had been dragged by cougars or bobcats. There were rifles and bows and knives scattered and starting to rust. There were so many dead that not even the wolves and coyotes and bears had been able to eat them. The sun had blackened everything but I could see that none of the people had been scalped. I could not think of who had done this to them.

Most of the horses had been driven off by the wolves, or eaten, but a few dozen of the most loyal or helpless grazed the periphery; there was a big dun mare still saddled, though the saddle had rolled all the way under her belly and she could barely walk. I nickered and rode up next to her and she stood resigned to whatever I might do. I cut the cinch and at the sound of the saddle hitting the ground the mare stepped away, then shook herself and broke into a trot. She had an army brand on her hip, though she had been wearing an Indian saddle, and I wondered about the things she had seen.

One of the tipis had been sealed shut, rocks and brush piled around it, and without dismounting from my horse I took hold of the flaps and cut the ropes. Inside there were two dead vultures and dozens of small bodies, carefully placed in rows and stacked on top of one another. Whoever had put them there was too weak to bury them, or maybe they had been dying too quickly; it was either smallpox or cholera or some other disease and I turned my horse and kicked him and went back to where the others were waiting for me.

"They still had their hair?"

"Yes," I said.

"How many?"

"Hundreds. Maybe thousands."

"I think around one thousand. Did you touch anything?"

"Not really. A tipi that was in the sun."

He squinted and looked around. It was a pleasant little canyon. "I guess there are worse places to die."

"Who were they?"

"I think that is Kicking Dog's band. Tenewa Comanche. They are outside their territory so something was not going well when they put their camp there, they were running from something. *Tasía,* probably." He dotted his face with a finger. "The gift of the great white father."

I RODE MY horse into the middle of the stream and scrubbed his feet and legs with sand, then did the same to my own body. I slept by myself that night, a good distance from the others. A few days later, before we reached camp, I went to the river to scrub myself again and asked Nʉʉkaru to bring me a bowl of yucca soap and place it on the ground. I cleaned the horse again as well.

When I reached the village they were preparing a big celebration and scalp dance. One of the medicine men took me into a tipi and made me strip. He swallowed breaths of cedar and sage smoke, blew them onto me, then rubbed my body with leaves. I told him I had already used soap, but he figured the smoke was better.

A few weeks later a group of Comancheros came through the camp and said they had seen more Indians killing buffalo. Toshaway told me we were going on another scouting trip. I acted enthusiastic.

"Give me one of the Tonk rifles," I said.

He must have thought something would happen because he handed it over without comment, along with a dozen of the paper cartridges.

At night we had fires but only in gullies and far away from any trees so there was nothing to show the light. Finally the scouts came back and reported a party of Indians cutting up buffalo: they appeared to be Delawares, who, though the Comanches would never admit it, were the best hunters of all the eastern tribes, good trackers and men to be taken seriously.

We decided to make a cold camp and sleep before we laid into them. The Delawares made a cold camp as well, though they did not know they'd been seen, and I thought of them out there in the dark, they'd once been the kings of the east as we were the kings of the west, but now they'd killed twenty buffalo and couldn't even have a fire to celebrate.

The light was flat and gray and a slick mist was rising from the grass. There were horses going in all directions and everyone shouting and I was staring at one man who had taken four or five arrows but stood calmly tamping a charge into his musket. Someone came from behind and pinned him with a lance. It was Nuukaru. There was something about the man squirming on the ground but Nuukaru didn't seem to mind.

The rest of the Delawares were quickly unroostered, but one managed to make a clear swing. I had stayed on the outskirts and he went right past me; he might as well have been standing still, though he didn't react to the shot and with the smoke I wasn't sure I'd hit him.

I watched him ride off. I knew what I had to do. There was no time to reload the rifle, and even with all the fighting I knew Toshaway and Pizon were probably watching me. While I was thinking this, the two of them finished killing the man they had started to kill, saw the escaping Delaware, and took off after him.

I fell in behind. I had never whipped a horse so hard but the four of us were strung out in a long line across the prairie with the Delaware at the head. He was riding a legendary animal, putting ground on us with each step, he was nearly a half mile ahead, but there was nowhere to hide, no canyons, no forest, just open prairie, and we began to close. Then Toshaway's pony stumbled and collided with Pizon's and I went around them.

As for the Delaware, I could see a shiny slick down his back where my ball had gone in and I whipped the horse even harder, though I had no plan for what I would do if I caught him.

Then he was on the ground. There was a gulch he'd tried to jump and the horse had thrown him. He was lying in the tall grass.

I was on him before I knew it and I nocked an arrow but it went several feet wide. I tried to nock another but my hands were shaking and the horse was skittering so I slid off onto the ground.

The Delaware hadn't moved. I felt better about everything, I was looking down at my string, trying to get the arrow set, and I looked up to see him spin and draw and shoot in the same movement.

There was an arrow sticking out of me. It seemed like I ought to sit down. Then I was looking at myself; then I decided there was nothing wrong. I grabbed the arrow and pulled it out.

Later I realized that the Delaware was so weak he hadn't been able to fully draw his bow. My quiver strap had stopped his arrow—but right then I picked up my own bow, which I had dropped, aimed carefully, and shot the Delaware in the stomach. The arrow went to the feathers.

He was looking around for his quiver. It had gotten separated in the fall. I shot another arrow, then a third, which went between his ribs. He was tugging at the one where it was stuck into the ground and I knew he would send it back to me. I shot the rest of the arrows I was holding and he gave up, though he was not quite dead. I knew I should go and thump him but I didn't want to get any closer, I was ashamed of his breathing and gurgling, of my bad shooting, of being afraid of a man who was nearly dead, and then someone kicked me in the backside.

It was Toshaway and Pizon. I hadn't heard them come up.

"*Ku?e tsasimapʉ.*" Toshaway nodded at the Delaware.

"Do it quickly," said Pizon. "Before he dies."

The Delaware was lying on his side and I rolled him onto his belly. I put my foot on his back and grabbed his hair and he raised his arm to stop me, but I cut all the way around. He was slapping at my hand the whole time.

"Snap it off," called Pizon. "One big motion."

The scalp came off like a cracking branch and the Delaware lost his fight. I walked a few yards and looked at it: it could have been anything, a piece of buffalo or calf hide. The sun was coming up and my leg began to hurt: I'd cut myself on my own arrow spikes where they'd come through the Delaware's back. He gave a last moaning rattle, and, looking at him there on the ground, stuck through from every direction with my spikes and the grass matted with his blood, it was like a haze clearing from my mind, like I'd been dunked again, like I'd been chosen by God Himself. I ran over to Toshaway and Pizon and grabbed them.

"Fucking white boy," said Pizon. But he was smiling as well. He turned to Toshaway. "I guess I owe you a horse."

THERE WAS A big dance when we got back, eight scalps had been collected, but before it began, Pizon told the story of how I'd gone after the Delaware alone, like a proper Comanche, with nothing but my bow, and he said we know what a great talent Tiehteti is with his bow.

There was general laughter, which annoyed me. But this is serious, he continued, this was not some filthy *Numu Tuuka,* but a warrior, and Tiehteti's only weapon was one he cannot yet use from his horse. And to be shot in the heart, only to have the arrow refuse to go in? What does that say about Tiehteti?

For the rest of the night the medicine man who'd cleansed me of smallpox told everyone that he had given me his bear medicine, as only that could have stopped the arrow, but no one believed him. I knew the Delaware was almost dead when I reached him, that he had taken a ball in the lungs and been thrown from his horse onto the rocks, that if I had caught him five or ten minutes earlier he would have driven his arrow to my spine. That even in his final condition, if the buffalo-hide strap of my quiver hadn't been hanging just so, the spike would have reached my heart. But by the end of the night those details meant nothing, and this was the point of the scalp dance, we were eternal, the Chosen People, and our names would ring on in the night, long after we'd vanished from the earth.

SOMETIME BEFORE MORNING I opened my eyes. I was lying in the yard of our old house and there was an Indian standing over me. I was watching the arrows go in but decided not to believe what I was seeing; I remembered I'd hit my head and was probably confused. The Comanche was young and there was something familiar about him and after a time I began to recognize his face.

WHEN MORNING CAME I could still feel the hollow where the arrows had gone. The sun had risen and was shining directly through the open door of the tipi and Nuukaru and Escuté were outside smoking. I went and sat with them. The three boys who had taken me hunting, all of whom were still better hunters, riders, and bowmen than I was, came over and said hello, but didn't sit—I was now their superior—and then Nuukaru waved them away. "You're done with those kids," he said.

Escuté called his mother to bring us something to eat and then there were sugarberry cakes, which were hackberries and tallow mashed together and cooked over a fire. Nʉʉkaru and I thanked her. Escuté just took the food and ate. He must have seen the way I looked at him because he said: "We could get killed every time we leave camp. They all know this. Half of us will be dead by the time we reach forty winters."

A short time later Fat Wolf, Toshaway's eldest son, came by with his wife.

"So this is the famous white boy?"

Escuté said, "You're a man now, Tiehteti, and I'm sure Fat Wolf appreciates the respect but you don't have to stare at the dirt."

Fat Wolf leaned over and gripped my chin, then his hand softened. "Don't listen to my asshole brother. I always put him in a bad mood." He pointed over his shoulder. "This is Hates Work. Obviously you've noticed her before, but as you are a man now, you may talk to her, and take note of her unfortunately soft hands."

Hates Work, who was standing a ways back from her husband, smiled and waved, but didn't say anything. She was by far the most beautiful Indian I'd ever seen, in her early twenties with clear skin and shining hair and a good figure; it was widely thought a tragedy that she would soon be ruined by children. Her father had asked fifty horses as a bride-price, which was outrageous according to Nʉʉkaru, but Toshaway, because he spoiled his sons terribly, as anyone spending time with Escuté might notice, had given the fifty horses and the marriage had been approved.

Fat Wolf himself was as tall as his father, but while his face was young, he already had the thin arms and heavy paunch of a much older man. He looked as Toshaway might if Toshaway had stopped hunting and raiding. I nodded at Hates Work and tried not to show too much interest.

Fat Wolf had lifted my poultice and was touching me gently, the open skin and bone, the cut still weeping. "Motherfucker," he said. "I have never seen a wound like that on a living man." He looked me up and down. "My father talked about you, but he likes everyone and we thought he was going soft. Now we see he was right. It's no small thing." He took me by the shoulders; he was a very touchy Indian. "You ever need anything, you come to me. And don't hang around my brother too much, he's a bitter little fuck." Then he walked away with his pretty wife.

"What a fat fuck," said his brother, when the pair were out of earshot.

"Escuté has been hoping that Fat Wolf will send her his way, but Fat Wolf is not interested in sharing yet."

"I get plenty of *tai?i* on my own. I don't need a handout from the fat one." He looked at Nuukaru: "You, on the other hand . . ."

"I get plenty."

"From old women, maybe."

"Like your mother."

"I wouldn't put it past you," said Escuté.

It was quiet. I'd invented a number of stories about the various girls I'd been with, but Nuukaru and Escuté knew better than to ask.

AFTER LUNCH I went to the stream to clean my trophy. I scraped the inner skin to remove all the meat and fat, rinsing it in the water, rubbing it with a coarse stone and rinsing it again, teasing off the silverskin with my fingers, repeating until the inner scalp was white and full and soft. Then I took a wooden basin, filled it with water and yucca soap, and carefully washed the hair, separating the strands, trying not to pull too hard, as if the Delaware might still feel what I was doing, teasing out each burr and grass seed, the dandruff and dried blood. I rewove his braids, replacing all the beads, which were turquoise and red glass, in the same places he had put them. I made a paste of brain and tallow and rubbed it into the inner skin, allowing it to dry and then rubbing

in more of the paste. I stretched it on a willow hoop to dry, then carried
it back to the tipi to hang in the shade.

THAT NIGHT WE stayed up late talking. I'd hung the scalp above my
pallet and I watched it turn all night in the warm air from the fire. The
embers went dark and we all drifted off and there was a rustling at the
tipi flap and the sound of someone trying to come inside and I heard
the other two wake up as well. By her hair I could tell the visitor was a
woman, but otherwise it was too dark.

"If you are here for Escuté, I am over here."

"And Nuukaru is straight ahead of you, on the other side of the fire."

"You are both dreaming," said the woman. "Forget I am here."

"The wife of Fat Wolf. You are joking me."

"Where is Tiehteti?"

"He is right here," said Escuté. "You are talking to him right now."

"Is he in here or not?"

"I don't know. Tiehteti, are you here? Probably not. I saw him heading out to the pasture; Fucks a Mare was going to show him something."

Hates Work said: "You are a serious asshole, Escuté."

"But funny?"

"Sometimes."

"Nuukaru, I have bad news. For the one-thousandth time, a woman
has come to the tipi and she has no interest in you."

"Fuck off," said Nuukaru.

"As for Tiehteti," he pronounced, "it is time for him to become
a man. It is a process that requires physical contact, and so at some
point, unless you would simply prefer to watch a master at work, you
will have to tell this woman, who is among the most beautiful of all
Comanches, though also the laziest, where you are located in the tipi."

"I'm over here," I said quietly.

"Nuukaru, you skinny pervert, don't think you can lie there and
masturbate; get up and give Tiehteti his privacy."

"*Noyoma nakuhkupa.*"

"I would prefer not to," said Escuté. "For I am wise, and a great leader, and one day I'll be your chief."

He and Nuukaru took their blankets and left.

"Tiehteti? Say something so I can find you."

"Follow the wall to the right," I said.

I felt her touch my pallet. It was too dark to see her, or to even know who she was except by her voice, but I could hear the rustling as she took off her dress. Then she slipped under the robe. Her skin was smooth against me. She began to kiss my neck and drift her fingers along my stomach, I tried to touch her, but she put my hand back and continued to rub my belly, then my thighs, it seemed I ought to be doing something, I tried to reach between her legs, touched hair, but she stopped that hand as well. I began to feel docious. Nothing was expected of me; she was a grown woman and she had the reins.

She was of this same opinion. She ran her fingernails up and down, across my chest and down my legs, while slowly kissing my neck. This went on much longer than I thought it properly ought to, but finally she climbed on top of me and then I was inside.

There was a noise. Escuté poked his head into the tipi.

"How long, wife of Fat Wolf? One minute? Or, let me guess, he is already *pua*."

"Out," she said. "Go masturbate yourself with Nuukaru."

She kissed me on the nose. She was leaning over me, being very still. I wanted to start moving but she held me in place.

"How does that feel, brother-in-law?"

I made some noise.

She moved her hips. "Should I do this?"

"Yes."

"Hmmm. Maybe not."

I didn't say anything.

"I think we will just stay like this," she said.

I cleared my throat.

"It feels good to me also," she said.

This seemed like an unbelievable coincidence. At some point she began to move slowly. She was leaning forward and our foreheads were touching and she was holding my hands. Her breath was sweet. "Hates Work is not my real name," she said. "My name is Single Bird."

BY THE TIME Nʉʉkaru and Escuté came back, I had slept with Single Bird five times. I expected Escuté to have something to say but he didn't; he and Nʉʉkaru whispered something to each other and then Nʉʉkaru went to his pallet but Escuté, instead of going to bed, slipped over to us very quietly. He felt Single Bird's hair, and then he gently felt my face, and then he patted me on the chest and said something in Comanche I did not understand, and Single Bird murmured something in her sleep, and Escuté leaned forward and kissed her hair and patted me again and then kissed me on the forehead. Then he went back to his pallet.

I was awake. I woke up Single Bird and we did it again.

IN THE MORNING, when the faintest of gray light was coming through the smoke flap, I felt her get up. I pulled her back.

"No," she whispered. "It's already late."

"Tell me why they call you Hates Work."

"Because I only do the work of ten men. Instead of fifty." She leaned over and kissed me. "Don't look at me in public. This will probably never happen again. This is the first time my husband has sent me to anyone, and I don't know what kind of mood he's going to be in when I get back."

A few hours later, Nʉʉkaru and Escuté and I were sitting around the fire, eating dried elk and watching the bustle of the camp. Something was wrong with Escuté; normally he did his hair carefully into an a fan on the top of his head but that morning he had not even painted himself.

"Is Fat Wolf going to be angry at me?" I said.

"He's going to cut your dick off. I hope it was worth it."

"Don't listen to him," said Nuukaru. "Everyone wants to sleep with Hates Work and you're the only one who has, except the guy who paid fifty horses for her."

"My father paid fifty horses, not my fat brother. If it was my father getting her I wouldn't care."

"Escuté is especially pissed, as you can tell."

"Why shouldn't I be? Where are my fifty fucking horses if I wanted to marry? Meanwhile, Hates Work gets sent to Tiehteti."

"Who do you want to marry?" I said.

"No one. That's the point. Who the fuck can I marry now that the fat one has taken the best-looking girl anyone has ever heard of?"

"Her sister is not bad," said Nuukaru.

"I am fucked, is the point. He is a fat coward but I still end up looking like the bad one. Eight of the horses that went to her bride-price were horses I gave to my father. When was the last time my brother even went on a raid?"

"You should stop," said Nuukaru.

"I don't care who hears me."

"You will later."

We sat for a while. I couldn't see what Escuté had to worry about. He had six scalps and while he was shorter and slimmer than his father and brother, he was nicely built and had an easy way of moving and all the young Indians, men and women alike, looked up to him. Then I thought maybe he was right: Hates Work was his only real equal in the band.

"There is a very beautiful captive owned by Lazy Feet, the blond one? The German?"

"Yellow Hair," I said.

"Yes, her. She is the equal of Hates Work."

"I'm not marrying a fucking captive. No offense, Tiehteti."

"We're all from captives at some point," said Nuukaru.

"Yes, but still I am not doing it."

"You weren't angry last night," I said.

"No, I wasn't. I'm not angry at you, Tiehteti; I'm glad you got a taste, you deserved it. It's just my father, because the fat one is the oldest, he can do no wrong, and fifty fucking horses, he didn't even try to negotiate."

"We all know you'll be a chief," said Nuukaru. "Everyone knows that. Your brother won't be. He's just a man with a rich father."

"Yes, and if I get killed on a raid before I get to be a chief? While my father supports the fat one and buys him a few more wives?'"

"Then I'll make sure you don't get scalped."

"Unbelievable," said Escuté, and shook his head.

"You still have a father," said Nuukaru. "This is something to be grateful for."

"Your father died well and he wasn't scalped," said Escuté. "He is already at the happy hunting grounds."

"Thank you, Escuté, and where is that, exactly? I've heard it's beyond the sun somewhere, in the west. You know it's strange, because sometimes I get the urge to ask my father's advice on various matters, or feel his hand on my shoulder, but everyone assures me he is in the west, just past the sun, though Tiehteti, who does not know our ways, tells me that if you follow the sun to the west you eventually reach a limitless expanse of salty water, rather than a land where horses run fast enough to fly, where it is neither hot nor cold, where game impales itself on your lance and is magically roasted and you eat everything with an accompaniment of the richest marrow."

"I'm sorry," said Escuté. "I have no right to complain."

"Ah. For once your lips move and there is truth."

"On a different matter," I said, "do you think it's likely I'll see Hates Work again?"

"Knowing my brother, no."

"Impossible to say," said Nuukaru. "But it would be an extremely bad idea to think about her at all, as Fat Wolf might be sensitive about it. That was incredibly generous, what he did, and he may have done it just to look good."

"She enjoyed herself, I think."

Escuté shook his head. "Be careful, boy."

"She enjoyed herself because her husband gave her permission. If it ever happens without his permission, or he even suspects it has happened, he will cut off her nose and ears and slash her face. And you will develop similar problems yourself."

"In your favor," said Escuté, holding up a hand, "your accomplishments notwithstanding, he still considers you to be extremely young, and not so much of a threat. So it is possible."

"You are better off thinking about her sister, Prairie Flower, who is unmarried."

"Also not as lazy. Or as good-looking, for that matter."

"But still very pretty. And intelligent."

"And thus pursued by plenty of men with more to recommend them than you have, who have killed more than one enemy and stolen many horses."

"Not to mention Escuté fucked her, so she almost certainly has a disease."

"Perhaps," said Escuté, "you should concentrate your efforts on your riding and shooting, which are known to need attention, and consider this as you might consider a visit from the Great Spirit."

"Scalps and horses, my son."

I didn't say anything.

"But if some other girl decides to come to your tipi at night, of her own free will, and manages to make it past Nuukaru and I, which is unlikely, then you can safely fuck her. While the opposite situation—let's say you have been talking to a girl, and she has given you certain signals, such as letting you put a finger inside her while she is out gathering firewood, and, being certain she likes you, and being desirous of a respectable place to make love to her, you decide to visit her tipi one night—"

"You will be instantly killed by her father," said Nuukaru. "Or some other family member."

"Who will then give Toshaway a horse in compensation for your death."

"In short," said Nʉʉkaru, "until they get married, the women get to be with whomever they want and are the only ones allowed to choose. Afterward, if they behave like that, they get their noses cut off."

"So what do I do now?"

Escuté was shaking his head. "Listen to the white one. He lost his virginity only eight hours ago."

"Horse and scalps," said Nʉʉkaru. "Horses and scalps."

CHAPTER FOURTEEN

JEANNIE McCULLOUGH

I n 1937, when she was twelve, a man named William Blount, along with his two sons, disappeared from his farm near the McCullough ranch. The farm itself was dried up, the family living on relief flour and rabbit meat, and Blount's wife said her husband and two boys had gone onto the McCullough's property—which still had plenty of water and grass—to get a deer to feed themselves. Neither Blount nor his sons ever came home and his wife claimed to have heard shots from the direction of the ranch.

Everyone knew what happened if you trespassed on McCullough land. Both roads to town wound through its quarter-million acres and if your car broke down, you were better walking ten miles along the road than cutting through the pastures, where fence riders might take you for a thief. After the Garcia troubles, the ranch had been declared a state game preserve, which meant that in addition to the vaqueros, the McCulloughs had game wardens—technically employees of the state—as additional security. Some said they buried a dozen people a year in the back pastures, poachers and vagrant Mexicans. Others said it was two dozen. *Those people are just talking,* is what her father said. But she could see that her brothers, who treated the vaqueros as family, were not comfortable around the fence riders.

The day after the Blounts disappeared, Jeannie answered the front door to find the sheriff standing there alone. He was originally from up north; suspected of being a half-breed Indian, he was a tall thin man with a sunburned face and hawk nose. He had been elected over Berger, her father's man, by pandering to the Mexicans. Berger had hunted their land and borrowed their horses; Van Zandt only came when there was trouble. Or, said her father, when he needed money.

On the staircase landing, right under the big Tiffany window, was a daybed where you could lie and read. You could also hear downstairs without being seen. She lay there, with the sunlight coming through the window, the portraits of her family along the staircase: the Colonel leaning on his sword, in the uniform of the Lost Cause; the Colonel's dead wife with their three boys. Both the wife and one of the sons (Everett, she knew) were illuminated by an otherwordly light; Peter (disgraced) and Phineas (whom Jeannie liked) looked normal. Also along the stairs were marble cherubs and busts. She listened to her father and the sheriff.

"I didn't want to call," said Van Zandt.

Her father said something she couldn't hear.

"Folks are saying we ought to be searching for these Blounts."

"Evan, if we let ten deputies on our land ever'time some greaser disappeared . . ."

"This is a white man and two boys and folks are pretty worked up, even the Mexicans. I haven't seen anything like it."

"Well, it is nothing new," said her father. "There are plenty around here who won't like me unless I lose money to them in every horse trade."

Relations between the McCulloughs and the citizenry had been strained for some time. A third of the town was out of work; a few months earlier it had come out that her father had blocked the construction of a new state highway through their lands—the road would have cut thirty miles off the trip between Laredo and Carrizo Springs. The *San Antonio Express* picked up the story. It was the same thing they were saying about the King and Kenedy ranches: Another Walled Kingdom. Common men not welcome.

"It's this goddamn Roosevelt," said her father. "You mark my words, that was the last free election we will ever see in this country. We are on the verge of a dictatorship."

THE NEXT DAY a crowd gathered at the main gate. They stayed there all day. Her father did not go down to talk to them; instead he distributed the ranch's half-dozen Thompson guns among the hands who knew how to use them.

"Stay off your porch tonight," he told her. "Stay away from the windows and don't turn on any lights."

"What's going to happen?" she said.

"Nothing. This has gone on plenty of times before."

She went to bed early, climbing the stairs to the east wing, where the children slept. All the bedrooms had their own sleeping porches and she turned out the light, debated a few seconds, then, disobeying her father's orders, went out to her porch and got quietly into bed. The stars were bright as always and she lay listening to the crickets, the hoots of owls, lowing of cattle, whippoorwills, a coyote. There was the creaking of the windmill that fed the house cistern, but she barely noticed. The tree frogs were thrumming, which meant rain. She heard a rustling from the next porch—her brother Paul.

"Is that you?"

"Yeah," he said.

"What d'you think's gonna happen?"

"I dunno."

"It's nonsense about those Blounts, isn't it?"

He didn't answer.

"Isn't it?"

"I'm not sure," he said.

"Are Jonas and Clint in bed?"

"They're with Daddy."

"Can you see down to the gate?"

"Stop asking questions."

It was quiet and then he added: "I can't see anything."

"What'll happen if they come through?"

"I imagine Daddy will shoot them. I saw them carrying the Lewis gun a few hours ago."

Her father must have called the governor because the next morning a company of Rangers drove down from San Antonio. The day after that he agreed to let the sheriff search the property, all quarter-million acres. The Blounts were never found, but she knew as well as anyone it would have been like needles in a haystack.

OF THE FOUR children, only she and Jonas liked school. Paul and Clint found it boring; their father had no use for it either; the compulsory attendance laws were another sign of the government reaching into his pocket. The school was in McCullough Springs, named after her great-grandfather. After the Blount incident her father set out to mend relations, agreeing to pay for a mural that had long been planned for the school, a pastoral scene showing Americans and Mexicans working together to build the town, but when the mural was finished, it showed skeletal Tejano farm workers stooped in an onion field, eyes bulging, a few ragged crosses in the distance. A *patrón* bearing a passing resemblance to Jeannie's father sat astride a black horse, keeping watch. The mural was painted over and Jeannie's father gave up trying to be nice to the townspeople.

The McCulloughs paid most of the school's expenses, though the Midkiffs and Reynoldses chipped in as well. The children of Mexicans attended free, though never for very long; they came and went throughout the year, a month here, a month there, the truant officer never went after them. There was no point trying to be friends; they would disappear for half the year and when they came back she would have to start all over. The children of the white farmers were better, but when they visited the ranch she could see how they wished they lived there instead of her, and an uncomfortable eagerness would come into their manner. Eventually she had stopped being friends with anyone. The only person she had much in common with was Fannie Midkiff, but she was three years older and crazy for boys. She was bound for a sorry end, they all said, Midkiff or not.

BEFORE THE COLONEL died, so long as he had the energy, she was allowed to sit with him and do her studying. The Colonel spent his mornings on the west gallery, out of the sun, and his evenings on the east gallery, also out of the sun. The visitors never stopped: a man from the government (a Jew, they said) came with a recording machine and the Colonel would talk into it for hours. There were daybeds on the galleries so he might sleep whenever he wanted; he slept and slept, that was what he did mostly; *One day I will sleep forever,* that is what he told her.

He never slept for very long, though. He was always up in time to shoot a snake trying to get across the wide dirt yard, hoping to reach the cool under the porch. *Someday we will live in a house that doesn't have a damned dirt yard,* said her grandmother. *That will be the day we get snakebit,* said the Colonel.

If Jeannie happened to be nearby when the Colonel woke up, he would send her for ice. Or mint; he had planted a patch around one of the stock tanks. He seemed to live off juleps. She would crush the mint at the bottom of the glass and add three spoons of sugar and fill the glass with ice. Sometimes, before he added the whiskey, he would let her suck on the sweet minty ice.

When it was not too hot, she and the Colonel would go on walks, shuffling through the tall grass under the bright sky, stopping to rest in an oak mott, or a copse of cedar elms, or along the streams if they were running. She was always missing things: deer, a fox, the movement of a bird or mouse, a flower blooming out of season, a snake den. Though she could see twice as far as he could, she felt blind around him—she noticed practically nothing except the sun and grass. She often wondered if he were making things up, but every time they went walking, he recovered some keepsake—the bleached skull of a possum, a shed antler, a bright wingfeather off a yellowhammer woodpecker. He walked very slowly and often had to stop and lean on her for support. If it were not too dry when they came on a snake den, he would send her back for a jug of kerosene to pour down the hole, but it was dry most of the time. Sometimes when they stopped to rest he would ask her to dig a thorn out of his hard yellow foot. He didn't wear boots; he could no longer keep his balance in them. He wore only Indian moccasins. Indians—the real Indians from the reservation in Oklahoma—would give him things like that, and when they left, he got a sad look and would be short with her father or anyone else who bothered him. Jeannie was his favorite, it was plain to everyone, and her father pretended not to care, though she knew he did.

If the Colonel was busy and she did not have schoolwork, her job was to gather the milch cows from the pasture and milk them, smelling their sweet breath and listening to the sound of the pail, tinny at first, then soft as it filled with milk. Her brothers hated the job—it was not proper work for a vaquero, being swished in the face by the cow's dungy tail—but there was a satisfaction at seeing the animal's relief, the sounds she could make with the streams of milk, playing them against the sides of the pail. It was not a song, but it was something like one. The milk was taken to the kitchen, strained, and either put into the icebox or left out for the cream to rise and be skimmed off. The domestic staff were allowed to have all the skimmed milk they wanted, but everything else was for the family. They always had more milk than they needed and often entire buckets would clabber and one of her brothers would carry it out to the bunkhouse for the vaqueros. It was something she missed later in life, clabbered milk with brown sugar and fruit. When pasteurization came along, they said clabber wasn't safe, though she'd been eating it all her life.

When she was not gathering the milch cows she was looking after the dogies; technically this was her brothers' job as well, but they rarely attended to it. When a calf was orphaned, the hands would drive it to the pens near the house. Jeannie would tie a cow to the fence, then splash the cow's milk on the dogie's head. She allowed the cow to smell her own milk on the orphan, then brought the dogie to the cow's udder. Usually the cow would kick the strange calf away, and Jeannie would have to wait a while before repeating the process. Sometimes the cow gave in immediately and allowed the dogie to suckle; other times it took days. Clint and Paul were always buying horses with their dogie money; no one knew what Jonas did with his. She gave hers to her father to hold, and when she was twelve she opened an account in San Antonio, depositing nearly ten thousand dollars.

WHEN SHE COULD not sit on the porch with the Colonel, her other favorite place was the old Garcia house, which, though the Garcias were long dead, was still called the casa mayor. She had known from a young age what happened to them.

"Pedro Garcia didn't have any sons to work the ranch," her father said, "and his daughters all married bad men who ran Pedro into debt. The bad men started stealing our cattle and then they shot your uncle Glendale."

"So we went and shot them back."

"No, the Texas Rangers went to their house and tried to talk to them, and we went along with the Rangers. But the Garcias started shooting at the Rangers."

There was nothing higher in her mind than a Texas Ranger. "I am glad they are dead," she said about the Garcias.

"They were good people who had bad luck," he said. Then he added: "Bad things can happen to good people."

Daughters—that was one bad thing that could happen to you. Once she had overheard her father telling a reporter, who was visiting for the occasion of the Colonel's hundredth birthday, saying: "First you pray for sons, second you pray for oil. You look at the Millers over in Carrizo, they used to own eighty sections, but they had nothing but she-stuff to pass it to."

She went right up to her room and at supper she pretended to be sick. After that she had not minded when the Colonel talked bad about her father.

THE GARCIA HOUSE had been built in the 1760s, one of the first settlements in the area; it sat on a rise over the Nueces River valley where, even with the rest of land dried up, a spring still flowed from the rocks. The house, which resembled a small castle, was built of heavy stone blocks. There was an observation tower, nearly forty feet high, for keeping watch over hostile territory, and the casa mayor's windows were tall slits, too narrow to climb through. There were plenty of gun ports as well, which she imagined had spit death at heathen Indians.

The roof was long collapsed and inside the casa mayor, mesquite and huisache grew up among the debris, along with a few oaks and hackberries that were already higher than the walls. From the outside, the casa mayor now looked like a walled garden, a safe and inviting place, though it was not. The floor was dirt and there were rusty nails and springs and bits of jagged wood, not to mention the thorns of the huisache. She was not allowed inside but she went anyway, picking her way carefully to the tower. After clambering over more half-burned beams and thorny brush, she could reach the stone staircase that wound around the inside of the tower, all the way to the top, though there was no longer any platform. She would stand on the narrow top stair, in the sun, looking out over the country as it descended to the Nueces River, then back toward her own house, and beyond that McCullough Springs, with its two- and three-story buildings and big stone bank. When the Colonel first moved here he had lived in a jacal, and then a house made from timber. That house had burned after the Colonel's wife died and he'd built another one from stone.

She had to squint to ignore the farmers and laborers like ants in the fields near the river, and she would avoid looking toward her own house and the town, and try to see the land as it had once been. A poor man's paradise—that was how the Colonel described it. But she preferred to imagine herself a princess, courted by all the sons of hacendados; there would be seven and she would have no interest in a single one and would lock herself in the tower and refuse to eat, until the poorest and ugliest of the seven revealed himself to be a prince in disguise, whereupon they would sail away to Spain, where it was cool and the servants would feed her plums.

Other times she pretended to be Mrs. Rosalie Evans, the Englishwoman her father always talked about who, just a few years back, had barricaded herself in a tower just like this one, and, in the name of democracy, had shot it out to the death with the Mexican communists who had come to take her land.

When she got too tired standing in the tower (there were only the narrow steps, a four-story plunge just beyond) or her eyes hurt from the glare, she would strip off all her clothes and sit in the spring, the best on the McCullough property. The vaqueros gave the casa mayor a wide berth and she knew she would never be discovered.

Mostly the spring ran down over the rocks toward the river, but it had once been dammed, and off to one side was a stone spillway that carried water to a cistern under the house. She could hang her head through the opening and smell the damp. From the cistern another stone trough carried the overflow to a bathing pool below the house and from there a third spillway diverted to a sink for washing clothes or pots, and from there the water would flow to a large earthen terrace, now overgrown with mesquite and persimmon, which had once been the kitchen garden. It was like the Roman ruins they showed in schoolbooks, but here she could walk along the edge of the old bathing pool, imagining it full of cool water, and sit in the shade of live oaks. In the distance were rolling hills and oak motts and buffalo, she imagined, grazing along the river. Though of course there would be danger; she would want a pistol for Indians. She could not imagine a more perfect life.

In the pasture below the house were more stone walls and rubble, the remnants of a church and other important buildings, the purposes of which were now a mystery. Many of the old *corrales de leña* still stood and the Garcias' spring still flowed, but someone had knocked out the dam so the water no longer reached the spillway. The casa mayor had gone dry like everything else. The stream now flowed in its original bed, down past the old church, where occasionally, especially after a hard rain, it would dislodge interesting things. Small bits of tin whose purpose she could not identify, uncountable shards of colored glazed ceramics, broken cups the Colonel said were for drinking chocolate. Antler buttons, brass screws, various coins and fragments of bone.

Only the children had interest in the casa mayor. The Mexican hands, if forced to fetch cattle from the pastures nearby, always crossed themselves. They could not help being ignorant Catholics. And the Garcias had not been able to help being lazy, cattle-stealing greasers and she felt sorry for them, even if they had shot her uncle Glenn.

Occasionally, it seemed strange to her that lazy greasers would construct elaborate stone houses, complete with cisterns, bathing pools, and various gardens, but on the few occasions those thoughts rose to the surface of her mind, she reminded herself that people often did strange, unaccountable things, like the Brenners, whose two sons had been shot robbing a bank in San Antonio, or the Morales family, who had worked for the McCulloughs three generations until their daughter ran off to become a prostitute. So Clint told her. He had scratched his name into the soft caliche walls of the casa mayor, C-L-I-N-T, in letters as tall as he was.

ONE SCALDING-HOT DAY during the summer, when there was no school, and she was bored with swimming in the stock tank, she and Clint and Paul rode up to the hacienda.

They took a meandering route, passing along the way a spring none of them had ever seen before, not as large as the one by the casa mayor, but a spring nonetheless, which flowed into a stream lined with persimmons, grapes, and oaks. They rode to the edge of a swimming hole—where it was clear you might gig as many frogs as you wanted—

noting the place so they could return to it later. There were stream-beds all over the ranch, but they were mostly dry, filled with sand, their courses marked with the skeletons of dead trees. Irrigation, the Colonel said. It had dried everything up. Which was another thing about the old Garcia place—all the springs there still ran, it was the best-watered section of the entire ranch.

Jonas, her oldest brother, was not with them. He was about to go away to college in the east, and as punishment, their father did not let him take a single day off the whole summer. Paul and Clint, the middle children, had decided not to work in the heat. Years earlier, she had asked Clint if he thought their father should get another wife, so they would have a real mother, and Clint had said we already had a mother, except you killed her. By being born, he added.

The only satisfaction she got was hearing Clint whipped for a very long time. Still she knew it was true. Their mother had died giving birth to her. God's will, her father said. Though another time he said it was because he hadn't gone to church.

She imagined if she had a mother, what that would be like. They would go burying things and digging them back up. Once, in school, she had buried a thick silver ring the Colonel had given her, as deep in the sandbox as she could put it. When she came back a little while later, Perry Midkiff was digging it up. Their teacher was standing there.

"That's mine," said Jeanne Anne, pointing at the silver ring.

"No," the teacher said, "he found it fair and square."

"But I put it there."

"Why would you put a ring in the sandbox?" said the teacher. She was young and fat and had no chin to speak of—she would die an old maid, everyone said.

"I wanted to discover it," Jeannie told them, but even as the words came out, she knew they made no sense. She had lost the ring forever.

★   ★   ★

THERE WAS PLENTY to dig for at the casa mayor, in the dirt inside the walls, or out in the yard, or down around the old church and the fallen-down jacals of the dead vaqueros. It was rare that some piece of treasure was not unearthed. There was a crumbling Spanish breast-plate that her brothers broke into pieces trying to dig out. Plenty of old weapons, so rusted they were barely identifiable: a rapier, a lance head, hatchet and knife blades, a single-shot pistol with the lock broken off.

That particular day, walking along the streambed by the church, they came to a fresh cutbank where the earth had caved. There was a flat piece of wood lying just under the dirt, and Clint, sensing treasure, dug it out and flung it away before leaping back suddenly. Looking up at them, with the bright sun striking it directly, was a human skeleton draped with tattered cloth. Clint reached in and plucked up the skull. It was small—smaller than a muskmelon—and colored a deep yellow. She had thought all bones were white. There was a gold necklace that Clint removed as well. "It's a girl!" he exclaimed.

Clint made a show of looking at the skull for a while, then tossed it away into the grass. She wanted to touch it but could not. Paul put the skull back in its proper place, put back the coffin lid, and kicked dirt and rocks overtop.

"The animals will just dig it up again, jackass."

"There's nothing to eat in there," said Paul. "We're the only ones who care."

Back in the shade of the spring they stripped, though they were all too old now to remove their underclothes. They sat in the cool water, looking out over the pastures and the low crumbled walls of the old church, the Nueces far beyond.

"How old was she?"

"Half-grown," said Paul.

"Around your age," said Clint.

After a time they got cold; the temperature of the water never changed, no matter how hot the weather. They ate lunch and sat on the warm flat stones. Not far from the church, a group of cows had been standing in the shade, watching them, and now a bull came into the lower pasture, sniffing the air and following a particular cow. They watched the cow run, stop and look over her shoulder, then run again. Jeannie had a terrible premonition that the animals would step into the coffin, but they did not go anywhere near it.

"They are all like that, aren't they?" Clint was saying. "They run away but really they are begging for it. Soon he will get what he is after. And she as well."

Jeannie laughed nervously and squeezed her legs closed. Underneath the hair there were awkward flaps of skin and underneath those, a tiny opening that she knew a man was supposed to fit into, though she could not understand how or why she would ever let that happen, except by some strange agreement, the way she had once allowed Paul to borrow her horse.

"See," said Clint. He nodded at her. "She knows what I am talking about."

The cow had run partway up the hill toward them, then seen them and stopped. The bull caught up to her and she had not run and he quickly jumped on top of her.

"Look at that fuckin' hammer," said Clint.

They could not see well but it was clear the bull had put something into the cow and was moving it in and out. Finally he slid off her and stood panting and blowing.

"One of these days some big bull is gonna be doing that to you."

"Leave her be," Paul said.

Clint punched him but Paul just sat there. Poor gentle Paul. A few years later she would put his death notice on the dresser of his room, where his bed was still neatly done, his bookshelf still full of dime westerns, his school picture still dusted every week by the maids. *Small-arms fire, Ardennes Forest.* January and the snow waist-deep, and Paul, who had grown up in the Wild Horse Desert, had not even had a proper coat.

Clint had died first, but in Italy. Her brothers had both traveled a long way to die, but that evening, years before either of them had left the ranch forever, Clint had come to her and, without saying anything, had handed her the necklace from the young girl's grave.

Clint the Cruel. That was her name for him, though she knew it would have hurt him. He made a hobby of trapping birds and small animals, skinning and stuffing them until they did not resemble animals, they were like small lumpy pillows; he had them all over his room. At fourteen, he was an excellent hand, but her father cared only for Jonas. He was the oldest. Clint was a better rider, a better roper; he threw like the old Mexicans—overhand or under, no windup, no extra movement—and he rarely wasted a loop. He could pluck a calf from the herd before it even knew he was there. He was always first to tail a big bull or climb on a gut-twister; she had seen horses sunfishing, trying to turn themselves inside out; they could not get Clint off their backs.

It didn't matter. Jonas was the oldest and her father paid more attention to Jonas's various failings—too numerous to list—than to Clint's triumphs. One day the ranch would belong to her father, and after that it would belong to Jonas. Everyone knew it, including Clint, who had spent two days sick in bed after drinking a bottle of their grandmother's blackberry cordial.

But Jonas was leaving at the end of the summer and had told her, privately, that he was not coming back. Though she had not believed him at the time.

TECHNICALLY JEANNIE HAD another family, another set of grandparents from her mother's side. But the other grandmother had died long before Jeannie was born; she might as well have never existed. Her other grandfather died when Jeannie was eight. He was a farmer who had come down from Illinois to buy land the Colonel was selling on promotion. Maybe if his daughter—Jeannie's mother—hadn't passed Jeannie might have known him better, but the few times he had visited, he had been so quiet and deferential that he had seemed no different than a stranger. He had not tried to make any claim on her or any of her brothers, and once, after he left the house, her father called him a man who knew his place.

Much later, it had occurred to her that, scientifically anyway, she was a closer relation to this quiet farmer than she was to the Colonel, but she quickly put the thought from her mind. When he died, it was the last she heard of her mother's side of the family. She did not see much point to them; even the poorest vaquero was higher than a farmer. She was more interested in her uncle Glenn. He had still been a boy when he was first shot, and she imagined she would have done the same thing herself, bravely alerting her father of the Mexicans to their rear, then clutching her heart and dying painlessly. Of course, Glenn had not died. But she would have. They would have named the school after her, and put up a statue, and her teacher would be sorry for letting Perry Midkiff steal the Colonel's silver ring.

AFTER THE COLONEL passed, her grandmother moved to Dallas, returning to the ranch a few times a year to make sure things were still in order. Jeannie had not expected to miss her. Her grandmother insisted that she wash and dress for supper—which her brothers did not have to do—scrubbing the dirt off Jeannie's hands, cleaning under her nails with a steel pick. Though she also threatened Jeannie's brothers with a quirt if they treated her improperly or said something a lady wasn't supposed to hear. But her grandmother was not home very often.

And so, as the only woman in the house, she was entirely unprepared for what happened when she was twelve, which had sent her running for her father and nearly stepping on a snake. He understood the situation so quickly, before the words had even come out, that she realized he must have known something like this would happen. He began ringing frantically for a maid. The two of them stood in silence. Her father, she saw, was more embarrassed than she was and she knew she was lucky this had not happened in front of her brothers, or in school, or in church; in fact it could not have happened at a better time, walking by herself, examining the tracks by the stock tank.

"Gramammy didn't say anything about this?" He called again for help. "Where is everyone?"

She didn't know.

"Well, from a scientific point of view you are a female. And your body is preparing itself so that eventually, many years from now, as a grown woman, you can get married."

She knew he did not mean married. As she looked at him, shifting his weight from one foot to the other, his white shirt stained with sweat, it occurred to her that she could no longer entirely trust him. The Colonel had been right; the only one you could depend on was yourself. She had always known it on some level or another and at this realization all the shame faded away from her; she was embarrassed only for her father, who despite his height and big hands was completely helpless. She excused herself and went into Jonas's old room and took an undershirt from his dresser, which she cut up to line her shorts.

When she went back downstairs a maid was waiting and, after inspecting Jeannie's handiwork and judging it suitable, explained as best as she was able, half in Spanish, half in a coded Catholic English, exactly what was happening, no, it would not stop, and then the two of them went to town to get supplies.

CHAPTER FIFTEEN

DIARIES OF PETER McCULLOUGH

SEPTEMBER 5, 1915

Glendale has been home two weeks, but he is pale, weak, and still fighting off some infection. Tomorrow they will take him back to San Antonio. Charlie's arm is better, though not entirely, and there is an image clinging to my mind, which is both of my sons laid out together in one casket.

AFTER A LONG absence, the dark figure has returned. I see him in the shadows of my office; he follows me around the house, though he has not yet begun to call to me (I once saw him rise from the middle of the flooded Red, his arms open for me like Christ). I have unloaded all my pistols. No longer the energy to be angry at Pedro and my father. Visited the graves of my mother and Everett and Pete Junior (snakebite, which I cannot blame on the Colonel, and yet I do).

Of course he senses something wrong. Appears to not know what. A few times he has found me reading in the great room and stopped as if waiting for me to speak. When I did not—where would I even begin?—he shuffled on.

★   ★   ★

A MAN OF Pedro's intelligence could not have overlooked it. So my father's voice—the one inside my head—tells me. The same voice says Pedro had no choice—his daughters had married those men, they had become his family, fathered his grandchildren. And if Pedro had no choice, then we didn't either. That is my father's logic—there is never any choice.

Meanwhile my old acts of cowardice continue to haunt. Had I married María (for whom I briefly harbored feelings), instead of Sally (my proper match) . . . who was thirty-two and twice jilted, who loved her life in Dallas, whose bitterness was apparent from the moment she stepped from the train, who came because her father and my father and her own biology gave her no choice. *I was so lonely when I met Peter,* that is the story she tells of our courtship. Our fathers arranging the breeding as if we were heifer and bull. Perharps I am dramatic; in truth our first years were quite pleasant, but then Sally must have realized that, just as I always said, I really had no intention of leaving this land. Many families of our stature, she rightly pointed out, maintain more than one residence. But we are not like other families.

THERE ARE MOMENTS I see José and Chico and (impossibly) Pedro himself on the other side of the river, shooting at us. Other moments I remember the event as it truly happened, a half-dozen riders in the dark, dodging into the brush, hundreds of yards away. Perhaps Mexican because of the cut of their clothing, perhaps not.

Being at the rear, higher on the riverbank, I had the best vantage. If I'd taken more time with my shooting, or dismounted . . . but I did not want to hit them. I thought I might push death aside, if only for a moment, so I held over their heads and emptied my rifle, nothing but sound and fury, the extreme range absolving me of marksmanship. Had I simply adjusted the ladder on my sight . . . one of the men I intentionally missed likely shot Glenn. The incident might have ended there. Though it is unlikely.

★ ★ ★

I CANNOT HELP having sympathy for the Mexicans. So far as their white neighbors are concerned, they come into this world coyotes in human form, and when they die they are treated like coyotes as well. My instinct is to root for them; they despise me for it. I see myself in them; they are insulted. Perhaps you cannot respect a man who has what you do not. Unless you think he might kill you. A preference for hardhanded authority seems bred into them—they are comfortable with the old relationships, *patrón* and *peón*—and any attempt to change these boundaries they find undignified, or suspicious, or weak.

TO BE A simple animal like my father, untroubled by consciousness, or conscience. To sleep soundly, at ease with your certainties, men as expendable as beef.

WHEN I SLEEP I see Pedro, neatly arranged with his vaqueros in the yard. Eyes open, mouths gaping, the flies and bees swarming. I see him in bed, his daughter dead at his feet, his wife dead at his side. I wonder if he saw them shot down. I wonder if he recognized the men doing it as his friends.

SEPTEMBER 17, 1915

Sally has moved into her own room. Glenn continues to recover in San Antonio; we drive there alternately to be with him. Pilkington has no explanation. The vaqueros suspect dark forces, a *bruja* at work.

Today Sally began a conversation at supper:

"Colonel, what did you used to offer for a bounty on wolves?"

My father: "Ten dollars a pelt. Same for a panther."

"What would be a good bounty on Mexicans, you think?"

"Don't," I said.

"I'm just asking, Pete. It is a reasonable question."

"I don't think you'd have to offer a bounty," said Charles.

"So is ten dollars too much? Or not enough?"

"I would prefer not to talk like this. Today or ever."

"I do not even know if you are upset about this, Peter, I can't even tell. Can anyone else? Does Peter look bothered?"

Everyone was quiet. Finally the Colonel spoke up: "Pete has his own way of handling things. You can leave him be."

She got up and took her plate into the kitchen, with a furious look at my father. Me, she already hates.

TRYING TO CONSOLE myself that we aren't alone in our suffering. Two weeks ago the railroad bridges to Brownsville were burned (again), the telegraph lines cut, two white men singled out from a crowd of laborers and shot in the middle of the morning. About twenty Tejanos killed in reprisal—twenty that anyone heard about. The Third Cavalry has been in regular fights with the Mexican army all along the border, shooting across the river. Three cavalrymen killed by insurgents near Los Indios and, across from Progreso, on the Mexican side, the head of a missing U.S. private was displayed on a pole.

In better news, the air smells sweet and the land is already coming back to life. The rain continues to fall and there are adelias and heliotrope, the hummingbirds everywhere in the anacahuita, bluewing butterflies, the scent of ébano and guayacan. The clouds glow at sunset and the river shimmers in the light. But not for Pedro. For Pedro, it is only dark.

OCTOBER 1, 1915

Woke up in a chair next to Glenn's hospital bed, thinking if I stayed there long enough my mother would come and rub my neck. I have always depended on other people to drive out the ghosts. When I shaved, the face I saw in the hospital mirror was not quite mine; it was as if there was some defect in the glass, my features crooked, out of proportion, like a dead man's.

OCTOBER 3, 1915

Back at home. Judge Poole visited from Laredo to tell me Pedro Garcia was eight years delinquent on his taxes. I knew what he was angling for. I was overcome with shame. I could barely hear what he said, my ears were throbbing.

The judge was looking at me.

"That doesn't sound right," I said.

"Pete, I hold the Webb County tax register and I have checked with Brewster in Dimmit."

"Well, I still don't believe it."

Poole sat there quivering like a bucket of clabber. He knew I was calling him a liar, but as I'm the Colonel's son he elected to overlook it. He repeated that the State of Texas was offering to sell us all the Garcia land, nearly two hundred sections, for back taxes. "Sheriff Graham has already taken possession of the property for the court."

"I thought notice of tax sale had to be posted."

"It *is* posted. It is on the courthouse door, in fact, but I do not think anyone will see it, as there are some other things posted on top of it. I do not see why any Yankee speculator ought to get into a bidding war over land that ought rightfully to belong to you."

Like all adulterers he is as passionate as a drummer, as sure of himself as Christ making his long walk . . . that the Yankee speculators were scared off long ago by all the shooting meant nothing to him. But there was no way out . . . I apologized and said my mind was still not right due to worry about Glenn. He nodded and patted my hand with his slippery claw.

I hoped my use of Glenn's name in such a mercenary fashion would not get me condemned to the flames, though if it allowed me to escape Poole's company, I might have agreed to it. I excused myself, but before I could leave (my own living room) Poole mentioned that a small consideration for his advocacy might not go unappreciated. I was thinking one hundred dollars but he read my mind. Ten thousand sounded fair, didn't I think?

Poole could have given the land to anyone, but Reynolds and Midkiff (along with all the other cattlemen in Texas) are known to be having money troubles and with the Colonel spending so much money buying up oil rights, we probably appear rich. Everyone loves the underdog. Until they have to take his side.

I AM CURIOUS if Pedro did miss some tax payments. A year, maybe. Eight is not possible. He knew what happened to Mexicans who didn't pay their taxes, though he did not know that the same thing might happen to Mexicans who did. I can hear the Colonel—no land was ever acquired honestly in the history of the earth—but it does not make me feel any better.

Total price for the Garcia sections: $103,892.17. About what the land was worth when the Apaches lived here.

OCTOBER 27, 1915

The Colonel insisted I ride with him to the Garcia compound. When we dismounted he produced several jugs of coal oil from his saddlebags.

"I don't think so," I said.

"I should have done this fifty years ago, Pete. It is like killing all the wolves but leaving a nice den for other wolves to return to."

"I won't let you burn their house."

"Well, I won't let you stop me."

"Daddy," I said.

"Pete, it has been too long since we had a real talk and I know I am hard on you. And you are mad at me for the oil leases. I should not have gone behind your back. I am sorry but it was the only way I saw of doing it."

"I do not give two shits about the oil leases."

"Well, they were necessary," he said.

"We are surviving just fine. Unlike some of our neighbors."

"You know I was fond of old Pedro."

"Not fond enough, apparently."

It was quiet for a long time.

"I don't have to tell you what this land used to look like," he said. "And you don't have to tell me that I am the one who ruined it. Which I did, with my own hands, and ruined forever. You're old enough to remember when the grass between here and Canada was balls high to a Belgian, and yes it is possible that in a thousand years it will go back to what it once was, though it seems unlikely. But that is the story of the human race. Soil to sand, fertile to barren, fruit to thorns. It is all we know how to do."

"The brush can be removed."

"At enormous cost, which used to go into our pockets."

"And still we are not doing badly."

He shrugged. "Pete, I love this land, and I love my family, but I do not love cattle. You grew up with them. I will not say I grew up with the buffalo, because while it is true it is also an exaggeration, but I will say that to you there is something sacred in a cow, and in the man who raises and cares for them, but me, I can take them or leave them; it was a business that I undertook to support our family, and I have seen so many things disappear in my lifetime that I cannot bring myself to worry about this one. Which brings me around to my point. What were our losses this year, in one pasture, to the Garcias?"

"Daddy," I said again, a strange word to come from the mouth of a man who is nearly fifty, but the Colonel continued:

"In the west pasture alone, in this year alone, we lost forty thousand dollars. In the other pastures, maybe eighty thousand. And I would judge they have been robbing us for quite a while, at least since the first of the sons-in-law showed up. Now there has been a drought these four years, but does a drought reduce your calves fifty percent? Not if you've been feeding like we did. Do you suddenly lose thirty percent of your momma cows? No, you do not. That is the hand of man. You figure in the increase, they have stolen close to two million dollars from us."

"Don't forget the increase on the mules."

He shook his head and looked off into the distance and it was quiet for a long time. Of course I did not have to acquire this land, as he did. Of course I take it for granted in a manner that seems unthinkable to him. The Garcia sections will double the size of our ranch; this at a time when other cattlemen are struggling. It is an enormous coup, from a certain perspective, and I wonder if he is capable of seeing any other. Then he was talking.

"You've never had any problem standing up to your own family, Pete. But you have a hard time standing up to strangers. That has always been your problem." He wiped his forehead. "I am going to burn out this roach nest. Are you going to help me or not?"

"What's the point of having all this?" I said.

"Because otherwise it would be someone else. Someone was going to end up with this land, maybe Ira Midkiff or Bill Reynolds or maybe Poole would have gotten half and Graham would have gotten a quarter, and Gilbert would have gotten the other quarter. Or some new oilman. The only sure thing was that Pedro was going to lose it. His time had passed."

"It did not just pass of its own accord."

"We are saying the same thing, only you don't realize it."

"It did not have to happen that way."

"Matter of fact it did. That is how the Garcias got the land, by cleaning off the Indians, and that is how we had to get it. And one day that is how someone will get it from us. Which I encourage you not to forget."

He took up two coal oil jugs, one in each hand, and made his way slowly up the steps. The jugs were heavy and he was struggling; he nearly dropped them.

As I watched him I realized he is not of our time; he is like some fossil come out of a stream bank or a trench in the ocean, from a point in history when you took what you wanted and did not see any reason to justify.

I realize he is not any worse than our neighbors: they are simply more modern in their thinking. They require some racial explanation to justify their theft and murder. My brother Phineas is truly the most advanced among them, has nothing against the Mexican or any other race, he sees it simply as a matter of economics. Science rather than emotion. The strong must be encouraged, the weak allowed to perish. Though what none of them see, or want to see, is that we have a choice.

I heard my father knocking things around inside the house. On a horse he still looks like a young man; on the ground he carries the weight of all his years. Watching him shuffle with the jugs of kerosene I could not help feeling sorry for him. Perhaps I am insane.

I followed him into the house. I could knock him over and take the kerosene away. But it was too late. This was only a formality.

Inside everything was covered with dust that had blown in the open doors and windows, the tracks of animals were thick, the blood dried to an indistinct black stain. In the living room, my father had pushed the furniture into a pile and sloshed oil over it. I followed him into the rest of the house, into the bedrooms and then Pedro's office.

He pulled all the papers from their cabinets, old letters, stock records, deeds, certificates of birth and death for ten generations, the original land grant, back when this area was all a Spanish province, Nuevo Santander.

After everything was doused in coal oil, he struck the match. I stood watching the papers curl, the fire spreading across the desk and up the wall onto a large map of the state, drawn when all the sections had Spanish names. I heard someone calling my name—Pedro. Then I realized it was my father. I went to look for him and when I walked out of the office the entire house was filled with smoke; he'd lit fires in the other rooms.

I bent beneath the smoke, looking into Pedro and Lourdes's bedroom. Their bed was beginning to burn; the canopy caught and flared and the light filled the dark room. I wondered how many generations had been sired there and knew the Colonel must have thought the same thing.

Through the flames I saw a dark shape calling me forward and only with effort did I turn and make my way toward the sunlight. When I reached the outside my father was already limping down the hill toward the Garcias' stock buildings, a jug of fresh coal oil in each hand.

CHAPTER SIXTEEN

ELI/TIEHTETI

The Buffalo

The Comanches owned all the territory between Mexico and the Dakotas, the most buffalo-rich land on the continent. The northern bands hunted them seasonally, but the Kotsoteka, whose home territory was the center of the range, hunted year-round. In summer they hunted the bulls, because they were fattest, and in winter they hunted the cows. Until the age of three summers, the meat of either animal was equally good; older than that and the cows tasted better. Old bulls were mostly killed for their hides.

The animals were hunted with either a lance or a bow. Using the lance required a bit more backbone; you had to match speed with the buffalo and drive the lance, one handed, through the ribs, through the lights and into the heart. At the first prick the animal would turn and try to gore you or crush you against the other running buffalo. The only safety was to go all in, give yourself totally to the lance, to use the animal's own weight to drive the point deeper. Unless you were crushed first.

The average buffalo was twice the size of a cow and as mean-spirited as a grizzly. They could jump over a man's head if they wanted, though they rarely did, and if your horse stumbled, or stepped in a prairie dog hole, you could lay money that there would be nothing left of you to bury, as buffalo, unlike horses, would go out of their way to trample you.

The bow gave more wiggle room, as the animal could be killed from a short distance, a few yards, shooting the arrow at a steep angle behind the last rib. Just the same, as soon as the buffalo felt it'd been stuck, it would turn and try to gore you. The best horses would veer at the sound of the bowstring, and this quarter-second gap was usually enough to keep you alive.

Until the big Sharps rifles came along, the buffalo had to be killed while running, from behind and to one side, and so a group of riders would whip the animals into a stampede, and then, by running their horses in front of the lead animals, turn the herd and force the buffalo into a mill, a running circle. Then the hunters would begin the killing.

When as many animals had been killed as could be cut up in a day, the herd was released from the mill and would disappear across the prairie. The fallen buffalo were butchered where they lay, though butchering is not the right word. The Comanche were like surgeons. The skin was cut carefully along the spine, because the best meat and the longest sinews were just underneath, and then the hide was peeled off the animal. If the village was close, by this point a group of optimistic children would have gathered and would be pestering the butcher for a piece of hot liver with the bile of the gallbladder squeezed over it. The stomach was removed, the grass squeezed from it, and the remaining juice drunk immediately as a tonic, or dabbed onto the face by those who had boils or rashes. The contents of the intestines were squeezed out between the fingers and the intestines themselves either broiled or eaten raw. The kidneys, kidney tallow, and tallow along the loins were also eaten raw, as the butchering continued, though sometimes they were lightly roasted, along with the testicles of the bull. If grass was scarce the contents of the stomach were fed to the horses. In winter, in the case of frostbite, the stomach was removed whole and the frostbitten hand or foot thrust in and allowed to warm; recovery was generally complete.

If water was scarce, the veins of the animals were opened and the blood drunk before it had time to clot. The skull was cracked, the brains stirred on a rawhide and eaten as well, being fatty and tender; the teats of any lactating cows were cut and the warm milk sucked directly from them. If the brains were not eaten immediately they were taken to tan hides; every animal has enough brains to tan its own hide, except the buffalo, which was too large.

Once emptied, the stomach was rinsed, dried, and used as a water bag. If there were no metal pots, food could be cooked in the stomach by filling it halfway with water and adding hot stones until the water boiled. Another popular water carrier was the whole skin of a deer, which, if it were to be used for that purpose, was cased and removed whole, and the ends sewn shut. But we are talking about the buffalo.

Once the organ meats were consumed, the hunters retired and the women took over the harder work of butchering. The meat was cut from the bones in three- to four-foot lengths. The strips were placed on the clean inner skin of the recently killed animal and when the animal's skin was completely full of its own meat, it was wrapped up, tied, put on a horse or travois, and taken back to camp to be dried. After which it was packed into *oyóotʉ*, or rawhide containers, and sewn shut with the animal's sinew. Once dry, the meat would keep indefinitely.

The tongue, hump, side ribs, and hump ribs were all choice cuts and were usually saved for barbecue. The bones were cracked and cooked and the buttery marrow, *tuhtsohpeʔaipʉ*, scooped out to be used as a sauce alone, or, as previously mentioned, mixed with honey to make a sweet sauce, or cooled and mixed with pounded mesquite beans for dessert.

The shoulder blades were turned into shovels and hoes. The smaller bones were split, fire hardened, and whittled into needles or awls, or into knives, arrowheads, and scrapers. The hooves were boiled to make a glue used for saddle making, attaching sinew to bows, and nearly everything else. Every brave kept a small amount of this glue for emergency repairs. The horns were used as carriers for the fire drill, and, of course, for gunpowder.

The droppings, as a fuel source, improved every season they sat on the prairie, burning longer and slower and more evenly than mesquite. When dried and powdered, the droppings were also used to pack cradleboards for both warmth and moisture absorption, though cattail down, when available, was considered superior.

From the sinew along the spine, as well as the fascia under the shoulder blades, along the hump, and in the abdomen, all manner of thread, bowstring, and bow backers were made. Threads, ropes, and lariats were woven from the long tufts of hair on the head. Pipes were made from the thick ligament in the neck. Arrow straighteners were made from the center bone of the hump, though many preferred to use their teeth.

Scabbards were made from the tail skin, handles for knives and clubs from the tailbones; the trachea was cut and tied to make containers for paints, clays, and makeup. The hard yellow paste inside the gall was used for war paint, the udders dried to be used as dishes and bowls (pottery being fragile, heavy, and generally useless to horse-mounted people). Any unborn fetus was taken and boiled in its sac, and, being more tender than veal, was fed to babies and old people and those with bad teeth. While the pericardium was used for sacks, the heart itself was always left where the buffalo had fallen, so that when the grass grew up between its remaining ribs, the Creator would see that his people were not greedy and ensure that the tribes of buffalo were replenished, so that they would return ever after.

CHAPTER SEVENTEEN

JEANNIE McCULLOUGH

The Colonel died in 1936. Jonas left for Princeton the next year, returning only twice and fighting noisily with her father both times. He was no longer mentioned in the house. Her grandmother, too, had disappeared, but she had not died, only moved back to Dallas to be with her other family.

Her father and brothers took their supper in the pasture or ate it cold after working late. The three siblings would come home from school; her brothers would change quickly and ride out to meet their father; Jeannie would continue her studies. Every Saturday a tutor would drive in from San Antonio and assign her extra work. Her grandmother had insisted and her father agreed to anything that kept her occupied. One day she would rebel; she would do only half of what was assigned. She already knew what she would skip: it was Latin, it was definitely Latin, and the tutor would stare down his long sweaty nose while she triumphantly proclaimed she had not translated a word of *Suetonius*.

When her schoolwork was done, the silence in the house would begin to weigh on her, and she would put on her boots and clomp around just to hear the noise they made, then eat supper alone on the gallery. She would listen to the president's radio address and sometimes, if she were especially annoyed, she would leave it on so that when her father came home, he would have to go out to the porch and turn it off. It gave her satisfaction, knowing how angry this made him.

By that time she'd given up working in the pastures. She knew she might be good at it if she continued to try, but the work was hot and long and boring and besides, no one wanted her there. Even the Colonel, who had founded the ranch, had not thrown a loop in the last thirty years of his life—he saw no point to cattle except the tax breaks. Oil was what one ought to be interested in, and now, whenever her great-uncle Phineas came to visit—always with a geologist in tow—she would sit in the backseat while Phineas and the geologist rode up front, talking about shale and sand and electric well logging, which got the geologist very excited. He did not mind that Jeannie was only thirteen; he was happy to ramble on about everything he knew. She could see it pleased Phineas that she listened. The oil business was booming; there were parts of South Texas where you didn't need headlights to drive at night, there was so much gas being flared, the fire lighting the sky for miles around.

Her grandmother returned every so often, smelling of ancient perfume and peppermint drops, her stern face pointy above a black dress, it was always black, as if she were in mourning for something no one else understood. Nothing could be to her satisfaction: the maids were scolded, her father was scolded, her brothers were scolded; she went down to the bunkhouse and ordered the hands to wash their sheets. Jeannie would be prescribed a long bath to open her pores, which, according to her grandmother, were growing larger each month.

After she'd soaked her face, conditioned her hair, dried herself off, and dressed again, she would sit in the library on the couch while her grandmother cleaned under each fingernail, filing off the rough edges, pushing back the cuticles and rubbing cold cream into her skin. *We will make a lady of you yet,* she said, though Jeannie had not thrown a rope in over a year and the calluses were long gone from her hands. Every third visit she would bring her entire wardrobe to the library so that her grandmother might assess the fit of her dresses—*that one makes you look like a servant girl on the prowl.* The offending articles would be packed into a box that her grandmother took to Dallas for tailoring.

Her grandmother always had news from the city, which Jeannie found immensely boring, except for the stories of good girls being ruined, which had begun to feature prominently in her grandmother's lectures. Still, she no longer fell asleep during these talks; there was a comfort in being told to stay out of the sun—*your freckles are bad enough*—to watch what she ate—*you have your mother's hips*—to wash her hair once a day and to never wear pants. Then her grandmother would take up Jeannie's hands, as if something might have changed in the ten minutes since she last touched them, but no, there were her stubby inelegant fingers, which no amount of piano lessons could ever fix. Her grandmother's own fingers were knobby and arthritic and resembled the claws of an animal, but they had once been the hands of a lady, no matter how many years she had wasted on this ranch.

A MONTH OR so after she finished the eighth grade, her grandmother, after giving the usual news from Dallas, informed Jeannie that she had been accepted to the Greenfield boarding school in Connecticut. Jeannie had not known she'd applied. *You leave in six weeks,* her grandmother said. *Tomorrow we'll take the train to San Antonio and get you some proper clothes.*

Her protests, which went on the rest of the summer, meant nothing. Clint and Paul considered it pointless to resist; her father was pleased that there might be a better place for her, going so far as to invoke Jonas as a reason she might be happy up north.

I'm not Jonas, she protested, but everyone knew this was only partially true. Her grandmother gave her pearls and four sets of kid gloves, but this did nothing to assuage her anger; she did not even look at her father when he put her on the train north. She did look at the pearls for a long time that evening, after closing the curtains to her sleeping compartment. They were worth twenty thousand dollars, her grandmother had said; she would not have any granddaughter of hers looking common.

★　★　★

JONAS WAS SUPPOSED to meet her at Penn Station but was an hour
late. In which time she stumbled in on a man, his pants down and his
rear end very white, pushing up against a woman in a red bustle in
the far stall of the ladies' toilet. She rushed out but after five minutes
realized she had no choice and went back into the same restroom,
choosing the stall farthest from the man and his friend. Miraculously,
her luggage was not stolen. *I hate it here,* was the first thing she said
to Jonas, who got her luggage properly stowed and then took her to
lunch. They walked among the tall buildings. *Don't look up so much,*
he said. *You don't want to be a tourist.*

But she couldn't help it. Pictures didn't capture the size of the
buildings, which leaned ominously over the streets, ready to fall and
crush her at any moment, if a taxicab didn't get her first. The din of
all the trucks and shouting people left her ears ringing and she had a
rushing in her heart that didn't go away until she was well north of the
city, on the train to Greenfield, back among trees and pastures. There
were a few stray cattle and sheep grazing in the distance, Holsteins and
Jerseys, *at least I know about that,* she thought, it would be something
to talk about with her new classmates.

THERE WERE NUMEROUS things that appealed to her about
Greenfield. The old stone buildings with their steeply pitched roofs
and tall ivy walls, the sunlight like a gauze across the landscape—what
passed for summer was like winter in Texas—the dense forests and
rolling fields at the edge of the campus. She had not known there were
so many shades of green, she had not known there was so much rain
and moisture on earth. The campus was only forty years old, though
it might have easily been four hundred, the way the vines had taken
over the buildings and trees brushed the windows in the breeze. In the
few moments she had to herself each day, it was hard not to feel like
someone important, as if she were only steps away from being swept

up by some prince, or prime minister's son, who, she now knew, would be English instead of Spanish, though other times she wondered if she did not want to be swept up at all, if perhaps she would be a prime minister herself—it was not inconceivable, times were changing. She could see herself behind a great wooden desk, writing letters to her loyal citizenry.

She did not have much time alone. The days were rigidly ordered: wake-up bell followed by breakfast and chapel, followed by classes, lunch, classes, athletics, dinner, and study hall. Lights out at eleven P.M., a monitor stalking the halls to enforce it.

Her roommate, a small Jewish girl named Esther, cried herself to sleep every night and at the end of the first week, when Jeannie returned from dinner, Esther and all her things were gone. Her father had owned factories in Poland, but he had lost everything to the Germans; the tuition check had not cleared. Jeannie was moved into a nicer room. Her new roommate was a girl named Corkie, who was shy but pleasant, and, unlike Esther, seemed comfortable at their new school. She knew everyone, though Jeannie sensed that she did not have many friends. Corkie had shoulders as thick as a cedar chopper's, and she was tall, and she went about everything with a kind of resignation: to her long face that would never be pretty, to the red bumps above her lip, to her split and frazzled hair. From the way she dressed—in drab, frumpy clothes— and the inattention she gave her appearance, Jeannie thought she must come from a very poor family, and so she went out of her way to be nice, bringing Corkie desserts she'd smuggled from the dining hall, as she had once carried the buckets of clabber to her father's vaqueros.

That Monday, when asked at lunch who her new roommate was, she told them Corkie Halloran.

"Oh, you mean the Mighty Sappho?"

That was Topsy Babcock. She was small and pretty with pale blond hair and skin to match, a smile that turned on and off like a traffic switch. Sometimes the smile meant approval, other times disapproval— she was not a person you wanted to disappoint. The others at the table laughed at Corkie Halloran, and Jeannie laughed with them, though she did not know why.

"She was at Spence but they say she was spending a little too much time with one particular girl, if you know what I mean."

"They should have sent her to St. Paul's—she would have fit in perfectly!"

Everyone thought this was hilarious. Jeannie just nodded.

THE NEXT WEEKEND Corkie invited several people to her parents' house, which was only forty minutes from school. To Jeannie's surprise, many of the people who had made fun of her at lunch went along: Topsy Babcock, Natalie Martin, Kiki Fell, and Bootsie Elliot. Jeannie expected some old jalopy, or perhaps a truck, but instead they were picked up by a uniformed driver in a seven-seat Packard.

Kiki said: "You're the one who got stuck with that Jewish girl, aren't you?" She was the dark-haired version of Topsy, though her hair was cut just below her ears, almost as short as a boy's, and it was said she'd had a surgery to make her nose smaller. Since arriving at Greenfield Jeannie had spent more and more time in front of the mirror at bedtime, inspecting herself. Her nose had straightened considerably but her eyes had no character, they were the color of fog or rain. Her chin was pointy, her forehead high, and the scar across her eyebrow—which she had always been proud of because it was like the scars her brothers had—made her look like a man. It was a deep scar, you could not miss it.

"McCullough . . ." Topsy was saying. "That's Jewish, isn't it?"

The other girls tittered, except Corkie, who looked out the window.

"I don't think so."

"I'm kidding. Of course it's not."

Jeannie was quiet the rest of the drive. There were very few houses. The roads were small and winding and yet they were paved. There were tall hedgerows, red barns, the ubiquitous stone walls. Everything was in shadow, the sun came weakly through the trees and the sky felt small and closed in. There was a chill in the air, though it was only September.

Topsy and Kiki and Bootsie had gone to primary school together; the others seemed to know each other in the same ways, she guessed, that she knew the children of the Midkiffs and Reynoldses. The second silent girl in the car, Natalie, had long chestnut hair and a large chest that she slouched to conceal. She made a point of looking out the window, not making eye contact with Jeannie, though, like everyone else, she smiled at whatever Topsy said.

It was a relief when the car turned into a stone gate and made its way up a long driveway with big trees on both sides. There were acres of grass, she had never seen so much green healthy grass in her life; she tried to calculate the number of head you could support here (an acre per head? It seemed possible) but knew better than to say this out loud.

At the top of the hill the house appeared. She began to feel embarrassed. It was not any larger than the Colonel's house, but it was more grand, with arches and pillars and towers, dark granite, marble statuary, a look of weathering as if it had been standing since the time of kings.

"What does your father do?"

The girls all looked at her. Corkie gave her a look as well and she knew she'd made some sort of mistake. But it was too late. Corkie said: "He goes to his firm in New York and he plays racquets at the club and he rides and shoots a lot. And he works on his novel."

"What kind of firm is it?"

"You know . . ." Corkie shrugged.

Bootsie Clark said: "Poppy's father rides and shoots as well, I imagine." Poppy was what the others had decided to call Jeannie. "He's a cowboy. Isn't that right?"

"Cowboys are hired men."

"So what does your father call himself?"

"A cattleman." She was about to add, *but that's not where our money comes from,* when the other girls cut in:

"Does he go on those epic rides, then? Up to Kansas?"

"Those ended in the eighteen hundreds."

"That's too bad," said Bootsie. "They looked very exciting."

She was not sure if it was worse to respond or to let it drop. "They didn't really drive them like in the pictures. They had to walk them or they'd lose all their weight."

"How does Corkie's house look?" said Natalie, changing the subject. "I guess yours must be bigger."

"Not really."

"Of course it is. We hear everything is bigger in Texas."

She shrugged. "It's not as nice as this, though. It's not nearly as green."

"How many acres do you have?"

It was a rude question—the last thing you would ask someone in Texas—but she knew she had to answer. "Three hundred ninety-six sections."

"That's not so much," said Topsy.

"She said sections, not acres."

"How much is a section?"

"They don't even call them acres. An acre is too small."

"How much is a section," Kiki asked, for the second time.

"Six hundred forty acres."

For some reason this caused all the girls, with the exception of Corkie, to break into hysterical laughter. Corkie was watching the driver, waiting for him to open the door.

"Are you going to be a cattlewoman as well?"

"I don't think so."

"What are you going to be, then?"

"She's going to be someone's wife," said Corkie. "Just like the rest of us."

THAT AFTERNOON, THEY went riding. Below the main house was a stable with twenty or so horses, an immense corral that they called an arena, and a large pasture. It was all set in a manicured wood but she did not ask where the property ended. There were men in the shadows, cutting branches and loading them into a cart.

She was wearing jodhpurs and knee-high boots borrowed from Corkie's younger sister. She felt ridiculous, but everyone else was dressed the same way. She presumed they were going for a long ride, four or five hours, and she wished she had eaten more at lunch.

"I imagine you must have horses," said Natalie.

"Yes," she said. "Do you?"

"There isn't really enough room for them in Tuxedo Park." She shrugged.

"There's room for Jews, though," said Topsy.

"Topsy and Natalie were neighbors with the girl you roomed with."

"Her father bought a house there ten years ago," said Topsy, "but they wouldn't admit him to the club, so his family couldn't so much as dip a finger in the lake. If they ever heard them splashing around down there, someone would call the police."

"Tell her about the wedding."

"They had a wedding last summer, and all the kids in Tuxedo Park went and turned the signs around, so none of the guests could find their house. Completely ruined the ceremony." She smiled. "The problem is when people think that just because they have money . . ."

Jeannie nodded. The horses were brought out. They were sorrels, smaller chested and longer legged than cow horses.

"I had them put my sister's saddle on this one," said Corkie. She handed the reins over. "You're about her height." The saddle was simple, without a pommel or high cantle, and when Jeannie climbed up, the stirrups felt short and awkward, as if they had been set for a child.

The horse was tall and long legged, near sixteen hands; it looked like a fast horse but it did not look nearly as fast as it really was. It was so much more powerful than a cow horse that it felt closer to an automobile. With a cow horse (quarter horse, these girls called it) there was a negotiation, there were times you let the animal have its way, but this horse was both fast and anxious to please; giving it its head just confused it, like letting go of the steering wheel of a car. It seemed—like everything else in these girls' lives—to have been created just to serve them.

She found she barely needed the reins; the horse responded if she even tensed her legs; he was so responsive, in fact, that he was difficult to ride at first. She wondered if she was a sloppier rider than she thought. She was uncomfortable in the saddle and when they hit a gallop she had a hard time maintaining her seat. They were going fast down a groomed path and there were a series of hurdles ahead; Corkie went over the first one and Jeannie got a bad feeling but followed anyway. There was nothing to worry about. The horse cleared the gate without any input from her at all.

After an hour the rest of the girls were tired and decided to return to the stables. She put her heels in and brushed through a small gap between Topsy and Bootsie, hoping to spook them, then passed Corkie as well. The horse was enjoying itself, so she did a hot lap of the corral (*arena,* she corrected herself), which was nearly a half mile in circumference. It was a good horse; it did not want to stop and she was overcome with sadness, for the life it lived in this corral and these few miles of manicured trail, ridden by these girls who spent longer getting dressed than they did in the saddle. A pointless existence.

By the time she'd cooled the animal down and walked back to the stable, the other girls were waiting and their horses were already being curried by the groom and his children.

Bootsie was saying: "She does ride like a cowboy, doesn't she?"

"Does it feel strange, not having a handle to hold?"

"You don't touch the saddle horn," said Jeannie. She knew she'd looked awkward at first, but she thought she'd recovered well. It was plain she was a better rider than any of them, perhaps even Corkie. It was equally plain that none of them would admit it. Or they would find some way to turn it into an insult. She had an impulse to get back on the horse, gallop into the woods, and begin her long journey back to Texas. Certainly no harder than anything the Colonel had done. Her father would pay for the horse.

"Then why is it there?" said Bootsie, still talking about the saddle horn.

"It's for holding your tools. Tying your rope to and such."

"Well, you looked uncomfortable. I'm sure you'll get used to it."

"I'm a better rider than all of you," she said. She felt her face get hot; she had been pressed into saying something she wasn't sure of. "Except Corkie," she added.

"Still," said Bootsie. "You looked strange."

"That was nothing compared to what we do at home."

"Because it's bigger down there, I'm sure."

"Because we're roping big animals and trying not to get gored by their horns."

"I believe she said we'd be gored," said Topsy.

"She meant bored. To actual death."

"I'm going inside," said Corkie. She was standing against the stall door, looking tired. "Dinner will be ready soon."

THAT NIGHT, SHE couldn't sleep, and after a good deal of wandering down dark hallways, she found her way to the kitchen for a glass of milk. She had just gone into the icebox when she heard someone behind her.

"You're not supposed to be in here," said a voice. It was one of the maids.

"I'm sorry."

The woman's face softened. "You just ask, sweetie. We'll bring you whatever you need."

After drinking her milk she decided to go outside. It was dark, but there was a light on at the stable and she made her way down the hill in the wet grass—wet, everything here was wet—she was not sure what she had in mind. To talk to her horse, sneak him out for a night ride, to ride away and never come back. As she approached the stable she saw the light was coming from an upper window, in what she had presumed was the hayloft. There was a person moving behind a thin curtain, the faint sound of music. She was close enough to smell the stalls. The person passed behind the curtain again and she realized it was the groom. He lived with his family above the horses. She watched as he sat down in an armchair and appeared to close his eyes, listening quietly to the radio. She could not believe it. Even the lowest hands, who did nothing but stretch fence all day, slept in the bunkhouse. They did not live with animals.

She felt very tired and turned to go back to the house, her legs cold and damp from the dew. It was only September, it was just the beginning. *Things will get better,* she told herself. She thought of the Colonel being held by the Indians; if he had survived that, she could survive this, but even that did not feel true, it was just words, it was a different time.

Back in the main house, she heard a noise and saw a light at the end of a corridor and made her way toward it. It was a library or study of some sort; a fire was going and there was a person sitting in a leather chair, smoking a pipe. She approached and when she got close enough the man looked up at her.

"Excuse me," she said.

It was Corkie's father. He looked almost like a boy in the dim light; he must have been very young when his children were born. He was very handsome. Much more so than his daughter. He took off his reading classes and she saw his eyes were wet, as if he was upset about something. He rubbed them and said, "You're the gal from Texas, right?"

She nodded.

"How are you finding it here?"

"It's green. The grass is nice." It was all she could think of and then she was afraid to say anything else.

"Ah, the lawn," he said. "Yes, thank you." He added: "My great-grandfather spent some time in your state before it was admitted to the Union. In fact he was instrumental in that process. But then we had the Civil War, so back he came. I've always wanted to go and see it myself."

"You should."

"Yes, one of these days. It seems to be where everyone goes to make money now. I suppose I should see it."

She was quiet.

"Well." He nodded. "I ought to get back to work." He put his spectacles on. "Good night."

THE NEXT MORNING, after breakfast, Corkie whispered that she ought not talk to her father while he was working in the library.

"He's finishing his novel," she said. "He's been writing it a long time and he can't be disturbed."

She nodded and apologized. She was trying to recall if she'd ever seen her own father crying. She hadn't.

THE NEXT WEEKEND she took the train to see Jonas at Princeton. The ride was pleasant and she felt very grown-up, in a strange land traveling by herself. She did not think she could ever get used to how green everything was. And yet everywhere you stopped, there was a faint odor of mold, of decay, as if no matter what you did, the trees would come back, the vines would grow over, your work would be covered up and you would rot into the moist earth, no different from anyone who had come before you. It had once been like Texas, but now it was just people, endless people; there was no room for anything new.

Jonas met her in the train station and she hugged him for a long time. She was wearing her pearls and a nice dress.

"How are you doing up there?"

"Oh, fine."

He fingered the pearls, was on the verge of commenting, then decided against it.

"You'll get used to it," he said. "It's better that you're here than being stuck in McCullough or Carrizo. You're not going to learn anything down there."

"The people are cold."

"They can be."

"I sat on the train with two men and neither of them even said hello to me. It was like that for a whole hour."

"It's different here," he said.

Later they spent time with Jonas's friends: Chip, Nelson, and Bundy. It was only two in the afternoon, but they had all been drinking. Chip burst out laughing when he heard Jeannie's accent. He was soft around the middle, not exactly fat, just soft everywhere, with a deep sunburn and a confidence out of proportion to his appearance.

"Goddamn, McCulloughs. You two *are* from Texas. For a while we didn't believe you—this one hides it so well." He pointed at Jonas. Then he cocked his head and narrowed his eyes, assessing Jeannie. "Bundy, this one doesn't appear to have a drop of the tar baby, either. We must be sitting with the only pure-blood southerners who ever lived."

She reddened and Bundy touched her shoulder. "Don't worry about him. We're all so inbred we don't know how to act when someone new comes in."

Chip was not through with her: "What are your opinions on this war, Mizz McCullough? Should we send in the Marines or wait?"

She must have had a blank look.

"The one Hitler started? Last week?"

"I don't know," she said.

"My God, McCullough. What the hell are they teaching you at Greenfield, anyway?"

"The blessed M-R-S," said Nelson.

"Dump that bunch of slags and go to Porter's." He waved his hand. "We'll get it arranged. You are not going to learn a goddamn thing at Greenfield."

It had gone on like that for hours. She knew nothing the older boys hadn't heard before, nothing they hadn't already considered. Finally she and Jonas went for a walk around campus.

"They're just kidding around, Jeannie."

"I hate them," she said. "I hate everyone I've met here."

She had thought they would spend the evening together but Jonas had work to do. Next time, he said, she could stay in his room and meet more of his friends. They were good people to know—it would be nothing to get her into Barnard when the time came. But for now he was exhausted and behind in his studies. *Because you have been drinking all afternoon with your friends,* she thought.

She considered mentioning that she had spent three hours on the train coming to see him, and would now have to spend three hours going back to Greenfield, but she was too angry to say anything. When she got to New York it was already dark and the train to Connecticut did not leave for some time. She walked around outside the station, looking in the pawnshop windows, getting bumped by all the people walking, men staring at her in ways that would have gotten them shot or at least held for questioning in Texas. The newspapers were all screaming about the war, the Germans had taken Poland. As miserable as she'd been at Greenfield, she'd only faintly registered the war's existence, and, even now, it seemed more important that she make her train.

She did not get back to Greenfield until just before lights-out and as she'd forgotten to eat, she had to go to bed hungry. The next morning Corkie let her know they'd announced the fall dance. She would need to invite a date, preferably several. Even Corkie, who did not care about those things, had already drawn up a list of two dozen young men, intending to write invitations to all of them. Jeannie excused herself, then went to the library and spent the day there.

It would be a disaster. Not only did she have no one to invite—the only boys she'd met here were Jonas's friends—but the previous weekend, when the girls had gotten into Corkie's parents' wine and danced afterward, she had not known any of the steps. Charleston, hat dance, waltz, box step. She had not known any of it. Corkie had tried to show her, but it was pointless, utterly pointless; it would take years, years to learn these things, it would be utter humiliation. Even riding with these girls—the one thing she had nearly mastered—had been somehow degrading.

Meanwhile, the rest of them were already talking about the dances they would attend later, the big ones around Christmas; at fourteen they were now old enough. She realized that her classmates had spent their entire lives preparing for this moment; while she had been off visiting Jonas, they had spent the day shopping for dresses with their mothers. And of course they all knew dozens of eligible boys, who would all have to come several hours from other schools.

That Saturday she packed a small overnight bag, telling Corkie she was going to visit Jonas again. She took the train into New York and went looking for a bank—she did not have enough money to make the trip she wanted to make—but it turned out that banks were closed on weekends. All of them? Yes. Finally she walked into one of the pawn-shops near the train station. The man inside was in his fifties, looked as if he didn't eat much or see the sunlight, and spoke in a heavy foreign accent. She had never seen a Jew like him. She handed over her grand-mother's pearls.

"Are they real?"

"Of course," she said. He looked past her, to the street outside, to see if anyone was waiting for her. Then he put the pearls in his mouth as if he planned to eat them. Instead he rubbed each one against a front tooth. Afterward, he looked them over with a magnifier.

"Did a policeman send you in here?"

"No," she said.

"I am interested in why you brought these here."

"I saw the window." She shrugged.

"They're yours to sell."

"Yes."

He looked at her, but he didn't say anything.

"What sort of hat is that?" she asked, trying to be polite.

He said something that sounded like *hichpah*. "I'm Jewish. Unfortunately a bad one, working on the Sabbath. Don't worry, I won't eat you. But I can't buy your pearls, either."

"I don't have any money. I went to the banks but they're closed and I have to get home to my family."

"I'm sorry."

They stood looking at each other and finally he told her: "I'll go wake up my brother. But he is just going to tell you the same thing."

Another man, much more nicely dressed, came in from the back. He looked over the pearls, and ran them over the edge of his teeth, then looked at them with another loupe, then under a very bright light, and then under what appeared to be a microscope.

"Obviously these are worth several thousand dollars . . ."

"They are worth twenty," she said.

"They are worth eight," he said. "On a good day, to the perfect buyer."

"That would be fine."

He smiled. "I can't buy them from you. You're too young. I'm sorry."

She felt her eyes get wet. She wanted to take the pearls back and run out into the street, but instead she made herself stand there so they could see that she was crying.

"You're too young," he repeated.

"I don't care. I'm not leaving."

The two of them looked at each other and began to discuss things in a foreign language. Finally the better-dressed one said: "We can give you five hundred dollars. I'd like to offer more, but I can't."

Through her tears she said: "I will take a thousand."

THAT NIGHT SHE was on a train to Baltimore. Four days later, when her grandmother picked her up in San Antonio, she told her the pearls had been stolen.

IT WAS NOT a story she had told many people and even Hank had never grasped its significance. It had been the turning point of her life, in some sense its most important moment; she had seen the world and retreated, while Jonas, for all his other failings, had not. There were times she imagined how she might have turned out had she stayed in the North. Like Jonas, she knew, settled and comfortable, she would have been someone's wife. And that was not who she had wanted to be.

And yet Jonas had four children who adored him, a dozen grandchildren. Her houses, all three of them, were empty. Pointless monuments. Her life's work would pass to a grandson she barely knew—who would likely crumble under its weight. *It is not fair,* she thought. She wanted to weep.

She looked around her. She was certain now. There was a smell in the room, it was gas.

CHAPTER EIGHTEEN

DIARIES OF PETER McCULLOUGH

NOVEMBER 1, 1915

Phineas came down from Austin. We are the darlings of the capital for killing nineteen of our neighbors and getting two family members shot in the process. Phineas talking about a run for lieutenant governor.

Glenn is home, but still sick. He and my brother talked for a long time. The boys have always liked Phineas; to them he is a younger version of the Colonel, the pinnacle of manly attainment. Of course I do not dare tell them what I suspect, though I am not sure he would extend me the same courtesy, were the situation reversed—he would probably take me out to a pasture and shoot me.

How two men from the same stock might be so different . . . my father likely reckons my mother snuck off for congress with some poet, scrivener, or other nearsighted sniveling half-man. I have always seen myself as two people: the one before my mother died, fearless as his brothers, and the one after, like an owl on some dark branch, watching the rest move about in the sunlight.

How he and Phineas can stand in front of a hundred men and never once wonder what they are thinking—I can barely eat dinner without considering if I've been talking too much or not enough, drinking too much or not enough, making as little noise as possible with my knife and fork, paying mind to the clunk as I set down my water glass. And yet when I crossed the wall at the Garcias', I forgot myself.

HAVE BEEN TENDING their grave, unbeknownst to everyone. That day, after I left, they were all buried in a single pit: mother, father, daughters, grandchildren, assorted employees. No marker and, owing to the caliche, the hole was not very deep so I have been piling rocks and dirt on top. Old Pedro, who sent a priest to his vaqueros after every miscarriage, who always paid for a lined casket and a Christian burial. I still imagine the house as it has always been; each time I am freshly shocked, the charred walls, the birds flying freely where there was once a roof. The wood was old and seasoned and the fire burned hot. Little left inside but nails and bits of glass and metal. Even staring directly at it, part of me believes it is an illusion.

Perhaps this is why I am constantly disappointed—I expect good from the world, as a puppy might. Thus, like Prometheus, I am unmade each day.

PHINEAS AND I rode out to see what was left of the casa mayor; he explained he had already been talking to Judge Poole about the Garcias' "tax problems." I waited for him to acknowledge the chicanery, but he did not. He does not trust me entirely. No different from the Colonel.

When we reached the house Phineas was shocked. He sat there on his horse while I dismounted and went to pay my respects at their grave. He must have realized what I was doing so he left me alone. As I passed their spring I saw that someone had thrown a dead dog into it. I roped the animal and pulled it out.

"See clear to the goddamn border, can't you?"

It was an exaggeration but I got the meaning.

"You know, Pete, you might want to stay away from here for a while. I don't like looking at this myself and you . . ." He shook his head.

"Pedro Garcia was a friend."

"That's what I mean," he said.

I walked off behind the house, where I could sit on the patio and look over things. A few minutes later he came and found me.

"You shouldn't hold this against Daddy."

"How would that be possible?"

"This would have happened anyway. And of course, Pedro wasn't eight years behind in taxes. But there are things he could have done . . ."

"Such as?"

"Marrying his daughters right? I guess he thought he was making them happy, but . . ."

"If they'd married whites, you mean."

"Why not? All the old families did it. They saw the writing on the wall and married their daughters off to the proper people." He shrugged. "It's Darwin at work, Pete. Dilution is what the situation called for, but Pedro decided to double down."

I thought about Pedro encouraging me to call on María. I began to get a sick feeling.

"You and Daddy see eye to eye on a lot of things."

"There is not a moment of my day I am not thinking about this place."

"You are here twice a year," I said.

"You think a bank in Austin wants to lend a half-million dollars to a ranch it's never seen, and doesn't know anything about except it's already mortgaged out its asshole? Or Roger Longoria in Dallas? You ever wonder why your credit comes on such good terms from him? Or why it even comes at all? Or how it might be that the cattle business is collapsing all around Texas but somehow money comes easy for us?"

I decided to change the subject. "Meanwhile Daddy goes and spends the money on oil leases."

"Daddy can smell a change coming like a buzzard can smell a dry canteen. He's got more sense than both of us put together and if he had any ambition, he'd be governor."

"That I highly doubt."

He shook his head. Any word against the Colonel is like a word against God, or rain, or white men—the good things of the earth.

"I have spent most of my life trying to figure out what goes on inside your mind," he said. "First I thought you were slow and then I thought you might be red. Finally it occurred to me that you are just a sentimentalist. You believe in the open range, the code, the nobility of the sufferin' cowpoke and the emptiness of bankers' hearts—all stuff you picked up from Zane Grey . . ."

In fact I have not read Zane Grey, though I do not mind Wister, but explaining these distinctions to my brother is pointless.

" . . . you know in the old days, when Daddy needed stock, he found them in the bushes or paid some half-breed a dime a head to steal them. If a slick calf was found, it got branded, if a piece of land caught his eye, it got fenced. If there was someone he didn't like, he ran them off. And"—he looked at me meaningfully—"if someone stole your cattle, you crossed the river, burned their entire fucking village, and drove all their animals back to your pastures."

"That does not appear to have changed much."

"It *has* changed. You now need an adding machine just to figure out if you're getting enough beef per acre to cover your payroll. You've got a quarter of your labor going into brush, another quarter into screwworms and fever ticks. And when you're worrying about that kind of piddling bullshit . . ."

I put up my hand to stop him. "This is what we have, Finn. We can complain about it or we can keep working, and I would rather keep working. Daddy wants to think we are sitting on a sea of oil, but we are not; we are sitting on a bunch of expensive and utterly worthless leases on land we don't even own." I thought it was well played but he was smiling. Through sheer willpower I forced myself to stay where I was.

"When did they find oil in North Texas, Pete?"

Something they have always done: call me by name, as if disciplining a child. And yet still I feel compelled to answer them, as if, despite decades of evidence to the contrary, I might explain my point of view.

"Twelve years ago," he said, when I didn't respond. "And now half of our oil comes from there. Spindletop was only two years before that. The biggest fucking oil well in human history, before which the Rockefellers, Mellons, Pews, all those eastern cocksuckers, they made hundreds of millions in Pennsylvania. Pennsylvania! There are two buckets of oil in that entire state. Christ, Pete, the Hughes bit, what was that, 1908? Before that, a drilling rig was not so different from what the Romans used. Do you follow?"

Looking over the grave of the Garcias I did not tell him that 1908 was also when they found the caves at La Chapelle, when they found an apelike man, a Neanderthal fifty thousand years old, who had been carefully buried in a sepulcher, a haunch of meat and several flint knives left to protect him in the afterlife. That is how long we have been hoping for a next world. Since before we were truly men.

" . . . this is like the cattle business in 1865. There's nowhere to go but up. We find oil in even a couple of acres, our costs will be covered."

I walked back to my horse, silently, and he did the same. We made our way down the hill, through the old Garcia hamlet, the ruined church and old graveyard, the burned tower of the casa mayor still the highest point on the land. We drifted slowly toward the river, not speaking, my brother riding a few paces behind.

Finally he caught up: "You know, I've always been glad you like living here. When you left for the university I thought I would be stuck taking care of this place, but then you came back. And I have always been grateful for that, because this place is too important to have someone running it who isn't family. That is what I wanted to say. I am grateful you are here."

"Thank you."

"Just remember that you are not out here alone, and that I am thinking about it same as you."

I did not say anything. Phineas inherited my father's great ability to make any compliment sound patronizing. Then I said, "What's going on with Poole? I am trying to figure out how this land deal won't come back to bite us."

"Back taxes."

"Tell me."

"Back taxes," he repeated. "And possibly the judge has an itch to leave Webb County; we're looking into a position for him on the Fifth Court. But you can dig all you want. The Garcias owed taxes, and if it was not in the books before, it is there now, and there is nothing more to it."

OTHER NEIGHBORHOOD EVENTS:

October 18, a train attacked by sixty insurgents near Olmito (five killed).

October 21, army detachment at Ojo de Agua attacked by seventy-five insurgents (three killed, eight wounded).

October 24, second attack on the Tandy Station railroad bridge.

October 30, Governor Ferguson rejects calls for more Rangers. Reason? They are too expensive. Raising taxes out of the question.

Which is perhaps for the best—for every insurgent they kill, a hundred more are converted to the cause. The Tejanos do not mind the army, but they hate the Rangers.

NOVEMBER 15, 1915

Now that we have clear title to the Garcia land, it is just as my father supposed—we look like benevolent kings. Where Pedro was tight-fisted, we employ half the men in town. Anyone who wants work now has it: clearing brush, digging irrigation, rounding up twenty years of maverick longhorn bulls. Two men have been gored and Benito Soto died of heatstroke but people are at the gate every day wondering if we are hiring. Despite the sheriff's warnings, I am allowing some of the Mexicans to be armed. Just working for a gringo can get you shot by the *sediciosos*.

How we can appear to have clean hands, despite what happened, I find baffling. And depressing. As if I alone remember the truth.

MOOD MUST IMPROVE. Record year for rain—twenty-one inches already. The faster we get the brush out, the more grass will start. There is a pall of smoke over the town from all the brush being burned, and in that smoke I see nothing but good. The ashes will fertilize the soil and it is well known that the bluestems and gramas germinate best if they are heated.

Some bitterness in town (among whites) that no one else was offered the Garcia land. Bill Hollis's widow was one of the lead rabble-rousers. She has no real means—she could not have afforded to buy even a quarter section, let alone two hundred—but she senses the unfairness of it. Dutch Hollis, Bill's brother, apparently has not been sober since his brother died.

Will suggest to the Colonel that we offer Marjorie Hollis a generous price for her house, just to get her out of town. And perhaps we know someone a few counties over who might be induced to offer Dutch Hollis work. Certainly it cannot be good for him to remain in this town, our big white house on the hill, his brother's grave . . .

Such is the way I deal with things. But the Colonel has never had any trouble knowing people dislike him.

JANUARY 1, 1916

Sally has decamped to Dallas with her father and sisters, taking Glenn and Charlie with her.

After they left I went to the graves of Pete Junior, my mother, and Everett. Seeded with rye to keep them green. The birds will probably get most of it. Not sure if cemetery so close to the house is good or bad.

In the afternoon went to the casa mayor. The Garcias' grave has sunk in quite far. Spent three hours scraping dirt to fill it; did not return until well after dark.

Meanwhile the bandit raids continue: three ranches hit in the Big Bend. The Twelfth Cavalry, after several months of heavy losses, crossed the border and burned two Mexican towns.

JANUARY 4, 1916

Sally and the boys are back. She accused me of feeling more for the Garcias than she did for our own son. Asked me why I go back there so often.

"Because no one else will."

"Those greasers shot Glenn," she said. "I want you to think on that."

"Well, we killed them. All nineteen of them, not one of whom was present when Glenn was shot."

"That doesn't make us even," she said.

"You're right," I said, "but we do not have that many family members, do we?"

"I wonder if I am beginning to hate you. But then I wonder if you would even notice."

"If you hate me it is because I have morals."

That left her speechless. I went to my office and put a few logs in the fireplace and pulled the sheets over the couch.

It is only now, since we have been sleeping apart these three months, that I wonder how I ever managed to have any feelings for her at all. She is still pretty, charming in her way. But if she has ever had a thought that did not in some way involve herself, I have not heard of it.

CHAPTER NINETEEN

ELI/TIEHTETI

1850

By summer we knew that the Penateka, the largest and wealthiest of all the Comanche bands, had been mostly wiped out. The previous year's smallpox epidemic had been followed by cholera—all spread by the forty-niners, who shat into the creeks—and a hard winter had finished off the survivors. By the time the first meadowlarks appeared, the Penateka—with the exception of a thousand or so stragglers—were rotting into the earth.

We moved our camp far north, into what was then still New Mexico, to get away from the sick Indians and the disease-carrying whites still crossing along the Canadian toward California. We were now in the territory of the Yap-Eaters and I had a hope I might run into Urwat and be able to pay him back, but I never saw him, as the Yap-Eaters had gone even farther north, into Shoshone territory.

Despite the extermination of ten thousand Comanches, the plains had never been more crowded. The displaced tribes—from the easterners like the Chickasaws and Delawares to the more local Wichitas and Osages—continued to be resettled in our hunting grounds. The buffalo were scarcer than anyone could remember and the spring hunts had not yielded enough meat or hides to carry us through the year. Toshaway and the other elders decided to put in all our chips;

planning the largest raid in the band's history, which would bypass most of the settlements in Texas and go straight down into Mexico. Because of the size of the raid and the long distance, a number of women and boys would go along to keep the camps, and three hundred people in total, including Toshaway, Nʉʉkaru, and Escuté, rode out in July and did not return until December.

I was left in the main ranchería, where, with the men gone and the buffalo scarce, the younger boys, whether they had gotten scalps or not, were kept patrolling and hunting all the time. There was a sense things were changing for the worse. The camp felt empty, everyone was missing a family member or two, and a general downheartedness had settled. The only good news was that the market for captives had improved—a white person could be sold back to the government at any of the new forts, sometimes for three hundred dollars or more. We bought several whites from the Yap-Eaters and took them to sell to the New Mexicans, who eventually sold them at the forts.

HATES WORK NEVER came back to my tipi, but gradually other girls began to, because their *notsakapu* or lovers were off raiding, and I was known to be a solitary type who didn't talk to the other young *tekʉniwapʉ*. Scalp or not, I was still a captive, and the other men saw nothing to gain by talking to me.

So the women would find me while I was out hunting or taking a nap and tell me things they didn't want anyone to hear. Who was sleeping with her friend's husband or with the *paraibo*. Who was planning to defect to the Yap-Eaters or start a new band. Who was going to elope with her *notsakapu* because his parents couldn't afford her bride-price, who was tired of being the third wife of some fat old subchief—who, by the way, was lying about something he'd done in combat—who had caught *pisipʉ* from a married man, was it worth paying for a cure?

* * *

ONE NIGHT SOMEONE came into the tipi and sat by the opening, looking for my pallet in the darkness. There was a sweet smell I didn't recognize, like honey, or maybe cinnamon.

"Who is it?" I said.

"Prairie Flower."

I poked the embers to get some light. She was possibly not as pretty as her sister, Hates Work, but she was so far above my bend that I guessed she had come to talk.

"I'm tired," I said.

She ignored me and took off her dress. She fell asleep so quickly afterward, nestled into me, that I wondered if that was all she wanted in the first place, someone to sleep next to while her boyfriend was off with Toshaway and the others. I fell asleep but only halfway. It was too dark to see her face, but she was warm and sweet-smelling and her skin was smooth. I lay for a long time breathing into her neck. I wanted to rut but I did not want to wake her up. Then I must have fallen asleep because later she was shaking me awake. She was putting her clothes on.

"Don't expect this ever to happen again, and don't tell anyone, either."

I wondered if I'd done a bad job. "That's also what your sister told me," I said.

"Well, I am not a slut like she is, so you can expect I'm telling the truth."

"She was also telling the truth."

"Then you are one of the lucky few who has only had her once."

"Huh," I said.

She adjusted her dress. "That's not true, really."

"You can get back under the robe," I said. "We don't have to do anything."

She thought about it, then did. I gave her as much space as I could.

"Good night," I said.

"It's been hard for you, with everyone being gone?"

"It's been hard for everyone."

"But you especially. Nuukaru and Escuté are your only friends."

"That's not true."

"Who else, then?"

I shrugged. "What do you smell like?" I said, trying to change the subject.

"This? Cottonwood sap. The bud sap, you can only collect it in spring."

"It's nice," I said.

It was quiet.

"People are stupid," she said. "Everyone is from captives."

"I guess not everyone looks like it."

"What about Fat Wolf?"

"No, not really."

"Poor Tiehteti."

"Poor nothing," I said.

"Okay, I'm sorry."

"Time to sleep."

"I wonder when you'll stop being so nice."

"Time to sleep," I said again.

"You are nice," she said. "It's obvious. You don't order people around, you mostly skin your own animals, you—"

"Ask that *papi bo?a* how nice I am." I pointed above the pallet, where the scalp of the Delaware was hanging.

"It's a compliment."

A short while later she put her hand on my thigh. I was not quite sure what it meant. She moved her hand slightly higher. "Are you still awake?"

"Yes."

She pulled me on top of her and hitched her *kwasu* up. As usual it was too quick and then it was awkward as she tried to keep moving. I started to roll off but she held me.

"It's okay," she said. "Everyone is quick with me at first."

I was annoyed at how sure she was. Then I decided I wasn't. I fell asleep. When I woke up she was gone, but she came back the next night.

DURING THE DAY we wouldn't speak but at night, after the fire had died to nothing, I would hear her rustling at the tipi flap and then she would be in my bed. By the third night I had memorized every inch of her, as if I were blind as a pup, though there were moments, if her hair was different, or her smell was different, when I was not sure it was her. The Comanches took this uncertainty for granted, which worked mainly to the advantage of the women, who could satisfy their needs without risking their standing, and less so for the men, who were often not sure who they'd conquered, or if maybe they had been conquered themselves and had done it with someone they hadn't wanted to. All skin was good at night, blotches invisible, crooked teeth straight, everyone was tall and beautiful and it was a fine kind of democracy; the women would not admit their names, and so a breast or ear or chin would be kissed to determine its shape, or the curve of a hip or collarbone, the softness of a belly, the length of a throat, everything had to be touched. The next day we would make a shape from the pictures we had gathered with our hands and mouths, watching the girls go by in the sun, wondering who it had been.

It had always been this way. There was a story about a beautiful young girl who was visited every night by a lover (which, as men, we were not allowed to do, but this had taken place in a different time) and, as her passion turned gradually to love, she began to wonder who this lover was; she knew every part but not the whole, and as time passed she became obsessed with knowing, so she might be with him during the day as well as night, that they might never be separate. One evening, just before her lover came to her, she blackened her hands with soot from the fire, in order that she might mark his back and have her answer. In the morning, when she rose to get water for her family, she saw her handprints on the back of her favorite brother, and she cried out and fled the tribe in shame, and her brother, who had never loved anyone more, ran after her. But she would not slow down, and he could not catch her, and the two of them streaked across the earth until finally she became the sun, and her brother the moon, and they could only be in the sky together at certain times and were never again allowed to touch.

As for Prairie Flower, she had something serious with a boy named Charges the Enemy, who was five or six years older than me but had gone on the long raid with Toshaway, Pizon, and the others. She was around sixteen, which the Comanches considered a marriageable age, but the fifty-horse price set for Hates Work had scared off most of Prairie Flower's suitors, which she considered a temporary advantage, as she knew that no men in the tribe could afford her, though she also knew that as soon as we became prosperous again, she would be purchased by some fat old chief, and her life as she knew it would be over.

Most of the girls quietly worried about this. Prairie Flower's hope was to remain unmarried until the age of twenty, a year longer than her sister, before some old man decided he would buy her as a wife. Charges the Enemy did not have fifty horses, or even twenty—he had about ten, she thought—and his family did not have many more; her father would never consider him a suitable match. In fact there were no young warriors with the capital her father required, Toshaway's generosity being an unheard-of exception, and so Prairie Flower was doomed to be the third or fourth wife of someone she would never love, the lowest in the domestic order, and once married she would live out her days scraping hides like a common *na?raiboo*.

MEANWHILE, I HAD made friends with the bow. With buffalo in short supply, I was killing a deer, elk, or antelope every other day for camp meat, though like everyone else, I was riding farther and farther to find the animals. At one point in August I was gone for nearly five days and realized I could simply ride east until I reached the whites, but as I sat there looking out over the plains on my horse, leading a mule loaded with meat for the tribe, it occurred to me that I had nothing to go back to, no family except perhaps my father, who, if he was still alive, had made no effort to find me. Many of the white families were actively seeking their children and news of rewards spread quickly among the tribes. A month earlier, a free Negro from Kansas had ridden into the camp, taking everyone so completely by surprise that it was decided not to kill him. His wife and two children, also Negros, had been taken, and he was hoping to buy them back.

We did not have them but we knew they had been seen with another band to the west, and, after feeding him and allowing him and his horses to rest two nights, we directed him toward the *Noynkanʉʉ*. The only non-Indians we universally hated were the *Tʉhano,* or Texans, whom we always killed on sight. Other whites, or Negroes for that matter, were mostly judged on an individual basis, and if a man did something especially brave or clever—like surprising a camp full of Comanches in broad daylight—he would not only be allowed to live, but be treated as a guest of honor as long as he wanted to stay. Toshaway's father informed me that before the *Tʉhano* came, the Comanches had had nothing against the whites—we had traded with the French and Spanish for hundreds of years—and that it was only the arrival of the *Tʉhano,* who were greedy and violent, that had changed this. The whites knew this and a Texan, if caught by the Indians, would claim he was from New Mexico or Kansas. Coming from Texas would get you roasted over a slow fire. Even a knife was considered too quick for a Texan.

I stood there watching a blue front blow across the plain and decided to make my way back to camp. It occurred to me that I had not thought about going back to the whites in several months, and what I would be returning to was most likely an orphanage, or a job as a servant, and while the tribe considered me a grown man, the whites would have not thought any such thing. And of course there was Prairie Flower, who denied there was anything serious, but still came to my tipi every night. If I saw her carrying water, I would carry it for her, or help her collect firewood, or skin a deer I had killed for her family. Her father did not approve of me, though I was technically Toshaway's son, he preferred Escuté, who was older, and not white, and not a captive.

Most of the boys were embarrassed for me, especially because they knew that the moment Charges the Enemy returned, Prairie Flower would forget I existed, and Charges the Enemy, while he would probably not kill me, would certainly hurt me badly, a likelihood they repeatedly reminded me of, urging me, if not to stop seeing her, to at least not humble myself in public. But if I'd once thought her the inferior of her sister, I now thought the opposite. Prairie Flower was as light on her feet as a fawn, her eyes and cheeks and chest not as exaggerated as her sister's, but much finer, as if the Creator decided there ought to be nothing extra. I didn't mind humbling myself.

In the end, there were other things to worry about. We had enough to eat but it was the same every night; we were short of all our trade goods, of sugar, corn, and squash as we had no spare horses or hides to trade for them. We were short of lead and powder and screws to repair our guns; we were in cold, dry, unfamiliar country. The sense of order continued to slowly break down, as young boys who ought to have been playing were depended on to hunt, and old men were stuck doing the work of women. And perhaps it was this general lowness that had led Prairie Flower to first visit my tent. Or perhaps it was because in June, when it was presumed the raiders had reached Mexico, she had a series of dreams in which she had seen Charges the Enemy's scalped corpse, which was not something she could have told any other Comanche, as it was very bad medicine. If for some reason she had decided to share her dreams, many of the older people in the tribe would have blamed her for being a *bruja* and she would have been driven from the band or killed. Of course if anyone had witched Charges the Enemy it was me, though I did not believe in those things, and besides felt bad for him, as he had taken me hunting a few times, so I did not want to see him scalped, maybe just captured by the Mexicans, and put in prison, and kept there forever.

All in all, it was the greatest summer I had ever had, and despite everyone's blue mood, I was content in a way I had never been. I might be killed any day, by whites or hostile Indians, I might be run down by a grizzly or a pack of buffalo wolves, but I rarely did anything I didn't feel like doing, and maybe this was the main difference between the whites and the Comanches, which was the whites were willing to trade all their freedom to live longer and eat better, and the Comanches were not willing to trade any of it. I slept in the tipi when it was cool and in a brush arbor when it was warm, or under the stars, went hunting or wandering when I wanted, and had a girl, even if she also considered herself the girl of someone else. The only thing I really missed was fishing, as the Comanches would not eat fish unless they were starving. Though even on my hunting trips, when I could have fished, I didn't.

In October the older men of the tribe decided we ought to move south, into familiar territory, as winter would be much worse here, and food more scarce. Despite the fact the raiders had not yet returned, which was beginning to worry everyone, we packed the camp and left detailed instructions, in the form of hieroglyphs carved into a tree, about where we were headed.

We set up close to our old campsite, ten miles north of the Canadian, expecting it to be occupied, as it was close to several well-known Indian trails, but it was empty and the grass was tall. It had been a wet year and there was plenty of forage to get our horse herd through the winter, which was a good sign, but no other horses had been grazing there, which was a bad sign, and the tribe went further into a depression, the consensus being that an enormous number of Comanches must have been destroyed, not just the Penateka, for a campsite this good to have gone unoccupied since we had left it.

WHEN THE RAIDING party finally returned in December, the only good news was that Toshaway, Escuté, and Nuukaru were still alive. They were all so pale and had all lost so much weight that when they first rode up, everyone thought they were spirits. Toshaway had nearly lost a foot to frostbite. Escuté had taken a ball through the shoulder early in the raiding and spent three months riding with it broken. He could barely raise his bow arm.

In June, they had captured eight hundred horses but there had been an ambush—the army and the Mexicans were working together now, instead of killing each other as they had always done—and nearly half the Kotsoteka warriors were killed or scattered. The army, along with several Ranger companies, had chased the remaining warriors deep into New Mexico.

While this was happening, the women's camp, which had been waiting for the warriors to return from Mexico, had been attacked by Mescalero Apaches, and either wiped out entirely or carried away as captives. The remaining bodies were so scattered by animals it was impossible to count them. Toshaway's daughter was among the lost, and of the three hundred Kotsoteka who'd ridden out, less than forty had returned, and, while no one would mention it in the same conversation, nearly a thousand horses had been lost as well, which meant that we had no surplus to trade and the winter would be even worse than expected. From that day until early spring, all the other noises were drowned out by crying and wailing, and half the women in camp had cuts on their faces and arms, many of them clipping off whole fingers to honor their dead family members.

Prairie Flower stopped seeing me for a while, as Charges the Enemy was known to have been killed, but had fallen behind the enemy lines so quickly that his body had not been recovered and was presumed to have been scalped and desecrated. She barely ate or left her tipi, but as they were not married, she could not even mourn in public, or tell anyone she had known when it happened, that she had witnessed his death just as clearly as if she had been there to see it.

CHAPTER TWENTY

JEANNIE McCULLOUGH

1942

Phineas called her to Austin a week after she finished high school. It was May and already hot, one hundred in McCullough, ninety in Austin, it would be nice to make a trip to Barton Springs, to lie in the grass and watch the people swimming—flirting couples, young men and their footballs—to spend the day by herself in a place she was not known. She wouldn't, of course. There were people you could never figure—her great-grandfather for instance—but that was not her. *I am boring,* she thought. *Predictable. But brave in my own way, brave despite* . . . she did not like to think of the North, she did not like to think of her time there. She had been miserable and she had left. She did not mind taking risks when she wanted something, though no one else understood this. When she wanted something, she was truly brave. And yet no one else knew. So it didn't matter.

The train made its way to Austin. There were more cars on the highway, double or triple what she had seen in her childhood, most Texans now lived in cities, they said. You would not have known it in Dimmit County. She watched a truck with a half-dozen Mexicans in the back, their knees scrunched around a pile of scrap iron, the driver weaving and changing lanes, one miscalculation and they would all be spilled to the pavement. She wondered why they allowed themselves to be treated that way. They're animals, is what her father said. On Election Day he would take her down to the south end of McCullough, dusty streets, tin shacks, wreaths of chilies and goat meat hanging with the flies buzzing everywhere. Her father would hand out slabs of beef from an ice chest in the back of his truck, cases of warm beer; he would pay their poll taxes and show them how to mark the ballot. *Gracias, patrón. Gracias.* They were more gracious than niggers—that was another thing he always said.

The windows in the train were open and her face was cool in the breeze but she was sweating under her dress, under her arms. It was the time of the year the heat became its own entity, a creeping misery. No. It was like a sledgehammer on the head of a steer. It would only get worse until September. From the other side of the car, three soldiers were stealing glances, one of them was much older, the other two were Mexican, barely her age, afraid to look. Most draft boards had not yet begun to call up whites, though some, like her brothers, had volunteered.

She studied her reflection, imposed as it was on the dry rushing landscape beyond the window. *I am pretty,* she thought. There were prettier, but she was well above average. *Phineas will offer me a job.* A sort of special adviser, a confidante. But that was not possible, either. She was not even qualified to be a secretary; you needed shorthand for that. There was nothing she really knew how to do, nothing she did well, she was a dabbler. Pointless. If she vanished from the earth that instant, it would not have made a lick of a difference to anyone.

Maudlin, maudlin. She leaned her head against the glass and felt the shaking of the train. *That's not even your word,* she thought, *that's from Jonas.* She could see the hills to the north, the Llano uplift. The Colonel had known those things: this rock is ten million years old, this other two hundred, here is a fern contained in stone. The soldiers were staring at her openly now. When she was young, a year or two ago, she would have turned and stared them down, but now she let them drink her up, have their fantasies, or so she imagined. In a few months they would be off to war, and many would not come back, their final rest in a foreign place. Perhaps all three of them, their lines come to an end. She wondered who would survive, she guessed the bigger one, though you could not tell. It was not like the old days, it was a falling bomb and a hundred dead at once, all mothers' sons. An emotion came over her, and she wondered if she might give them something, cigarettes or a soda pop, but those were just tokens, money would not help them. There was only one thing and she allowed herself to think about this for a while, shifted her legs and adjusted her dress, it was just a thought, out of the question, she had never given herself to anyone. But what did it matter, truly? There were times she was desperate, absolutely desperate to be shed of her virginity, but no, she thought, impossible, it could not be some pimple-faced soldier, or that older, more scary one with the patch of razor burn along his neck as if chafed by a rope. He will be the one to die. She felt it instantly. It excited her. It was all very dramatic.

Then she felt guilty. She thought of her brothers, who were still in America, training in Georgia. Clint would do something to show off and be killed. Paul would be more careful, though easily convinced to do something risky, especially if a friend were in trouble. She prayed he would have no friends. Otherwise he would surely be killed. It was Jonas: he was the only one among her brothers who acted like a rich man's son. He would not take any risk if someone else might do it instead. And he was an officer.

Outside, the grass was already brown from the heat. To the south, the flat Texas plain stretched down to Mexico; to the north the escarpment began. A yellow tint of summer haze. A mule pulling a plow. She did not know why, it was plain to see there would be no rain for weeks, the dryness made you wonder if it would ever rain again.

Her uncle Phineas was a powerful man, head of the Railroad Commission, more powerful than the governor, they said. He was not really her uncle, but great-uncle, and he determined how much oil could be pumped in all of Texas. Somehow that controlled the price. She supposed it was like cattle. In a drought everyone had to sell quickly so the price went down, though when beef got scarce the price went up again. Except the packers were now interrupting this—buying cheap from distressed ranchers while raising the price on the other end—telling the city buyers, who did not know better, that a drought meant scarcity. The packers were where the money had gone; it was no longer made on grass, but in cement buildings. Armour and Swift. Her father hated them. Meanwhile Texas made more oil than anyplace on the earth. You did not hear people who made oil complaining very much.

SHE OPENED HER eyes. She was on the floor of the great room, watching the fire. Her arm, the skin old and so thin the light seemed to pass right through it, the watch askew on her wrist. Perhaps she might inch just one finger? No. Her eyes moved around the room and settled on a globe next to the divan. It was no older than she was, but many of the countries had already ceased to exist. No hope for a single person. She could see that the mortar had begun to crumble in the fireplace; the stones would soon come apart. *When did that happen?* she wondered, and then she thought: *I did not expect to live this long myself.* Except that was lie. She had always known it was the others who wouldn't make it.

Death the common companion; it was not like the settled places of the North. Jonas sensed it and saved himself. *You did not know better. Or did and thought you could escape it.* She watched the ember on the hearth. She wondered if she had really known that about Paul and Clint, or if it was another trick of the mind, the memory recording something that had never been true, like a magnetic tape that had been tampered with.

PHINEAS HAD BEEN good to her. It was hard to imagine the power he'd had: as OPEC would years later, the Railroad Commission controlled the price of oil in the entire world. Phineas had become enormously wealthy. He could make or break any oilman in the state, any politician—you might drill all the wells you wanted, but you could not pump a drop without his say-so.

The commission's offices were in a drab state office building; the only thing giving it away were the cars—Packards, a Cadillac Sixteen, Lincoln Zeyphrs, and Continentals. Phineas had a corner office, the walls lined with his trophies, the Colonel's Yellowboy Winchester, a brace of Colt Peacemakers, plaques from the Southwest Cattle Raisers and the Old Trail Driver's Association. There were pictures with elephants and lions and antlered game of every description, he had hunted on five continents. There were pictures with Teddy Roosevelt in Cuba, Phineas smiling broadly, more sure of himself than the old man.

He was seventy-five now and, when seated, still gave off an impression of power. He looked nothing like the Colonel: a tall man with thick white hair, expensive suits, beautiful secretaries. He did not wear cowboy boots or a bolo tie—those were affectations of a later generation—he was more like an eastern banker.

But his health was failing. His legs were swollen, his heart unsteady. He would never live to see his father's age, that was plain.

Jeannie watched the secretary as she left coffee and a tray of kolaches. A brunette with violet eyes, high cheekbones, a perfect figure—she would never be pretty enough. Phineas asked about the news from Paul and Clint, congratulated her on finishing school. Did she have plans? Not really. She settled into a chair overlooking the capitol and downtown Austin. She was only five hours from the ranch but it was a different country entirely.

When the secretary had closed the door, something in Phineas's manner changed and she knew he meant to talk business.

"I suspect it is obvious to both of us that the ranch is losing money."

She nodded, though it had not been obvious: beef had been climbing steadily since the war began.

"I lived on that land before it was settled," he continued. "I buried my mother and father and brother there. And now my nephew—your father—is running it into the ground. He is content to burn through our money as if a fresh supply will come up like grass in the springtime. Why the old man left him majority holder, I have no idea." He leaned back in his chair. "Have you seen the books?"

"I don't think so," she said.

"Of course not." He beckoned her around to his side of the desk, where a ledger was sitting open. He pointed to a number: a little over four hundred thousand dollars. "Last year's cattle sales. It seems like a large number, and it is, because your father sells a lot of cattle. But the next thirty-seven pages are debits." He skipped forward, first a page at a time, then two or three at a time, until he reached the end. He pointed to another number, just under eight hundred thousand dollars. "The ranch's expenses are nearly double its income."

There is some mistake, she thought, but she kept quiet. Instead she asked: "How long has it been like that?"

"Oh, twenty years, at least. The only thing keeping us in the black is the oil and gas, but the wells are old and shallow and the Colonel, quite wisely, leased only a few thousand acres, trusting that we would lease the rest at higher prices. Which we have not yet done."

He paused again.

"For reasons I do not quite understand, our state has a club of wealthy children who like to play at being cattlemen. As if the term can even exist today. Bob Kleberg has put it in your father's ear that with technology, better bulls, and a few bump gates, he can make money selling beef, which is a feat Kleberg has not even managed on his own land. As you may or may not know, the King Ranch, all million acres of it, was on the verge of bankruptcy until Humble Oil loaned them three million dollars. Which was a pity, because I had made Alice King a very generous offer. And I have always liked the coast."

He looked for her reaction but she sat quietly, so he continued.

"Your father is counting on the fact that I will not be around for-ever, because he thinks that once he gets my money, his problems are over. What he does not seem to realize—or care about—is that even *with* my money, the ranch will still go bankrupt—it is just a question of how many millions your father will go through until it does."

She knew then why she had been called: he wanted her to betray her father. To her surprise she did not object to this as much as she might have hoped. Her father, for all his rough-and-tumble image, was a dandy. She had always known this, perhaps because the Colonel was always pointing it out. Earning money was the furthest thing from her father's mind, he wanted to be on magazine covers, like the Colonel had been. She had always known that the Colonel did not respect him and now she saw that Phineas—the other famous member of the family—did not respect him, either.

"Shall we get lunch? Or can you handle a little more business?"

"I'm fine," she said.

"Good. Tell me what you know about the depletion allowance."

"Nothing," she said.

"Of course. That's what your father knows about it as well. The depletion allowance is one of the things that makes the oil business as far from the cattle business as the North Pole is from the South. At the moment, it says that if you drill for oil, you can write twenty-seven point five percent of your proceeds off as a loss."

"Because you spent money to drill the wells?"

"That is certainly what we tell the newspapers, though in general we have already written off about sixty percent of those costs as intangibles. The depletion allowance is something entirely different. Every year a well produces oil, even though it is putting money into your pocket, it is simultaneously reducing your tax burden."

"You're making a profit, but calling it a loss."

She could see this pleased him.

"It sounds dishonest," she added.

"It is the opposite. It is the law of the United States."

"Still."

"Still nothing. The law was put there for a reason. People will raise cattle even though they will lose money doing it—you do not need to incentivize the cattle business. Oil, on the other hand, is expensive to find and even more expensive to get out of the ground. It is an enormously risky enterprise. And so if the government wants us to find oil, it must encourage us to do so."

"So we should drill."

"Of course we should drill. How your father can still be thinking about cows is a mystery. Every bit of profit we made in the old days was based on overstocking, on using up a thousand years of grass in a decade. The way we used to fill those pastures, it was like those file cabinets there, touching on both sides, it was mining for grass. But, as you must know from listening to me this long, facts are boring, especially to men like your father. Because what does every coonass wildcatter do when he makes his first million? He buys a ranch and stocks it with Herefords, in the same way he acquires a Packard or a beautiful wife. Though he does not expect any of them to be profitable investments.

"In the meantime, the rest of us have no choice but to exist in the present. I'm getting calls from the secretary of the navy, who is telling me he does not want a single production control in place. He wants drilling, drilling, and more drilling—the only thing we have over the Germans is our oil—they are building a pipeline from here to New Jersey, where all the refineries are, and they want every goddamn drop we have."

He was looking out the window; he was talking again but she could not follow the thread—it was more taxes—and she was beginning to feel sick, she could not bring this up to her father, it was out of the question. *This war won't last forever*, that was what her father was always saying, *things will go back to the way they were.* She wondered what it must be like to be her father, taking himself so seriously, imagining himself a kind of royalty, though from a country no one had heard of. Of course, in his defense, people had lately begun to agree with him. The Colonel had been dead long enough that her father was now interesting to reporters;

they would visit and he would tell them the Colonel's stories, jumbled together with his own, the time he and the Colonel had charged a house full of Mexican horse thieves during the bandit wars of 1915. It was said he had once shot a man in cold blood.

Regardless, her father *was* part of a dying breed, for better or worse, most of the old-time ranching families had gone bankrupt. Most people now lived in cities—she could still not get her head around that one—the days of the frontier were gone, long gone, though there were those who preferred not to admit it. As for her father, with his heavy face, his big hands, he had finally become what he had hoped for since childhood, the representative of a bygone era, an emissary from a lost time. That he himself had not lived during this time was irrelevant—he would take the reporters out to the corrals and put on a show, rope and cut for them, he had begun to keep older, gentler horses just for visitors, which would have been unthinkable in the old days, because horses cost money and they were for work, not play.

An automobile horn on the street brought her back. Phineas was still talking.

" . . . even if most of the Hill Country still doesn't have electricity, even if one does encounter the occasional bucktoothed child on a donkey, this war has dragged the rest of the world into the modern age. The Polish cavalry smashed itself against German tanks, every cannibal in the South Pacific has now seen a Zero, and if there was doubt in any mind that the era of the horse was over, that question is now settled."

She nodded. It was obvious even to her.

"Jeannie," he said, "it will not be long before we look back on this time and think we barely used any oil at all. Which is why we need to get some wells sunk on that land. I am tired of lending your father money."

THE NEXT DAY she took the train home. It stopped for a long time in San Antonio, the air still, the sun beating against the car. She lay against the window, trying to breathe slowly, thinking of cool things, the stock tank, the spring at the casa mayor. There were soldiers everywhere, Mexicans sweating through their uniforms, heads hanging numbly, sweat pooling, their only hope that the train might move again, they were like steers on their way to Fort Worth. Thousands had been abandoned to the Japanese, who were cutting off their heads with swords. Though MacArthur himself had escaped. A little too proudly, she thought.

She searched their faces but they were all looking down. The walking dead. How many were not even men yet? She was tired of being alone, she imagined her father's angry face, *I gave it to a soldier*, the great burden carried away. Clint and Paul had gone to a house in Carrizo. Her father had known about it beforehand. *But I am not allowed.*

When she was younger and found her father working in his study she would sit next to his chair and read, or hang around his neck and look over his shoulder, and finally he would turn and silently give her a kiss, the signal to leave him alone.

That was all he had. A hug and a kiss. Though he would kiss a horse as well, give months to understanding it, more than his own daughter.

Phineas was just using her, that was true, but he had always made time for her, even when she was young; she must have been tiresome and yet he'd made a point of teaching her things. To her father, she was just in the way. An inconvenience. A thing that might have been a son.

It was all an exaggeration, it was not the entire truth, but it made her furious, the nights she'd spent alone in the house, her father and brothers in the pastures. Things had improved since Clint and Paul left, but still. *He loves you*, she thought, *but he prefers not to think about you.* What did he prefer? Horses. Cows. Women, perhaps, though if so she hadn't heard about it. She decided if she ever had children, she would not leave them alone for a single minute.

"I won't have children anyway," she said out loud.

The Negro porter in the doorway looked up, then looked away, embarrassed. The train began to move. She wondered what she would say to her father.

★   ★   ★

WHEN SHE WAS sixteen she had kissed one of the vaqueros, out in the stables he was supposed to be cleaning; they had stood there for ten minutes, she could feel his tongue move lightly inside her mouth. She spent the whole night thinking about him, his cheekbones and soft eyelashes, but when she went to see him the next day, he would not let her near. A week later he was gone. She knew they had not been seen; it was as if her father had merely sensed it—as if he had sensed something was making her happy—and ruined it.

Meanwhile he did not care if the family declined. He cared only for himself. Eventually they would be bankrupt and all they had ever done would be forgotten; they would be no different from the Garcias, the children of strangers in their ruined house, a young girl in a grave. She leaned against the train window and listened to the tracks rumble beneath her, it would all come to an end.

No. She would not let it. She did not know how she would stop him, but she was as sure of this as she had ever been of anything; Phineas was old, her father was a fool, and Jonas cared only about himself. Paul and Clint were happy savages, running around without a thought in their heads. *It is up to me,* she thought. *I will have to do something.*

JORGE PICKED HER up at the station in Carrizo. She didn't feel like talking so she rode in the backseat, which she didn't normally do, she wasn't inclined to make people feel like servants. But Jorge wasn't bothered. He seemed relieved, even. He liked being alone with his thoughts just as she did, going for a drive to think, his own life, same as her, working through problems in his mind. Somehow this embarrassed her.

As they came up the caliche driveway, the house appeared at the top of the hill, the sun blinding white on the limestone, the dark green oaks and elms, the sky a hot pale blue. The third floor would be unbearable, the second floor only slightly better: she would be sleeping on her porch tonight, ice water on the sheets and two fans blowing. There was a black coupe parked in front that she recognized as her grandmother's. The driver, a white man, was sitting on the porch by himself, far away from the vaqueros who were noisily taking their supper.

The curtains were drawn against the sun; the house smelled of hot stone. She went upstairs and changed out of her sweaty dress, fixed her hair and face, then went down to join her father and grandmother in the dining room.

Her father smiled and got up to kiss her hello and she knew immediately something was wrong. She wondered if one of her brothers had been hurt, then reminded herself they had not even left the country yet. Of course that meant nothing: one of their vaqueros had lost his son in basic training, run over by a jeep on a military base. It all went through her head in an instant; she dismissed it just as quickly. They would not be sitting for supper if something had happened to Paul or Clint.

Her grandmother, weaker even than Phineas, did not get up; Jeannie greeted her and kissed her cheek.

"How was your trip?"

"Hot," she said.

"And Phineas?"

"He's well."

Her father, who had no use for Uncle Phineas, said, "Your grandmother was just telling me she's spoken to the people at Southwestern in Georgetown."

She nodded.

"You can start there in August."

"Oh, I'm not interested in that," she said cheerfully, as if they were asking her opinion.

A look went between her father and his mother and he said: "Jeannie, it's unpleasant, but we all have our jobs in life. Mine is to make sure this ranch stays above water. Gramammy's there is to make sure I don't make any mistakes." He smiled indulgently at her grandmother. "Yours is to get a proper education."

He does not respect her, she realized. All the air went out of her; her talk with Phineas was just talk, it meant nothing. She felt cold. She would end up at Southwestern; she would make the best of it.

"You won't have to go so far away this time," her grandmother was saying.

Later she would not recall making any choice, the words seemed to come out on their own: "I am not going to be a secretary."

"You don't have to," said her father.

"Or a teacher."

"We all have our obligations, Jeannie."

"Phineas and I were just talking about that same thing," she said brightly. She took a drink of water.

"Well, it is true," he said.

"He showed me the ledger."

Her father was beginning to say something else but then her words caught up with him. She intended to stare him down but couldn't and instead she spoke to her plate. "In fact, the ranch is not above water. It is quite the opposite."

She looked up; her father's face showed nothing. Out of the corner of her eye, she saw her grandmother trying to get her attention.

"I know what we lose on the cattle."

"Well, you shouldn't spend so much time listening to old Phineas," he said. He tried to smile again, but couldn't.

She began to feel sick; she wondered if she had caught a fever on the train.

" . . . this ranch is not the right place for a young lady with your talents," her father was saying. "You'll report to college, which is an opportunity I myself never had, at the end of summer."

"Your life is no harder than mine," she said. "You ride a twenty-thousand-dollar horse but you act like we live in the poorhouse. We lose four hundred thousand dollars a year on your cattle. Phineas says he's tired of lending you money. Something will have to be done."

There it was: she'd declared her betrayal. He was saying *you will leave the table, you will leave the table right now* and she said: "I will not." She couldn't have anyway; she was sure her legs would not hold her. "Every day you pretend you are supporting the family, when all you are doing is spending the family's money."

"It is my money," he said. "It is not your money; you have no say in this, you are a child."

"It is the Colonel's money. You did not earn a dime of it."

"You will stop."

"We have not had supper in two weeks. Why? Because you are playing with your horses. Before that it was almost six weeks. The oil is the only thing allowing you to do this."

She expected to be slapped, but her father seemed to calm down and he said, "The oil pays for improvements to the land, honey. It pays so we don't have to sleep in the mud at roundup, so we can just drive home and sleep in real beds at night. And that airplane, because we can't hire enough men to check those pastures from horseback anymore."

"Then perhaps we should stop doing roundup altogether," she said. "As it would save us a great deal of money."

Then he got up. He squared himself and stepped toward her, but nothing happened. He turned and walked out of the room. She could hear his footsteps slow as he reminded himself the house was still his, his boots went down the hall, past the parlor and into the foyer, then out the front door, slamming it behind him.

"That was very stupid," said her grandmother.

She shrugged, wondered if she'd destroyed everything she knew; then had a feeling it had never mattered anyway. The day before, an hour before, to speak to her father, to speak to anyone like this would have been unthinkable.

"I didn't realize you were afraid of him," she said. "Is it because the Colonel didn't leave you anything?"

Her grandmother ignored her. "You can't stay here, Jeannie. Especially after this."

Jeannie had a feeling she would be content if she never spoke to her grandmother again, or to anyone else in the family.

"Your father is not going to let you run this ranch."

"There *isn't* any ranch. We're living on minerals and borrowed money."

"Did Phineas write you that little speech? Because if you think a woman will have any place in his schemes, you're mistaken." She got a nasty look. "In more ways than one."

"I guess we'll see." She was thinking about her father, how thin he was; she knew he no longer slept through the night.

Her grandmother set down her knife and fork, arranging them carefully and smoothing the tablecloth, and took a sip of her sherry. "I have always known that you find me tiresome," she said. "You think it is my nature, or my disposition, or you have likely never thought about it. But when I decided to move here, I found I had a choice between being liked and having a say. That's the choice you'll have to make as well. They will either love you and not respect you, or they will respect you and not love you."

"Things are changing."

"It may appear that way, but when the war is over, the men will come back, and it will go back to the way it has always been."

"I guess we'll see," she repeated.

"This place," said her grandmother. She waved her hand, dismissing not only Jeannie but everything else, the house, the land, their good name. "I'm a member of the wealthiest family in four counties, but they still give me dirty looks when I vote."

It was quiet. It occurred to Jeannie that for years she had wanted nothing more than this—for her grandmother to treat her like a confidante, a real person—but now she wanted nothing of the sort. She guessed she ought to feel privileged; instead she was embarrassed. Embarrassed that her grandmother was bullied by her own son, embarrassed that she would complain about her sex; what should have been sympathy somehow turned to anger, her grandmother ought to be out among the right people, solving the social problem, for if not her, then who? It was weakness, the entire family, and she felt a lifetime of fear and respect burn off as quickly as it had for her father. She sat up straight, smoothed her dress, she would be alone in life, that was clear, but right now she did not mind.

"You are not going to find a husband here who understands that we are halfway through the twentieth century. Do you understand?"

"I'll end up like you, you mean."

"That's exactly what I mean. Married to men like your father or your grandfather or your brothers. To the sort of men who would choose to live out here, you will just be a place to get warm."

"That's not going to happen."

"You won't have a choice, Jeannie."

CHAPTER TWENTY-ONE

DIARIES OF PETER McCULLOUGH

MARCH 10, 1916

Yesterday Pancho Villa crossed the border into New Mexico, killing twenty. Today, hardly a white man to be seen without a pistol or slung rifle, even to buy groceries.

The Germans have promised to reinforce Mexican troops with German infantry should they choose to cross the border. Whole town in a frenzy; we are only ten miles from the river.

I do not point out there is little likelihood of the Kaiser sending troops to McCullough Springs when he is losing them ten thousand a day in France. I do not point out that the number of Americans killed in Columbus is the same as the number of Tejanos shot in bar ditches on any given night in South Texas. I do not point these things out because everyone seems happy with the news of this new threat; neighbors who didn't speak are suddenly friendly, wives have new reasons to make love with their husbands, disobedient children do their schoolwork and come home early for dinner.

FOUR MEXICANS FOUND shot outside town, all teenagers. No one is sure who they are or who killed them. The vaqueros think they are *fuereños*, men from the interior of Mexico, though how they can deduce this from a bloated corpse is beyond me. Incident not mentioned in newspaper.

If it were four dead mules, there would have been an investigation, but there is nothing except general grumbling about the burial costs.

MARCH 14, 1916

Yet more blood on our hands and Charles has been taken to Carrizo. He was in town buying supplies when he ran into Dutch Hollis. Though it was only noon, Dutch was quite drunk and in front of a lunchtime crowd of onlookers accused our family of various crimes (of which we are certainly guilty), including engineering the death of the Garcias to gain their land.

After a short struggle Dutch got the better of him; Charles went to the truck and returned with his pistol. Dutch may or may not have reached for his knife (a folding jackknife in a pouch, same as all the men here carry). Charles shot him in the face.

Our caporal Garza arrived in time to see the final act: *Madonna, you should have seen it, his hand did not even tremble.* He related this expecting I would be proud.

Shortly after getting home, Charles saddled his horse and rode for Mexico. The Colonel and I caught him a few miles short of the river and convinced him to come back.

"It'll be all right," I said to him, as we returned.

He shrugged.

"We'll muddle through." He did not say anything. I felt the old impotence rising within me—what was the point of my even existing—or so everyone else seems to think.

"He had it coming," said Charles. "He's been talking like that all over town."

"With his brother dying . . ."

"His brother? How about *my* brother?" He kicked his horse and caught up to the Colonel, who was riding ahead of us. They nodded to each other, did not speak, some wordless understanding, the same as my father and Phineas. My skin began to tingle . . . it occurred to me that I was the one who ought to be fleeing to Mexico. . . .

Was he right? He and Sally seem to think the same way . . . is a near death equal to a death?

When we returned to the house, Sheriff Graham was waiting. Charles, bluffing over, turned white. Graham told us there was no hurry. He was thirsty.

The four of us spent the rest of the evening on the gallery drinking whiskey and watching the sunset, the three of them sitting together and chatting easily about how to best handle the incident, the sky going its typical blood red, which to me alone seemed symbolic, as I was sitting off a small distance from the others.

To listen to the three of them talk about the death of Dutch Hollis, you might have thought there had been some accident, a lightning strike, flash flood, the hand of God. Not my son's. *Had to do it, acted on instinct,* the sheriff just nodding away, sipping our whiskey, my father refilling his glass.

Considered interrupting them to note that the entire history of humanity is marked by a single inexorable movement—from animal instinct toward rational thought, from inborn behavior toward acquired knowledge. A half-grown panther abandoned in the wilderness will grow up to be a perfectly normal panther. But a half-grown child similarly abandoned will grow up into an unrecognizable savage, unfit for normal society. Yet there are those who insist the opposite: that we are creatures of instinct, like wolves.

Once darkness had fallen and all were convinced of my son's righteousness, Graham drove Charles back to Carrizo, all agreeing it was best if Charles spent a night in jail for appearance's sake. Glenn meanwhile has been keeping his distance. He is confused by Charlie's actions, to say the least.

MARCH 15, 1916

Went to see Dutch Hollis's body before they bury him. He was lying in Graham's back shed with several blocks of ice. He was unshaven, had not been washed; his face and clothes were filthy and clotted with blood and, like all the dead, he had lost control of his waste. Not long ago, twenty years maybe, he was a child reaching for his mother . . . a boy becoming a man . . . I had a sudden memory of him playing the fiddle, together with his brother, at the Midkiffs' house. I peered into the dark spot, just at the edge of his eyebrow, an intricate machine, broken forever; there had been words and music . . . we had put a stop to that.

There was something shiny inside his shirt, a woman's locket . . . I lifted it but could not quite make it out in the dimness. I broke the chain, jerking his head in the process. Then I left the room quickly and walked back into the light.

When I got home (heart racing the entire time, as if I'd committed some great felony, as if the crime was not killing him but taking his locket), there was no picture, no message, no piece of hair: the locket was empty. I took it to the Garcias' and buried it there, along with our other victims, the whole time expecting I was being followed, the criminal feeling lingering. There are those born to hunt and those born to be hunted . . . I have always known I was the latter.

MARCH 16, 1916

Charles has returned, but he is not allowed to leave any of the four counties in which our property extends. He strides about with his chin up; I find it difficult to look at him. Judge Poole assures us there will be no indictment. In fact he and the sheriff and my father went calling at the homes of those likely to be empaneled.

Would like to report I have been torn between a hope he might receive punishment and hope he'll be exonerated. I have not. I want only for him to be acquitted. And yet his crimes multiply . . . this the son I raised with my own hands.

Have been in to buy supplies, keeping my hat pulled low, terrified the entire time I would run into Esther Hollis, Dutch and Bill's mother, but this evening, with enormous relief, I remembered that she has been dead several years.

No one seems particularly bothered, least of all the Mexicans. The *coraje,* they say, the heat and dust and thorns. Even horses get it. For the grandson of a great *patrón*—a man with blood—to get the *coraje,* it is only to be expected. Especially when a man slanders his family. And in public . . . In truth it was the only reasonable action.

Meanwhile both Hollis brothers now lie rotting. Impossible to believe we are truly in God's image. Something of the reptile in us yet, the caveman's allegiance to the spear. A vestige of our time in the swamps. And yet there are those wish to return. Be more like the reptile, they say. Be more like the snake, lying in wait. Of course they do not say *snake,* they say *lion,* but there is little difference in character between the two, only in appearance.

MARCH 24, 1916

Grand jury refused to indict.

APRIL 2, 1916

Despite Dutch Hollis, despite the Garcias, our name carries more weight than ever. Where I expect bitterness, I receive respect; where I expect jealousy, I receive encouragement. Do not steal from the McCulloughs—they will kill you; do not slander the McCulloughs—they will kill you. My father thinks this the proper state of affairs. I tell him this is the tenth century of the second millennium.

In the end it is as he says—they think we are made of different stuff. If it ever occurred to them that we eat and bleed the same as they do, they would run us down with torches and pitchforks. Or, more accurately, holy water and wooden stakes.

★ ★ ★

IN NEWS OF the broader suffering, Villa's men attacked the barracks at Glenn Spring yesterday. My sympathies for the Mexican people aside, my father and I are both anxious for the arrival of our Lewis gun, which fires ten .30-caliber rounds per second. A true blessing for the few holding out against the many. Due to war in Europe they are running a severe backlog.

Serious talk that the Mexican government is planning an assault on Laredo—Carranza's troops are massing across the river. The Mexicans believe we ought to hew to the original border (the Nueces). Texans believe the border belongs another three hundred miles south, somewhere around Durango.

SALLY WANTS TO move to San Antonio or Dallas or even Austin—anywhere but here.

"We are perfectly safe," I told her. "Neither the Huns nor the Mexican army will be approaching our gate anytime soon."

"That is not what I care about," she said.

"Is this about the boys?"

"It's about all three of them. The two living and the one buried."

"They will be fine."

"Until they do something like this again. Or until someone's brother finds them."

"There are no more Hollises left. We have seen to that."

"There will be someone else," she said.

Considered mentioning this was her reward for marrying into the family of the great Eli McCullough, but said nothing. All the energy had left me.

"My nephews in Dallas have guns," she said. "They use them to hunt deer. They go to school, they chase after the wrong sort of girls, but . . ." She choked up. "I went to see the boy . . ."

"Dutch?" I said gently.

" . . . they had him laid out in a shed behind Bill Graham's office. It was a disgrace."

I did not say anything. Things have been so bad between us for so long and every time I have had hope, she has smashed it. I looked away from her and closed myself off.

"You might be staying here alone, Pete. I have lost all the sons I care to lose."

CHAPTER TWENTY-TWO

ELI/TIEHTETI

Spring 1851

To white ears, the names of the Indians lacked any sort of dignity or sense and made it that much harder to figure why they ought to be treated as humans rather than prairie niggers. The reason for this was that the Comanches considered the use of a dead person's name taboo. Unlike the whites, billions of whom shared the same handful of names, all interchangeable in the end, a Comanche name lived and died with a single person.

A child was not named by his parents, but by a relative or a famous person in the tribe; maybe for a deed that person had done, maybe for an object that struck their fancy. If a particular name was not serving well, the child might be renamed; for instance, Charges the Enemy had been a small and timid child and it was thought that giving him a braver name might cure these problems, which it had. Some people in the tribe were renamed a second or third time in adult life, if their friends and family found something more interesting to call them. The owner of the German captive Yellow Hair, whose birth name was Six Deer, was renamed Lazy Feet as a teenager, which stuck to him the rest of his life. Toshaway's son Fat Wolf was so named because his namer had seen a very fat wolf the previous night, and being an interesting sight and not a bad name it had stuck. Toshaway's name meant Bright Button, which had also stuck with him since birth, but that seemed a strange thing to call him so I thought of him as Toshaway. Spanish-sounding names were also common, though they often had no particular meaning—Pizon, Escuté, Concho—there was a warrior named Hisoo-ancho who had been captured at the age of seven or eight, whose Christian name was Jesus Sanchez, and, as that was all he would answer to, that was what he was called.

Many Comanche names were too vulgar to repeat in print and thus, when the situation required, were changed by whites. The chief who led the famous raid on Linnville in 1840 (in which a group of five hundred warriors sacked a warehouse full of fine clothing and made their escape dressed in top hats, wedding gowns, and silk shirts) was named Po-cha-na-quar-hip, meaning Cock That Stays Hard Forever. But neither this nor the more delicate translation, Erection That Will Not Go Down, could possibly be printed in newspapers, so it was decided to call him Buffalo Hump. He was thusly referred to until he died, many years later, attempting to learn farming on a reservation, having lost both his land and his good name to the whites, though in his own mind he remained Cock That Stays Hard Forever.

The medicine man who, along with Quanah Parker, led the entire Comanche nation against the whites in the Red River War of 1874 was named Isahata?i, meaning Coyote Pussy. The newspapers called him Ishtai, Eshati, and Eschiti, no translation offered. Toshaway had a nephew called Tried to Fuck a Mare, a name acquired in adolescence, and Hates Work, as previously mentioned, was originally called Single Bird. The Comanches were a good-natured sort and names were accepted with humor, though after Tried to Fuck a Mare got his first scalp and it was decided to change his name to Man on a Hill, he was not heard to complain.

BY FEBRUARY THE tribe was starving. There had not been a big buffalo kill in over a year, and most of the local deer, elk, and antelope had been hunted down over the winter. The few animals still alive moved only at night, surviving on twigs and dry brush. By then we had taken to tracking packrats back to their nests and eating their stashes of dried fruits and nuts, along with the rats themselves if we could catch them, and everyone in the tribe knew that the very young, the very old, and the sick would soon begin to die, and they would have, had we not discovered a buffalo herd beginning to drift north.

Everyone took this as a sign that our bad luck had ended, and the Creator-of-All-Things had forgiven us. By the time the first Spring Beauties appeared we had replenished our stores of meat and hides and begun to look forward to the summer, when the weather would be warm, though this also meant that the women in the band were put to double work preparing all the hides, so that they would be ready by the time the Comanchero traders arrived.

IN MAY IT was time to go raiding again. A third of the band had been killed the previous year, most of its horse wealth lost, and if this summer's raids were not successful, it was not clear how much longer we would survive. Toshaway would go again, though Escuté, who still could not quite draw his bow, was ordered to stay in camp, and I would be sent in his place. Nuukaru was also going but, unlike the other young braves, he was quiet about the deeds he would commit.

"Don't look so down in the mouth," said Escuté. "You can bring back a beautiful Mexican girl and listen to me fuck her."

Nuukaru shook his head.

"Let me guess. You have a bad feeling."

"Stop," he said, indicating me.

Escuté looked over: "This one always has a bad feeling. Don't listen to him."

"I had it about the last one, too."

"Ah, the great *puha tenahpu*. I had almost forgotten."

"Things are changing," he said. "Whether or not we admit it. The Penateka . . ."

"Fuck the fucking Penateka. They were the white man's *tai?i* and they got what was coming to them."

"They were four times our size."

"And they were the white man's bitch and got all his diseases."

"Ah, of course. The ones who make the greatest-ever raid on the whites were also his bitch."

"Ten winters ago."

"They had horse herds as thick as buffalo."

"Nʉʉkaru, we had one bad year, and you are a gloomy cocksucker, and you might ask to stay behind because if you continue to talk like that, instead of singing the *woho hubiya,* someone will shut your mouth with a tomahawk."

"If we have another raid like last year," said Nʉʉkaru, "there will be no one left to shut my mouth at all."

"Ignore him, Tiehteti. This is what gets people killed." He shook his head. "You will bring back a thousand horses and a hundred scalps and fifty Mexican slaves. That is what you will do. Talking about it is a waste of time."

"All right," said Nʉʉkaru.

"My arm hurts so bad I can't sleep but you don't hear me whining like a child. Kill some Mexicans, die a hero, I don't give a fuck, but this talking is pointless, you might as well cut your own throat, and the throats of your people while you're at it."

"WE ARE PLANNING to avoid the whites," said Toshaway, "but . . ."

"You don't have to worry about me," I told him.

"Good." He looked out across the village, noticeably smaller than it had been the previous year. "I wish you had been born twenty years ago, Tiehteti, because those were real days. The buffalo wolves used to follow us on our raids because they knew they'd get something to eat." He scratched his chin. "But perhaps those times will return."

WE DESCENDED FROM the plains and the land became mesas and canyonlands again, there were trees, mostly cottonwoods and oaks, the grass was tall and the blanketflowers were thick, patches of color going on for miles.

Toshaway had relatives along the San Saba headwaters and while looking for them we found a freshly raided Comanche camp, around seventy bodies, all scalped. There were a few warriors, but mostly it was women and children and old men. Toshaway had found his relatives. They were a splinter band of the Kotsoteka. Many of the women and girls had been treated the same as my mother and sister, cut up in the same way as well. We spent the day burying them.

"Their men must still be out," said Pizon.

There were boot prints everywhere, boots made in Austin or San Antonio or somewhere in the east. There was a strange litter of musket balls on the ground and the hoofprints of shod horses. The tipis, weapons, and camp equipment had all been thrown into a fire and burned. I was dauncy with shame, but the other Comanches kept their faces hard, and the only thing said was that a few years earlier, the nearest white settlements has been hundreds of miles away, and it was a bad sign that they had found this camp.

"How many whites are there?" said Toshaway. "Do you know?"

"They say about twenty million."

He grunted and looked at me.

"Come on."

"It's a fact."

"Okay, Tiehteti."

We rode in a wide circle around the camp, taking a break from digging. It could not have been a Ranger squad because twelve men could not kill seventy-three Comanches, even women and children. Toshaway guessed three hundred riders, but there were so many tracks on top of each other, as they had spent at least a day raping and sacking the village, it was hard to be certain.

I thought about my father's tracks, he had a strange duck-footed walk and his left foot stuck out more than his right, and for a tall heavy man he had very small feet. I decided not to look.

At the top of a hill we found ruts as if a pair of wagons had been parked. The grass was burned down to the dirt.

"Strange," said Toshaway.

"Those were cannons," I said. "That's why the grass is burned."

"Those are very heavy, no?"

"A mountain howitzer can be pulled behind a horse. The army used them against the Mexicans all the time."

The hill was maybe a furlong from the village and I knew the musket balls littering the ground must have been canister. A mountain howitzer loaded with canister was like two hundred rifles firing at once, or as my father used to say, like the hand of the Lord Himself.

"Tiehteti, it is very strange. For instance, how did they get into position without being noticed? And why would they have brought cannons all this way unless they were sure that Indians would be here? That is what I find strange." He shook his head. "Someone was leading them."

"They put the guns in place in the dark."

"Of course in the dark. But still. They knew Indians were here." He stood looking down at the ruins of the camp.

"Unfortunately most of the men seem to have fallen into their cooking fires and I could not tell if my cousin was among them. Though I did recognize his wife and two daughters."

By then the other men were washing the ash and gore off in the river. Before we left, we hacked a flat place into a cottonwood and carved a note in hieroglyphics, telling what had happened, and how many we had buried, in case there were other members of the band who had not yet returned.

THE NEXT NIGHT we saw campfires in the distance, fires as only the whites made them, twice as large as they needed to be, nearly two dozen in all. It could only be the army, as there were not that many Rangers in the entire state of Texas.

There was discussion about whether to steal their horses but we

decided to keep going. It would be safer to get them from the Mexicans, and instead of sleeping we rode all night to put distance between
us and the soldiers. We crossed the Pecos without seeing anyone
else, though there were recent tracks of shod horses, a small party
of travelers. There was a debate about following them but the army
was still close and it was again decided to wait. Climbing out of the
Pecos Valley, the land became flat and dry. Long patches of caliche,
clumps of oaks, mesquites, and huisache, the occasional cedar. We
didn't relax until we'd reached the Davis Mountains, where there was
another debate about using the standard route past the old Presidio
del Norte, which was well watered and had good grass and involved
the least climbing, or going farther east into the mountains, where
it was steeper and less watered but also less traveled. The younger
men—who needed scalps—were annoyed we hadn't taken on either
the army or the travelers whose tracks we'd crossed, so it was decided
to go past Presidio.

We stayed at a distance from the town, dropping gradually into
the valley, then the river itself, and then back up into the mountains. A
day's ride from the border was a latifundio that was known to have a
thousand horses.

THERE WAS A small village attached to the latifundio and we left the
remuda with a half-dozen young Indians to guard the animals. Most
were better hands than I was at riding and shooting, but that did not
matter, because I had gotten a scalp and they hadn't.

The rest of us picked the best horses, covered our faces and bodies
with red and black and yellow paint, put on silver and brass armbands
and bracelets, and tied feathers to the manes of our horses. Toshaway
made sure I got a medicine hat with a large brown shield and I spent
a long time painting it. I emptied my bowels three times, though the
last time it was all water. I kept my eye on Toshaway and Nuukaru.
Toshaway was laughing and joking with various people, making sure
everyone was ready; Nuukaru was keeping to himself, and looked seri-

ous, and I also saw him go into the bushes and then a second time a few minutes later. I tried to eat some pemmican, but my mouth was too dry. I decided that was fine. If you were hit in the guts you did not want them to be full.

The sun was close to setting when a bell in the hacienda began to ring, probably the supper bell, but the Comanches thought we'd been spotted and then everyone was on their horses, moving toward the village and the ranch. Shields were adjusted. A few riders carried cut-down shotguns or repeating pistols, but most had their bows ready with a half-dozen arrows clenched in the hand that held the bow, the seventh arrow nocked, quivers adjusted so they could get to more arrows when they needed them. Reins were tied short so they would not be in the way. You were expected to steer only with your knees.

We came at them with the sun behind us, making our way quietly through the brush until we were nearly at the edge of the village. Then we kicked the horses into a run. There was a small open area to be crossed and there was whooping and ululating as if we were celebrating a great occasion, white-clad Mexicans fleeing for the chaparral, a general cry of "*Los bárbaros,*" a single puff of gunsmoke from between two houses, another musket pointing from a window. I aimed just to the left of the barrel but the horse was running too fast and I missed. I fumbled away my rifle and took out my bow and we were into the village, a wide main street with white adobe houses on either side; I wondered how many people there were and saw more puffs of gunsmoke but all I heard was the whooping and ululating and I started to think I would not be hurt. Everything was moving slowly. I could see each stone and clod of dirt, arrows falling toward men on rooftops or behind walls, a boy holding an escopeta sprinting down the street in front of us, his hat fell off, his arm went back to reach for it and an arrow stuck into him, then a second arrow hit and then he turned suddenly and dodged between two houses.

Then we were at the end of the village. There was only one street so I turned around and went back down it. An old man stepped out with a pistol; he was pulling a careful bead and I felt the wind as the ball went. Before I could get my bow aimed the horse changed course and ran him over and I could tell by the sound that he would not be getting up. Then I was going by a long adobe wall and there were puffs of clay the whole length and I realized people were shooting at me. Somehow I was at the front, but the arrows were still going past on both sides and then I reached the end of the village again.

A man wearing the black coat of a hacendado was crouched behind a mesquite, calmly letting off a repeater. I shot two arrows but they went rattling off the branches and then another arrow came from behind me and cut through a small opening and the man fell backward. There was a *whoopwhoopwhoop* and Toshaway shook his bow, then turned away to look for more people. I realized I had not been shooting enough. I stopped to situate my arrows. My shield popped me in the nose; there was a white-shirted man surrounded by a cloud of gunsmoke and I shot a quick arrow. He dropped his musket and took a few drunken steps, then ran into the chaparral with the arrow wagging in front of him. I shot another into his back, which didn't slow him down either. He disappeared. I noticed I'd been standing still. I kicked the horse and we went back down the street.

There was no longer a charge as much as a general melee. Arrows kept flying past me; people kept falling over; I would look at someone— they would get hit by an arrow—I would look at someone else—they would get hit as well. I was beginning to feel like the hand of God Him- self, then remembered my shield and got it up and moving just as it was knocked into my head again. I tried to wipe my eyes and kicked the horse just as the shield was hit a third and fourth time. I was row- ing it in huge circles; I crouched and reached the end of the village and charged directly into the chaparral to gather myself up.

A woman with a child appeared in front of me; she was running blind and the horse turned to trample her. I kneed him away, miss- ing her, then made a big circle in the brush and headed back to the village. By now the street was nothing but bodies and dismounted

Comanches taking scalps. Most of the riders had gone somewhere else. There was shooting a few hundred yards away, at the main ranch house. A person with a musket came out from behind a wall, looked around, and sprinted for the chaparral. I cut his shirt with an arrow but he kept running and I knew I'd been missing most of my shots. I sat there a minute and nothing happened. I rode toward the shooting.

A dozen Indians had surrounded the house and were shooting arrows and occasionally a rifle toward it. The inhabitants were alive and well as there were regular puffs of smoke coming from the gunports and windows. On a stone patio, two men were lying next to a stub-barreled cannon, a ramrod and barrel of powder turned over next to them.

The main body of Comanches was off rounding up the horses, and I got a strange feeling watching the siege of the house so before I could be recruited I rode off to help gather the animals.

WE RODE ALL night but everyone was in a good mood, a thousand horses stretched out in front of us, enough to get our band back on its feet. I thought about the man I'd shot in the back and stomach and the other man I'd run down with the horse, and the others I had shot at but was not sure if I had hit. I figured it was possible they were all dead. None of them had given me the feeling of the Delaware and I wondered if I would ever have that again. I told myself they were just Mexicans and they would have done the same to me. My father always said the Mexicans had as much fun torturing people as the Indians.

Around midday we were into the foothills, driving the horses up a dry streambed. At the top of the hill, opposite the side we'd climbed, we stopped to collect our thoughts. I rode to find Toshaway and found him standing with Pizon, refilling his waterskin at a stream and cursing the Indians who had driven the horses through the water instead of along the banks.

"Ah," said Pizon. "The Great Tiehteti."

"He who charges at the front."

I started to grin.

"Oh, that was quite beautiful, Tiehteti, you charging through the middle of them like that, missing with every arrow you fired, then meanwhile every single one of them was trying to kill you, and they were missing as well." He chuckled and shook his head. "It was something to behold."

"I did hit one of them," I said.

"Are you sure?"

"Yes, in the stomach. And in the back. And I killed another one with the horse."

"Did you scalp them?"

"No, I kept going." I couldn't quite remember why I hadn't scalped them. "The one had a musket," I said.

"Oh, a musket."

"Pizon and I were maybe ten paces behind, but it was as if all the rays of the sun were shining only on you, you were like the prize that every man in that village wanted and they had no eyes for the rest of us."

"And you were riding so fucking fast."

"That's what you said to do."

"If you are attacking, you don't ride faster than you can shoot."

"Don't worry, we killed them all for you. And Saupitty and Ten Buffalo killed the ones we didn't see. What a beautiful fucking massacre."

"How is it possible I missed?" I said.

"I would say that you shoot like a woman," said Pizon. "But it would not be fair to the women."

"Tiehteti, if you are charging directly toward someone, it does not matter that you are moving. But if they are off to your side, it matters a lot. If your horse is running, you aim one step behind your target if he is close, so the arrow will be carried into him, but if he is far away you might aim five steps behind, though of course it depends on the angle, and on the wind, and how fast you are moving. When the horse is running, you have to remember the arrow is falling both down and forward. Last night you shot ahead of every target, as if you were aiming directly at them."

"I was," I said.

"Fuck it," said Pizon, "he deserves a scalp anyway. I have never shot so many people in my life who did not even know I was there." Then he added: "You are fucking brave, Tiehteti. I was very worried for you. And Toshaway is right, you cannot shoot for dogshit." He saw the look on my face. "At least not from a horse. I have seen you shoot from the ground, and you are okay. But perhaps for the rest of this year, when we return, you will practice only from horseback and only at targets that are to one side of you."

"And perhaps we will make sure you have a few pistols in the future. The white men all have them now anyway. It is not such a crime to use them."

"I've been trying to ask for one."

"If I had given you one, where would you be with the bow?" He shook his head. "You are very good with the pistol, we all know that, but there is no point practicing what you are already good at."

We stood there. I filled my *pihpóo* with the muddy water. To the north we could see the river and the mountains rising up from it, blue and purple with the distance. Then Nʉʉkaru came bounding over the rocks, followed by another young *mahimiawapi*.

"We are followed. Maybe a hundred men, maybe more."

We stood looking at him.

"Did you hear me?" he said.

"You are like a little girl, Nʉʉkaru."

"We need to get moving," he said.

"Where the fuck did a hundred men come from?" said Pizon. "There are not one hundred horses left in this entire province."

"A hundred, fifty, there are a lot of men. I am not sure how else to explain it."

"First it's one hundred. Now it's fifty. Soon it will be five old men herding goats."

"Toshaway," Nʉʉkaru said, "bring your spyglass, but you won't need it."

He ran back up the hill.

Pizon looked at the boy who'd come down with Nʉʉkaru. "Is he just being a woman?"

"I can't see if it's men or horses, but there was a lot of dust." Then he added: "His eye carries farther than mine, though."

"Probably some asshole driving cattle."

"They are following our route."

"It's a dry riverbed through chaparral. With a spring at the top of the hill. Every animal within five miles is going to use this path."

"I think they are men, Pizon."

Pizon dismissed him. "Do not let yourself become like this, Tiehteti. There are many things to worry about, but when you think every bush is hiding something, you soon become tired, and then you will not see the man who really is waiting to kill you."

He spat into the dirt.

"*Yee*, this is making me crazy. When we get to Presidio, it will be time to worry."

No one said anything.

"You fucking kids."

Toshaway came back.

"*Tʉyato?yerʉ*, the young ones are right. When we reach the river, you'll take the horses and the north trail, the rest of us will make tracks going west."

Pizon looked at him.

"They are right. It is far and the dust is thick, but they are men, and they are chasing us for sure."

WHEN WE REACHED the river it was dark and we were barely a few miles ahead of them.

The water was shallow; the summer rains hadn't yet come. That was lucky and the moon was not up yet, which was also lucky.

Pizon and twenty or so others took the horse herd downriver, directly through the middle of the water. They would ride that way before turning into the Texas mountains. The rest of us rode up and down the banks trampling their tracks, leaving obvious sign pointed upriver and also directly up the opposite bank, any direction except the one they'd taken. Then we headed upriver.

"We're the bait," I said.

"If they are stupid they'll presume we crossed directly and they will enter the rocks on the Texas side and become confused about where we went. If they are smart they will presume we went upriver."

"What if they go downriver?"

"Let us hope for the sake of our band that they do not do that."

"So they will follow us."

"Most likely."

When we reached a point where the ground was rocky, we climbed out of the water in single file and, after a brief discussion about where to meet, split into three groups heading in different directions. Toshaway and I continued west, along with a few others.

"If they are Mexicans, maybe they do not follow us," he said.

The moon had finally come up and we could see where we were. Then there were sounds and a dozen riders were coming upriver and then another group came out of the brush and the shooting started and didn't stop. I took off into the chaparral. When I looked back the only one still mounted was Toshaway; he had another Indian riding double behind him. I stopped in a thicket with my rifle pointed toward a gap, watching as the men approached the opening and squeezing the trigger as they passed. One of them doubled over and I turned and rode straight into the thorns; there was a lot of shooting and bullets cracking branches all around but they couldn't see me and I didn't slow down. After a few minutes I couldn't hear anyone. It was a miracle my eyes had not been torn out by the brush. I continued uphill another half mile or so, then circled and waited.

There were a few shots down toward the river and I stopped to recharge my rifle then rode toward the noise. Then I saw a man crouched in the brush. It was Toshaway. He was naked and his breech-cloth was tied around a wound on his leg. All he had was his bow and a handful of arrows; his knife and pistol were gone. He mounted behind me and kicked the horse and we were moving again.

"Are you shot?"

"I don't think so."

"Then your horse is."

He was right. Its flank was streaked in blood, which I had mistaken for sweat. "You're a good horse," I said.

"Use him up, but do it gently."

"How's your leg?"

"It must have missed the artery or I would not be alive."

We rode for two hours, climbing into the barren mountains, keeping to the drainages to stay hidden. Whatever water had carved them was long gone; the streambeds were as dusty as the flatlands. We stopped at a ridge top. While I was watching our backtrail, Toshaway slashed the needles off a pear pad, split it, and packed it into his wound. I tied the poultice on with his breechcloth. The muscle was badly bruised. Behind us the mountain dropped steeply toward the river; we had not made much distance but we had climbed a lot. I could see riders moving where the moon came off the water and I knew they could see us against the pale rocks.

"Now we ride."

"Does it hurt?"

"Does it hurt. Oh, Tiehteti."

There was shooting along the river—they had found someone from the band. The noise slowed and then stopped. I wondered who it was.

"Keep going," said Toshaway.

* * *

BY THE TIME the sun came up, the horse was nearly dead. Toshaway was pale and sweaty and we were looking north into a dry basin that went on for dozens of miles.

"How is your water?"

"The *pihpóo* was shot at the river."

"Very bad," he said.

The horse was lying on its side. There was no hope for it.

He cut a vein on the animal's neck and drank for a minute. Then he made me do the same. The horse didn't protest. Toshaway began to drink again. My mouth was full of hair and my stomach was full of blood and I wanted to air my paunch. He made me drink some more. The horse's breathing got quicker.

"Now we walk," he said. "And hope the buzzards don't lead our friends to the *tusanabo*."

I inspected my rifle and saw the lock was wrecked so I threw it into the brush.

"Those were fucking Indians leading them," he said. "Lipans. And there were white men as well." He shook his head. "The Apaches sucking the cocks of the Mexicans who are sucking the cocks of the whites. The world is against us."

BY AFTERNOON WE had dropped into the basin. From the top we could see a tree line farther north—a stream—but to reach it we would have to cross miles of open ground, no cover but cane cholla and giant dagger. Anyone looking would see us right away.

"Unfortunately I do not think I will make it if we skirt the edge."

"We'll cross the flat."

"No," he said. "Give me a few of your arrows. You will take the long way and stay hidden."

"We'll cross the flat," I repeated.

"Tiehteti," he said. "It is good to give your life, but not for a dead man."

"We're crossing the flat," I said.

By late afternoon we were in the shade along the creek. It was not much more than a muddy trickle and as gyppy as I'd ever tasted, but we both lay drinking for several minutes. I left Toshaway and went off with my bow to see if I could find a deer or something we might eat and also we needed a stomach for a water carrier.

I had been sitting in the willows, hoping to see some game, when I noticed a man on a bay horse picking his way up the stream. He was leading a small paint that was saddled and covered in handprints, similar to the horse Ten Buffalo had been riding.

The man was white and wearing new buckskin and there were scalps on his belt. I began to shift my weight. Then he stopped. He was staring at my footprints in the mud. I had been drawing my bow so slowly he would not have seen it even if he'd looked directly at me, and the way the light came through the leaves there was a pattern all over him and I found a bright spot and popped my fingers. He saw the arrow and then his horse turned and pitched through the bushes. There was more crashing. I moved about another ten yards and nocked another arrow and waited. I thought I could see his horse just past the trees. Finally I circled around.

He was lying in the grass in the shade. He had pulled out the arrow and it was still in his hand and something made me think of my father, but there was only a slim resemblance, dirty black hair and bloodshot eyes and pale skin under his hat. He looked right at me but it was an illusion; I counted the scalps tied to his saddle and then rolled him onto his belly to take his.

In addition to the two horses, he had a pair of brand-new Colt Navys, a .69 rifle, a nearly new gun belt, a powder flask, a knife, a heavy bullet pouch, three water gourds, and a wallet full of food. I notched the arrow with an X, then stripped off all his clothes and bundled them in case Toshaway wanted them.

THE SON 249

The paint was grazing at the edge of the stream. I nickered and it came immediately. I was no longer sure it had belonged to Ten Buffalo but it was wearing a Comanche saddle and there were red and yellow handprints all over it.

I was looking out over the mountains to the north where I could see trees and good grass; it would be nothing to ride away, there would be no more ambushes, I could reach Bexar in eight days. But the feeling soon passed and I went to find Toshaway.

WE SAT EATING the man's dried beef and drinking his clean water and eating the dried plums and apples he'd been carrying as well. I was starting to feel good about things when Toshaway decided it was time to cut the bruised parts out of his leg. He had split and cut more pear pads and gathered up creosote leaves for a poultice and mashed them with water and soaked two clean pieces of the man's shirt. Then he sat down near the stream.

"Don't be a fucking butcher," he said, "but don't take your time, either."

He put a stick in his mouth and I took up my scalping knife and cut around the bullet hole. His eyes rolled and the stick fell out of his mouth. I finished cutting, then rolled him over and cut out the bruise from the other side. Then I pushed the pieces of the man's shirt through the wound and drew them out. I was packing it when he woke up. Piss continued to run out from between his legs, but he did not seem to notice. The wound was bleeding freely and he told me that was a good sign. When I had packed it full and covered it with the split pear pads, we tied a tight bandage with another piece of the scalp hunter's shirt.

As we were sitting there he told me he knew on the night I was captured that I had been the one to shoot Skulking Bear, but he had not told anyone else in the tribe.

"It did not make sense to me, either," he said. "I knew you had done it and yet I did not tell anyone."

I was quiet.

"I knew what you had in you," he said. "Now everyone else will see it as well."

I wasn't really listening. I was thinking about the night I was captured, about my mother and brother and sister. He saw something in my face and told me that his grandfather had been a captive Mexican—the tribe was all from captives—it was the way of the Comanche; it had kept our blood strong all these years.

WE CONTINUED TO ride and change his poultice. A few days later we found a honey tree and filled our wallets from it, eating some but saving the rest to pack his wound, resting while the sun was up and traveling only at night.

By the time we reached the plains, two weeks later, there was still a gash in his leg, but the redness and swelling were gone. In another two weeks we were back in camp.

CHAPTER TWENTY-THREE

JEANNIE

Spring 1945

I t was a bad storm, a gully washer, the rain coming so fast the ground had no time to absorb it, the clouds so heavy they blotted out the light. By noon it was completely dark. The lightning was echoing through the house and she was sure it was a gunnery raid, a mission from the Kaufman air base gone off target. She watched fire leap through a patch of cedar close to the house, entire trees erupting ahead of the flames; a great sheave of rain put it out.

Her father had been out in the far pastures. He did not return for supper but a few hours later his horse showed up at the gate, alone and still saddled. It was even darker now; she could barely see her own feet. There was no chance of going after him, but it was not cold, and he was resourceful, and she expected he would show up sometime in the morning, soaked and footsore but otherwise intact.

Still, she slept in fits, waking every hour or so until at some point she looked out and saw the moon. The vaqueros were all waiting downstairs; her horse was already saddled. At first light they followed the dim tracks of her father's grullo, nearly obliterated by the rain but, when she put herself in the right mind, clear enough to follow.

The tracks led to a big arroyo but they did not continue on the other side. The light was spreading across the horizon and the birdcalls were starting up as if nothing had happened. Jeannie and the older vaqueros continued the search, the horses and most of the men held back so as not to trample any sign, but even later, with the sun risen, there were no tracks.

Her father, upon reaching the arroyo, must have dismounted. Or more likely, he had come upon it at speed, blinded by the rain and dark, and been thrown. There was only a thin trickle of water now, but high along the banks, fresh grass dangled from the sycamores. A man might have been carried miles. Dozens of miles.

FOUR DAYS LATER, one of the Midkiff vaqueros found him at a water gap, the white sole of a foot showing under the brush and flotsam. No one told her; the telephone rang and then Sullivan got into his truck and went to town and when he returned, there was a box on the front seat with her father's clothes. They were filthy and torn but she recognized his shirt. She picked it up, thinking to bring it to her face, then dropped it. It was crawling with blowflies.

Clint had died at Salerno, Paul at the Battle of the Bulge, even though she had prayed every night, even though she had not missed a Sunday of church. When Clint was killed she had continued to pray for Paul and Jonas, and at some point, months before his death, she had begun to pray for her father as well. Now she wondered if she had somehow killed them. One seemed as likely as the other. She decided she would stop praying for Jonas, and he had lived.

BECAUSE OF HER father's condition, the funeral was planned for the next day, and as she lay in her bed that afternoon, exhausted but unable to fall asleep, it occurred to her that the ranch still needed to be run, that there was no one left but her.

She allowed herself a few more minutes, then drew a bath, scrubbing herself thoroughly, though without wasting any time, as she imagined a mother might wash a child. She put on her black dress, then decided against it; she could not afford to be worrying about her clothes. She changed into blue jeans and old boots and knew her grandmother would not have approved, though of course she was gone as well, dead the previous year. She put on a bit of makeup—almost as bad as the pants. But her eyelashes were blond, like the rest of her—they made her look too young. *Where is Jonas?* she thought.

No work had been done in four days; everyone had been looking for her father. Now all thirty of his employees—vaqueros, fence riders, the windmill monkeys—were gathered around the bunkhouse, sitting on the porch or under trees in the shade, speaking quietly and wondering what was going to happen.

She told them nothing would change, that if for some reason she were not around, their paychecks would be distributed by Mrs. Wright, the bookkeeper. Everyone will be paid for the past four days, she continued, and tomorrow will be a day off. But between now and then, the water gaps need tending, the Midkiffs have some of our stock, and anything else the storm broke, you just get to fixing it, you don't have to ask.

She did not tell them that she did not have the authority to sign their checks. She spent the rest of that day and night alternately worrying that no one would attend the funeral and wondering where her father kept his will. Their lawyer tore his office apart but found nothing; around midnight Jeannie found the document in an old file cabinet. It had been updated several times: once for Clint and once for Paul, but the newest version, dated only a few months previous, which had doubtless caused her father much anxiety, named her sole inheritor of his share of the ranch. Jonas got a share of the minerals but that was all.

A feeling of happiness overtook her; she could not help smiling, then laughing, and then felt terrible. Still, Phineas would be overjoyed—the entire property was now split between them. Jonas would not care too much; he was trying to make his way back from Germany, though the flights were infrequent and always full and a ship would take weeks. She went back to worrying about the funeral.

Outside several fires had been built, calves and goats and hogs set to roasting. Trips had been made to Carrizo for beans, corn, coffee, and two dozen store-made cakes. A hundred cases of Pearl beer and four cases of whiskey. The house felt more alive than it had in years; the cooks were up all night, doing whatever it was they did, and the maids were as well, changing all the linens in the guest rooms, getting the folding cots out of storage, making the house ready for company.

PHINEAS ARRIVED WITH a sizable entourage; there was a trickle, then a flood, of people from Austin and San Antonio and Dallas, from Houston and El Paso and Brownsville, the other South Texas ranchers, newspapermen, nearly five hundred people in total, which at first caused her to weep—her father had been more appreciated than she had ever realized—but as the day went on she saw that most had come out of politeness, not for her father but for her, or for the family, for the idea of the McCulloughs. The local Mexicans, who had mostly hated her father, and not without cause, they all came as well, because that was what you did when your *patrón* died.

THE LAST TIME the house had been so full was at the Colonel's funeral, but that had a different feel altogether, of genuine misery, the end of something, of grown men who could not stop crying. The faces now were somber but not troubled, the conversation easy. Her father had not mattered. It was not fair but the more she thought about it, the more condolences she accepted, the more she heard the circumstances of his death whispered around the room, the more furious she got. He had died stupidly. From stubbornness and poor judgment. The vaqueros had all lit for home as soon as the storm blew in—lightning killed more cowboys than guns ever had—but her father, with his notions, had wanted to finish his count. *I don't mind getting a little wet*—those were his last words.

She circulated through the house, hundreds of people, thanking them for coming and insisting they eat, the smell of beef and cabrito and roast pig, unending dishes of beans and sauce and tortillas, gallons of beer and sweet tea. She was in and out of the kitchen; yes, another calf should be knocked in the head—on the coals immediately—yes, another run was needed to Carrizo—no telling how long people would stay. Sullivan periodically appeared and pressed a cold glass of tea into her hand. She had sweated through her dress. She went up to change but there was nothing else; of course she had only one black dress. She hung it in front of the fan in her bedroom, wiped herself down with a wash towel, then stood in front of the fan herself. She made a note to check Sullivan's salary; his people had worked for the family three generations; her father had been stingy. She was tempted to rest but knew she would fall asleep.

Back downstairs she continued to move through the crowd, barely hearing what people said. There was Uncle Phineas in the corner, leaning on his cane, holding forth with a group of young men. He was so clearly enjoying himself that she turned away when he called to her.

The vaqueros and the Mexicans from town stood deferentially, speaking quietly, but the men from the cities—all in riding boots and stockman's hats—clomped and talked noisily like they were family. It made her feel weak. The Colonel would not have stood for men like that. She wished that one of his old friends might show up—as a few still did, once in a while—and, for the sake of the Colonel, empty a six-gun into the ceiling to clear out the house.

But even that was a fantasy. From what she had known of cowboys, even the old ones, they tended not to do well in crowds, they tended to be polite and deferential, and most could not have even looked these new men, these city men, in the eye.

JONAS MISSED THE burial but came home from Germany anyway, where the war, for all practical purposes, was over. She practically smothered him when she picked him up; she was not sure what to expect—a thousand-yard stare, deep scars, a limp—but he looked fit and healthy and had a confident stride.

The first thing he said, when he walked into the house, their steps loud in the cavernous great room, with its stone walls and thirty-foot ceilings, was, "We need to get you the hell out of here. You won't have a normal life. The war will be over in a few weeks and I could get a job for you in Berlin. It would probably be as a typist or something but we could live together."

She was not sure how to respond—it was appealing but also entirely wrong—she was not going to be a typist. It was her brother who ought to be coming home, not her going to some foreign country.

"Or hell," he was saying. "We've got money. You don't have to work at all, just come live."

"How is it there?"

He shrugged.

"I guess you've seen terrible things?"

"No worse than others."

She wanted to ask if he had shot anyone, or seen anyone shot, but he seemed to sense the question was coming and stood abruptly, walking to the other end of the room, looking at the old drawings, the marble statues and figurines, shaking his head, picking things up and putting them down.

"Would you like something to eat?" she called.

"We probably better go to the grave. I can't stay long."

This didn't make any sense—he had traveled a week to get there—and she decided to ignore it, not being sure he was in his right mind.

"Do you want to drive or ride?"

"Let's ride. It's four years since I've been on a horse."

OVER SUPPER, WHICH he was now calling dinner, he had asked, in a way that struck her as too direct: "Are there any men around here you like?"

No. In fact the year before there had been another vaquero, less handsome than the others, with a squishy sort of nose; they had kissed behind one of the brush corrals and later lain together by the springs at the old Garcia place. He had been more aggressive than she wanted—the few men left seemed to get their way far too quickly—but that night, when she was reflecting on it alone, she was sorry she'd stopped his hands. These chances only seemed to come at great intervals, and so a few days later, when they agreed to meet again, she had carried an ancient condom—found in Clint's room, of course—tucked into a pocket in her dress. She had waited an hour, then two, lying by herself under the trees, in the soft grass overlooking the old church.

Her vaquero had not shown up. Again it was no mystery what had happened: the young man's friends, afraid of her father, afraid for their own jobs, had warned him off. She had cried for days—even for this man, whom (snobbishly, she knew now) she had considered below her, she was not good enough. She had always thought herself a prize: blond, petite, not as shapely as some but certainly with a woman's shape; her button nose had straightened out, her eyes had gotten bigger, and in a certain light she wondered if she might be beautiful. But most of the time she was at least pretty, far above average, and while it was true that there was a Mexican girl in Carrizo who was prettier, that girl was very poor.

And yet . . . she was nearly twenty, she was supposed to be out living, she was supposed to have suitors and she did not, with the exception of a few men from town who may have thought they were courting her, but, so far as she was concerned, weren't. She did not think of herself as rich, but she knew that other people did; she did not trust any of the whites from town; they saw her in the wrong way. The vaqueros she knew and trusted well enough—it was against their interest to damage her reputation—though apparently they did not trust her, or they did not respect her, or perhaps they sensed her desperation.

As for Jonas, she barely recognized him. His face had filled out, his frame as well; there was no longer anything of the boy. He spoke too fast, like someone raised in the North, and he cursed constantly, like someone raised in the North; he seemed entirely too sure of himself. Over dinner he got drunk on whiskey and they talked and built an enormous fire, of the sort their father would have found wasteful, but when they finally decided to go to sleep, Jonas refused to go up to his old room—making a show, she thought—and instead he took a blanket to a couch near the fire. She went to her bedroom and as she sat there in her nightgown, she knew she would be responsible for losing everything. Jonas had absolved himself—he cared nothing for the house or their legacy. Though of course he had been cut out of much of it. It must have stung him, their father's final insult, though he had still left Jonas half his minerals, which, in the end, mattered more to her brother than the land ever could have.

The next morning they took their breakfast in the great room, where they could listen to the radio.

"Will you stay here until the fighting is done?"

He shook his head. "I remember Daddy turning that off every time FDR came on." Pointing to the radio.

She wondered if she would have to defend her father for the entire visit. Though as it turned out, it was for the rest of their lives. "He didn't do that once the war started," she said. "On D-day he let everyone off and we all sat here and listened, and he drew a big map, and he would say that is Paul's division, the Eighty-Second Airborne, who have landed there, and that is Jonas's division. He made all these notes for everyone to see. He was proud of you."

"Well, he was wrong because I didn't land until the second day. And Paul didn't land on a beach at all, he dropped in by parachute in the middle of all the Germans."

"I don't remember all the details," she admitted.

"Do you remember him saying that FDR's election was the end of American democracy? Or that the Dust Bowl was a communist invention?" He shook his head. "I don't know how we came from him."

"He wasn't so bad." She had not remembered her brother as so cold, but then maybe she had never really known him. She closed her eyes.

"I remember him saying that we lived on the Frontier," Jonas continued, "Frontier with a capital *F*. I told him the frontier had closed

before he was even born, and then he would lecture me about the tradition we were carrying on. I would tell him there *was* no tradition,
there could *be* no tradition for a thing that had lasted only twenty years.
Anyway . . . I don't know what this place will become, but right now I
can't see the point. It's not settled enough to have any culture, but it's
not wild enough to be interesting. It's just a province."

She didn't answer.

"You should sell it. Keep the minerals but make a clean break. We
could get you into Barnard easy as that."

"I'm not moving to the North," she said quietly.

"You were a kid then."

"I'm happier here."

"Jeannie." He put his hand to his forehead as if what she had said
was the stupidest thing he'd ever heard. "Everything we were taught
was either a lie or a bad joke. It was always Yankees this or that, the
worst sort of people, all full of shit, and then one day it occurred to me
that if Daddy hated them so much, that was probably where I belonged.
Meanwhile he was worse than anyone I met at Princeton, born into
money but always complaining about how poor and put-upon he was.
And the way he was with the Mexicans?"

She didn't say anything.

His eyes were closed. "I was so fucking stupid when I got there."

HE STAYED ANOTHER week, until they were both sure the estate
was in order. By then all the anger had gone out of him. He changed his
will to leave her everything in case something happened; he signed a
power of attorney. She felt closer to him than she ever had; she had lost
her father but regained her brother. And then he got on the train east,
toward the war, and she did not see him for three more years.

STARTING THE DAY Jonas left, and continuing for how long she
didn't know, she kept hours like a cat, sleeping three-quarters of the
day, waking in the middle of the night, pacing the empty house, crying

herself to sleep on the sofa only to wake a few hours later with the sun in her eyes. Going back up to her room with its heavy curtains, finding breakfast or dinner on a tray outside her door, cold eggs, cold meat, visiting the bathroom.

There was nothing for her to do. No job, nothing useful to which she might attach her mind. Once a week, on what she knew must be Thursday, she found a clipboard on the dining room table with all the employee paychecks attached, which she signed individually and left by the door. She thought of her father and cried, she thought of her brothers and cried, she was vaguely aware that time was passing, she wondered why Phineas wasn't calling her, why he hadn't invited her to live with him. Often she could not tell if she was crying about this, or about her father, or her brothers, or even her great-grandfather, gone almost a decade but more tender toward her than her father had ever been.

A month might have passed. It might have been two. But she woke up one morning as the sun was rising, and accepted, with total certainty, that no one would ever look after her again.

A WEEK LATER a man from Southern Minerals showed up, wanting to talk about her future.

"I've been stopping by awhile, but they always said you were indisposed."

He acted as if they were old friends but she crossed her arms and stood square in the door. He promptly offered a million dollars plus 12.5 percent to lease her property, with the exception of the acreage that Humble had already drilled. He knew her entire story. He knew her brothers had died in the war, that her father had died in the accident, that Jonas had gone back to Germany.

"You can move to the city." He quickly adjusted: "Or raise your steers. Life won't have to be hard anymore." He gave her a sympathetic look.

She was not looking at him; she was hoping one of the vaqueros would ride past.

"You sound like a minister," she said.

"Thank you." He smiled and went back to talking about grass, and the weather, and how the cattle were doing, and after a time, when she had thought of what to say, she interrupted him.

"Do other people still sign at eighth royalties or is it just widows and orphans?"

He smiled again, saw right through her, saw the planning that had gone into her rudeness. He was standing closer now and she resisted the urge to step back—that would mean giving up the threshold—and then there was the heat; the natural thing was to invite him out of the sun. She decided she did not care how close he stood; she would not budge. But at the same time she wondered if this was stupid, if she was misjudging the situation entirely. She wondered if all the maids had left; she wondered how he had gotten through the gate.

He was so close she could smell his breath, and she felt a growing alarm at how alone she was. All the hands were out in the pastures— miles from earshot—and Hugo, the cook, had gone to Carrizo for supplies. She was alone and this man thought nothing of her whatsoever.

"I believe I'm getting tired," she said.

He nodded but kept right on talking; he took off his hat to mop his forehead and she saw he had no tan line: an office man. He mentioned for a second time that it was no place for a girl to be alone and a tingling began in her neck and spread to her fingers; perhaps it was too late. He would take whatever he wanted. Her mouth went dry and she summoned up the effort to say, "If you do not leave I will call the sheriff."

He stood as if this statement required further consideration, or maybe just to show that he was only leaving because he felt like it. Then he reached forward and squeezed her shoulder and wished her a good afternoon.

After closing the door she went straight to her father's office, passing dozens of open windows, French doors with useless locks—there were any number of ways to get into the house—he was likely going around the back.

In her father's drawer she found his Colt pistol, but after pulling back the slide in the manner she'd been taught, the magazine fell out onto the floor and bounced under the desk.

She unlocked the large closet where the rest of the guns were kept and found the .25-20 she had hunted with as a kid. Her brothers thought it weak medicine but she had killed two deer. She found the proper shells, prepared the rifle, and went back to the hallway. It had taken minutes. It was ridiculous. If the man really had followed her, he would have gotten her ages ago. She felt a fury building at Jonas, at her father, at . . .

There was something outside—the landman's Ford—it was already at the front gate. She watched him, a distant speck now, open the gate and drive through. She felt very tired. She wanted to lie down.

Instead she loaded several revolvers (the automatic she no longer trusted), put them into a basket, and walked around the house distributing them as if they were flowers: one in the big vase next to the front door, another on a shelf in the kitchen, a third next to her bed, the fourth next to her favorite couch in the great room.

She went out to the gallery—where she could see a long way over the hills, nearly to the main road—and began to analyze what had happened. Calling the sheriff was wrong. It was the vaqueros you would call. The thought of someone killing the landman made her heart light, cleared her mind in a pleasant manner. She sat and watched the clouds and thought of what it might look like. He would go down like a steer or hog, right on his chin. She wondered why her hands were shaking. *I am going crazy,* she thought. She left the gallery and wandered through the house, stopping in front of the hall mirror. It was a joke, the guns were a joke, she was a child playing at grown-up things. She wondered again if she was going crazy.

It was a relief when she heard the cook come in and begin chattering to one of the maids. She was not sure if she had been talking to herself or not, if the maids had heard her. Everyone had been right—Jonas, her father, her grandmother—she did not belong here.

She saw the first of the vaqueros' trucks crest a distant hill, trail-ering the horses from the pastures. Then the second truck, and the third. She felt everything get lighter. It was as simple as that. She would tell them. What would come of the landman, she didn't care—*I don't,* she thought, *I really don't*—this was not the North, where you went around accosting people. Even loading the guns had been wrong; she needed a wall of armor around her, of men, like her father had kept.

Sullivan, the vaqueros, they would all know what to do. She decided to act before any further consideration weakened her; he was probably not such a bad man, she had probably misread the entire thing, she was young and alone (*he accosted you,* she reminded herself). Yes, that was it. The man would pay some price. Even Jonas would agree with that. He would not be killed, but it would be something unpleasant. She was not sure what. She didn't care. She reminded herself of the way he had grabbed her and then, before she could change her mind, she was out the front door, ignoring Hugo's calls about supper, making her way down the path toward the bunkhouse.

CHAPTER TWENTY-FOUR

DIARIES OF PETER McCULLOUGH

MARCH 25, 1917

Drought is back but cattle remain high due to war. Woke up after a night of vivid thoughts, pulled the curtains expecting the green country of my youth and of my dreams. But with the exception of the area immediately around the house, there was nothing but sparse brittle grass, thorny brush, patches of bare caliche. My father is right: it is ruined forever, and in a single generation.

Meanwhile he has hired promoters to bring in northern farmers. The trains are specially chartered and the Yankees will be shown the best farms (irrigated), the best houses (ours, as it is the most ostentatious), and offered used-up hardpan at five hundred times what the current owners paid for it. I have been ordered to make myself scarce.

For two months the Colonel has been diverting water from the stock tanks onto our lawn (we now have one, instead of a dirt yard) and the stream that runs below the house, past Everett's pasture, has been dammed to flood the lowlands one looks over from the gallery. Ike Reynolds came to complain that his water dried up, but the Colonel explained his reasons and Ike left convinced.

Even the springs at Carrizo are barely flowing; it is said this is a result of the irrigation. The resacas have all gone dry. The entire earth, it seems, is being slowly transformed into a desert; mankind will die off and something new will replace us. There is no reason that there should only be one human race. I was likely born a thousand years too early, or ten thousand. One day those like my father will seem like the Romans who fed Christians to the lions.

APRIL 6, 1917

Heard Charlie and Glenn and my father talking this evening, walked into the great room to see what was about, they all three looked at me and went silent. Of course I left. The generations pass, nothing seems to change, the silent understanding between the others and my father, wordless looks that have always excluded me. Wilson declared war on Germany today.

APRIL 9, 1917

Charlie and Glenn came to me. They have both decided to join the army. I told them it would be better to wait until the end of the year when it would be easier to find hands to replace them. They were unconvinced. "We have plenty of money to hire people," said Charlie.

Sally has been in her room all day, unable to get out of bed.

They could not have picked a worse war to join. Machine guns and half-ton shells. I had always thought the Europeans returned to the Stone Age when they landed in America, but apparently they never left it. Seven hundred thousand dead at Verdun alone.

What we need is another great ice to come and sweep us all into the ocean. To give God a second chance.

APRIL 12, 1917

The boys took the train today to San Antonio. Sally is packing a bag to stay with her family in Dallas. Told me this is the reason she wished we had daughters. I told her I agreed with her.

"Come with me," she said.

Could not explain to her why I could not survive Dallas.

☆   ☆   ☆

AN OMINOUS SIGN: immediately after seeing Glenn and Charlie off, received a call from the postmaster. The Lewis gun has arrived. After several mint juleps with the Colonel, decided to test the gun.

We took the largest drum—nearly one hundred rounds—and after laboriously loading it and figuring out the winding mechanism, which is much like a pocket watch, we were ready to send some prickly pears to the next world when the most unfortunate group of javelina on earth walked into view.

They were nearly a quarter mile away but the gun was advertised as effective at three times that distance for "area fire." The Colonel could barely make them out so he suggested I do the shooting while he looked with field glasses. I was lying on the ground behind the gun while he stood next to me. I saw a shadowy figure waving in the distance.

We elevated the sight and I fired a quick burst, perhaps five rounds.

"Son of a bitch, Pete, you missed 'em by near thirty yards."

"Must be the wind." My ears were ringing. I pretended to adjust the sight.

"All right, they're back to rooting. You gonna shoot or piss your pants?"

I aimed into the sounder of pigs—which at that distance looked like a brown patch against the green of the brush—and pulled back the trigger. It was like holding on to a locomotive. One does not aim so much as direct the gun like a fire hose.

"Left," he was shouting, "right, right, walk 'em right . . . now left, more left, left left *left left*!" I did as he asked, seeing the bullets kick up dirt among the running brown shapes.

"Put on that other drum, there are some still kicking."

I attached the second drum.

"Son of a whore," he was saying, "I wonder is that really four hundred yards . . ."

I drowned out his talking with the noise of the gun.

★   ★   ★

WHEN WE WENT to pack our things, my mare, who is used to me shooting deer, quail, and turkey from her back, was bug-eyed. She knew something unnatural was afoot. My father's horse was nowhere in sight and it took nearly half an hour to find him.

Before heading home, we rode out to inspect the damage. The javelina were spread over a large flat section of caliche, splayed in all manner of disassembly. It looked as if someone had put dynamite inside them.

"Good," my father said, surveying the damage. He rode around nodding. Then he said: "You think the Germans have these?"

"They have thousands," I told him.

The Lewis had cooled enough to strap it to my saddle. Of course the Germans have machine guns. But it is not my father's nature to look to that side of things. We began to ride back to the house.

"I remember when a five-shot Colt was a weapon of mass destruction. Then you had maybe twenty years and there was the Henry rifle, load it on Sunday and shoot all week. Eighteen shots, I think."

"Life gets better and better," I said.

"You know I always thought those books would take you somewhere. I was sad when they didn't."

"They have," I said.

"I mean away from here. You think I don't *sabe* but I do. My brother was exactly like you. It runs in the family."

I shrugged.

"Wrong place, wrong time . . . wrong something."

"I like this family and I like this place," I told him, because for some reason, at that moment, it seemed true.

He started to say something, then didn't. As we rode back through the sun and the dust, toward our great white house on its hill, he seemed to relax, to settle into his saddle; I could tell his mind was wandering, doubtless over the many things he has done for which the entire world admires him.

I began to think of how often he was home during my childhood (never), my mother making excuses for him. Did she forgive him that day, at the very end? I do not. She was always reading to us, trying to distract us; she gave us very little time to get bored, or to notice he was gone. Some children's version of the *Odyssey*, my father being like Odysseus. Him versus the Cyclops, the Lotus Eaters, the Sirens. Everett, being much older, off reading by himself. Later I found his journals, detailed drawings of brown-skinned girls without dresses . . . My assumption, as my mother told us that my father was like Odysseus, was that I was Telemachus . . . now it seems more likely I will turn out a Telegonus or some other lost child whose deeds were never recorded. And of course there are other flaws in the story as well.

APRIL 13, 1917

This morning, Sally found me in my office, where I had slept. She had brought a tray of coffee and kolaches. I presumed she wanted something. She has not yet left for Dallas.

"How was your new gun?" she said.

"I guess the Colonel is quite fond of it."

"Is it the one we use or the one the Huns use?"

"Ours, of course."

"But the Huns have them too."

"Of course," I said again.

"Well, I hope you had a good time with it." She shook her head. "The whole time I was listening to that gun I could only think about Glenn and Charlie."

"I know."

She stood there, and I noticed the lines around her eyes, deeper every year, like my own. She looked like my mother in that light, her pale hair and skin . . . but unlike my mother, there is always a wheel turning somewhere in her mind. Though today she looked tired of thinking. I went forward and held her.

"I'm not sure I can stay here anymore."

"You've been saying that."

"I really mean it."

I shrugged and released my grip, but she pulled me tighter.

"We have to stick together," she said. Then she added, "You haven't touched me in weeks."

"You haven't touched me either."

"I have. You just haven't noticed."

"Our children will be fine."

"Pete," she said, "is there anyone you ever have honest conversations with?"

I wasn't sure what she was getting at. "There isn't anyone else."

"So start with me," she said. "Tell me exactly what you're thinking. Not what you think I want to hear, but the truth."

"You are talking crazy."

She looked at me. "I know I don't do much for you. I know I never have."

What would I tell her? That I have always known I belonged here? That one day some action will be required that will prove my life's value? A forty-six-year-old man, waiting for fate to take over . . . it likely already has.

"You promised me a place in the city when the children left."

"I know," I said.

"I still have a few years I could salvage. A few men still find me attractive. If you want me to move to San Antonio by myself, tell me. Otherwise I am willing to split our time between here and someplace civilized, if you will just come with me some of the time."

"This place will fall apart without me," I said. "And the Colonel cannot be left alone."

"You are worried about your father."

"He is eighty-one years old."

She shook her head. She looked out the window for a long time. "Is that your final decision?"

APRIL 15, 1917

Sally departed for the train station. We have made love four times in the past two days, more than the past year in total. Deep depression when I dropped her off, pointlessness of living alone . . . several times allowed the car to wander without my hands on the wheel . . . but that was not it, either. Somehow this was required. The greater plan. Strange tingling along my scalp, as before we rode on the Garcias, as on various days in my younger life, such as when Phineas stepped forward to take the halter of that black horse. My father had wanted me to do it, but in front of all those people, I could not touch it.

When I got home it was dark and the house was also dark, quiet, and empty. Added another item to the list I began in Austin, originally titled "The Seven Types of Loneliness" (a man and woman sitting close, boy holding his mother's leg, a cold rain, the sound of crows, a girl's laughter down a stone street, four policemen walking, a thought of my father); of course the list has reached several hundred now. I ought to have burned it years ago, but instead I add another item: "A quiet house."

Tomorrow will release all the staff except Consuela and one or two of the maids. They should have no trouble finding work—men are being drafted left and right—I will give them three months' pay.

I tried to fall asleep but after a few hours I got up and walked around turning all the lights on. I could hear the wind rattling windows on the other side of the house. Finally I couldn't stand it and walked out to see if my father was still awake.

Chapter Twenty-five

ELI / TIEHTETI

Fall 1851

Pizon and the others, driving the thousand stolen horses, had reached camp a week before us, and stragglers continued to trickle in. We had lost eleven members of the band but the raid was quietly considered a success. Though we knew that if we continued to have these sorts of successes, there would be no Indians left to ride the horses.

Smaller raids continued all summer, mostly put on by young men who needed horses and scalps, both for marriage and because otherwise they had no status. The army had nearly finished a second line of forts—from Belknap to Abilene to Mason—but many settlers had already leapfrogged this second line. To the old-timers, the most ominous sign was the bee trees, which seemed to precede the line of settlement by a hundred miles or so and now reached nearly to the edge of the Llano. We were happy for so much honey, but we all knew what it meant.

The Comancheros had figured out we were prosperous again, and I convinced Toshaway to double the price of the horses we traded. Previously, a good horse might be traded for a handful of glass beads or a few yards of calico, but now we wanted more ammunition and gun parts, more steel arrowheads, and more food. I stayed in camp and

272 P H I L I P P   M E Y E R

hunted and broke horses, but mostly I spent time with Prairie Flower, who was no longer embarrassed to be seen in public with me, as my stature was now equal to Nuukaru's or even Escuté's, even if my abilities were not.

THE MOST IMPORTANT event of late summer was the capture of a young buffalo hunter, who, along with the rest of his party, had misjudged the degree to which the army and Rangers could protect him. We caught them in the lower reaches of the Palo Duro and after a brief fight his companions were all killed. He crawled out from under their wagon with his hands raised and, knowing what would happen to him, I immediately nocked an arrow, but Pizon shoved me and it went wide.

The hunter was in his late twenties, with blond hair and beard and blue eyes and an innocent sort of look. I was happy to get his rifled Springfield and Minie ball molds, but the real prize was the man himself. Because he was alive and uninjured and so close to our camp, it was decided to bring him in to be tortured.

This caused great excitement and all work was stopped for the day. It was as if the circus had come to town, or a public hanging called among the whites. He must have seen what was going to happen because he begged me to help him but there was nothing I could do, and a few of the newer captives, whose position was less secure, stomped on his face to show their loyalty.

The torture of a captive was considered a high honor for the women of the village and all the female elders were gathered along with the younger ones. Prairie Flower was upset that she had not been selected. After stripping him naked, tying his hands and feet to stakes, spread-eagled so he was just barely suspended in the air, they poked fun at his pale hair and his privates, which were shrunken with fear; one woman sat on top of him and pretended she was going to rut him, much to the delight of everyone. Most of the village was gathered, with children sitting or standing on shoulders, the same as would witness a hanging in town. The women built four very small fires, one each at his hands and feet. Fuel was added carefully, keeping the flames to a minimum, only building them hotter when he stopped shouting, which indicated the nerves had died. They would increase the heat by adding one very small stick, at which point he would begin to sing again.

He shrieked himself hoarse and the children mimicked him with great joy. By late afternoon he was barely making a sound and I wondered if he'd ruptured his vocal cords. At supper he was given broth and water, which his body accepted gladly, though he must have known why we were giving it to him. Later they fed him again. I walked by, thinking he was in a stupor, but he recognized me and begged me to kill him—one Christian to another. I stood there thinking, knowing what I would want done for me, and then Toshaway caught me as I was returning to the tipi.

"I know what you are thinking, Tiehteti. Everyone will know and the penalties will be severe. More than you think, probably."

"I'm not thinking anything," I said. "He's killing our buffalo."

"All right," he said. "All right, Tiehteti."

PRAIRIE FLOWER WAS on fire that night. I did my best but after the second time I was less interested. She was rubbing herself against me and finally I stopped her.

"Usually I can't get rid of Nɯɯkaru and Escuté," she said. They were out on a raid, so we had the tipi to ourselves. "But now the one time I could use them . . ."

"I'm sure others are still awake, if that's what you really want."

"You know I don't." She cuddled against me. "What's wrong?" she said.

"Nothing."

"It's the white man, isn't it?"

I shook my head.

"Okay," she said. "I apologize for my horniness."

"Just give me a minute."

"Don't worry."

"I'll try," I said. But I couldn't.

In the morning, just after breakfast, they cut off his hands and feet because the nerves were all dead, and when the screaming began to abate, they moved the fire under the stumps where the nerves were still fresh. Fewer people were watching now, and though the sound of the man's screaming filled the camp, it had already started to seem normal.

Toshaway told me this had once been a regular event, but over the years, as they began to raid farther and farther away from camp, the risks of bringing back a full-grown male prisoner just to torture had not been worth it.

"I am going out to hunt," I said.

He looked at me.

"I'm fine," I told him.

When you don't want to see snakes you find them everywhere and when you want one you can't find it. Certain men milked rattle-snakes for war arrows, but I fumbled my equipment so much I had not wanted to risk it. Still, I had milked snakes, and after spending most of the day looking, I finally found a big *wutsutsuki* late in the afternoon, on a high rock in the sun. When he had stopped thrashing I cut off his head and wrapped it in a piece of buckskin.

The second night, the buffalo hunter was given broth and more water. By then he had only fifty or so fans, sitting around eating and watching him. I went to bed like normal and then waited until I couldn't hear any more talking. The night was overcast and nearly black, which I took as a sign. I made my way quietly to where he was staked out.

He made a sound when I approached; he might have been saying please; he might have been saying anything at all.

It was a stupid plan; it was dark, there were small sharp teeth, and it was messy, but I used the back of my knife to milk the snake's head over his mouth. It was only a drop or two but he began to kick. "Let it pass through you," I said. "You don't have to hold on to it." I made a cut on his throat and milked the rest of the venom into that. I could tell I'd nicked my hand.

His breathing was already starting to change.

I walked away and washed myself in the stream.

When I got back to my tipi, Prairie Flower was in my bed, as excited as the night before.

When we were done, she said: "Where were you?"

"Just walking."

"You were wet," she said.

My arm was tingling. Finally I asked her: "That didn't bother you, what they did to that man?"

It came out louder than I wanted.

"It's just because he is white."

"I don't know."

"It is not good to discuss this with anyone."

"I'm not. I wouldn't."

"Even me," she said.

It was quiet.

"I know you're not weak. Everyone knows you're not weak." She was measuring her words. "Toshaway says you'll be chief one day. They're making you a buffalo robe, but it was supposed to be a surprise."

"I was just asking how you felt."

"They're making a robe that shows how you killed the Delaware, how your magic protected you from his arrows, and then how you saved Toshaway from the soldiers. It's supposed to be a surprise, though." Then she said, "That man was white. You need to think about that."

"We didn't do those things where I grew up."

She rolled away. "You know I was not always Kotsoteka," she said.

"No."

"When I was *tuepuru*, maybe six years old, the Texans attacked my band. My brother made my sister and me go into the river and swim away. They shot my brother's head off in the water, and they shot at me but missed. The next day my sister and I went back to our camp and found my mother, along with one hundred other dead women and dead old men and dead children. The Texans had cut off my mother's head and put it on a stick in the ground and they had taken a *tʉtsuwai* and put it all the way up between her legs, and there was so much blood we knew they had done it while she was still alive. But there was no blood around her neck so we knew that was not done until after. That is why I grew up *Pena tʉhka* but now I am Kotsoteka."

"The same thing happened to my mother and sister," I told her. "And my brother."

"Tiehteti," she said, "this cannot happen." She reached for her things and began to dress and I decided I didn't care. And of course she was right: she was allowed to talk about her family, I was not allowed to talk about mine, because unless your family was Comanche, it was as if they had never existed.

"You can stop me if you want," she said.

I didn't say anything and I heard her make a little sob and then I grabbed her and pulled her back down.

"I won't talk about it anymore," I said.

She shrugged. She slipped out of her clothes but we just lay against each other and eventually she fell asleep.

I stayed up thinking, trying to figure if the tingling in my arm was spreading to my side or if I was imagining it. Then I was thinking about my father. In the early forties, there had been so few victories over the Comanches that when they occurred, the news spread to the entire state. In all those years there had only been one fight in which so many Comanches had died, which was Moore's expedition on the Colorado. Moore had claimed that over one hundred fifty braves had been killed, but there had always been talk that it was mostly women and children, that the braves had been out hunting when the raiders hit the camp. My father had ridden with Moore, and sometimes talked about the raid, but no differently than he'd talked about anything else. It was just something that had happened. Little Indians became big Indians. Everyone knew it.

Prairie Flower kissed me in her sleep. "You are good," she murmured. "You are honest and good and you are not afraid of anything."

THE NEXT MORNING the buffalo hunter was dead. His face and neck were bloated, but no one seemed to notice. Mostly they were disappointed. It was another sign the old ways were being lost: in the past, a captive might have been kept alive two or three days longer.

But if anyone suspected me, nothing was said. Prairie Flower and I spent every night together and Toshaway said if I wanted to borrow some horses to offer as a bride-price, they were free for the taking. He cleared his throat then, and mentioned, in a quieter tone, that fifty horses would be far too high. Times had changed.

I was given the buffalo robe they'd made for me, and my own tipi as well. It was turning out to be a good year. Fall had come and the rains were heavy and the heat had left the plains. The nights were crisp and the days sunny, the hunting good, and I began to make my plans with Prairie Flower.

A FEW WEEKS after the buffalo hunter died, people began to get sick.

CHAPTER TWENTY-SIX

JEANNIE

Summer 1945

VE-day came and for a few weeks it seemed everything would be different and then it wasn't. Her brothers did not return, the vaqueros went about their business without her—she did not see the point of helping them lose money. Several times she packed a suitcase, feeling desperate enough to take up Jonas on his offer, but she could never reach him before she changed her mind, she was sure that if she found him in Berlin, it would be no different from Princeton, he would abandon her some way or other.

Mostly she was bored. She made runs to Carrizo for the cook (always managing to forget a thing or two), she made trips to San Antonio, where a few dressmakers knew her and promised to introduce her to young men, but never did. She visited with Phineas, always expecting an invitation to stay with him, in his grand house overlooking all of Austin. She thought they might sit on his gallery and talk long into the night, but he was a private man (*you are a grown woman,* is how he put it) and so she roomed at the Driscoll instead.

It was a good year for the land. The grass had stayed green. With so much good grass she knew she ought to buy a few hundred stocker animals, but the cattle were a luxury, the horses were a luxury, even the grass was a luxury: the poorer ranches now looked like patches of dirt. Anyway, she preferred grass to cows.

Once a week she would saddle her father's horse, General Lee, and take him out on the land. Sullivan objected—he'd wanted to shoot the animal—and he was probably right. A few times General Lee had nearly gotten the best of her. He would stand quietly, allowing himself to be saddled, and then, just as she mounted, he would begin to kick. He did tend to buck a straight line, but he had thrown her more than once. You ought to be grateful, she told him. I am the only reason you are still alive.

But he was not grateful. He must have known she did not appreciate him, or that her feelings were mixed, or maybe, like her, he was simply bored, because he had no job and no prospects and when you went on like that too long, habits tended to grow on you.

Texas had once been full of wild horses, five million, ten million, no one knew. But they had mostly been rounded up and shipped to the British during the Great War. Between the war and the rendering plants, Texas had been just about cleaned out of ponies. In her childhood, most of the old cow horses still went to East Texas to become plow horses, but the tractors had changed that. Old horses now became feed for other animals.

Oil was what mattered. The Allies had burned seven billion barrels during the war; 90 percent of that had come from America, mostly from Texas. The Big Inch and Little Big Inch: they could not have invaded Normandy without them. The Allies had sailed to victory on a sea of Texas oil.

She sometimes wondered about that—if the pipelines had not been finished—if the liberation of Europe had been canceled—maybe Paul and Clint would still be alive. Or maybe the war would still be going on. Maybe Jonas would be dead as well. That was what they always said—if this or that terrible thing had not been done, the war would never have ended.

She was not sure she believed them. They sounded like men who'd been thrown from horses because they'd wanted to get off anyway. And as for the war ending, it turned out the Russians were as bad as Hitler.

No, she would not go to Europe. She would not follow her brother around like a stray. Something would change, she could feel it.

SINCE THE VAQUEROS had done their work on the landman, there had not been any other callers, but one day there was a letter from a manager at Humble Oil. He wanted to take her to lunch.

They met in town and he was nicely dressed with fine features and gray hair that was neatly parted. He was handsome and tan and she liked him immediately and right after they ordered their steaks he offered four million plus 25 percent royalties.

It was double the offer from Southern Minerals but after pretending to think it over carefully she said: "What else will you give us?"

He held the same sweet expression.

"I know that you put in bump gates for people, but we already have them."

"What else would you like?" he said.

"What if I asked you to clear all the land within"—she thought of a large number—"five thousand feet of each well?"

"You want us to root plow your mesquite."

She nodded.

"You want us to root plow five hundred sixty-eight acres of mesquite around each well."

Was that the real number? She had no idea. She had no idea how he'd calculated it without pen and paper. But she knew she couldn't reveal her ignorance so she said: "Actually we want you to clear the acreage around each drilling site, whether it's a good well or not."

He laughed, reminding her of Phineas. "Honey, you realize there's a lot of proven land in South Texas, and no one else is asking for these improvements."

"I know you paid three and a half million plus royalties for the King Ranch," she said. "And that was ten years ago, with nothing proved, and I know all the work you've been doing to their land, because we are friends with Bob Kleberg."

It was quiet and it continued to be quiet. Outside it was busy, people dressed in city clothes, shopping or out for lunch. She started to apologize, she'd pushed too far, but of course this man wanted something from her, same as the other one, and she made herself sit as if the silence was perfectly natural. She could sit without talking for a hundred years. The man was looking out the window. She took note of his bright eyes, his small features—a man's features, but finely done—he had clearly taken more from his mother. He was quite a striking man. It occurred to her that he was just as aware of this as she was. He seemed to decide something. Now he was judging.

"I wish we could do better, but . . ." He put up his hands.

"What if we just connected to your pipeline?"

"That is funny," he said.

"Well, there is very little oil going through it at present. It will likely rot."

"If you're planning on drilling your own oil, Ms. McCullough, let me assure you there is no faster way to go bankrupt, and you'll end up living in one of these houses with the niggers and the never-sweats. If you take our offer, that land will be supporting your family for the next few centuries and you will not have to dirty a finger except to sign the lease."

She knew he was wrong but she didn't know why and she knew if she said another word her ignorance would be laid bare, if it had not been already. She collected her purse and shook his hand and walked out of the restaurant before their food even came. It was a three-dollar steak and she wondered if she ought to leave money. No. She slowed her pace, making her way down the street in the town named after her family, the shade of the awnings, parked cars, the sky looking bright between the brick storefronts. Four million dollars. It did not seem meaningful to her. In truth she felt more guilty about the three-dollar steak.

Then she began to feel stupid. She was not a grown-up at all, she was a girl, the accountant said she would owe the government five million dollars in estate taxes—that had not seemed real, either. They could get an extension but they would have to drill, and soon; it was a question of finding the right people. Phineas had told her not to worry, but she had not been worrying anyway.

The road turned back to dirt. She passed the houses of the Mexicans, their filthy alleys, doors that didn't close properly, people living ten to a room, slabs of meat hanging in the sun, collecting flies. She was sure she ought to turn around, to catch the man from Humble before he left.

But she was still walking. It was brush and farmland. Her feet, in her good shoes, sank into the dust; they would be ruined. It was stupid talking to people without Phineas around. It was stupid what she'd said about the pipeline. She should not be taking these meetings alone. But that made no sense, either. Phineas would not live forever, he was no different from her father.

Ed Freeman was in his onion field, tinkering with his irrigator. Did he still owe her father money? She waved and he looked as if something might be wrong—as if he might be required to help her. She continued along the bar ditch, sweat running down her back now.

Her father had allowed her to hate mathematics; he'd told her it didn't matter if she were good at it or not. He had been wrong about that as well. It did matter. What had the man figured—five thousand times five thousand? No, it was a geometry problem. *I haven't the faintest,* she thought.

She watched a car pass, roiling up the dust, a white man taking four Mexicans to work. License number 7916. Seventy-nine times sixteen. It seemed impossible. She did not see how the man had done it. And yet he had.

AS SOON AS she got home she had called Phineas and told him what happened, including what she'd said about the pipeline. He told her not to worry: she hadn't said anything they weren't already thinking. She felt relieved but Phineas was still talking. He was inviting her to Austin. He had someone for her to meet.

CHAPTER TWENTY-SEVEN

DIARIES OF PETER McCULLOUGH

APRIL 17, 1917

"Would you ever go into farming yourself, Colonel?"

"Sure," he says. "Natural progression of the land."

There are perhaps fifty of them, all in their Sunday best, eating tenderloin and drinking claret in the great room, listening to the Colonel expound on the wonders of our southern climate. I consider leaving my shady spot on the gallery to tell them that his policy was to shoot at any farmers who tried to toll us on cattle drives. And has said his whole life that grubbing in the dirt is the lowest form of human existence. He blames this on his time with the Indians, though it is common among all horse people, from landed cattleman to poorest vaquero.

" . . . the winter garden of Texas," he is saying, "two hundred eighty-eight growing days . . . you'll never lift a hand to shovel snow again." Scattered applause. "Further," he says, "you will find the proportion of advanced females greatly reduced compared to what you are used to in Illinois." Laughter and more applause. I close my ears; I decide to go for a walk.

Naturally they will only show the farms that are doing well; none whose water was too salty for irrigation, none of the farms on the old Cross S land, subdivided less than ten years ago, most of which are reverting to the lowest class of scrub rangeland. The soil as dead as anything you might find in Chihuahua.

APRIL 18, 1917

Ran into Midkiff's son Raymond at the store. He was driving a few critters along the road after the hailstorm this afternoon when he saw the caravan of Illinois farmers pulled over under some trees.

They were standing in the road examining hailstones the size of oranges, remarking how they might have been killed. One of them called to Raymond to ask if this weather was unusual.

"Sure is," he told them. "But you should have been here last year, when it rained!"

When the Colonel returned he was furious and told me we needed to fire the limp-dicked droop-eyed son of a bitch who was driving brindle calves on the lower road.

Explained we could not fire Raymond Midkiff. He said that was fine—we would shoot him instead. Reminded him the Midkiffs are our neighbors.

Naturally, all the farmers thought Midkiff was joking. The irrigated fields are quite lush. They have no mental ruler to understand the country here; a few of them were overheard repeating the old saw "if you plow, the rains will follow." I wonder what century they are living in.

ALL OF IT, for some reason, makes me feel almost unbearably lonely ... but I have always been a keen student of that emotion.

APRIL 19, 1917

The entire Pinkard Ranch—over one hundred sections—has been sold and divided. The family is moving to Dallas. I went to visit with Eldridge Pinkard. He could barely look at me. We are nearly the same age—his father settled this country not long after the Colonel.

"The bank would have taken it one of these days, Pete." He shrugged. "Even with beef where it is, this drought ... I had to pull the money out before there was none left."

"Heard you bought a little in the cross timbers."

He chuckled bitterly: "Two whole sections."

"Probably run a few head."

He shrugged and scuffed the dirt, looked out over what had been his pastures. "Before you get to thinking I am too badly looed . . ."

"I don't," I lied.

"You do, but I appreciate it. I wasn't going to say this to any of you who's staying, but you and me have known each other since there was Indians."

"Sure," I said.

"I was mighty down in the mouth about this until I got to talking to Eustice Caswell. On the draft board?" He shook his head. "Pete, a year from now all the good men'll be overseas. I can't even take a piss without some bond salesman drumming me for ten dollars. And . . . truthfully I am jealous of some of those boys who are shipping out, because by the time they get to France, they will have seen more country than I've seen in my whole life. And once I realized that, I got to seeing this as the last clear swing I'd ever get. And that I was a fool if I didn't take it."

"I guess."

"It ain't like our daddies grew up here, Pete. It ain't like people have lived here long. This is just the place they happened to stop."

"The fences got all of us," I said.

He looked as if he might cry, but he didn't, and then I saw that he was not happy, but he was not sad, either. The idea of moving away from here appealed to him. "You know if I was staying, I'd build roads through the whole place, get to where I could run it with a quarter of the hands, drive ten minutes instead of riding four hours, eat home every night, do the feeding out of trucks. You could get it pretty well oiled, if you put your mind to it. But even so . . ." He lifted his boot and ground it down on a mesquite seedling. "Let's face it, Pete. This land is niggered out. I wish they'd taken pictures when we were kids, because I want to forget it ever looked like this."

★　★　★

WHEN I GOT home, my father revealed he has known about it for months—he picked up half the minerals underneath the Pinkard land. I asked how we were going to pay for it.

"I decided to sell the pastures across the Nueces."

"Where are we going to keep the bulls?"

"After the promoter's cut we're clearing $31.50 an acre. We can fence off whatever we want. This pays for the minerals under the Pinkard, plus half the Garcia acquisition."

"You can see those pastures from every high point on our property," I said.

"So what? We'll look at the pretty farmer girls."

"What if I refuse to sign the deed?"

"You can refuse whatever you want," he said.

Except I cannot. I signed as he knew I would. I console myself with the fact that the Nueces pastures were not exactly convenient, anyway. The Colonel consoled me by pointing out we kept mineral rights. "Anymore, the surface ain't worth two shits," he said. "Luckily them ignorant Yankees were too busy carrying on about their college to figure that out."

Fine except the Nueces pastures were the only sensible place to keep the bulls. It will be much harder to control breeding now, more work for us, more work for the vaqueros, and much more expensive.

As for the minerals, there has been a good deal of drilling along the big river; trucks and roughnecks no longer garner any notice. Lease prices have tripled. But still the closest strikes are at Piedras Pintas, far to the east, which produce only a few hundred barrels a day under pump. The rest is just gas, which for now is useless.

APRIL 26, 1917

The Colonel, who has been gone a week, returned today from Wichita Falls with a nearly new rotary drilling rig on several old trucks. He claims to have gotten a good price. *Feller who owned it went bankrupt,* he told me, as if this were a selling point.

Accompanying the Colonel is a very drunk man who claims to be a geologist. A second drunk who claims to be a driller. Drunks number three through five are the floor- and derrickmen. They look to have been sleeping in hog wallows.

"Where did you get all that?" I asked him.

"Wichita Falls," he said, as if I didn't know where he'd been.

"We puttin' in more windmills?"

"Don't you worry about it."

He and the geologist went to explore in the sandy Garcia pastures. The rig builder, toolie, and driller retired to the Colonel's porch to drink.

MAY 4, 1917

Having come up with nothing better, they have located a spot to drill, barely half a mile from the house, based on a foggy recollection of a seep my father might have seen fifty years ago, which has not been seen since.

"That's an interesting spot," I told him, "where we can see and hear it from the house. I guess you couldn't find anywhere else in almost four hundred sections."

"That's what the doodlebug told me. Always listen to the doodlebug."

There are times I can't tell if he thinks I'm a simpleton, or if he really is one himself.

MAY 27, 1917

Panic sweeping through the Mexicans. Six of our top hands, including Aarón and Faustino Rodriquez, informed me they are resigning and returning to Mexico—they do not think it will be safe for their families.

Reason: The good people in Austin just approved funding to expand the Ranger force. Number of Rangers on border will increase to eight hundred (currently forty).

I tried pointing out to the vaqueros that Mexico is a war zone. They don't care. Safer than here, they say.

Freddy Ramirez (our segundo who first caught the Garcias stealing cattle) also put in his notice. The factories in Michigan are still
hiring Mexicans. Or so he has heard.

I tried to make a joke about it: "Michigan? *Muy frío!*" Rubbing my
hands on my arms.

He did not find this funny. "The cold we can survive. The *Rinches*,
maybe not."

MY FATHER DOES not care that we are losing seven of our best
hands. After putting half our employees to work assembling the derrick and getting supplies to the drilling site, the real work has begun.
Din is oppressive. Where there was once the sound of cattle, a creaking
windmill, it now sounds like a train station, though the train never gets
closer, or farther, or quieter. Because of the heat all the windows are
open. I walk around with cotton stuffed in my ears.

JUNE 19, 1917

Drilling continues and so far nothing but sand. Meanwhile,
because of the sale of the Pinkard Ranch, and other smaller ranches
like it, the town is nearly unrecognizable. Trucks and vegetable pickers
instead of horses and vaqueros. Gilbert's store selling fertilizer by the
ton. Went there to buy some digging bars, a few shovels, and a case of
.30-cal gov't for the Lewis gun.

"Is that my price as well?" Everything was three times as expensive
as it had been.

"Nah. I figure the few of us left ought to stick together." He pretended to do some figuring on a pad and reduced the bill by half. It
was still a 20 percent increase over the previous month. I decided not
to mention it.

"Who's left?" I said.

"Far as the greasers, none of them. About ten families, Vargases,
Guzmans, Mendezes, Herreras, Riveras, I don't even fuckin' know
who else—all happened the same day, it seemed like—they sold their

lots to Shaw who owns the rooming house, bought a few old trucks, and headed to Michigan, forty or fifty of them in one caravan. Cleaned me out of coats and blankets. They say Ford hired two thousand Mexicans in one factory. Which is pretty funny when you think about it, greasers building cars and all."

Considered mentioning that several of the "greasers" (Vargas and Rivera, at least) had gone to college in Mexico City while Gilbert and his cross-eyed brothers were diddling heifers in Eagle Pass.

"Even old Gomez sold out. Everything in his store for cost. I got crates and crates of metates, chorizo, horsehair bridles, and hide ropes. Plus his *curandero* shit. You believe that? You are looking at the new town *curandero,* right here."

The thought of any Mexican trusting Niles Gilbert to sell them medicine was depressing. I paid the bill and tried to hurry out, but not before he added: "Funny thing is, I do miss all those people, which I never thought I would say, given all the trouble they caused."

Fine sentiments for a murderer. I suppose I am no better.

DESPITE THE DISAPPEARANCE of the last of the original Mexican families (many of whom have been here five or ten generations—longer than any white), a new crop has arrived to fill their places. They speak no English and will be easy prey for men like Gilbert. Still, it is better than northern Mexico, where a state of open warfare persists. *Dunno what they're complaining about,* said my father. *At least there's no taxes.*

After I got home, I rode out to help rotate the beefs off the number 19 pasture. We are getting everything cross-fenced, and as Pinkard said, this place *is* beginning to run like a well-oiled machine. But when does the soul go out of it? That is what no one seems to know.

JUNE 20, 1917

Need a new truck. Have settled on a Wichita. The 2.5-ton would be a dream. Cannot decide between the worm drive and the chain drive.

Considered a Ford (they now make the Model T cars in Dallas) but everyone who owns a Ford has had a shoulder dislocated (or broken) when the starting handle kicked back. You can judge a Ford driver by the cast on his arm—that is the old joke.

You cannot build junk and expect to survive in today's world. People want things that last.

JUNE 21, 1917

A poor Mexican woman came to the door today. Was surprised she was bold enough to come through the gate. She looked familiar but I could not place her, presumed she was the wife or sister of one of the hands. She was thin and pale, wearing only a shift and a thin shawl over top, and when the wind blew her dress against her body I could see her legs were nearly skeletal.

"*Buenas noches,*" I said.

There was a pause.

"You don't recognize me." Her English was perfect.

"I guess not," I said.

"I am María Garcia."

I stepped back.

"I am Pedro Garcia's daughter."

CHAPTER TWENTY-EIGHT

ELI / TIEHTETI

Fall 1851

At first it was just a fever but then the spots appeared and everyone panicked. A quarter of the band struck their tipis, gathered their horses, and left the camp within a few hours. A few days later, the people who'd first taken sick were covered in boils, their faces and necks, arms and legs, the palms of their hands and the soles of their feet.

The medicine men built sweat lodges along the stream; people were dunked in the cold water, put in the sweat lodge, then dunked again. It wasn't long after that that people started to die; soon all the medicine men were sick as well.

The whites had been variolating their children for a hundred years, but by the time of statehood, you could find the vaccine in most cities. The Germans had paid a doctor to come to Fredericksburg and my mother had taken us there to get our shots.

Prairie Flower was one of the first to get sick. She hadn't touched the dead man, but I had. I hoped it was just a fever, but then her mouth felt strange, there was a kind of roughness around her lips, which I tried to smooth away.

☆   ☆   ☆

A FEW WEEKS into the epidemic, a pair of young Comanches in their best war paint rode up to the camp calling out that the raiding party, including Escuté and Nʉʉkaru, had won a great victory, many scalps and horses, not a single man lost.

The messengers stopped at the edge of the village and Toshaway, who had the first of the red marks on his face, limped out to meet them, carrying his bow and quiver.

"The band is sick," he said. "You have to go somewhere else."

The messengers protested; they didn't want to be denied their victory, and finally Toshaway told them he would shoot anyone who came into the camp, including his own sons, as it would be a more merciful death than the *tasía*.

Later that day the raiders appeared. They rode to within a few hundred yards of the camp and the people who were still able came out to wave their good-byes. Toshaway stood leaning on his bow. Two riders broke from the group and everyone squinted to see who they were. It was Nʉʉkaru and Escuté. They came within fifty paces and then Toshaway nocked an arrow and fired it into the ground in front of them.

"We'll wait for you in the Yamparikas' territory," said Escuté.

"We will not see you there," said Toshaway. "But I will see you in the happy hunting grounds."

Another young *tekʉniwapʉ* came forward.

"I have stated my mind," said Toshaway. "I will kill any man who comes into this village."

"Where is Gets Fat?" said the young man.

"She's sick," said someone.

He continued to ride forward.

Toshaway shot an arrow past his head.

"You can kill me if you want, Toshaway, but either way I am going to die in this camp with my wife."

Toshaway thought about it. Then he aimed his bow at the other raiders.

"The rest of you will leave now," he said.

A few of the other *tekɯniwapɯ,* not sure what they ought to do, not wanting to look like cowards, began to ride forward, but Escuté and Nɯɯkaru held them back. Even the very sick had come out from their tipis; they gathered at the edge of the camp and began to call out to the young men, first telling them to stay back and then telling them things they wanted them to know, family news, old secrets, things they should have said a long time ago, things that had happened since the raiders had gone.

Finally, after all the messages had been shouted across the distance, the riders kicked their horses and began to ululate and the entire band, for the last time, called back with their own war whoops, until they filled the air, and the riders shook their bows and lances, and turned their horses, and disappeared across the prairie.

BY THE FOURTH week the boils covered Prairie Flower's entire face—there was nothing left I could recognize, she had become the sickness itself. Each morning our pallet would be soaked from her breaking sores; but finally the boils began to shrink and scab and it seemed she would heal.

"I am not going to be beautiful anymore," she said. She was crying.

"You'll still be beautiful," I told her.

"I don't want to live if my face is ruined."

"You'll heal," I said. "Don't pick."

That night her fever broke and she began to breathe easily. I watched her for a long time. When the sun woke me up my arm was numb—all her weight was on it—and when I tried to wake her she wouldn't move.

IT WAS A clear warm day but only a few people were about. Toshaway was lying in his hammock, eyes closed, face to the light. The bumps on his skin were just starting to swell.

"Do I look bad?" he said.

"I've seen worse."

"Yes. And soon I will look worse." He spat. "Tiehteti. What an absurd way to die."

"The strong always survive."

"Is this known among the whites?"

"Yes."

"You are lying."

"Maybe not," I said.

"Now it's only maybe." He closed his eyes again. "It's not dignified."

I wasn't sure if he was talking about my lie or the sickness.

"When I was younger," he said, "the son of our *paraibo* became very sick. He had always been small but he was growing thinner every day, and no matter what medicine was made, he did not get better. Finally the *paraibo* asked if I might do him a favor. He made a purification ritual, washed and dressed his son for battle, gave him his own shield, the chief's shield, and then we all went to a mountain, and my friend and I did battle with the chief's son, just the three of us alone, and we killed him. And in that way, we took a pointless death and made it into a brave death."

"I'm not going to kill you."

"You could not anyway," he said. He grinned. "At least not yet."

"But someday." I didn't mean it, but I knew it was what he wanted to hear.

"Come over here, if you don't mind touching me."

I sat on the ground.

"You smell," he said.

"Prairie Flower just died."

"Ah, Tiehteti." He took my hand. "I am so sorry. And meanwhile you have been letting me talk." He began to cry. "I am so sorry, my poor son. I am so sorry, Tiehteti."

AFTER I BURIED Prairie Flower I began to go to the other tipis. There was a surplus of the dead. Pizon died that afternoon and I helped his son bury him. A week later I buried his wife and two weeks later I buried his son. Entire families passed in the same night and now I went tipi to tipi, tying the flaps shut if I had buried everyone. I buried Red Bird, Fat Wolf, Hates Work—whose dead face I kissed, imagining the scabs were not there—Lazy Feet and two of his slaves, Hard to Find, Two Bears Walking, Always Visiting Someone, Hisoo-ancho and his three children, whose names I never learned, Sun Eagle, Big Fall by Tripping. Black Dog, Little Mountain and her husband. Lost Again, who died in the arms of Big Bear, who was not her husband. I buried Hukiyani and In the Woods. Humaruu and Red Elk. Piitsuboa, White Elm, Ketumsa. The other names I didn't know, or had forgotten.

I SLEPT IN my own tipi but spent my days with Toshaway. He and his two wives were all sick, the three of them on one pallet. There was a good supply of firewood and it was warm.

"Come over here, Tiehteti," said Situtsi.

I did. I sat with my back against their pallet, and my feet near the fire, and she stroked my hair. I began to close my eyes. Watsiwannu was asleep, closer to the end than the others. Toshaway was murmuring. I couldn't tell if he knew I was there. But a little while later, he said: "Tiehteti, the next band you go to, if this happens to them, I want you to ride to the whites and tell the army where their camp is, and tell them to bring the mountain howitzers. Do you understand?"

"Yes."

"That is an order," he said. "From your war chief."

I nodded.

"Will you go back to the whites now?" said Situtsi.

"Of course not."

"Do the whites get this disease?"

"Yes, but they make medicine on people who do not have it, and it keeps them from becoming infected."

"This was done to you?" said Toshaway.

"When I was a child."

"So what do you think of the Comanche medicine?" he said. Then he began to laugh. Then Sitʉtsi began to laugh as well.

"You will lead our people to a good place," she said.

"Do not let him get ahead of himself," said Toshaway. "First he must dig." He lifted his head to look at me. "That is your only job. You must dig."

MANY OF THE captives had begun to flee, stealing horses and disappearing across the plains. No one was strong enough to stop them.

As for me, I dug. I wore out all our bone shovels and then I dug with lance shafts, tipi poles, and anything else I could find. I might have dug for weeks, or months, it got colder, the nights were freezing but the daytime sun kept the soil soft, and so I dug. Some of the Comanches who'd recovered from the sickness began to dig alongside me, the color gone from their faces in patches. Some of the survivors hunted so we could keep digging, others did nothing, still waiting to die with their families, until they did not, and so they joined us.

WHILE DIGGING THE grave for Toshaway and Sitʉtsi, in a place far from the camp, an overlook I'd spent weeks thinking about, I found a small black-and-white cup. It was made of pottery and beneath it, as I dug deeper, I came to a flat stone and beneath that was another stone, and the more I dug, the more stones I found, until the stones turned into a wall, and then a corner of two walls, and then I stopped.

Neither the Comanches nor the Apaches before us had ever built houses of stone, and no horse people would have made pottery. The Caddo and Osage had never lived this far west, and neither had the whites or Spaniards, and I realized I had come on the remains of some ancient tribe that had lived in towns or cities, a tribe so long extinct no one remembered they had ever lived.

I decided to take the cup to ask Grandfather but he was dead, and then I thought I would ask Toshaway but he was dead as well, and I nearly put it down but couldn't, I couldn't stop turning it over in my hands, and then I knew why, because it had lain there a thousand years or more and it made Toshaway and all the others seem very young; as if they were young and there was still hope.

CHAPTER TWENTY-NINE

JEANNIE McCULLOUGH

1945

Thehe man Phineas introduced her to looked like a share-cropper—a deep tan, high cheekbones, and a raw, under-fed look—except for a widow's peak he might have been a half-breed Indian. He was leaning against the file cabinets in Phineas's office, trying to act older than he was, and when she came in, he nodded as if he had not seen anything interesting and turned back to her great-uncle. There was something in his manner that made her wonder if this young man had some private relationship with Phineas, if maybe he was part of the reason she was never allowed to stay at her great-uncle's house. She decided she didn't like him.

"Hank is a driller," said Phineas. "And Hank is looking for work."

Hank nodded to her again but didn't offer to shake her hand. He and Phineas continued a conversation they were having about rocks and well logging or something equally boring. She half listened and walked around the room, but they continued to talk and she began to wonder why she had been invited, she looked at pictures of Phineas with her family, Phineas with various famous people. The driller wore a white shirt and dark trousers, which were clean but had seen better days; leather work boots, because, she guessed, he had no proper shoes. Still, she found that she wanted him to notice her; he was not properly handsome but there was something. *You have been living by yourself too long,* she thought.

On the other hand, there were few men whom Phineas treated as equals; for some reason this driller was one of them, though she could not understand exactly why. As for the driller (Hank, she thought), he continued to take no notice of her at all. A secretary walked in, a beauty like all the girls who worked for Phineas, dark hair and creamy skin and all her assets on display in a tight green dress; she went out of her way to touch Hank's hand as she filled his coffee, but Hank acted as if she didn't exist, and Jeannie forgave the girl her good looks and became sure that there was something between this young man and her uncle. Finally they finished talking and Phineas swiveled his chair.

"We're hiring Hank," he said. "He'll be heading down to the land with you today."

THEY DROVE BACK to McCullough Springs in Hank's old truck. It was hot and noisy; she hoped he wouldn't notice how much she was sweating. *He is just a driller,* she reminded herself. And not all that good-looking, either; she was far out of his league. He had a flat nose that might have come from being punched, or might always have been that way. A bit of the cur dog in him, her grandmother would have said, and yet he had a sort of physical confidence that could not be faked, she had seen it in the best vaqueros, there was a swagger about him as if, despite his size, whatever you or anyone else could do, he could do it better. He reminded her of Clint: the sort of man to whom things came easily, who was good at everything he tried.

Hank was twenty-four and had spent the war (and all the years before it, back to early childhood) looking for oil with his father, who was now dead. They had been worth several million at one point, but their last few gambles had not paid off, and then his father was killed in a blowout, leaving Hank in a tight spot. He owned his own Cummins power rig and six-wheel-drive International, knew of dozens of good roughnecks looking for work, but at the moment he barely had money for gas.

"I could rent my rig out," he said, "but then what would be the point?"

He wasn't looking for a reply.

"You got brothers or sisters?"

"Three brothers," she said, "but two died in the war."

"I've got two sisters."

Something must have occurred to her because he said: "In case you're wondering, I tried to enlist in '42, but they turned me down for color blindness."

She nodded and looked out the window, watched the brush and baked earth pass outside. Everyone who hadn't served felt compelled to give you their tale of woe.

"Meanwhile I never knew I was color-blind, I see the same as anyone else. A few months later I went to the station in Houston, but I still couldn't make out the numbers in the test, so they flunked me again, only this time I went back and borrowed the book when they weren't looking." He looked at her. "I figured it didn't cost much."

"Probably not," she said.

"Anyway I memorized the numbers and had to drive to New Mexico so they wouldn't remember they'd already seen me. This time I passed the test, but I must have done it too quick, because they started showing me the pages in a different order and I didn't get a single goddamn one of them. They knew what I'd done and told me if I ever tried again they were going to have me arrested for interfering with the war effort."

"That is some story."

"Interfering with the war effort, you believe that?"

"I believe it was a blessing."

"Try going four years where everyone thinks you're a communist or some other type of shirker. I was about to go to Canada and join up there. I probably should have but Daddy talked me out of it."

"A lot of men in oil and gas were exempted," she said. "We couldn't have won the war otherwise." ·

"Well, I didn't intend to be one of them."

She started to say something else, but he rolled down the window so all the wind came in.

By then they were south of San Antonio, into the great flat plain. She squinted against the glare; the noise made it hard to think. Hank kept the needle at eighty and she wondered what would happen if they lost a tire. She watched the way he drove, the muscles in his arms going tight and then loose again, his jaw working; it was plain he was a man whose mind was always running. She thought about her father, who thought he was a good driver, but was not. Hank kept the truck on a very straight line; he was going too fast but they were not jerking around the road. She wondered about her brothers, what they might say if they could speak, if their opinions might have changed on the war. She supposed it would not be any different. Once men got an idea, they did not seem to care if it killed them or not.

"Well, I am glad you are here," she said, once he rolled up the window. He nodded; perhaps he no longer remembered what they had been talking about. Or perhaps he did not agree. Long before they reached McCullough Springs she was wondering what it might be like to live in the big house with him. Her suspicions of his relationship with Phineas did not seem to be correct; he seemed entirely masculine. But otherwise nothing special. She was not sure why she felt so drawn to him. *You do not meet enough men,* she decided again.

Still, she pretended to sleep so that she could watch him without his knowing it. She could not help the feeling that she had been waiting for him, not someone like him, but him exactly, that she had been waiting without even knowing that he existed. And then, a minute later, she would resolve to get an apartment in Dallas or San Antonio so she would not be so alone. She supposed this man reminded her of her father and brothers; he had that sort of confidence, though he did not have their vanity—he'd worn work boots into the office of the most powerful man in Texas. *He is like the Colonel,* she told herself. The Colonel had not come from anything, either.

When they reached the ranch, they sat at the gate until she realized that he expected her, as the passenger, to get out and open it, even though she was a woman. Then they were climbing the hill. The enormous white house appeared; she wondered if he would find it too much. He didn't seem to notice. He might as well have been pulling up to an old shack. They parked in the shade and went inside, though she saw him check his boots at the threshold.

"I'll have someone get your bag and show you to your room. Then we can have supper."

"I'd like to study the maps your uncle gave me," he said. "While that drive is still fixed in my mind."

"There are lots of tables in there," she said, pointing to the great room.

She went upstairs and read in the sun with the noise and cool of the air conditioner blowing. Her father had been against them. She had a pleasant feeling and then she thought she was kissing one of the vaqueros; when she opened her eyes she could still hear the peculiar sound their lips had made. Then she was awake. She went downstairs and found Hank eating alone in the kitchen; Flores had fixed him a steak.

"You might have called me," she said.

"I figured you wanted to eat alone."

"We consider it normal to eat with company."

"I didn't know if I counted as company."

"Well, you do," she said.

"All right. In that case I am sorry I missed dining with you, Missus McCullough."

She turned her back on him and got a glass of milk from the icebox.

"I will make it up to you."

"You will indeed," she said.

She didn't want to look at him but she could tell he was grinning. "I will show you to your room now," she said.

She took him upstairs, past the enormous dark paintings of the Colonel and his children, past the Roman busts and drawings of Pompeii and silver knickknacks on all the marble, finally to the guest rooms on the opposite side of the house. Something told her he was used to sleeping in his truck and she said, "I hope you find the accommodations adequate."

He shrugged and she got annoyed again.

"Well, good night," he said. "You are not as bad as I first thought." He smiled and she found she didn't like it; it was too direct. She hurried away down the hall.

THE NEXT MORNING he laid out the maps in the dining room. "From what your uncle said, the most obvious faults are over here on the eastern part of the property. That is where we'll want to start."

"Then the easiest way will be to ride. Otherwise we will be walking through a lot of brush."

He did not react to this.

"I'll find you some proper boots," she added. "I doubt yours will fit in the stirrups."

"I will be honest," he said. "Horses don't like me much. And I guess I have never cared for them, either."

"That is very strange."

"I suppose it is for you. But I prefer my truck. It doesn't make my eyes itch and I know it won't kick me."

"Where are you from again?"

"The moon."

"I am going to teach you to like horses."

"You can try," he said. "But if I am kicked, it might decrease my affections for you."

He looked away and cleared his throat noisily.

She looked away as well. She had never met anyone so direct. She felt a prickly sensation. She worried that Flores had heard, then she decided she didn't care. "You will not be kicked," she whispered. "Nor will your affections decrease." Her neck got even hotter.

"You are probably right," he said.

"About which?"

"I guess we will find out."

But once they were driving, he seemed to lose all interest. He looked straight ahead and off to his left and off to his right but never at her; he was looking at things outside. She thought about what she had said: it had been too much. She had been too direct. A despair came over her, yes, she had been too forward, she had not known what to say. Now he thought she was a different kind of girl than she really was.

"I have never been with a man," she said. "In case you were getting the wrong idea."

He began to laugh, then stopped himself.

"I didn't want you getting the wrong idea," she insisted.

"You aren't used to talking to people, are you?"

She looked out the window. For a moment, idiotically, she thought she might cry.

"It's all right," he said. He reached over and squeezed her hand, then took his own hand back just as quickly. "I'm the same way."

THEY SPENT THE entire day driving the ranch's dirt roads. He would skid the truck to a stop, then climb out and stand on the roof.

"What are you looking for?"

"The escarpment," he said. "But there is so much goddamn brush."

"There's brush everywhere."

"That's what I just said."

"It's not just on our land."

He continued to look. "I forgot my binoculars," he said. Then he added: "For someone who owns this much country, you are one sensitive individual."

She didn't answer.

"But at least you have good roads. Half the time I drill in Texas I have to bushwhack through three miles of mesquite."

"We ought to just drill near the Humble fields."

"That is a good idea," he said, "except they have been tapping them for twenty-five years. And if we find something they will just have incentive to get those wells reworked, and take even more oil, and your uncle will be mad at me."

"So we're just going to start drilling in the middle of nowhere?"

"You know how you are with horses?"

"Yes."

"I am that way with oil."

"So you have convinced my uncle."

He grinned. "We'll get a shot truck in here and narrow things down."

"I suppose that will be expensive."

"It will be a lot less than a dry hole."

SHE SLEPT IN her bedroom and he slept in his. She did not want him to get the wrong idea, though on the other hand she did. She left her door open, just a crack, just in case he came. Which of course was ridiculous. He didn't even know where her room was and he was not going to come find it in the dark. "You are a slut," she said out loud. Though of course it had been two years since any man had touched her. And compared to her mother, who was already having children by now . . .

She was awake most of the night. She saw herself marrying him, she saw him using her and throwing her away. She decided she didn't care as long as he wasn't rough. Then she was thinking about the glorious life of men—to go off and have whatever experiences you wanted, whenever you wanted to have them—meanwhile here she was, nearly twenty and still a virgin, her only prospect asleep on the other side of the house. He acted as if he liked her but then suppose he didn't. It was too awful to contemplate. She looked out the window and waited for the sun to rise.

CHAPTER THIRTY

DIARIES OF PETER McCULLOUGH

JUNE 22, 1917

I stood there with the door open, expecting her to draw a pistol, or rush with a knife, but she didn't move. She was smaller than I remembered, her clothes ragged, sun-beaten, beyond worn, her skin leather over bone, scabs on her face where she had fallen or been struck. Her hands hung at her sides as if she did not have the energy to lift them.

I tried to recall her age, thirty-three or -four, except she would be older now . . . I remembered her as a pretty girl, small with dark eyes; she now looked her mother's age. Her nose had been broken and it had set crooked.

"I came to see our house," she said. "I was hoping to find my birth certificate." She shrugged. "Of course they assume I'm not a citizen when I try to cross."

I looked away from her. There was something troubling about her accent—she had spent four years at a women's college—compared with the way she looked.

"You may have trouble finding it," I said quietly, referring to the birth certificate.

"Yes, I saw."

Still I could not look at her.

"I'm very hungry," she said. "Unfortunately . . ."

Every time I tried to lift my eyes, they wouldn't. It was quiet and I realized she was waiting for me to say something.

"I'll try at the Reynoldses'," she said.

"No," I said. "Come in."

SHE HAS BEEN living in Torreón for two years with a cousin, but the cousin was a Carrancista and the Villistas had come to his house and killed him, then beaten up María and the cousin's wife, perhaps done worse. What money she had was long spent and she had been on the road for nearly a month. Finally she'd decided there was nothing else to do but come back here. She reminded me, several times, that she was an American citizen. I know that, I told her. Though of course she looks as Mexican as anyone else.

Was it polite to offer condolences for her family? Probably the opposite. I didn't say anything. We stood in the kitchen as I heated beans and carne asada, some tortillas Consuela had made, my hands shaking. I could feel her eyes on my back. The beans began to burn and finally she pushed me aside. I smiled at her, I didn't usually do this sort of thing, but she didn't smile back. As the beans were stewing she cut some tomatoes and onions and a few peppers and mixed them together.

"If you will excuse me, I am quite hungry."

"Of course. I have a few things to do upstairs."

She nodded, not taking her eyes off me, not touching the food until I'd left.

I SAT IN my study as if all the life had been sucked out of me ... all the energy I'd once had, my years at university, smashed against the rocks of this place. I nearly picked up the phone to call the sheriff to come remove her, though what my reason would be, I couldn't say. We had killed her family, burned her house, stolen her land ... she ought to be calling the sheriff on us ... she ought to have shown up at our door with a hundred men, rifles cocked.

I considered climbing out the window onto the roof of the gallery—it was only fifteen feet to the ground—I could drop to the grass and walk away, never to come back.

Or I could simply wait until someone, perhaps my father, more likely Niles Gilbert, would take her outside, walk her into the brush, snip the last frayed end. I see Pedro, the tear weeping from beneath Lourdes's eye, I see Aná's head tilted back, her mouth wide as if trying to scream even in death.

I decided I would tell her. I had done my best—perhaps she had been watching? I had stood between the two lines and the shooting had begun anyway. I went to the safe and counted out two thousand dollars and put it into my pocket. I would drive her to the hospital in Carrizo or wherever her birth had been registered, procure the necessary papers, and help her on her way, polite but firm; there was nothing for her here.

SHE WAS TRIMMING the skin off a mango.

"What are your plans," I said, as gently as possible.

"Right now I am planning to eat this mango. With your permission, of course."

I didn't say anything.

"Do you remember the times we sat out on our portico?" She continued to peel the fruit. The knife slipped but she continued as if nothing had happened.

"Do you want a bandage?"

"No, thank you." She put her thumb into her mouth.

I looked at the table, then around the room, at the patterns in the tin ceiling. Her shoulders were shaking; her head was down and I couldn't see her face. But there was nothing I could say that wouldn't be taken the wrong way.

It was like that until I decided to put the dishes in the sink.

"Of course I shouldn't be here," she said.

"It's not inconvenient," I told her.

"It was inconvenient to my cousin."

"Do you have other family?"

"My brothers-in-law. I'm hoping they're dead but they are the type to survive."

Of course it was obvious what any normal person would do. We had provided a place to live for numerous of my father's old friends, decrepit herders from another age, men who had no families, or who no longer had anything to say to their families; dozens of them had lived out their last days in our bunkhouse, taking their meals with the vaqueros, or with us, depending on how close they had been to my father. But this was a different matter. Or so it would be said.

"I live here alone," I told her. "My father has his own house a little ways up the hill. My wife has left me; my remaining sons are in the army."

"Is this your way of making a threat?" she said.

"It's the opposite."

"I imagined you might shoot me," she said. "I imagine you still might."

The sympathy began to go out of me. I continued to wash the dishes, though they were already clean. "Then why did you come?"

No answer.

"You're welcome to stay the night. There are plenty of spare rooms on the second floor, just go up the stairs and turn left and pick one."

She shrugged. She was sucking at the pit of the mango, the juice had run down her scabbed chin. She looked like she belonged on a stoop in Nuevo Laredo, the old combination of hopelessness and rage. I began to hope more than ever that she would turn me down, that a meal in the house of her enemy would be enough.

"Okay," she said. "I will stay the night."

JUNE 23, 1917

My bedroom did not feel secure so I lay back down in my office, door locked. I loaded, unloaded, then reloaded my pistol. I listened for her footsteps in the hall, though the runner was thick and I knew I would likely hear nothing.

Around midnight I unloaded the pistol a second time. Of course I am no different from the others, the same dark urges inside me. I was not afraid of her physically. It was something much worse.

AROUND FIRST LIGHT, I drifted off. Then the sun was coming in; I rolled over and fell back asleep. In the distance was a sound I had not heard in a long time; when I realized what it was I woke up immediately and got dressed.

Downstairs, Consuela was standing at the entrance to the parlor, watching. She saw me and walked away as if I had caught her at something.

María was sitting at the bench, playing the piano. She must have heard my footsteps because her back went straight and she missed a few notes, then continued playing. Her hair was down around her shoulders, exposing her neck; I could make out the vertebrae easily. What she was playing, I didn't know. Something old. German or Russian. I stood a few paces behind her; she continued to play without turning. Finally I went to the kitchen.

Consuela looked at me. "Should I prepare breakfast for her?"

I nodded. "Is there coffee?"

"In the pot. *Frío*."

I poured a cup anyway.

Consuela busied herself chopping nopales, tossing them into the pan with butter.

"Does your father know?"

"He will soon enough."

"Am I to treat her as a guest or ... ?"

"Of course," I said.

I wondered how well she had known the Garcias. But of course the Garcias were wealthy and Consuela is a servant. The sun had been up two hours and was filling the house, the warm air coming through the windows. I was four hours late for work. I went to the icebox and pulled out a few chunks of cabrito, then wrapped them in a cloth with a tortilla.

"Let me heat that," she said.

"I better go," I said. "I'll see you at dinner."

"Should I watch her?"

"No," I said. "Just give her whatever she wants."

I DIDN'T GET home until well after dark, when I knew Consuela would have gone back to her house. I could smell that someone had been cooking, but the plates had all been cleaned and put away. María was at the table, reading a book. *The Virginian,* by Wister.

"Do you like this one?" she said.

"It's not bad."

"The strong white man comes to an unpopulated wilderness and proves himself. Except there has never been any such thing."

We sat there with nothing to say. Finally I decided to bring it up.

"Everything happened pretty fast that morning."

She went back to the book.

"I think it's best we talk about it."

"Of course you do," she said. "You want to be forgiven."

The night air was blowing through the house. There was a screech owl outside and the windmill, and, in the distance, the sound of my father's drilling rig. I sat and listened.

"I'll leave in the morning. I'm sorry I came."

I felt myself relax. "All right," I said.

LAY AWAKE SEVERAL hours. Am courting disaster, some cataclysm I cannot imagine; I feel it as the old man knows rain is coming. I want only for her to disappear ... the thought itself relaxes me. All my noble thoughts vanish—when kindness is truly needed it is scarce as the milk of queens. It seems that any moment a company of *sediciosos* might kick down the door, carry me off to the nearest adobe wall ...

But that was not what I was really afraid of. I had a memory of Pedro and I sitting on his portico. Aná came out and brought us sweet tea, but when Pedro drank, the tea ran down his shirt and onto his lap;

there was a hole under his chin I had not noticed. Then I was standing with my father and Phineas, on one side a deep green pasture, the
smell of huisache, the shrubs all around us dotted with gold. In front
of us an old elm tree . . . a man on a horse, a rope slack around his
neck, people expecting something of me; I could not do it, though it
was a simple enough action. Finally Phineas slapped the horse across
the hams and the man slid off the back, twisting and kicking, his legs
searching for purchase, but there was only air . . .

Humiliation of failure, jealousy of Phineas. And yet I knew I could
not have done it, no matter how many chances they might have given
me. They were trying to harden me; all wasted effort.

I opened my eyes. I was cold. The wind was blowing through
the house, two or three A.M., the windmills creaking, coyotes yipping. I thought of a fawn running in panicked circles, then went to
the window and stood looking, there was enough moonlight to see far
out over our pastures, ten miles at least. Nothing in sight that did not
belong to us.

Finally I got dressed. I made my way to the hallway in the west
wing of the house, stepping quietly, as if meeting for an assignation,
though it did not matter . . . we were alone. I noticed that my breath
was foul, my hair and face greasy, the smell of old sweat, but I continued down the hall. A prowler in my own house. Past the busts on their
pedestals, the drawings of ruins . . . another portrait of my mother, past
Glenn's room and Pete Junior's room and Charlie's room . . . finally I
heard a fan blowing behind one of the doors. I knocked softly.

I knocked again and waited and then knocked a third time. Then I
opened the door. The bed was empty but the sheets were mussed and
it was dark. I went to the window and she was standing on the roof of
the gallery, at the very edge.

"Come back from there."

She didn't move. She was wearing a nightdress Consuela must
have given her. For a moment I thought she was sleepwalking.

"Come here," I repeated.

"If you're going to kill me . . ." she said. "I don't care but I am not just going to walk out into the *brasada* with you."

"You should stay here," I told her.

"Imposible."

"Stay until you're well."

She shook her head.

"I wanted to stop you before you left. That's all I wanted."

"In order that you will have done something kind." She looked at me, shook her head, then looked out over the land. She was looking toward her old house, I realized. I worried she might step over the edge. She said, "Today in the kitchen while your back was turned, I thought about how I might put the chopping knife into your throat. I thought about how many steps it was and what I would do if you turned around."

"Stay," I said.

She shook her head. "You don't know what you're asking, Peter."

JUNE 24, 1917

In non-Garcia-related news, the vaqueros complain that the noise of the drilling is ruining the cattle. They do not see this year's calf crop being a good one if the animals are subjected to all that noise.

I went to my father to ask how deep they intend to drill. He told me to the center of the earth. I ask if he knows that our aquifer is shallow, and our water some of the best in this part of Texas, and that if he leaks petroleum into it, we are done for. He tells me these men are experts. He means the ones who sleep in hog wallows.

IT OCCURS TO me that we are entering an era in which the human ear will cease to distinguish sounds. Today I barely heard the drillers. What other things am I not hearing?

WHEN I RETURNED to the house for dinner, there was the sound of the piano before I even reached the door. I removed my boots and left them outside so she would not hear me enter, opened and closed the door very softly, then lay on the divan listening to her play. When I opened my eyes she was standing over me. For an instant I imagined her as she had been ten years earlier: her round face, dark eyes. Then I looked at her hands. They were empty.

"I am going to eat."

"Alone?"

"I don't care," she said.

She heated up what Consuela had left for us. When we finished I asked her again what had happened that day.

She acted like she hadn't heard. "Would you mind if I cooked a little more? I can't stop thinking about food."

"There are always things in the icebox," I said.

She took some cold chicken and began to eat. She tried to be dainty but I could tell it took a lot of effort, I was full but she was starving.

"Tell me."

"You think that talking about this will allow me to forgive you."

"I haven't forgiven myself," I said quietly.

"Telling you changes nothing," she said. "Just so we are clear."

I nodded.

"Fine. So, when they came into the house, they shot everyone, whether they were already on the floor or standing up. Someone shot my niece, who was six, and then, like a coward, I went into my room and hid in my closet. After that I remember sitting on my bed and someone removing my shirt and realizing they are going to rape me before they kill me, then I saw it was you. I thought you were going to rape me and somehow it was much worse.

"Then you walked me through the house. I saw into my parents' room, my mother and father dead, my sister lying with them, then in the *sala* were Cesár and Romaldo and Gregorio, Martin and my nephew, and their families. I could see the front door was open, and the sun was coming through it and I began to hope I might live, but when we reached the portico I saw the entire town had gathered. Then I wished I hadn't hidden in the closet. I nearly took your gun.

"After that I was at the Reynoldses' house. They thought they were rescuing me, they thought they were doing me a favor. They fed me, allowed me to bathe, gave me clothes, a room with clean sheets. Meanwhile, my own house, with my own bed and my own clothes, was just a few miles away. But it was already not mine."

"No one wanted it to happen."

"These lies come out of your mouth so easily," she said. "You yourself, I believe you had reservations, perhaps a few others . . . the Reynoldses, obviously . . . but not anyone else."

She looked at the plate in front of her. "And still I am hungry. That is what I cannot believe."

It was quiet and finally she said, "Can we go outside? I get spells of hot and cold, and now I am very hot."

We went onto the porch and looked over the land. It was an unusually cool day, a pleasant evening, with the sun just going down. I considered remarking as much, then decided against it. I could hear the drilling going on from the other side of the hill.

After we'd sat awhile, she said: "I've spent a long time thinking about what happened. And the longer I thought about it, the more I began to think that things had just gone very badly wrong, of course the shooting of your son—it was Glenn?"

"Yes."

"And how is he?"

"He is alive."

"I am glad."

I felt my face get hot. For some reason this—Glenn still being alive—embarrassed me.

"One of yours hurt, eleven of mine dead . . ." She put up her hands, as if balancing scales. "We have all suffered, the past is the past, it is time to move on."

I didn't answer.

"That is what you think, isn't it? Your child injured, my family exterminated, we are even. And of course you are the best of them; the others think okay, a white man was scratched, there is no amount of Mexican blood that can wash out that sin. Five, ten, one hundred . . . it's all the same to them. In the newspapers, a dead Mexican is called a carcass"—she held up her fingers—"like an animal."

"Not all newspapers."

"Just the ones that matter. But of course I'm no better; for a long time, I had fantasies about nearly every white person in town, burning them, cutting them. I remember very clearly Terrell Snyder staring at me with a grin on his face and the Slaughter brothers as well . . ."

"I don't think the Slaughters were there," I said.

"They were, I saw them clearly, but that is irrelevant. I decided I would stop being angry and perhaps accept that the entire situation, everything that had happened, was bad luck. In fact I became certain of it. We had known your family for decades, it didn't make sense. You in particular we knew very well; I could not imagine you plotting against us. I began to think that perhaps I overreacted by fleeing from the Reynoldses' house.

"And so when my cousin was killed, I decided I would come back. I crossed the river and reached our pastures and felt more alive than I had been in months. I decided to walk all night. I had a story prepared if I met one of your fence riders, though I hoped I would not, as I knew that, depending on their mood, my story would not matter. But . . . there was no one. This I also took as a sign.

"I knew what condition the house would be in. The stuffing would be pulled out of chairs, bird droppings, dirt everywhere, our papers shredded by mice, and of course the old pools of the blood of my family would not have been cleaned and the bullets would still be in every wall. It would look exactly as I had left it, except that it would have aged two years.

"When I reached our lower pasture, by the old church, the sun was coming up and I could see the house had been burned. But still I thought no, empty homes are often vandalized, lovers go to them, the poor occupy them, the dry climate—even a cigarette might have started a fire. I went through one of the doors, made my way through the rubble to my father's office, where I knew all our papers were kept, in metal cabinets that would have resisted any fire. The cabinets were buried under debris, like everything else, but after some time I uncovered them. My birth certificate, perhaps some money, stock certificates, things like that. But do you know what I found?"

I looked away.

"Nothing. They were empty. The papers were gone. Every single document and letter, every record had been removed. And then I knew it had been intentional. It was not enough to exterminate my family; it was also necessary to remove every record of our existence."

"No one wanted that," I told her.

"Another lie. You of all people, you have already forgotten that you are lying. Your lies have become the truth."

I decided to study a green lizard scuttling across the porch. Sometime later I heard a sound; her breath was rattling like a dying man's. I had a terrible feeling but I watched her and she continued to breathe; she was asleep. I watched her for a long time after that and when I was sure she was not going to perish, I went inside and got a blanket and put it over her.

Chapter Thirty-one

ELI/TIEHTETI

Late Fall/Early Winter 1851

After we buried the last of the dead, the fifty of us still alive had gathered the few remaining horses and were making our way southwest, mostly on foot, hoping to find the buffalo, or to at least cut their trail. There was no fresh sign. It was clear the *nʉmʉ kutsu* had not been in the area for over a year.

No one knew where the good grass was or where the buffalo might be headed. Later we found out they had stayed north, with the Cheyennes and Arapahoes. Meanwhile, the snow was beginning to fall and there was not much to eat.

With the exception of Yellow Hair, myself, and a few old Comanches who'd been exposed in previous epidemics, there was no logic to who had survived. The *tasía* had killed the weak and the strong, the smart and the stupid, the cowardly and the brave, and if the survivors had anything in common, it was that they had been too lazy or fatalistic to run away. The best of us had either fled or died in the plague.

No one spoke. There was nothing but the wind, creaking of packs, the travois poles scraping over rocks. If we did not see enough deer or antelope, we would kill a horse, further slowing our progress. There was no plan except to find the buffalo; we did not know what we would do if we ran into the *Tuhano* or the army; there were less than ten of us who could still fight; many of the children had gone blind.

One day, as we watched another norther blow in, the sky behind us the color of a bruise, a cold I knew would cut through my robe, it occurred to me that I had missed seeing many of the children at breakfast. I could not recall seeing them the previous night, either. I looked behind me and made a count of our long slow column and it was true. Half the children were missing. Their mothers had taken all the blind ones out onto the prairie and killed them, so that the rest of us would have enough to eat.

That night we ran into a group of Comanchero traders who saw our fire in the storm. They were loaded down with cornmeal and squash, powder and lead, knives and steel arrowheads, woolen blankets. We had nothing to give them. Apparently all the other bands were decimated because they decided to keep us company a few days. They gave us a few sacks of cornmeal but we had no hides and our few remaining horses could not be traded.

As they began to repack their mules, a sense of despair came over everyone; a few people sat down in the snow and refused to be consoled. The night had cleared and I walked away from the fire to look at the stars. There did not seem to be much point in continuing. The few people like me, who could still hunt, could simply ride away, but that was out of the question. I was standing there thinking when our surviving chief, Mountain of Rocks, came up next to me.

"I would like to speak quickly, Tiehteti."

"All right," I said.

"Obviously," he said, "we may not make it through the winter."

"I can see that."

He looked out over the prairie, now covered with a light dusting of snow, which would soon turn into several feet.

"There is a way for you to help."

I knew what he was getting at. The government was still paying high prices for returned captives.

"You yourself may survive this winter here. Most of us will not. Maybe none of us will. But if you return to the *taibo* . . ." He shrugged. "You can simply come back once the traders are paid."

I didn't look at him.

"It is your decision, of course. But there is talk that you might volunteer to do this, especially given the sacrifices that many of the families have already made." He meant the children. "Still, you are one of us and we would prefer if you stayed."

FOR THE GERMAN girl and me, the Comancheros left twenty bags of cornmeal, forty pounds of *piloncillo,* ten bushels of squash. Twenty pounds of lead, a barrel of powder, some gun lock screws, a thousand-pack of steel arrowheads, a few rough knife blades with rawhide handles. It was considered quite generous, though the traders had no doubt they would make a large profit, as I was still young, and the German girl still pretty, her face unmarked. Many captives, especially women, were returned with ears and noses cut off, faces branded, but Yellow Hair looked unscathed, and it was obvious that she would be beautiful once cleaned up. I was asked a few questions in English, to see if I still knew how to speak it, which I did. After nearly three years living among the wild Indians, that was not common, either, and by any measure our return would look like a great success and the Comancheros would be well paid.

Mountain of Rocks asked me to leave him my Colt Navy, one of the two I'd gotten off the scalp hunter, but it was out of the question. I had buried the other with Toshaway. And I did not like the look of the traders, or Mountain of Rocks, for that matter.

THE FIRST NIGHT Yellow Hair stayed close to me, away from the Comancheros.

"Don't let them touch me," she said.

"I won't."

"Make them think I'm your wife."

"They're trying to get money for us," I said. "I don't think they'll do anything."

"Please," she said.

The next night I knew she was right: one of them kept sitting closer until finally he put his arm around her. He was a big man with a large gut; he looked like an unwashed version of St. Nicholas. I stood up and pulled my knife and he put up his hands, laughing at me.

"You look a little young, but I won't fight you."

"We don't have to fight for her," I said. "We can just fight."

He laughed some more and shook his head. "Boy, I can see you are holding on to her like death to a dead nigger. I already said I won't fight you. I'm going to sleep." He got up and went to his pallet under the wagon.

That night she slept in my robe. I hadn't touched a woman or even myself in nearly two months, because all I could think about was Prairie Flower, and her ruined face when I put the dirt over her.

But spooning with Yellow Hair, part of me seemed to forget all that. I could smell her sweet unwashed hair, and finally, when I couldn't stand it, I began to kiss her neck. I wondered if she was asleep but then she said: "I won't stop you, but I don't want to do that right now."

I kissed her behind the ear and tried to make out that I had just been being brotherly. She moved my rutter so that it was not poking into her. We fell asleep.

The next night she said: "We can make love if you want to but you know I was raped by maybe ten men in our band. I tried to talk to you about it many times."

I felt so ashamed that I pretended to be sleeping.

"It's okay," she said, patting my hip. "I doubt they would have let you into the tribe if you'd been nice to me."

"I'm sorry."

"Just don't let these men rape me. I don't think I could stand it."

On the third night I asked her: "Do you think I am not attracted to you because you slept with all those men in our band, or do you just not want to sleep with me?"

"I don't want to sleep with anyone," she said. "But especially not these Comancheros. St. Nicholas showed his cock and balls to me and they are covered with a disease."

On the fourth night I persisted: "But what about me?"

"Would you kill these Comancheros if I asked you?"

"Yes."

"In that case I'll sleep with you. But we have to be quiet so they don't hear us or you might end up having to kill them."

"I'll kill them," I said, though in truth I thought it was unlikely, as we represented a year's wage for them.

She looked at me. She was a sensitive one. "Forget it. I'll sleep by myself." She got out of the robe. "I'd rather be raped than have sex with a liar."

"I'll protect you," I said. "Let's not do anything. I'm sorry I mentioned it."

The last time I asked her anything about sex was: "Did you ever get pregnant?"

"Three times, but they all came out after a couple of months."

"How?" I said.

"I beat myself in the stomach with rocks. Also, no matter how hungry I was, I would not let myself eat."

"If you'd had a baby, they might have made you a tribe member."

"That would have been great except every night I was there, all I dreamed about was going home."

"To where?"

"Anywhere there were white people. Anywhere I wouldn't have to live with men who'd raped me."

I should have felt sympathy for her, but it just made me angry. I missed Toshaway more than I missed my own parents and the thought of Prairie Flower made me so empty that I wanted to put my gun to my head. I rolled over and went to sleep.

We rode together for three weeks, sharing the same robe so the Comancheros would think we were married, and every night I expected we would make love, as we slept spooning in the same robe, but it was true what she had told me, she had no interest at all. Even the one night we drank whiskey with the traders and she let my hands wander more than normal and I thought this is the night I might get inside her, but soon realized she was breathing very deeply and was no longer awake. I let my hands wander over her a little longer. The Comancheros knew their buyers, they were feeding us four or five times a day and Yellow Hair was looking healthier every minute, her ribs softening, her breasts and hips filling out, though still she cried every night in her sleep.

"I guess if I had a fantasy," she told me, "it would be to rape all the men who raped me. Bring them back from the dead and rape all of them, over and over. With a big jagged stick, I mean. I would push it in and out and I would not stop until I was good and ready."

I didn't say anything. I thought about Toshaway and Nuukaru and Pizon, and Prairie Flower and Fat Wolf and Grandfather, and Hates Work, who was really Single Bird, Escuté and Bright Morning, Two Bears, Always Visiting Someone; I guessed I might kill Yellow Hair quite happily just to have a single one of them back.

But she did not appear to notice. "I've actually thought about it quite a lot," she said. "I mean raping them. It was what got me through the day sometimes."

She was smiling.

"But now I don't have to think about it anymore."

I didn't talk to her that night, or the next day, either.

THE LAST WEEK we spent on wagon roads, passing villages, settlements, the first white people I'd seen in three years who hadn't shot at me. Yellow Hair waved at everyone. But the whites did not think it was a special occasion, seeing other white people. The land was settling up.

When we reached the Colorado, close to Austin, I could not believe the roads; they had doubled in width and the ruts were all filled. Yellow Hair was happy, unusually talkative, and she had kissed the traders on their cheeks and thanked them and cuddled very close to me during supper. I could see their looks of jealousy, but St. Nick kept them in line. He knew what we were worth. He offered me a spare cylinder for my pistol if I would let him wash and cut my hair, which had grown halfway down my back. I thought about it, then agreed.

When we went to bed that night, Yellow Hair allowed me to put myself partway into her but she was very dry, and after moving around for several minutes she got no better, and I was so ashamed I removed myself.

"Go ahead and finish," she said.

"I can't with you not wanting to."

She shrugged. "I really don't mind. You kept your word."

I thought about it and then got out of the robe, stood up, looked at the sky, and finished myself off. The grass was not even covered with frost, it was so much warmer in the hill country than on the plains. I got back into the robe with her.

"You're a good man," she said. "I've never known anyone like you."

THE NEXT DAY we rode into Austin. We were taken to the house of a merchant the traders knew and then to the state capitol. A bunch of white men came and asked our names. It took most of the day but eventually three hundred dollars each was raised for us; the traders were paid and rode off without a word to me, though they tried to kiss Yellow Hair good-bye. She turned away from them. Now that we were in public, she would not even allow them to touch her.

Her real name was Ingrid Goetz. The word spread and various wealthy women adopted her. When I saw her the next day she was wearing a blue silk dress, her hair washed and braided and pulled into a bun behind her head. Meanwhile I had refused to let them touch me—I was wearing buckskin leggings and a breechcloth, no shirt, and while they had insisted on holding on to my revolver, I would not let them take my knife, which I kept tucked into my belt.

And so I slept on a spare cot at the jail while Yellow Hair stayed at a plantation east of town, the home of the U.S. representative and his wife. After a few days there was a reception for us at a judge's house, a Georgian-style mansion near the capitol with a nice view over the river. The judge was a big redheaded man who could have hoisted a barrel in each arm, though his hands were soft as a child's. He'd been educated at Harvard in his youth, then became a senator in Kentucky, then swore off politics entirely and moved to Texas to increase his fortune. He read a lot of books and his words ran eight to the pound, but he had a good spirit and I took to him right away.

Yellow Hair and I made quite a pair. She looked like she'd lived in town all her life; I'd taken a bath and lost my long braids but otherwise I looked like a feral child. Several reporters gathered and they asked if we were husband and wife and looking at her, with her hair washed and her face clean, she struck me as even more beautiful than I had ever thought and I wanted her to say yes.

Everyone else wanted her to say yes as well, as it made a good story, but Yellow Hair was a selfish creature. No, we were not connected in any way, I had simply protected her honor from the Comanches, she was returning with her honor intact thanks to me, honor honor honor, she still had it, that was all.

I was speechless. No one except the Yankees believed a word of it. The Indian's appetite for his female captives was well known to all Texans.

WE WERE FED big meals with fresh bread and beef and a roasted turkey, which I would not touch, as the Comanches thought that eating turkey made you a coward, and staring at the bird I was reminded of Escuté, who liked to tell the joke, *if eating turkey makes you a coward, what does eating pussy make you?* There was also roast pig, which I would not touch, as the Comanches knew it was a filthy animal. I ate about five pounds of beef and two rabbits and it was commented what a good appetite I had. Yellow Hair ate a small amount of bread and turkey and, looking at me directly, helped herself to several servings of pork.

That night, despite the breezes flowing through the house, it felt so hot and still, and the beds so soft and smothering, that I went outside and slept in the judge's yard. Yellow Hair, meanwhile, was already telling people that she had come from an aristocratic German family, though, as they had all been killed, there was no way to verify it. I was certain she was lying, as I knew where her family had been living, and the others doubted her as well, but no one was going to say anything. They had never seen a female captive returned in such good condition. You did not look a gift horse in the mouth.

A few days later, the judge gathered several of the town's influential people in his yard for a barbecue, along with a few reporters from the East. I was asked to dress in my garb and do some tricks. Of course most of what an Indian knows cannot be shown in a circus, like how to follow game, or read a man's mood from his footprints, so I asked for a horse and galloped it up and down the yard bareback, while shooting arrows at a hay bale. The judge had first suggested I shoot a stump but that was out of the question, as it would ruin my arrows, and as both they and my bow had been made by Grandfather, I had no desire to damage them except on a living target. I sat there on the horse and people gave suggestions. The judge pointed out a squirrel that was high up in a live oak and I shot it off the branch and then shot a dove off a different branch. The onlookers applauded. Not far from them was a black eye in the grass that I knew belonged to a rabbit so I put an arrow through that as well. Several of the eastern reporters looked sick at the rabbit shrieking and flopping itself into the air but the judge laughed and said, *He's got quite an eye, doesn't he?* Then his wife gave him a look. He called an end to the demonstration. The Negroes stomped on the rabbit to quiet it and trampled the divots in the lawn as well.

We sat and drank tea and finally they got to quizzing me about Yellow Hair, or Ingrid Goetz, as they insisted on calling her. During my demonstration she'd claimed to have a spell and they'd taken her back to the plantation. Of course I knew better.

The judge, who was sitting in, said: "Did you know her well?"

"We were captured at the same time," I said.

"So you did know her."

"Somewhat."

"And it's true she wasn't misused?" said the reporter. He was from the *New York Daily Times*.

I considered throwing her under the wagon, because she clearly wanted nothing to do with me, but I couldn't. "For sure not," I said. "They never touched her. She was a member of the tribe."

"That is somewhat unlikely," said the judge. He looked embarrassed but continued: "If that is true she would be the first case I have ever heard of, as most female captives are misused by the entire tribe. And often by any visitors to the tribe as well." He coughed into his hand and looked at the ground.

"That is not what happened to her," I said. "A lot of the braves wanted to marry her but she wouldn't allow them. She was kept separate from the men."

The judge was giving me a strange look.

"I guess there was one young chief who wanted to marry her but he was killed in a battle with the army and maybe that broke her heart."

"Was she ever attached to this chief, matrimonially or otherwise?"

"No," I said. "The Comanches are real strict about that stuff."

"Poor girl," said the reporter. "She might have ended up a queen."

"Probably would have."

The judge was staring at me, as if trying to deduce why I would tell such an outrageous lie.

"I guess that proves the red man can be noble if he wishes it," said the reporter from the *Daily Times*. He looked at the judge. "Contrary to what I am told."

The judge didn't say anything.

"It is as plain as day," said the reporter. "If the Indians were left in peace . . ." He shrugged. "There would not be any trouble with them."

"May I ask where are you from?"

"New York City."

"I know that, but what tribe are you from? The Senecas? The Cayugas?"

The reporter shook his head.

"Or perhaps you are Erie, or Mohawk, or Mohican, or Montauk or Shinnecock, or Delaware or Oneida or Onondaga. Or, my favorite, Poospatuck? I suppose they are your neighbors. Do you attend their scalp dances?"

"Come off it," said the reporter.

"There are no Indians left in your part of the country because you killed them all. So we find it interesting you have such a fascination with making sure we treat ours humanely. As if, unlike the savages your grandfather wiped out, ours are thoughtful and kind."

"And yet look at this woman. She was taken as a prisoner, but not mistreated."

The judge began to speak, then thought better of it. After a time, he said: "So it seems."

Two weeks later, Ingrid Goetz was traveling east with that same reporter. I never saw or heard from her again.

AROUND THAT SAME time Judge Black came to me and told me my father was dead. He had been killed somewhere near the border, riding with a Ranger company. A woman claiming to be his widow, who had seen the announcement of my return in the newspaper, had written the judge and offered to let me stay with her.

From what anyone knew, my father had signed back with the Rangers after coming home to find his house burned and his family dead or missing, and while he had survived his first two years, he had been killed the third. The Texas Rangers in those days had a 50 percent fatality rate per tour; they lay buried all over the state, three or four to a grave. My father had been killed by Mexicans. That was all anyone knew.

I took my bow and a pair of trousers the judge had bought for me, so I would not be mistaken for an Indian, and went walking by the river. I expected to blubber, but nothing came out, and then I wasn't sure if I was betraying Toshaway or not and I decided to stop thinking about it. That night I had a dream in which my father and I were standing together by the old house.

"You couldn't have caught us," I was telling him. "No one could have."

But then he was gone and I was not sure if I was saying that to him or to myself.

THE JUDGE CLAIMED it was no problem but I could tell I was disturbing his household, as his three daughters had taken to painting their faces and making war whoops and practicing their ululations. His wife suspected this had something to do with me. She was the type who liked saving people but she had so many rules I couldn't keep them straight.

I took to excusing myself after breakfast and spending the day along the river, looking for things to shoot. The judge made me promise to wear the white man's clothing. He was worried I'd be killed by a citizen.

I was careful to hunt the birds I knew his wife liked and one afternoon I returned and laid out four ducks and a pheasant for the servants to pluck.

"Good day at work, I see." The judge was sitting on the gallery, reading a book.

"Yessir."

"It will be difficult to get you into a proper school, won't it?"

I nodded.

"I have always found it interesting that white children take so quickly to Indian ways, while Indian children, when brought to be raised in white families, never take to it at all. Not that you are a child."

"No sir."

"Of course there is no doubt that the Indian lives closer to the earth and the natural gods. There is simply no question." He closed his book. "Unfortunately there is no more room for that kind of living, Eli. Your and my ancestors departed from it the moment they buried a seed in the ground and ceased to wander like the other creatures. There can be no turning back from that."

"I don't think I'm going to school," I said.

"Well, if you stay around here, at some point you will have to. Especially in m'lady's house. It's not quite proper to have wild Indians sleeping under one's roof."

I considered pointing out that I had two scalps under my belt, that I was a better hunter, tracker, and horseman than any white man in town. The idea of putting me in a school, with children, was ridiculous. But instead I said: "Well, maybe I should go check in with my father's new wife." She lived in Bastrop, which had never really settled up.

"No hurry," he said. "I enjoy your company. But even there, if you want to have a future, you'll have to acquire some education, however painful that might be."

"I could sign with the Rangers right now," I said.

"Of course. But I think it might be in you to do something more important than living among outlaws and mercenaries."

I got sore at this but kept quiet. I tried to consider by what measure I might be thought to need further education. It was just that the whites were crazy for rules. And yet they were in charge. And I was white myself.

One of the Negroes brought us cold tea.

"Something's been bothering me," he said. "Ingrid Goetz wasn't really treated any differently than any other captive, was she?"

"She was treated just as you thought she was."

"So you made that story up to protect her?"

"Yes."

He nodded. "Glad to see your time with the savages has left your humanity intact, Master McCullough."

"Thank you, sir."

"One other thing."

I nodded.

"M'lady's favorite Persian cat is missing and she is worried you might have had something to do with it."

"Absolutely not."

"How are the Indians on cats?"

"I never saw one. Plenty of dogs, though."

"They eat the dogs, don't they?"

"That's the Shoshones," I said. "A dog or coyote is sacred to a Comanche. You would be cursed."

"But they do eat human beings occasionally?"

"That's the Tonkawas," I said.

"Never the Comanches."

"A Comanche who ate a man would be killed by the tribe immediately, because supposedly it becomes an addiction."

"Interesting," he said. He was scratching his chin. "And this Sun Dance they all talk about?

"That's the Kiowas," I said. "We never did that."

SHORTLY AFTER INGRID left, two more captives, sisters from Fredericksburg, were brought in by traders. There was a big fuss until people got a look at them. One had her nose cut off. The other seemed normal but her mind was gone. There was a big announcement in the paper but no one knew what to do with them; they were not talkative and very upsetting to be around so they ended up living in the spare house of the minister, behind the church. I went and visited them at the judge's request, to try to communicate with them, but as soon as I spoke to them in Comanche, they didn't want anything to do with me. They both drowned themselves a few weeks later.

Which, of course, saved everyone a good deal of trouble, as proper society now regarded them to be roughly the same as whores, being they'd been raped by buck Indians. And, unlike a whore, who might renounce her immoral choices and properly redeem herself, these women had no power over what had happened to them, and thus had no power to undo it, either.

I WAS ALREADY getting tired of the judge's house and had taken to sleeping outside. I'd gotten in small trouble for borrowing a neighbor's horse and for shooting various of the neighborhood hogs full of arrows, not to mention that all the other petty larcenies, which had nothing to do with me, were now attributed to my presence.

I admitted to the judge that the Comanches hated swine and I guess I'd inherited that from them. I was severely understimulated. I had no idea what white children did to occupy themselves. They go to school, he told me. I told him the slaughter of the pigs would look like nothing if I was put into school. Which of course was an exaggeration—I would simply walk out. Meanwhile the judge told the neighbors that the state would reimburse them, as I was still adjusting back to civilized life.

One afternoon he sat me down: "Master McCullough, I don't mean to suggest you aren't welcome in my house, but it might be time to pay your father's new family a visit down in Bastrop. M'lady believes this might do you some good, if you know what I mean."

"She doesn't like me."

"She admires your spirit greatly," he said. "But one of the Negroes discovered a few items that he believed to be human scalps and reported as much to m'lady."

"The niggers went into my bag?"

"They are naturally curious," he said. "My apologies."

"Where is it now?"

"It has been deposited above the stables for safekeeping. Don't worry, I told them they would be whipped if even a single item was missing."

"I guess I will leave today, then."

"No need for that," he said. "But soon."

I gathered my things and asked the Negroes to return the scalps they'd stolen, along with my madstone.

Then I went and found the judge in his study and thanked him and made him a present of my butcher knife and beaded sheath. I had liberated a better one, a fine bowie knife, from one of the judge's neighbors who had kept it in a glass case: supposedly it had been owned by Jim Bowie himself. I would have given it to the judge, but I did not want to get him in trouble. As for my Indian knife, the judge asked: "This ever raise any hair?"

"Some," I said.

He raised his eyebrows.

"Only Mexican and Indian," I lied.

He looked at the knife.

"I'll have a display case made for it. I know just the man to do it."

"Whatever you like," I said.

"I'm honored to meet you, young man. You're headed for great things if you don't get yourself hanged. I think you'll find that not all servants of the law are as liberal minded as yours truly; that judge in Bastrop is a real prick, in fact, he's one of my greatest enemies and I would not mention our friendship to him if you can avoid it."

That night I left for Bastrop, over the judge's objections, as he said I ought to catch a wagon in the morning. I could see the mistress felt guilty about having me removed, and the children, when they found out I was leaving, wept and could not be consoled; their eldest daughter jumped on me and began kissing my neck and crying hysterically.

But I felt free again, as the judge's forty acres, though he was quite proud of it, seemed to me like a postage stamp; I was used to having twenty or so million at my disposal. And Austin was overrun with people, five thousand and climbing; it was impossible to walk along the river without being interrupted by the clinking of horsebells and the cries of boatmen. Anyone could see there were too many pigs for the tits.

CHAPTER THIRTY-TWO

JEANNIE McCULLOUGH

I t was near first light when she fell asleep and sometime later she heard him calling. She opened her eyes. By the sound of it he was right outside her door and though she'd been thinking about him all night, she found herself afraid and not sure what to do so she stayed quiet. She could hear him there in the hallway.

Finally she got the nerve to call out, "I'll be down in a minute. Tell Flores to make you coffee."

She heard him go downstairs. Then she was sorry. She told herself it was only because she didn't want him seeing her like this, puffy faced and without makeup, but she knew that wasn't true. *I'm a coward,* she thought. She washed and put her hair back and made herself up. Then she went to the kitchen.

"How'd you sleep?" she said.

"Pretty good, I guess."

If the comment hurt her, she didn't show it.

After breakfast, he went to fiddle with the maps and as she was carrying the lunch basket out to the truck, her eye caught on the serving cart with its bottle of whiskey and silver cocktail shaker. She put them into the basket, chiding herself the entire time, wondering how she might explain it if she were somehow caught, or if he objected, but it occurred to her there was no one to catch her, and this made her feel both better and worse, and then it seemed to her that as far as Hank was concerned, things could not move quickly enough. She went back to the kitchen and wrapped a block of ice in some towels and she needed sugar as well. She could always get rid of it if she changed her mind.

As they were driving away from the house, she said, "Pull up next to that stock tank."

He complied. She got out and picked a big handful of mint and put it in the basket. "What is that for?" he said.

"Refreshments."

"I will take your word for it."

A few hours later, when he was satisfied he had seen enough of the country to take a break, they ate lunch at the stream by the old Garcia house. Along the stream were a few young cottonwoods; she excused herself and picked her way down the steep embankment and plucked a handful of the buds, then walked back up to see him. She scraped the sap of the buds with her fingernail.

"Here," she said.

"What is it?"

"Just smell it."

He gave her a skeptical look and then she put her hand near his face.

"Whoa," he said. He seized her arm and pulled her whole hand in and they sat like that. She could feel his breath on her wrist.

"I wish I could smell that the rest of my life."

"It's the sap of the buds," she said. "You can only get it a few times a year."

"What's it taste like?"

"Try it."

"Off your fingers?"

She shrugged. She watched him . . . hoping for . . . she didn't know. But he put only the tip of her finger into his mouth, then removed it quickly.

"Smells better than it tastes," he said, and laughed.

She sat there hoping he would kiss her, but he didn't move, in fact he let go of her wrist.

"This is country," he said, looking out over the savannah.

She forced herself to nod. Something had settled over her which blotted out the light.

"The company is not bad, either."

She nodded again. They could hear the stream running and the locusts.

"And if you are telling me that I am hard to beat as well, I agree with you."

"I didn't say anything at all," she said.

"That is what I am choosing to hear."

"Well, you have not said anything like that to me." Thinking, *He is an idiot*. She was in no mood for clever talk, the moment had passed, it was ruined.

"You are a beautiful girl." He reached his hand toward her cheek, then stopped. "But . . ."

"I am going to make us those refreshments," she said, though she was not sure she wanted to.

"We ought to get moving," he said. He sat up and began to gather his things. "It might be difficult for me to explain how bad I need this work."

He started to stand but she took his hand and pressed it to her mouth.

"You do not know very much about your uncle, do you?"

She shook her head and kept hold of him.

"He will have me hanged. After I am shot and stabbed."

"He will not," she said. "You will remain on the blanket." She felt jittery; she hoped it didn't show.

"I am the dumbest man alive." But he stayed where he was.

She retrieved the julep fixings from the truck, mixed the mint and sugar and a good deal of bourbon in the shaker, crushed it all together and added the ice. She had forgotten to bring glasses. She supposed he would not mind. She sat down again and passed him the shaker.

"That is a rather large refreshment," he said. She noticed that in her absence he had spread the blanket out neatly, and moved it farther into the shade, and she was jittery again.

"I forgot the cups," she said. "We will have to share."

"I have no objection."

"I doubted you would. This is my great-grandfather's recipe," she added.

He took a big sip. "That is a delicious julep." He coughed. "My Lord. Be careful it doesn't put hair on your chest."

"I have been drinking these since I was a child." She took a sip, and then another, and felt it go to her head instantly.

"Oh my," she said. She lay back.

"You okay?"

She nodded.

"You look to be in distress."

Still, he hesitated. He wasn't like the others. She felt the annoyance coming back and then she decided she liked it. She took his hand and pulled him over. They kissed for a long time, in what she thought was a very considerate way; he mostly stayed to one side of her. Then she was waiting and wanting for his hands to wander but they didn't. She began to move her hips and then he stopped kissing her and the feeling of embarrassment came back; she had somehow gone too far again.

"What's wrong?" she said.

"I believe we should continue our search for oil and I also believe that your great-uncle will kill me."

He does not mean kill, she thought, *he means ruin,* and it was depressing to hear people worrying about money; she felt herself get cold inside. She did not want to look at him. She decided that if she never saw him again, she would not mind. Maybe that wasn't fair. She made herself say, "He won't hear a word about it."

"Thirdly, though it is against my own self-interest to mention this, I can take one look at that house and see I am not right for you."

She knew what he meant but she pretended not to. She felt tired, enormously tired, she was tired of these men being nice to her, she wanted him to lift up her dress or push her against a wall, she wanted him to stop asking and stop talking. "Do you have a bad reputation?" she made herself say.

"I have no reputation. I've spent my life chasing oil instead of chasing tail." Then he added: "Unfortunately, and my dad was more the type to dip me in the water than send me to the whorehouse."

"It decreases your risk of a disease."

"Yes, though it increases my risk of losing a limb."

"Is it really that dangerous?" A stupid thing to say: obviously it was dangerous, he'd just lost his father. But she found she did not care at that minute, she did not want to go in this direction, she did not care about his father or anyone else.

"It's getting safer all the time."

"You could do anything you wanted," she said, "it is plain to see just watching you."

"I happen to like doing this."

It was quiet.

"Just so you know, my being broke is a temporary situation. Though fortunate for your family."

She pulled him over and kissed him again. They stayed like that for a while, but still his hands didn't wander, it was frustrating, she was ready to give herself to him, she had a feeling she might not ever see him again, she wondered if there was something about her, about her body or about her face or just something else entirely, that men didn't like.

Perhaps they sensed her inexperience, perhaps they thought she would not be good at it, or that it would mean too much to her; *it means nothing*, she wanted to tell him, *it feels like a curse to me and I want to be rid of it*. Or perhaps they did not think about her that way at all. Perhaps she was simply someone nice to talk to. She began to feel cold again.

"I guess we have to get back to work?"

"We should," he said.

"Okay," she said. "Great. That is a great idea." She sat up and gathered her things quickly and walked to the truck ahead of him. She could feel his eyes on her, he did not know what he'd done wrong, but she didn't care. She wanted to go home.

THEY SPENT THE rest of the day driving, stopping every so often so he could make marks on his maps.

"How do people find their way around here?" he said. "It all looks the same."

"It doesn't look the same at all," she said.

"Perhaps I'll get used to it."

"How long will you be down here?" She did not care, she was just asking.

"If we find oil? It could be years if I am not hanged from that oak tree in front of your house."

"That is a cedar elm," she said.

"We will see."

"Do you always talk so much?" she said.

He blushed and looked out his window and it got quiet and awkward again. She considered asking to be dropped off at the house but instead she said, "Did you ever go to school?"

"To a certain extent."

"What does that mean?"

"I am a proud graduate of the sixth grade."

"I guess it's better than nothing."

"Even that is an exaggeration, unfortunately."

"You seem to be able to read and write."

"As we say back home, there are coonasses and then there are coonasses. I am the first type."

That night they took supper with the vaqueros. Hank spoke to them in Spanish. She could tell they liked him, though they were suspicious, and also, she could see, jealous, which surprised her. Her feelings came back. But when supper was over and all the maids and Flores and Hugo were cleaning up, he excused himself. "We need to get an early start tomorrow," he told them. "Good night." Not a word to her. She went to bed furious.

THE NEXT MORNING they were driving and she ordered him to stop to collect more mint.

"You are intent on making sure we don't get any work done, aren't you?"

"You'll be here a year."

"If your uncle doesn't throw me off."

"Fine. I don't care what we do."

"Don't sound disappointed."

"Too late," she said.

"Are you really?"

"Yes, I am."

"I didn't know."

This made her furious. "You are quite stupid."

He reached over and tried to take her hand. At first she didn't let him.

THAT AFTERNOON THEY laid a blanket out in the shade. She encouraged his hands to wander, which they did, but then there was the natural pause and it seemed to not go any further. She felt her interest peak and decline, all the heat seemed to go out of her, as if she were already feeling a disappointment that had not arrived. She decided to think about it mechanically, a problem she might solve, and she made herself sit up and unbutton Hank's shirt, though she was not sure exactly how to get it off his back, and then she undid his belt and the buttons of his pants. He didn't stop her but he gave her a questioning look. She nodded. Then he took over and a few seconds later he was entirely naked. And then she was as well. He was suspended in the air over her, looking at her breasts, at the rest of her body, she guessed he was enjoying it but he might also have been judging, either way it was uncomfortable and she pulled him on top of her.

They lay there, sliding a little, then more, and after a time it was unbearable, she began to push against him much harder, she was not sure how to get what she wanted, she lifted her hips, and then again, and then suddenly he was inside her. It had not hurt at all. In fact it was the opposite. She pulled him closer and then it hurt, though it stopped again immediately. It was like a paper-thin wall between what pinched and what felt exactly as she'd hoped. Then he began to take over and she forgot herself for a moment, then remembered again and began to wonder if the only reason they made such a big deal about the pain was to keep you from doing it every minute of your life.

She could see the trees above her, then she was not sure, it did not seem like she was any particular place at all, she wondered if she was bleeding, *there will be blood,* they said, *blood blood blood,* as if this were the worst thing on earth, she wanted to laugh, she must not laugh, it would not be taken the right way. She was in and out of her body, in and out of sleep, here and then somewhere else, and then here again. On a blanket with a man on top of her, a rock or stick or something hard in her back. She pulled him tight against her. It went on a long time until he pulled out of her suddenly. She knew why but she was still sorry.

Then he said, "Sorry," as well.

"For what?" She kissed his neck.

"It'll be better next time."

"I liked it."

"It will be better."

"Go back in," she said.

"Give me a few minutes." He rolled off and lay next to her with his leg over her.

She began to move her hips. It felt like she was breaking some rule and she was happy. "Can you use your hand?" She had a feeling she was being greedy, but he happily complied.

She could feel it building, it was much better than anything she'd tried herself, but before she finished he climbed on top again.

"Go slower and take longer strokes," she told him.

He did and she felt a sort of heat washing over her, like someone had dipped her in a warm bucket *(red paint,* she thought, *it feels red),* she could feel it spreading from her waist.

Later it began to feel very good again and he pulled out of her just as suddenly. She held him so he wouldn't go away. He tried to lift his head to kiss her neck. She could see he didn't have the energy. He was like a person drunk or asleep, he moved his mouth from her ear to her shoulder without actually kissing her. He had nice breath. She held him tighter.

"Did you?" He said, after a minute.

Had he really not been able to tell? She was hurt and then no, she was just being sensitive. It was likely normal.

He was talking again, "Do you think . . ."

"Shhhhhh," she said. "Shhhhhh shhhhhhhh shhhhhhhh." She still felt like she was underwater, or in a warm bath. She woke up a short while later, her heart was beating strangely, it was not hers, but his. *Blood,* she thought again, she found this hilarious, people were stupid, she could not believe it, *silly,* she thought. She began to stroke his back, she kissed his hair. He sighed but didn't wake up. There was a breeze and she could hear the trickling of the water from the spring where it ran down the hill past the old church, where her brothers had found the grave, *all gone,* she thought, *all dead,* she watched the sun flickering. *If I died . . .*

A short while later Hank was inside her again but now her bladder was full. He continued to move but she wanted to get up. She was not exactly sure what to say to him and she began to wonder if she'd given away something valuable, the most valuable thing she had, without asking for a single thing in return, without even asking for a promise. She wanted to stop him and be reassured, but this was not a good idea, he might say anything now.

As if he'd been reading her thoughts, he seemed to wake up and all his weight came off her.

"Was I smothering you?"

"No," she said.

He rolled off slightly, she sighed as he came out. They lay together, legs entangled, for a long time, until finally she had to get up or there would be a real accident, there was no getting around it.

"Where are you going?"

"I need a minute alone," she said.

"For what?" Then he realized.

She slipped her dress on and her shoes and scooted off to the other side of the house.

When she came back to the blanket he was still naked, lying with the sun spotted all over him. It was nice in the shade. She ran her hands over his chest. It was bony, though he had muscle there, his shoulders were thin as well, though ropy, there was just nothing extra anywhere on his body. She traced the thin line of dark hairs from his belly button down below his waist, his . . . (*penis,* she thought), there were a variety of words but she was not sure which was correct in this situation, it was lying against his leg, much darker than the rest of him. It was covered with a dried-up film, and there were spots of that on his belly as well. She touched him and he flinched.

"Does it hurt?"

"Surprised me, is all."

It seemed small now. Very small. She nearly said something about this, then decided against it.

"What do you think Phineas would say?" she asked.

"That is a very scary thought."

"I think he will be happy," she said.

"You are probably the only person in Texas who thinks so. But . . ." He shrugged. "I imagine he knew this would happen. Or something like it."

"Though maybe not so soon."

"I cannot see how he would approve of me for you, but he is no dummy, either. I was surprised when he asked me to drive you home. That did not make sense to me. I took one look at you and thought . . ."

"What," she said.

"I thought you would never speak to me, that's all."

"Why would he have sent us down here together?"

"I think the main reason was I am willing to work cheap."

"He is not stupid," she said.

"Oh, he is definitely not stupid. I have no doubt about that."

"I mean he likes you. He does not like many people."

"Huh."

"And maybe because we're both orphans."

"I'd never thought of it that way."

"Really?"

"No," he said.

It was quiet.

"It's up to you how you're going to feel about that stuff," he said. "People have it a lot worse."

"You don't really like me," she said.

"You're right. I can't tell if I like you or not."

She pushed him.

"You look nice in the sun."

"I feel nice," she said. She had taken her dress off again. The sun was nothing but spots on the other side of her eyelids. "I could lie here forever."

THEY MADE LOVE again that night and then went off to their bedrooms on opposite sides of the house. She did not want Flores suspecting anything, though why this concerned her, she wasn't sure, she lay there and felt slightly guilty, again wondering if she'd made a mistake.

But when morning came her first thought was of him, of why he was not in bed with her, and she hugged her pillow toward her and lay half on top of it, then kissed it, imagining it was his neck. Then she got a strange feeling. She wondered if she ought to stay home today. To lock herself in her room and not come out . . . it was an extravagance, something she might use up, she should not waste it all at once. Yes, it was certain, she should not see him. It would not do to get used to him.

Time was passing and she realized that he must be waiting for her downstairs; she got a nervous excited feeling and made herself up quickly and hurried to meet him.

They ate breakfast slowly, both struggling for things to talk about while staring intensely at Flores's back and willing her to leave as soon as possible. Finally Jeannie had told her, in what she hoped was an innocent voice (though it was not, it could not be), that she and Hank would clean up.

When Flores was gone they pulled each other's clothes off in the pantry, they tried it first standing up, but it was not satisfying and finally she was on the floor, among the bags of beans and flour, she felt a brief cold flash as if her father was seeing and judging her and then she decided she would do as she pleased.

SIX MONTHS LATER the first drilling rig was up and running. After all the shot testing, Hank decided the best place to start was in one of the old Garcia pastures. He insisted (disgustingly, she thought at first, then endearingly) on putting the samples of rock into his mouth; he plucked them right from the shale shaker. They were starting to taste like oil, he claimed, and if she wanted to learn the business, she would have to learn how it tasted. He offered her a crumbly piece of limestone from several thousand feet below the earth. It was wet with drilling mud, she smelled it, it was sulfurous and disgusting. She touched it to her tongue and wanted to gag immediately; it did taste like oil, but it tasted like other things as well, like something bitter or rotten, it had been in the damp earth for eighty or a hundred million years.

Near the end of the day the big Cummins diesel had suddenly changed pitch, the drill string gave a little hop and then dropped into the hole and then the derrick, the entire steel superstructure above them, gave a loud groan as if suddenly burdened.

"Not good," Hank said.

The engine was running with less strain, it was quieter, but the hands were suddenly moving with purpose. There was a movement high in the derrick; the derrickman had come off the monkey board; he was half jumping, half sliding down the ladder. He brushed past her, running down the stairs toward the mud pits; a short time later, the mud motor got louder.

Nothing seemed to have changed but everyone was running around like a circus. It was amusing. She leaned back against the railing.

The piperacker and tongman were cutting sacks of yellow barite powder and dumping them into the mud pits; the derrickman was pumping mud from the reserve.

Now she could see a change: the return mud pipe, which had been flowing smoothly out onto the shale shaker all day, began to burp and sputter. The drilling mud was what kept the drill string in the hole; the drilling mud was the only thing keeping gas from blowing out of the wellbore.

She began to get nervous. A minute later there was a popping noise and mud blew out over the top of the traveling block. There was a sulfur smell and Hank pointed at her and said: "Get out of here."

"Why?"

"We're getting kicked."

Then he stopped paying attention to her again. She was not sure if he was treating her like a girl. She decided she would not be treated any differently. She stayed where she was. She would never learn this if she went running off every time things got complicated.

"Get off the rig," he said again, but she didn't. He declutched the drill string and dropped the rams. More drilling mud blew out over the traveling block, spattering her dress and shoes.

"Get the fuck off the rig, Jeannie." He shoved her roughly to the edge of the stairs. She looked back at him and finally went down. He was ignoring her again. She sat on a rock a few yards away. She was scared, though she was not sure of what. On the other hand if something happened . . . it was fine. She would be there with him.

After ten or fifteen minutes, the burping stopped. Mud began to flow into the pits again. The men began to laugh and the way they were clapping each other on the back, all talking very fast and grinning uncontrollably, she knew they had all been afraid. There were hundreds of empty Baroid sacks blowing around in the wind.

Hank waved to the motorman to shut the engine down and the hands all sat by the doghouse. One of them lit a cigarette, but Hank reached over and plucked it out of his mouth and crushed the ash carefully into the dirt.

"Maybe we can hold off on that cowboy shit, you think?"

The man nodded.

Then he turned to Jeannie: "Next time I ask you to leave, you leave."

"How am I going to learn if I leave when things go wrong?" she said.

"You would not have learned anything. This would have been a fireball they would have seen from town."

The roughnecks were slumped on a bench in the doghouse. The derrickman was pacing back and forth, cursing the mud pumps.

"What about the rams?" she said.

"Sometimes the gas is coming up no matter what. You can do everything perfect but you can't always stop it."

After that she did not want to be away from him. If he was on a well that blew out, she would be on it as well. She would not be alone again.

CHAPTER THIRTY-THREE

DIARIES OF PETER McCULLOUGH

JUNE 25, 1917

Tonight she found me in my office. I had given her one of the trucks to take to Carrizo, half expecting she would never return.

"Did I scare you?"

"A little," I said. I realized I had indeed been expecting her to disappear, which had made me feel both relieved and depressed.

She looked around. "All these books. And you sleep here?"

I nodded.

"Because of me?"

"I got in the habit before my wife left," I told her, which was not entirely a lie.

She took a seat on the sofa. "Look at me," she said, holding out her hands. "I'm like a dead person. I can't stand to even look in the mirror."

"You just need to eat and rest."

"I can't stay that long," she said.

"I already told you I don't mind."

"But I do."

It was quiet and she looked around again.

"How old are you?"

"I am eleven years younger than you are," she said. "Though I now look older."

"You are still very pretty." It was not true, not really, and yet all the blood went to my face. If it is possible to make an improvement in four days, she had. Her skin was no longer dry, her lips less cracked, her hair washed and shining. But she didn't appear to notice my compliment.

"You know I imagined telling you all these things for years now, but when I see it hurts you, I feel guilty. Then I am angry at myself for feeling guilty. And yet the past two nights, I have slept very well here. Which also makes me feel guilty. I guess I am the coward after all."

"That's ridiculous," I said.

"You're not in a position to judge."

She continued to look around the room, at all my books, floor to ceiling, and her eyes got soft again but I could not help the feeling she was not long for this earth; I had seen dead people with more weight to their bodies.

"There are many farmers here now?"

"Yes."

"And the other Mexican families? The ones who were here?"

"Some of them went to Michigan to work. Some disappeared. Some are dead."

She asked which ones. I opened my journal and told her what I had written, though I mostly knew it from memory.

Killed in the riots: Llewellyn and Morena Pierce, Custodio and Adriana Morales, Fulgencio Ypina, Sandro Viejo, Eduardo Guzman, Adrian and Alba Quireno, all four of the Gonzalo Gomezes, all ten of the Rosario Sotos except the two youngest, who were adopted by the Herreras.

Fled during or after the riots: the Alberto Gomezes, the Claudio Lopezes, the Janeros, the Sapinosos, the Urracas, the Ximenes, the Romeros, the Reyes, Domingo Lopez, unrelated to Claudio, Antonio Guzman, unrelated to Eduardo (killed), Vera Florez, the Vera Cruzes, the Delgados, the Urrabazes.

"There may have been others I have not heard about."

"Well, you wrote them down," she said. "That is something."

"There are more," I said.

The ones who had moved to Detroit for work: the Adora Ortizes, the Ricardo Gomezes, the Vargases, the Gilberto Guzmans, the Mendezes, the Herreras (including the two daughters of Rosario Soto), the Riveras, Freddy Ramirez and his family.

"Do you own all our land," she said, "or was it split with the Reynoldses and Midkiffs?"

"Just us. And some farmers from the North." Which was true, but also a lie, and I was sorry I'd said it.

"For taxes, I guess."

"They said your father was in arrears."

"He was not. Obviously."

I looked out the window.

"There is so much anger in me," she said, "that I sometimes cannot understand how I still breathe."

JULY 1, 1917

María Garcia has been here ten days. According to Consuela, when I am gone she wanders the house or sits on the gallery staring out over the land that used to be her family's or plays the piano that used to be my mother's. When I come back from the pastures she is usually playing the piano—she seems to know it is a kind of present for me.

After supper I find her in the library. We both like the same places in the house—the library, the parlor, the west side of the gallery. The small protected places where you can see a long way, or hear if someone is coming.

When I ask about her plans she says she would like to continue to eat, and when she is done eating she will make other plans. She is already looking better, gaining weight, the years dropping off.

"When it becomes inconvenient," she tells me, "I'll be on my way."

I don't tell her it is already inconvenient, that my father has already demanded that she leave. "Where would you go?"

She shrugs.

Then I say, "How's old Mexico these days?" as if I don't know the answer.

"They pick you up on the street, or when you are coming out of the movies, or from a cantina, and say here is a gun, you are now a Zapatista or a Carrancista or a Villista, depending on who catches you. If you protest, or if they find out you were on another side, they kill you."

"You must have friends from university?"

"That was fifteen years ago. And most of them left when things got bad."

"Michigan?" I regret saying it immediately.

"Those are not my people." But she shrugs and I can see she forgives me.

I look at the light coming in on her hair, which shines, and the line of her neck, where there is the faintest hint of sweat. It occurs to me that she has very nice skin. She leans back into the stream of air from the fan, kicks her foot up and down, looking at the slipper on it, which she must have gotten somewhere in the house.

"I'll be fine," she says. "It's nothing for you to worry about."

JULY 2, 1917

Went to see my father to discuss the matter further. The drillers have run out of coal for their boiler and the silence is a relief. Forgot what silence sounded like.

The Colonel was sitting in the shade on the gallery of his house, which is more like a jacal. It does not have nearly the view of the main house, but it is in a copse of oaks, with a live stream running past it, and is ten degrees cooler than any other place on the ranch. He still sleeps in a brush arbor at night (though he has run an electric wire and keeps his Crocker fan blowing) and refuses to use an indoor toilet, preferring to squat in the bushes. Walking around his house is a bit like walking through a minefield.

"This heat," he said. "We should have bought on the Llano."

It was 110 at the big house, 100 at his jacal.

"We'd have to shovel snow," I said.

"That is the problem with having a family. Take a man like Goodnight, does whatever the hell he wants, moved himself right up to Palo Duro when the Comanches left."

"Charles Goodnight has a family. A wife, anyway."

He looked at me.

"Molly."

"Well, he never talks about them." Then he changed the subject: "There is a man coming here in the next few weeks, name of Snowball. He's a Negro I knew from the old days. He may be here awhile."

I cleared my throat and said: "There is also the matter of this Garcia girl."

"She is not as good-looking as her mother. I will say that for her."

"She is pretty enough."

"I want her making dust as soon as possible."

"She's sick."

"It's not in the best interest, Pete."

"The best interest."

"There are three events regarding this woman. The first is her brother-in-law shot your son. The second is that, with a half-dozen law enforcement officers present, we went to capture the guilty parties. Unfortunately things did not go as hoped."

"That is an inaccuracy, at best."

He waved his hand furiously, as if my words were a stale odor. "The final thing is her father's land was put up in a tax sale by the State of Texas, which would have happened sooner or later, whether they were living on the property or not, as they had not been paying their taxes."

I snorted.

"It is in the records."

"Which makes it all the more likely to be a lie."

"Pete, there are many things I have wanted to save: the Indians, the buffalo, a prairie where you could look twenty miles and not see a fence post. But time has passed those things by."

How about your wife, I thought, but I remained silent.

"Give her some money and get rid of her. By the weekend."

"She will leave over my dead body."

He opened his mouth but nothing came out. By his color, he must have been very hot.

"Now don't go getting up on your ear," I heard him start, but I was already walking away, my hands hidden in my pockets as they were shaking. They did not stop shaking until after I got back to the house.

CALLED SALLY, HOPING she might be a voice of reason. We had not spoken in a month—she does her communicating through Consuela—and she was surprised to hear from me. Says she has no interest in returning to McCullough Springs. Greatest mistake of her life. We discussed Charlie and Glenn, who are still in training. We both agreed it was unlikely they would ever make it to the war. I suspected Charlie would be disappointed by this, but I did not say it.

After a time she mentioned that she spent two weeks in the Berkshire Mountains in Massachusetts with a "friend." She wondered if I had heard anything of it, if perhaps that was the reason I had called. Ridiculousness of asking her opinion about María Garcia suddenly apparent; I became annoyed at myself for calling her, annoyed at my own desperation. But she thought I was annoyed at her tryst and immediately became conciliatory.

"I'm sad you're not here," she said. "It would be more fun if you were."

"I'm just working."

Silence.

"Are we separated?"

"I don't know."

"But we are taking some time away from each other."

"I don't care what you do," I told her.

"I'm just asking. I'm trying to figure out our status."

"You can do whatever you want."

"I know you don't care, Peter. You don't care about anyone but yourself and your sadness. That is what you care about the most, making sure you are as unhappy as possible."

"The things you do haven't bothered me before," I said. "I don't know why they would now."

"I am trying to figure out how it's possible that I still love you, but I do. I want you to know that. You can still save this whenever you want."

"That's nice," I told her.

Silence.

"Say," she finally said. "How is that drilling going?"

WENT DOWN TO see about dinner.

"Your father says I am not to cook for her," said Consuela.

I shrugged.

"I'll make extra for you," she said.

Of course there is no one to talk to, even Consuela; I know what her answer will be. What anyone's answer will be. The right thing is to get rid of her. Perhaps for her own good.

AFTER A TEN-MINUTE search I find her in the library. The nicest spot in the house, as most of the windows face north and there are a few seeps hidden among the rocks to keep the view green.

"What's wrong?" she says.

I shrug.

"I saw you walking back from your father's house."

I shrug again.

"Of course. Consuela's given me a few things, I'll get them together."

"Didn't your family have a bank account?"

"They did," she said, "and what little I could withdraw I used to live."

"Is there really nowhere else?"

"Don't worry about me."

"He's always done this," I say, referring to the Colonel.

"The land makes people crazy."

"It's not the land."

"No, my great-uncle was the same. A person to him was an obstacle, like a drought, or a cow that would not do what he wanted. If you crossed him he might cut your heart out before he came to his senses. If his sons had lived . . ." She shrugs. "Of course we didn't belong here, my father was two years into university when his uncle died. But . . ." She shrugs again. "He was a romantic."

"He was a good man," I say.

"He was vain. He loved the idea of being a hidalgo, he was always telling us how blessed we were to live on the land. But really, there was no *we*. It was only him. He could not accept that his neighbors might one day kill him, and so he kept us all there, despite the risks, which we were all aware of."

It gets quiet.

"You don't belong here, either," she says. "You've probably always known it and here you are."

Not always, of course, but perhaps since my mother died. Though I cannot tell her that story; it does not compare to her own. Instead I tell her another:

"I remember when I was a kid, we caught this boy who my father thought had stolen cattle from us. He was maybe twelve or so, but he wouldn't tell my father anything so my father threw a rope over the top of the gate, put it around the boy's neck, and tied the other end to a horse. When they let him down he started talking. He scratched a map in the dirt and said the men we were looking for were white, that they'd made him come along because they didn't know the land."

She nods. I can't tell if I should continue or not. But I do:

"I was taking the noose off him when my father slapped the horse and the boy went back up in the air."

"And then?"

"He died."

"Did they catch the others?"

"He hanged the ones he didn't shoot."

"The sheriff?"

"No, my father."

THERE WERE NINE of them but the last four gave themselves up and my father stripped the saddles off their horses and found a proper cottonwood and hung them with their own ropes. I held the camphene lamp while Phineas put the nooses on. At first Phineas was nervous but the last man he noosed he told: *It'll all be over in a minute, partner.*

That is real kind of you, said the man.

My father said: *Either way you're hanging, Paco. It's just whether it's now or in a few weeks in Laredo.*

I'll take the few weeks. Spit popping in his mouth.

You ought to be happy we aren't skinning you, said my father.

MARÍA HAS COME to sit next to me. The sun is going down, the light in the room is dim. She brushes a hair behind her ear and I swallow. Her eyes are soft. She touches my hand. "You should stop thinking about it," she says.

I can't. But that is difficult to explain to people, so I don't say anything.

PHINEAS STOOD BESIDE one of the horses and slapped it, then moved down the line to slap the next one. When the last man dropped it was quiet except for the ropes creaking and the men gurgling and shitting as they pedaled their legs. They were still kicking when my father said: *There's some nice saddles here.*

"PETER?"

Her hand is covering mine and I am afraid to move.

"That is in me somewhere," I say.

We sit there like that and I wonder if something might happen but we both know there is nothing right about it.

CHAPTER THIRTY-FOUR

ELI McCULLOUGH

Early 1852

I arrived in Bastrop and found the address of my new home, a rickety frame house with multiple rooms added, built before statehood when materials were thin. But there was a large front yard with flowers and grass and a whitewashed fence.

My stepmother was in her forties, with a harsh expression and a tightly tied bonnet. She looked like she'd been raised on sour milk and when the Indians thought of white people, she is the person they imagined, from the look she gave, she did not exactly think me nickel-plated, either. Her two sons were both taller than me and they smirked. I made up my mind to bash their heads.

"You must be Eli."

"Yes," I said.

"Well, we found some clothes for you. You can change out of those things. You better give that pistol to Jacob."

The taller one was reaching for my Colt. I slapped his hand away.

"We lock our guns up here," she said.

I slapped his hand away again.

"Mother."

She looked at me for a long time and then said: "Let him be."

I had a pallet in the same room as the other two boys, who were eyeing my bow, knife, pistol; everything I owned. As soon as I'd been given the tour I went on a walk, and, after losing my stepbrothers, who were trying to follow me, I buried the pistol and everything else I cared about in my bag, taking only my bow and arrow and a small wallet of things I did not think would interest anyone.

On the way back I saw my stepbrothers walking in circles, trying to cut my trail, considered ambushing them but decided against it, and made my way back to the house.

That night we had salt pork, which I would not touch. I ate most of the corn bread and all the butter, though. The family was originally from East Texas and did not believe in buying wheat. The fact they had butter was a small miracle.

I could not fault my stepmother as she had bought me a new set of clothes, including shoes, and the next morning I was dressed up like her sons, tripping over my shoes the first time I walked in them, which inspired great hilarity in everyone but myself.

The state was paying for my schooling, on the judge's orders, and there was one room and a very young teacher trying to teach two dozen children of all ages. After sitting a few minutes I stood up so I would not fall asleep. I felt sorry for the other students, who could not imagine saying no to this teacher or anyone else; they were going to spend entire lives doing things just like this. I felt so sorry for them I nearly burst out crying. The teacher forgot how nice she was and came after me with a paddle and I let her chase me awhile before going out the window.

I spent the rest of the day building snares and setting them, walking in and out of people's barns. I stole a mare, rode her for an hour, and returned her to her stall. I watched a pretty older woman reading a book on her back porch, her fine brown hair going gray, just wearing a shift on account of it being warm. She adjusted one breast and then the other and then reached up under her shift and left her hand there, which was too much. I ran off and had a few moments to myself. I thought I could probably make it in Bastrop.

When I got back home, my stepmother was waiting.

"I heard you left school," she said, "and I heard you were seen on Mr. Wilson's horse and I heard you were walking around the yard of the Edmunds, looking in their windows."

How she had learned this I did not know. I expected her to check my hands for the mark of Onan. Then I noticed a strange smell. Something was burning and I went to the fireplace and saw that some person had put my moccasins, bow, arrows, and loincloth into the flames.

"The man who built that bow is dead," I told her. "It cannot be replaced."

"You need to put those days behind you, Eli."

If she had been male I would have killed her and not thought another thing about it. Later I would consider this and decide we were both lucky.

"Jacob and Stuart brought your shoes back for you."

"I'm not wearing those fucking things," I said.

I went to my pallet and took the wool blanket off it, then went into the kitchen. I took a knife and some things I found in the drawers, a ball of sisal, a needle and thread, a half loaf of corn pone.

"Eli, you may take whatever you want," said my stepmother. "It all belongs to you. This is your home now."

It was a queer way to act. She was either softheaded or a Quaker.

I WAS SURE I'd be followed by my stepbrothers so the trail I left them led right to a patch of quicksand. From there I made some footprints that led to a rattlesnake den. Finally I went to the tree where I'd buried my things and dug up my bag, which contained my revolver and various other pieces of gear, all in fine condition.

After walking another hour I found a high overlook with a stream running in front of it and plenty of shade. I made a fire and fell asleep wrapped in the blanket, listening to the wolves howl. I howled back and we went on for a while like that. I kept my Colt under my knees,

Indian-style, but I knew I was not going to need it for anything, the country was too settled up.

The next morning I hacked down a bunch of saplings with my stolen bowie knife, which was indeed a very good knife, heavy but nicely balanced; even after batoning through some of the saplings it was not dulled at all. I wondered if Jim Bowie had actually owned it but by then for him to own all the knives attributed to him he would have had to live a thousand years. I made a drying rack and a frame for a brush arbor. But there was not much point in working so hard. I lay down in the sun and looked out over the green hills; I had forgotten how warm it was in the lowlands. I thought of all my friends buried up on the snowy Llano, cried for a while, and fell asleep.

That afternoon I shot two does and skinned and flayed out the meat and hung it on the racks to dry. I teased out the long sinew from the backbones and cleaned and washed the stomachs. One of the legbones I sharpened into a passable scraper and fleshed both the hides. By then the sun was almost down so I built a fire and had a fine supper of venison rubbed with cedar berries, and marrow mixed with dried sugarberries. The next day I decided to find a bee tree.

After a week I'd built another bow and a dozen arrows so inferior to the one Grandfather had made me that it put me into a conniption every time I drew it. I made a new pair of moccasins and a breechcloth, then went back into Bastrop. I walked directly to the backyard of my stepmother, where my stepbrothers kept the hogs they had threatened to feed me to. I shot all the hogs full of arrows.

Their mutt was easily converted with the gift of a bloody piglet, after which we were friends for life. He followed me back into the countryside where my brothers were afraid to go, as they'd been told they would be stolen by Indians. Of course the Indians would not have stolen them; they were more the type to be knocked on the head.

I stayed out a month, missing Toshaway and Prairie Flower and all the others. I guessed Nuukaru and Escuté were out there somewhere in the snow, but how I would find them, I had no idea.

★   ★   ★

I WENT BACK to town often, mostly to steal things that seemed interesting, like horses, which I rode for a while, then left them tied wherever I got tired of them. I let myself into people's houses and enjoyed fresh-baked pie and roasted chicken and all the other bounties of civilization, but when the sun got low I always headed back where I belonged.

It did not take long to figure out that the nicest house in town belonged to a judge by the name of Wilbarger, who was the enemy of my friend in Austin. I would sit in the trees overlooking his backyard, listening to the stream there. Occasionally his wife would come out and read books on the porch. She was the woman I'd seen in the shift, very pretty, somewhere in her forties, but very thin and sad. Everything about her was pale. Her hair, skin, eyes. I did not see how a creature like her might survive in such a sunblasted place, and the servants must have agreed because they were always looking in on her, as if they expected her to die or run off at any moment.

A few times a week she would go walking by herself in the woods, which was safe for someone with sense, but probably not for her, so I would follow at a safe distance. She would walk a stream until she guessed she was alone, then strip naked and swim in some convenient hole. She had a few favorites but they all got more traffic than she supposed. The first time I saw her go under she held her breath so long I nearly dove in to pull her out. She and the judge had as much in common as a Thoroughbred and a cross-eyed donkey.

After swimming she would lie on the rocks in the sun and I would squint to get my look. There were wisps of gray in the hair she had, which was something I had not thought about. I felt certain the judge had not been in there recently. All thunder and no lightning.

AT THE EDGE of town one afternoon I was stopped by a man who identified himself as the sheriff's deputy. He was not pointing his gun but he said he needed to take me in for some questions. I could have slipped him but I was bored and I wondered what jail would be like.

It was not bad. The judge's wife came and cooked for me every day, three meals with pie. Of course I recognized her and she was even prettier up close than from a distance. She was tall and thin with gray eyes and delicate bones and a pleasant manner; one look and you knew she was an import. The local women, most of whom could have wrestled a razorback hog, must have hated her. She had an accent that made her hard to understand but I knew my brother would have liked it. She was English, they said.

Judge Wilbarger, whose Thoroughbreds I'd been riding some nights, came and gave me a lecture on morality.

"I understand you have been through a hard time," he said. "But we cannot have you stealing horses and killing people's livestock."

I nodded.

"I've hanged men for stealing horses."

I nodded again. I hadn't actually stolen any horses, just borrowed them and returned them, probably better behaved than they'd been before I got to them.

"If you are caught breaking the law again, you will be severely punished. This is your only warning. Tell me you understand me, boy. I know you speak English, you were with those Indians not even three years."

"The wind blows softly through the flowers," I said, in Comanche. "Also, you smell like a buffalo's cunt."

"Speak English," said Wilbarger.

"I have stimulated myself to your wife over thirty times."

"English, boy."

Then I didn't say anything.

Finally he got up. "You're smarter than you act, boy. You can be tamed and I will do it if you make me."

They held me three more days but after Wilbarger left, the sheriff let me out of the cell to walk around.

"Don't piss him off," he said. "They told me you came in with scalps but you are gonna get yourself in a tight you can't get out of."

I shrugged.

"Those *were* Indian scalps, weren't they?"

"One was a white man," I said, in English. "But he had been living in Mexico."

He looked at me and burst out laughing. I started laughing as well.

"Is it true all they had you doing all day is riding and shooting?"

"There was a lot of rutting as well," I said.

"Some old fat squaw, I imagine."

I shook my head. "You are only allowed to do it with the young ones. Once they get married they are off-limits."

I could see this idea appealed to him but he did not believe me.

"The one who popped my cherry was twenty and the others were even younger."

"Son of a bitch," he said. "Maybe they will kidnap me."

Then I felt low speaking that way about Prairie Flower. And Hates Work, Big Water Falling, and Always Visiting Someone. It occurred to me that they were the last people in the world who had actually loved me. I got up and went over to the window. I could feel myself getting dauncy.

I heard the sheriff go back to his desk and move some things around and then he came up next to me. He handed me a glass of whiskey.

"So what the hell happened?" he said. "Why'd you come back?"

"Everyone died," I said.

THINKING ABOUT THE Indians had put me in a state and when they let me out I went back to my stepmother's house, thinking I would make good with her, but no one was home. I felt low and I was tired of being by myself. Still no one came home. I got restless. I went to my stepbrothers' room, where I found several nice steel fishhooks, which I pocketed, and a large collection of wrinkled pornographic postcards, which I left in the kitchen for my stepmother. Then I took all their gunpowder and percussion caps and headed back into the woods.

I SLEPT UNDER the brush arbor or under the open sky, set traps, caught raccoons and tanned their hides, killed deer and tanned them as well. I found a pool by an old beaver dam where the water was brown from oak leaves and I buried the hides in the mud under the water. After a few weeks the hair slipped and they were nicely tanned, just stiff.

Among the whites in town I was as popular as the tax collector. I knew they wouldn't put up with much more horse stealing and stock-killing so I mostly stayed where it was natural. But eventually it got to where the deer and wolves did not cut through my lonesome, not to mention I was in a fierce rutting mood, so I went back to check on the judge's wife.

Eventually she came out on the porch. One of the Negroes brought her tea. I was in dire need of stimulation and afterward I fell asleep. When I woke up she was not on the porch and the sun had sunk a good ways. The judge had a few shoats and piglets in a pen and looking at them I got very hungry, I had forgotten to eat for nearly a day. I arrowed one of the piglets but despite all the squealing no one came, I took my time and went into his smokehouse and got a big helping of salt and carried the piglet back to camp.

A few hours later I was lying there, my belly full of the crispy meat, watching the sun go down from my perch. I could not remember why the Comanches hated pork so much. It was likely the best thing I had ever tasted. The wolves howled and I howled back and they howled back at me.

* * *

THE NEXT MORNING the wife went on her daily walk to the swimming hole, but instead of following her I waited until her two Negroes went out on an errand, likely to hump, then slipped into the kitchen. I liberated a bottle of sweet wine and several cigars, smoked one of the cigars and nearly threw up. I was sure I would be sick. I lay there on a couch while my head spun. It was a nice house with wood paneling, thick rugs, paintings everywhere. The couch was firm like no one had ever sat on it.

When I opened my eyes someone was standing over me and I was running before I even woke up. I was nearly to the door when I stopped.

It was the judge's wife.

"You don't have to run," she said. "You looked so peaceful that I didn't want to wake you."

I didn't say anything.

"It is nice to see you again," she said. "I mean, not behind bars. Though I've also seen you out in the yard."

I didn't want to evidence against myself, but I didn't want to lie, either. I stayed quiet.

"So. How is the wild Indian?"

"I am fine," I said.

"People say you're very dangerous."

"Only to hogs."

"Are you responsible for our missing piglet?"

"Depends who's asking."

"We were just going to eat her anyway. Or was it a him? I can't remember." She shrugged. "You can sit down, you know. I'm not going to tell anyone you were here."

"That is all right," I said.

"Did you eat it? They say you just like to kill them."

"That one I ate."

"Well, I am glad."

I didn't say anything.

"You really should have a seat. I can see you were smoking one of Roy's cigars. They're awfully strong."

At the mention of the cigars, I began to feel green at the gills again. I decided I would stay a few minutes. If the judge came home, I would kill him and go back to the Indians.

"What are you doing here?" I said.

"This is my house."

"I mean in Bastrop."

"The judge was the business partner of my first husband."

"Did he pull stakes?"

"He caught the fever in Indianola. The heat here was quite a shock. As were the insects."

"They are worse in Indianola," I said. "Along with everything else."

"I suppose you could slather yourself with mud."

There was something about the way she looked at me and I went and sat on the couch. She sat down as well.

"Are you going to call for the sheriff?"

"I'm thinking about it. You're not going to scalp me, are you?"

"I'm thinking about it."

"How old are you?" she said.

"Nineteen." Of course I was only sixteen but on account of being in the sun I never had carbuncles.

"Did they treat you badly?"

"The sheriff?"

She thought this was funny. "The Comanches, of course."

"They adopted me."

"But you were of a lower caste than a natural-born, no?"

"I was mostly the same. I was a member of their band."

"That is very interesting."

"My Comanche family died," I said. "That's why I came back."

Her face went all motherly. She really was a sweet woman. But before we got too far down the path of righteousness I said, "I'm going to drink some of the judge's port wine and then I'm going to steal one of his horses. Do you want some or not?"

"I could have a drink with you," she said. She wrinkled her nose at me. "But would you object to a bath?"

"Are you gonna give it to me?"

She acted surprised but I could tell she wasn't.

CHAPTER THIRTY-FIVE

JEANNIE McCULLOUGH

They heard it before they saw it, but when it finally appeared over the trees, it was clumsy and ponderous and not much to look at and most wished they had not taken off work. The sheriff and his men backed everyone out of the way, and, when it was safe, the helicopter dropped through the air until it settled in the dirt next to Hollis Frazier's spinach field.

A tall man with a big nose uncurled himself from the machine and, once the dusty crowd had formed around him, stood on a wooden box and began to speak. Someone else distributed peaches from the Hill Country. The man insisted that Coke Stevenson was giving away the state to big ranchers and northern oilmen, with nothing left over for the workingman. It occurred to her that she would have been nervous to speak in front of four hundred strangers, but it was plain he was not nervous, he was enjoying it, and he turned his megaphone on a group of people at the outskirts of the crowd and urged them to come in and hear him. Bullshit Johnson, they called him.

Watching him shake hands with all the shorter men around him, she knew Phineas was right. She had met Coke Stevenson, a nice man who did not particularly care what your opinion was. He had his own moral compass; a do-gooder, the sort of man you hoped your children would become. The man she saw in front of her was so happy in the crowd, so happy to be watched and paid attention to, there could not be room inside him for anything else. There wasn't an oilman in the state who didn't back him.

"I have something for the future senator," she told the aide, hoping he would notice this flattery.

He didn't. He looked her over and said, "You can give it to me." He was sweating in his black suit, a northerner, with thick plastic glasses, a man no one had ever liked, who was beginning to come into his own. It was a look she would take for granted among people who worked in Washington.

The man took her envelope and she thought of his boss and she thought of Coke Stevenson, and then she thought about what Phineas had told her before she sat down to write the checks. *The problem with most people is they don't give enough. They all want to be ambassador, but when it comes to giving money they think a hundred bucks is plenty and are surprised when they never hear back.* In her envelope were four checks for five thousand dollars each. One from herself, one from their lawyer Milton Bryce, one from their foreman Sullivan, and one from a vaquero named Rodriguez. Sullivan and Rodriguez made less than five thousand a year put together; she'd had the money deposited in their accounts the previous day. Any one of the checks would have bought a new Cadillac and the aide read each one carefully, making sure they were properly filled out. Then he led her over and whispered something to his boss.

Johnson's face lit up; he was a natural. He nudged a few people and the crowd parted, big ears, big nose, bushy eyebrows, he towered over everyone else.

"You must be Phineas's niece." He hadn't stopped smiling since he landed.

"Yes," she said.

"Well, he has spoken about you often and I am pleased to meet you. Tell him I miss those fishing trips."

"Yessir," she said again.

Someone was grabbing at his sleeve.

He grinned at her. "Back to work. But I will be seeing you again, young lady."

After the congressman was back in the helicopter, the aide found her and said: "Since you're at your limit, next time pay cash. It's going to be a tight race and we need all the help we can get." He handed her a peach.

She considered it as she walked back to the car. It was runty and bruised, barely fit for hog feed, and dozens more just like it lay scattered in the dirt.

WHEN WAS THAT? Forty-seven or -eight. She couldn't remember exactly. To say he was elected was not exactly accurate. Though at least Box 13 had come from Jim Wells County, not Webb or Dimmit. Those years had blurred together. They'd gotten enough wells sunk on the ranch to start a capital flow, then agreed there ought to be no more drilling there. She and Hank had bought a house in Houston. Rented a small office. Then a bigger one. Then they bought a bigger house. The way the economy was going it was impossible to lose money no matter what you did.

In the three years she and Hank had been together, she had expected they might settle into a pattern, boring but stable, they would begin to track like tires settled into ruts. But that had not happened. Their lives were changing too quickly, their business growing five- or tenfold each year, it was hers as much as Hank's. She was not surprised at her own abilities, which she had always taken for granted, but his, which seemed to have no limit, and she was beginning to wonder if he might surpass her—a thought that was liberating and disturbing at the same time. She'd never considered that she might be looked after, that she might have a normal life and not have to worry so much.

Most of the men she'd known were fools like her father and brothers, their lives shaped by a willful ignorance they mistook for pride. That ignorance guided every moment of their existence and until now, she had never doubted that she saw more clearly, more honestly, than any man she had ever met, with the exception of the Colonel and perhaps Phineas. And now there was Hank.

Though he was not perfect. He had no patience for things he found foolish, even if those things were important to others. There was a coldness about him that was almost northern. That awful writer from New York had come to visit and she had not wanted to meet the woman alone, but Hank had made sure he was out of town. Jeannie, meanwhile, had stupidly agreed to meet the writer at the ranch, an eighthour drive from Houston—they didn't own a real plane yet—instead of insisting on meeting at the office. The woman was writing a big novel about Texas; she had already seen the Klebergs and the Reynoldses and had just come from the opening of Glenn McCarthy's hotel. And she had won the Pulitzer Prize; it seemed a good idea to be in her favor.

They sat down for an early supper; Jeannie instructed the maids to put out the good plates and silver. She noticed the woman appraising those things, she was taking in everything, like a poor relation about to come into an inheritance. She was tall and gangly as a teenager but her hair was gray and frizzy like birds had made a nest of it, and like many northerners, her confidence was out of step with her appearance.

"You're the millionaire teenager."

"I'm twenty-two," she said.

"But you got the money when you were a teenager."

"That's true," said Jeannie. "Though I never thought of that as being of any consequence."

"Oh, it is," said the writer. "It most certainly is." Then she added: "How very Texan."

She could not tell if this was meant as a compliment.

"Were you very lonely out here?"

"I have a husband now," said Jeannie, "and most of us don't live on our land anymore. We're all city people now." She wished Hank was with her; he would know the proper way to deal with this woman; she worried she would end up saying something she did not mean.

"The house is decorated unusually for this area," said the writer.
Jeannie shrugged.

"Very tastefully, I'd say. It looks as if it's been here forever."

She shrugged again. She was not going to feed the woman any more gossip. "My great-grandfather was a brilliant man."

The woman nodded. Jeannie could not understand what was so important about her. Even her hat was ridiculous. Everything about her screamed she was from somewhere else, she was obsessed with how much money and land all the families had, with whatever dirt might be scraped up on them.

The maids brought supper out. Jeannie had considered carefully what ought to be served and, after ruling out anything elaborate that might imply she was seeking the woman's approval, had decided on fajitas.

Flores was a good cook; she'd rubbed the steak with salt and hot pepper, charred it over mesquite, and served it with heaping sides of guacamole and salsa and fresh tortillas.

When they finished, the hands were getting in from the pastures and taking their places at the long table behind the main house. Flores began to carry out their meal, chatting with them in Spanish. The author watched through the window.

"Do you want me to introduce you?" said Jeannie. "Those are the people who do the work these days."

"I don't think I speak their language, darling. But I do think I'll go out for a cigarette."

"I need to freshen up," said Jeannie.

When she returned from the toilet, she found the writer standing next to the window in the dining room, a strange look on her face. "Jeannie," she said, indicating the vaqueros with her chin, "they are eating the same thing we did."

THE WOMAN'S BOOK had come out and later was made into a movie starring James Dean. It was one long exaggeration. It made everyone look like clowns, as if they had stumbled dumbly into wealth, as if the state was nothing but backwoods tycoons without two brain cells to rub together.

And yet most of the oilmen had liked it. They began to invent over-the-top mannerisms, throwing silver coins out of the windows of their limousines, taking twenty-thousand-dollar baths in champagne. Maybe it was no different from any other time. The frontier was not yet settled when Buffalo Bill began his shows and the Colonel always complained about the moment his cowboys began to read novels about other cowboys; they had lost track of which was more true, the books or their own lives.

JOHNSON LOST BY a few hundred votes. But he became senator anyway and Jeannie began to expect his calls. He called on the Murchisons, on Cullen, Brown, and Hunt. There were very few oilmen he did not call on. Sam Rayburn was House Speaker; Rayburn and Johnson were the only thing keeping the Yankees from overturning the depletion allowance and as they would later need Congress to be Republican, the oilmen of the time needed Johnson and Rayburn in charge, they needed the House to remain Democratic, and they gave generously to keep it that way.

They were all gone now: Hank, Johnson, Rayburn, Coke Stevenson, Murchison, Cullen, and Hunt . . . soon she would join them. She supposed she ought to be happy: nearly everyone she had ever known had passed over to the other side. But she was not happy at all. She was going into a darkness from which she would not return. That others had gone before her did not make any difference.

She was not a good Christian; that was the problem. The true believers all had their motives, things they had wanted, but not gotten in this world—money, happiness, a second chance—but she had those things or did not need them and had always known that the greatest of her gifts was her ability to see things just as they were. To see the difference between her desires and reality. And the reality was that her life would end just like Hank's. She would not see him again: what made him Hank had stopped existing the moment he died. They now said that even the tunnel of light was just a trick of the neurons. There was only the body. She hoped she would be proved wrong, but she doubted it.

She looked around at the ancient carved furniture and the high cold ceiling and the logs burning without any heat. It might be a sort of purgatory. She would not mind that, remaining like this forever, reliving pleasant memories. She closed her eyes and she was in Washington visiting Jonas. There was someone he wanted her to meet and they had spent the afternoon on his boat in the Chesapeake Bay.

Her legs were tan, not a vein to be seen. She was wearing a white-and-yellow sundress and sitting in a wooden Chris-Craft; Jonas was driving and the man, pale and thin-haired and going pink from the sun, was flirting with her. A pleasant feeling. Not something she would have indulged back home, but here on the bay, under a sky that was blue but not hot, on the water that was clean and cool, she did not mind it.

It was the first time she'd been away from her children in over a year. Though she sensed she was carrying one inside her. Benjamin, probably. She was not showing—the pleasant man had no idea. He was short, soft in the gut, the opposite of Hank, but he was funny and she found him attractive. Though it might have simply been that she was treated better; women still had their place here, but it was not quite as small as in Texas. A Yankee might forget to hold the door, but he might also forget (or pretend to forget) that he was your superior. She began to imagine a life.

Then something passed between the man and Jonas and then he turned to her and was not smiling.

"I hate to get down to business, Jeannie, but I fear our friend the driver"—he indicated Jonas—"has some pressing business back in the city."

She shrugged as if she didn't care, though she would have been content to spend the entire day out on the water, away from her children and the telephone.

"What do you know about Mohammad Mosaddegh?" he said.

"I know we should have been more careful of him."

"What if I told you that he is not long for the throne?"

As he allowed her to process this she realized she might say any number of things. She decided to say nothing. She was glad Hank was not with her.

"Anglo-Iranian will get back some of what they lost," he continued, "but it won't be like before. Times have changed."

She sipped her drink.

"The majors will get the biggest piece, but right now we're trying to assemble a coalition of the willing. We need good people who have resources available immediately."

"Because it won't look good if you give it all to the majors."

"That is correct," he said. "And this is America. We like to look out for the little guy." He went back to looking over the water. "Nice day, isn't it?"

She knew that Hank would have pressed the man for numbers, for percentages, but that was not the right approach; she simply had to agree and to trust in this man and in Jonas.

"We'll take as much as you can give us," she said. She considered asking him what the time frame might be, but that would be even worse than asking for the size of the piece. She felt another wave of relief that Hank was not with her.

"You know Sedco?"

"I know Bill Clement."

"Get with him when you get back to Texas. Tell him I sent you."

Jonas turned the boat toward Annapolis; Jeannie and the man went on talking about other things. Their knees brushed, then brushed again. She expected he might ask her for a drink when they reached the dock, decided she would turn him down, but was hurt when he didn't. Of course it was for the best. She called Hank from her hotel and told him in a coded manner that they ought to free up as much cash as possible. They were both used to calls like that, they both knew better than to ask for details over a telephone.

By then it had been clear for decades that the future was overseas. The first well drilled in Iraq, in 1927, when it was still called Mesopotamia, had come in at ninety-five thousand barrels a day. A big Texas well, even then, produced five hundred, maybe a thousand, and everyone knew it was only a matter of time. The Persian Gulf was where the real oil was. If that well in Iraq had come in ten or twelve years earlier, the Ottoman Empire would not have collapsed. The world would be an entirely different place.

By the 1950s, domestic drilling was a tough business. It cost a fortune, the wells produced less, and once you found the oil, there was no guarantee you'd be allowed to remove it from the ground. The government was planning a war with Russia and they wanted plenty of domestic oil in storage if that happened. The best way to store oil was to leave it where you found it. Strategic reserves, they called it. Good for the government, bad for the oilmen.

There was no good answer. The hot oil days of the '30s—filling tankers at night and running them over the border to avoid production quotas—were long over. You had to go overseas. All over the old Ottoman Empire, you could pull oil out of the ground for pennies a barrel. There wasn't much infrastructure yet, but that was just a matter of time.

CHAPTER THIRTY-SIX

DIARIES OF PETER McCULLOUGH

JULY 4, 1917

When I am in my office I leave the door open so that I might hear the faintest noise of her footsteps around the house. If I hear someone on the stairs I walk casually down the hall to see whom it might be, heart rushing . . . but it is generally Consuela or her daughter.

Have not been out to pastures in several days. Told Sullivan I was buried in paperwork. Since then have been inventing tasks for myself so I can remain in the house.

When I do hear footsteps I rush for my door. If she is not in the west hallway (I am at the end of the east hallway, on the other side of the staircase) I will walk to the middle, hoping to catch her on the stairs or in the foyer below. Then I will stand, pretending to investigate the stained-glass window I have been looking at for thirty years, as from this vantage I can see anyone who passes the main entryway or goes from one side of the house to the other.

María's footsteps are easily discerned from the vaqueros' but I am constantly fooled by the light feet of Consuela and her daughter Flores. And by Miranda and Lupe Jimenez. If they see me, they look away— they all now suspect I have designs on them, though in fact I am hoping they are someone else.

If several hours (which feel like weeks) pass in which I have not seen her, I'll pick up a few worthless papers and stroll around the house as if on an errand, and, if the door to the library is open, I will go and pretend to find some book or pamphlet, for instance, *The Record of Registered Brands (1867)*—or something equally useless—but of course María does not know better. She thinks I am being diligent, and we'll speak for half an hour, and then she'll apologize for interfering with my work and take her things and go elsewhere, while meanwhile all my blood, or whatever vital force that is in me, sinks down into the earth.

Today I was in the kitchen, eating a plum, and she walked in and asked what I was doing and without answering, I impulsively offered her the plum, from which I had already taken two bites, and without hesitation she took it and had a dainty bite, looking at me the entire time. Then she abruptly left. I put the plum to my mouth and held it there until common sense forced me to eat the rest of it.

I cannot imagine making love to her. It seems disrespectful somehow. Every evening she plays the piano; I have moved the divan into the parlor (it properly belongs there, I lied to her) so that I can close my eyes and feel how close she is. She seems to think this a proper time for us to keep company, as she never tries to escape. Cannot stop reliving the moment in the library (her hand on mine), I curse myself for not responding, for not returning her touch or even leaning against her—this is likely the reason she has not done it again. Or perhaps she was simply being sympathetic, and the world I have invented for us exists only in my own mind. Just the thought leaves me hollowed out.

July 6, 1917

My father's deadline for María to leave has come and gone. Was beginning to feel better until he found me this morning.

"Pete, I am going to Wichita Falls. I will be back in one week, at which point the Garcia woman will have made her absquatulation. I have always let you do whatever you want, but this . . ." He looked around my office, as if the right words might be found among my books. " . . . this is not adjunctive to the forwarding of the design."

"What are you doing in Wichita Falls?" I said.

"Don't worry your head over it."

"There is nothing she can do to us."

"This has gone on long enough. There is one person on earth who cannot be here and you have brought her into this house."

"You are not going to change my mind," I said.

"Every day I see you now you're out on a dike. You think I don't notice that for ten years you don't bother to wash and now you're wearing collars?"

I didn't say anything.

"This ain't a grass widow you get to tap free, son. This one will cost us the ranch."

"You may leave now," I said.

He didn't move.

"Get out of my office."

LATER I COME across María in the library. I am pretending to look for a book, when she says, apropos of nothing: "How is your work going?"

"I'm not really working," I say.

She smiles, then gets serious again.

"Consuela tells me things."

"Whatever she is telling you, I won't let it happen."

"Peter." She shrugs and looks out the window, past the trees. I look at the skin along her neck, her collarbones, the edge of one shoulder, I look at her arms, still thin. " . . . I shouldn't be here anyway. This is the last place I should be, in fact."

"I'll take care of my father."

"That's not what I mean."

"Where else do you have?"

She shrugs and it is quiet and I watch her face changing. After a moment she decides something. "Do you have time to sit? If you are not really working?"

She is on her chair facing the window. I go to the couch.

"Don't worry about my father," I say.

She stands up and comes over and sits next to me. She touches my wrist.

"Sooner or later, I'll have to leave. Days or weeks, it doesn't matter."

"It does to me."

She touches my cheek. We are so close and I wait for something to happen, but it doesn't. When I open my eyes she is still looking at me. I lean forward, then stop myself; she is still looking at me, and I kiss her, just barely. Then I lean back. I am seeing spots.

She puts her fingers through my hair.

"You have good hair," she says. "And yet your father is bald. And he is short, and you are tall."

I can feel her breath.

"You will forget me," she says.

"I won't."

I wait for something to happen. We're leaning against each other. I work myself up and turn to kiss her again, but she only gives her cheek.

"I want to," she says. But then she stands up and walks out of the room.

CHAPTER THIRTY-SEVEN

ELI McCULLOUGH

1852

A few weeks later Judge Wilbarger's wife and I were lying naked on her couch, in my mind to spite the judge, in her mind because she was high on laudanum and being naked on the couch was a comfortable place to be. She had sent the Negroes to Austin on errands. She had the sort of face you saw in old books; it was pale and very delicate and I guessed that at one point she'd been the kind of woman that men would have killed to be with. And I guessed that she knew this, and knew it was not true anymore.

"How old are you, really?"

"Nineteen," I said.

"I don't care, you know. I just want to know more about you."

"Seventeen," I said.

She looked at me.

"Sixteen."

"Will the number keep going down?"

"No, it's sixteen."

"I'll take that. It's the perfect age."

"Is it?"

"For you it is."

She was quiet. I wondered how it was that a woman like her would ever end up with a man like the judge. I wondered if she had loved him. Then I was thinking about the Comanches.

"Are you mad at me?"

"No," I said. Then I said, "Why don't you go back?"

"To England? I'm very respectable here." She laughed. "No, of course I'm not. But what would I do there?"

"Better than Bastrop, probably."

"Probably."

I was looking at her smooth belly and wondering if she'd ever had children, but something told me not to ask, so instead I said, "I don't understand why you won't go back. Even I don't like this place."

"It's complicated," she said. "I can't explain it."

IN THE MEANTIME, being in town so much, I began to see the same kid over and over until I was sure he was following me. I knew his name was Tom Whipple; he was thirteen or fourteen, but barely five feet tall and lazy eyed to boot. Finally I caught him waiting for me around the judge's house, which I took for a bad sign. I followed him home and waylaid him in the woods behind his house.

Though I had him on the ground, for some reason he didn't look afraid. "You're the wild Indian," he said.

"I am."

"Well, the Indians killed my father. I guess now you'll kill me, too."

"You have been following me," I said.

"They say you go around stealing horses from people."

"I borrow them."

"They say you kill people's chickens and hogs."

"I quit doing that weeks ago."

"They say that someone is going to shoot you."

I snorted. "Well, I would like to see them try it. I could whip every one of these alfalfa desperados."

"My Daddy was a Ranger," he said.

I'd been in town long enough to know this wasn't true; his father

had been a surveyor, and the whole party had been killed by Comanches. Or so it was told. Most people couldn't tell an Apache from a
Comanche from a white man dressed in buckskin.

It was quiet.

"Show me how to steal a horse," he said.

THE NEXT DAY I told Ellen about Whipple lurking around the
house. We went out her back door and cut through the woods until
we were out of town, then went to a swimming hole I knew about. I
brought a pair of deer hides for us to lie on.

"These have a smell to them," she said. "Are they very fresh?"

"A few weeks."

"My little savage." She was lying with the sun on her, her legs
spread, her arms at her sides. There was a breeze but the rocks underneath us were warm. I could see the waving green of the cypresses and
the bare branches of the oaks, and the sky in the narrow place above
the stream. It had been like this every day for a month, and it would
stay like this until the summer. It was not a bad life.

"Have you ever had another affair?"

"You *are* a man, aren't you?"

"I guess."

"Men always want to know."

"Why shouldn't we?"

"Do you want the real answer or the nice one?"

"The real one," I said.

"You're my first. I have never felt as good as the way you make me
feel."

I got up.

"I'm sorry," she said. "I thought being half Comanche you
wouldn't mind it."

"I don't care."

"Come back." She patted the ground next to her and I did what
she said. After we lay awhile longer she said, "You know there are

times I think I might open my legs for nearly anyone, just to keep from going crazy. There are times when I think I would open my legs for Henry."

"They will sure as shit lynch you."

"Over a black man, yes. Do you know he won't even look at me?"

"He's a Negro," I said.

"But still he won't look at me. He knows they would kill him for it, so he's afraid of me. I feel sick about it all the time. He is more scared of me than Roy."

I was quiet.

"If I ever move back to England, that will be why."

I slid up next to her and lifted one leg and eased inside. Then I had the urge to stop and hold her. She wanted me to continue with the rutting. When we finished she fell asleep. I sat up and looked around, watching the stream going over the rocks. There was a mockingbird going through its songbook.

When I opened my eyes it was late.

"When are Cecelia and Henry getting back?"

"I don't know," she mumbled. "I sent them to Austin."

"We should get dressed."

She didn't move. Her long hair, which wasn't quite gray and wasn't quite brown, was tangled all around her.

"You know if you keep sending them on errands like that, one day they will run to Mexico."

"I certainly hope so."

"And you know they know about us."

"I certainly hope not."

"Of course they do."

"Well, Roy will shoot us both."

"They'll never tell."

"Why not?"

"Well, they like you better than him, for one. And for two, they're niggers."

"What does that mean?" she said.

"You know." I watched as she put on her underthings.

"Not really, I'm afraid."

I knew I was in the right but still I felt my bristles go up.

"If you don't like the judge, why don't you just leave him?"

She was shaking her head.

"It's not as hard as it sounds."

"Sure," she said. "I suppose we could run away together."

"We should."

"You don't know what you're saying, honey."

She pulled back her hair and tied it and then went into the bag for her laudanum.

"You think you're a bit superior to me, don't you." She held her fingers together. "Just a tiny bit."

I shrugged.

"Well, you're right."

She offered me the laudanum. "Would you like to try some?"

"Not really."

"Good," she said. "Good for you."

She took the trail back to town and I waited half an hour or so then walked out after her. There was another set of footprints across the rocks.

THE JUDGE'S THOROUGHBREDS knew me so well that it was not really stealing. Tom Whipple knew nothing about horses. The first time I took him into the stables, they nearly kicked him through the wall. I helped him onto the saddle, then got up behind him.

When we got back, Whipple was so excited he couldn't stop talking, and, as we snuck away through the woods, it occurred to me that he was going to do something stupid. I watched his feet as he walked ahead of me.

✫   ✫   ✫

A FEW DAYS later he tried to catch his neighbor's horse, a hog-backed Belgian draft animal, and instead caught a load of turkey shot. Luckily the barn door stopped most of it. But that did not stop him from blabbering.

I EXPECTED ELLEN to see me in jail but she didn't. When I mentioned her, the sheriff just shook his head.

"Son, I am tryin to figger how you could have picked a worse person to connubiate with."

I didn't say anything.

"Were you drunk?"

"Sometimes."

"Them aborigines must have scrambled your head, boy. I really had my hopes for you."

"Is there gonna be a real trial, you think?"

"If there is," he said, "it will be the shortest one in history."

CHAPTER THIRTY-EIGHT

JEANNIE McCULLOUGH

She was sitting on the couch, watching Susan suck her blanket and Thomas, with his cowlick and overalls and fat little arms, his red bandanna, she wanted to eat him up. He was trying to make a tower from blocks. The sun was on him and she continued to watch and after the tower collapsed for the twentieth or fiftieth (or hundredth) time, she winked out. Later she came to. Thomas was arranging the blocks; Susan had fallen asleep. It seemed that the rest of her life, before she'd had children, had been a dream. Did she even have a mind at all? She was like an animal chewing its cud.

Now she was awake. She was bored but there was something else, a restlessness so intense that she could not physically sit still any longer, she got up and paced the room and then, glancing behind her quickly— the children still in place—she went out the glass door to the backyard and walked a lap around the high wooden fence. The grass was thick; it was humid under the trees. She could make a drink.

She returned to the patio and watched her children from the other side of the glass. Of course she loved them, but there were times, she did not want to say it, there were times when she wondered what would happen if they simply stopped existing. *There is something wrong with you,* she thought. *There is something very wrong.* She'd tried to broach the subject with Hank, but it had not gone anywhere; he'd had no idea what she was talking about, and she'd ended the conversation before indicting herself any further. Hank spent only fifteen or twenty minutes a day with them alone. Though in his own mind, he looked after them from the time he got home until the kids went to sleep: his idea of looking after them was simply being in the same house. She spent as much time with the kids in one day as Hank spent in an entire month. She could not help doing the calculations.

She'd been low since the birth of Thomas, their first. She'd gotten lower when the doctor insisted, six months into the pregnancy with Susan, that she stay home as much as possible. She had begun to wonder about the point. The same as when her father died. Something was wrong with her, here she was surrounded by her growing family, her beautiful healthy children, asking about the point of being alive.

It was beautiful, it was natural, but of course it was something else, something you could never say or they would lock you away forever, it was another creature taking the blood right out of you. She was there in the hospital and then it was as if some malevolent spirit had settled inside her, something had risen and taken hold, one minute she was herself, the next she'd been snatched and pulled under, she had no say, she had never understood how small she was. It was not something you could explain to other people. She had survived.

A feeling of being tricked came to her constantly, betrayed by her own body, she had thought it existed for her own enjoyment and she was angry and jealous of Hank, who had paid no cost, who, as she lay in the hospital bed, held her hand and looked lovingly into her face and told her to *breathe, breathe;* meanwhile she was on a plane that had lost its engine, plummeting toward open water, toward annihilation, breathing was the last thing on her mind. She had not stopped being angry about that, either. His sure advice on matters he knew nothing about.

She was being unreasonable. There was no point thinking about it. She stood on the patio, watched her children through the window a few moments longer, wondered what she would say if a neighbor saw her or the nanny came downstairs or Hank came home. She went back inside. She called the nanny on the intercom and asked her to pack a bag for Susan. Thomas was old enough to be looked after; Susan she would take to the office. She still went in a few times a week to visit her old life. *You are being a baby,* she thought.

She put Susan in the front seat of the Cadillac and felt an immediate relief, even before she left the driveway. Susan began to cry. Jeannie lifted her and held her in her lap as she drove. Twenty minutes later they were in front of the office, and after a long elevator ride she handed Susan off to the secretaries, who were happy to have her, happy to hold a child, happy to avoid work, she didn't know and didn't care, she only wanted to be alone.

She went into her office and shut the door. It was hot, pleasantly so—it was all windows. It was a green view over the city, which was growing, growing, the East Texas country was lush and wet, it was the Deep South. Hell in the summer. She loved her children. She had expected something different. She had expected them to be like her brothers, or like foals or calves, helpless at first, but quickly capable of looking out for themselves.

What she had not expected was so much need. They said it was love but it was not love at all, if she was honest, they had taken far more than they could ever give. Perhaps they had taken everything. "That is wrong," she said out loud. "I am wrong for thinking that." She sat there, not daring to breathe, looking out over the skyscrapers, filled with people, she could see them bustling, sitting in their offices. There was no one like her. *You are pathetic,* she thought, *think about your own mother.*

In the other room, she heard Susan begin to cry; the sound brought her out of the chair, she was moving toward the door before she even knew what was happening. But of course the girls could handle it. She went back to her desk—stacks and stacks of papers—it was ridiculous, she had no context for any of it, she began to read at random. A landman's report, a geologist's report, a deal long gone bad. It was hot. The questions were pointless. She'd known what she was getting into (*except I did not,* she insisted, *I did not know*), her life was ruled by the needs of others; the only need she could not indulge was the one she felt nearly every day, to get into the car and begin driving and never stop.

Sometime later she woke up sweating. The sun was still coming in. She wondered if the air-conditioning was on. She shuffled the papers, throwing out the old ones, but it was pointless, it would take her months to catch up. She went to the divan and fell asleep again. Then it was past five. Nothing had been done.

She checked her face in her compact: puffy, the fabric had marked her, there was a pretty girl in there somewhere, with good cheekbones and perfect skin and a nice mouth, but it was not visible in the mirror; all the color was gone except for under her eyes. Her teeth were yellow, her hair was like something dried up in the sun.

She winked out again. When she came to it was dark. She touched herself up and she went back out into the office.

Susan was asleep in the remaining secretary's lap. Everyone else had gone home and the girl was not moving, just sitting there, looking helpless.

"I'm so sorry," said Jeannie.

"Oh no, I love her," said the girl, and she did. She was perfectly happy to be sitting there with an infant on her lap; she looked as angelic as the child and somehow this made Jeannie feel even worse.

"Thank you for looking after her. You have no idea what a relief it is."

The girl just looked at her. It was true—she did not have any idea. She would be happy if she had a baby like this, happy to have a husband to go along with it.

Luckily, Hank was up in Canada again. At least she was spared him seeing this. He, along with Herman Jefferson, their geologist, and Milton Bryce, their lawyer, was always telling her she didn't have to worry about coming in. Things had been running fine without her, running fine for two years. They were too delicate to say it, but what they meant was, *You are not needed. Our world has continued without you.*

Though hers had not. *I might as well be dead,* she thought.

WHEN HANK GOT back from Alberta, she told him it was time to add a second nanny, and maybe even a third, if they were to have another child.

"That's silly," he said. He buzzed about the kitchen, fixing himself a sandwich, moving with his usual efficiency, everything put back in its place.

"Why does it matter?" She thought he was talking about money.

"It matters," he said. "I don't want our kids being raised by people they won't know when they get older."

"So stay home and raise them."

He looked at her to see if she was being serious.

"You don't have to work," she said. "We will never need money."

He was annoyed. He took a bite of his sandwich and washed it down with milk.

"I can't do this by myself anymore. I'm serious."

"That's ridiculous."

"Then I guess I'm ridiculous."

"No, I mean it's ridiculous to say you're by yourself. You have Eva all day and I am home by six every night."

"What if I were to point out that they are half yours," she said. "And that you might take half care of them."

"I do my share," he said, and by the funny way his voice broke she could tell he really believed it.

"You do," she said, "but it is not half, or even a quarter, it is more like one percent. I appreciate that you leave your door open but that is quite different from sitting all day with them, alone."

He didn't say anything.

"We will get another nanny. Nothing will change for you."

"Out of the question," he said.

"I will not be leaving the business."

"You already left it," he said. "You barely know anything that is going on."

It occurred to her then that he was no different from her father, which was maybe an exaggeration, or maybe not, maybe he just put a nicer face on it.

"I don't feel like a person anymore," she said.

"Well, that is nice to hear from the mother of one's children." Now he would not look at her.

"I feel like it's me or them," she said.

"I don't know what's gotten into you." Even through his tan she could see his neck was red. He put down his sandwich and walked out of the room, then out of the house.

She heard him start the car and pull out of the driveway.

Of course she began to cry. The truth was much too far. She should never have said it. She went out into the yard and sat in the green darkness. What he wanted, what everyone wanted, was that she stay at home and never have a meaningful thought again while they all kept doing exactly as they pleased. It was insane. Hank, Jefferson, Milton Bryce—she hated all of them, actually hated them at that moment—she didn't care what they thought of her.

The decision was made. She was not going back. An arrangement would be figured out, she was worth fifty million dollars and it was insane, actually insane, that she should be trapped here, or anywhere else, by children, her husband, this situation, she was not sure how to properly describe it, but it was all of those things, and it was over.

She heard the car pull into the driveway. She stayed in the yard where it was dark. Inside, she watched Hank come down the steps into the living room, past all the new furniture, two hundred thousand dollars' worth—her money—she watched him go to the bar and pour a whiskey and stare into his glass. Then he went to the window and looked out. It was too bright in the house for him to see her; he was looking only at his own reflection. His coarse sharecropper's face and his thick hair and the lines already around his eyes, yes she loved him, but she stayed where she was. He would have to choose.

HE WAS A good man. But in the end, the money was hers, and without that, she was not sure he would have given in.

It did not seem right, having to bargain with her own husband, having to manipulate him, but maybe he'd been doing it to her the entire time, even if neither one of them had realized it.

THEY HIRED TWO more nannies, and she went back to work. They thought she was a bad mother. She overheard the secretaries, of course they were all unmarried, of course they were all jealous, of course they would have slept with Hank in a heartbeat—a wealthy, good-looking man. Women pretended sisterhood until it counted; they acted as if they cared nothing for men they were actually in love with. Naturally, she made sure that every girl they hired was so unattractive that Hank would have to be extraordinarily drunk to even consider them. *We have the ugliest secretaries in the world,* he always said.

Still. They thought she was a bad mother. She tried to forget it.

Chapter Thirty-nine

DIARIES OF PETER McCULLOUGH

July 7, 1917

Slept only a few hours, thinking of her on the other side of the house. She did not report for breakfast and if she left her room at all, she must have done it quietly as an owl. When I went for lunch I found dishes in the drying rack, freshly washed; she had been there, I had missed her. Lost interest in eating and returned to my office.

Picked up and set down at least two dozen books. Considered, then dismissed, calling Sally. Overcome with need to tell someone about this. If I could climb to the roof and announce it with a bullhorn . . .

But I am happy simply knowing she is in the same house. If there is any question of whether it is better to love or to be loved . . . the answer is obvious. I wonder if my father would agree. I wonder if he has ever felt this way; like all men of ambition I suspect he is incapable of it. I want to weep for him. I would trade everything in this house, everything we own, to keep feeling this, and at this thought, I do begin to weep, for my father, for María, for the Niles Gilberts and the Pedros.

FORTUNATELY OR NOT, I was pulled from this morass of emotion by events that required my action. Around two P.M. there was a loud noise. When I got up to investigate I could no longer see the top of the derrick sticking up over the brush.

As it turned out, the driller had hit a gas pocket and lost control of the rig. One of the hands rode the derrick to the ground; by some miracle he is still alive (they say drunks fall better). By a second miracle the gas did not ignite and by a third miracle (from the common perspective) there is oil now flowing steadily into our pastures, down the hill and into the stream.

By evening the entire town had arrived, looking at the fallen derrick where it lay in a swamp of oily mud. It was plain this was a coup of monstrous proportion, that what few worries we might have had are now over, we are even further removed from the daily lives of the citizenry. But the townspeople did not seem to understand this. They almost seemed to think it was *their* good fortune. People were dipping cups into the mud to taste the oil as if it were coffee.

It is as my father says. Men are meant to be ruled. The poor man prefers to associate, in mind if not in body, with the rich and successful. He rarely allows himself to consider that his poverty and his neighbor's riches are inextricably linked, for this would require action, and it is easier for him to think of all the reasons he is superior to his other neighbors, who are just poorer than he is.

As the crowd pressed around the fallen derrick, the lake of oil growing larger, the driller, whose back teeth were still well afloat, could not decide whether or not to ignite the well. Gas can travel hundreds of yards aboveground, flashing at the smallest provocation; it is not uncommon for spectators to be immolated in this fashion, hours or even days after a well comes in.

After more whiskey to clear his head, he decided not to flare the well. The oil was flowing, not gushing. There could not be much gas. Or so he reckoned. I reckoned he was drunk. I told everyone to stay clear of the well, though when I saw Niles Gilbert and his two porcine offspring clomping out of the viscous mud, having stood nearly at the mouth of the burbling black spring, I began to wish for a divine spark. It occurred to me, as I watched the oil flow down the hill, that soon there will be nothing left to subdue the pride of men. There is nothing we will not have mastered. Except, of course, ourselves.

THE VAQUEROS ARE using horses and fresnoes to build a dyke, but they are losing the battle. A jimberjawed Yankee farmer offered to rent us his new Hart-Parr tractor. Had he been born here, he would have simply driven it over, but being from the North he thinks only of what fattens his pocket. After some consideration I agreed to pay him. The oil is flowing strongly into the stream—the fresnoes are not designed for emergency work.

Nonetheless everyone was in a good mood and proceeded to get drunk, including the fallen derrickman and the partially crushed floorhand. People from Carrizo began to show up, though what attraction there was—a black pit, a sulfurous stench, even more money flowing into their wealthiest neighbor's pocket—I did not understand. The Colonel appeared at midnight, having driven all the way from Wichita Falls at sixty miles an hour, blowing out a tire from the speed.

He found me in my office. Through the windows came a faint odor of brimstone, as if Old Nick himself were having a smoke on our gallery. By sheer coincidence, I am sure, this is also the odor of money.

"Son," said the Colonel. He hugged me. He was already as drunk as the others. "From now on, you can pay for all the brush-clearing you want."

Not a word about María. In a moment of panic I went and checked her room: she was asleep in her bed, sighing about something. I watched for a long time until she stirred.

JULY 8, 1917

This morning I find her waiting for me downstairs.

"Very exciting news, no?"

I shrug. I am only thinking about what she's lost; I'm happy the oil was found on our land, instead of hers.

"Will you have much work today?"

"I don't think so," I say. "I have some errands in Carrizo, if you want to come."

She agrees, which puts me in a good mood about everything, even the steady stream of cars going to and from the drilling site, the gates left open—fifty heifers found on the road this morning.

When we get to Carrizo there is nothing in particular either of us want to do. On a whim we decide on Piedras Negras for lunch (Nuevo Laredo is brought up; María does not want to go there). It will be a three-hour drive; we will be home late; we do not discuss this. She ties her hair back to keep it out of the wind; I steal glances, her warm mouth, dark eyelashes, the fine hairs at the nape of her neck.

When we finally reach the town, around four in the afternoon, I am nervous, wondering about the Carrancistas, Villistas, Zapatistas, but María does not seem concerned. We ignore the shoeshine boys and lottery vendors and find a cantina where we sit on the patio under an arbor. We order *arrachera* eels, grilled fish, *tortillas sobaqueras*, chopped avocados and tomatoes. She has a tequila sour; I have a Carta Blanca. We cannot fish all the food; she stares at it. We hesitate at ordering more drinks. We hesitate again at the car.

Instead of heading home we drive farther into the country to see the old San Bernardo Mission. It is a small old ruin, a single story, nothing on the scale of the cathedrals of Mexico City, but in its time it was the upper reach of Spanish influence here. All the northern expeditions left from and returned to it; you could sense the relief the riders must have had when the mission, with its dome and archways, appeared on the horizon. And the fear they must have had when they left it. This land was far more dangerous than New Mexico ever was.

It occurs to me that the San Bernardo is not much older, fifty or sixty years, than the Garcias' casa mayor. I become quiet. María either reads my thoughts or thinks my silence is due to something else, because she takes my hand, and puts her head against my shoulder.

"It is nice to be out of your house," she says.

We walk slowly, small steps, waiting for something important to be said. She does not let go of my hand, but she will not look at me either.

"And your wife? When will she return?"

"Never, I hope."

"Will you divorce her?"

"If I can."

"She is the beautiful woman in the pictures."

"She comes from a good family."

"She looks it."

"You know she married me because her family is bankrupt. She thought she was marrying a younger version of my father, but unfortunately that is my brother Phineas."

"Perhaps she preferred you because you are handsome."

"Certainly not."

"Certainly," she says. "Your brother has a weasel face."

"My wife wants me to be a different person." I shrug. "I am happy she is gone."

We continue to walk. I expect her to let go of my hand, but she swings our locked arms back and forth, as if we are children, and holds on firmly.

When we reach the car she says: "We will be very late driving home, no?"

Some part of me, the part that takes over when there is something at stake, says: "I'm expected back."

"Oh," she says, and looks away.

She sits in the car, arms crossed, looking out over the mission and the *brasada* to the south, while I get the engine started.

When I get in with her, I swallow and say: "Perhaps it will not be safe to make the drive after dark."

"Perhaps not," she says.

We find a hotel by the railroad depot.

"How is this?"

Now she won't look at me. We are silent as if we are an old couple having a fight. It's cooler and the ceiling fans are turning but I feel the sweat running down my back. Every noise amplified, my boots scuffing the floor, the counter creaking when I lean to sign the register. I hesitate, then write Mr. and Mrs. Garcia. The clerk winks. Our room is on the second floor. We walk up the stairs, silent, then into the room, silent.

"Well?" I say.

She sits on the bed and looks at everything but me. The furnishings are cheap; someone has carved their initials into the headboard.

"This is wrong," she says. "We should go back."

I blurt out, "*No quiero vivir sin ti.*"

"Say it in English."

"I will not live if you leave me," I say.

She goes back to looking at the floor, but I think she is smiling. "I wondered if your hesitations were because of the way I look."

"No," I say.

"This is when you tell me I'm beautiful," she says. She laughs. She pats the bed next to her. "Come over here."

"I love you," I say.

"I believe you," she says.

July 9, 1917

We are on the bed facing each other, her leg is thrown over me, but we are not moving; she is lying sleepily against me. I watch my finger go along her arm, her shoulder, her throat, then back down her arm. The glow from the railroad comes through the window.

"Touch my back," she says.

I spend a long time drawing lazy shapes, then kiss her to let her know my intentions. She pulls me on top of her and sighs. She begins to move her hips.

Afterward we fall asleep like that. When we wake we do it again.

"I would be happy if we never left this bed."

"Me too," I say.

She kisses me and then again and again and again and I close my eyes.

In the morning, when the light comes through the curtains, I wonder if the spell will have passed, but she looks at me with the sun shining brightly on us and puts her head against my neck. I can feel her there, breathing me in.

CHAPTER FORTY

ELI McCULLOUGH

It was not long before Judge Wilbarger was making arrangements for a necktie social, because once Whipple blabbered, the slaves were blabbering as well and then the whole town caught the whispering fever; everyone knew I'd been pirooting the judge's wife eight and ten times a day, drinking his wine, stealing his horses, feeding his cigars to the hogs. It was reckoned a miracle he had not shotgunned his untrue companion, though it was equally reckoned that someone would have to meet Old Scratch in her place.

I had hopes I might win on popularity, but that was youthful ignorance, as the whites had no love for horse thieves and hog killers, even good ones. The only thing that saved me was Judge Black in Austin, who got the statehouse involved, and accused Wilbarger of mentally abusing me, a helpless returned Indian captive, son of a martyred Ranger, and so the trial and hanging were put off until Wilbarger found a way to get rid of me, namely mustering me into a Ranger company. Which, in those days, was considered near the same as a neck-lining.

THE IDEA OF riding with the Rangers appealed to me the same as riding with the Comanches would have appealed to my father, but the seriousness of my situation was made plain. I was taken to Austin in bracelets and released into Judge Black's custody, though I was only there for a few hours. He had a small bay waiting for me, a good saddle, a second Colt Navy and a Springfield carbine. The children came and saw me but his wife would not, and the judge was down at the mouth, and nothing I could say would make it better.

I MUSTERED INTO the company at Fredericksburg, near our acre-ocracy, which my father had deeded to my stepmother. Rangering was not a career so much as a way to die young and get paid nothing for doing it; your chances of surviving a year with a company were about the same as not. The lucky ones ending up in an unmarked hole. The rest lost their topknots.

By then the days of the ace units, under Coffee Hays and Sam Walker, were over. Walker was dead, killed in Mexico. Hays had given up on Texas and gone to California. What was left was an assortment of bankrupt soldiers and adventure seekers, convicts and God's aban-dons.

At the end of each tour, the ones who survived were given a square mile of unclaimed land somewhere in the state. It was a sharecropping of blood, in which we killed Indians and took a por-tion of their lands in payment, but like any other share work, you always came out a loser. The safe land was all claimed and the only acres still redeemable would not have value for decades. And so the vouchers were always traded for equipment, mostly to specula-tors who lived in big houses and offered us horses or new revolv-ers, picking up the land for ten cents on the dollar. Our only other remuneration was ammunition, which we got in unlimited supply. Everything else—from corn bread to side meat—we were expected to forage or otherwise annex.

WE DUNNED THE state for powder and lead and spent a few weeks training before riding out. All we did was shoot. We set up a fence post and the captain told us we were not leaving until everyone could hit the post five out of five times from horseback, at a lope at least, a gallop being better, with no preference for handedness, those appendages being considered disposable.

After those few weeks it was clear that a gun fit my hand better than a bow. Those who afforded it carried two Colt Navys, as reloading in those days took several minutes. A few of the men carried Walker Colts, which were twice as powerful but also twice as heavy, and had to be carried in saddle holsters, rather than a belt holster, which was not safe if you were separated from your horse. Not to mention the loading lever would sometimes drop and jam the cylinder; despite all that has been written about them, there was a reason not many Walkers were made.

MY FIRST TOUR we did not see a single Comanche. We saw their tracks and leavings, but could not catch them. Being better raiders they were better at avoiding raids, being better trackers they were harder to follow, and so my fears that I would one day see Nuukaru or Escuté over the barrel of my Springfield turned out to be laughable.

With the exception of a few tired Lipans and Mescaleros, most of what we caught were Mexicans and vagabond Negroes, or starving Fort Indians whose skills had rusted by close proximity to the whites. Meanwhile, any outlaw group worth its name carried an old bow and arrow and after making their killings they would shoot a few arrows into the victims, so the Indians would get blamed for whatever they'd done. Wherever you looked, the red man was at a discount.

When game was scarce or settlers stingy it was normal for us to go hungry a few days, so whenever we recovered a big lot of property, say horses or cattle, unless we recognized the brands we would take a detour to sell them in Mexico, along with any saddles and guns. To the settlers we sold scalps, lances, bows, and other Indian accoutrements that people wanted to hang as trophies. Ears were especially popular.

Despite this pilferage we usually rode home with empty pockets, our gear was always breaking and our horses dying and it all had to be replaced in the field. The legislators encouraged our thieving ways, *plunder the plunderers*—which of course was the same as stealing from our own people—but so far as the elected ones cared, anything not recorded in the register did not count as a tax increase, which was all that mattered to their owners, the cotton men.

As for the cotton men, they admired and respected the state's public servants, who unlike them worked for glory rather than money. They passed this wisdom to the cattlemen, who passed it to the oil-men. It was a smooth-working system, as any foolish servant who suggested he might be paid in dollars, rather than pats on the back, was tarred as a Jayhawker or Free-Soiler, or, worse, an Abolitionist, and run out of the state.

IN THE RANGERS there were a number of former captives, some of whom were glad to get back at their old captors, though mostly they had joined for the same reasons I had, namely that the habits of whites had stopped making sense. They felt crowded in cities or even settlements, they longed for their old lives on the plains, and the closest they could get to their old lives, and their old friends, was to chase and occasionally kill them.

My second year I rode with Warren Lyons, who had spent ten years among the Comanches. After getting into a fight with some chiefs, he'd defected back to the whites, checking in with his birth family only to discover he had nothing left to say to them. Then he signed up with the Rangers. The men were not sure if he was a genius or mass murderer.

Thirteen of us rode out in May, and in June we lost an Ohioan to fever and in August our captain caught a ball along the lower San Antonio–El Paso road. Lyons was elected the new captain and we continued to range in the area between the Davis Mountains and the border. One day in September we were looking for some Mexicans who had stolen horses from Ed Hall, nooning on a nice ridge a day or so east of Presidio. A spring came out of the rock, as they did in those days before all the water was used up, and the country dropped below us to the green flats of the river, with the Sierra del Carmen showing blue in the distance. It was a peaceful scene. The last time I'd been there, with Toshaway and Pizon and the others, I had not had time to notice it.

We lunched on fresh venison, ate some fruit we'd gotten off the settlers, and were generally enjoy our jobs when Lyons spotted eight riders making their way toward us on the Mexican side, heading for one of the fords on the old Comanche war trail. He passed me the spyglass. I could barely make out their colors, but there was something about them and I was sure they were Comanches. They were driving a small *caballada*, maybe two dozen horses.

"What do you think?" I said to Lyons.

"I'd say they are *Numunuu* for damned sure," he told me.

"The numbers aren't exactly on our side." There were only eleven of us. Unless you were fighting two or three to one, someone was going to get shot.

"They're probably tired. They don't have many horses."

"That doesn't mean they're tired."

"It means things went bad."

I went back to tell the others. There was whooping and excitement; Comanches were as rare as elephants and everyone wanted to bag one.

Lyons was collecting himself in an orderly fashion. Meanwhile I was jumpy as I'd ever been, which was odd because we'd been getting in a fight once a week. We dropped from the bench down a cottonwood-lined drainage, sticking to the damp sand so as not to kick up any dust.

The Comanches had only two muskets between them and we decided to sneak just within gunshot of the ford and get as many as we could with rifles before they could close the distance. I wondered if Lyons was as rattled as I was. The others had their sap up, having never fought anything but Fort Indians.

When we got near the river I checked my guns a third time and put a fresh cap on my rifle. The Comanches were still on the other side of the water. We were ghosting through the rocks and willows and they hadn't seen us and I knew if we could catch them in the river it would be a slaughter. I thought about Toshaway again.

When I turned to look for Lyons, he had thrown off his boots and was donning a pair of moccasins he'd pulled out of his saddlebag. He'd been with the Comanches almost a decade, he still talked to himself in Comanche, he didn't even think of them as Comanches but as *Numunuu,* and I realized why he wasn't nervous about taking them on when we were nearly evenly matched in numbers: he was heading back to fight alongside his old friends.

I unshucked my pistol; he stood up and walked straight into the muzzle.

"What the fuck are you doing, McCullough?"

"What the fuck are *you* doing?" I kept the gun pointed.

"I like my moccasins to fight in," he said. He pushed the barrel away. "You got real troubles, McCullough. You got 'em all down but the nine."

I COULD HEAR them laughing and talking, we were waiting for them to all get clear of the brush so we could lay a clean volley into them, but then Hinse Moody and the other half-wits fired their rifle shots and called out their war whoops and hubbed themselves in, kicking their ponies and charging down the hill. The Comanche was the wall-hanger; no one wanted to miss his chance.

The Indians took to the rocks and when Moody and the others got to pistol range the arrows started coming in.

After ten minutes, two of the Comanches made a break for the river. Moody and the others had gone down in the first volley and most everyone else had gotten a dogwood switch in the meantime. Except Lyons. He fought like a purebred *Numu,* rolled off to one side of his grullo, shooting under the animal's neck. His horse looked like a pincushion when it finally gave up; the Indians must have picked him as a turncoat because they were all shooting for him. When his horse went down I expected him to cover behind it, but he dodged through the arrows and was not even touched; they were clattering off the rocks all around him and he was closing on the Indians by himself.

There was a shadow in the brush I had a feeling about; I put a shot into it, adjusted a half foot, put another shot in, adjusting and putting a ball here and there until the gun was empty. I had barely got the first cylinder charged when Lyons went running up the left.

It was quiet. The arrows had stopped coming and my ears were ringing and there were horses squealing and snorting. Someone was moaning and calling for his wife. Other than Lyons and myself, there were only three on our side still up and they were dug in way behind me. Lyons was way ahead. My horse was down and I was happily covered behind it, but I made a rush and closed six or seven yards. Then Lyons made a rush. I watched the pile of rocks where the Indians were, but I'd lost my hat and the sun was glaring. I made another rush. Nothing happened. I made a longer rush and an arrow came out of the willows and clipped my thigh. I saw Lyons charging in, heard him shoot his gun empty, then made myself get up. I was not sure where I ought to be aiming. Lyons came out of the bushes.

"Well, I think that's all of them."

"How 'bout down there?"

"Well, go look. But I counted five dead ones, plus the two that ran off."

"There's one more by the water," I said.

"Then there's your eight."

I didn't feel so sure. "Do you have any left?"

He shucked the pistol and pulled out his second and checked it. "Two. Should be enough for some dead Indians." Then he turned around: "Hey, you fucking women."

The other three were eighty yards behind us.

"Move up the right." He pointed toward the river.

Though the two of us were standing out there in the open, they all made the shortest possible rush and ducked down again.

"Who the fuck is that in the way back?" said Lyons.

"I think it's Murphy and Dunham. And maybe Washburn behind them."

"What a bunch of cockchafers." He looked over. "You might want to check that leg."

I did. By miracle of a quarter inch, the spike had turned to the outside of the hip instead of going inside where the big artery was. I made a wide circle of the rocks. Lyons went overtop. I could feel the blood running into my boot. But there were no more Indians and their horses were grazing along the water.

"You want us to come in?" shouted one of the laggards.

I looked at Lyons. "Not yet," I shouted back.

We moved carefully among the fallen Comanches, some lying in deep slicks of blood while others looked asleep, a lucky ball to the neck, a clean, dry end, we lifted their faces and checked them carefully and Lyons must have seen someone he recognized, because when we called the other three in, he didn't share in any of the scalping or stripping; he went off by himself and didn't talk to anyone.

Just when we were starting to gather the dead, MacDowell, one of the men we thought was down for good, stood up. He had been hit in the head by a fragment and after he collected his senses he was able to ride. I bandaged my hip—considered again what a miracle it was that the arrow deflected away from my innards—and got our five dead loaded. We took them to Fort Leaton, where they had shovels.

THE NEXT MORNING, three of the four remaining Rangers, Murphy, Dunham, and Washburn, turned their badges in to Lyons. "We don't want none of the aborgoin horses," said Washburn. "We just want to keep the guns and scalps and such."

"Keep 'em," said Lyons.

"You startin' to miss your turpentine?" I looked at Washburn. He was a cross-eye from East Texas and he had stayed a hundred yards behind us during the fight.

"There ain't pay enough for this," he said. "Even a clay-eater like me can tell that." He indicated the others: "Dunham had ran with Hinse Moody since he was eight years old. You even know that?"

"No," I said. Dunham was already walking off. I didn't know why I was taking the blame.

The three deserters went to attend to their packing, which left only me, Lyons, and the young horse thief MacDowell. He had a good nature and I was happy he had made it. Later we stood on the parapet and watched them ride off toward the mountains, but they felt us looking and put the gaffs to their ponies.

"Well," said Lyons. "Looks like our take just doubled."

We spent the rest of the day scrubbing guns and fixing tack. Two of the horses we'd got off the Comanches had U.S. markings; we traded them to Ed Hall so he could sell them in Old Mexico. I got a beautiful pumpkin-skin gelding, which I later lost in a card game.

Ed Hall said, "How many do you think got away?"

"Two."

"You sure you boys won't stay awhile longer?"

"You'll be fine," I said. "Just invite 'em for dinner in front of your cannon."

He chuckled: "I don't think they'll fall for that one twice."

Of course it was not his cannon; it was Ben Leaton's. Leaton had died a few years earlier and Hall had married his widow but was having trouble filling his shoes. Leaton had been a scalp hunter extraordinaire and I'd always suspected he ran the party that had nearly got Toshaway and me. He was most famous for inviting a group of Indians to dinner, then slipping out halfway through the meal to touch off a cannon he'd charged with canister and hidden behind a curtain. The shot obliterated the unsuspecting Indians along with everything else in his dining room. No one stole his horses after that.

WHEN WE GOT up in the morning we found that MacDowell died during the night.

"I'm cursed," Lyons told me.

"I think MacDowell was cursed worse than you." I was in no mood for his antics. My leg was throbbing and I hadn't slept and I was too tired to dig another grave.

"No," he said. "I mean I've always known it, that everyone around me will die and I will never even get a scratch."

"I'm the same way," I told him.

He looked at me. "Just in the six months I've known you, you've been stuck with two arrows."

"But not seriously," I said.

"Still. There's a big fuckin' difference."

I could not make him understand that there was no difference at all. He quit the Rangers a year before we mustered out to join the Confederacy. Then he moved to New Mexico and died despite his luck and good health.

AFTER SELLING THE horses and captured guns and saddles in Austin, Lyons and I split the money and he rode out again toward the border. I kitted myself out in a new shirt, pants, and hat, dropped my guns off to get the timing fixed, and went to pay the judge for the horse and pistol he'd given me two years earlier. He would not take it, but he was happy to see me, he said, looking and acting like a white man. I had dinner with his wife and three daughters, who were happy to see me also, and I could tell his wife was warming up to me.

"I just knew this would be good for you," she said. "I knew it would help civilize you just a little bit."

I didn't tell her I was doing the same thing I'd been doing with the Indians. The oldest daughters were making eyes at me, and that was not bad, except that it put me in a certain mood and within a few days I'd emptied my pockets.

The city was above my bend. It was nothing but guttersnipes and gaycats, whoremongers and Sunday men. I sold my derringer pistol for a dozen doses of calomel, poured in both ends, as I thought I'd caught the French pox. Then I pawned one of my Colts and got the cheapest room I could find, waiting for another patrol to be funded by the Chosen Ones.

A man found me at the rooming house. He handed me a rawhide wallet like he was making a delivery I was expecting. I took the bag but didn't open it, and I reached toward my back pocket until I remembered I'd sold my derringer. The man had a weak chin and four days of stubble and a rotting hat pulled to his eyebrows. He looked like a mortuarian's assistant.

"I saw Sher Washburn the other day," he said. "He mentioned he had rode with you and I thought I knew your name. Then I found I had wrote it down."

I looked at him.

"Your daddy talked about you a fair bit. We all knew."

"Who are you?" I said.

"I rode in from Nacadoch. I'm trying my hand at granging up there but I have kept this a long time to give to you."

Inside the wallet was a scalp vest. Dozens of scalps, some with the hair on, others with the hair off, sewn together in a careful pattern. They all looked dark.

"Oh, they're all Injun," he said. "You can be goddamn sure of that; I probably helped your daddy with about half of 'em." I handled the vest; it was soft and finely made and I thought of Toshaway, who had his own shirt made of scalps. I had buried him in it.

"Can I give you something for it?"

"Nope." He shook his head and went to spit and then stopped himself.

"Let's get into the air," I said.

We walked toward the edge of town.

"You know he went after you, don't you? He was always worrying if you knew that. They got as far as the Llano before they lost the trail."

"Huh," I said.

"Oh, he went after you all right."

We reached the water and stood there and there was not much to say. A few boatmen were poling supplies for the settlers upriver. I took out my piece of thick and offered it and he cut off a chunk and put it in his lip.

"Your daddy was somethin' else," he said. "He could smell the Indians better than a wolf."

"What happened to him?"

He was looking over the water. "I remember you could stand on Congress and hear billiards in one ear and whoopin' aborgoins out the other. There was thirty, forty houses, maybe. And now look at it." He looked behind us at the town, where there were now thousands of people. Down on the riverbank, the ferryman was doing a brisk business.

"What happened to him?" I said again. He was quiet and I thought of my father coming back to his house and wife and daughter and then I thought of him riding out after us. I watched the water. I could feel my fear drifting away from me.

The man just stood there. He never answered.

CHAPTER FORTY-ONE

J.A. McCULLOUGH

She knew she was not alone, there was someone in the room, the person responsible for her condition. *I'm living through my own death,* she thought, and let herself drift. *A cold place. An old pond. But the mind,* she thought, *the mind will survive,* that was the great discovery, it was all connected, it was roots beneath the earth. You had only to reach it. The great hive.

She was not sure of herself; she felt like a child. The mind was just . . . it was the soul, they had always said it. The body shrank, it shrank and shrank while the soul grew and grew until the body could no longer hold it. You could build a pyramid or vault but it did not matter, the body shrank and stooped, they were right, she thought, they had been right all along, it was an error, the worst of her life. *You have to wake up.*

She opened her eyes but she was not in the room, there were colors, a landscape, a green plain going on as far as she could see and in front of her, an immense canyon drifting among clouds in a bright sky. *This is not my memory,* she thought, *this belongs to someone else.* She could see a coyote padding in a bar ditch, scents sounds it was taking in everything; she thought of a lock, a gate, a man shooting a gun.

She opened her eyes, latched on to the room, counting the chairs tables drawings, embers on the hearth, she was back in the house in

River Oaks. Hank was by the window. He was angry about the children. Or something else: the television. The president had been shot and his wife was climbing over the seat.

"H.L. fucking Hunt," Hank was saying, "we just killed the president."

There was a voice, hers: "They say Oswald was working for the Russians."

This is not real either, she thought. Hank had died before JFK. She was mixing things up.

But Hank did not appear to notice. "Hunt has a thousand people waiting for him at the airport with signs saying TRAITOR and YANKEE GO HOME. A few hours later, they shoot him."

"It's a little obvious," she said.

There was the fireplace burning. Hank was looking out the window, but what he saw she couldn't say. "When God dumps a lot of money in your lap, you start thinking you are closer to him than other people."

Then he was kissing her. It went on, he didn't notice that she was old, that she had lost her teeth. Then they were making love. She winked out, then came back again.

They were standing by the bar.

"Are we in on anything with Hunt?"

"No," she said.

"That is a relief." He sipped his whiskey. "If he weren't such a hick, he'd be dangerous."

"You're a hick, darling."

"I'm a hick with an art collection. A hundred years from now, we'll be the Rockefellers."

Of course it was not the Rockefellers he meant. It was the Astors. Or the Whitneys. As for their collection, half of what they'd first bought was fake and it had taken her the rest of her life to replace them with the originals.

★   ★   ★

As for JFK, it had not surprised her. The year he died, there were still living Texans who had seen their parents scalped by Indians. The land was thirsty. Something primitive still in it. On the ranch they had found points from both the Clovis and the Folsom, and while Jesus was walking to Calvary the Mogollon people were bashing each other with stone axes. When the Spanish came there were the Suma, Jumano, Manso, La Junta, Concho and Chisos and Toboso, Ocana and Cacaxtle, the Coahuiltecans, Comecrudos . . . but whether they had wiped out the Mogollons or were descended from them, no one knew. They were all wiped out by the Apaches. Who were in turn wiped out, in Texas anyway, by the Comanches. Who were finally wiped out by the Americans.

A man, a life—it was barely worth mentioning. The Visigoths had destroyed the Romans, and had themselves been destroyed by the Muslims. Who were destroyed by the Spanish and Portuguese. You did not need Hitler to see that it was not a pleasant story. And yet here she was. Breathing, having these thoughts. The blood that ran through history would fill every river and ocean, but despite all the butchery, here you were.

CHAPTER FORTY-TWO

DIARIES OF PETER McCULLOUGH

JULY 13, 1917

Four days since we returned from Piedras Negras. Of course they noticed our absence—my Chandler was gone overnight—but nothing was said. María believes we were missed in the bustle.

Landmen have flooded the town; strangers appear at our door at all times of the day and lights burn at my father's house all night. Both the Midkiffs and Reynoldses have been selling leases, but my father has turned down every offer that has come our way. I went over to his house to talk to him and found him sitting naked in the pool by his spring. His eyes were closed. In the water he looked like a small pale imp.

"I dunno why this heat never got to me before," he said.

"You are getting old," I told him.

"So are you."

"We ought to sell some leases and forget about this."

"That girl still in the house?"

I didn't answer.

"You know, if I hadn't kept your mother locked up I would swear you got made by an Indian."

"You wouldn't have been home to notice if I had," I said.

He considered that, then changed the subject.

"Let them find some more oil and then we'll consider selling leases."

I sat down on the rocks.

"It's all right, son. You're a good cattleman. But you don't know a goddamn thing about making money. And that's why you got me."

"Thanks for the reminder."

"Do some figuring on what our minerals are worth at a hundred an acre, which is where Reynolds and Midkiffs are selling."

"Tens of millions," I said.

"Then figure what they'll be worth at a thousand an acre. Or five thousand."

"Why do you even care?" I said.

"This is what is going to happen. A couple dozen drillers and oilmen are going to spend the next year or two proving our leases. That is when we will sell."

I want to believe he is wrong. Unfortunately, I know better.

"What's happening with that girl?" he said, but I was already walking away.

WHAT IS HAPPENING with María is that we have both been sore for days. The first night after Piedras Negras I slipped quietly from her room, but within an hour I'd returned and since then we have not spent more than a few minutes apart.

This morning I woke just after sunrise. I lay there, listening to her breath, taking in the odor of her hair and skin, dozing, then waking up to look at her again, washed over in the light and the pleasant feeling of being near her.

It occurs to me that I have not seen the shadow in several days; I have not thought about Pedro's ruined face or Aná's scream. In a moment of sheer perversity, I try to call the images back to mind, but I cannot.

☆　☆　☆

I HAVE ALWAYS known I am not the sort of person other people are inclined to love. They are blind to what I see in myself; with a glance they decide that my judgment ought not to be trusted. My singular luck, so far as they are concerned, was to be born into this great family; elsewise I would be some scrivener, renting a dim room in a filthy city.

It occurs to me that María may wake up one morning and see me as the others do, that her love may prove deciduous, though so far it is nearly the opposite; I see my own childish gaze reflected in hers, I catch her looking at me when my back is turned, I wake up and she is leaning on an elbow, watching me. We are drunk on each other. As for my so-called ailment—which I had presumed was a symptom of age, and Sally had presumed was yet another symptom of my unmanfulness—there has been not a single sign. If anything, the opposite: my body is possessed by an unending desire to be connected with her (just the thought . . .); we never separate after making love and she will often roll on top of me and fall asleep while we are still attached.

This morning she read to me from the Song of Solomon; I read the second of the Heloise and Abelard letters to her; when we are together it seems our mere existence is a transcendence of all that is wrong with the world, but as I sit now I wonder if there is some darker element, a man having relations with someone who is not his equal, though of course she is, in every way except in power, which means she is not. She is free to go and yet not free, as, aside from our room here, she has no place to call her own.

"WHERE DID YOU go?" she says, when I return.

"To my office."

"You were gone so long."

"I'll never do it again."

"Do you ever write about me?"

"You are most of what I write about," I say. "What else would I write about?"

"Since when?"

"Since the first day."

"But then you were unhappy. Perhaps you should destroy those pages."

"I was confused," I say.

"I've been thinking about the story of your father and the dead men . . ."

I hesitate for a moment; this could be nearly any story of my father. Then I realize what she is talking about.

" . . . and there is one I'd like to tell you. Perhaps you wouldn't mind getting your journal?"

"I have a strong memory."

"But a lazy body."

"No, it's true. My memory is my curse."

She runs her fingers through my hair. I get up and get my journal, just for her sake. On the way to my office I pass Consuela straightening up my bedroom, where I have not slept in five days. She doesn't look up.

HE WAS A Coahuiltecan, the last living one on earth. His people were older than the Greeks and Romans; they'd been living here five thousand years by the time the pyramids were built, and to them, all the other races of the earth were like scurrying ants, who appear in the first warm days but die off in the first frost.

But finally their own winter arrived. The Spanish appeared and then the Apaches, who continued the work of the Spanish, and then the Comanches, who continued the work of the Apaches, until, by this day in the spring of 1836, this man was the only survivor.

On that day my great-uncle Arturo Garcia saw the Coahuiltecan kneeling in his pasture, looking for something, and as the Indian was nearly blind, Arturo went to help him. After several hours in the buffalo grass and nopales he found the missing item, a marble of black obsidian, which Arturo presumed had mystical properties. Arturo had been born on this land, as had his father, and he knew that no rocks of that nature are found in the area.

Arturo was a wealthy young man, with a remuda of blooded horses, a beautiful wife, and a sixty-league grant from the king of Spain himself. His house was full of silver, pieces of art, and the weapons of his family, who had been knights in the olden times. Every morning he woke before the sunrise and watched the light come in, illuminating his land and his works and all he would leave for his sons.

Arturo had blood, and was known to cut out the hearts of his enemies, but he was also the sort of man who—despite having one hundred men working for him, a small town to look after, a beautiful wife and four children—would help an old Indian look for a marble.

Of course he didn't believe in seers or oracles; he was not a stupid peasant. He and his brother had both attended the Pontifical University, his ancestors had founded the University of Sevilla, he had grown up fluent in French and English and Spanish. But that day he was not feeling so intelligent. The Anglos had, against all odds, won the battle against his people at San Jacinto, and he was worried for his family.

The victory made no sense. On one side was a professional army, a powerful and ancient empire on which the sun never set, and the other a pack of ignorant barbarians, condemned criminals and land speculators. Though Texas had briefly been open to the Anglos, the borders had been closed since 1830, and yet they continued to illegally sneak into the state to take advantage of the free land, free services, loose laws. It was not unlike what happened on the fringes of the Roman Empire, when the Visigoths overran the imperial army. Perhaps God curses the proud.

Arturo asked the seer if he could put a question to him, and the seer said of course, but there was no guarantee of any answer.

Arturo said: "Will I lose my land?"

The seer said: "Go away, do not disturb me with questions of a material character; this is a place of the spirit, of philosophy, of the nature of the universe itself."

(This is not really what the Indian said, I interrupt.)

(The fact that he was an Indian has no bearing on his intelligence. She puts her finger to my lips.)

That night he couldn't sleep, thinking about all he had to lose. He returned to the seer the following morning.

"Seer, will I lose my land?"

And the seer said: "You have the best horses for five hundred miles, the biggest house, the most beautiful wife, an ancient lineage, and four healthy sons. I am a blind, penniless Indian. You should be the one giving me the answers."

"But you are wise."

"I am old. So old that I remember playing at your house before it was there."

"I suspect you are mistaken," said Arturo. "That house has stood nearly a hundred years."

"Nevertheless, I remember. There was an enormous rock I used to sleep on with my wife and all my children, for it was very warm, even in winter, as if it went down to the center of the earth. It must have been removed, as it was a growing rock, and became a little taller each year."

Arturo knew there had been such a rock. The top had been blasted off and the house was built over what was left. But as the years passed, the rock had begun to grow, cracking the plaster and bowing all the floors, so that a marble placed in the center of the room would roll toward any of the walls. Finally the floor was removed and the rock hammered and chiseled away. But there was no way for the Indian to have known this. Arturo said: "Old Man, I have done you a favor, and now you will kindly do me this favor as well. Will I keep my land or not?"

The old Coahuiltecan did not take a single breath for ten minutes. Then he said: "You will not like my answer."

"It is as I suspected."

The man nodded.

"I must hear it."

"I am sorry but you will not keep your land. You and your wife and all your sons will be killed by the Anglos."

THAT EVENING ARTURO stood on his portico, watching his sons play in the grass, his beautiful wife standing near, his vast pastures where his vaqueros and their families tended his herds.

He could not understand why a man like him, a good man, should suffer such a terrible fate and that night he took the most ancient weapon of his family, an *alabarda* that had seen combat against the French, the Dutch, and the Moors, and honed the edge so fine that it would split a hair. The next morning he returned to the camp of the old Coahuiltecan, where he cut off the man's head with a single stroke. But even as the head lay there, detached from the body, it looked at him and uttered a curse.

(But the lungs, I say. Without the lungs there can be no air . . .)

(The finger goes again to my lips.)

A few months later, deciding on the course of maximum caution, Arturo sent his family to Mexico City for their safety. But before they could even cross the river, they were waylaid by white militiamen, who committed enormous outrages upon his wife as she lay dying and murdered Arturo's four sons as well.

Arturo resolved to never marry again, and did not. In 1850, after the second war, he went to Austin and paid all his property taxes, and it was only because of his mastery of both written and spoken English, which exceeded that of every Anglo lawyer in the capital, that he was allowed to retain any property at all. Half his lands were immediately confiscated because the Anglos claimed the title was flawed, though they could not point out how, or where.

TWENTY YEARS LATER he disappeared, murdered with all his vaqueros. My father, who was his nephew, inherited the property. My mother wanted no part of it. She wanted him to sell the land to the Americans.

"But they are murderers," my father said.

"Better to sell to them than live among them," said my mother.

But my father began to go crazy thinking about the vast pastures he might own and six months after Arturo's murder, he and my mother moved here, along with a dozen vaqueros he hired in Chihuahua.

The house was untouched, the family treasure still intact. After reading my uncle's journals, he went and dug up a skeleton at the place they described. He reburied the man, whose head was indeed detached, at the most peaceful place he could find, under a persimmon tree next to a spring, with a good knife and a sack of beans to carry the man through his journeys in the next world. He was certain this would lift the curse and keep our family safe.

(She looks at me. "As you can see, it did not do any good.")

CHAPTER FORTY-THREE

ELI McCULLOUGH

1854–1855

That winter, instead of being sent down to the border, we were sent north to range the breaks from the Washita to the Concho. Winter was usually when the Indians holed up, but the previous year, the government had settled five hundred reluctant Comanches on the Clear Fork of the Brazos and another two thousand Caddos and Wacos on a larger reservation farther east.

As was normal, the reservations were short of food and the attempts to teach the Indians our superior white ways only convinced them of the opposite. The crops they grew were killed by drought or eaten by grasshoppers; there were more of them squeezed into a smaller space than they'd imagined humans could live. Locals complained about the reservation Indians stealing livestock; Indians complained the settlers were stealing horses and grazing their stock on Indian pastures. But we never caught any Indians, and the whites we caught we couldn't do anything about.

MEANWHILE, THERE WERE houses going up within gunshot of the caprock. The settlers had pushed far beyond Belknap, Chadbourne, and Phantom Hill, a hundred miles past where the army could protect them. They did not care that there was only one Ranger company patrolling the entire eastern Llano. As for the legislature, lice-ridden clodhoppers did not vote or donate to political campaigns, so their problems, quietly viewed to be of their own causation—though necessary for the betterment of the state—were ignored. No new taxes. Rangers cost money.

One night in April we'd made camp on a mesa. Unlike the other ranging companies we were careful with our fires, building them like the Indians did, in arroyos or depressions away from any trees that would reflect their light. We could see thirty or forty miles, an expanse of badlands going on in every direction, the river snaking between mesas, buttes, and hoodoos, uncountable side canyons and rolling hills, motts of juniper and shinnery oak. The land was greening up, the hackberries and cottonwoods along all the streams, the grama and little bluestem on the river flats, and it was pleasant with the red rock buttes and green valleys and the darkening sky overhead. The Dipper was riding high and though we had not caught a single Indian in six months, the weather was warming and we were not going to lose any more toes. We were all ready to turn in when we saw a glow off in the east, in a small valley, that grew brighter the longer we watched it. Five minutes later the horses were saddled and we were making our way off the mesa, toward the fire.

The house was still burning when we reached it. There was a charred scalped body in the doorway; we could see it had been a woman. Off in the brush we found a man stuck with arrows. The arrows had two grooves and the moccasin prints narrowed at the front and I knew it was Comanches. The homestead had not been there long—the corral posts were still leaking sap—and there were the framed beginnings of a smokehouse and stable. Yoakum Nash found a silver locket and Rufus Choate found a barlow knife and after drinking our fill at their spring and making a quick scout for other valuables, we cut stick and rode after the Indians.

Their trail was clear enough, and a mile or so along it we came on a young boy with his head caved in, barely starting to stiffen. When we hit the river the tracks crossed and recrossed in every conceivable direction and the captain put me out front. All the trails were too obvious. I took us up the middle of the water until there was a long patch of rocky ground. I knew they'd taken it and sure enough, where the rocks ended, the pony tracks began.

The grass was high and the tracks were clear but there were not enough of them. They aimed toward a bluff, which the others presumed the Indians had climbed to watch their backtrail, but it was too early for that so I led us back to the river, losing another half hour. Then we found a pale blue dress in the rocks. It was something a teenager would wear, too small to have fit the burned woman, who was tall and chunky.

"Well, it appears we have a live one," said the captain.

"Maybe," said McClellan. He was the lieutenant. "Or maybe they just threw her off in the brush like the other one."

I knew she was alive. They had taken her and her brother, but her brother was too young, or he had cried or been noisy and she was smart enough to take a lesson from that, despite what they had done to her before tying her to the horse.

We stood on the banks another minute, collecting our thoughts, looking around at the hoodoos and canyons and tall grass and cedar; the Indians might be anywhere. It would not take Napoleon to make an ambush in country like this and we all wanted to stay in the flat open plain along the water.

After a few more miles we came to a bend thickly overgrown with cottonwoods and there was something about the light. The sun was coming up behind us. The captain and I eased forward and he looked through his glass while I looked through mine; there were some specks along the red rock, maybe five miles out.

"You seeing horses?"

"Yup."

"Do they know we're following?"

"I don't think so."

The sun was rising into their eyes but we turned around and cut through the brush anyway, keeping the trees and buttes between us and the Indians, gaffing hell out of our ponies. But when we got another look at them again, this time from the top of a small mesa, they'd put even more distance on us.

MIDWAY THROUGH THE day our horses were blown. The Comanches would have changed mounts twice and the captain was reckless, leading us through funnels and thickets at top speed. "They don't want a fight," he said. "They just want to get away."

Meanwhile we were getting close to the Llano and the badlands had narrowed to a single canyon a few miles wide. Blocks of stone the size of courthouses had tumbled from the upper walls; there were forests of petrified stumps and logs, herds of pronghorn watching from the ledges. The Indians would have to climb out.

We were getting close to the canyon mouth and as we emerged from some cottonwoods, there they were, only a half mile ahead but six hundred feet above us. One of them turned to look and waved his arm. I was squinting through my field glass. It was Escuté.

I couldn't make out his face, but I could tell by his straight back and crooked arm and the way he'd done his hair, which was unlike most Comanches. I wondered if Nʉʉkaru was with him. It occurred to me that Nʉʉkaru might not even be alive.

Then a flat crack rolled across the valley.

One of our men had a Sharps rifle with a tang sight, but he must have missed the Indians by a comfortable margin because they continued to wave as they disappeared over the ledge.

After three hours of riding into box canyons and other dead ends, we found the trail the Indians had taken. There was bear grass and juniper hanging above us, water splashing over shelves of rock nearly too high for our horses to climb. A few men with bows, firing down into the chasm, could have easily gotten all of us, so we moved slow. Our arms were shaking from keeping the pistols up. The ravine ended in a cul-de-sac. There was a wall covered with drawings and carvings, snakes and men dancing and horses and buffalo, a shaman in a head-dress, the swirling figures you see when you fall asleep.

It had the feeling of a sacred place and we expected the Indians to appear above us and rain arrows from every direction. Then there was a rustling or whirring all around us and Elmer Pease began shooting. The rest of us jumped behind the closest rock.

There were no arrows. Instead there was a kind of dervish hanging in the air, a small tornado, though there was no wind, it was some kind of Indian spirit, and it floated about for a long time before moving back down the canyon, where it vanished.

The captain came out from behind his rock. "McCullough and Pease, get up behind that face and see if the path goes anywhere."

An hour later we were on the Llano. The Comanches' trail was faint but clear. In the tracks I saw three riders split west from the group, driving a dozen unsaddled ponies, leaving a large, clearly beaten trail, a diversion. The main body had continued north in single file, their tracks nearly indistinguishable among all the buffalo sign and rocks. I thought about the girl they had taken. Then I thought about Escuté.

"Here they go," I said. I pointed toward the diversion.

AFTER FIVE OR six miles it petered out. I guessed they had been dragging brush and dropped it. Or they began to ride single file. Or they knew tricks I had never learned. We turned and followed our back-track; we were six hours behind them and they all had fresh mounts. I got off my horse and stood looking around in the dirt, ignoring the trail they had left across the rocks, invisible to everyone else, but clear enough to me, a faint disturbance, scuffs here and there in the dust.

"I'm about stumped," I said.

The captain looked at me.

"We could split up and see what we find."

"We aren't splitting up," the captain said.

"We know they didn't go west and they probably didn't go south, either."

"You don't see anything?" he said. "Anything at all?"

"There's no tracks," I told him.

He didn't believe me but there was nothing he could do. We went north along the caprock, putting the spurs in and hoping to get a glimpse of them against the horizon before the sun faded. I watched as we rode, our track slowly diverging from Escuté's until finally we were on a different course entirely.

THE CAPTAIN DIDN'T trust me after that, but it didn't matter. Two months later, we made an unplanned resupply trip to Austin and he found his wife entertaining a sutler. The captain's pistol misfired and the sutler stabbed him to death.

After the burial we went to the jail and took the sutler into custody. The sheriff handed us the keys.

"You ain't gonna do nothin'?" the man said, as we marched him past the sheriff. "Just let them hang me, is that it?"

As we led him out into the sunlight, he protested that he'd been one of the filibusters to survive Mier, but we pointed out that was a long time ago, and in another country, and it was time to acknowledge the corn.

A few blocks from the capitol we stripped him, cut off everything hanging between his legs, then fixed him with a riata and dragged him up and down Congress. By the time we strung him up he had stopped kicking. I thought we ought to scalp him, but everyone else thought he made a fine blossom just as he was and there was no sense cuttin' it too fat. We went to the tavern and I was elected captain over McClellan. I waited till they were good and damaged and then went back to scalp the sutler. I had always been fond of the captain.

WITH THE EXCEPTION of Nuukaru and Escuté, I had no doubts about my loyalties. Which were in the following order: to any other

Ranger, and then to myself. Toshaway had been right: you had to love others more than you loved your own body, otherwise you would be destroyed, whether from the inside or out, it didn't matter. You could butcher and pillage but as long as you did it for people you loved, it never mattered. You did not see any Comanches with the long stare— there was nothing they did that was not to protect their friends, their families, or their band. The war sickness was a disease of the white man, who fought in armies far from his home, for men he didn't know, and there is a myth about the West, that it was founded and ruled by loners, while the truth is just the opposite; the loner is a mental weakling, and was seen as such, and treated with suspicion. You did not live long without someone watching your back and there were very few people, white or Indian, who did not see a stranger in the night and invite him to join the campfire.

People came and went in the Rangers. I was not always elected captain, but I always had a slot to ride. I looked after the new arrivals, whether they were younger or older, and I was beginning to see my life laid out in front of me, one year no different from the next; the faces around me would change, I would put them into the ground or give them a clap on the back as they mustered out, then I would go and see to my equipment, drop my revolvers off at the gunsmith, my tack at the saddlemaker, buy a new shirt and pants, then trade my land vouchers for a horse or whiskey or something useful.

Then I shaved off my six-month beard, figured out what company was riding out next, and put my name back on the list.

CHAPTER FORTY-FOUR

J. A. McCULLOUGH

I t was dark, it was loud, she could not make out where she was, there was the sound of water, a rushing like standing in the tides. Two people arguing: *it is a girl,* said one, *this one will be a girl,* then another voice, which she recognized as her father's, saying, *okay, honey.* The drumming of a heart, the swell of breathing. She couldn't move. There were children's voices. *My brothers,* she thought.

Then she wasn't sure. There were voices in Spanish and in another language she didn't recognize, though it made a kind of sense. A burning feeling. The grass was tall and the sun was in her eyes and there was a man with a dark beard and shining helmet looking as if he wasn't sure what to do. He stepped forward and stuck something into her again. It caught; he pulled it out and tried again and this time it went all the way through and then the man and the sun were nothing but black spots.

She opened her eyes. She was back in the enormous room. *There have been times before this one,* she thought. She felt a relief come over her; it was the beginning of something, not the end, she had been wrong all along, wrong her entire life.

Then it was gone. She'd made it all up. It was nothing but the mind inventing stories. Anything that did not involve its own end. The house vanished, dust blowing, she could see into the stars . . . she willed herself back into her thoughts.

✳ ✳ ✳

THE TRUCK WAS going too fast, fishtailing through corners, as if the driver thought he was on tarmac instead of dirt. Something was wrong, she knew immediately, though the vehicle was just a speck still, a mile or more away, an immense cloud rising behind it. Someone had been hurt; that was plain. *Do not let it be Hank.* It was more a feeling than a thought. She stood in the great room and watched the dust come closer. *If it is not Hank, I will never miss a day of church.* Then this seemed overdramatic, a ridiculous promise, they had run out of beer for all she knew. Still, she had a feeling.

She picked up the phone and called the doctor before the truck arrived, before she even knew for certain. "This is Jeannie McCullough," she said. "I think someone's been hurt at our place here, I think they were bird hunting."

She went out onto the gallery. One of the hands saw what was happening; he was riding toward the gate to intercept the truck. He rolled off his horse and pushed the gate open just as the truck shot through and then she had a different feeling, that a mistake had been made, that the man should not have let the truck through at all; she was suddenly very cold and wanted to go upstairs.

When the pickup came to a stop near the gallery, she ran down to meet it. There was Hank in the cab with one of the insurance men. All the worry went out of her, she felt foolish, she felt *thank God thank God,* she was smiling, she was a ridiculous person, but then the two men jumped out without looking at her and she saw she'd been wrong.

Then she was behind the truck. There was Hank, his face white, his shirt heavy and dark, bright handprints over the paint, all over the windows, the third man was holding Hank in his arms and crying. *That is okay,* she thought. *There is more blood in him than that.* She climbed into the bed, it was littered with quail, the man did not want to let go, he was holding on to Hank so tightly; *honey,* she was saying, *honey can you hear me*; his eyes were closed but then he opened them. She put her face to his; someone was saying they were sorry they were sorry. *Hank it's me. Open your eyes.* He did; he saw her. He was trying to smile and then nothing happened. His eyes changed.

A few moments later Hank's dog arrived; it had run the entire way from the quail fields, it leaped into the truck and began licking Hank's face and barking, trying to wake him up, tugging at his shirt and barking; it would not be pushed away. "Get this fucking dog out of here"—that was her—"someone get this fucking dog." The pointer bit someone's hand, then went back to licking Hank's face, the barking was never going to stop and finally the insurance men got hold of it and lifted it off the truck. "Shhhhhh," someone was saying, "shhh shhhh shhh," but she didn't know if they were talking to her or Hank's dog.

No, she thought now, *no no no*. She did not want to think about this. She wished she had been struck down before she had even looked out the window. The pointer would not leave her side. She flew with it everywhere and eight years later, when it finally died, she had been incapacitated with grief, she had not been able to go to work, it was like losing her husband a second time.

He was a great man. There were men who were born like that, the hand of God all over them, Hank had been one. Losing him . . . she was choking. When people spoke she was underwater. She heard them and didn't. She would think about something else. She could still feel pain, she knew she was still alive. Was it true what they said, you were like a butterfly stretching its wings, one day you were trapped here, the next you weren't? She didn't know. She did not want to forget. *I want to remember,* she thought. *I will remember I will remember I will remember.*

CHAPTER FORTY-FIVE

DIARIES OF PETER McCULLOUGH

JULY 22, 1917

Drilling begun in the Reynolds and Midkiff pastures. Not a single room available in town. The streets are packed with men, trucks, carts, stacks of equipment; there are people sleeping in tents and ditches. Niles Gilbert is letting his pig stall for eighty dollars a week. As usual I expect anger at our skyrocketing fortune; of course it is the opposite. They see our prosperity nearly as their own, as if rent for a hog sty is no different from a few million dollars in oil.

And—for the time being—everyone *is* making money. Selling clothes, old tools, food, water, rooms, renting use of their cars, trucks, mules and carts, horse teams, and backyards. Grover Deshields has stopped tending his crops and is instead driving around on his tractor, charging ten dollars (a week's wages) to pull stuck trucks out of bogholes in the drilling fields. It is rumored he waters the bogholes at night. Someday this boom will end. Though not for us.

There are now four derricks, in various states of assembly, visible from our back ridge. My father's driller is not impressed. He thinks there will soon be a hundred or so. This despite the fact that the only other oil around here was found at Piedras Pintas. There are the Rieser and Jennings fields, but they are only gas.

∗   ∗   ∗

AS FOR MARÍA, I have stopped even pretending to go out to the pastures. Sullivan finds me in the evening and gives me a report of the day's activities. He has nearly caught us several times. . . . I expect the novelty of her to wear off but it has only gotten more intense. If I spend even an hour apart from her I can't think of anything else, I forget the names of people, what I am supposed to be doing, any reason I have for being.

I want to know everything. The way a child learns the world by tasting it . . . I want to take every part of her into my mouth; I find myself wondering about her former lovers, how she was with her sisters, her father, her mother, who she was at university, where the separate parts of her come from.

I AM UP before the light and she is still sleeping, relaxed, her hands thrown behind her head, face to one arm, her knees leaning in as if she has fallen asleep on a beach . . . I watch the sun brighten as it touches her, the smooth skin along her neck (a red mark I clumsily left), an ear, the hollow behind her cheek, her chin (slightly pointed), her lips (slightly chapped), while her eyes, which are nearly black except for a few flecks of gold, flicker in a dream. Without waking, she realizes I am not lying next to her and she reaches for me and pulls me over.

Still the shadow has not appeared. Have begun to look in all the dark places, out of the corner of my eye, but . . . nothing. Pedro—I can only recall his face as a younger man, and Lourdes, too, as a younger, more beautiful woman, as if, in my mind, they are aging in reverse.

JULY 23, 1917

A rush of air from the north, high of eighty degrees. We wake up alert and clearheaded—we must be outside. As there is an unspoken agreement about spending any time near the Garcia land, we pack a basket into the Chandler and head for Nuevo Laredo. As I drive, she encourages my hands to wander; we make a brief stop along the way. I consider the fact that I have never done this before—never made love to a woman outside the confines of a bedroom. I wonder if she has, feel briefly jealous despite my former sentiment about her old lovers, but the feeling passes and I am content again.

When we reach Nuevo Laredo the ugliness of the city is somehow overwhelming.

"This will not do," I say.

"We will make it beautiful for everyone else," she says. She leans her head against my shoulder.

We are looking for a cantina (or hotel, she reminds me) but as we approach the *plaza de toros* there are several drunk Americans, well dressed, calling loudly after the Mexican girls; one of them stares into the car, says something to his friends about María. I nearly stop to have a word, but she tells me to keep driving. We make another slow circle through the town, past the Alma Latina, where a trio of mariachis sit with no one to play for, and then somehow our eyes seem to catch on all the *congales,* and we decide instead to drive along the river.

After we have put a good distance between us and the city we stop where a small hill affords a good view over the savannah. There is an old long-armed oak with soft grass underneath.

We are lying on a blanket, looking out over the endless land and sky, when María says: "I like to imagine this at the beginning of time, when the grass was very tall and there were wild horses."

"Horses have only been here a few hundred years," I say.

"I prefer to forget that."

"It's buffalo you would see."

"Except there is little to like about a buffalo," she says. "What is the point of a buffalo?"

I shrug.

"But you prefer them. Okay, I will imagine buffalo instead, though they are hairy, smelly, inelegant, and have horns."

"They belong here," I say.

"In my mind, the horses do as well. And if the horses do not, I do not. And if I do not, you do not. In your world there is nothing but buffalo and sad Indians."

"And then a gallant Spaniard appears on horseback. And shoots them."

"It's true. I'm a hypocrite."

I kiss her neck.

"My father thought there were still mustangs here. He said he often saw their footprints, without shoes."

"It's possible," I say.

"I used to dream about them."

I think of all the mustangs we shot. But Pedro had done it too. Everyone had done it.

I look around. At the bottom of the hill is a stream that feeds the Rio Bravo. Along the water are persimmons and hackberries and pecans, cedar elms. I can hear green jays calling.

We lie and make love in the sun, despite the fact that we can see, in the distance, the workers moving in the onion fields along the river. María finds them picturesque; I can't help feeling sorry for them.

"Are you sure you want to be with me?" she says. "I think you would prefer a revolutionary."

I kiss her again.

"I am just old and sentimental," she says.

"Younger than me."

"Women age in dog years."

I look at her.

"Even me," she says. She shrugs again. "But for now I think our wine has gotten hot."

She stands and walks down the hill to put the bottles in the stream. I worry she'll catch a goathead, but her soles are tougher than mine. I watch her disappear over the hill, her small hips swaying, the scars on her back, her hair curled on top of her head.

When she is gone a few minutes I guess she might be relieving herself, but when she still doesn't return I decide to find her, consider putting on my boots, don't, then make my way through the tall brown grass, worrying about snakes and burrs and thorns. I find her lying in the creek. Her hair is loose and streaming around her, the stones white beneath her. I take three or four bounding steps and then she looks up.

"I have always liked being outside," she says.

She pats the water as if it is our bed. I lie down in it. I notice how white and freckled I am, tan only at the arms, scraggly hairs every-where . . . but then that feeling passes.

We lie as if we are the first people on earth, or the last, the sun coming down on us, the water cold, our every action of the utmost importance, as if, like children, we know that no one else really exists.

Finally we climb the hill to the blanket. The sun dries us and she curls against me and falls asleep. There is nothing missing. I wonder if I have ever been this happy and then I wonder again about my father, if he has ever felt anything like this. Even as a young man, I cannot see it. He is like my brother, a gun aimed squarely at the world.

CHAPTER FORTY-SIX

ELI McCULLOUGH

O ur commission ran out in 1860. The state was split over secession, with the cotton men and everyone who read their newspapers in favor, and everyone else against. But the Rebels needed Texas; without our cotton, beef, and ports the Confederacy could not stand.

That summer, Dallas burned. As in any conspiracy of prophets, a series of miracles surrounded the fires. The first was that all the buildings had been empty—not a single soul hurt—though an entire block had been torched. The second miracle was there were no eyewitnesses. The third and final miracle was that even though there was nothing an Abolitionist liked better than the sound of his own voice—every time an oxcart or soapbox caught fire in Kansas, a dozen Free-Soilers would turn themselves in, hoping to be hanged for their crimes—no soft sister came forward to claim the Dallas fires. The cotton men had burned their own buildings to bring us into the war and before the sun came up the next day, their newspapers were blaming escaped slaves and Yankees, whose next step would be to burn all of Texas, right after they got done raping all the white women.

By the end of summer, most Texans were certain that if slavery was abolished, the whole of the South would Africanize, no proper woman would be safe, amalgamation would be the order of the day. Though in the next breath they would tell you that the war had nothing to do with slavery. It was about human dignity, self-governance, freedom itself, the rights of the states; it was a war to keep us free from the meddling hand of Washington. Never mind that Washington had kept us from becoming part of Mexico again. Never mind they were keeping the Indians at bay.

It is worth noting that even then, no one thought slavery would last forever. The tide was strongly against it, not just in America, but all the world over. But the plantation owners figured if they could get another twenty years out of the institution, it was worth convincing everyone to fight. That was when the acquisitive spirit began to wake inside me. There was no point being a small man.

AFTER THE SECESSION vote, the state began to empty out. Half the Rangers I knew lit for California—they were not going to die so a rich man could keep his niggers. Close on their heels was any Texan who had ever said a word against the slaveocracy, or the cotton men, or was suspected of voting for Lincoln. And plenty of secessionists left as well. Over many of the wagon trains headed west, away from the war, the Confederate flag could be seen flying proudly. They were in favor of the war as long as they did not have to fight it themselves, and I have always thought that is why California turned out the way it did.

WHILE NOT EXACTLY sound on the goose, slavery struck me as the natural state: we had slaves, the Indians had slaves, you shall enjoy the spoils of your enemies, which the Lord your God has given you. The faces of Christ and his mother have adorned many a sword; all the heroes of Texas had made their names in the fight against Mexico. For them the war had been a golden arrangement and I could not see why this one ought to be any different.

IF YOU WEREN'T lined into a Texas cavalry unit, you'd be drafted and sent east to fight afoot, and so any right-thinking man who didn't have a horse quickly begged, borrowed, or stole one. I signed with the Mounted Rifles under McCullough (no relation) and we were put under Sibley and sent to take New Mexico from the Federals.

Things went agee from the start. Our leader, Colonel Sibley, found the march considerable boring, and a few weeks into it, he retired to the bed of his wagon, accompanied by two prostitutes and a barrel of who-hit-John. There was an uproar from the fire-eaters, who imagined they were fighting for human dignity and freedom from the northern elite, but more cat wagons were requisitioned and the complaining stopped. The rest of us were already calling ourselves the RMN men— Rich Man's Niggers—in honor of those brave souls who'd inspired our fight for freedom. As for Sibley, as long as he shared his whiskey, we did not mind him.

THE NEWSPAPERS SAID we'd have an easy fight against the Yankee farmers but it was not long before we detected a miscalculation. There were not many grangers to be found among the New Mexicans. In fact they appeared to have grown up the same as we had, hunting and fighting Indians, and after a few months they got behind us and burned our whole supply train. Sibley became down in the mouth and retired again to his whore-equipped ambulance; the rest of us took a vote and decided to return to Texas. The newspapers said that since New Mexico was teeming with aborigines, we didn't want it anyway, and thus our retreat was more properly considered a great victory.

RICHMOND WAS FIFTEEN hundred miles away; they mostly forgot we existed. Belts were tight—the new governor was inaugurated in homespun—but everyone had enough to eat. Except for the shortage of young men on the streets, and occasional news of Yankee ships sunk in our harbors, you would not have known a war was going on at all. Being now a lieutenant I could come and go as I pleased, but there were not many places to go. The Comanches had taken back a smart sprinkle of their old territory; the frontier had collapsed several hundred miles. On every stretch of lonely backroad where the Indians didn't lurk, you'd find the Home Guard. There was a fifty-dollar bounty on Confederate deserters, and if they didn't know you personally, they were likely to tear up your leave papers, put a noose around your neck, and take your carcass to trade for their pieces of silver.

Judge Black had plenty of pull, so I stayed at his house when I got bored with the barracks, drinking his claret, sleeping in his office, calling for sandwiches on the dumbwaiter. I read a few books but mostly I drank whiskey and smoked cigars and planned my future. It had become clear to me that the lives of the rich and famous were not so different from the lives of the Comanches: you did what you pleased and answered to no one. I saw myself finishing out the war as a captain or major, at which point I'd go into cattle or shipping. One thing I knew: I was done working for other men.

As for the judge's three daughters, one had died of a fever and the other two were still unmarried. The elder was twenty-two, a cremello like the judge, fair of skin and temperament, with my brother's tendency toward books and deep thoughts. There had been some scandal associated with her, but no one would discuss it. The younger was more proper, in the exact form of her mother, a dusky beauty with a taste for the finer things and impeccable public behavior.

I abused myself thinking about them, but the judge had expectations that his daughters would marry Harvard men, or sons of Sam Houston, or at least sons of bankers. I was an unreliable lieutenant, whose time on earth would likely be short, and it would not do to make any investment in me. So when the door to my room opened and closed quietly one night, I wagered it was Millie, the quadroon who'd just been added to the judge's household.

She came and sat on the bed. I looked at her in the light from the window. It was Madeline, the older daughter.

"I didn't think you'd mind," she said.

I didn't. She had pale skin and red hair; her face was covered in freckles but she had big green eyes and a soft mouth. Everything about her was finely done, and though in the past I'd found kissing girls that pretty to be like biting into a green persimmon, I patted the mattress and she lay down next to me.

Her breath was sweet, which I guessed to be from her mother's sherry. When she saw I would take no initiative, she straddled me. It was not long before I determined that she had waylaid her maidenhead sometime in the distant past.

Unfortunately I felt cowardly as a Dutchman. The judge would never forgive me; at best he'd expect me to marry her. Not to mention she was drunk, and, I thought, slightly crazy; there was no telling how the story might play when the sun rose. She detected my cowardice and lay on top of me. Unlike most of the women who consented to my company in those days, she was sweet and clean. I ran my fingers through her hair—finer than corn silk—but I did not think she'd appreciate the comparison so I kept it to myself.

"Am I not pretty enough?"

"You're too pretty," I said.

"But . . ." She touched me and reminded me of my failure.

"There is a lot on my mind," I told her.

"Because you're going back to fight this awful war for the slavers."

"It's for Texas," I said.

"Texas is not Jefferson Davis," she said.

"This is not good talk."

"Who will hear me?"

"I can hear you."

"Don't be silly. Texas is worth fighting for, but not the slavers. And I am not sure there is a difference right now."

"This is some house to be a Free-Soiler in," I said.

"I told my father he was a coward and the reason slavery hadn't ended was that men like him didn't speak up. And men like you, who are going to fight for it. Though of course unlike him, you have no choice." Then she said, "Do you have syphilis?"

"No," I said.

"He has been warning me against you since I was twelve."

"Did he say I had the pox?"

"He said if I looked the word up in Johnson's there would be a picture of your face."

I was quiet.

"I am joking you," she said. "I was just wondering. Given your history."

"Well, I don't have it," I said.

"I'll lay with you despite your pox. I love you and now you're going off to die."

I did not know what to make of her.

"Well," she said. "Do you love me?"

"Jesus," I said.

"I'm kidding." She sighed. "All right, I'll go."

"I'm going to die of old age," I said.

"Don't be hurt."

"I'm not."

"You shouldn't be afraid of him."

"I'm not afraid of him. I'm afraid of what will happen if you spend too much time with me."

"Well, I'm sure you would like that honor, but you're about five years too late. As I'm sure you've heard." She began to move her hips. I allowed my hands under her shift. I knew even then I was not doing right. I will not lay it on anyone else. But I told myself she was a young girl and whatever affection she possessed would be gone by the time the dew burned off the morning grass.

For most of the night we were enthusiastic and in the morning she snuck back to her room. I expected a speech about us being married in the eyes of God, as that was the price of milk in those days, but all she said was: "My mother and father are going to San Antonio."

That night we did it several more times and each time I took precautions.

"You're afraid you'll have to marry me," she said.

"I don't mind marrying you." I hadn't thought about it until that moment, but I knew it was true and I didn't regret saying it.

"Well, that is a very sweet way to put it."

I ignored her. "Nothing's going to happen to me," I said. "You don't have to worry."

"You really shouldn't talk like that."

I nearly told her that there were things God and I had buried the hatchet on, though it was just as likely Old Scratch. But I decided to keep quiet.

A FEW WEEKS later we got orders to ride on Kansas. The judge summoned me to his office. He was unbarbered and his hair was askew and I could see he'd slept in his clothes. He was a big man in every way and except for his ginger color I had never noticed anything to link him to his daughter. But now I saw that Madeline had his eyes and his large mouth, and something about this made me happy.

"You are nearly a dead man," he told me. He took a pistol from a drawer and thumped it on the table. "I tried to get her to admit that you'd abused her honor, but she insists you have not. Is this true?"

"Yes," I lied.

"I told her you had syphilis and her face would be marked by pox."

"That is not true, so far as I know."

"I told her you laid with whores."

"I'm leaving," I said. "You shouldn't worry about it."

"I'm not," he said, "but I am very worried for my daughter. I am terrified for my daughter, in fact. I don't approve of this. I approve of you but not with Madeline. Unfortunately she gets what she wants. You will marry her."

"I intend to."

"Good man," he said. "Good man."

The whole time he hadn't looked at me. He was staring out the window. I knew what he was trying to find: the exact moment in time he'd made his first mistake. Was it taking me in when I came back from the Indians, or was it saving me from the hanging in Bastrop, or was it allowing me to come around all those years since, the whole time against everyone's best judgment? His eyes were wet.

"Say something terrible, Eli." He began to straighten the papers on his desk, pushing them into neat stacks, and then he stood up and picked up an armful of books that had been sitting on the floor as long as I could remember. He carried them to the shelves.

"Don't make my daughter a widow." He looked at a title and shelved it and looked at the next one and walked a few steps and made a space.

I was nearly to the door when he called after me: "You have to understand I wanted something different for her, Eli. You're a good man, and I love you like my own son, but I know the life she will have with you."

He continued to shelve his books.

"I wanted her to marry someone with a house in a city, some banker or clerk or Yankee. I didn't want her living in a cabin and dying in childbirth or from drinking bad water or being kicked by a horse or scalped or shot." He shook his head. "My daughter . . ."

"I promise."

"You can't," he said. "You can't make a promise about what other people will do to her."

CHAPTER FORTY-SEVEN

J.A. McCULLOUGH

S he was back in the office in Houston. Milton Bryce in his thick lawyer's glasses, already combing his hair over, telling her to make an offer on Brown and Root. But there was very little oil flowing anywhere; she couldn't see the point in a pipeline company.

"They also do dams, military bases, things like that," Bryce was saying. "A lot of work for the Corps of Engineers. You know Herman Brown died . . ."

"I heard that."

"And now George is trying to get out of the business. I mean now. This week."

Something about his insistence put her off; she stopped listening.

"It's clean and you could probably get the whole thing for forty. If I had the money myself . . ."

She made a note to look into it, but a few days later, Ed Halliburton scraped together an offer, despite the fact that, along with the rest of the industry, his well-cementing company was hitting bottom. George Brown sold out for thirty-six million dollars; within a decade the company was grossing seven hundred million a year, building bases for the army in Vietnam.

It was hardly her only mistake. For years after Hank's death, she'd felt the need to calculate and recalculate every risk, as if everything she did was being recorded for others to judge, as if her most private thoughts would become public. She became deliberate to a fault, building cases for every decision, she was never not reading, she was never not thinking; it was unusual for her to have a conversation that she had not already rehearsed in her mind, and there were times she convinced herself that not even Hank could have kept pace. Though in more sober moments, she knew there was something missing. The men around her were always sure they were right, even when there was no good reason. That was what mattered. Being sure of things. If you were wrong, you just defended your position even more loudly.

Meanwhile, everyone was stealing from her. T.J. Block, their partner on several drilling projects, had for "purposes of convenience" moved into Hank's office. In her haze she had signed off on new leases, not having the energy to look into them herself, though the problem was also Hank: he had made so many verbal agreements, had his fingers in so many projects, so many promises . . . she could not keep track. She could not tell when someone was lying to her. She was being charged twice for the same orders of casing pipe and drilling mud, she couldn't tell if it was her drillers ripping her off or the suppliers or both, everyone saw an opportunity, there were offers to buy her out. Hank's sisters sued her for half the company and her own employees thought she was stupid; they were slow to follow orders, seemed to think she could not tell the difference between a good job and a bad job, they were reluctant to start big projects that they were certain she would abandon. There were casing problems, cementing problems, flow problems, the equipment broke constantly . . . to Hank they had given their best, to her they gave nothing.

Of course, they all assured her this wasn't so. She was not sure if she was being paranoid or going crazy or was just in over her head and ought to sell the company to T.J. Block, who acted like it was already his. Everyone seemed to know things she didn't; she wondered if her phone had been bugged.

So far as everyone was concerned it was Hank they had worked for.

She was nothing more than an appendage, a pretty blond housewife who—instead of opening a clothing boutique or horse stable or something sensible—had decided to amuse herself at her husband's office.

She began to suspect she might really crack up, that she would have to take the kids and leave Houston and move back to the ranch, and then she and Milton Bryce were going to lunch and instead of stopping to park she kept going. Down the street and out toward the countryside.

"I was not hungry anyway," he said.

She continued to drive out of the city until there was nothing but tall straight pines and oaks, the light coming green over the road. She said, "Who is definitely *not* stealing from me?"

He was quiet and then he stayed quiet . She wondered if he had turned against her like the others.

"Bud Lanning is not bad," he finally said.

"Bud Lanning ordered four thousand feet of casing pipe to finish a two-thousand-foot hole."

"Gordon Lytle?"

She had made a mistake.

He mashed his hair over.

"What do you think of Mr. T.J. Block?"

"He is fine," said Bryce. "Except for being a liar and a thief."

She felt herself smile and the relief came over her and then faded and then she was furious. They continued down the road in silence.

"You didn't ask," he said. "And it's not really my place to offer these opinions."

"What if I just fired everyone right now?"

"You'll want to change the locks first. And you'll need to hang on to at least one of the secretaries. Maybe two."

She turned the car around at a logging road and headed back to town.

They spent the rest of the afternoon walking around the Museum of Fine Arts. Finally she decided she could hold down a sandwich.

Even that turned out to be too ambitious but nonetheless, that night she had the locks changed and in the morning, as people began to show up at the office, she fired them all except Edna Hinnant, the secretary.

THE NEW EMPLOYEES were better and yet . . . in order to be respected she had to know their jobs as well as hers; if she did not understand fracture flow and jet perforation versus gun perforation and different methods of sand consolidation and acidizing and propping agents . . . she wanted only to sleep but there was so much to review, more than would ever have been expected of Hank. She felt herself wavering again; there was no point in working so hard at something that no one wanted her to be doing.

Later she would realize that it was simply that she'd had nothing else. Her children were not enough and she had always known she was nothing like her grandmother, nothing like the other women in the neighborhood, whose lives were sunk into their outfits and fundraisers, who might spend a week trying to get the seating at a party just right. She had always seen herself a certain way; the fact that others felt entitled to an opinion on the matter—on who she ought to be—should not have come as a shock, though it did. While other women got prescriptions for Valium, she got one for Benzedrine, and every time she felt herself fading or she wanted to stay in bed or take a long lunch she reminded herself of the Colonel, who had kept working until he was ninety years old.

Endless reports, mental exercises to keep her mind fresh. Any numbers she saw—a license plate, house number, street sign—she would multiply, divide, manipulate in some way, 7916 Oak Drive, seventy-nine times sixteen, which was eighty times sixteen minus sixteen. Twelve hundred eighty. Minus sixteen. Twelve sixty-four.

As for the men around her, they remained polite while resisting everything she did. She convinced Aubrey Stokes to sell her a lease instead of passing it up to the majors, but just as she was about to hang up the phone, he said:

"I'll get some papers over there this afternoon. Just to make sure we're on the right page."

She was too surprised to reply.

"Nothing personal, Jeannie."

But it was personal. There wasn't a single oil operator in the state who didn't consider his word as good as his bond, who didn't look down on the easterners and their endless need for lawyers and documents. But men who'd taken Hank's word would not take hers. They acted as if she'd landed from outer space or they sweetly ignored her attempts to talk business and turned the conversation toward her family and her health (she was under a lot of pressure); they did not trust that she could be relentless or focused when nature demanded she stay home with her babies.

She took all the pictures of the kids out of her office. She could not have people suspecting she was thinking about her family when she ought to be thinking about work, and equally—though it took much longer to admit this to herself—she could not disturb the fantasy that these men had about sleeping with her. She wouldn't, and didn't, but you did not want them thinking that door was closed. You did not want pictures of your kids.

After she fired everyone she spent seven days a week in the office and, knowing she would need the same of Milton Bryce, tripled his salary and gave his wife a credit line at Neiman Marcus. As for her children, Tom and Ben sensed they would have to bear up. Susan was lost for good. The boys had always been well-behaved and self-sufficient; Susan had been a colicky baby and as a toddler she was always sneaking into bed with Hank and Jeannie, claiming she'd had a bad dream. By the age of four or five, if she were not getting enough attention she would reach for something convenient, perhaps a vase, perhaps her water glass, and, while pretending to inspect it, drop it to the floor.

Hank had known how to deal with her. He had patience and an ability to compartmentalize that Jeannie could not muster. His mind was a neatly ordered place and if Susan threw a fit he could give her his complete attention and then forget her the moment he walked out the door. *The nanny is taking care of her—there is no more need to worry—* that was how his mind worked, it was switches inside a computer. But Jeannie, even after getting to the office, would stay angry with her daughter for half the days. She took the fits personally, she took her daughter's softness personally, there were strains of weak blood in all families, there were those who sat and soaked in their own problems and those who got up and helped themselves. Jeannie, at her daughter's age, had taught herself how to ride and rope, she had taught herself to compete with men on their own terms. Her daughter competed by being loud and disruptive, an impossible princess; even before her father died she saw him as a saint and her mother as something else; whatever Jeannie did it was never enough.

Of course her daughter was only being what a girl in Texas was supposed to be. It was Jeannie who was the odd one.

CHAPTER FORTY-EIGHT

DIARIES OF PETER McCULLOUGH

AUGUST 1, 1917

Most of the drillers are progressing twice as fast as the Colonel and his alcoholic henchmen. At least forty rigs visible from the road. Quiet nights are a thing of the past.

The town is overwhelmed not just with drillers and landmen and speculators, but now with the men who build storage tanks and dig trenches, who haul pipe and wood and fuel, who repair tools and other equipment. Everyone is working at twice last year's wages.

In news of the dead: a man's body was found behind the Cabot Inn (what Wallace Cabot is now calling his house). A moonshiner's still exploded in the tent city. A roustabout sleeping under a truck was crushed.

Our driller claims this is nothing. Wait till all the rest of those rigs get running, he said. It will be a river of blood and bodies.

I ask María what she thinks of all this. She says she is trying not to.

AUGUST 3, 1917

My father sold twenty-eight hundred acres of leases under the old Garcia pastures to Magnolia Oil. Nearly a thousand an acre. Drillers on the Midkiff and Reynolds pastures are getting shows a few hundred feet beneath the surface, and the Colonel's rig (now staffed professionally) hit a good show of oil at eight hundred feet. That or my father spiked the well corings. Regardless, it appears that our money worries are over for the next ten or so generations. This depresses me enormously.

Naturally Magnolia wants to drill near the house, where my father's discovery well was (the only one actually flowing), but I said I would not allow it.

That area is now a half-mile pit of stinking black sludge. Sullivan and I rode past it today. He is bitter about the oil, and worried about his job.

"You know I am glad about this oil," he said. "But I can't even get a glass of water in town without someone trying to charge me for it."

"Well, now we can afford to get all this brush cleared off, get these other pastures cross-fenced . . ."

"What's the point of getting the brush off if we have to look at this shit all day and listen to those drillers all night. Not to mention they leave every goddamn gate open."

We continued to look at the oil spill.

"Think he'll sell the cattle?" he asked.

"I won't let him."

"That's what I've been telling the boys. He's always had his mind on other things but you . . . you are not the type to let that happen."

It is quiet and I consider that Sullivan has not said a word against my father in the thirty years I've known him.

"We've got twice as many head as we did two years ago," I said. "We've got twice the work." The reason for this occurred to me and I winced. I began to wonder where María was.

"But the cattle won't make money like this stuff. That's what everyone is worrying over."

"Well, they shouldn't."

Then I added: "Have you heard about this Garcia girl?"

He didn't answer. I wasn't sure if he was chewing his thoughts or if he hadn't heard me. We continued to ride and then he said: "I believe everyone has heard of her, boss. In these three counties, anyway."

"It's a difficult situation."

"That is putting it lightly."

"What do you reckon about my wife?"

"Maybe she'll get kicked by a horse. Or fall into a river."

"My luck has never been that good."

"That is true," said Sullivan. "If anyone will fall into a river, it will be you."

August 4, 1917

Today, for the first time, we go to McCullough Springs together. At first she keeps a comfortable distance, as if she is an employee, but I take her hand. We have lunch at Almacitas, drink Carta Blancas, linger in the street holding each other. I am not sure I have ever felt better. Though part of me wonders if we are doing this as a bulwark against the tide that is rising around us. As if we might stop it with love. Which, of course, is ridiculous.

TONIGHT WE ARE sitting in the library, my head in her lap, when I say: "Why didn't you ever get married?"

She shrugs.

"But really."

"I had lovers, if that's what you're asking."

It isn't, and it gives me a bad feeling to think about, but I persist.

"I won't give myself to anyone who doesn't respect me," she says. "I would rather be dead."

"They couldn't have all been so bad."

"I should have been born a man," she says.

I pinch her thigh.

"They expect you to look at them adoringly, regardless of what they have done, and if they don't expect you to wash their clothes, they expect you to keep after the woman who does." She shrugs. "And the Mexicans are the worst. A Mexican man will take you to a place, say a nice hotel, or a nice view in the mountains, and show it off as if he made it. And part of him really believes it."

"It's bravado," I say.

"Regardless," she says. "He believes it. And that is why I never married. And never expect to."

I give her a hurt look.

She leans over and kisses me. "Except to you, of course."

I nuzzle into her lap and wrap my arms around her waist. But when I look up at her again, she is staring out the dark window, and doesn't appear to notice me. "There is another story," she says.

LONG AGO, HERE in the Wild Horse Desert, there was a young vaquero, very handsome, though very poor, who was in love with the daughter of a Tejano rancher.

This girl, who was almost too beautiful to look at, was desired and courted by every rancher's son on both sides of the river, though being of pure heart, she was more interested in horses than men, and dreamed only of a certain stallion that ran with the wild mustangs. This horse was unusual in both his pure white color and his size, sixteen hands. In addition to his perfect form, he had the toughness of a paint, the speed of a Thoroughbred, and, like the girl, he was coveted by every man who had ever seen or heard of him. But none could ever catch him.

When the young vaquero learned how much the girl loved this horse, he decided to make her a present. For months he studied its tracks and discovered its secrets. Then he waited all night at a hidden watering hole, and when the stallion came in, he roped it. He fed it plums and persimmons and chunks of *piloncillo*. He repeated this process for many weeks until the horse allowed himself to be stroked and touched, and then led with a halter, and then saddled. But even then he would stand only in one stirrup, never trying to mount the horse, until he knew the horse would not mind. And in this manner he broke the horse to the saddle without breaking his spirit.

After more gentling, the vaquero brushed and groomed the white stallion and rode him to the house of the Tejano rancher, where he called softly to the rancher's daughter. When she opened her window

she recognized the vaquero instantly, and the horse as well, and knew
that this was the man she would marry. They shared one chaste kiss,
but agreed to find a priest before they did anything else.

Unfortunately they were not alone. The fat son of an Anglo rancher
had seen the entire thing, because when he was not forcing himself
upon servant girls he was hiding in the bushes outside the window
of this beautiful Tejana, watching her disrobe and doing unspeakable
things to himself.

(Was this in your mother's version of the story, I ask.)

(She ignores me.)

He returned to his father with news that the most beautiful girl
anyone had ever seen was about to marry a common vaquero. And
then he and his father laid an ambush.

With their specially made rifles they waited until the vaquero's
back was turned and then murdered him, and, for the rest of their days,
told all their friends of the beautiful shot they made, at a very great
distance, on a Mexican.

But when they reached the body of the young vaquero, the white
stallion had returned to protect him. He bit and kicked at the rancher
and his son and so they murdered him as well. Then they cut off the
vaquero's head.

The ranchero's daughter, when her vaquero did not return, took
her father's pistol and murdered herself. But God does not allow noble
beings to be separated, and thus the vaquero can be seen on his horse
at every full moon, with his head in his lap, riding his ghostly white
stallion with the other mustangs, looking for the spirit of his intended.

(I believe you have the story wrong, I tell her.)

(How so?)

(That is an old folktale of ours as well, I say.)

FOR MANY YEARS there was a black stallion, not white, that ran
with the mustangs and carried a ghostly rider on its back. The sight of
the rider made the mustangs stampede, and thus people always knew

when the black stallion appeared, because it sounded like a tornado had touched down in the desert, thousands of mustangs galloping across the caliche.

Very few men ever got close to the horse and its rider, but the few who did said he was sitting normally, except that his head was not attached. His head, along with a sombrero, was strapped to his lap. And so for many years, the cowboys shot at the ghostly rider, but the bullets went through his body like a paper target, and he continued to ride.

Finally, a few cowboys decided to solve the mystery. They waited all night at a watering hole, and when the black stallion and the headless rider appeared, they shot the horse.

On the back of this beautiful mustang there was an old dry corpse tied upright with rawhide, the head tightly bound to his lap. After many months of inquiry, it was discovered that a young Mexican by the name of Vidal, who was a notorious womanizer and horse thief, had met his end.

The men who caught him were Creed Taylor and Bigfoot Wallace, legendary Texans about whom many books have been written. They were great practical jokers, and so to make an example out of Vidal, they cut off his head and tied both his head and body to an unbroken black stallion that had been caught in a trap with other mustangs. They released the stallion and his headless rider, who confused and terrorized the populace for over a decade.

"YOURS IS THE true one," she says.

"It's an old story," I say. "It's well known."

"Of course," she says. "There are many convincing details. First, there is a dead Mexican who was a horse thief, as all dead Mexicans are. Second, there are two famous Texans, who decided, after killing a man, that they would decapitate him for fun. Third, they decide that merely decapitating this man is not funny enough. It will be hilarious if, instead of burying him, they tie his body to a wild horse."

"Hmmm," I say.

"And the final convincing detail is that a group of Anglo cowboys, when faced with the task of capturing a legendary black stallion, instead of roping him, or building a simple trap, decided to shoot him, because it required the least effort."

"That is why I don't tell stories."

"No, it was educational."

"Yours is the one our children should hear."

"No," she says. "Our children should know the truth." Then she kisses my forehead and strokes my hair, as if I am a child myself.

CHAPTER FORTY-NINE

ELI McCULLOUGH

1864

At the beginning of the year there was a shakeup and most of the RMN men were sent east. They tried shipping me to the Frontier Regiment, but I didn't feel like riding against the Comanches and I didn't like McCord, either, and so as punishment I was sent to the Indian Territories. Most whites didn't want to work with Indians—they were considered only a step above Negroes—but I suspected it would be high living and I was right.

Of the five civilized tribes, two—the Creeks and Seminoles—had sided with the Union. The other three—the Cherokee, Chickasaw, and Choctaw—were fighting for the Confederacy. There was a brigade of Cherokee under their own general, Stand Watie, and a Choctaw brigade under Tandy Walker. I was given the temporary rank of colonel and put in charge of a battalion of ragged Cherokees. They'd signed enlistment papers the same as whites, but they didn't believe in boots or uniforms, or remembering their orders, or fighting when they were outnumbered. They believed in eating well and staying in one piece, which made them just about useless, as far as the army was concerned.

By then, we were getting most of our equipment from Union supply trains. We wanted Union-made pistols, which had steel frames instead of brass, and we wanted their repeating rifles, Henrys and Spencers, though we were happy with their Enfields as well. We wanted their wool pants and blankets, their field glasses, their saddles and tack, their horses and ammunition, tinned beef, coffee and salt, quinine, factory-made shirts, their writing paper and sewing needles.

Our only orders were to disrupt the enemy's rear, which meant riding into Kansas or Missouri, burning barns or bridges or just stealing chickens. Eventually, when our bellies were as empty as bankers' hearts and there was nothing left to plunder from the locals, we would go south to resupply.

It was a familiar way of living and I did not mind it one bit, sleeping outside and roaming where I wanted, and I did not mind being with the Indians, either, who, civilized or not, lived closer to the natural ways than most whites. But in summer I got a few days' leave and decided to head back to Austin.

I was heating the axles the whole way but when I came across the hill and saw the judge's house, I reined up short. I wasn't sure why I'd come home. I could remember sitting on a horse in my Comanche gear, shooting arrows for the reporters; in the backyard there were hackberries thirty feet tall that I remembered as seedlings. I suddenly felt old, and I nearly turned around and rode north again, but Madeline was standing in the doorway of the guesthouse, so I got off and fixed my horse to the snubbing post and went to her.

She was holding Everett. He was nine months old, or it might have been eight, or eleven.

"Daddy's back," she said.

He looked like he might cry and she looked like another person— she'd aged ten years since the war started. She'd had no trouble getting back her old figure, and looking at the dark circles under her eyes and her skin that bruised at the lightest touch, I knew I'd made a mistake for the ages.

We went inside and she put my hands on her chest and then I was in a fierce rutting mood. But once we made it to the bed, I could tell she wasn't.

Still she wanted me to do it anyway but right before we started she said, "Put it there instead," and raised her legs a little higher. "I don't want my milk to get thick."

"Does that feel good?"

I nodded.

"As good as . . ."

"Sure," I mumbled.

"It feels good to me, too. It also hurts, though."

I took it out. She rolled over and examined me.

"I thought it would be filthy." She looked closer. "It does smell."

"I better wash I guess."

"I thought you would like it," she said. "Did you?"

"Sure," I said.

The Negroes had kept some water hot so I walked over to the main house and took a bath. When I came back she was dressed again.

"Is it the baby?" I said.

"Probably."

I looked around the cottage. It was small and dark. I told myself that I loved them.

"I feel a little far away from you, maybe."

"I'm right here," I said.

"You're gone and then every few months you're back for a few days and we do it and then you're gone again. I feel like a cow."

"You're beautiful."

"Not the way I look. I mean you come home and leave and that's all there is to it."

I started to say something but she interrupted. "My father could get you something here. I know he told you that. I see officers around town all the time and there must be men on the coast who see their families all the time as well."

"That wouldn't be fair."

"To the army or to me? To a bunch of men you've known a year, or to me? You like to pretend it's not a choice but it is, Eli."

"Why are you mad?" I said. "I just got here."

"I'm trying not to be."

Everett was glaring at me. "I made you," I said.

"That's just his normal face," she told me.

THAT AFTERNOON, AFTER we'd been to see the judge and his wife, we were back in bed. Madeline had stolen a bottle of sunflower oil from the kitchen.

"You don't want another Everett," I said. "Or a little sister for him?"

"I do," she said. "One day I really do, just not by myself."

She looked at me and took my hand in both of hers and kissed it. She was a beautiful woman. I reminded myself she was plenty strong.

"Do you ever think about what my life is like here?"

"I imagine it's hard," I said, though I didn't.

"It is hard. I'm stuck in this house with a little animal who can't even talk to me. Sometimes I wake up and think today will be the day that I forget how to speak."

"Isn't it nice to have the baby, though?"

"Of course it is," she said. "But not any nicer for me than it is for you. When he's crying I sometimes want to leave him in his crib and run as far away as possible."

I didn't say anything.

"Sorry. I'm tired of playing the long-suffering wife. I thought it suited me and now it doesn't. I will do all the work of raising your son but if you think I am going to be silent about it you have another think coming."

"Can't the niggers look after him?"

"My mother keeps them busy enough," she said.

"You know when I'm not here I'm either sleeping in the rain or living off wormy biscuits. Or people are shooting at me."

"I feel like your mistress," she said. "So don't pretend it is nothing but misery, because I know you, Eli, and I know you wouldn't be doing it if it were."

Then we were both quiet. She looked like she was going to cry. "I don't want this to be your last memory of me."

"Nothing's gonna happen."

"And please stop saying that."

"All right," I said.

"At first I thought there was another woman up there. Now I wish that's all it was."

CHAPTER FIFTY

J. A. McCULLOUGH

Things had gone wrong from the start. She'd walked onto her plane and her pilot was missing and his replacement—a woman—had a certain look. For the first time in her eighty-six years, decades of flying ten or twenty times a week, she wanted to get off the plane. Of course everything was fine. The woman was an excellent pilot, she'd flared so perfectly that Jeannie had barely been able to tell they'd touched down. But still there was that feeling.

Later she was sitting on the gallery, the sun was going down and it was quiet and she had begun to weep, the entire sky from front to back was red and purple and fiery orange, one day soon would be her last, perhaps this one, everything was so beautiful she could not bear the thought of leaving it. Then Frank Mabry had made his presence known. He took off his hat and waited for her to acknowledge him. She wondered if he were blind, or deaf, but he was just stupid. She ignored him, but still he would not leave, he stood there like a scolded dog and waited.

"Ma'am," he said, after a minute.

She nodded. Dabbed at her eyes.

"I was wondering if you'd thought about what we talked about last time."

"No," she told him. She had no idea. He flew the small helicopter they used on roundups. She dabbed her eyes again and hoped he would drop dead but he didn't retreat, he seemed to have a sense that he might yet be able to weasel his way into her good graces.

"How long have you known me, Frank?"

"Thirty-four years. And in fact that is just it. I have been wondering if something . . . were to happen, if any arrangements had been made, any considerations, for the people who had been in your employ so long."

She wondered what he was talking about. Then she understood. "Please leave," she said.

He clomped away. She hoped he might be kicked by a horse or that his truck would flip or that the rotor might fall off his little helicopter. She watched him drive away, had the sense everything was ruined, and went up to bed without dinner.

THE NEXT MORNING she woke up earlier than she wanted. Normally she turned on the computer, checked the oil and S&P futures, where Asia had closed and Europe was trading, but this morning she had no interest. She dressed and padded down the long hallway, the light just coming in on the dark wood and busts of old Romans, but instead of going downstairs she stood at the top and watched the sun come up through the stained glass. There was something about it. She'd seen it thousands of times but now there was something different. *You're being sentimental,* she decided. She began to make her way down the stairs.

In the kitchen she made breakfast but when she went to put her plate away, she found the dishwasher full of clean dishes and glasses. Not hers; she'd only been here a night. Someone—some employee—must have thrown a party, she didn't remember being asked, *no,* she thought, *I was not asked,* of course it was Dolores, who ran the house, no one else would have dared.

Dolores had worked for her thirty years and they'd always maintained a tactful sort of friendship, hugs and air kisses, J.A. making the occasional showing at Dolores's family gatherings, birthdays or graduations, a benevolent presence. Certainly she had helped them live far above what was normal in Dimmit County. And, unlike Mabry, Dolores *was* being taken care of, though she did not know it yet.

She felt a heat rising in her; she should not be having these feelings. They were no longer healthy. She pulled back into her mind. The anger went out of her, the sun came brightly through the windows, she could see hummingbirds just outside and the scent of vanilla—the agaritos were blooming—but it didn't matter, everyone was against her, they all saw the end was near. She wondered if she should have remarried. Which was ridiculous—Ted had died years ago, another husband to bury—but still, she had not led a natural life.

Your pills, she thought, *and your drink.* But even the small container seemed like too much effort. She wondered when Dolores would come, she would mention the incident but make it clear all was forgiven, she could have parties but only with permission. The light was spreading through the house, across the old rugs and dark floors, the portraits of her father and grandfather and great-grandfather along the main stairway; of course there ought to be one more, the person who had run the ranch longer than her father and grandfather combined, but one did not hang a portrait of oneself. And there was no one behind her to do it. Her grandson: perhaps he would be happy. That was all she could hope for.

The front door opened and closed and Dolores appeared at the end of the dining room, a tiny figure, out of proportion to all her surroundings. There was a long minute as she walked closer; she was carrying a new white handbag and when she reached the near end of the dining room, she smiled and said, "Good morning, Mrs. McCullough."

"Good morning," she said. "How was your little party?"

The woman looked away. Jeannie could see her mind working. "Party?" she said. "It was not a party, it was just a gathering, it was not planned."

This was clearly rehearsed and she became angry again: "Well, let me know next time. It is still my house."

Dolores continued to look away and then Jeannie felt bad; what would it be like to be nearing the end of your life, still being scolded? She came around the counter, intending to hug her, to show this was nothing serious, they were old friends, but if Dolores noticed her intention she didn't let on. She said, "I'll go see about your room," and turned back toward the stairs, giving Jeannie the feeling that she, not Dolores, was the one who ought to be apologizing.

And there was that feeling—that Dolores no longer thought it worth hiding what they both knew, which was that in most important ways she no longer needed J.A. McCullough. Within her own community, Dolores was considered wealthy, a matriarch, people calling on her for favors, at every holiday there were cars parked on both sides of the road to her house.

In the old days it would have been the opposite. Jeannie would have been the one with the house full of lively children, weddings and birthdays and graduations to plan, while Dolores would have lost most of hers—perhaps all of them—to dysentery and malnutrition, to over-work and bad doctoring and the *coraje* and jealous husbands (they used to butcher each other, she thought, it was always in the paper that some *peón* had woken up and found he'd cut his wife's throat). But now ... now ...

The sun was bright. Soon it would be summer and the light would extinguish everything, all the colors. But for now it was green and cool. She had a feeling, which became a clear thought, that she would not live to see it. She looked at her hands. Something was moving in the corner. She felt cold.

AFTER HANK DIED, there were times when the face that stared back at her in the mirror meant exactly nothing; given the right circumstance she would have obliterated it like a fly on a window. But they had not let her alone. If there was anything you could say about oilmen, they knew about suffering and loss; most were only a generation or two out of some tarpaper shack and for weeks after Hank died they had not let her alone. No matter how much she wanted silence there were people in the kitchen, living room, guest rooms, there was food out, servants she didn't recognize, strangers coming and going, the kids going to school, coming back, how she didn't know.

The Texans had been relentless; they might hate the blacks and Mexicans, they might hate the president enough to kill him, but they had not let her alone, they had cared for her like a mother or daughter, men she barely knew, men whose absence from their offices cost them thousands of dollars an hour, and yet she would come downstairs and find them asleep on her couch, and call their drivers to pick them up.

Though of course it was these same men who had nearly refused to do business with her in the years that followed. It was better not to think about. It was all forgiven, they had all gone back to the earth, they had lived only to die.

TED HAD COME into her life a few years after Hank left it. He was older and he came from an even older family, he spent most of his time playing polo—when he was not running or swimming—though he gave off the aura of someone who had done a lot of drugs, a man going to seed.

Not physically; at fifty he was over six feet, with a thirty-two-inch waist and the rugged looks of his ancestors, though his calluses were particular to polo mallets and dumbbells and he had never broken a bone in his life, most of which he had spent chasing women. But as if a switch had turned, he'd decided to settle down. He was smart, though it took her a long time to realize it, he paid attention to her in many ways that Hank had not and she had slowly come to see that Hank, as good as he was, had lived mostly for himself, though neither one of them had known it at the time.

And Ted, just in this difference, had given her hope, that she had not totally figured out life or people, that things might be different; it was a pleasant feeling. It mattered to Ted how she looked, he noticed all her haircuts and new clothes, he knew the difference between a mood he could talk her out of and one he couldn't. He didn't fawn, but he noticed. And yet he was not a serious person. He was an aging playboy who wanted company; who had grown tired, she guessed, of putting on an act for every waitress or stewardess who caught his eye. He'd decided he was old, and he wanted to be around his own people.

The boys liked him well enough. They did not quite take him seriously, though he was good to them, and filled a role she could not, taking them shooting and riding; he was too lazy to hunt deer but enjoyed hunting quail. The boys never seemed to learn anything from him; neither their riding nor their shooting improved in his presence, but he did not demand anything of them, either, and nights she would come home and find them sitting together on the sofa watching television, Ted with a bottle of wine, the boys with their pop, *The Avengers* or *Bonanza,* none of them with anything to say, but as happy as a pile of dogs in winter.

As for Susan, she had begun to summer in Maine with Jonas's children, three months of blessed silence and privacy and after the second summer she came back asking to leave Kincaid and go away to Garrison Forest, like Jonas's daughters. The idea that her daughter might disappear from her life for eight months was not entirely appealing, though it seemed better—barely—than having to put up with her. By then Susan was not just needy; she was a saboteur. She would go through her mother's things, she would walk into their bedroom when she knew Ted was there, she would pretend to sneak to the kitchen for a snack, wearing only her T-shirt and underpants.

"That girl is a handful," Ted told her.

"She will be lucky if she isn't pregnant by her next birthday," Jeannie said.

"I think you will be the lucky one."

Of course he was right. But somehow, even then, it had not felt that way.

Ted didn't have children of his own; she might have given him one while it was still possible, but neither one of them had been willing to commit to that. Mostly what Ted wanted was a family, without having to raise it himself; a woman who had her own money, a woman who accepted him as part of her pack, but otherwise asked nothing. She would never have guessed it, but she'd been more happy with him, more settled than she'd ever felt. Of course she could not help but be drawn to people like Hank, people with their own fire, but no matter how much they thought they loved you or their family or their country, no matter how they pledged their allegiance, that fire always burned for them alone.

CHAPTER FIFTY-ONE

DIARIES OF PETER McCULLOUGH

AUGUST 6, 1917

Sally called to say she will be coming to visit. "Don't worry about your little *pelado*," she told me. "I won't interfere."

For a moment I saw everything falling in around me. I didn't say anything. Finally I told her, "There is no reason for you to be here."

"Except that it is my home. I would like to visit my own home. All sorts of excitement going on, I hear."

"You are not welcome," I said, though I knew it was pointless.

"Well, get that idea out of your head. Because I am coming back."

MY FATHER WAS sitting on the porch with the driller and a few other men.

"I just spoke to Sally," I said.

He gave me a look.

"And if anything happens, I will make certain things known."

"I'll see you boys this evening," he told the men. They got up as one and left.

"Whatever you are about to say, do not say it. In fact do not even think it."

"Stop her from coming."

"I have nothing to do with that," he said.

I shook my head.

"Anyone but that girl, Pete. In fact I would like it if you got every wetback in town pregnant, because unless I am given a proper Good-nighting, my days of prodding are over, and I could use a few more heirs."

"We have nothing to worry about from María," I said.

"I know that."

"Then tell Sally to stay away."

"You know, if you were a Comanche you could just cut Sally's nose off, and throw her out, and get married to the new one."

"Her name is María."

"Unfortunately you are not a Comanche. You are subject to the laws of America. Which means you should have gotten rid of Sally before signing this other one on."

"I'm embarrassed for you."

"The feeling is mutual," he told me.

"So your wife is returning?"

I look at her; there is no point denying it. "Don't worry about her," I say.

She shrugs. I can see she has been crying. "I knew it had to end sometime."

"It doesn't," I say.

She turns from me.

I try to hug her but she shakes me off. "It's fine," she says.

"It's not fine."

"I will be fine."

I realize she is not even talking to me.

AFTER SHE FELL asleep I took a bottle of whiskey and walked out into the chaparral until I reached Dog Mountain, which is nothing more than a large hill, though it is the tallest around. At the top is a large rock with a backrest cut or hacked into the stone and I climbed up and lay against it. The house was a mile or so behind me; I could see a few lights, but otherwise, it was dark.

When I had sat long enough I began to get a strange feeling. This has always been a warm place and men had likely sat on this exact rock for ten thousand years at least, as it provides the best view of the surrounding country. How many families had come and gone? Before there were men there was a vast ocean, and I knew that far beneath me there were living creatures turning to stone.

I thought of my brother, who has always pitied me for my temperament, who spends his life inside, obsessed with his papers and bank accounts. When the agarito ripens he can't smell it, when the first windflowers bloom he will not see them. As for my father, he sees everything. But only so he can destroy it.

August 7, 1917

Sally arrived this morning. She kissed me politely on the cheek, then greeted María. "Nice to see you again, neighbor." Then she laughed and said: "This heat can make for strange living arrangements."

She said she would take a bedroom on the other side of the house and had her things brought up there.

Meanwhile, I was supposed to spend the day with Sullivan, as we have hired a crew to do more cross-fencing.

I intended to tell him he would have to do it without me, but María assured me it would be fine.

"Your wife and I are going to have to be alone at some point. Better sooner than later."

We met the crew at the gate and drove to the middle of the ranch, explaining what we wanted done. Gates here and here and there . . . after a few hours I was so antsy my hands were shaking. I told Sullivan I had to go.

Back at the house, Phineas's Pierce Arrow was parked in the driveway. I got a terrible feeling. Phineas, Sally, and my father were all sitting in the parlor, waiting.

I went from room to room, calling for her, the kitchen, the great room, the library, then searched every closet. Consuela was in my bedroom, stripping the sheets off the bed. She would not speak. I went back downstairs and found the three of them still sitting there.

Sally said: "María has decided to go back to her own people."

"I am her people."

"Apparently she felt differently."

"If you hurt her," I said, "either one of you," looking at Sally and my father, "I will kill you."

They looked at each other and something crossed their faces, some expression of humor. If I'd had a pistol, they both would have died an instant later. There was a red mist and I took my jackknife out of its sheath, opened it, and stepped toward my wife.

"I will cut your fucking throat," I told her. She smiled and I stepped closer and she lost all her color.

"And you," I said, pointing the knife at my brother. "Did you know about this?"

"Pete," he said, "we offered her ten thousand dollars to move back with her cousin in Torreón. She decided to take it."

"Her cousin is dead."

"She knows other people down there."

"Where is she now?"

"She's in a car."

"Son," said my father, "it's for the best."

I went upstairs to my office. I loaded my pistol and was making my way down the hall when I saw the dark figure, leaning on the banister, waiting for me. The sunlight was on him and I stood for a long time watching: first he had a face like my father's, then it was my own, then it was something else.

I went back to my desk.

Waiting for them to make the car ready. Leave for Torreón in an hour.

CHAPTER FIFTY-TWO

ELI McCULLOUGH

June 1865

The Federals stuck to our tracks all winter and by Christmas we'd lost half our number. It was plain that if we didn't leave Kansas we would all end up either shot or hanged; Flying Jacket and the remaining Cherokees decided to absquatulate west to the Rockies. The five RMN men—Busque, Showalter, Fisk, Shaw, and me—decided to go with them. The last we'd heard was Sherman had taken Georgia. If there were other bands of Confederates, we'd stopped running into them.

THE CHEROKEES COLLECTED a few Ute scalps but we avoided the Federals entirely, camping at tree line and generally sticking to the owl-hoot trail until one afternoon in the Bayou Salado we chassed into a small regiment. Normally this would have sent us scurrying over the next ridge, but there were two dozen wagons for only a few hundred men, and they all had eight-mule hitches, and this was not lost on Flying Jacket, either. We hunkered in the rocks and watched them.

"They are pulling something heavy," he said.

I stayed quiet. I knew exactly what they were carrying but unless Flying Jacket agreed with me, it was pointless. He was near fifty and he'd insisted on being called a colonel and that's why they made me one as well. He wore his jacket with the oak leaves even when it was a hundred degrees out.

"They're going to the assay office in Denver," I said. The war had been nothing like I thought—even the judge was nearly bankrupt—but the longer I watched the wagons, the more I wondered if something might yet be saved from the wreckage. I thought about Toshaway and the raid we'd made into Mexico and I could not see why this was any different.

"If they're not carrying hides," Flying Jacket was saying. "Or timber. Or, who knows, perhaps they're simply that strong now. Perhaps they ride this way for fun."

"Well, they won't make the pass at that pace. They'll have to camp on that bench."

We continued to watch. The men riding the wagons got off to walk as the road got steeper. It was gold country and they were pulling something heavy. Of course, it could have been anything. But Flying Jacket was coming around.

"I hope we don't go in and find it's just a pile of rocks."

"If we do," said Flying Jacket, "it will just be a continuation of my entire life."

He called a few Cherokees over and they talked. Then he turned back to me.

"This cannon they are pulling?"

"Probably a mountain howitzer."

"With canister shot, if they are worried about being robbed."

"Yes, but they only have one shot, and they will be firing into their own men."

"And yet it is strange," he said.

THEY MADE THEIR camp where we thought they would. There were butterflies in the grass, a hundred-mile view of the mountains, a cold stream running past them. We were at the tree line. It was rocks and dust. The Union men were relaxed, taking their time to set up their tents, making bets on the bighorn sheep, which were white dots on cliffs high above them. A few had Sharps rifles. Once in a while one of the white dots would come tumbling off the mountain, looking like a falling snowman.

ALL THE BOYS were against it. Except for Showalter, who was down with the Indians, we were on our bellies in the rocks, passing the field glasses back and forth.

"This might be a persimmon above our huckleberry," said Fisk.

"Well," I said, "it's what the Indians want, and it's what Jeff Davis wants, and it's what we're going to do."

"Listen to the fire-eater. The living legend."

Shaw said: "May I humbly suggest to the boss that his attitude is outdated. By about four years."

I passed the glasses to Fisk. He was the oldest of us; he had a big family back in Refugio.

"This is a dumb idea." He began to wiggle back down through the rocks.

"Where are you going?"

"I gotta write a letter," he said.

"Same here," said Shaw. "Let me know if y'all change your mind. Otherwise you'll find me and my horse heading down that draw we came up."

I looked at him.

"I'll be back at the camp," he said. But he wasn't smiling.

Then it was only Busque and me.

"What do *you* think," I said.

"I think it's stupid."

"It'll be high livin' if it goes off."

"You know they'll find some way to take it off us."

"That is a sorry attitude."

"It's time to piss on the fire and call the dogs, Eli. For all we know, Jeff Davis is already a cottonwood blossom."

I didn't say anything.

We continued to watch the bluecoats, who had stripped down to their underwear and were lying in the grass, enjoying the sun, gambling on saddle blankets or writing in their journals. Others were skinning the sheep, getting a fire going.

"I feel sorry for those Indians," said Busque.

WE WATCHED AS the Federals ate their supper, we watched them watch the sunset, we could still see them even as the first stars came out, passing around a bottle, enjoying their jobs, acting like there wasn't any war.

Most of the tents were in a small depression, their wagons and horses on the outskirts. Around midnight we shot arrows into their pickets. Then we stampeded the horse herd through the tents and it became a proper massacre; the Federals were easy to pick out as they were all wriggling under collapsed sailcloth or looking about confusedly wearing bright white union suits. We came into the bowl from all sides, shooting with our repeaters while the Cherokees raced around, ululating and smashing heads with their flint axes. Most of the Yankees died before they even knew who was tormenting them and I began to feel sorry for them, it was not even an honest fight, and then Flying Jacket was trying to get my attention.

A dozen of the Union men, all in their underwear, had escaped to the rise where the cannon was parked. They were fetching things from a wagon, making no attempt to stiver off, and I thought they had lost their heads. Then their gun started up and I knew why they hadn't run.

One aimed it while others worked to feed it or watched the flanks and the gun was popping so fast it was like twenty men shooting at once.

Some Cherokees made a charge on horseback and then there was a second charge. The gun had not stopped firing since it started and Shaw and Fisk and I hunkered in some scraggly brush on the other side of the meadow. The Federals were on a rise directly across from us and in the grass below were dozens of trampled tents and dead and dying men and horses and the sound of moaning like a cattle auction.

They ran out of targets. They began to work over the wounded. The moon was bright and Fisk shot a man standing near the gun and then the branches overtop of us were swaying and crackling and Shaw said, "Leon's hit," and went quiet.

There would be a shot from our side and the Federals would see the flash and put twenty or thirty rounds in and get their credit. Shaw's face was dark and I reached for Fisk. He was wet. One of the Cherokees broke cover but the gun caught him, then came back to me. I pushed up against a rock no bigger than a saddletree and the bullets were slapping against it, something punched my arm, my face was stinging, and then they were working the bushes over my head. The ground all around me was flat and open and I knew my medicine had run out. I tried to remember the death song. I'd forgotten it.

The gun stopped again. Flying Jacket was yelling something. I looked for a ditch or rock or dead horse. There was a flipped wagon but it was too far, and there was an Indian behind the wagon shooting his bow nearly straight up, and then more Indians were doing the same and the air above the gun began to shilly and waver, as if there were heat from a great fire. The loaders were shrieking and calling out and then all the Indians were shooting and the gunner was alone firing blindly into the dark.

THE CHEROKEES WERE moving among the tents, finishing off the wounded with clubs. There was an occasional shot farther down the valley.

I bandaged my arm, then I found Busque and Showalter. We went to the gun. The ground around it was stuck with hundreds of arrows— the Indians had shot them almost straight up so that they would fall on the Federals from above and there were scattered bodies with the switches sticking into them at strange angles, into the tops of their shoulders and heads.

One of the bodies began to move. A man slid out from under it. He appeared to be unhurt.

"I surrender," he said. He held up his hands. "Are you bandits?"

"We're with the Confederate States of America," I told him.

He looked at us strangely. Then he said: "I'm a civilian. I'm a sales representative."

Busque said: "What does that even mean?"

"I represent the Gatling company. We're not under contract with the army, but we offered a few production samples for their use, as I . . . as I believe we had difficulty contacting your government."

The remaining Cherokees were beginning to gather.

"How does that gun work?" said Busque.

"It's actually very simple. You take a standard paper cartridge, insert it into this carrier . . ." He picked up a small metal cylinder from the ground, where hundreds or thousands were littered. "The cartridge and carrier unit then fit into this hopper at the top of the gun, like so."

Flying Jacket had come up.

"Who is he," he asked. "A deserter?"

"He works for the company that made the gun. He says he is a salesman."

Flying Jacket cocked his head as if thinking. He said something to his men. Six or eight of them rushed forward and stabbed the sales representative to death.

THE INDIANS ATTEMPTED to take the gun apart so that it couldn't be used again. But they couldn't make sense of it in the dark and instead began to bash it with rocks.

Flying Jacket took me aside and led me to the other wagons, where a crate had been pried open.

"This is heavy but it does not look like gold. It looks like wheat."

"That's gold dust," I said. "That is gold for sure."

"There is a lot of it."

"How much?"

"Hundreds of sacks like that one. Hundreds at least."

The sack looked to be about two pounds.

"We'll have to bury some of it and come back later."

"Why?" he said.

"It'll be tough to move it all."

He looked at me.

"What?"

"Eli, did the sight of that gun not convince you of anything?"

"No."

"I believe that you are not telling the truth. Did you know of the existence of this type of gun?"

"Not exactly."

"So you did."

"I didn't know they were in production."

"But you knew the other side would eventually have them. A gun with which one man can kill forty."

I looked off into the dark valley below us and the mountains beyond it. I wondered if we would make it home.

"Ah, Eli. Our band is nearly a thousand women, children, and old men. When we began this trip there were nearly two hundred warriors to support them. It was not enough. Now there are perhaps forty."

"It's a tragedy," I said. "I am extremely sorry."

"It is an even greater tragedy that we are on the losing side of this war. The land we have been given by the federal government, which was not very good, and which we hoped to improve by fighting, we may lose entirely. Just to see that gun fired it is clear."

I shrugged.

"And these men! Look at how fat they are, and how good their horses, when we are starving and our horses starving as well. And the ammunition they carry . . ."

"It's always been like this," I said. "We were always the underdog."

"We are done fighting," he said. "I'm sorry."

"That is a poor decision."

"Your government will not even exist a year from now, Eli. You are five white men . . ."

"Now three."

"Three. I am sorry for your loss of two men, but when this war is over, you three will be able to do whatever you like. But I will be stuck on the reservation, along with my family, paying the price for supporting the wrong side. As will all my men. Who, when they are finished burying their brothers, will likely come to the conclusion that the best action is to kill the three of you. Both because you led us to this gun, which you did not bother to tell us about, and also because when whites steal something, it is no problem—whites can steal from each other—but if Indians steal something it is another matter. Do you understand? Indians who steal gold will not be forgiven." He shrugged. "And yet we need this gold."

I didn't say anything.

"This was a great battle, Eli. The last we will ever win. After this there will be only losing. And I think that if I were you, I would get off this mountain as soon as possible."

"You're their chief," I said.

"Unlike your people, we are democratic. Each man is free. My word is simply advice, not law." He patted my shoulder. "I am telling you this because you are the best white man I have ever known. The thought of you living gives me great pleasure."

"Me too," I said, but he ignored me.

"It will be best if you ride all day and all night, at least for the first few days."

I turned to go. He had loaded sacks of the gold into a rawhide parfleche. "Magic will not touch you, Eli. I saw it from the first time I met you. But of course that is also a curse." He handed me the bag.

"WHAT DO YOU think," said Busque. Rummaging in the moonlight, he and Showalter had each found a clean Union uniform, which was not hard to do as most of the bluecoats had died in their underwear. They packed the uniforms into their saddlebags.

"We're going to California," said Showalter.

"I'll report you as killed in action."

"Asshole," said Busque, "the action is over. Those bluecoat motherfuckers all had Henrys and Spencers and that fucking automatic gun. Not to mention those Yankee boots they were all wearing. I would have killed any one of them just for those boots."

"And this fucking gold," said Showalter. "Our guys are getting paid in scrip that'll be worthless by the time the peaches come in."

"I'm a colonel," I said.

"Eli, very shortly we will have lost the greatest war in history; in fact it is possible we have lost it already, and that the news has not reached us yet. I don't plan on being put in a Union prison camp, or shot by the Home Guard between now and then, or, even worse, dying in the final battle for a house of bullshit."

I didn't say anything.

"If you go back to Austin you'll be shot for desertion. And the war will end anyway, whether you're alive or dead. Come out west and send for your family."

"I can't."

"You think we lived this long because of what great soldiers we are? Is that what you think?"

I didn't say anything.

"You're a real sonofabitch," he said. "I always wondered about you."

"Girls," said Showalter, "you think these prairie niggers are gonna let us into any of that gold?"

★　★　★

THERE WERE OVER two hundred Union dead, mostly in their underwear. Usually the time after a fight felt like after a deer hunt, but now I began to get a terrible feeling.

Twenty-eight Cherokees had been killed outright and at sunrise, fourteen of the wounded would be shot by their friends. We buried Shaw and Fisk, whose faces were staved in. I thought of Fisk's children, and the children of all the other men, they were all somebody's darling.

From the supply wagons I loaded up on salt pork and cartridges for my Henry rifle. Flying Jacket allowed Busque and Showalter a bag of yellow dust apiece. They were happy and I decided not to tell them what I'd been given earlier.

His men wouldn't look at us. They all thought we'd known about the gun and the three of us trotted off down the mountain, leaving the Cherokees with the gold and all the Federals' weapons, ammunition, and horses. Just off the road was a dead man in his long underwear, and farther off the road, at the edge of the stream, was a second one.

I could not shake the feeling I'd stepped over some line over which I would never return, but maybe I'd crossed it years earlier, or maybe it had never existed. There was nothing you could take that did not belong to some other person. Whatever strings that held me had been cut.

"Stop fretting," Showalter said. "As soon as the sun comes up and they see all their loot, they'll want to take it and run. They'll forget we exist!" He grinned at me.

"You're probably right," I said.

Busque stayed far ahead. He hadn't looked at me since the burial.

AT THE BASE of the mountain, when we reached a long stretch of rock, I split off on my own, promising to see them in California when the war ended. It was the end of the RMN. I said a few words to distract from what was showing on my face.

We heard the shots as the Cherokees finished their wounded. I watched Busque and Showalter disappear to the west and then I pried the shoes off my horse and looped around the base of the mountain, staying under cover, changing direction every time I crossed a stream or patch of rock. I guessed Busque and Showalter wouldn't be careful about their tracks. I hoped the Indians wouldn't find them, but I knew better, the people around me did not live long, the Cherokees would catch the others, but not me, I was as sure of that as anything.

A MONTH LATER I got to Austin. The war had been over since spring.

CHAPTER FIFTY-THREE

J.A. McCULLOUGH

She was a slut or a dyke or a whore. A man trapped in a woman's body; look up her skirt and you'll see a cock. A liar, a schemer, a cold heart with a cunt to match, ridden hard and put up wet, Though she shouldn't take it personally. No one meant anything by it.

To be a man meant not living by any rules at all. You could say one thing in church and another at the bar and somehow both were true. You could be a good husband and father and Christian and bed every secretary, waitress, and prostitute that caught your eye. They all had their winks and nods, code for *I fucked that cheerleader or nanny or Pan Am stewardess, that maid or riding instructor.* Meanwhile, the slightest hint she was anything but a virgin (excepting the three children), would get her banned for life, a scarlet letter.

Not that she was complaining, but it had never stopped being strange that what was praised in men—the need to be good at everything, to be someone important—would be considered a character flaw in her. This had not been the case when Hank was alive. Perhaps they thought her ambition came from him, perhaps they did not mind a woman if she was under the control of a man.

But why did she care? Most men bored her, people bored her; she'd spent fifteen years watching Hank's mind grow and change and constantly being surprised. She was not going to give up her freedom for anything less. In the first few years after Hank's death, she'd slept with only a handful of men and of all of them the only one she'd fallen for was married, and as far as the others, her feelings had faded, or turned off abruptly; they were not Hank, could not be Hank. Most nights, if she had the energy, she reached for her massager and fell asleep.

Yes, she was jealous, there were two sets of rules, a man could have mistresses and abortions, sleep with every cheerleader on the Dallas Cowboys . . . to be free that way, to do whatever you wanted, though it was not just about being free, it was about being desired. No matter how old, fat, or ugly you were—you were desired nonetheless. She could not think about it without feeling like a failure, as if she had to live her life in a sort of cage, a narrow and particular path, watching the others sprint about like a pack of children, or dogs, breaking the rules, going in circles, this way and that.

She was not a prude. She'd used a few men for sex, or tried to, but each time it was less than she wanted, it was something half-complete, and even men did not not enjoy being treated that way, no matter what they told their friends, *you acted like I was some kind of vibrator,* one had told her, they were sensitive creatures, monsters and sensitive creatures, they were whatever they wanted to be.

AND YET THEY had begun to accept her. They were all getting old, they were all getting rich, she didn't know, but they had begun to treat her like the lady who'd been on the cover of *Time,* the woman you should have known way back, when she was a looker, a man-eater. Of course, she had never been a man-eater; of course, even at fifty, she was still striking. But that was not part of the agreement. The agreement was she was old and fat, just like them, though being old and fat did not matter for them.

Lucho Haynes invited her to his hunting camp, and she'd immediately turned him down. It was Lucho, not Clayton Williams, who'd come up with the idea of the Honey Hunt: prostitutes hired by the dozen and set out in the woods with a blanket and cooler—as a bird handler would place pheasants before a hunt—at which point Lucho and his friends would go out and find them.

She mentioned the invitation to Ted.

"Well, I doubt they'd rape you or anything," he said. "They probably have younger girls for that."

"Sex could be an interesting novelty," she said.

He faked a hurt look, then went back to his magazine. "I would not mind trying it later."

"Fat chance."

"Well, if you are seriously interested in my opinion, I think it's a terrible idea. They'll figure out some way to humiliate you or it'll happen naturally without them even planning it, because they aren't so stupid that they can't see what you really want."

"Which is what?"

"To be like them," he said. "To be accepted into their little club."

"There is no club," she said. "And if there is, I am in it."

"I suppose that is true."

"That is ridiculous."

"No, you're right. I don't know what I was talking about."

The next day she called Lucho and told him she was coming.

THE CAMP WAS three hours northeast of Houston, deep into the Pineywoods. There were families living in shacks, fields of wrecked farm equipment, it was as poor as Mexico, poor as the last century. In her trunk were three days' worth of clothes and a pair of shotguns: a 28 gauge for quail, a 20 gauge if she needed something heavier, and her normal revolver under the driver's seat.

She made her way down the sandy road, the car fishtailing the entire time. The vegetation was thick, vines hanging, smells of flowers she didn't recognize, she thought of white sheets, her father, old longleaf pines and white oaks and magnolias a hundred feet tall. It was like going back in time, mosquitoes and dragonflies and the air so wet and heavy—it did not seem possible this was Texas.

By the time Lucho showed her to her cabin, the sun was going down and most of the men had returned from fishing or shooting. She was wearing heels and a skirt and blouse and cursing herself for forgetting the bug spray. None of the men appeared to have showered or shaved in several days. The average oilman's ranch had a main house of limestone with heavy wood floors and leather furniture; the lodge here was a crude plank structure with stapled screen windows and unfinished walls. It might have been the hunting camp of some backwoods mayor, jury-rigged electrical cables, old refrigerators and televisions. She knew all of the men present, Rich Estes, Calvin McCall, Aubrey Stokes, T.J. Garnet, a half-dozen others, all dressed in their oldest clothes, pale legs under Bermuda shorts, bellies hanging. She had brought jeans but decided not to change—the worst thing would have been to give off the impression that she cared to fit in, to let them know how flattered she was. They were all good men, but they were the type who demanded submission.

Dinner was beans and tortillas, beef or cabrito, piles of fried catfish caught that morning, a platter of fried squirrel riddled with number-six pellets; if you counted what these men might have been earning had they not been hunting and fishing, it was probably the most expensive meal ever eaten. Travis Giddings was picking out the squirrel heads and methodically sucking them, his shirt covered in gravy. Drinks were Big Red or sweet tea or Pearl beer, but mostly whiskey in a paper cup. Then there were trays of peach cobbler and buckets of ice cream. But there was no loud talk, no cursing; it was like a locker room when the teacher walks in. She let slip that she would only be staying a night or two at most, saw the relief. Lucho began passing a handle of whiskey; she put the bottle to her mouth, lifted it high and held it for a long time as if she intended to drink the whole thing. Of course she kept her tongue pressed to the rim, letting barely any into her mouth, but there were cheers and laughter and within a few minutes a stream of *fuck*s and *shit*s like a dam had broken, *everyone likes the drunk girl,* she thought. Maybe that was not fair.

She pretended disgust at the mess, laughed at the dirty jokes, and when four women showed up (strippers? prostitutes?) she didn't react. Lucho gave her a look and she knew it had not been his idea; she winked to show he shouldn't worry. She was safe—any one of these men would have jumped in front of a train for her—but they were not above making her feel uncomfortable. She wondered who had ordered the girls, maybe Marvin Sanders, who had never really liked her, or maybe Pat Cullen, or maybe it was Lucho himself, whatever he was pretending now. Maybe they had invited her to test her. Or maybe they had presumed she could handle it, or maybe they had not thought of her at all.

Sitting in the dirty armchair, watching the girls circulate, the lights dim, the windows open, a record player going with Merle Haggard, she sipped from her 7 and 7, drunk despite her best efforts. Everyone looked terrible; everyone said what they meant. It was a pleasant feeling of companionship; she had known these men for decades. Many of them had sat with her when Hank died, and despite their behavior since, here she was, safe and protected. She began to relax and then Marvin Sanders looked at her and said something and then the girls looked at her, too. There were three bottles of whiskey circulating. She wondered if any of the men were doing harder stuff, though this was not that kind of place, and these were not, for the most part, those kinds of men. Drinking until your car went into the bar ditch or you blacked out at the controls of your Cessna: yes. Smoking reefer: no. One of the girls was standing next to her, a brunette with theatrical black eye makeup, wearing nothing but a bra and panties. Then she was sitting in Jeannie's lap. Jeannie could feel the girl's crotch rubbing somewhere above hers, it was soft and entirely wrong, she wished she had put on pants or something thicker. She started to push the girl off, then stopped, everyone was watching, the girl was watching, did she care what Jeannie wanted? No, the man who was paying her had told her to do this; the girl would see it through. It went on a half minute, then a minute; there was cheap vanilla perfume, there was a strange intensity in the girl's eyes. *She is enjoying this,* Jeannie thought, and then the girl kissed her, openmouthed, hard and fake, all for show. Jeannie turned her head. She wondered how much the girl made in a year. What she would do if she knew how much Jeannie made. Then the song ended and the girl climbed off. Jeannie winked at her in solidarity, but the girl ignored her; she was already looking around the room. *I was prettier than you even ten years ago,* she thought, but she knocked that from her mind, the girl was not the problem, it was Marvin Sanders, red-faced and fat; his comb-over flopped to the wrong side, his pants covered in cherry soda, a ridiculous figure, though it did not matter, he was rich and could buy whatever he wanted.

Not much later she got up and yawned and said it was getting late for an old lady. Everyone stopped what they were doing and shouted good night, raised their drinks. It was very early but no one protested. As for the girls, they ignored her.

She walked in the dark toward her cabin, the pines enormous above her, everything closed in. She wondered if Hank had done things like this; of course he must have, it was likely he had touched plenty of strippers, he'd spent weeks with other operators at their hunting camps and private islands, for all she knew he became an entirely different person. He certainly would not have gone to bed early—it would have been a mark against him—and she was suddenly sure that he had slept with another woman, absolutely sure, he could have done so, at no risk and no consequence, hundreds or perhaps thousands of times, the code of silence would never be broken. She wondered why she had never realized this. A loneliness came over her.

Why it might disturb her so much, he had been dead twenty years, it made no sense, she listened to the cicadas whirring, laughter and music from the main house, who was she to say who her husband had been? She sat in her underwear on the strange, hard cot. She wondered if she ought to get dressed and drive home, home to Ted, who had asked her to marry him twice now, she would see if he was still up for it. She was tired of being alone.

She lay back down. Too drunk, too far to drive. She fell asleep and the next morning washed her face in the stream, put on makeup in the dull cracked mirror, dismissed the thought of marrying Ted, and spent the morning shooting grouse with Chuck McCabe. After which she got in her Cadillac and headed back to Houston. No one asked why. They pretended they were happy she had come.

She was driving. It was hot and she had a sudden memory of the branding fire, defying her father and all the rest, and now here she was, forty years later, desperate to belong. They had broken her. She had given up. She should have given Ted a child, she had been selfish, her entire life for her father and for Hank, but you could not measure yourself against the dead, they retained their perfection while your flesh got weaker and weaker.

And her father had been weak himself, and even Hank, she could see that now. He had been an idea longer than a real person, but he was only an idea, he was no longer real, she had not done badly, there was no one like her. That ought to count for something. She was not like other women. A dozen lifetimes of tennis or polo could not have made her happy, and, as for a child, if Ted had asked she would have given him one. But he had wanted children like he wanted everything else, it was an old song somewhere in his mind, dim and faint. Though he had been right about this. She should not have come. It was a mistake, an enormous mistake, she would learn from it.

CHAPTER FIFTY-FOUR

DIARIES OF PETER McCULLOUGH

AUGUST 8, 1917

Hot. Blew two tires driving fast on the rocks. Half a day lost; believe we will reach Torreón tomorrow. Sullivan and Jorge Ramirez are with me. Jorge knows the area somewhat. He is very nervous—if we get stopped by the Carrancistas it will be a dice roll on whether we live or die.

I do not particularly care. It feels as if someone might push a finger through me. There is nothing inside.

AUGUST 9, 1917

From some workers along the road Jorge acquired sombreros and proper clothing, which we change into, giving the men our own. Anger at Americans high here especially given Pershing's recent expedition (*la invasión,* they call it). We pass donkeys dragging lumber and mules laden with pottery and thick-footed men padding slowly in the heat, all in white except for the blankets across their shoulders. There are children wearing nothing but hats and ragged blankets that barely reach their waists and we stop often for herds of sheep and goats and bare-ribbed cattle that see no reason to move out of our way.

I asked Sullivan and Jorge if they thought it possible that Phineas had María hurt or worse. Sullivan vigorously denied. Jorge silent. I pressed him and he said no, he did not think so.

Sullivan pointed out that Phineas is preparing to run for governor, and Sally's father is an important judge. Suggested it was probably because of those reasons they wanted María gone. I pointed out there were other reasons as well.

In Torreón, which is bigger than I thought, we drove until we found a cantina Jorge judged to be safe (what logic he used is beyond me) and spent a few hours sitting in the back corner (after $150 bribe to owner) while Jorge went out to scout. We were both wearing the soiled white shirts and pants of workers, reeking of the sweat of other men. Sullivan kept his .45 on one empty chair and the carbine on the other. I had my pistol under my shirt but doubted I would have the energy to use it. Sullivan sensed this and it angered him.

When Jorge had not come back for several hours, Sullivan pointed out, though he said he had promised himself he would keep quiet, that ten thousand dollars is a lot of money. Enough to start an entirely new life. *I am nervous here, boss, to tell you the truth. The longer we stay here, the lower our odds of staying above the snakes.*

Am not sure what I am supposed to feel. Jorge finally returned and we ordered food. He had found us a good hotel.

Did María know this would happen? Was she waiting for it? I find it unlikely—she just as well expected to be led into the *brasada* and shot.

But it is the unstated question for the rest of the day. There are no signs of her that Jorge was able to detect—she might have come through last night, or might not.

I watched as Sullivan and Jorge silently pondered what they might do with ten thousand dollars. Five years' wages. They would leave me, certainly. I see it on their faces about María. I cannot explain the situation. No longer certain I know it myself.

That she was desperate remains unsaid; that she had everything to gain and nothing to lose also remains unsaid. That she is ten years my junior and beautiful; no one mentions that, either.

AUGUST 10, 1917

Car stolen. Barricaded in hotel room. Waiting for Phineas to wire money for a new vehicle. They now know Jorge's face and it is dangerous even for him to go outside. Strangely we see a European photographer walking around in the streets; no one seems to harass him in the slightest.

AUGUST 11, 1917

Phineas and my father apparently making calls: chief of police this morning brought a suitcase full of pesos and a 1911 Ford he is willing to sell. I point out that his price is the same as for a new Ford on a dealer lot. Sullivan and Jorge give me a look to shut the hell up.

Jorge's arm nearly torn off by the starter handle, but we get police escort out of town. They encourage us to make the most of our journey today, it being Sunday, as the people will be taking their leisure. No one seems to know anything about María.

AUGUST 13, 1917

Drove to San Antonio to talk to Pinkertons.

"You want us looking in every city in Mexico."

"Yes," I told him.

"That is impossible. It is financially impossible and it is logistically impossible. There is a war going on there."

"Give me a figure."

He put up his hands. "One hundred thousand dollars."

I didn't say anything.

"I am taking you at your word when you say you want us looking everywhere. There are ways to do it for a tenth as much."

"Will that get me the same result?"

"Either way, the result will likely be the same."

"Let's do it," I told him.

He looked at the desk. "Everyone knows your family, but . . ."

"My family is not to know a word about this."

"What I was getting at is that we will need the money up front, Mr. McCullough."

I took out the checkbook, the money I have been socking away for myself, all I have ever put aside. I thought: I will never be free if I write this.

"I can give you eighty thousand today. The rest I can bring you next week."

"Just so you know, you are wasting your money. Villa is still running around in the north, Carranza and Óbregon have the middle, and Zapata has the south. Even if she is still . . . in good health, finding her will be extremely difficult."

"I am well aware of that."

I wrote the check. A drop of sweat smeared the numbers.

"Are you sure you want me to take this?" he said.

August 18, 1917

Sally asked when I was going to accept the reality of our situation. I told her I said prayers every day that she would roll her Packard into a ditch. She laughed and I pointed out I was not joking.

After she collected herself she said she was willing to spend only half the time here, and half in San Antonio, just for appearance's sake. I didn't answer.

This afternoon she returned to my office with a bottle of cold wine and two glasses. Admitted she had not been perfect, though I had not been either. She wants to start over. A second marriage, of sorts.

I told her I did not want her around, now or ever, that I would sooner lie with a rotting corpse.

"You were with the girl a month," she told me. "It is time to grow up."

"That is the only month I have ever been happy."

"Well what about the boys?" she said.

"The boys do not respect me. You have taught them that. You and my father."

She smashed the glasses and stood leaning in the doorway, as

María used to do. After she left I looked at the jagged wineglass and wondered what it would be like to push it into her neck. Then I was nearly sick. Follow your footprints long enough and they will turn into those of a beast.

I think about María. I tell myself she was a luxury, like fruit out of season, lucky to have but temporary.

AUGUST 19, 1917

They have buried me alive.

CHAPTER FIFTY-FIVE

ELI McCULLOUGH

1865–1867

The best of the Texans were dead or had left the state and the ones who'd run things before the war came back. The cotton men wept about paying their slaves, but they kept their land and their Thoroughbreds and their big houses. There is more romance roping beefs than chopping cotton, but our state's reputation as a cattle kingdom is overboiled. Beef was always a poor cousin to the woolly plant and it was not until thirty years after Spindletop that even oil knocked King Cotton from his throne.

I moved back in with the judge but I could barely stand to be in town, with the better classes strutting around in carriages and the errant freedman or Unionist to be cut down from the trees every morning. It was more and more like the Old States, some neighbor's nose in all your business, who did you vote for and which was your church, and I considered buying a parcel along the caprock, where the frontier was still open, though the judge was dead set against it. I pointed out the Comanches were on their heels; it was just a matter of time. And we did not have to move there; I could simply buy it. But the judge reckoned the temptation would be too much, and he was likely correct, as I often sat on his smoking porch wondering about Nuukaru and Escuté and if I ought to ride out and find them. Likely they were already in the

Misty Beyond, but had it not been for Everett I would have left Madeline all my money and lit off to find out.

It was an idle period. I put on a bloom and my pants got small and I developed a taste for nose paint I never shook. The judge encouraged me to find a regular job but I had money in the bank and I was determined to make it work for me—as it did for the better classes. I tried to buy back my father's headright, which was now well settled, but it had already been split into four parcels and the new owners wouldn't sell and all my other plans fizzled. My best days were behind me, that was plain.

Meanwhile, the judge thought the opposite. He had moved to Texas to watch it settle up, and now that he'd gotten his wish, he was planning a run for Senate. It was touchy business as Custer's troops were occupying the capital and no one knew what would happen when they left. The judge rolled the dice and announced on the Republican ticket, which his friends had counseled him against, though he would not hear them. He thought times were changing. A few weeks later he was found shot by the river.

Whatever had been left in me after Toshaway was buried along with the old ram. I refuted my kinship with other men. If anyone knew who did it, they were not saying, and I began to plot a campaign of murder among the Roberts, Runnels, and Wauls, felt the old holy fire begin to spark, but Madeline detected my plan and her words got the better of my judgment. The big house was sold and we moved to the farm at Georgetown. The slaves were now called servants and they worked on shares.

Madeline's mother and sister felt content to lie around crying about the judge, but so far as they were concerned my job was to sit on a pot-gutted horse watching the freedmen as they trudged up and down the rows of cotton. The days of high living were over; we survived on venison, side meat, and the holy trinity. But I was not content to see the great house fall. And I was not cut out to be an overseer. And the Comanche in me held grubbing in the dirt to be lower than hauling slops. And I wanted to make my money work.

For twenty-eight cents an acre I picked up sections in LaSalle and Dimmit Counties. I considered parcels on the coast but the Kings and Kenedys had already driven up the prices, and the Nueces Strip was rich, well watered, and so cheap I could acquire a proper acreocracy. There were bandits and renegades but I had never minded packing my gun loose, and in that part of the state a man with a rope could still catch as many wild cattle as he wanted, which sold for forty dollars a head if you could get them north. It was not panning for gold, but it was close, and I rode out to save the family's good name.

THERE WERE FORTY-EIGHT souls in the entire county, the nearest being an old Mexican named Arturo Garcia. He had once owned most of the surrounding country but was down to two hundred sections, and the same day I met him he tried to outbid me on a four-section parcel that linked all my other pastures. My ranch was useless without it. I went to the commissioners' office and offered forty cents an acre, a gross overpayment, which they accepted.

"Happy to have you in the area," said the commissioner.

"Happy to be here."

"We are trying to move folks like Garcia out, if you know what I mean."

I looked at him. I was thinking I could have bid less for the land but he mistook my meaning.

"Not just because he's Mexican. My wife is Mexican, in fact. I mean because he associates with known thieves."

"That is interesting knowledge."

"I'm guessin' you got a gun?"

"'Course I do."

"Well, I wouldn't stray too far from it."

I would like to say otherwise, but this only convinced me I had come to the right place.

CHAPTER FIFTY-SIX

J.A. McCULLOUGH

Once again she was a fool, they all knew it, even Milton Bryce. Domestic oil was a dead end, you lost money on every barrel you pumped. But she had a feeling. That was what she told them. Then she put it out of her mind. It was the biggest bet of her life and she was at peace.

She was happy with Ted, she was happy with her children, they were all doing well, even Susan and Thomas. Ben had finished at the top of his class and gone off to A&M. He did not care much for sports but he was conspicuously bright, interested in others, a good listener, the opposite of his siblings, who seemed to believe they had some special arrangement with fate (Susan) or were barely aware of anything outside themselves at all (Thomas). Susan had survived a single semester at Oberlin before moving to California; she would be unreachable for months and then the phone would ring at three A.M. and there she was, asking for some outrageous sum of money. Though she seemed happy. Jeannie would agree to the sum and Susan would tell of her adventures. As for Thomas, the oldest, he continued to live in her house. She was happier about this than she liked to admit, she knew she ought to push him out, but—his eccentricity—it seemed better for him to be close to home. There was the example of Phineas, but Thomas was not him.

Thomas was content to live with his mother and she was content to have him, he had a car, a large allowance, trips with his friends. He'd been a gorgeous child and it had ruined him; even now he expected to be the center of things. A man in love with his own face, that was how Ted put it, and she supposed she couldn't blame him, he really did look like a young Peter O'Toole, the fact of which he was enormously proud, so much so that she was often tempted to point out that Peter O'Toole did not live with his mother.

As for his eccentricity, he hid it so well that she sometimes wondered if she were mistaken, though other times she was certain, and scared, and waiting for him to be caught in public. In truth, there was not much to be worried about. Everyone knew Tom McCullough, and Texans were good at ignoring things they didn't want to see, it was a leftover from the frontier days when you couldn't choose your neighbors.

Yes, her children were happy. It was a real pack, even Susan. These were good years. And perhaps because of this she continued to unwind her properties, to undiversify, she sold the steel company and the insurance company she had bought with Hank, most of the real estate, she plowed it all into oil, domestic acreage, which everyone was happy to sell her. It happened so easily she sometimes wondered if she was walking into her own suicide—financial suicide, at least—which would leave her family greatly diminished.

She wondered if it was the same liberated feeling that allowed her father to blow his inheritance on the ranch. Though her father was an actual fool. This was something else. She had gone touring around the Middle East with Cass Rutherford and while he found nothing amiss, in fact he thought things were getting better—the infrastructure, the competence of their drillers and geologists—she found the whole thing disturbing. Twenty years earlier, it had been men on camels. Now it was housing blocks, trash everywhere, people staring you down on every street corner. That was the problem with television—everyone saw what you were taking—what these Arabs saw was rich foreigners buying up their oil at ten cents on the dollar. By the end of the trip, she felt so corrupt and depressed that she'd considered getting out of the business altogether.

After a few weeks at home she came to her senses, but the uneasy feeling remained. Something was going to happen and the overthrow of Mosaddegh was a miracle unlikely to ever be repeated. And so she had begun to look at domestic acreage. She was a fool, though later they would call it women's intuition, though it was not, it was just a question of seeing what was actually in front of you, instead of what you wanted to see.

Oil went nowhere. Then Bunker Hunt bet big in Libya and got massacred and the Egyptians went into Israel and the embargo hit. The boom had lasted ten years. And still this dissatisfaction. She had won her bet but they would not recognize her. *They* being . . . she was not sure. The world? Her dead father and brothers and husband? *You expect a medal,* she thought. And she did. It was not entirely unreasonable, some notice from the other operators, a bit of recognition, a mention of her alongside the Richardsons and Basses and Murchisons, the Hunts. She was certain—ragingly certain—that if Hank had pulled off what she had, his name would have been included. Maybe she had a victim complex. That's what they wanted her to think.

She focused on her home life, maybe for the first time ever. Here was her medal: a happy house, happy children. Ben and Thomas and all their friends, who, like them, had gotten exceptions from the draft. They made her house their own, drinking and swimming at all hours, it was like being an older sister, young people drunk in the kitchen, drunk in the yard, they would tell her their problems.

THEN, QUICK AS that, as if a single twig had been holding it all up, it was over. Ben was down at the ranch; his truck went into a bar ditch. Milton Bryce had gone with her to see him—he did not look himself, she was not sure how, he had only a single black eye—they had parted his hair wrong—she walked out of the room and they had handed her something sweet—a Coke?—and then she was thinking of her brothers and then she remembered nothing.

They had buried him and then nothing more was expected, she had sat down in the old familiar house and everything became gauzy and unreachable. She had allowed, in some far corner of her mind, that something might happen to Thomas or Susan—their judgment was terrible, the risks—but Ben had been the linchpin, the steady soul. And if he . . . she had a feeling she would lose them all. She had failed in some fundamental way. They had been right about her all along.

Thomas also seemed to sense this, to sense that his brother's death was her fault, that there was some power she had failed to exert, over the driving habits of young men, or the sharp curve in the road, or the bar ditch that flipped the truck. One day he went out and never came back. Susan called to say that he'd arrived in California; he'd driven all night. Gone forever, as it turned out. She sold the house in River Oaks and moved in with Ted.

She could admit it was different from losing her husband. She knew she would survive, she knew she would recover, *do not take this as a lesson,* Jonas told her, but she did, she had expected too much, and if it was not a lesson, then what was the point?

EVEN IF GOD existed, to say he loved the human race was preposterous. It was just as likely the opposite; it was just as likely he was systematically deceiving us. To think that an all-powerful being would make a world for anyone but himself, that he might spend all his time looking out for the interests of lesser creatures, it went against all common sense. The strong took from the weak, only the weak believed otherwise, and if God was out there, he was just as the Greeks and Romans had suspected; a trickster, an older brother who spent all his time inventing ways to punish you.

She was bitter, Ben had changed her, first for the better and then for the worse, she was furious and defeated, when she was not too low she assembled a vast dissertation, praise from various figures, approval from the Colonel, success in business, the covers of magazines, her marriage and worthy lovers and her saving of the McCullough name, it buoyed her for a time, it held her above the darkness, but always, always, she plunged. None of it mattered.

The boom continued. *Time* magazine came around again: now she was the woman who'd predicted the embargo. Incidentally, was she a feminist? No? Back on the cover she went, not entirely defeated, though it was not the same, not the same. A publisher approached her about a memoir, something inspirational for other people, women, they meant, your life story, the way you think and solve problems, something for the young to take inspiration from, though likely they meant housewives.

But what would she say? That the Colonel had been right? That you could only depend on yourself? It would not exactly fill a book. She tried anyway, and for a time a dream came back to her from youth, sitting behind a desk, answering letters from all her subjects, the cameras lingering on her every word, she wrote about her father and two brothers and the mother she had never known, her husband and son, where should she stop, children in the graveyard, the dead pouring forth until she set the papers aside. She knew why the Colonel had hated talking about the old days. Because the moment you looked back, and began to make your tally, you were done for.

By '83 THERE were wildcatters going bankrupt left and right, but for Ted and most of their friends, the boom had been nothing more than a period of unusual wealth, in which the royalty checks they all lived on had been preposterous instead of merely large.

Jonas was fine, frugal as always; no belt tightening necessary. He still commuted down to Boston a few days a week in his old Volvo, maybe from Martha's Vineyard, maybe from Newport, maybe from his lake house in Maine, though if he really did anything at his legal practice, she didn't know. Mostly he seemed to wake up at the same time every morning, spending hours writing lists of what needed to be done: *winterize boat, paint railings on porch* (he considered himself handy), *call about*

Volvo noise, Bill squash (racquet), porch screens, tuition, Bohemian Club, reservations at . . . He got great satisfaction crossing things off his list; sometimes he would write things he had already done (*breakfast with Jeannie*) just to cross them off again.

She considered selling the ranch, keeping the house but selling the land, she had no family left in Texas; in Midland you could buy a Rolls-Royce or office building or even a Boeing for pennies on the dollar, there wouldn't be work in the oil business for a long time, that was clear. It was time to sell. There was no point being so far from her only living brother and her children.

She and Ted were at the ranch, fighting about this very thing (one did not sell land, he thought), when Consuela came to tell her there was someone at the door.

IT WAS A Mexican woman around her own age, wearing a dress and jewelry as if expected for a party. Jeannie hadn't yet showered that day; she brushed back her hair and smoothed her blouse and felt short.

"I am Adelina Garcia."

This meant nothing.

"I am Peter McCullough's daughter."

This meant nothing as well. Then it did. She reached for the doorknob.

"Peter McCullough did not have any daughters," she said. "I'm afraid you are mistaken."

"He is my father," the woman repeated.

When Jeannie didn't react, the woman got an imperious look. "You are my niece," she said. "Regardless of our ages."

Maybe it was the language barrier, but she could not have picked a worse thing to say. "Well you have met me. And I am busy." Jeannie closed the door. The woman stood on the porch a long time then walked slowly back to her car. Jeannie wondered how she'd gotten through the gate.

It was an old trick. Though usually you heard about it through a lawyer. Still, she felt unsettled, and back in the library, she lost all her strength and collapsed against Ted. He leaned around her to see the television.

"Anyone important?"

She felt sick; something told her to follow the woman but she could not make herself get up.

"What do you want to eat?" he said.

"That was a Mexican person claiming to be my relative."

"Your very first?"

She nodded.

"Welcome to the club."

She sat there.

"Call Milton Bryce," he said, not looking up from the television. It was *Dallas.* People were obsessed with it. "Call him right now if you're really worried about it."

But she was not sure that was she was worried in that way. She decided to think about it. She waited until dinner and decided it was nothing.

WHAT ELSE MIGHT she have been? She had plenty of friends from old families who were always carrying on about how helpless they were, no driver's licenses or social security cards, the worst sort of bragging, they were helpless, absolutely helpless, and proud of it.

The things that made them happy meant nothing to her. She was a leftover from another time, maybe, like her great-grandfather. But even that was not true. She was not like him at all. She'd had no imagination, she'd chased only what she could see, she could have done more.

She had a feeling she ought to apologize, but to whom, and for what, she didn't know. She looked around the room. It was still dark. When it finally happens, she thought, I won't even know it, and then she wasn't afraid.

CHAPTER FIFTY-SEVEN

ULISES GARCIA

There had always been a rumor that they were descended from wealthy Americans, it was a story his mother liked to tell about his father's side of the family. His father had died when he was two. The Dirty War was going on, and the last anyone heard of his father, he was being taken into a police station.

After that, they had moved around a lot, finally settling in Tamaupilas with his grandparents. His grandfather worked on a ranch, tending the fences, repairing the windmills and outbuildings, more time on a truck than on a horse, but this is what vaqueros did now. In America, the cowboys now flew helicopters. Or so it was said.

His grandfather had worked for the Arroyos his entire life and was no richer now than when he started; the Arroyos had owned the land since the 1600s and paid as if no time had passed since. Sitting at the fire with the old-timers, he could see his entire life from birth to death, it was good work, he was lucky to be born into it; his friends would end up in the refineries, or selling trinkets to tourists, or with the narcos.

Still, there were nights he woke up thinking he was as old as his grandfather, he would turn on the light and go to the mirror and look at his face. He was dark, people thought he was mulatto, he had a soft nose and a heavy brow.

In winter the men would trickle back from the north with thousands of dollars in their pockets and some would blow it all—a season's work—in a night or two of gambling. His grandfather just shrugged. Mercedes Arroyo would spend three thousand dollars on a scarf, what was the difference?

As for Ulises, he watched the Arroyos' pretty granddaughters come and go, their drivers and BMWs; when they passed he smelled perfume from inside the cars. The house was full of stuffed jaguars and elephants, exotic rugs, bathrooms done in gold, but he'd only heard this; he'd never been allowed inside.

His mother went to work in Matamoros and he stayed with his grandparents. One day he was going through a suitcase she had left, which was full of her junk, old pictures and keys, birthday cards from people he didn't know, letters, faded receipts, his father's university ID, and then, in its own paper bag . . . his grandmother's birth certificate. The document was in Spanish but the name of the father was not: Peter McCullough. And there were letters written in English.

He knew that his grandmother had tried to get in touch with the American side of her family, but they had spurned her, and then his father had tried as well, and also been sent away, and he could not imagine how the McCulloughs (he now knew their name) had done this. He tried to imagine their point of view, a person showing up on your doorstep and asking for money. The details mattered; it would have to be handled a certain way.

He began to daydream about visiting them, and being received, and given land, and made wealthy. Of course they would not simply do this for no reason; he would show them that he knew cattle, he knew their business, he was not simply some freeloader, he was a hard worker, and then, once he had proven himself beyond question, he would make a formal presentation.

Those daydreams had gone on for several years; they were straight out of a telenovela and he was not clear when they had materialized into a firm plan. But in September of 2011, he crossed the river and rode onto the McCulloughs' ranch. His grandfather knew someone on an olive plantation on the Mexican side, just a few miles upriver from the ranch, and he and this old man had waited for a dark night and crossed. After that it was easy. He was not some pollo, he was a vaquero, and he belonged.

HE FOUND THE white foreman and offered to give up his hand-tooled saddle if any bronco in their remuda could throw him. The fore-man burst into laughter, then explained they did not have any broncs in the remuda, it had probably been half a century since they had broncs. They did their big roundups with helicopters and bought most of their horses as three-year-olds from other ranches.

But he could see the foreman was impressed with his appearance, he had not thrown Ulises off the ranch immediately, he'd carefully inspected his tack, his chaps. Ulises threw a few loops for him, caught a calf by the neck and then the foreleg. *I roped an eagle in flight once,* he said. It was not exactly true—it had been a turkey. But he could see the man liked his face. *I can also use a welder.*

He spent the rest of the day in the man's truck, helping with chores, repairing a fence, running a tractor with a bale spike. At the end of it, the man said:

"Two fifty a week. *La Migra* mostly stays off the property, but if you stick your nose out and get caught you'll spend a few months in the pokey. Normally we'd never do this but we are shorthanded and getting shorter."

He noted this, but decided not to ask why.

"If you're still here after a few months, we can talk about apply-ing for a permit. Though none of us are sure if this place will even be around that long. I lost two guys this week alone. So if you've got other prospects, I suggest you follow them."

HIS SALARY WAS not much by *norteamericano* standards but he had nothing to spend it on. On smaller ranches the ICE agents came and went daily but the McCulloughs kept their own security and *La Migra* was rarely around. It was dangerous to leave the property, though: the white-and-green trucks were everywhere; it was a bit like being under house arrest.

He had a bunk and a few nails to hang his shirts. When he wasn't working he sat around watching TV with the other vaqueros. When they wouldn't let him watch the American programs—they did not care about their English—he borrowed a rifle and went out into the *brasada* and shot an occasional javelina or rabbit, or trailed the big-racked deer that were everywhere. They were too valuable to kill; the Americans would pay thousands to shoot them.

He snuck to town once a month and sent his grandparents half his salary and bought a new shirt, though he had to ask for the hanger it came on. At Christmas he spent a long time looking at some Lucchese handmade boots but decided on Ariats, as they were a quarter the price. He also picked out a Leatherman tool. He felt rich. Then a white man with a gun walked into the store and everyone got quiet. Some kind of deputy. Ulises stood by the cash register, waited for his items to be bagged, watching the man's reflection in the window. He felt disgusted as he walked out. He paused near the trash bin, considered throwing away everything he'd just bought. It could not be worth this.

It will be better when you get your permit, said Romero, when they were back in the truck. *No estoy recibiendo mi permiso,* said Ulises, but Romero pretended not to hear. He had worked for the McCulloughs five years but still got stopped by the ICE, who pretended not to recognize him. Ulises could see the pride he took in the new white truck, though it was not his any more than the ranch was, and it struck him that Romero was a fool and he was a fool as well.

THE OLD LADY was dying and had no one to take over the business. Her daughter was a drug addict and her son, it was said, was not fully a man. There had been a grandson everyone liked, but he had drowned in three feet of water. The other grandson visited the ranch with his friends: they wore sandals and never shaved and were constantly smoking *mota*. One look and you knew why the vaqueros were leaving. This place would die with the old lady.

HIS PLAN WAS ridiculous. The old lady rarely visited the ranch and the foreman, who was likely looking for another job himself, forgot his promise to apply for a permit. But still it was better than the Arroyos. So he stayed.

CHAPTER FIFTY-EIGHT

DIARIES OF PETER McCULLOUGH

SEPTEMBER 1, 1917

The shadow follows me everywhere; I see him in the corner at supper, biding his time; he stands behind me as I sit at my desk. As if a great fire were burning in front of me. I imagine reaching for it . . . letting the flames carry me off.

I ride to the casa mayor and put my ear to the rock. I hear the bell of the church, children calling, women's shoes.

A memory from the day after the killings:

My father postulating, absentmindedly, that María's survival was a kind of tragedy. Had she died, all the Garcias' anger and sadness would have disappeared from the earth. His words have become a moving picture, playing over and over in my mind. I imagine putting a revolver to his head while he sleeps. I imagine the well shooter parking his truck next to the house, setting a match to the nitro bottles.

Of course this has always been inside me. It was only waiting for a moment to escape. There is nothing wrong with my father: he is the natural. The problem is those like myself, who hoped we might rise from our instinctive state. Who hoped to go beyond our nature.

SEPTEMBER 4, 1917

It came to me this morning: she is dead. I paced my room but then I was sure of it, she is dead, I have never been so sure of anything in my life.

My father came to find me in my office.

"You know I am sorry," he said. "You know it hurts me to see you like this."

I didn't respond. I have not spoken a word to him since that day.

"There are responsibilities," he told me. "We don't just get to act like normal people."

Still I ignored him. He walked around my office, looking at my shelves.

"All right, partner. I'll leave you alone."

He came forward, raised his hand to put it on my shoulder, but something in my face . . .

"It will get better," he told me.

He stood there another minute like that. Then I heard him shuffle down the hall.

OF COURSE IN person . . . the idea of hurting him is repulsive. Because, unlike him, I am weak. He did not mind trading a wife and a few sons to get what he wanted . . . each of us walks in his own fire for his own sins, lies down in his own torment. Mine the sin of fear, timidity . . . I might have carried María away from this place . . . it did not even occur to me. Held by the chains of my own mind.

My sun has set, the journeying ways have darkened. The rest of my life hangs above me like a weight; I remind myself that my heart for a brief time ran feral . . . my most preposterous thoughts came true.

Perhaps another great ice will come and grind all this into dust. Leaving no trace of our existence, as even fire does.

SEPTEMBER 6, 1917

Sally continues to make overtures. As if I will simply forget what she has done. It is only because I no longer defer to her that she is interested in my company. Today she asked if I would continue looking for María. Then she asked, *Would you look for me if I disappeared?* She is baffled. She did not see María as entirely human; she does not see herself as having done anything wrong. Like stays with like—that is her only principle.

I content myself to think that one day we will all be nothing but marks in stone. Iron stains of blood, black of our carbon, a hardening clay.

SEPTEMBER 7, 1917

This family must not be allowed to continue.

CHAPTER FIFTY-NINE

ELI McCULLOUGH

In 1521 a dozen Spanish cattle were landed in the New World; by 1865 there were four million living wild in Texas alone. They did not take to domestication; they would happily stick a horn through you and go back to chewing grass. Your average hayseed avoided them as he might a grizzly bear.

But they could not help being herd animals. Once you had a big enough bunch even the mossy horns would fall in. Starting from nothing it might take a year to build your brand, roping and cutting and marking seven days a week, and if you weren't gored or trampled there was always a neighbor who found it more enjoyable to spend that same year grinning up at the sun; all he had to do was come into your pastures one night with ten of his boon companions, where, in a few hours, he could take your entire year's work and make it his.

FOR ROOM, BOARD, and a sliver of the future profits, I hired two former confederates, John Sullivan and Milton Emory, along with Todd Myrick and Eben Hunter, who had spent the war dodging the Home Guard in Maverick and Kinney Counties. They knew the land better than I and were not allergic to sweat or blood. All knew Arturo

Garcia and hated him, but as it was common to dislike Mexicans in those days, I did not think anything of it.

YOU BEGAN A cattle drive owing your hands a year's back wages and after borrowing money from everyone you knew. The brutes were gently walked and allowed to graze and drink at will, so they would not drop even an ounce of weight. They were treated as precious eggs. Meanwhile, a storm might cost you half the herd.

The life of the cowboy has been written about as if it were the pinnacle of freedom in the West but in fact it was a sleepless drudgery almost beyond imagination—five months of slavery to a pack of dumb brutes—and had I not been riding for my own brand I would not have lasted a day. The fact the country was tame enough to drive valuable property across tells you all you need to know; the days of Bridger and Carson and Smith were long gone, the land was already going domestic.

We lost two of the thirty-dollar men when their horses went off a cliff in the dark. The others we released in Kansas. They were happy to see the big city and look for other work; they had more money in their pockets than they'd ever seen. On 1,437 head I cleared $30,000 and two hundred Indian ponies no one wanted. We drove the ponies back down the Chisholm and I stopped in Georgetown to see the family while Sullivan, Myrick, Emory, and Hunter took the ponies back to the Nueces.

Madeline was still living on the farm with Everett, Phineas, and Pete. Her mother, still a known beauty, had remarried and there were dining room servants again.

WE WERE IN the kitchen in the sun. The money was in the bank and I was happy to be home, happy to be looking at my pretty wife. She had a white hair among the red ones on her head. I leaned and kissed it.

She smacked her hand there. "Is it one of the gray ones?"

"More white," I said.

She sighed. "Now you're going to miss me even less."

I kissed her again.

"Do you miss me?"

"Of course."

"Sometimes I'm not sure if you even like me."

"That is crazy," I said, though I knew what she meant.

"I mean, I know you like the idea of me. But I am not sure you like the thing itself."

"I love you."

"Of course you do. But that is different than liking me."

It was quiet.

"The year before last, when we were all together here, I still think about that. I don't want another bite of venison in my life but when I think about it, it was the happiest time I've ever had."

"We were broke," I said. "There was no future in it."

"Well, one day I'll be dead. There is no future in that, either."

I looked at her with the sun coming in and her elbows on the white-washed table. Her hair went softly over her shoulders and I looked at that and her red lips and high cheeks and pale chest still heavy under her dress. I thought any man would be happy to have her in any way he could.

"Let's go to the bedroom," I said.

She gave me a tired smile. "Okay," she said.

Then I was looking at her in the white sheets. Her eyes were closed.

"I needed that."

"Me too," I told her.

She shook her head. "You don't need anything." She pushed the sheets off herself and lay there in the sun. I ran my fingers up and down.

"If you keep doing that I am going to want you again."

I kept on but I wondered what was wrong with me. She saw and crawled over and took me into her mouth. I wondered how or where she had learned it. Then I was ready again. As we were doing it I almost told her that if she had to do it with someone else I wouldn't care but then I changed my mind again. I tried to slip off but she held me where I was.

"Ten years from now we'll have the biggest house in Austin."

"And then you'll come back from the middle of nowhere?"

"Yes." I kissed her on the neck.

"I think you like the middle of nowhere."

"I like people, I just don't know how to make money where they live."

"Well, soon you won't have to."

"Soon I won't."

"That's right," she said.

WHEN I GOT back to the ranch Todd Myrick was dead in the yard and Eben Hunter was on the porch. They had been there for days. I went looking for Sullivan and Emory. In the lower pasture were more buzzards and by his lathyness I realized the man I was looking at was Emory.

Sullivan was at the Brackett army post. He had been shot through the lung but he had lived this long, and they were optimistic. He was a big man with a strange high voice he would pass along to his son. I asked him how he was feeling but he did not want to talk about that.

"It's a real piece of pudding how we were gone five months, then happened to get visited right when we got back," he said.

"And expecting us to have a wallet of money from a cattle sale."

The thieves had pried up the floorboards and tore the cupboard off the wall but there had not been any money. I had put it in the bank.

"A thinking man would allot upon your Mexican neighbor." He had to breathe awhile. "The buckras here paid him a visit, but it did as much good as a dog smelling his own piss."

"We get any of them?"

He looked out the window and I knew I shouldn't have asked.

"All I care about is you keep breathin'."

"Emory got a couple shots off. That boy was always quick."

I offered my handkerchief but instead he took my hand and held it. My throat got thick. I was thinking about the others. Then it was quiet.

Sullivan let go of my hand and took my bandanna. "I'm not leavin' this county without naturalizing at least a few of them. I wondered if you might stake me until then."

I SPENT THE day burying Emory, Myrick, and Hunter. Then I went to see Arturo Garcia.

He lived in a big white house that looked like a fortress of old. There was a long covered porch around the front and he came out to greet me. Through the open door I could see the house was filled with gold-framed paintings and weapons, furniture of the sort kings owned.

He was sorry for my loss. By some miracle his stock and horses had not been touched. I wanted to ride his fences and look for my two hundred Indian ponies, but I knew they had already gone to Old Mexico.

"What bamboozles me," I said, "is to get to my pastures, they must have passed pretty close to your house. Unless they wanted to ride twenty miles around. And to get my stock out, they had to lead them through your pastures again. Which is obvious because the tracks are all still there."

"It is big country, Eli. I am sorry."

"They also knew within a day that we'd got back."

"Eli, I will say this once, because I know you are upset, but the fact that I live on the border, and am Mexican, does not mean I had anything to do with stealing your horses, or killing your men."

"I didn't say it did."

A young white man came out of the house wearing bright yellow trousers and a blue silk shirt. His boots were spit shined and he had a pistol on each hip. He looked like a stage actor, an easterner's impression of a badman. "Jim Fisher," he said. "Very sorry for your loss, sir."

Then other men were coming from the pastures. I took my leave and spent a few nights sleeping in the brush, far from my house, thinking it over.

There were no other neighbors, no roads going in or out.

* * *

LET ME SAY that Garcia being Mexican had nothing to do with it. White or Mexican, the bigger a rancher was, the more liable he was to run his neighbors out. Your slice of pie is one less I can eat myself, that was his attitude, and for every orphan he helped in public there were ten he made in private.

Garcia had lost half his estate. That the state had stole his land I do not deny. But I had nothing to do with it and furthermore he was not the first to have lost it. He figured there was nothing I could do. I would dig out sooner or later.

Except I was not playing a lone hand. There was a twisting *barranca* to climb from his back pasture, where the walls were steep and you could only ride single file, a place where two men with ten-shot Winchesters, if they were patient, might stop any number of others. When Garcia died he was speaking in a language that was not English or Spanish or even Comanche, it was like nothing I had ever heard. Still, I understood him. He thought he was cursing me but it was nothing I didn't know already.

When Sullivan healed to ride the distance we hired a half-dozen sympathetics and drove Garcia's horses and cattle to New Mexico. Every unmarked calf and colt we drove into my pastures. I should have burned that house then, and salted the earth, because a year later, his nephew came and picked up where his uncle had left off.

CHAPTER SIXTY

J.A. McCULLOUGH

T o lie around and do nothing but think—if you'd asked her yesterday she might have wanted a year of it; now all she wanted was to get up. It was bright again in the room, the sun was coming in, but something was wrong: tables and chairs had been flung, pictures were off the walls, busts and pedestals scattered about. Aphrodite was facedown in the corner. The roof would fall in and animals would build their nests.

I am not really seeing this, she thought. She decided to ignore it. She decided to be glad to be in this room, the one place her father hadn't had the gumption to redecorate, he had filled the rest of the house with Remingtons and Russells and Bierstadts. But the Colonel would not have abided that. For him, this was what success looked like: dark wood, old sculpture, Eastern money. Which was trying to look like European money. Of course that had changed. The Italians now made movies about cowboys.

Even before the boom ended she had begun to diversify again, oil was overheated, every housewife in Midland was driving a Bentley. Along with most everyone she knew, she got into the savings-and-loan business. The S&Ls had been deregulated, allowed to loan money in commercial real estate, oil, and gas, the ceiling had been removed on the interest that could be paid to depositors. She bought a small one, offered high rates to attract depositors, then used the money for real estate projects in Houston and Dallas, taking a ludicrous up-front fee. But then real estate crashed along with oil, and Southsun was bailed out, which she felt guilty about, though not so guilty she wanted to lose the hundred million dollars herself. She thought she might have to testify in Washington, but she didn't.

MEANWHILE THOMAS WAS making plans to come out to all his old friends, to everyone he'd known in Houston, she had discouraged him, she had relentlessly discouraged him, there was not a single bit of upside to his plan. He would only be making things harder on himself. He never saw those people anyway.

"Why should I have to hide who I am?" he said.

She was so surprised she couldn't think of anything to say. He was finally standing up for himself, she ought to support him. And yet, she was not sure, it was a cry for attention—to identify yourself in public by what you did in your most private moments—it was wrong, entirely wrong, he ought to look to Phineas, who had taken the world in his fist and crushed it.

She had made some error. Neither of her children had any confidence, they were both muddle-headed, Susan in her addiction to gurus and therapists, Thomas in his liberal politics, his insistence on coming out. They could not seem to grasp that what mattered was what you did. Not what you said or thought about.

The coming-out had been a nonevent. She had sensed his confusion, she had felt terrible for him, he had thought it would be important, a pivotal moment, but nothing had changed, he was the same person.

It was not fair of her. She did not know what he'd been through. She had begun to wonder again if it was her fault, both her children had become unhappy, she guessed because neither one had ever engaged in any meaningful endeavor. She had flown to see them, a formal proposal, a few million each, or twenty, whatever they needed, whatever they wanted to do—a gallery for Thomas, a vineyard for Susan—there was no reason to start small. They were confused. She had always left them alone. And then they saw. They understood. She considered them failures, she considered them trivial, she was trying to save them from themselves.

BY THEN SUSAN had two young boys, Jeannie barely saw them, it was as if her daughter, without ever hinting at it, knew this was the only war she might ever win with her mother. But then Susan's boyfriend, father to neither of the two children, ran off somewhere and Susan was calling to ask if she might move to Texas, though she didn't actually mean that, what she meant was could her mother look after the children while she went off to hunt another man.

Jeannie was delighted, though she tried not to show it. The boys were six and eight, but had little recollection of ever meeting her. Ash was pale and blond, Dell a pure Spaniard; they looked like exactly what they were, boys with different fathers. She loved them. They had not seen the ranch since they were very small and she took them over it in a helicopter, the vast kingdom, they were its princes.

"One day this will belong to the two of you," she said.

"Mother," said Susan.

"One day this will all be yours."

She loved the boys. They sat there in front of the television, she bought a few tame ponies they enjoyed riding, but in general both were possessed by a clumsiness, a wariness, as if the physical world were conspiring against them. She could not help comparing them to her brothers, even to Ben and Thomas. It was likely an illusion. It was likely her failing memory. She loved them anyway; sitting there on the couch watching jangling cartoons, she forgave Susan everything she had ever done.

But the slackening. By five she and her brothers were throwing loops. By ten she was at the branding fire. Her grandchildren were not good at anything and did not have much interest in anything either. She wondered if the Colonel would even recognize them as his descendants, felt briefly defensive for them, but of course it was true. Something was happening to the entire human race.

That is what all old people think, she decided.

She took them on walks for as long as they would put up with her, *this is a javelina track, this is a deer track, that is a green jay. That is a kettle of buzzards and there is where a rabbit has been making his run and here is where a hawk ate a woodpecker.*

WHEN THE FIRST men arrived, she told them, there were mammoths, giant buffalo, giant horses, saber-toothed tigers, and giant bears. The American cheetah—the only animal on earth that could outrun a pronghorn antelope.

Her grandsons listened politely. Maybe they sensed where the story was going; where all her stories went. The American cheetah had disappeared and antelopes had gotten slower—the laggards got to keep breeding. People had become slower as well.

They went inside to watch television. She sat on the gallery alone. McCullough land, as far as the eye could see. There was no reference. There was the Colonel of course, but what kind of man had it taken to thrust a spear into a twenty-thousand-pound animal? The bears were twice the size of a modern grizzly, they must have died horrible deaths, as many words for courage as an Eskimo had for snow. For suffering as well. *That is who we came from,* she thought.

They'd left nothing but tracks and bones. In Australia, frozen into rock, there were the footprints of three people crossing a mudflat. At twenty-seven miles per hour—all three moving as fast as the fastest man on earth today. They were speeding up when the tracks ended.

WHAT SHOULD SHE tell her grandchildren? There were too many facts and you could arrange them in any order you wanted. Eli McCullough had killed Indians. Eli McCullough had killed whites. He had killed, period. It depended on whether you saw things through his eyes or the eyes of his victim as he pulled the trigger. Dead people did not have voices and this made them irrelevant.

She didn't know. Perhaps he had sown the seeds of his own ruination. He'd provided for all of them, and they'd become soft, they'd become people he never would have respected.

Of course you wanted your children to have it better than you had. But at what point was it not better at all? People needed something to worry about or they would destroy themselves, and she thought of her grandchildren and all the grandchildren yet to come.

CHAPTER SIXTY-ONE

ULISES GARCIA

The ranch made all its money from oil and gas, and the men from those companies were always driving around checking the wells and tanks and pumps. They were mostly white and their soda cans were always found along the roads. The vaqueros did not care for them and every time they saw a piece of surveyor tape marking some turn, they would stop to cut it down.

But the work was not bad; there was something to be said for air-conditioning when you wanted it, and the money, compared to Mexico, was unbelievable. In late January he'd gone to a rodeo with the other vaqueros, all of whom had work permits. They had been reluctant to take him—a truck full of Mexicans was a prime target and if they were caught they would lose their permits—but he pretended not to notice their hesitation. He quickly realized that three-quarters of the men in the competitions did not live or work on ranches—they competed at rodeos for fun.

He and Fernando got third in the team roping; he was going to collect his ten dollars when he saw a pair of ICE men talking to the promoter. He walked the other way. He waited in the brush outside the parking lot and watched for Fernando and the others to come out.

No one spoke on the ride home. It was no small thing to have a work permit; even being around them, he was putting them in jeopardy.

He was going stir-crazy. He could not even leave the ranch. One Sunday he rode up to the old Garcia place; it was just crumbling walls now, but it had once been a big house, a fortress even. There was still a spring running nearby, and trees and shade, and a view. He entered the ruins of the house and knew instantly, felt in his gut, that his people had lived here. Though Garcia was not exactly an uncommon name.

A truck came up the road, and he slipped out of the ruins and considered hiding; he felt as if he were doing something wrong. Though of course he was not. He might be trailing a lost cow.

The man who got out of the truck was short and baggy, old pants and an old shirt and thick glasses, the look of a person who spent all his time alone. The other hands had mentioned that Mrs. McCullough was paying someone to write a history of the ranch. He had never met a writer, but he thought this man looked like one, like he had not washed his hair or his glasses in a long time. Ulises introduced himself.

"I like to come up here and eat lunch," said the man. He seemed embarrassed to be breathing. "It's about the best view on the property, plus"—he indicated the spring—"it's nice to be near water."

After they had been sitting and talking, Ulises asked: "So what happened to the people who used to live here?"

"They were killed."

"Who killed them?"

"The McCulloughs. Who else?"

CHAPTER SIXTY-TWO

DIARIES OF PETER McCULLOUGH

SEPTEMBER 15, 1917

Feel my heart growing moderate. An even worse punishment. The might-have-beens filling in my years.

I think of my son's wounding, his near-death, as an excuse for other deaths. Both my children in some barracks, waiting to be sent overseas. This house nothing more than a mausoleum. Just in recorded history the polestar has changed four times. . . . yet men insist we will endure on this earth.

SEPTEMBER 18, 1917

Went out to help the vaqueros check the fences after last night's rain. In an arroyo, sticking out of the bank, I found a bone so ancient it had completely turned to stone; it rang like steel when I struck it.

SEPTEMBER 20, 1917

Ab Jefferson at Pinkerton came by today in person. Pretended it was a social call. We went for a drive and he informed me that in Guadalajara there are three possible María Garcias, all recent arrivals. Gave three addresses.

I had to pull the car over. He patted me on the back.

"It's one of the most common names in Mexico, Pete. They are probably farm girls."

"It's a start," I said.

"Do you want me to send someone?"

"No," I said.

Wrote letters to each of them, begging them to take me back. Lay on the sofa all day. The shadow is no longer standing over me. He has retreated to one of the corners.

CHAPTER SIXTY-THREE

ELI McCULLOUGH

Early 1870s

Beef was up four straight years but in '73, with the economy falling over, most went back to killing steers for hides.

I would not allow it. By then I owned 118 sections in fee simple with another 70 on lease. I held my stock. Our losses we kept to a minimum as we shot any mounted rider inside our fences. It was all according to Gunter.

Those afoot we let pass: it can never be said I denied an honest man his day's work. It was known in Carrizo that any man who found his family short rations could entitle himself to one of my calves, so long as he left me the hide. Only bullets and walls make for honest neighbors and a single night in my pastures would net any rustler a year's wages, a year of my own life. If they had built a cow-proof fence between us and the river . . .

There are plenty of old pistols still to be found in the brush country. Bone rots faster than iron. It was all according to Gunter.

MADELINE AND THE children had moved to a big house in Austin. The children had schools and tutors and I would have sooner burned the ranch than had them out to it, though Madeline had been asking for a proper house on the Nueces, so that we could all live together. I put it off. There were no schools. And she would not have cottoned to our treatment of fence crossers.

ONE DAY A black mood came over me for no reason, I was ornery as a snake and could not stand for anyone to look at me. I went off by myself. I guessed it was the heat.

The next morning they were shouting it in the streets: Quanah Parker and the last of the Comanches had surrendered. There were barely a thousand left on earth—the same number that had lived in Toshaway's village—and now the whole of Texas was open to the white man. I told Madeline I needed time alone, saddled my horse and went up the Colorado. I was riding and riding, but no matter how far I got there were hog callers and boatmen. I rode well into the night until finally it was quiet. I climbed a ledge and built a fire and howled out to the wolves. But nothing howled back.

That I had done wrong was plain. I was not thick enough to believe I might have saved the ponies from Ranald Mackenzie's troopers, but you could never say for certain. A single man can make a difference.

I thought how I might have gone back to the *Numunuu* when the war started. It hit me that fifteen years had passed since. I could not believe it; I could barely name a thing I'd done. I sat there looking out over the cliff, running it through my mind. It was not that I did not love my family. But there are things no person can give you.

Then I could not stand looking at my fire; I kicked the logs into the river and watched their spark quench. Then I rode home. I arrived well into the black morning, filled a lamp, and went into my office.

I took out my ledgers and securities and laid them on my desk. Deposits, shares in the Pacific Express, a steel concern in Pittsburgh, a sawmill in Beaumont. I considered how good the rains had been and the pastures I had just leased and all the new cowbrutes the green grass would nurture. I sat in my chair and thought about these things. I began to feel at ease.

CHAPTER SIXTY-four

J.A. McCULLOUGH

Ted had not left her so much as asked to be released. There had been some final revolution of the blood and he'd gotten tangled with a woman half his age. She was angry, she was worried about him, about the convenience this woman—a schoolteacher—might see in him. Which only made him furious. You could have kept me, he said, you could have kept me a hundred or a thousand different times. But of course she could not have. It was not in her.

It was true that she was lonely, that she was occasionally struck by a physical need that she had not felt for him in decades, but mostly there was a lightness. She wondered what was wrong with her. She had always been a person who did not need much affection, she did not need much from other people, but of course there was the downside; she did not have much to give, either.

Her worry that Ted might be her last lover turned out to be ridiculous. There were other companions, men who could have, and still did have, younger women, but they were companions nonetheless; there were things they could not share with young people, and she suspected, though not a single one had admitted this to her, that decades of being the less attractive partner might take a toll. She wondered what it would be like to look into the mirror and see yourself, white haired, slough skinned, your wilting everything and uncountable skin tags, right next to some perfect young specimen of the human race.

She was not sure. She had not compromised. She had not compromised and in that way, she'd escaped. *I am the last of my kind,* she thought, *the last the last the last* . . . but even that was a kind of vanity, there could be no last of anything, there were uncountable billions to come.

Milton Bryce became a widower, there had been another chance, she had known him nearly fifty years, and they had talked about it, how the two of them might form a sort of partnership, they had kissed but not otherwise touched, they were both into their seventies, he was a good man, but there was not a drop of fire in him. It was better to be alone. She was not some spinster. There were things she had not done, perhaps she had missed out, but the Colonel had not remarried, either. There was a reason for that.

Maybe if she'd gotten sick she would have felt differently. But even then she would not have wanted a lover taking care of her, even after two decades she had not liked using the toilet in front of Ted, had not liked brushing her teeth in front of him and when she got out of bed she always put on a nightgown, it was not modesty. It was just that without keeping something to yourself, the only thing left was comfort.

SHE HAD ALWAYS suspected (*known,* she thought) that she might outlive Thomas. There were people with a will to survive, people who might drag themselves across a desert, but Thomas was not one of them.

At a certain point, she had begun to think he would dodge it, he had been with the same partner (*lover,* she thought, *husband*) for over a decade, then quick as that, his partner was dying and they all knew what that meant for Thomas. It did not make her special. All stories ended that way. And yet it seemed to her that she had willed her son's fate, that by somehow suspecting it, considering it, she had witched it up out of the future, where a child's death was supposed to remain.

As for the man Thomas lived with—Richard—she had never cared for him. He was not sure of himself and he compensated. Thomas and Susan both found him hilarious, but he was not and she hated the sight of him at the hospice, *you have killed my son,* that was all she could think. She had to fly back to Midland in the morning. "When will you be here again?" Thomas asked her. *For the funeral,* she thought. Richard hated her even as he was dying; she hated him right back. But there was something in her son's face.

"All right," she said. "I'll be here tomorrow."

She'd been trying to unload some acreage in the Spraberry to Walt and Amos Benson. They wanted to take her out at $16.26; she was looking for $19.00. It was high but things were happening.

"Come out to the ranch," they said. "We'll get the quail opener."

There was nothing she would have liked better; the Bensons were old friends, Walt's wife had died a year earlier and there had always been some spark . . . but she couldn't. She had to go back to San Francisco. She did not want to tell them why.

So she had flown back and spent the night in the hospice, staring at the gaunt-faced man in the bed, knowing she would be looking at her own son there soon enough. The man's parents had not been told. She wondered if she ought to find out who they were and call them. She decided she should, they had a right to know, but then she wasn't sure, and then she had never been more afraid of anything, she made one bargain after another, her own life, all her money, speaking to God the entire night. None of it meant anything. She would lose her son. In the morning she slept two hours on her Gulfstream and woke up in Midland to meet with the Bensons again. She told them that Saddam Hussein was going to invade Kuwait.

"Is that what your price is based on?"

She was too tired to explain.

"Honey," they said, "what's wrong?"

She wanted to go to their ranch, she wanted to sit on their patio and drink wine with Walt, she wanted to stop thinking about her son. Instead the driver took her back to the airport.

All of this for money. Money she did not need, money her daughter did not need, money her son did not need. No one she knew needed money. And yet, apparently, she would do anything for it. She would spend her days in Midland and her nights in San Francisco. She was crazy. She agreed to the Bensons' price.

Walt invited her to the ranch again. They looked at each other a long time, here was her chance, she'd rejected him years earlier, he would not try again. Instead she went back to San Francisco, got a room at the Fairmont, and stayed two months helping Thomas clean out his condo, agonizing over Richard's awful paintings. And Thomas had lived. He had gone on the drugs and they had saved him. He went back to calling her Mother; he called her Jeannie only when he was mad.

She knew that other people felt sorry for her. She knew that her life looked empty, but it was the opposite. You could not live for yourself while also living for others. Even lying here she was free. She was not in some hospital where they kept you alive when they shouldn't, where you had no say over your own end.

She was back in the enormous room. The light was blinding now, the sun was shining directly through the roof, the furniture askew, everything in shambles, but she did not mind it.

There was a scent in the air, soothing and oversweet and she recognized it: balm of Gilead. Cottonwood buds. Were they blooming? She couldn't remember. She could not remember the day or year. She and Hank had planted a row of saplings around the stock tank, they were now enormous, a grove of cottonwoods. She had left things better than she found them. She remembered the Colonel rubbing the sap into her fingers, she remembered how the smell lingered all day, every time you lifted your hands to your face, every sip of water, you drank in that smell. The Colonel had showed her and she had showed it to Hank. Now they were waiting for her. She could feel it.

CHAPTER SIXTY-FIVE

ULISES GARCIA

He had heard and then seen her jet land yesterday; it was quite a sight, a plane that looked as if it might carry thirty or more people, landing to discharge a single person. It was a Gulfstream. The same one the *narcotraficantes* preferred. A car picked her up from the runway.

Even watching her from a distance gave him a nervous feeling. He had worked all day, but had not been able to eat lunch.

Later he saw her being driven around the ranch, sitting in the back of her Cadillac. Her chin held high, surveying all she owned. Near dinnertime he had made a point of passing by the house, just to get a glimpse of her, when he noticed an old person sitting by herself on the vast porch, looking at some papers.

He rode up and tipped his hat. "Good evening. I am Ulises Garcia."

She looked at him. She was annoyed at being interrupted. But he smiled at her and finally she couldn't help herself. She smiled back and said: "Hello, Mr. Garcia."

He couldn't think of anything more to say, so he wished her a good night and rode off cursing himself.

☆　　☆　　☆

THE NEXT DAY the plane was still there. The sun was going down and he was heading back to the bunkhouse. He supposed it was now or never. Of course if she rejected him, he would have to leave. It was a good job, Bryan Colms liked him, the other hands liked him, even if they thought he was a showoff.

Of course he was a coward if he didn't try. After dinner, he changed into his good shirt and packed his papers into a small leather bag his grandfather had given him.

CHAPTER SIXTY-SIX

DIARIES OF PETER McCULLOUGH

OCTOBER 13, 1917

Received two telegrams from Guadalajara asking me to come down, but neither is the real María. Today a letter arrived. Very short.

"Received your note. Good memories but see no way of continuing."

I wait until I am certain Sally is out of the house, then call Ab Jefferson and tell him what happened.

"We could bring her up here easy," he says.

"How would you do that?"

"It has been done, Mr. McCullough."

Then I understand. "No," I tell him. "Absolutely not."

IT IS NOT much of a plan. Composed a letter to Charlie and Glenn explaining as best I could. Do not expect they will forgive me—especially Charlie. He is the Colonel's son as much as mine. Tomorrow is a Sunday so I will have to wait.

OCTOBER 14, 1917

Woke up this morning with a happiness I have not felt since she left, replaced slowly by the old feeling. Did not know I had so much fear in me.

If she consents to see me it will not be the same, she was a refugee then—we will be like old friends who no longer have anything in common. Our bonds revealed as illusion. Better not to see it. Better to hold on to something I know is good.

OCTOBER 15, 1917

Did not sleep last night. Packed three changes of clothes and my revolver. In a few minutes I will pass through the gates of the McCullough ranch for the last time. One way or the other.

The bank in Carrizo will not have what I need so I am going to San Antonio. Ronald Derry has known me twenty years—he will not question me. Unless he does. Two hundred fifty thousand dollars for oil leases. *Oil leases,* I will say, *you know these farmers, they all want to see cash.*

Then I will cross the border. Of course the money is not mine. If they decide to call my father . . .

I HAVE NO illusion about my chance of reaching Guadalajara alive. I am of sound mind and body. This is my testament.

CHAPTER SIXTY-SEVEN

ELI McCULLOUGH

With the surrender of the Comanches, an area as big as the Old States opened to settlement and every easterner who owned a whaling ship or hotel began to fancy himself a cattle baron. There were Frenchmen and Scots, counts and dukes in scissortail coats, peacocked Yankees with their faces shining like new mirrors. They overpaid for range, overpaid for stock, overpaid for horses, they were trying to catch up to the rest of us. Meanwhile the southern grasslands were already run-down; the smart stockmen drove their herds to Montana to get fat on what grass remained.

Half the cowhands were Harvard men in lisle thread socks, with mail-order pistols and silver-decked tack bought straight from a leathershop drummer. They'd come west to grow up with the country. Meaning see the end of it.

I said I would sell out by '80. The part of me that was still alive hated the sight of cowbrutes, hated chewing every waking minute on how I would profit or lose by them. The rest of me couldn't think of anything else. How to protect them, how to get the best price for them, and, when the money had gone out of them, how I might make it another way. I was caught in the thorns of my own undertaking, unmaking, I considered the beasts more than my own wife and children, I was no different from Ellen Wilbarger with her laudanum. She had not needed it until she tried it, but soon saw no other way.

MADELINE THOUGHT I was interfering with some senorita. She gave me too much credit. The problem was much bigger than any girl.

BY THEN I had moved them to San Antonio, but I still spent my time in the *brasada* or along some dusty waterhole and Madeline was not any happier. She told me to get a proper house built on the Nueces or else. I told her I had only a few years left—I could feel it doing something to me.

"Like what?" she said.

I started to tell her, but couldn't. Old Nicky himself had pinched my jaw shut.

She paced the living room. She'd fallen in with some other grass widows and had taken to wearing paint; just a touch but I noticed it. The servants were off being servants and the boys were in the yard.

"I hate this house," she said.

"It's a hell of a nice house," I said. It was a big white one in the Spanish style, big as the one she'd grown up in, with a good view of the river. It was two years' wages and a sizable note to match.

"I would rather be living in a hut."

"We'll be out soon enough," I said.

"Why not now?"

"Because."

"We do not have to live in the biggest house. Now or ever. I believe you have confused me with my sister."

She smiled but I wanted to keep it serious. "Three years," I told her. "Come hell or high water I swear I will not touch a cow after that."

"That is the same as never."

"There is no school."

"We will build one. Or hire a teacher. Or we keep this place and go back and forth and hire a teacher half the time." She threw up her hands. "There are any number of ways," she said. "We are not exactly building a railroad."

"Well, it's a waste of money to build a place and leave it."

"The fool who buys the land will also buy the house. Meanwhile I am here with your children, who spend all their time pretending they *are* you when they don't really know you."

"It's not the right place," I said. "I am sure of it."

But she was already not listening. I could see her thinking. "The representative is going back to Washington," she said. The representative was her mother's new husband. "There is a nice house for sale next door to theirs. Which is where I am taking the children unless you convince me otherwise."

I walked away from her and stood by the window. The best part of me knew I ought to let her go but I could not get the words to my mouth. Outside, Everett was wearing my old buckskin shirt. He had a feather in his hair and he was stalking the other boys. I had been promising to show him how to make a bow for so long that I realized he had stopped asking me. Pete and Phineas were digging at something in the yard—they didn't have the fire of a firstborn. I had also promised Everett I would let him ride with me a few days during roundup. In truth I liked that the boys were in school. I had not wanted to start them on the outdoor life; soon it would be fit only for hobbyists and outcasts.

Madeline was still talking. "Or," she was saying, "you can move us to the Nueces."

I didn't say anything.

"Wonderful. September, then."

"That is barely enough time to build a dugout."

"Then hire twice as many men. Or ten times as many. I don't care. But three months from now the children and I will not be living in this house."

★   ★   ★

IN ABILENE A new tailor opened shop every week, and, after making a drive, most of the hands would sell their horses, buy suits, and take the train home. The ones who'd seen a Ned Buntline or Bill Cody show would brag on the incident for months, as if the shows were more real than their own lives. The others passed the winter reading Bret Harte.

The drives got shorter. The International and Great Northern surveyed a line through our pastures. The grass was disappearing but it didn't matter—the railroads brought the farmers and nesters, people who wanted to live in towns—the land I had bought for a quarter was worth forty dollars an acre when they built.

Had it not been for the children I would have moved to the Klondike. The country was ruined, as a woman would have been after riding the cat wagon. I had never known it could fill up. I had never known there were so many people on earth.

CHAPTER SIXTY-EIGHT

J.A. McCULLOUGH

She'd come into the great room to see her father sitting next to the fireplace. He didn't notice her—she remained in the shadows—he was sitting in a chair he had pulled onto the stone hearth, reading from a leather-bound notebook. When he finished a page, he would tear it out, lean forward, and drop it into the flames. There were three other notebooks—they appeared to be some sort of journal—on the floor next to him. She watched for several minutes. Finally she walked over. "What are you doing?" she said.

He was sweating and his face was pale as if he had a fever. For a time he didn't speak.

"Your grandfather was a liar," he finally said. He looked as if he would tear up and then sat there like that and she was reminded of the father of her school friend, who had also sat weeping in front of the fire, and she wondered if it was something that fathers did.

He collected himself. "I should get some work done." He stood and picked up all four of the notebooks and tossed them among the burning logs. Then he kissed her on the head. "Good night, sweetie."

When she was sure he was gone, she took the poker and pulled the journals out. The flames had barely touched them.

She had not shown her brothers, or anyone else. She had known better. She had known she was the only one who could be trusted with them.

JONAS HAD BEEN acting strangely all day; after school, instead of going out to the pastures to meet their father, he had gone up to his room. She had watched him at dinner, there was something wrong with him, probably the flu. He barely touched his food.

The dishes had been cleared away and Paul and Clint had gone to the library to play cards. She went out to her sleeping porch to read and looked out into the dark and saw a figure walking down the hill toward the stables. His shoulders were hunched and his head was down as if he was embarrassed and she knew immediately it was Jonas.

Even later, she was not sure why she followed him. She walked to the stables and sat in the dark, watching. A light went on. She wondered if her brother was meeting a girl; she wondered who the girl was. But then he was leading all the horses out to the pasture, slapping to get them moving.

She went closer and watched through the cracks in the boards, standing in the dark night, as he dragged hay bales down and stacked them under the loft. When he was satisfied with the pile he'd made, he took a jug of coal oil and poured it over the hay.

"What are you doing?" she said. She opened the door.

He was looking at her and she stepped into the light.

"Jeannie," he said. He looked stricken.

"What are you doing?" she said again.

"This is the only way he'll let me leave."

She had not understood.

"Daddy," he said. He shrugged. "I thought I would see what happened when I start costing him real money. That's always been the way to his heart. You can tell on me if you want, I don't care."

"I won't tell," she said.

"Then go through the stalls and make sure I didn't leave any of the horses. I'm not thinking straight right now."

She had walked through the stable, checking each stall.

He had made a torch out of a stick and an old shirt and she watched through the door as he doused it in kerosene and lit it. Then he threw the torch onto the pile. There was a noise and it was bright. He came out and shut the door behind him. They sat on the hill and watched as light began to come through all the cracks in the building, as if a small sun were rising inside it. Smoke began to pour out into the night and her brother stood up and held her to him and then he took her hand and they walked quietly together back up the hill toward their father's house.

CHAPTER SIXTY-NINE

ULISES GARCIA

He had shaved and his hair was wet and neatly combed. He was wearing a fresh shirt and pants. The shirt was brand-new, as were the trousers; his boots were polished. He brought his leather bag with all the birth certificates, and his great-grandfather's old Colt revolver, which no longer worked but was clearly engraved *P. McCullough*.

He walked around the porch, looking for her, and saw a pair of open glass doors.

He walked up to them and there she was, sitting in a chair, reading. She recognized him.

"You must be looking for Dolores."

"No," he said.

"I like to have a fire when I come here," she said. "Even if I have to leave the door open so it doesn't get hot."

"It seems nice."

She waited for him to say something else.

"I work for you."

"I remember."

A long time seemed to pass before he could say anything. His head felt light.

"I'm the great-grandson of Peter McCullough," he said. "I wanted to work for you because . . ." He couldn't say the rest; it would make him sound like a crazy person.

Her face showed nothing.

From his leather bag, which he had also cleaned and oiled before coming over, he removed all the letters and papers. He took a few steps into the room and handed her everything, then stepped back. He looked around as she read. The room was enormous, thirty meters by forty, he guessed. The ceilings were ten meters tall, a beam construction like an old church. The room itself might have contained three of the houses in which he'd grown up, and he began to think about the Arroyos' house.

She read the first few pages, but then she was going through the papers faster than she could read them.

"We are family," he repeated.

Her eyes showed nothing, but he could see that her hands had begun to shake.

"I'm afraid I'll have to ask you to leave," she said.

He pointed again to the papers.

"You will leave this house right now," she said. "Mr. Colms will have your check."

He was about to say more but she was not paying attention. As if he were not there, she casually pushed herself up from her chair and walked to a low marble table and picked up the phone there.

She dialed and their eyes locked.

"This is Mrs. McCullough. There is a man in my house who refuses to leave. Yes, he is here right now in the room with me."

She nodded at him and waved him out. He could feel his body begin to move, toward the door.

"His name? Martinez, or something."

It felt like he'd been splashed with hot water. He marched forward to take back the papers, but she misinterpreted him, she backed away too quickly and tripped over her own feet, he reached to catch her but she twisted away and fell in front of the fireplace. Her head made a noise on the stone hearth. The phone went out of her hand. He could hear someone talking on the other end.

"Mrs. McCullough?" He was whispering.

She did not respond. Her eyelids were trembling, they were not quite closed and not quite open.

"I did not touch you," he said to her.

She said nothing. She made no move, her eyes were open now but they did not fix on anything and he knew that she was going to die.

He collected his papers and put them into his case, looked around to see if he'd forgotten anything else, then walked toward the door. He had killed her. Not by touching her, just by existing.

He went outside but in the distance he saw one of the ranch trucks cresting the hill and came back in. Of course they would find him, they would figure it out, they had ways of doing that. He had not touched her. *You are a Mexican in the house of a rich lady,* he thought. *They will not care if you touched her or not.*

He waited for the truck to pass outside and wandered through her house, looking for another exit; what a house it was, the rugs so soft his feet made no noise at all, art and statues everywhere, dim light, it was like something from the movies. He shook himself out of this, reached the kitchen; beyond it was a door that led outside.

His mouth was dry. He went to the sink and drank from the tap, he had not touched her. *They will kill you,* he thought. *They will not care.* This was obvious.

The water was helping. His heart began to slow. He smoothed a few drops from his shirt, thought of all the ways he might explain himself, but no one would believe him, he would not have believed himself.

Later he was not sure how he came to this solution, but it occurred to him this quickly: there was an immense gas stove and he dragged it away from the wall. The gas came right from the property, that was what all the hands said, directly from the ground beneath.

He took his Leatherman from his belt, reached behind the stove, and unscrewed the copper line.

Out on the porch, he closed the door quietly behind him. All around the land spread out in the dusk, there was nothing in sight that did not belong to the McCulloughs.

He considered stealing a truck but that would leave him afoot once he reached the border. He could see the lights in the housekeeper's cottage, in Bryan Colms's house, in the bunkhouse; he began to walk toward the McCulloughs' private stable, praying there was no one there, but there were no vehicles, and when he reached the stable he left the lights off.

He had been inside before to muck the stalls and he knew which horse he wanted. He put on a bridle, threw a blanket over her, and saddled her quickly. Bryan Colms insisted on calling her a gray, but she was white, of course.

Then he led her out of the stable, downhill, away from the house, and put his heels to her. The stirrups were short.

He had not made it far when there came the loudest noise he had ever heard. The horse took the bit in its teeth, but he didn't care, as long as he was heading toward the river. He hazarded a look behind him; there was a dust cloud all around the house, though it was still standing. Then there were flickers and he saw the flames. A few miles later he looked back and the light had spread from one side of the horizon to the other.

WHEN HE GOT to the river he reined up to look around. The sky was enormous. The lights of America, which had blotted out the stars, had faded. His legs were beginning to seize and his abdomen and back were cramping as well. "You're a strong horse," he said. He kissed it on the neck.

Then they eased down the bank. It was easy to cross, the river was shallow; it was no longer even a river.

What had the historian said? Nineteen or twenty people. He had stopped by the man's house and the man had shown him the picture they had taken of the Rangers and townspeople posing with the bodies of his family.

"Who are they?" he had asked. "Who is who in the picture?"

The historian had shrugged. "No one knows. No one knows what any of the Garcias looked like."

The white men were standing in the sun, their faces clear, while the faces of the men on the ground might have been molded from clay. The historian had shrugged again and shown him some other pictures, Colonel McCullough's dugout, long-dead cowboys, horses and old cars. To him, the picture of the dead Garcias meant no more than these other things.

Ulises had not been able to stop thinking about it, it was like discovering a cancer in your own body, the thought of the uncles and aunts, great-aunts and -uncles, an enormous family, wiped out. He continued to ride. But of course he had equal blood from both sides. He was not some victim. One half of his family had killed the other. Both of those things were inside him.

The Americans . . . he allowed his mind to roam. They thought that simply because they had stolen something, no one should be allowed to steal it from them. But of course that was what all people thought: that whatever they had taken, they should be allowed to keep it forever.

He was no better. His people had stolen the land from the Indians, and yet he did not think of that even for an instant—he thought only of the Texans who had stolen it from his people. And the Indians from whom his people had stolen the land had themselves stolen it from other Indians.

His father had come to this woman asking for help and the woman had denied him. His grandmother had come and had been denied. And now he had been denied as well. Yet this same woman had given twenty million dollars to a museum. Millions for the dead, nothing for the living, it was people like her who ended up in charge. He had to remember those things. He was still young. He would remember.

In the meantime he would go back to his grandfather, and then, he thought, to Mexico City, where there were no problems with the cartels. Business, politics, he didn't know, but it was as he'd suspected, the days in which you held your head up because you were a man, because you had roped an eagle, those days were gone. The Americans, it seemed, had known this.

He would go a few more miles and rest for the night. After that . . . he didn't know. But he would be someone. No one would forget his name.

CHAPTER SEVENTY

J. A. McCULLOUGH

She had seen the Garcia boy come in; she had known him from across the room. She had known from the moment he spoke that he was telling the truth.

She no longer fit inside herself. All her life she had known she would ride off into the dark, but now the land was as green as it had ever been, the sun was running, she had been wrong, she could see her brothers far ahead of her. They were young, and she made up her mind to catch them.

CHAPTER SEVENTY-ONE

PETER McCULLOUGH

After four days of driving he reached Guadalajara. He stopped in front of her house, a small adobe structure with peeling yellow paint and a tended garden.

That night, after she had fallen asleep, he put on his pants and shirt and went out to make sure the car was still there. It was dark and quiet; most of the lights in the neighborhood were out. He had been surprised that so many had electricity at all.

He wondered if he had stolen the money because he was a coward, because he was worried about changing his mind. He decided it didn't matter. He went back inside to wake her up. They loaded the car and drove off into the darkness.

For a time they moved every few weeks, staying in hotels under different names. It was quieter in the south and they had one child in Mérida and a second near Oaxaca, but when the war ended he began to worry they would be found, and in 1920, after Carranza was deposed, they moved to Mexico City.

There was a new government and the city was overflowing. There were bankers and industrialists, exiles and artists, musicians and anarchists; there were cathedrals and sprawling markets and gaudy *pulquerías,* murals going up everywhere, streetcars running through the night. Motorcars jostled with donkeys and horsemen and barefoot peasants. He guessed it would drive him insane. It didn't. He would lean over the edge of their apartment building and watch the street; he had never seen so many people in his life.

"You don't like cities," she said.

"It's better for the children."

It was not just that. He was losing his memory; Pedro and Lourdes Garcia seemed impossibly young, likewise his mother and father; he could barely remember his own childhood; he could barely remember last year. If there was anyone watching from the dark corners, he never knew it. Each night after the sun set he would go and stand over the street and put his hands to the warm stone, a million lives passing just beneath him, millions more yet to come, they were all just like him, they were all free, they would all be forgotten.

CHAPTER SEVENTY-TWO

ELI McCULLOUGH

1881

I had told myself I would sell out by '80. The rains were good and my two-year-olds had brought $14.50 and then a German baron, looking to stock a range in Kansas, promised ten dollars for spring yearlings. The hands sold their horses and took the train home, but I wired Madeline that I would be delayed. I had built her the house on the Nueces but by then she had stopped expecting I would come home at all.

I rode the long way down, past our old hunting grounds. I shooed cows from our camp on the Canadian, where the dogwoods had grown up straight and tall, higher than a man could reach. I looked for days, but I could not find the graves of Toshaway or Prairie Flower or Single Bird. The ground had gone to rocks and the trees had all been cut for firewood.

As for my brother's grave, at times I have been certain the Indians led us up the Yellow House, and other times I have been equally certain it was the Blanco, or Tule, or the Palo Duro. I rode the length of the Llano, following the edge of the caprock, hoping I would be sparked, that I would feel the spot when I came to it. There was nothing.

★   ★   ★

I ARRIVED HOME to find my men all waiting for me on the gallery.

"Nothin' better to do?" I said.

Then I saw the house.

"What was all the shooting?" I said.

No one answered.

"Who did the shooting?"

THEY HAD BURIED them under a cottonwood on a hill overlooking the house. It had a good view of things. Madeline, Everett, and a hand named Fairbanks.

Madeline had been shot in the yard and Everett had been shot trying to pull her into the house and the three surviving hands, two of whom were shot as well, had driven the bandits back. All anyone knew was it was renegade Indians. No one knew which ones.

"Were they scalped?"

Sullivan followed me up the hill. He had a sense for things. I took a shovel and set to digging and when we could smell the grave gas and Sullivan saw I wasn't going to stop, he held me to the dirt. A penny for three measures of barley, hurt not the oil and the wine. My wife and son had not been scalped and neither Peter nor Phineas had been scratched.

THE ARMY THOUGHT the perpetrators to be a renegade group of Comanches. They had trailed them to Mexico but had not gone over the water. Sullivan led me to where the Indians had stood in the corral. It was Lipans. The toe of an Apache moccasin is much wider than a Comanche's, which comes to a point, and the fringes are shorter and drag less. The Apache has a bigger foot. And the arrows had four grooves.

There were three and twenty hands and they all stood up to ride. The oldermost was twenty-eight, the youngest sixteen, and to ride on a group of Indians—they had thought those days were gone forever. If you were free to go back in history, to fight the great battles of your ancestors . . . you should have seen their shining faces.

The party of Lipans split seven times on rocky ground and the trail was weeks old but if I ever believed in a Creator it was for this reason: it had rained before the Lipan attack and then gone dry, leaving their tracks as frozen into the earth as the marks of the ancient beasts. Twelve riders, tracks of the unshod ponies leading right to the water's edge.

We did not slow down when we reached the river. In Coahuila the tracks stopped; it was hard dry ground. I did not get off my horse. I looked into the book of the earth: I was Toshaway, I was Pizon, I was the Lipans themselves, afraid to stop looking behind me, knowing I'd killed where I should not and yet the ponies I'd taken would save my tribe another year.

The others saw nothing. A grieving man on a pale horse. They followed on faith alone.

By dusk we stood on a hill overlooking the last of the Lipan band. They had lived in the country five hundred years. We waited until their fires had gone dark.

We dynamited the tipis and shot the Indians down as they ran. A magnificent brave, his only weapon a patch knife, charged singing his death chant. A blind man fired a musket and his daughter ran forward, knowing the gun was empty; she swung it toward us and we shot her down as well. It was the last of a nation, squaws and cripples and old men, our guns so hot they fired of their own will, our square-cloths wrapped the fore-grips and still every hand was branded.

When the people were finished we killed every living dog and horse. I took the chief's bladder for a tobacco pouch; it was tanned and embroidered with beads. In his shield, stuffed between the layers, was Gibbon's *Decline and Fall of the Roman Empire*.

✷   ✷   ✷

WHEN THE SUN came up, we discovered a boy of nine years. We left him as a witness. At noon we reached the river and saw the boy had followed us with his bow—for twenty miles he had kept up with men on horseback—for twenty miles he had been running to his death.

A child like that would be worth a thousand men today. We left him standing on the riverbank. As far as I know he is looking for me yet.

MR
ATKINSON'S
RUM
CONTRACT

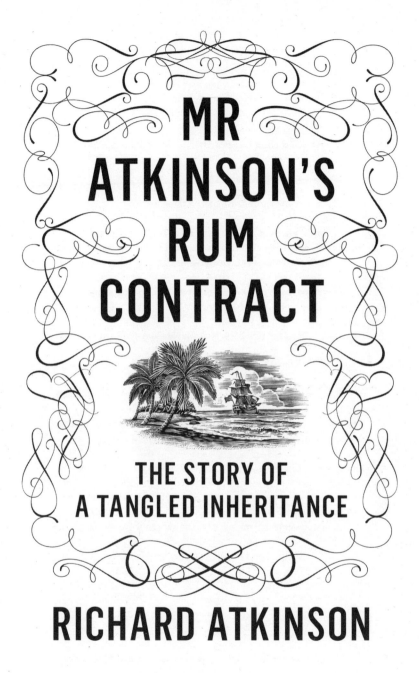

THE STORY OF
A TANGLED INHERITANCE

RICHARD ATKINSON

4th ESTATE • London

4th Estate
An imprint of HarperCollins*Publishers*
1 London Bridge Street
London SE1 9GF
www.4thEstate.co.uk

First published in Great Britain by 4th Estate in 2020

1

Illustrated maps by David Atkinson: handmademaps.com
Family tree diagram by Martin Brown

A catalogue record for this book is available from the British Library

ISBN 978-0-00-750924-9

Printed and bound in Great Britain by
CPI Group (UK) Ltd, Croydon, CR0 4YY

MIX
Paper from
responsible sources
FSC™ C007454

This book is produced from independently certified FSC paper
to ensure responsible forest management

Find out more about HarperCollins and the environment at
www.harpercollins.co.uk/green

In memory of my father,
and with love to my sister

CONTENTS

Family Tree viii
Maps x

The Atkinson family of Temple Sowerby

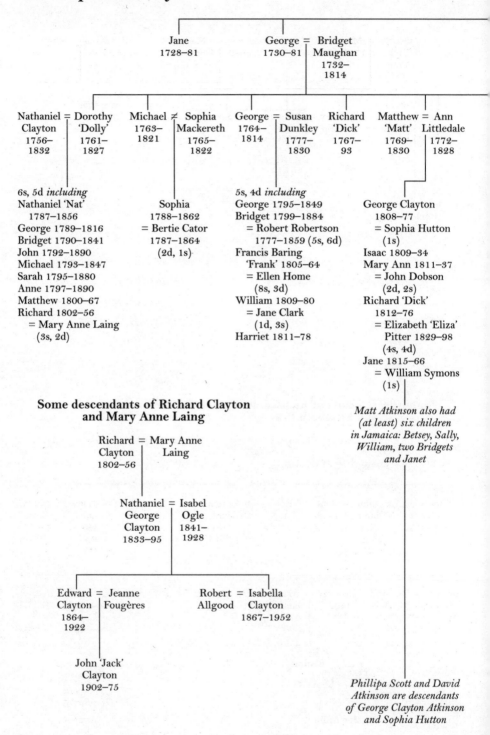

Jane
1728–81

George = Bridget
1730–81   Maughan
1732–
1814

Nathaniel = Dorothy
Clayton   'Dolly'
1756–   1761–
1832   1827

Michael ≠ Sophia
1763–   Mackereth
1821   1765–
         1822

George = Susan
1764–   Dunkley
1814   1777–
        1830

Richard
'Dick'
1767–
93

Matthew = Ann
'Matt'   Littledale
1769–   1772–
1830   1828

6s, 5d *including*
Nathaniel 'Nat'
1787–1856
George 1789–1816
Bridget 1790–1841
John 1792–1890
Michael 1793–1847
Sarah 1795–1880
Anne 1797–1890
Matthew 1800–67
Richard 1802–56
= Mary Anne Laing
(3s, 2d)

Sophia
1788–1862
= Bertie Cator
1787–1864
(2d, 1s)

5s, 4d *including*
George 1795–1849
Bridget 1799–1884
= Robert Robertson
1777–1859 (5s, 6d)
Francis Baring
'Frank' 1805–64
= Ellen Home
(8s, 3d)
William 1809–80
= Jane Clark
(1d, 3s)
Harriet 1811–78

George Clayton
1808–77
= Sophia Hutton
(1s)
Isaac 1809–34
Mary Ann 1811–37
= John Dobson
(2d, 2s)
Richard 'Dick'
1812–76
= Elizabeth 'Eliza'
Pitter 1829–98
(4s, 4d)
Jane 1815–66
= William Symons
(1s)

Some descendants of Richard Clayton and Mary Anne Laing

Richard = Mary Anne
Clayton   Laing
1802–56

Nathaniel = Isabel
George   Ogle
Clayton   1841–
1833–95   1928

Edward = Jeanne
Clayton Fougères
1864–
1922

Robert = Isabella
Allgood Clayton
         1867–1952

John 'Jack'
Clayton
1902–75

*Matt Atkinson also had
(at least) six children
in Jamaica: Betsey, Sally,
William, two Bridgets
and Janet*

*Phillipa Scott and David
Atkinson are descendants
of George Clayton Atkinson
and Sophia Hutton*

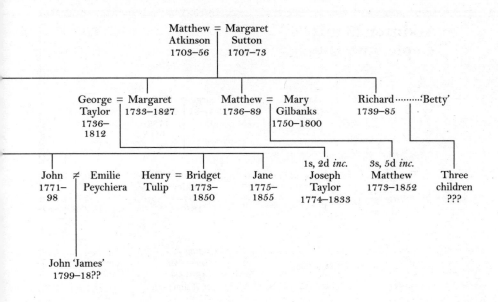

Matthew = Margaret
Atkinson   Sutton
1703–56   1707–73

George = Margaret   Matthew = Mary   Richard ········· 'Betty'
Taylor   1733–1827   1736–89   Gilbanks   1739–85
1736–   1750–1800
1812

John ≠ Emilie   Henry = Bridget   Jane   1s, 2d *inc.*   3s, 5d *inc.*   Three
1771– Peychiera Tulip   1773–   1775–   Joseph   Matthew   children
98   1850   1855   Taylor   1773–1852   ???
                                                1774–1833

John 'James'
1799–18??

Some descendants of Richard Atkinson and Elizabeth Pitter

Richard 'Dick' = Elizabeth 'Eliza'
Atkinson   Pitter
1812–76   1829–98

Elizabeth   John   = Jane   Richard = Margaret   John   = Constance   Catherine
'Lizzy'   Cunliffe 1853–   1854–   Hunter   Nathaniel   'Connie'   'Katie'
1850–1922   Kay   1922   1918   1861–   'Jock'   Banks   1860–
                 1849–   1951   1857–1931   1860–   1932
                 1915   1947

Kenneth = Dorothy   Geoffrey = Mary   George   John Littledale = Evelyn Hay   Bridget
Kay   Mitchell 1892–   Daintree 1886–   'Jack'   de Castañeda   'Biddy'
1881–   1879–   1961   1893–   1932   1888–   (née Cook)   1891–
1935   1955   1981   1973   1892–1976   1970

Carl = Renira   John   = Jane
Müller   1934–73 Chaytor

Jon Müller   Richard   Harriet

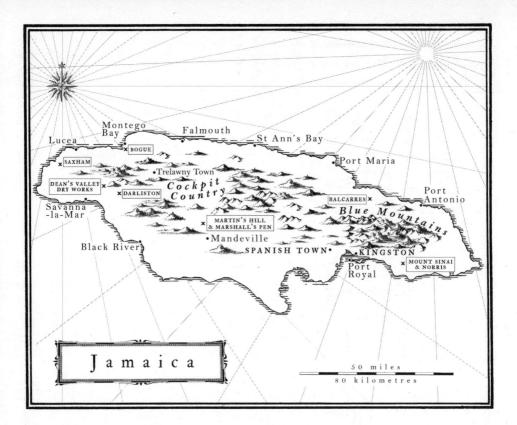

Jamaica

Montego Bay · Falmouth · St Ann's Bay
Lucea
× SAXHAM · BOGUE
× Trelawny Town · Port Maria
DEAN'S VALLEY × DARLISTON
DRY WORKS · *Cockpit Country* · BALCARRES ×
Savanna · *Blue Mountains* · Port Antonio
-la-Mar · MARTIN'S HILL & MARSHALL'S PEN
Black River · *Mandeville* · SPANISH TOWN · KINGSTON
MOUNT SINAI & NORRIS
Port Royal

50 miles
80 kilometres

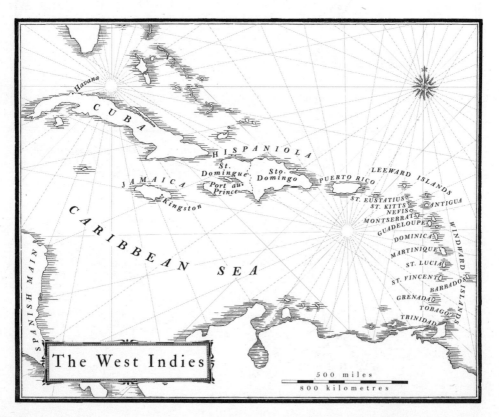

The West Indies

Havana
CUBA
HISPANIOLA
St. Domingue · Sto. Domingo
JAMAICA · Port au Prince
Kingston · PUERTO RICO · LEEWARD ISLANDS
ST. EUSTATIUS · ANTIGUA
ST. KITTS · NEVIS
MONTSERRAT · GUADELOUPE
SPANISH MAIN · DOMINICA · WINDWARD ISLANDS
MARTINIQUE
ST. LUCIA
CARIBBEAN SEA · ST. VINCENT · BARBADOS
GRENADA
TOBAGO
TRINIDAD

500 miles
800 kilometres

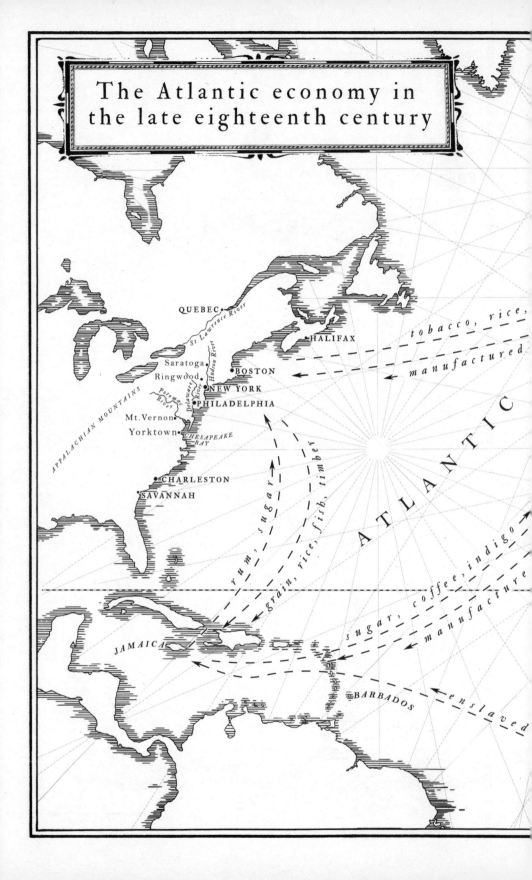

The Atlantic economy in the late eighteenth century

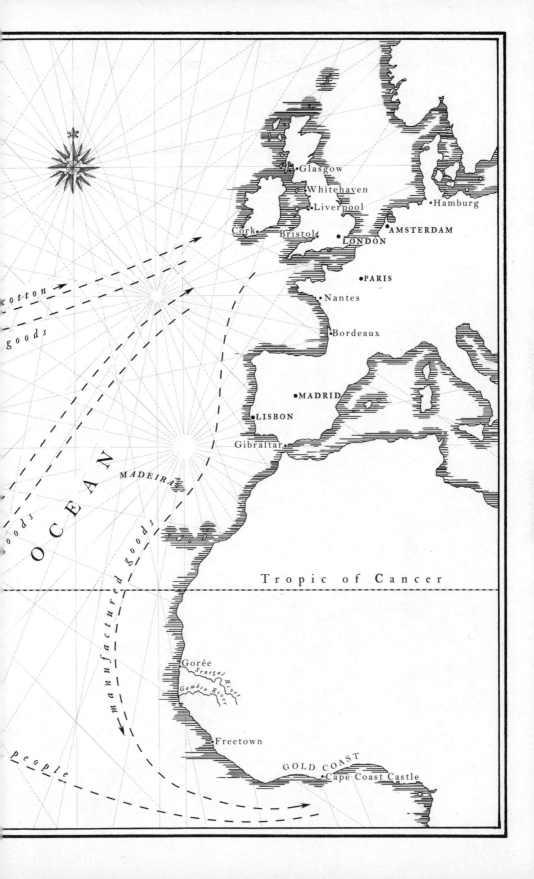

cotton

goods

goods

O C E A N

MADEIRA

manufactured goods

people

Glasgow

Whitehaven

Liverpool

•Hamburg

Cork•

Bristol•

•AMSTERDAM

LONDON

•PARIS

•Nantes

•Bordeaux

•MADRID

•LISBON

Gibraltar•

Tropic of Cancer

•Gorée

Senegal River

Gambia River

•Freetown

GOLD COAST

•Cape Coast Castle

'England is not the jewelled isle of Shakespeare's much-quoted message . . . it resembles a family, a rather stuffy Victorian family, with not many black sheep in it but with all its cupboards bursting with skeletons. It has rich relations who have to be kow-towed to and poor relations who are horribly sat upon, and there is a deep conspiracy of silence about the source of the family income.'

– George Orwell, *Why I Write*

PART I

The Temperate Zone

ONE

A Tangled Inheritance

SOME OF MY earliest memories are of Temple Sowerby House. I remember the line of tarnished servants' bells in the passage outside the kitchen door, the *tap tap tap* of buckets catching rainwater that dripped through the ceiling, the mint-green porcelain of my grandmother's 1930s bathroom suite; but most vividly of all, I remember the gallery. This was the light-filled corridor up narrow stairs at the back of the house, with three windows looking down on to the overgrown walled garden below. As a small child, on wet days – not unusual in this part of north-west England – I would run up and down the gallery, stomping on the floorboards, pausing only to examine the zoological specimens on display, which included two stuffed crocodiles, a rhinoceros horn and a narwhal tusk. I was particularly drawn to the glass domes filled with birds, their feathers all the colours of the rainbow, although I had no idea where they might have flown from.

This was the early 1970s, by which time dry rot was consuming the Georgian part of the house. In the entrance hall, burnt-orange brackets of fungus bloomed like a ghoulish botanical wallpaper; in the drawing room, many of the floorboards had been pulled up, and much of the ceiling plasterwork had fallen down. My grandparents, Jack and Evelyn Atkinson, had long since retreated to the rear of the building, the original seventeenth-century farmhouse on to which the handsome front wing had been added during more

3

affluent times. Here the parlour, with its low oak beams and red sandstone chimneypiece, and the kitchen, with its blue enamel range cooker, were the only rooms where they managed to keep the damp remotely at bay.

Jack was quite unfit to be the custodian of such a property. When he moved up to Westmorland from London in the late 1940s, having inherited the 200-acre family farm, he was nearly sixty. Too old and impractical to take the land in hand himself, instead he let it out, and was too soft-hearted to put up the rent for twenty years. As a result, my grandparents were always strapped for cash and invariably in arrears with local tradesmen, who made the classic mistake of confusing gentility with liquidity. They reckoned themselves too poor to have slates replaced or gutters cleared – which is how it came to be that water was coursing through the roof and walls. Even so, every Christmas they ordered a hamper from Fortnum & Mason, London's most exclusive grocer, to make sure they were adequately provisioned during the festive season.

Jack exuded old-fashioned charm; at eighty, as he ambled about the village, tipping his hat to the neighbours, his handsome features were still apparent. Evelyn, on the other hand, had the air of someone constantly disappointed by life, and there was little that did not provide the raw material for complaint. The pair of them rattled around the house, which was largely empty, since most of the contents – beds, tables, sofas, pictures, carpets – had been sold off long ago. They kept strange nocturnal hours, rarely going to bed before three in the morning, and rising in the early afternoon. Sometimes, after breakfast, Jack would wander down to the village shop, only to find that it had already closed for the day. Evelyn, who was obsessed by security – not that there was much worth stealing – roamed the corridors with a big bunch of keys, locking up behind her wherever she went.

My father John, their adored only child, used to dread visiting Temple Sowerby; as the next in a long line of Atkinsons who had inhabited the village for at least four hundred years, he was all too conscious that the house would one day pass to him. Already his parents had started offloading their money problems on to him, often sending begging letters that made him feel guilty and miserable. His salary as a book editor living in London barely met his own needs.

In October 1966 John married my mother, Jane Chaytor, who provided a much-needed burst of energy and hope. She took control of her in-laws' chaotic finances and arranged for a review of the farm rent, which at a stroke doubled their income. She paid their bills – they were amazed to find that the butcher would look them in the eye again. It was she who had the range cooker installed in the kitchen. Jack was captivated by his pretty, practical daughter-in-law, making it all too clear to Evelyn that she was exactly the sort of woman he wished he'd had the good fortune to marry.

A few weeks after I was born, in June 1968, Jack wrote to my father: 'Dear Old Boy, we were delighted with the photos; please thank Jane very much for them. Richard, understandably, didn't show much interest in the proceedings, but you looked, also understandably, as if you were holding the most precious bundle in the world. Quite right too.'[1] Two months later my parents took me up to Westmorland to be baptized in the church at Temple Sowerby.

AROUND THIS TIME, my father started waking in the night with a dull ache in his gut, and hospital tests revealed a tumour; but following surgery his prognosis seemed quite positive. My sister, Harriet, was born in the spring of 1972. That autumn, after four years of good health, my father developed jaundice; the cancer was back. Soon he was too weak to climb the stairs, and a bed was made up for him on the ground floor of our terraced house in Pimlico. He was a sociable man, and over the following weeks a succession of friends and colleagues came to say goodbye. He died at home on 24 February 1973. He was thirty-eight. His funeral took place a few days later, on Harriet's first birthday.

Three months later, Jack too was dead, and buried alongside his son in the graveyard at Temple Sowerby. Suddenly, following the custom of primogeniture, Temple Sowerby House was mine – not that I knew it. As for the farm, the line of succession was not so clear. Under the terms of my great-grandfather's will, written in the 1920s, Jack had been left a life interest in the property, which allowed him to enjoy the income it generated but prevented him from putting it up for sale. This same document stipulated that on Jack's death, the farm would pass to his eldest son or, failing that, his eldest daughter – but no such person now existed. What the will did not anticipate was the possibility that Jack might leave grandchildren who could inherit the farm. So instead the estate was split equally between the principal heirs of each of my great-grandfather's three children: the niece of Jack's elder brother George's late widow; the son of Jack's younger sister Biddy in South Africa; and me. In short, the premature death of my father, and the restrictive language of my great-grandfather's will, meant that the farm passed out of the family's hands.

The bleak practicalities of probate fell to my poor mother. Her first instinct was to hold on to the house, so I might one day have a chance of living there; but given that she had no money for repairs, the idea presented formidable difficulties. The most obvious solution was to pull down the rotten eighteenth-century wing and retain the relatively habitable oldest part. Following the local council's rejection of her planning application, however, my mother realized that only one viable option remained. After moving my grandmother into sheltered accommodation, and suffering many sleepless nights, she called in the estate agents. It was a conclusion for which I will always be grateful.

Temple Sowerby House was by no means an easy sell. Quite aside from its state of semi-dereliction, it had another major drawback. The busy A66 trunk road that crosses the Pennines, linking Penrith and the M6 motorway in the west to Scotch Corner and the A1 in the east, cut straight through the village, not twenty yards from the façade of the house. Just the thought of a thousand lorries thundering past every day was enough to deter most buyers. But finally, in the summer of 1977, the Atkinson family home was sold to a developer who envisioned for it a future as a hotel – the passing trade, for once, counting in its favour.

Apart from the crocodiles, which she banished to a Penrith sale-room, my mother put the contents of the old house into storage; in particular, the three oak court cupboards in the gallery, each carved with the year of its making (1627, 1658 and 1729), which were far too bulky to fit into our small London home. The Atkinson chattels also included two large blanket chests, two broken-down longcase clocks, a well-worn rocking cradle, a spinning wheel and a set of Chippendale mahogany dining chairs, as well as a bookcase full of well-thumbed eighteenth-century volumes on a variety of practical subjects, and heaps of Chinese blue and white porcelain plates, bowls and soup tureens, many of them chipped. Just as I am relieved that my mother got rid of Temple Sowerby House, I'm thankful she kept this motley assortment of objects – baggage they may be, but they are still my most treasured possessions.

My dad's death was the defining event of my childhood; not a day went by when I didn't somehow sense his absence. Because he had been an only child, there were no aunts or uncles to pass on Atkinson stories to my sister and me. (In fact, except for our elderly bachelor cousin in South Africa, who sent us a large, oozingly sticky box of crystallized fruits every Christmas, we were unaware of having any relatives at all on our paternal side of the family.) After the house at Temple Sowerby was sold, the only reason we had to stop off at the village – passing through in the car en route to holidays in the Lake District – was to place flowers on my father's and grandparents' graves. Although these visits lasted a matter of minutes, they loom large in my memory. Every time, as we approached, I would feel fluttering excitement; and every time, as we drove away, I would feel sadder and emptier than before. Temple Sowerby came to represent all that I had lost during my early years; it was a place where it seemed I would always have unfinished business.

WHILE I WAS growing up, people who had known my dad often told me how much I resembled him, so it was perhaps inevitable that I would follow him into a career in book publishing. In many ways I felt blessed to be like him, since it meant I always carried him around with me; occasionally it felt like a curse. In my thirties, I suffered from digestive problems that caused me much discomfort. Bowel cancer can run in families, and for several years I was sure that I was destined to follow my father to an early grave. When I finally celebrated my thirty-ninth birthday, in 2007, it felt as though a weight had lifted, even as another pressed down; for that year Sue and I finally grasped, after seven years of marriage, that we would never have children of our own. This was a fate I had not imagined, and I felt rudderless, as though robbed of my purpose. My emotions turned raw and unpredictable; for no clear reason, I would break down crying in the street. I now realize I was mourning the sons and daughters I would never know.

While my contemporaries looked to the future, and threw themselves into the all-consuming business of raising families, I turned towards the past, and decided that perhaps it was time I found out about those who had preceded me. One day, while rummaging around in my mother's house, I discovered, gathering dust on top of a cupboard, a scruffy old cardboard box which contained several hundred letters tied up in tight bundles with pink legal ribbon. Most of them were addressed to a 'Matthew Atkinson, Esq.' at Temple Sowerby and dated from the first decades of the nineteenth century. At the same time I came across a family tree, mapped out on a roll of graph paper about twenty feet long, which traced the Atkinsons back to the late sixteenth century. It was in my father's handwriting – I guessed he must have compiled it some time before his marriage, since right at the bottom I noticed he had added my mother's name, and then mine and Harriet's, in slightly different shades of blue-black ink. Looking over past generations, I soon realized how presumptuous I had been to assume that I would have children; while some branches of the family tree were ripe with offspring, others withered to nothing. Below the names of all those whose marriages had not borne fruit, my dad had written the sad little genealogical acronym 'd.s.p.' – *decessit sine prole*, the Latin for 'died without issue'.

I found the prospect of delving into the box of letters quite daunting, but one evening I took a deep breath and started reading.

Instantly I felt the exhilarating rush of throwing open a window to the past. Even so, my progress was slow while I got used to the handwriting. For every letter penned in an impeccable copperplate, another resembled a spidery scrawl. Sometimes the ink had faded to a ghostly sepia. Occasionally, to save the cost of a second sheet of paper, the correspondent had simply rotated the page ninety degrees and carried on writing, creating a dense lattice of words. No envelopes were used; sheets were simply folded, addressed on the front, sealed with wax and dispatched, often in evident haste.

I had observed on the family tree that my ancestors were quite unimaginative when it came to Christian names. George, John, Matthew and Richard had been standard issue for Atkinson boys since the seventeenth century. Right from the start, this small pool of names threw me into confusion, for I made the mistake of assuming that the Matthew Atkinson to whom most of the letters were addressed was my three-times great-grandfather, who had died in 1830. Only some months later did I gather that they related to another Matthew Atkinson, his first cousin, who had died in 1852; it would be several years before I discovered how these papers from a collateral branch of the family had ended up in my hands.

Matthew's correspondence mostly concerned business local to Temple Sowerby, and offered tantalizing glimpses of various trades – banking, farming, mining – which the family had been engaged in. Until then, I had always imagined my forebears as head-in-the-clouds types, rather like my ineffectual grandfather, but these Atkinsons were worldly folk. For the first time I was able to piece together the patchy outline of a family narrative. It appeared that something had occurred during the late eighteenth century to disrupt the fortunes of the entire family. Plenty of letters touched on legal matters, with frequent references to the labyrinthine affairs of a late uncle. And then I unfolded a document that made my jaw drop – it was a 'List of Negroes' giving the name, age, employment and value, in pounds sterling, of each of the 196 enslaved workers on a sugar plantation in Jamaica in the year 1801.

*

GENEALOGY IS ADDICTIVE, and I was soon hooked. I signed up to Ancestry, the online portal to an infinitude of parish records, electoral rolls, census lists and telephone directories, all just the wave of a credit card and the click of a mouse away. I spent countless hours googling 'atkinson' and 'temple sowerby' and 'jamaica', and any other combination of words that might summon up evidence of my ancestors. One day I typed 'atkinson' into the search engine of the National Portrait Gallery website (doubtful though I was that anyone to whom I was related would have earned a place in that august institution), and a result popped up for 'Richard Atkinson, Merchant', whose dates matched those of someone on the family tree – my five-times great-uncle.

I clicked through to this namesake's portrait. Instead of the conventional oil painting that I was expecting, what came up on screen was an engraving titled *Westminster School*, dated 4 February 1785, by James Gillray, the most savage cartoonist of his age. In the foreground, portrayed in the role of headmaster, sits the famous politician Charles James Fox, unmistakable with his bushy black eyebrows. William Pitt the Younger, the 25-year-old prime minister, is shown bent over Fox's knee, where he is being given a sound thrashing. Meanwhile a cohort of Pitt's 'playmates', held in place on the backs of prominent opposition figures, line up to await the same punishment, their buttocks bared. Poking out from the pocket of one of these miscreants is a piece of paper bearing two words, 'Rum Contract' – the detail which identifies him as Richard Atkinson. My head was spinning at the thought not only that a relative of mine should find himself in such rarefied company – but that our first encounter should take place at a moment when his breeches were hanging around his knees.

An internet search soon yielded a potted biography of this Richard Atkinson. He had been a West India merchant, director of the East India Company, Member of Parliament, alderman of the City of London, prominent early supporter of Pitt the Younger – and a major government contractor during the American War of Independence. His nickname, 'Rum' Atkinson, apparently originated from a notorious contract to supply a vast quantity of Jamaican rum to the British army headquarters at New York in 1776. He had died relatively young, in May 1785, unmarried, leaving behind an immense, self-made fortune.

BY NOW I WAS in the grip of an obsession, spending all my spare time online in pursuit of my ancestors. One evening during the autumn of 2010, I was browsing the website of Temple Sowerby House Hotel, which included a short page dedicated to the history of the place; and although it was a fairly unexciting account, one paragraph leapt out at me. This was a description of a 'fascinating Recipe or *Receipt* Book', written by Bridget Atkinson for her daughter Dorothy Clayton in 1806, which gave instructions, among other dishes, for collared eels, roasted tench and a sauce to serve with larks. I knew that this Bridget Atkinson was my four-times great-grandmother, as well as 'Rum' Atkinson's sister-in-law. My sister and I had inherited a number of her books – we knew they were hers because she always signed her name on the title page – including *Domestic Medicine: or, a Treatise on the Prevention and Cure of Diseases by Regimen and Simple Medicines,* by William Buchan, MD; *The Scots Gardiners Director, containing Instructions to those Gardiners, who make a Kitchen Garden, and the Culture of Flowers, their Business,* by 'A Gentleman, one of the Members of the Royal Society'; *An Account of the Culture and Use of the Mangel Wurzel, or Root of Scarcity,* translated from the French of the Abbé de Commerell; and *The British Housewife: or, the Cook, Housekeeper's and Gardiner's Companion,* by Mrs Martha Bradley. But this was the first I'd heard of Bridget having written a recipe book of her own. I publish cookbooks for a living; suffice to say my interest was piqued.

So I did something I'd never thought of doing – I stayed a night at the hotel. Arriving at Temple Sowerby around teatime, I parked near the maypole, beside the large stone from which John Wesley was said to have preached in 1782. It was a crisp November day. Across the road, the curtains of the hotel had not yet been drawn, and its brightly lit reception rooms radiated hospitality. Before

Plate I.   Frontispiece to the Compleat English Cook.

Jaques Le Sœur Inv.   Behold, ye Fair, united in this Book,   *B. Cole sc.*
             The frugal Housewife, and experienc'd Cook.

The frontispiece of Bridget's copy of The British Housewife.

12

checking in, I went for a short stroll, as far as the old tannery buildings at the other end of the village. Walking round the green, I found myself appraising Temple Sowerby as if visiting for the first time; with its handsome Georgian houses, coaching inn and red sandstone church, it seemed a delightful place. Much more peaceful than I remembered, too, since a new bypass had diverted all the lorries which had once rumbled through the village.

Over at the hotel, Julie Evans, one of the owners, greeted me warmly. She already knew about my connection to the house, and had reserved a room for me at the back, with a view down the garden. It was nice and cosy, in a chintzy kind of way, and the ensuite bathroom, with its Jacuzzi tub, was a definite upgrade from the spartan facilities of the Atkinson era. Even so, a small, churlish part of me resented the fitted carpets and double glazing, and yearned for the house of my grandparents. As a child, my favourite place had been the gallery, with its clattery floorboards and oak furniture, some of which now dominated my living room in south London. But it seemed that when Temple Sowerby House was turned into a hotel, in the late 1970s, the gallery had been carved up to make bedrooms, including the one I would be sleeping in. To describe my emotions as agitated would be an understatement; as I sat down to dinner, the only guest that night, I had never felt more lonely.

I had almost finished eating when Julie appeared, clutching a scrap of paper. 'I've just remembered something,' she said. 'A few years ago, this person came to stay, and she told me her ancestors used to live here. Perhaps you should get in touch?' She handed me the slip, on which was written an unfamiliar name – Phillipa Scott – along with a telephone number. I was intrigued.

Julie took pity on me after my solitary meal, and we chatted in the parlour. She and her husband Paul had owned the hotel for ten years, and she was clearly so fond of the place that I found myself letting go of the last of my proprietorial feelings. I'd brought a shoebox full of old family papers up from London with me, and we leafed through them together. Then I asked Julie the question I'd been burning to put to her since arriving – what could she tell me about this 'receipt book' that was mentioned on the hotel website? She left the room and returned a couple of minutes later, cradling an old quarter-bound book. She handed it to me; I opened it cautiously, not knowing what might be inside, and was amazed to find almost eight hundred recipes, handwritten in highly legible script.

It was evident from the sheer variety of meat, fish and game dishes in her repertoire that Bridget Atkinson had kept an excellent table. Many of her recipes included spices and flavourings that to this day carry a whiff of the exotic, such as cinnamon, ginger, nutmeg, curry powder, candied lemons and orange flower water. Although the instructions she gave were cursory at best, and her methods on the antiquated side – she was, after all, cooking over an open fire – many of the recipes, especially the puddings and preserves, seemed perfectly relatable to the present. I could imagine trying to make them at home.

Not so the recipes in the last third of the book, where Bridget offered remedies for every conceivable domestic situation or ailment: 'For Berry Bushes infested with Caterpillers'; 'To distroy Moths'; 'To prevent Milk from having a taste of Turneps'; 'A Pomatum for the Face after the Small Pox'; 'To draw away a Humor from the Eyes'; 'For worms in Children'; 'Against Spitting of Blood'; 'To prevent bad effects of a Fall from a high place'; 'To cure the Bite of a Mad Dog'; 'For Insanity'. Some of her preparations sounded downright lethal. On a loose piece of paper tucked into the book I found 'Mrs. Atkinson's Receipt', a concoction of rhubarb, laudanum and gin, all mixed into a pint of milk; it was not clear what condition it was intended for, but it seemed as though it may have been a case of kill or cure.

Bridget would have been in her seventies when she started compiling this volume for her daughter – it was odd to think she might well have written it in the same room in which I was at that moment sitting. For so long, I had associated Temple Sowerby House with death and decay; only now could I sense it as a bustling family home. In all my life, I had never coveted a single object so much as this wondrous book – so I felt crushed when Julie explained that it belonged to a private collector from Newcastle, and would soon have to be returned. I must have looked so downcast that Julie insisted I should immediately write to the owner, Miss Dunn, to ask whether I might buy the book; indeed, she thrust pen, paper and envelope at me, and promised to post my letter.

WHEN I OPENED the curtains the next morning, the sky was a brilliant blue; overnight had seen a heavy frost. After breakfast I walked across the road to the churchyard, crunching through glittery grass in search of Atkinson graves; then I set off for Northumberland, to spend a couple of nights with my godmother near Corbridge. My route over the Pennines took me on a zigzag road up the steep side of the Eden valley, through the ancient lead-mining town of Alston and across an ocean of bronze heather, dropping down alongside the South Tyne – a spectacular drive. That afternoon I had a couple of hours to spare, so I visited Chesters Fort, one of several Roman garrisons along Hadrian's Wall, now maintained by English Heritage. I knew from my family research that some cousins, the Claytons, had once lived in the big house near the ruins, and had been responsible for their excavation – Bridget's daughter, Dorothy, had married Nathaniel Clayton, the Newcastle lawyer who purchased the property.

Wandering around the neat stone footings, I struggled to imagine five hundred Roman cavalry ever having occupied such a peaceful spot. As drizzle hardened into rain, I took refuge in the small museum attached to the site. Near the entrance was a glass case devoted to the life of John Clayton, owner of Chesters for much of the nineteenth century. Among the objects on display was an old book which had belonged to his grandmother, Bridget Atkinson – as usual, her name was inscribed on the title page. Then something even more extraordinary caught my eye. It was the facsimile of a letter written by Bridget in January 1758, when she would have been in her mid-twenties, in which she was begging her sister to placate their mother, who was furious that she'd got married the previous Saturday without telling anyone. My heart pounded as I processed this – did it mean Bridget had eloped? *And how had the museum come by this letter?*

On my return to London, I wasted no time chasing up my leads – within minutes of arriving home, I had dug out the family tree and unfurled it on the kitchen table. First of all, I needed to locate Phillipa Scott, the mysterious woman whose details Julie Evans had given me. There she was, my fourth cousin – our last mutual ancestor was Bridget's son Matthew Atkinson, the one who died in 1830. I googled her, and soon landed on the website of a needlework expert living in Appleby, six miles from Temple Sowerby – with the same distinctive spelling of her first name, this was surely the right person. It was almost midnight on a Sunday, but the urge to make contact with this complete stranger was too powerful to resist. In a short email, I explained who I was and where I'd just been. About three minutes later, Phillipa's reply announced itself in my inbox. Hello! And, yes, she had stayed at Temple Sowerby House some years earlier, but also remembered visiting in the 1960s, as a child. 'Is it my imagination,' she wrote, 'or was there a crocodile on the top landing?'

Phillipa and I spoke on the telephone the following day, and for me it was a cathartic experience. We hit it off immediately, and discovered how much we had in common; although we belonged to different branches of the tree, we shared the same deep roots. We chatted for an hour, and afterwards I felt so overwhelmed with joy that I burst into tears. A few weeks later, Phillipa put me in touch with David Atkinson, her first cousin – my fourth cousin – who invited me to stay at his house in Cheshire so that I could search through his collection of family papers. He was trusting enough to let me carry away a suitcase full of them.

I also made contact with the curator of the museum at Chesters, Georgina Plowright, who delivered a surprising piece of news. She had recently unearthed a treasure trove of correspondence between the Atkinson and Clayton families, six large boxes spanning the eighteenth and nineteenth centuries, in the Northumberland Archives, buried among the papers of another family, the Allgoods of Nunwick Hall. (Apparently one of Bridget Atkinson's great-great-granddaughters, Isabella Clayton, had married an Allgood.)

And then there was Bridget's 'receipt book', the scent of which had lured me north in the first place. Two days after my return, I received a call from Irene Dunn in response to the letter I had written from Temple Sowerby. She told me she was a retired librarian with a special interest in books about food; she had found Bridget's manuscript at an antiquarian bookseller's in Bath about fifteen years earlier. It so happened that I had approached Irene at the perfect moment. She was now looking to downsize, and was tickled by the thought of selling the book to me, a descendant of Bridget. One bright Saturday in January I travelled by train up to Newcastle to meet Irene for lunch in a restaurant on the Quayside, and to carry my prize home.

SO THIS IS THE STORY of how I found my eighteenth-century family. It was as though Bridget's cookbook was the key I had been searching for, since doors immediately began to open. The thousands of old letters that fell into my lap as a result of my miraculous trip to Temple Sowerby – they were just the start. Within a few months I had located significant quantities of Atkinson correspondence in more than a dozen public archives and private collections on both sides of the Atlantic. My ancestors, it emerged, had occupied ringside seats at some of the most momentous episodes in British imperial history, most notably the loss of the American colonies, then the economic collapse of the West Indies. When they first sailed to Jamaica, in the 1780s, it was the most valuable possession in the empire; when they left, in the 1850s, it was a neglected backwater. Moreover, through the copious correspondence they left behind, I learnt the intimate details of their lives. Richard 'Rum' Atkinson, in particular, emerged as a brilliant but flawed man who amassed a fabled fortune as well as considerable power, but would have given it up in a heartbeat for the woman he loved.

It became obvious that I had stumbled upon the material for a book. Although I had edited a great many books written by other people, I had never planned to inflict one of my own on the world, being more than happy to remain on the other side of the publishing fence. But I found I couldn't ignore this story which kept me awake at night, so I started rising at six, to spend a couple of hours writing before leaving for the office. It was hard going, and on dark winter mornings it took every ounce of willpower to drag myself out of bed. I soon discovered – perhaps surprisingly, given my professional background – that I had little idea how to go about actually writing a book. So I signed up for an evening class in 'Writing Family History', and it was here that I had another stroke of luck – for the teacher turned out to be the acclaimed biographer Andrea Stuart, who was then at work on *Sugar in the Blood*, the story of her ancestors in Barbados, black and white. One Saturday morning, she took us on a tour of the National Archives at Kew, a vast concrete behemoth where we were inducted into the practicalities of archival research; it was time well spent, for I would become a frequent visitor over the next few years. Andrea encouraged me, at a stage when I really needed it, to pursue my own embryonic Jamaican story.

I look back on this as a strange, transitional period in my life; I felt like a kind of time-travelling commuter, secretly shuttling back and forth between the present day and the world of my eighteenth-century family. It was exciting, certainly, but also emotionally challenging, as I struggled to reconcile my inborn sympathy for these people, my ancestors, with their activities in Jamaica. I was never so naive as to imagine that those activities might be unconnected with slavery, but nor was I fully prepared for the degree to which they were involved. It was not a pleasant discovery.

My eyes were opened, too, to the nature of Britain's culpability. I learned that there were thousands of well-to-do Georgian families, like mine, whose wealth and prestige had derived from the blood, sweat and lives of enslaved Africans. Moreover, individuals from every rank of society had played their part in propping up slavery, from the royal personages who sanctioned the slave trade with West Africa in the first place, to the sailors who crewed the slave ships – even the ordinary working people who consumed the tainted sugar.

Here in Britain, we have tended to keep this disturbing aspect of our national story at arm's length; unlike the United States, where its divisive consequences are plain to see, slavery was not common-place on these shores. We proudly celebrate our great abolitionists, of course, but we would rather not know *too* much about what they were campaigning to abolish.

Sometimes, after yet another grim discovery in the archives, I wondered what kind of fool would knowingly implicate his own family by writing them into this shocking chapter of history. Yet my instinct told me to press on; in fact, I felt a powerful responsibility to do so. Clearly I could make no amends for my ancestors' misdeeds – but I could certainly attempt to make something positive out of what they had left behind. Since this mostly consisted of old letters, to tell their story made perfect sense to me. But it was essential that I should write it warts-and-all. 'Do not try and make all the ancestors goody two shoes when some were plainly not,' advised David Atkinson, whose messages were a tonic for my sometimes flagging spirits. 'Detach yourself – you have every right to portray some as villains, some as "not sures", some as feckless and some as the heroes. I suspect you might be torn on this – don't be. You have my blessing to treat some of them hard.'

To have my newfound cousins cheering me on was just what I needed as I embarked on a long voyage into our ancestors' past – one that took me all the way from London to the abandoned sugar plantations of Jamaica. But all roads ultimately led to Temple Sowerby, where so many Atkinsons were born and so many are buried. Their tangled inheritance may have scattered them around the world, but the evidence made its way back to that weather-beaten house in the shadow of the Pennines and, eventually, in the form of the curious miscellany of relics and papers that were my inheritance, into my hands.

TWO

The Tanner's Wife

THE RIVER EDEN carves a sinuous line down the valley that bears its name, past ruined castles and ruminating cows, swelling from the countless becks that drain off steep fells; by the time it flows under the red sandstone bridge at Temple Sowerby, it has completed almost half its ninety-mile journey. Cross Fell, highest of the Pennine hills, dominates the skyline at this point; it enjoys the rare distinction of harbouring a breeze with so much bluster that it has its own name. 'A violent roaring hurricane comes tumbling down the mountain, ready to tear up all before it,' was how one eighteenth-century traveller described the 'Helm' wind.[1]

From the summit of Cross Fell – assuming the absence of its usual cloud cap – you can see the hills of Galloway in southern Scotland. Two thousand years ago, the Romans built a wall to keep out the Caledonian people to the north, and legions of soldiers marched through Temple Sowerby on their way to forts along its route; a Roman milestone can be found in a layby just outside the village, although its inscription weathered away aeons ago. Scandinavian immigrants settled in the area during the ninth century. These hardy people left their linguistic imprint across northern England, not just in the words that evoke its landscape – *beck* and *fell* are of Norse origin – but also in its place names. *Sauerbi* is old Norse for 'farmstead on sour ground'. Even the Vikings, it seems, saw Temple Sowerby as a hardship post.

The first tangible evidence of the Atkinsons of Temple Sowerby can be found in the basement of the county offices at Kendal – this is where the records are kept for the historic county of Westmorland, which was absorbed into Cumbria in 1974. William Atkinson – my nine-times great-grandfather – was one of seventeen yeomen who in 1577 were granted thousand-year leases on their land in the village, along with 'reasonable common for the pasturing of their cattle', by the lord of the manor, Christopher Dalston.[2] It feels only fitting that I should examine the legal document in which my ancestors' earliest property rights were enshrined, but the large sheet of vellum is a brute to unfold, so defiantly springy that it resists my attempts to flatten it out. I must be firm with it, I realize, but not *too* firm, since the archivist is watching me like a hawk.

Eventually, after wrestling with it for a minute or two, I have it spreadeagled on the desk, its corners pinned down with iron weights. I now appreciate why calfskin has always been the material upon which parliamentary laws are recorded, for the document remains in superb condition, apart from two holes caused either by rodents or fire – it's hard to tell which. Next comes a still greater challenge – deciphering the script. At first I hold out little hope of being able to read the spiky Elizabethan handwriting. But soon I find that if I stare at them in an abstract way, shapes start to turn into words.

This lease marks the culmination of a conflict that simmered in Temple Sowerby for twenty years. Until the dissolution of the monasteries in the 1530s, the manor was held by the religious orders of the Knights Templar (who gave it their name), and then by the Knights Hospitaller, both of whom interfered little in the lives of the villagers. That all changed in 1543 when the Dalston family acquired the manor from the Crown. It was inevitable the tenants of Temple Sowerby would resent their first resident landlords in nearly four centuries, especially given that both Thomas Dalston and his son, Christopher, made it plain that they intended to claim the common land for themselves. William Atkinson was one of eight villagers who filed a writ against Christopher Dalston in 1559. Their case was rejected by the Lord President of the North at York; next, they took it to Court of Chancery in London.

The 1577 lease was the upshot of this litigation. Dalston gained exclusive use of half the common, and was ordered to grant his tenants possession of the other half. For their part, the villagers undertook to use Dalston's mill at Acorn Bank to grind their flour, and to pay for half of any necessary repairs. Although it was technically a compromise, they nonetheless saw the agreement as a victory against their overbearing lord. Christopher Dalston only conceded to these terms 'because he would be of quietness with the plaintiffs and no further be molested as he by a long time hath been'.[3] He never forgave his tenants their insolence; and they in turn fully reciprocated his ill feelings.

The first mention of the leather-tanning business that kept the Atkinson family busy for at least five generations is found in the will of William Atkinson, second son of William who signed the 1577 agreement. This William never married, and on his death in 1645 he left his elder brother John 'all my leather tubbes and barke and my apparel the bedstead I lye in and one feather bed and one nagge'.[4]

Temple Sowerby was well positioned for the trade in animal skins, being on a major cattle-droving route. Every year, between April and October, thousands of black cows funnelled through the village on their way from the breeding grounds of south-west Scotland to Smithfield market in London; plenty failed to last the distance, falling by the wayside due to lameness or sickness. The 'drovers' who herded cattle were tough individuals, and Westmorland was the harshest terrain they would cross – Daniel Defoe in 1724 described the county as 'eminent only for being the wildest, most barren, and frightful of any that I have passed over in England, or in Wales'.[5] At Temple Sowerby the drovers found a range of services, including a farrier for shoeing horses and cows, two inns and ample pasturage.

Two tanyards lay at a slight remove from the centre of the village – necessarily so, given the stench arising from the tanning process. First, any decaying flesh was cleaned off the raw hides, and any hair removed; next came the stage known as bating, during which the skins were softened in an ammoniac brew of watered-down pigeon shit shovelled from a large dovecote on site. They were then immersed in a succession of clay-lined pits filled with tanning liquor of increasing strength, the active ingredient being the tannin released by ground-up dried oak bark steeped in water. The overall length of the soak determined the toughness of the finished product, but generally lasted a year or more. Finally the cured skins were trimmed, shaved, greased, dyed, rolled, buffed and prepared for market. So many of life's necessities – belts, boots, buckets, harnesses, pouches, saddles, straps and trunks – were fashioned from leather. Its manufacture was by no means a noble activity; but it was a vital one.

THE HEARTH TAX return of my seven-times great-grandfather John Atkinson for 1670 declares just one fireplace – compared to Squire Dalston's nine at Acorn Bank.[6] John died in 1680, and what little I know of him comes from his will, a document noteworthy as the first (but by no means the last) record of friction within the Atkinson family.

The declarative language of John's will suggests it was dictated on his deathbed, the rather melodramatic custom of the day. So close to his final breath, you would hope that John might be making his peace with the world, but it seems he felt the need to mediate between his squabbling offspring. Thus, having apportioned his earthly possessions – he left forty shillings a year to his daughter Barbara, and the bulk of any 'goods and lands moveable and unmoveable' to his son George – John went on to specify some conditions. As long as she remained unmarried, Barbara was to be housed by her brother. 'If the sayd Barbry and Geordge cannot agre,' John went on, 'Geordge is to builde hir a chimley in the backe chamber and she is to live theire and if the sade chamber doe fall to decay then Geordge is to repare the same of his owne cost.'[7] Barbara never did marry, and I haven't been able to discover whether that extra chimney was ever needed. But when George died more than forty years later he left his sister £5 – so perhaps they managed to agree after all.

As I write, George's Latin textbook sits on the desk before me – it's the oldest object I own. Bound in scuffed calfskin, it contains almost five hundred handwritten pages of Latin grammar and syntax. Like the thousand-year lease, the script is in a distinctively Elizabethan hand, which is confirmed by the date: 'anno domini 1595'. For George, too, the book was a hand-me-down, as it predates his schooldays by several generations. Born in 1657, he was a pupil in the early 1670s, by which time the writing style had become rounder and, to modern eyes, much more legible. So how do I know that the book once belonged to him? The impulse to deface textbooks is hard-wired into every small boy's brain. George was no exception, and he wrote his name a few times on the flyleaf, along with this enjoyable doggerel:

> *Hic liber pertinet, deny it who can*
> *Ad Georgeum Atkinson, ye honest young man*
> *In opido Temple Sowerbie he is to be founde*
> *Si non mortuus est, if not laide in ye grounde*

The book is a yardstick of the Atkinson family's social mobility during the seventeenth century. George's grandfather John, who died in 1647, had signed his will with the rudimentary 'mark' of an illiterate man; John's grandson George, on the other hand, could read and write Latin.

History records neither how George met his wife Jane Hodgson, nor when or where they were married, but it must have been relatively late for both of them, since their first child was born in 1701, when he was forty-four and she was thirty-one. Jane came from Threlkeld, near Keswick, in the heart of the Lake District. Perhaps George encountered her on his way to take delivery of a consignment of raw hides at the port of Whitehaven; or maybe he knew her from expeditions to purchase oak bark, a commodity in which the coppiced woods of the Lakeland dales were rich.

The sandy incline known as Whinfell, just across the river from Temple Sowerby, was the most convenient source of the bark that was essential to the tanning process. Around thirty families, including the Atkinsons, cultivated a large open expanse of the fell, although the land was too scrubby – 'whin' being another word for gorse – to be much good. Beyond the villagers' strips, up the hill, lay Whinfell Forest, the domain of the Earl of Thanet. Since medieval times the forest had been renowned for the aristocratic sport of deer hunting, and for its 'prodigious oaks', including a trio known as the Three Brothers.[8]

Sadly, these giants would soon be slain. By the turn of the eighteenth century, Whinfell's oaks had been earmarked for the shipyards of the Royal Navy, which, having consumed vast tracts of ancient woodland in the south, was now sourcing its timber from further afield. Accounts kept by Lord Thanet's steward, Thomas Carleton, record the felling of fifty-four oaks at Whinfell during the winter of 1701, and twenty-three more the following spring. After being peeled and sawn on the spot, the timber was loaded on to sixty waggons that were dragged thirty miles up the old Roman road to Rockcliffe, at the mouth of the River Eden, where it was transferred to two barges and ferried round the coast to Whitehaven, to be warehoused 'till the Queen's Shipp Come for it'.[9] Meanwhile, the bark from these ancient trees was sold to a syndicate of five tanners, one of whom was George Atkinson.

Little went to waste in the rural economy. Animal hair, a by-product of the tanning process, was a commodity in its own right, used to add bulk to the mixture of lime, sand and water that made up plaster. Hair recycled from the tannery at Temple Sowerby found its way into the fabric of some of the area's finest properties; half a ton of the stuff was used in 1718 in the walls and ceilings of the Red House, Thomas Carleton's residence in Appleby.[10]

Over the course of his relatively long life, George's tanning business prospered, and he was able to buy two farms, one at Hilton Bacon, ten miles up the valley, the other at Hesket Newmarket, twenty miles in the other direction. By the time he was ready to be 'laide in ye grounde', when he was sixty-six, he had acquired sufficient property to provide for both his sons.

George's funeral was held on Whitsunday in 1723, and the parish record throws up a curiously intimate detail about his interment. A law had been passed in 1666 requiring corpses to be buried in woollen shrouds, rather than the linen sheets in which they had previously been wrapped; only victims of the plague were exempt. This was a protectionist measure, aimed at reducing linen imports from abroad, with a harsh £5 fine for non-compliance, payable out of the estate of the deceased. (Half the fine went to the informer, the rest to the poor of the parish.) Even so, some fancy folk were prepared to flout the law so that they could be interred in finer fabric. But the Atkinsons were plain people and thus – as the register certifies – George was buried 'in woollen only'.[11]

Following George's wishes, control of the tannery passed to John, his elder son. Matthew, the younger son, inherited the property beyond Temple Sowerby as well as bonds representing money owed to his father. A few years later, after his brother's premature death, Matthew took over the tannery.

SOMETIME IN THE mid-1720s, Matthew bought the farm-house in Temple Sowerby that would be home to the Atkinson family for the next 250 years, and he immediately embarked upon a programme of building works that included the addition of the upstairs corridor which became known, rather grandly, as the gallery. He married Margaret Sutton of Kirkby Lonsdale in April 1727; as though declaring his intention to establish a vigorous new branch of the family, Matthew ordered his and his bride's initials, and the year of their wedding, to be chiselled into the red sandstone lintel above the front door.

Through this entrance, a narrow passage opened into low rooms on either side. To the left was the main living space, with mullioned windows and a large fireplace, and a ladder leading to a loft. To the right, a cosy parlour led through to the smoky kitchen, where hams and other hunks of curing meat dangled from hooks in the ceiling, and peat smouldered in the hearth; also off the parlour, a creaking staircase led up to the gallery and the sleeping quarters. Matthew

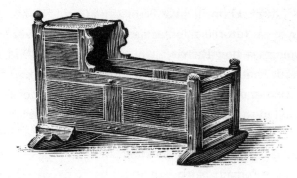

The oak cradle in which the Atkinson children spent their first years.

and Margaret's five children soon filled the house with noise: Jane, who was born in 1728, followed by George, Margaret, Matthew and last, but emphatically not least, Richard in 1739.

Details of their childhood must remain blurry, since the paper trail from this period is non-existent. Much of their growing up would have taken place outdoors, as there were always chores to be performed – cows to milk, pigs to feed, fields to dig, fruit to pick, wood to gather, peat to cut. Certainly, the boys fished in the nearby river; the shooting in the fields and woods around the village was off limits, however, since their father, not being a freeholder, did not have the right to kill game. Likely they played 'Scotch and English', a game in which the players of two teams launched raids into the territory of their opponents in order to steal their coats, meanwhile running the risk of being captured and taken prisoner. This 'active and violent recreation', which was popular in the border country, would have gained further significance for the village lads after 15 December 1745, when a Jacobite force passed through Temple Sowerby – one Atkinson legend tells of family members being forced to give up their pocket watches by the Scots rebels.[12]

What the Atkinson children received by way of education is a matter of conjecture. It's very possible the boys attended the excellent free grammar school at Appleby, but their names are nowhere to be found in the school's (extremely patchy) historical records. The Rev. Carleton Atkinson – no relation – who was a graduate of

Queen's College, Oxford, and rector at Temple Sowerby for forty years, may have tutored them at some point. They were all bright, but the youngest boy, Richard, was exceptionally so. It must have been obvious that his talents transcended the confines of the Eden valley, since somehow – I have no idea what chain of connections might have led to this – he landed a position as a clerk at the house of Samuel Touchet, a merchant of considerable influence based at Aldermanbury in the City of London.

Few traces remain of Richard's earliest years in London. The first evidence I have unearthed of his existence there comes at the end of a legal document relating to the transfer of some land in Temple Sowerby, which he witnessed in London on 14 September 1755.[13] This is also the first sample of his handwriting that I have come across. At sixteen, his signature had not yet developed its ultimate panache, but it already showed considerable self-confidence, underscored by a succession of delightfully superfluous loops – and only slightly undermined by a few blotches, which reveal its author not to be in full command of his ink.

The most conclusive proof of Richard's association with Samuel Touchet would be his contract of apprenticeship. Because stamp duty was imposed on the premium charged by a master, such contracts were registered by the authorities; details of all the apprenticeships entered into between 1710 and 1811 can be found in the National Archives at Kew, contained within seventy-nine bulky volumes that are also, mercifully, searchable online. But here's a puzzle. There's no evidence that Richard was ever apprenticed to anyone. Yet it was while they were both working for Touchet that Richard forged a lifelong friendship with a young man who definitely *was* an apprentice: Francis Baring, the son of a prosperous Exeter wool merchant. (Baring's widowed mother paid £800 for his seven-year apprenticeship, which started on 20 November 1755, when he was fifteen; the hefty premium reflected Touchet's prestige in the City.)[14] So how did Richard manage to get his foot in the door?

In his will, dated 6 March 1755, Matthew Atkinson bequeathed £200 to each of his two elder sons, George and Matthew, and £100 to Richard, which suggests previous expenditure on the latter's behalf. Matthew would die 'of a Jaundice' on 15 April 1756. 'He was not only one of the largest Dealers in his Way in the North,' noted the *Public Advertiser*, 'but also one of the most honourable.'[15]

THE MOTTO ENGRAVED on the face of the longcase clock in the gallery at Temple Sowerby was an hourly reminder of life's brevity – 'Remember Man / That Dye thou must / And after that to / Judgment Just' – and perhaps its message had rubbed off on George Atkinson, who was eager to enter the state of matrimony. He had been visiting his neighbour Biddy Shepard one day in 1756 when he first encountered Bridget Maughan, and was so taken with her that he soon found it convenient to call on her at home in Wolsingham, fifty miles away in County Durham. Theirs would not be a smooth courtship.

Bridget's father, Michael Maughan, had been a mining agent, prospecting for lead and copper on the Duke of Queensberry's estates in Lanarkshire, but died when he was twenty-six. His widow, Dorothy, who hailed from old Cumberland gentry, raised Bridget and her younger daughter Jenny at Kirkoswald, a village twelve miles down the valley from Temple Sowerby, in an extended family surrounded by cousins. Dorothy was a controlling mother who would resort to tears when other methods of coercion failed; as a result, perhaps, both girls were notably secretive when it came to matters of the heart. Apart from a stint at Mrs Paxton's academy in Durham, where they were schooled in the wifely arts of sewing and linen-dressing, the Maughan girls received no formal education. I would guess it was Dorothy who taught them to read and write, for Bridget's writing was almost identical to her mother's; furthermore, her spelling was wildly erratic, and she would remain more or less a stranger to punctuation her entire life.

In October 1755, when Jenny Maughan was nineteen and staying with friends in Newcastle, she fell in love with James Graham, and the couple were hastily engaged. Their idyll lasted a fortnight before Dorothy heard about it, pronounced Graham unsuitable, and commanded her daughter to sever the connection. Jenny's broken heart cast a long shadow over the family during the following months, and it was under its lingering influence that George Atkinson started courting Bridget, a compliment which she rewarded with a robust brush-off:

> Sir, I had your Letter and do remember what you said when
> you were at Wolsingham but you'll excuse me when I tell you
> I know your Sex a Little better than belive one word of it.
> When I was Last at Temple Sowerby I was told you courted
> Miss Thomson of Bowes and I belive it is so. I have the
> greatest reason to respect you for your great civility both to
> my Sister and myself. I shall always esteem you as a friend but
> no pitty for I am very sure your Heart is as safe as ever it was
> at Least for me.[16]

As a matter of fact, Bridget liked George more than she let on, but was afraid to encourage him, foreseeing her mother's disapproval. Dorothy, who was proud of her pedigree – which included a smidgen of Plantagenet blood – would no doubt say the Atkinsons smelled of trade, and an odoriferous one at that. Gentry they most definitely were not. There was, however, another reason for Bridget's guardedness during the summer of 1756 – for her heart was already under siege.

Earlier that year, Dorothy had moved to Wolsingham, the home of her parents-in-law, perhaps after falling out with one or more of her sisters. In these new surroundings, she might have felt that two unmarried daughters reflected badly on her; in any case, when a local gentleman started courting Bridget, Dorothy pressed her to accept his hand. So far as the daughter was concerned, though, the match was unthinkable. In the ensuing battle of wills, Bridget's friends feared she would be the one to give way first.

In August 1756, Bridget received a diverting parcel of books from her cousin James Tinkler, a merchant in London, accompanied by a letter full of family gossip and news of the opening salvos of a war with France. James was clearly worried about Bridget, for the letter to his 'Dear Coz' opened with the admission that he had been 'perplexed with a Thousand Fears' for her welfare. With regard to an ongoing commission, he could report only modest success: 'I have Collected a Few more Shells which I shall Send with the Other Things, and I Promise you I Lett nothing of that kind Slipp that I Can Procure. But it's now Fashionable for the Ladies to decorate their Rural apartments with Them, which makes them Both Scarse and Dear.'[17]

James Tinkler was not the only one with concerns about Bridget's beleaguered state of mind. By September, she had still not decisively turned down her suitor's proposal, and her standoff with her mother was now the subject of local tittle-tattle. 'How hard it is to think that people might be quite happy and there own parents make them quite miserable,' wrote Biddy Shepard, who knew that Bridget was soft on George Atkinson, and was keen to promote his suit:

> If you can only try for a littel bitt of More Spirit and Resolve to fight throw it and not Sink under the weight of what Some people would only Look on as trifels and who knows but you may yet make that worthy fellow happy that would be willing to be seven times hanged and let down agane for you, and if not him Some body else that disarves you. Never however throw your Self away on a *munkey* that all the World agrees is not worthy of you.[18]

*

TEA ARRIVED IN England in the 1650s, and was initially a luxury enjoyed only by the very rich. Over the following century, however, tea drinking turned into a British obsession, so much so that high-minded individuals began preaching against the moral consequences of the habit. One forthright critic of the beverage was the reformer Jonas Hanway, whose *Essay on Tea*, published in 1756, pinned many social ills on it, including rotten teeth, a soaring suicide rate and a loss of bloom in chambermaids. (He had a point about the teeth; the growth of tea drinking went hand-in-hand with a boom in the consumption of the sugar used to sweeten it.) The East India Company, as the holder of the monopoly on trade with the Orient, ought to have entirely fulfilled the nation's demand for tea; but the commodity was so exorbitantly taxed that around half of the leaves landing on British shores were imported illegally from the continent. James Corbet, a merchant and ship-owner from Dumfries, is known to have smuggled tea from the Swedish city of Gothenburg via the Isle of Man. His business ledgers record that George Atkinson – a regular visitor to Dumfries – purchased a pound of 'Singlo green tea' from him for 8s 6d on 30 September 1756.[19]

For George, the following winter was purgatorial, for he heard not a word from the object of his affection. On 4 March 1757, after months of silence, he could stand it no longer, and decided to enlist Bridget's sister Jenny to his cause, placing a small package addressed to her on a cart to Wolsingham. 'Good Tea I know is a thing not very common in your country, yet an article which I think Ladies ought always to be Indulged in,' George wrote in his accompanying letter. 'I have lately met with a parcell which takes my fancy vastly, yet knowing my Deficiency of Judgement in those things, I have sent a sample which I hope you'll give me your opinion of the first time I see you. I have every week since Christmas been expecting News from your Place of some Conquest this Winter,' he continued, a note of despondency creeping in, 'but I find you keep these things too closely amongst yourselves. Oh Jenny (as the Scotchman says) keep a good gripp of your heart, for after that's gone I now find (by Experience) uneasyness, Jealousy &c follows, and always assure yourself of this, that it's much easier for a person not in Love to persuade his Mistress he has a Passion for her, than for those who Loves with the greatest Sincerity.'[20]

Poor, lovelorn George – such an appeal carried its risks, but perhaps he felt he had little to lose. Certainly, his petition appears to have done him no harm. Over the following months, Bridget made it clear that one way or another, whether her mother liked it or not, she would marry George Atkinson.

On the morning of 7 January 1758, George rode out from Temple Sowerby, following the Eden ten miles downstream, past the ancient standing stones known as Long Meg and her Daughters, to St Michael's Church at Addingham. The village itself no longer existed, having been washed away when the river changed course in the fourteenth century; only the parish church remained. There he met Bridget, who was staying with her Tinkler relations in Kirkoswald and had stolen away for a few hours. Their wedding ceremony could not have been more discreet. At this solemn, lonely place, in the low midwinter light, they must have believed their secret to be safe.

They had hoped to keep it under wraps until Whitsunday, but news of their marriage somehow reached Wolsingham a few days later. Bridget, in palpable distress, dashed off a note to her sister: 'I beg Dear Jenny you will use your intrest to paceffy my Mother and to prevaill with her to alow me to come home a Little whille indeed my happyness depends upon it. I beg you'll write soon and tell me the worst.'[21] Her aunt Barbara Tinkler also wrote to Dorothy: 'Dear sister, Whether the News of your Daughter Bridget's being married to Mr. George Atkinson may be so Gratefull to you, as I could wish, I cannot Conjecture. But as I understand, She formerly acquainted you with her intentions I hope it will not be so Surprising to you. The man has a very good Character, and we all hope will make a kind and indulgent husband.' On the reverse, Bridget added a mournful paragraph of her own. 'Dear Mother,' she implored, 'till I have a Line from you I can never be easy. Alowe me once more to desire your Blessing and Leave to come over which if you do not grant will make me very unhappy perhaps to my Lives end.'[22]

MOTHER AND DAUGHTER made their peace. The *Gentleman's Magazine* recorded the match in the mercenary language of the day:

> Mr. Atkinson, tanner, near Appleby – to Miss Maughan of Wolsingham, Durham £3000.[23]

Bridget brought a tidy dowry to the marriage. George immediately set about enlarging the house at Temple Sowerby, which must have felt gloomy and old-fashioned. If his aspirations or his budget had been greater, he might have opted to pull the whole thing down and start again from scratch; instead he tacked on a symmetrical front extension built of brick, two storeys high and five bays wide. The new front door opened into a double-height hall; to either side was a well-proportioned reception room, and on the floor above were two commodious bedrooms. The old and new parts of the house connected to each other via a narrow corridor. The extra living space would soon prove its worth, but from an architectural point of view the overall effect was clumsy. It was as though two very different houses were huddled too close together, each treading on the other's toes.

While George supervised a succession of bricklayers, carpenters, plasterers and painters at Temple Sowerby over the spring and summer of 1758, Bridget stayed at Wolsingham, where she greatly missed her warm-hearted husband. George soon made a favourable impression among the Maughans' circle in Wolsingham by sending over some leather to help a struggling cobbler. 'He was stunned and could not tell how to express his gratitude and I hear says he never had so much given in his Life,' Bridget reported back. 'In short my Dear George has made a poor Family happy which is to me a greater pleasure than I can express, much more so than when you tell me you have Wainscoted the parlour to Oblidge me.'[24]

By the autumn, the house at Temple Sowerby was habitable. Newly installed as its mistress, Bridget duly received and then returned social calls from all the neighbours, which necessitated much sipping of tea. Such proprieties were especially tiring for her now that she was in the early stages of pregnancy. In mid-November, George wrote to sister-in-law Jenny at Wolsingham to say that while Bridget was well and cheerful, she was so busy completing her local visits before winter set in that she hoped her mother would forgive the lack of a letter that week.

In January 1759, the entire Atkinson family converged on Temple Sowerby to celebrate the feast of Twelfth Night. Matthew, who was George's partner at the tannery, had picked up a cask of West Indian tamarinds for Bridget at Whitehaven on his way back from a business trip to Dublin. Richard had come up from London, stopping off to meet sister Margaret (a woman of almost suffocating piety) and her husband George Taylor at Bowes in County Durham; the three of them had travelled together the last thirty miles over the desolate pass at Stainmore and down into the Eden valley. Two hours after the arrival of the Bowes contingent, Bridget wrote to Jenny with a pithy assessment of her youngest brother-in-law, whom she was meeting for the first time: 'Dicky is a very Smart Youth.'[25]

Over the winter Bridget kept Jenny occupied making baby clothes. 'As I knew you were very busy working for me,' Bridget wrote in late January, 'I shall say nothing about your not answering my Letter. I fancy you will be at a Loss for directions about the Little things. The Long Lawn I intend for skirts and some ordinary caps which you may border with what Leaves of the Cambrick of which you may make six caps, four Laced ones of the fine and two plain ones of the coarse. You need be in no hurry as I hope if all be well we shan't want them before May.'[26]

A boy was born in June 1759, but would die in infancy. A second child followed in February 1761, a girl called Dorothy. Two weeks after his daughter's arrival, George sent off a bulletin to Jenny, reporting on the happy progress of Bridget and 'her little Dolly'.[27] Alas, at this point in the narrative, the family correspondence dries up, a drought that would last more than a decade. To state the obvious: for old letters to provide the basis for a story, they need not only to have been written, but also to have been preserved. Now that George and Bridget were living under the same roof, they no longer had reason to write to one another; meanwhile most of the extended Atkinson family were in regular contact with each other in or around Temple Sowerby. Richard's communications from London were rare and wondrous happenings. 'I am glad that you have heard from Brother Richard,' wrote Margaret to eldest sister Jane on such an occasion. 'I think you are highly favoured.'[28]

As for the Maughan side of the family, they were touched by tragedy. Jenny never got over her forced separation from James Graham, and his death three years later – he left her his gold watch – further lowered her spirits. She died at Temple Sowerby in January 1762, at the age of twenty-five – a melancholy event that deprived Bridget of her only sibling and closest correspondent.

THREE

Atlantic Empire

LONDON IN THE 1760s. From the ashes of the great fire a century earlier had risen a sprawling metropolis of three-quarters of a million people; the gabled timber houses which kindled the devastation had been replaced by flat-fronted terraces of fireproof brick, while stone edifices such as the Mansion House trumpeted mercantile prestige on an imperial scale. The Lord Mayor was chosen each year from among the twenty-six aldermen of the City of London, an ancient office held in 1762 by William Beckford, the inconceivably wealthy owner of three thousand slaves in Jamaica.

London was a filthy place, notable for its pall of coal smoke that smeared the sky and caught in the back of the throat. Pedestrians took care to avoid treading in the contents of chamber pots strewn across the cobbles. 'Except in the two or three streets which have very lately been well paved,' observed a Frenchman visiting in 1765, 'the best hung and richest coaches are in point of ease as bad as carts; whether this be owing to the tossing occasioned at every step by the inequality of the pavement, or to the continual danger of being splashed if all the windows are not kept constantly up.'[1] The back alleys of the city clanked and clattered with the workshops of craftsmen – bootmakers, cabinet-makers, confectioners, cutlers, gunsmiths, haberdashers, hatters, mercers, milliners, perfumers, printers, saddlers, silversmiths, sword-cutters, tailors, watchmakers, wigmakers – while glass-fronted emporia lined its main thoroughfares.

'The shops in the Strand, Fleet-street, Cheapside, &c. are the most striking objects that London can offer to the eye of a stranger,' wrote the same Frenchman. 'They make a most splendid show, greatly superior to any thing of the kind at Paris.'[2]

Driving London's prosperity was trade, underpinned by the Navigation Acts. The first of these laws had been passed during the 1650s, to challenge Dutch commercial dominance, but they had since grown into the regulatory system that governed Britain's trade with the rest of the world. The guiding purpose of the Navigation Acts was to keep the benefits of trade within the empire, and they enshrined the basic principle that raw materials produced in the colonies, such as sugar, cotton and tobacco, could only be conveyed to Britain or another of her colonies in a British ship, while all foreign-produced goods bound for America or the West Indies had to be shipped first to Britain to be taxed, then carried onwards in a British ship. It was axiomatic that the role of the colonies was to generate wealth for the mother country.

The privileged status conferred upon British shipping by the Navigation Acts gave rise to a mighty merchant fleet; and nowhere was its strength more visible than on the four-mile stretch of the River Thames from London Bridge downstream as far as Deptford. In summer months the 'Upper Pool' near the Tower of London resembled a dense forest of masts, and it was often remarked that you might walk from one side of the river to the other, stepping from deck to deck.

On the north bank of the Thames stood the Custom House, the portal through which so much of the nation's taxable wealth passed in the form of sugar, coffee and indigo from the West Indies; tobacco, rice and cotton from America; timber, hemp and iron from the Baltic; and tea, silk and porcelain from China. The busiest period, from May to September, was marked by the arrival of hundreds of West Indiaman ships, heavy with muscovado sugar that would first be processed in one of the capital's eighty refineries, then stirred into the tea on which everyone was so hooked; there was often such a backlog that a cargo might sit around for two months before

The crowded quays fronting the Custom House.

clearing customs. Meanwhile, in the maze of streets behind the quays, hundreds of clerks sat hunched over ledgers in the dim light of their masters' counting houses, totting everything up.

Which is where young Richard Atkinson, albeit tentatively, enters the frame. Even by the standards of the day, his employer Samuel Touchet was a ruthless capitalist – not that this word had yet entered the lexicon. The eldest son of Manchester's wealthiest manufacturer of linen and cotton goods, Touchet had moved to London in the 1730s to gain better access to the market for the commodities needed by his family firm. The Touchets were early investors in Lewis Paul's roller-spinning machine, whose operation required so little skill that anyone would be capable of spinning 'after a few minutes' teaching', as the 1738 patent application boasted – 'even children of five or six years of age'.[3] During the late 1740s, Samuel Touchet was responsible for importing more than a tenth of England's raw cotton, and rivals suspected him of attempting to create a monopoly; by 1751, he and his three brothers together owned about twenty ships, some of which plied the infamous 'triangular' trade.

*

THE ROYAL AFRICAN COMPANY had been established under charter from Charles II in 1672, with the purpose of setting up trading posts and factories along the Gold Coast – modern-day Ghana – and exploiting the continent's ready supply of gold and slaves. By the 1750s, Britain had eclipsed Portugal to secure dominance in the slave trade; every year during that decade, British ships carried about 25,000 enslaved Africans across the Atlantic, destined for the colonies of the West Indies and the American mainland. The 'African trade' was largely accepted as a necessary evil; the economist Malachy Postlethwayt declared it to be of 'such essential and allowed Concernment to the Wealth and Naval Power of Great Britain, that it would be as impertinent to take up your Time in expatiating on that Subject as in declaiming on the common Benefits of Air and Sun-shine'.[4]

Brightly dyed, striped and checked cotton textiles, like those made by the Touchets in Manchester, were in great demand in West Africa. Indian fabrics were the benchmark against which all others were judged, but knock-off versions were fast gaining market share, and the Touchets' were among the best. (British manufacturers continued to use the Indian names – *calico* and *chintz* would enter the English language.) As Thomas Melvil, the governor of Cape Coast Castle, the principal British slave trading post on the Gold Coast, informed the Company of Merchants Trading to Africa in August 1754: 'If the Ashantee Paths open the Goods wanted will be Guns, Gunpowder, Pewter Basons, Brass Pans, Knives, Iron, Cowries, Silks. The Bejutapauts will go out. Of these Touchet's are here preferred to India.'[5]

At the same time, while merchants in Liverpool, Bristol or elsewhere packed their vessels with goods to be bartered for human cargo, West African men, women and children snatched from inland villages were marched to European forts on the coast, to be sold by their captors on to a Danish, Dutch, French, Portuguese or (most likely) British slave ship. It might take a ship's captain weeks, or even months, to purchase enough human cargo to fill its hold; two Africans per ton (bearing in mind that in shipping terms, tonnage

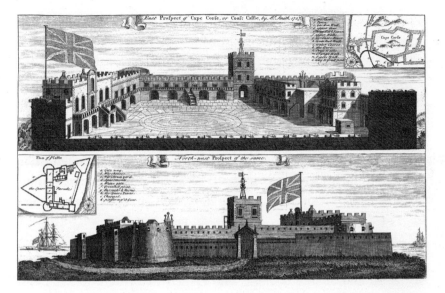

Cape Coast Castle, the main British slave trading fort on the Gold Coast.

is a measure of volume) was considered the 'right' load. The trans-atlantic leg of the voyage – known as the 'middle passage' – lasted around two months, and never was so much suffering crammed into so little space. Shackled and naked in the stifling heat of the ship's belly, unable to relieve themselves except on the bare boards where they lay, rolling in blood, vomit, excrement and urine, occupying less space than a coffin, it is hardly surprising that many captives sought to end their own lives. Some tried drowning themselves, others refusing food; but it was dehydration, caused by a water ration of just one pint a day, hastened by sickness and dysentery, that would prove most deadly of all. The crew simply tossed the corpses over the side without giving them a second thought. Roughly one in ten Africans died during the middle passage.

On arrival in the Americas, the survivors were prepared for sale. Their dark skin was slathered with a mixture of gunpowder, lemon juice and palm oil, then polished with a brush, to create the illusion of glistening good health. Grey hair was either shaved off or dyed black. The backsides of those suffering from dysentery were bunged with oakum, the tarred fibre used for filling gaps between timbers in wooden ships. Human cargoes were often sold by the method known as a 'scramble', in which the Africans were taken to a merchant's yard, the gates were suddenly thrown open, and the buyers rushed in, grabbing hold of their prey 'with all the ferocity of brutes'.[6] At this point, families were often separated for ever. Afterwards, the newly purchased men, women and children were branded with the initials of their master or estate, and assigned 'slave names' to strip them of their previous identities; the men were often given names of generals or gods from classical antiquity, such as Apollo, Brutus, Cupid, Hannibal, Jupiter and Ulysses, as if to mock their degraded state.

Once the ship's decks had been swabbed, then loaded up with sugar, coffee, tobacco and other commodities, it was ready to make the third side of the triangle, and return to Britain, to start this appalling cycle all over again. A triangular slave voyage typically lasted around eighteen months. The export of manufactured goods to West Africa, then the purchase of the labour with which to produce the raw materials, then the import of those raw materials from the Americas – as a business model, the diabolical logic of the triangular trade could hardly be faulted. Archive records indicate that ships owned by Samuel Touchet and his brothers took part in at least four triangular slave voyages. The first three vessels sailed to the Gold Coast between 1753 and 1757; there they embarked a total of 541 Africans, subsequently disembarking 455 in Jamaica.[7] The statistics of the Touchets' fourth voyage mark it out as a catastrophic venture. The *Favourite* sailed from Liverpool in January 1760, taking on board seven hundred Africans at Malembo in what is now Angola; by the time of its arrival at the sugar island of Guadeloupe the following January, only four hundred were still alive.[8]

TRADE AND WAR have always been energetic bedfellows. During the global conflicts of the eighteenth century, ministers regularly consulted merchants for their superior knowledge of distant lands, as well as their practical experience of shipping and finance. Meanwhile, for the business community, war represented opportunity. One manifestation of this murky symbiosis between merchants and ministers was privateering, an activity considered by some to be 'but one remove from pirates'.[9] At least two of Samuel Touchet's vessels carried 'letters of marque' – the licences granted by the Admiralty to British merchant ships, permitting them to seize vessels belonging to enemy subjects. One of Touchet's ships, the *Friendship*, was about to sail to the West Indies when it received its letter of marque in October 1756, shortly after the start of the Seven Years' War; the weaponry allocated to its crew of forty men included 'sixteen Carriage Guns, thirty six Small Arms, thirty six Cutlaus, twenty five Barrels of Powder, thirty Pounds of great shot and about fifteen hundred weight of small shot'.[10]

But Touchet had his eye on altogether greater spoils. He and a fellow merchant, Thomas Cumming, cooked up an audacious, secret scheme to invade the French colony of Senegal, fitting out and arming five ships at a personal cost of more than £10,000. Touchet's ships sailed from separate English ports on 23 February 1758 and rendezvoused at the Canaries; from here, by previous arrangement with his friend Admiral Anson, First Lord of the Admiralty, they continued in convoy with three warships. A bar at the mouth of the Senegal River proved impassable to the naval vessels, but Touchet's merchant flotilla landed two hundred marines and covered their march eleven miles upriver to Fort Saint-Louis. The French capitulated on 1 May. The adventurers returned laden with booty, including 400 tons of gum arabic – the sap of the acacia tree – a product essential in the printing of linens and calicoes, for which British textile manufacturers had previously been forced to pay premium rates.

So where, you might be wondering, has Richard Atkinson been all this time? There he is in the background, absorbing the rudiments of his trade; conversing with brokers and dealers at the Royal Exchange, or 'Change, the most cosmopolitan spot on earth; frequenting coffee houses, chiefly the Jamaica for West Indian business, Jonathan's for stocks and commodities, and Lloyd's for shipbroking and insurance; supervising the unloading of cargoes down at the

Some places well known to the young Richard Atkinson.

quays; and generating reams of correspondence. Sadly, little evidence of Richard's personal life has survived from his twenties. I imagine he was less raffish than his contemporary, James Boswell, who left behind a journal of his first extended stint in London that is replete with tales of encounters with writers and prostitutes – yet this is pure supposition on my part. It's ironic and not a little frustrating that Richard, whose professional life was taken up with the meticulous recording of the smallest details, should have proved so mysterious in his private affairs – but happily, this would soon change.

We might infer that Richard attempted to smooth off the rough edges of his northern diction, for in May 1761 he attended a series of talks given by the Irish actor Thomas Sheridan, held at Hickford's Concert Room on Brewer Street, on the subject of elocution. Sheridan, who was the godson of Jonathan Swift, not only advocated the 'polite pronunciation' of the court, but believed that regional dialects carried 'some degree of disgrace' about them.[11] 'The letter R,' he declared, 'is very indistinctly pronounced by many; nay in several of the Northern counties of England, there are scarce any of the inhabitants, who can pronounce it at all. Yet it would be strange to suppose, that all those people, should be so unfortunately distinguished, from the rest of the natives of this island, as to be born with any peculiar defect in their organs.'[12] The price of admission – one guinea – included an 'elegant Edition' of the lectures in a single quarto volume, and Richard's name is listed (as are those of 'Mr. Francis Baring' and 'James Boswall, Esq') among the book's six hundred or so subscribers.[13]

At the general election in the spring of 1761, Samuel Touchet was elected MP for Shaftesbury. Weeks later, a financial crisis almost engulfed him. As the merchant Joseph Watkins wrote to the prime minister, the Duke of Newcastle, on 28 May 1761: 'Private credit is at an entire stand in the City, and the great houses are tumbling down one after the other, poor Touchet stopped yesterday & God knows where this will end.'[14] Touchet's merchant house ultimately came crashing down in October 1763, with debts of more than £300,000.

After Francis Baring's apprenticeship expired in November 1762, he went on to set up a London office for his family firm. Business was precarious at first, and his mother Elizabeth, alarmed by his speculations, counselled him to 'let Mr. Touchet's example of grasping at too much and not being contented with a very handsome profit which he might have had without running such enormous risks, be a warning to you'.[15] Richard Atkinson, on the other hand, helped wind up Touchet's affairs – a task he was said to have performed 'with great ability' – before taking up a position as a clerk to the West India merchant Hutchison Mure, who was based at Nicholas Lane, off Lombard Street.[16]

SAMUEL FOOTE'S COMEDY, *The Patron*, opened at London's Haymarket Theatre in June 1764. It featured Sir Peter Pepperpot, a West Indian plantation owner with an 'over-grown fortune', drooling at the thought of a 'glorious cargo of turtle' and dreaming of a girl as 'sweet as sugar-cane, strait as a bamboo, and her teeth as white as a negro's'.[17] Such men were ripe targets for satire – although they usually had the last laugh, for their money bought them land, status and power.

Richard Atkinson's new boss, Hutchison Mure, was one of those men who sought to convert the base metal of their West Indian fortunes into the gilded trappings of the landed aristocracy. Hailing from the younger branch of a well-connected Renfrewshire family, Mure had come to London in the 1730s. After a short spell as a cabinet-maker, he entered the West India trade, having acquired some Jamaican property through his marriage. Soon, by his mid-thirties, he had made enough money to purchase the Great Saxham estate in Suffolk. His growing portfolio of Jamaican properties, meanwhile, included one called Saxham, after his English country seat, and another called Caldwell, after the Mure ancestral home in Scotland.

It seems that Mure, who is listed in the *Register of Ships* for 1764 as the owner of eighteen vessels, was an enthusiastic participant in the slave trade. Between 1762 and 1766, over the course of eight voyages, 2,959 Africans embarked on the middle passage aboard his ships, and 2,527 disembarked in the West Indies, all but 521 of them landing in Jamaica.[18]

The first of these voyages was the anomaly, in that it diverted at the last moment to Cuba, which on 14 August 1762 had fallen temporarily into British hands; Mure's ship, the *Africa*, landed its human cargo at Havana on 18 October. Two months later, presumably feeling flush from the profits that would follow, Mure commissioned Robert Adam to design a new house for him at Great Saxham. Adam dreamt up a vast Palladian villa with a *piano nobile* featuring a suite of rectangular, square, circular and octagonal state rooms – the plans are kept at Sir John Soane's Museum, and they are magnificent. For reasons unknown, however, Mure's palazzo never made it off the drawing board; instead he settled for the lesser option of incorporating some Adam interior designs into the old Jacobean house.

Now in his mid-fifties, Mure hoped to retire from active trade and live out the rest of his days in rusticated splendour. He was a practical man, and fascinated by agriculture; the philosopher David Hume, an old family friend, described Mure as 'a Gentleman of a very mechanical Head', as well as 'one of the most judicious Farmers and Improvers' to be found in the eastern counties.[19] And so his West India merchant house required a succession plan. Although one of Mure's three sons, Robert, was already a partner, he lacked the flair to head such an operation; but Richard Atkinson might just be the man for the job. In 1766, aged twenty-seven, Richard became Hutchison and Robert Mure's junior partner.

Mure, Son & Atkinson, as the new partnership would be known, began in the wake of the Seven Years' War, when Britain was for the first time the truly dominant global power. An almost indecent number of colonial territories had been seized from France and Spain during that conflict – to the extent that Lord Bute, the prime minister, realized that concessions would be necessary to avoid a peace so humiliating to the losers that they would soon be spoiling for another fight. The question was, which of the captured colonies should Britain keep, and which ones should be given back? The debate – on which much journalistic ink was expended – focused mainly on the relative merits of Canada versus the islands of Guadeloupe and Martinique.

The argument for holding on to the tiny West Indian territories and ditching Canada was obvious to most people – Guadeloupe's exports alone were worth twenty times more than the fur trade of 'barren' Canada. 'What does a few hats signify, compared with that article of luxury, sugar,' sniffed one gentleman.[20] But the West India lobby, not enjoying the competition provided by the former French islands – the wholesale sugar price had fallen 20 per cent since their capture – pushed hard for their restoration to their previous owners. The American colonists favoured the same outcome, albeit for different reasons. Benjamin Franklin, the agent of the Pennsylvania Assembly in London, wrote:

> By subduing and retaining Canada, our present possessions in
> *America*, are secured; our planters will no longer be massacred
> by the *Indians*, who depending absolutely on us for what are
> now become the necessaries of life to them, guns, powder,
> hatchets, knives, and cloathing; and having no other *Europeans*
> near, that can either supply them, or instigate them against us;
> there is no doubt of their being always disposed, if we treat
> them with common justice, to live in perpetual peace with us.[21]

In the end, the colonists prevailed. Under the Treaty of Paris, which came into effect on 10 February 1763, Guadeloupe and Martinique went back to France, while Cuba was returned to Spain; Britain held on to Canada, Florida and the sugar islands of Grenada, Saint Vincent, Dominica and Tobago.

The Seven Years' War had started in America, escalating out of all imaginable proportions from skirmishes in the Ohio valley between colonists loyal to the British flag and an alliance of French settlers and Native American tribes. Victorious Britain now found itself mired in a national debt of historic proportions, and unable to afford adequate protection for its newly acquired American territory, as was soon proved by a series of Native American attacks on

British forts and settlements to the south of the Great Lakes. As a result, in October 1763, George III issued a proclamation forbidding colonial settlement beyond a line drawn along the Appalachian watershed – much to the fury of land speculators who were intent on expropriating Indian territory.

Lord Bute resigned from the premiership after less than a year; George Grenville, who was said by the king to have the 'mind of a clerk in a counting-house', took over as prime minister and set about putting the nation's finances in order.[22] It would only be fair, he argued, for American colonists to help pay for the troops needed to defend the newly enlarged empire; while each Briton contributed about twenty-six shillings to the imperial coffers every year, each American gave about a shilling.

But American colonists always made a point of challenging the mother country's efforts to squeeze money out of them. The only revenue-raising taxes to which they would readily agree were those voted by their local assembly, while the only 'external' taxes remotely palatable to them were those used to regulate the trade of the British empire in its entirety, such as the import duties that fell within the Navigation Acts. Yet the Americans had signally failed to enforce the Molasses Act of 1733, which aimed through a duty of six pence per gallon to make molasses from the French West Indies prohibitively expensive, and thus tie the rum distillers of New England to the produce of the British sugar islands.

Grenville reckoned that if this duty were cut, making it cheaper to import French molasses legally than to pay the bribes and run the risks that attended smuggling, it would have the counter-intuitive effect of raising revenue; and so parliament voted to halve the tax on foreign molasses, to three pence per gallon, from April 1764. The Sugar Act sparked outrage in America. 'There is not a man on the continent of America,' fumed Nathaniel Weare, the comptroller of customs in Massachusetts, 'who does not consider the Sugar Act, as far as it concerns molasses, as a sacrifice made of the northern Colonies, to the superior interest in Parliament of the West Indies.'[23] A writer in Rhode Island's *Providence Gazette* ranted that

American interests had been trampled by a 'few dirty specks, the sugar islands'.[24] Their common hatred of the Sugar Act united the New England colonies for perhaps the first time, and set them on a collision course with the mother country.

BRITANNIA RULED the waves, for the time being, and her navy patrolled the waters of the North Atlantic and Caribbean, watching for French and Spanish attempts to violate her citizens' interests. To give one trivial example, tensions had long festered over British loggers' claims to the timber in the Spanish-held territory of Honduras. It is amid such rumblings that Richard Atkinson makes a fleeting appearance, in the earliest letter that I have found in his hand, dated 29 June 1764. He writes to the Secretary to the Treasury, Charles Jenkinson, with information from the merchant grapevine: 'As any Intelligence concerning the Bay of Honduras will I presume be acceptable I take the Liberty to send you an Extract of a Letter from the Same Hand as the former . . .'[25] The letter may not make for stirring reading, but it proves that Richard was already cultivating contacts at the very highest political level.

Meanwhile, George Grenville announced a new tax on the American and West Indian colonies. A stamp duty – such as had existed in the mother country since 1694 – would be payable on a range of paper items, from almanacs, newspapers and playing cards to conveyances, diplomas, leases, licences and wills. Each colony would appoint its own stamp distributor, who would take a small cut of the proceeds, but otherwise the tax would be largely self-regulating, since without its stamp any official document would be null and void. The bill passed through the House of Commons 'almost without debate'. Only Colonel Isaac Barré, a fearless orator whose left eye had been shot out during the capture of Quebec five years earlier, punctured the chamber's complacency with a 'vehement harangue' in which he argued that the very reason the colonists had emigrated to America was to flee such measures.[26] The king gave his assent to the Stamp Act on 22 March 1765. No one could have predicted its consequences.

Resistance erupted in Boston on 14 August, when the newly appointed stamp distributor for Massachusetts was hanged in effigy from the 'Liberty Tree'. It was unsurprising that the Bostonians should be foremost among the 'Sons of Liberty' – who took their name from a phrase used by Colonel Barré – since theirs was a literate and litigious mercantile community upon which the duty would weigh heavily.

By the time the Stamp Act came into force on 1 November, it was clear that the Americans' refusal to accept the duty would have a disastrous effect on trade, since without legally stamped port clearance papers their merchant ships might be seized at any time. Relations between the American and West Indian merchant communities were already frayed; now the mainland contingent resolved to cut off trade with all those sugar islands that submitted to the Stamp Act. The Jamaicans were the most acquiescent of all – they paid more stamp duty than all the other colonies put together. One Canadian newspaper, reporting an outbreak of yellow fever in Jamaica towards the end of 1765, quipped that 'the Inhabitants of the Town of Kingston fed so voraciously on the stamps, that not less than 300 of them alone died in the Month of November'.[27]

Although the Jamaicans certainly disliked the Stamp Act, pragmatism deterred them from rejecting it. Whereas the mainland assemblies resented being asked to pay for their own defence, the Jamaican Assembly actively volunteered a financial contribution, at the same time lobbying for an enhanced military presence on their island. The British sugar islands were surrounded by French and Spanish territories, and common sense dictated that these old enemies would soon seek to avenge their humiliation in the Seven Years' War. Most of all, however, the planters feared attacks from within. As the ratio of blacks to whites increased on the islands – in Jamaica it was roughly ten to one – so did the danger of slave insurrections. In November 1765, as the Stamp Act started to bite, an uprising broke out in the parish of St Mary, on the north side of the island; although it was soon quashed, it must have concentrated the colonists' minds.

Six prime ministers would hold office during the 1760s. The Marquess of Rockingham, replacing Grenville, adopted a more conciliatory tone towards the Americans – but it would be William Pitt's denunciation of the Stamp Act which finally persuaded Rockingham that repeal was the only way out of the crisis. Over three weeks, from 28 January 1766, a committee of the whole House considered the proposed repeal bill, with a succession of merchants coming forward to describe the negative impact of the Stamp Act on both sides of the Atlantic. The star witness was the 'celebrated electric philosopher' Benjamin Franklin, as the minutes describe him – his experiments concerning the nature of lightning had made him one of the scientific establishment's most venerated figures. Before 1763, Franklin testified, there had always been 'affection' among Americans for the mother country; but recently he had begun to be 'Doubtfull of their Temper'.[28]

Early on the morning of 21 February, MPs started bagging seats in the House of Commons in anticipation of the afternoon's debate. Pitt warned that parliament's failure to repeal the Stamp Act would lead to civil war, and cause the king 'to dip the royal ermine in the blood of his British subjects in America'.[29] For the time being, His Majesty's robes remained snowy-white; for both houses passed the repeal bill, along with a face-saving 'declaratory bill' that asserted parliament's right in principle to tax the colonies, and the king gave his assent on 18 March. American and West Indian merchant ships moored on the River Thames marked the news by hoisting their colours and blasting off their guns.

THE AMERICANS HAD MANAGED to overturn one piece of hated legislation; now they took aim at the Sugar Act. On 10 March 1766, at a gathering of colonial merchants held at the King's Arms Tavern in Westminster, the West Indian contingent agreed that the three pence duty that Americans paid on foreign-produced molasses could drop to a single penny. This was a massive climbdown on the West Indians' part; and yet, to their great dismay, when the American Duties Act passed into law in June 1766, it imposed a penny per

At its 'funeral', the Stamp Act is taken in a tiny coffin to a burial vault reserved for especially detested laws.

gallon duty on *all* molasses imported into the mainland colonies, thus eliminating any advantage possessed by the British sugar islands over the French. These reforms were too technical to be of much public interest, but they marked a further cooling in relations between the colonial merchant lobbies. By now the West Indians wholly distrusted the Americans, believing them to be motivated by treacherous ambitions to trade freely with the French.

Until the 1760s, the West Indian interest in the City of London had been informally managed. The Society of West India Merchants emerged as a lobbying organization sometime during this decade; its precise origins are obscure, since the minutes taken at its meetings before 1769 no longer exist. Under its chairman, Beeston Long, the society usually met on the first Tuesday of the month at the London Tavern, a dining establishment on Bishopsgate Street; attendance ranged from three (a quorum) to many more when feelings about some issue were running high. As the merchants tucked into turtle flesh – these gentle beasts lived in the cellars, in tanks painted with tropical scenes to make them feel at home – they chewed over the concerns of their trade. According to parliamentary records,

Richard Atkinson was among a delegation from the society summoned by Alderman William Beckford to the House of Commons in May 1766 in a last-ditch attempt to steer the arguments around the American Duties Act in the West Indians' favour.[30] The society's records show that during the 1770s Richard attended around six meetings every year; unfortunately the minutes are so cursory, and so devoid of descriptive colour, that it is impossible to gain much sense of his contribution.

The association between a merchant house such as Mure, Son & Atkinson, and the West Indian planters it served, rested on mutual confidence – not least because an exchange of letters between London and Jamaica often took four months or more. The merchant conveyed a planter's sugar crop back to England and brokered its sale, taking a 2½ per cent cut of the proceeds. It also sourced and shipped out any tools, provisions and other items required for the smooth operation of the planter's estates, subject to a mark-up; it recruited his overseers and book-keepers, and arranged their outward passage; it acted as his banker, paying bills of exchange drawn on his account, and advancing credit whenever necessary; it even oversaw the education of his children and ran his shopping errands. In short, it took care of his every need in the mother country.

But it was not quite a relationship of equals. So long as his account remained in credit, the planter maintained a degree of control; as soon as his expenses exceeded his remittances, however, the merchant gained the upper hand. The sheer precariousness of the sugar business – where hurricane, drought or rebellion could wipe out the year's produce at a stroke – drove many proprietors deep into debt, as what started out as modest loans ballooned into unsustainable mortgages secured against their property. The merchant could foreclose whenever he chose, and many men, including Hutchison Mure, were guilty of seizing clients' estates by this means.

John Tharp, who owned a number of estates in north-west Jamaica, retained Mure, Son & Atkinson as his London agents from 1765 to 1772. A cache of the firm's letters sent to Tharp's plantation house in St James Parish has survived, heavily watermarked and discoloured from years of storage in the tropics. Most of the correspondence is in Richard's handwriting, and it is illuminating about the seasonal rhythm of the West India trade and the volatility of the sugar market. The cane crop was cut and processed during the early months of the year. Gradually, over the summer, merchant ships returning from the West Indies appeared in the Thames, weighed down with their sticky cargo; if too many ships came at once, the glut drove down the price of sugar, while a scarcity early or late in the season pushed it upwards. The letters stamped on the large hogshead barrels in which the sugar was transported identified the estate on which it had been produced; its quality could be highly variable. 'Those of the Mark PP were much better than those of the same Mark last Year,' Richard wrote to Tharp on 13 July 1767, 'for these were only *very brown*, those of last Year were *black*.'[31] ('PP' signified Pantre Pant, a plantation that was managed by Tharp in the parish of Trelawny.)

Each autumn, Mure, Son & Atkinson sourced John Tharp's plantation 'necessaries' and other domestic goods, which were shipped out to Jamaica once the hurricane season had safely passed. In December 1767, in time for Christmas, the enslaved population of Tharp's estates were lucky enough to receive 1,107 yards of coarse Osnaburg linen and the needles with which to stitch the cloth into garments; meanwhile, for the master and his wife, there were tailored frock coats with gold buttons and braid, kid mittens, a 'very Neat Demi peak Sadle with red morrocco Skirts and doe Skin Seat neatly stitched stirups Leathers & Girths', a pair of brass pistols, a 'Copper Tea Kitchin with 2 heaters', twelve canisters of hyson tea, a 'Gadroon'd Cruit frame', a case of pickles containing 'Capers Girkins Olives Mangoes Mustard Oil Soy Wallnutt French beans Colly flower Anchovies', a hogshead of claret, casks of lavender and rose water, a selection of wallpapers, fine grey hair powder, guitar strings and the score of the *Beggar's Opera*.[32]

NO CENSUS EXISTS to permit more than a guess at how many black people were living in London at this time. 'The practice of importing Negroe servants into these kingdoms is said to be already a grievance that requires a remedy,' reported the *Gentleman's Magazine* in 1764, 'and yet it is every day encouraged, insomuch that the number in this metropolis only, is supposed to be near 20,000.'[33] This figure seems likely to have been an overestimate, but not wildly so. Among the wealthy, black servants had cachet, while black children were often treated as toys, to be returned to the colonies once they grew up or their owners tired of them. Samuel Johnson – who was more enlightened about these matters than most – famously employed a black manservant, Francis Barber, to whom he would leave the residue of his estate.

In clarification of the Navigation Acts' requirement that all merchandise must be transported to and from the colonies in British ships, the Solicitor General had ruled in 1677 that 'negroes ought to be esteemed goods and commodities' under the law.[34] But while the institution of slavery was woven into the fabric of colonial law, its status was not so certain in the mother country. According to one famous Elizabethan ruling, England was 'too pure an Air for Slaves to breath in', and many contradictory opinions had since been offered up.[35] In 1749, Lord Chancellor Hardwicke pronounced that a slave in England was 'as much property as any other thing'; whereas in 1762, Lord Chancellor Henley declared that 'as soon as a man sets foot on English ground he is free'.[36] It seems baffling that such men, the greatest legal minds of their time, could be so changeable in their judgements on a question that could surely be seen as none other than the choice between right and wrong.

In September 1767, David Laird, the captain of one of Mure, Son & Atkinson's ships, the *Thames*, was caught up in a dispute arising from the ambiguous status of a human 'commodity' destined for Jamaica. The episode had its origins two years earlier, however, when Granville Sharp, a clerk in the ordnance department based at Tower Hill, found a young black man of about sixteen injured outside the Mincing Lane premises of his brother William Sharp, a surgeon well known for treating the poor. It seemed that David Lisle, a lawyer who had brought the youth – whose name was

Jonathan Strong – from Barbados, had beaten him with a pistol so repeatedly that he had almost lost his sight and could hardly walk. William Sharp had Strong admitted to St Bartholomew's Hospital; Granville Sharp later found work for him as the delivery boy for an apothecary on Fenchurch Street.

One day during the summer of 1767, Lisle spotted Strong by accident and tricked him into entering a public house. There, backed up by two burly officials, he sold him to James Kerr, a sugar planter who was one of Mure, Son & Atkinson's clients. Kerr insisted he would only pay the £30 purchase price once Strong was securely on board the *Thames*, which was then preparing to sail for Jamaica. In the meantime the young man was thrown into the Poultry Compter, one of several small prisons dotted about the City. It was from here that, on 12 September, Granville Sharp received Jonathan Strong's letter begging for help.

Sharp called upon Sir Robert Kite, the Lord Mayor, in his capacity as London's chief magistrate, and requested that all those with an interest in Strong should argue their claims in open court. At the hearing on 18 September, Captain Laird and James Kerr's lawyer both insisted that the young man belonged to Kerr by virtue of a signed bill of sale. After heated debate, Kite stated that 'the lad had not stolen any thing, and was not guilty of any offence, and was therefore at liberty to go away'. Laird immediately grabbed Strong by the arm, saying that 'he took him as the *property* of Mr. Kerr', whereupon Sharp threatened to have him arrested for assault. Laird released Strong's arm, and all parties left the courtroom, including Strong, 'no one daring to touch him'.[37] Kerr subsequently pursued a court action against Sharp, seeking damages for the loss of his property; he persevered with the suit through eight legal terms before it was dismissed.

The thought that right here, on the streets of London, black people could have been lawfully snatched, sold and transported against their will to the colonies, seems almost unfathomable today; but such was the reality of the Atlantic empire. This particular incident was noteworthy only in that it galvanized the man who would come to be seen as the father of the anti-slavery campaign, twenty years before Wilberforce and Clarkson took up the cause. Granville Sharp subsequently became a formidable expert in habeas corpus, and his book, *A Representation of the Injustice and Dangerous Tendency of Tolerating Slavery*, would be the first major work of its kind by a British author. Which is how, in a blink-and-you-missed-it kind of way, Richard Atkinson came to be a bystander at the dawn of the abolition movement.

FOUR

Four Dice

THIS WAS AN AGE of polymaths, a time when gifted amateurs made strides in the fields of astronomy, botany, chemistry, mechanics and physics. Two of Richard Atkinson's closest friends in the early 1770s were George Fordyce and John Bentinck, both Fellows of the Royal Society, founded in 1660 for the purpose of 'improving natural knowledge'. Fordyce, a physician and lecturer in chemistry at St Thomas's Hospital, was also a member of Samuel Johnson's Literary Club, where his shambolic manner inspired various anecdotes. On one occasion, following a bibulous dinner, Fordyce was supposedly called out to attend to a fine lady. Unable to locate her pulse, he muttered under his breath 'Drunk, by God!'; the next day he received a letter from his patient containing £100, begging him not to disclose the intoxicated state in which he had found her. Bentinck, a naval captain, was also a skilled engineer, best known for developing a ship's pump that became standard issue throughout the Royal Navy. Some believed him underrated; Benjamin Franklin thought his 'ingenious Inventions' had not always 'met with the Countenance they merited'.[1] Captain Bentinck would die in his thirties, in 1775 – Richard was his executor.

Robert Erskine was another engineer who was much in Richard's orbit around this time. He had moved to London from Edinburgh in the mid-1750s, and for six years had used Hutchison Mure's premises as his postal address in the capital. Erskine's talents as an inventor seem to have been offset by bad luck in his financial dealings; in 1762 he was briefly committed to the debtors' prison. Soon afterwards he began work on a new pump, calling it the 'Centrifugal Hydraulic Engine'.[2] Only two were ever sold – one to the Venetian ambassador and the other for use in a salt mine belonging to the King of Prussia – and when Erskine fell out with an investor over their losses, Richard and his friend Captain Bentinck stepped in as arbitrators. Subsequently Erskine set up as a surveyor with a particular expertise in hydraulics, and established a practice at Scotland Yard in Westminster. By 1770, the year that he published 'A Dissertation on the Rivers and Tides, to Demonstrate in General the Effects of Bridges, Cuttings, or Imbankments, and particularly to Investigate the Consequence of such Works, on the River Thames', he had acquired some impressive clients, and his luck – like the tide – seemed to be turning.

Richard, however, had other plans for Erskine. Since 1765, Mure, Son & Atkinson had been part-owners of an ironworks at Ringwood, New Jersey, about forty miles north-west of New York. This enterprise had started at great tilt a few years earlier under its founder, Peter Hasenclever; by the summer of 1766 its assets included four blast furnaces, seven forges, ten bridges, thirteen mill ponds and more than two hundred workers' dwellings. Before long, Hasenclever had run through the £54,000 capital he had raised in England to fund the venture. He returned to London in November 1766 after learning that one of his partners had declared bankruptcy. In May 1767 Richard Atkinson was appointed a trustee of the business; Hasenclever was demoted to the position of agent, and soon resigned in disgust.

Following Hasenclever's departure, the ironworks struggled. The trustees' monthly letters of instruction to Reade & Yates of Wall Street, their New York agents, carrying Richard's signature as the managing partner in London, are a sorry catalogue of setbacks. Disobeyed instructions, delayed shipments, impatient creditors and accounting discrepancies – such are the perennial frustrations of long-distance business relationships. By January 1770 the trustees distrusted both the ironworks' managers, one of whom had been caught embezzling their money, and the other squandering it. 'An honest & a capable man is what we want,' they told Reade & Yates.[3] Robert Erskine answered such a description – but it is something of a mystery why he accepted Richard's invitation to cross the ocean to run a failing ironworks. Perhaps he perceived the American colonies as a place where he and his wife, who had recently lost their only child, might start again; maybe the salary of two hundred guineas, plus 5 per cent of the profits, was after years of financial troubles too powerful a lure to resist.

To remedy his lack of experience in the iron trade, Erskine gave himself a crash course in its practicalities during the autumn of 1770, when he spent two sodden months touring Britain's most prominent ironworks, including Coalbrookdale in Shropshire and the Carron Company in Stirlingshire. Often he turned up at sites unannounced, finding workmen more than happy to show him round in return for a few shillings. ('A very agreeable present to men who with families of 6 or 7 Children earned only 12s. a Week,' he would observe.)[4] Along the way, Erskine gathered dozens of lumps of iron ore which he boxed up and sent back to London for chemical analysis by George Fordyce.

Every few nights, by the guttering candlelight of his lodgings, he wrote a long letter to Richard in London, describing all he had seen; thirteen of these dispatches have survived, and they paint a vivid picture of iron production at the start of the industrial revolution, as the charcoal furnaces producing soft, malleable iron suitable for the blacksmith's forge were superseded by the hotter coke-burning furnaces of the coalfields. At Bersham in Denbighshire, for example, Erskine watched white-hot iron flowing from a furnace into the sand mould for one of fifty cannons ordered by the King of Morocco, protecting his eyes from the glare by 'Cutting a small hole in a letter and looking through it', and observed the barrel of another cannon being bored by a drill bit fixed to the axis of a water wheel, a procedure that 'made a very disagreeable noise which at a distance was much like that of Geese'.[5]

In late October, en route to Scotland, Erskine broke his journey at Temple Sowerby. During his stay, perhaps seeking respite from George and Bridget Atkinson's noisy brood, he worked out the height of Cross Fell, using his quadrant and a dish of mercury to provide a reflective 'false horizon'. It was a rare cloudless day. 'The Old Gentleman was so civil as to remain uncovered,' he told Richard, referring to the mountain, 'which was the more polite, as he had not been so long bare headed for many days before.' By Erskine's reckoning, Cross Fell stood 3,731 feet above the meadow by the bridge over the River Eden; while a benchmark chiselled into one of the quoins of Temple Sowerby church states the village itself to be 348¾ feet above sea level. He believed his measurement to be 'pritty accurate', but it turns out he was off by more than a thousand feet, for Cross Fell in fact stands 2,930 feet tall.[6]

During his final weeks in London, Erskine must have wondered whether he had made an error in accepting Richard's offer of employment, especially when turning down a commission from the Dean and Chapter of Westminster to survey their estates. In January 1771 he was elected a Fellow of the Royal Society; one of his nominees was Benjamin Franklin. Before sailing to America, Erskine wrote Richard a heartfelt note: 'I cannot have forgot the abject state to which I was reduced some years ago, nor can I ever fail calling to mind your kindness in suffering me to be a burthen to you. I am thus free in acknowledging my sentiments & obligations to prevent the most distant suspicion of ingratitude, which were it to rise in the bosom of such a friend would hurt me as much as anything I ever met with.'[7]

ALEXANDER FORDYCE was a banker well on his way to becoming one of the wealthiest men in the land; he was also the uncle of Richard's physician friend George Fordyce, although just six years separated the older man from his nephew. It was Alexander who, having witnessed the deft way in which Richard dealt with Samuel Touchet's unravelling affairs, had urged his associate Hutchison Mure to take on this impressive young clerk. Richard repaid the favour by offering Fordyce his unswerving loyalty.

Perhaps Fordyce saw something of himself in his protégé, for both men were the youngest children of provincial middle-class families. Fordyce had started out as the apprentice to an Aberdeen hosier, but soon leapt over the haberdasher's counter and moved to London, where he found work as the outdoor clerk to a well-known banker. He started gambling in the public funds and stocks, and made a small fortune in 1762, towards the end of the Seven Years' War, 'at the time of signing the preliminaries of the late peace, of which he gained intelligence before the generality of the bulls and bears at Jonathans'.[8] He was less risk-averse than his peers and, for a while, a good deal luckier.

By 1768, Fordyce was managing partner of Neale, James, Fordyce & Down of Threadneedle Street. It was said that his 'pride kept pace with the increase of his fortune', and when the firm moved to premises opposite the Bank of England, he insisted that his name should be listed first on the brass plate, even making hollow threats to terminate the partnership if his senior partners did not comply.[9] Fordyce stood for Colchester in the general election that year, and Richard canvassed alongside him for several weeks. After spending £14,000 on wooing the townsfolk – a lavish sum, even by the venal standards of the day – Fordyce lost by twenty-four votes, an outcome he attempted fruitlessly to reverse by raining down charges of bribery and corruption on his opponents. 'I really think we shall *force* the Mayor to return Mr. Fordyce,' wrote Richard from the battlefield, with characteristic vim.[10]

At the height of his pomp, Fordyce purchased a princely country house at Roehampton, nine miles south-west of London, filling it with fine furniture and works of art – Raphael cartoons and suchlike – that gave every appearance of riches and sophistication. He landscaped its spacious grounds, which adjoined Richmond Park, in the naturalistic style promoted by Lancelot 'Capability' Brown, felling an avenue of sixty mature elms using a contraption of Captain Bentinck's devising 'for drawing up trees by the roots' – after wrapping a long chain around the trunk, it took four men about twenty minutes to prise each tree from the earth.[11]

Now, to complete his ascent to the pinnacle of society, Fordyce was on the hunt for a suitably dazzling wife. His brother James, a Presbyterian minister, was courting the governess to the children of the newly widowed Countess of Balcarres. (James Fordyce's ponderous *Sermons to Young Women*, published in 1766, would later achieve dubious fame when Jane Austen had Mr Collins read them to the less-than-enthralled Bennet sisters.) Shortly after his brother's engagement, Alexander Fordyce called upon Lady Balcarres while passing through Edinburgh, and was struck by her second daughter, Lady Margaret Lindsay, an auburn-haired girl of fifteen. The countess, at first appalled by the thought of such a vulgar connection, was soon won round – the Lindsays were poor by aristocratic standards, and the pecuniary advantages of the match were obvious. (By supporting the Jacobite uprising of 1715, the third Earl of Balcarres had ended his days under house arrest, leaving his estates deep in debt.) Fordyce married his noble bride in June 1770 at her ancestral home on the Fifeshire coast; he was forty, she was seventeen. They set off for London the next day.

IT IS AT THIS POINT in the story that Richard Atkinson comes at last into sharper focus; because Lady Anne Lindsay, the elder sister of his patron's wife, was a dedicated lady of letters, and would go on to write about him at great length.

Anne Lindsay was a defiantly independent young woman who refused to conform to many of the conventions of submissive female behaviour. During her early years in Edinburgh, she had acquired a keen interest in literature and the arts, and a reputation as an accomplished conversationalist; she had also turned down a fair few proposals of marriage. She was thought very pretty, although perhaps not quite as arrestingly so as Margaret, from whom she had hitherto been inseparable. (The playwright Richard Brinsley Sheridan would call them 'Beauty's twin-sisters'.)[12]

Anne would later describe how, during the lonely months after Margaret's marriage, she daily climbed up to her little closet where, with pen in hand, she scribbled away 'poetically and in prose' in pursuit of 'artificial happiness'.[13] That winter Anne wrote a ballad that may have reflected her own ambivalent feelings about the state of matrimony. 'Auld Robin Grey' told the story of a simple country girl who, believing her true love to be dead at sea, marries an old man out of duty; a few weeks later her sweetheart returns from his unexpectedly long voyage. This bitter-sweet song would become famous – William Wordsworth called it one of the 'two best ballads, perhaps, of modern times' – although Anne was always reticent about revealing herself as its author.[14]

During the spring of 1771, when she was twenty, Anne left Scotland to take up residence with the Fordyces in London. After five days on the road, her carriage pulled up at a small door in Holywell Lane, a narrow street off Shoreditch. The Fordyces were away at the time, at their country house, and Anne was ushered into the drab apartment by servants. As first impressions go, this did not augur well; had she not known that her brother-in-law was in the midst of building a splendid mansion in Grosvenor Square, she later commented, she would have been mortified by these surroundings, which offered no clues of elegance, apart from a pair of beeswax candles on the table 'instead of the mutton-fats' she was accustomed to.[15] At noon the following day, Anne spied the Fordyces' coach with 'three well-powdered footmen behind it' pulling up outside the house; she ran downstairs, and the sisters tearfully embraced.[16]

She soon noticed a young man standing nearby, 'his arms crossed, and with an expression of benevolence, admiration, and what the French call bonté in his countenance'. From this moment on, Anne Lindsay and Richard Atkinson – who, at thirty-two, was twelve years her senior – would get along famously. She immediately felt him to be a 'sort of family friend', with whom she was on the same 'footing of ease' as if she had always known him: 'I was convinced I had done so, his countenance assured me of it; it was hearty, open, intelligent to the greatest degree, and it was impossible not to forgive the familiarity of his manners when ineffable good-humour and zeal was the basis.' Social deference was not one of Richard's habits. 'Zooks,' she recalled him saying, 'life is too short for bowing and scraping. When people esteem one another beforehand, it should make short work of the business of introduction.'[17]

Even so, an earl's daughter, arriving in London for the first time, was expected to observe certain formalities, foremost among them her presentation at court – it being reckoned 'improper' to be seen out in public until 'their Majesties had had the first glance'.[18] Until then, Anne had been quite innocent of the distinction drawn by fashionable people between 'the Man of the World and the Man of Business', but she now perceived the gulf dividing 'even the plain Country Gentleman' from the 'inhabitant of Cheapside'.[19] She also realized that her brother-in-law was a bore, and that the reason they did not receive many dinner invitations was because those who would have been delighted to welcome the sisters 'would not consent to pay the tax of his company for the *agrément* of ours'. The dinners hosted by the Fordyces were dreary affairs, generally attended by a 'few unpleasant men relieved only by the excellent Atkinson'. At one such gathering, Anne caught Richard gazing at her and Margaret with 'an expression that had an esteem and reverence in it, that I thought was almost accompanied with a sad feeling that such a pair should be no better associated'.[20]

DURING THE SPRING of 1772, Richard began to notice that Fordyce was preoccupied; on top of the 'hard bravery of manner and false spirits' that he habitually projected, a certain wildness in his behaviour suggested something was wrong.[21] When Richard voiced his concerns, Fordyce burst into tears and confessed to business problems, then tried to laugh them off. Pressed further, Fordyce revealed that only a miracle would prevent his bankruptcy.

Early on the morning of 9 June, Fordyce, without warning, told Margaret and Anne that they must leave town immediately; he then bundled them into the coach 'like frightened hares', slammed the door and ordered the coachman to deliver them to the country house at Roehampton.[22] That evening, he returned to Holywell Lane and packed up his papers. Richard stayed with him through the night. Fordyce left shortly after dawn, instructing his clerk to inform his partners that it was 'impracticable to carry on business'.[23] At noon on 10 June, the bank of Neale, James, Fordyce & Down stopped making payments.

While Fordyce lay low in an obscure corner of the city, Richard rushed to Roehampton. At about six o'clock he entered the parlour, finding Anne busy with her needles and silk; his face, she saw, was 'pale and haggard'.[24] He took her hand and was silent for a moment, before revealing that Fordyce was ruined, and that bailiffs would soon be arriving to take possession of the house. The sisters hurriedly stuffed their clothes into bed sheets and set out for London in two coaches, the second of which was full of dresses. Richard did his best to buoy their spirits, but Anne soon realized he was masking his own fears. When she asked whether he had been caught up in Fordyce's misfortunes, he replied 'no' with an agony that pierced her soul: 'I saw that ruin hung impending over his own head, and that he spared to Margaret at that moment the knowledge of what would have added to her distress.'[25] Fordyce's bachelor brother William, an eminent doctor, had offered the sisters sanctuary at his house in Sackville Street, off Piccadilly. In the gloaming of the physician's parlour, Richard at last explained what had led to this catastrophe.

During the Falklands crisis of 1770, when it had briefly seemed that a diplomatic standoff between Britain and Spain over those remote South Atlantic islands might lead to war, Fordyce had gambled heavily on the stock market, paying handsomely for inside information from secret negotiations that were taking place on the continent. The news with which his spy had set sail ought to have made him a fortune; but a thick fog descended at sea, forcing the ship into port for twenty-four hours. Fordyce lost his advantage, and instead incurred large losses. More recently, Fordyce had received letters from India, sent by the faster but less reliable overland route via Basra, Aleppo and Constantinople, describing events that were almost guaranteed to bring down the East India Company's stock price. He had quickly 'borrowed' an enormous quantity of stock and sold it short, intending to buy it back at a lower price and pocket the difference. But the stock price stubbornly refused to drop – instead it rose – so that when the day of settlement for Fordyce's transaction arrived, he had a 'difference of ten per cent to pay on half a million, some say, a million and a half, of India stock'.[26]

At the beginning of June 1772, the Bank of England, alarmed by a sudden decline in its gold reserves due to excessive demand from Scotland, announced that it would no longer accept many Scottish bills of exchange. These were the indispensable tools of credit of the time, pieces of paper on which one merchant made a promise to pay another a certain sum on a fixed date several months down the line. Bills of exchange were entirely transferable – they could be used by the recipient to pay a third party, or could be cashed sooner than the stated deadline, at a small discount, by a banker acting as a 'bill broker'. They kept the wheels of commerce turning; the economist Adam Smith would vividly describe the role of paper bills, in providing a substitute for gold and silver coin, as 'a sort of waggon-way through the air'.[27] Since much of the business of Neale, James, Fordyce & Down was with Scottish accounts, Fordyce could no longer obtain funds to cover his liabilities, and his opulent façade crumbled to dust.

RICHARD VISITED THE SISTERS the next morning, bringing the latest news from the City; so far there had been five major bankruptcies, and many more were expected. For now, Mure, Son & Atkinson held firm – but so closely intertwined were the affairs of the mercantile community that it was impossible to say whether it would survive. Later that day the wife of one of Fordyce's partners, unhinged by her nine children's reduced prospects, cut her own throat with a razor.

By now Fordyce was universally reviled, especially since it was rumoured he had hidden large sums from his creditors. With many bailiffs out to take him into custody, it was decided that the following Sunday, 14 June, by the light of the full moon, he would ride down to a port on the south coast and slip away to France; for his ledgers were in such disarray that to open them up to scrutiny at this point would only further blacken his name. On the continent he would have time to smooth out any irregularities within his accounts; and then, within the three months' deadline imposed by the bankruptcy laws, he could return to London and face justice.

Fordyce had not seen his wife since before the crisis began, and a last visit was fixed for ten o'clock on the night of his departure. Margaret begged Richard to be present – both sisters had come to rely upon his support – but asked him to delay his arrival by half an hour so that Fordyce, who would doubtless be in great distress, might have time to compose himself. When Richard turned up at Sackville Street – tactfully late as requested – he found the sisters, as well as William and George Fordyce, anxiously waiting in the parlour. At last there was a hammering at the front door, and Alexander entered in a mood of such exuberance that 'had a cannon-ball swept us all low, the company would not have had their powers more annihilated than by his manner'. Watching Fordyce drain great bumpers of port, as though celebrating some triumph, Anne wondered whether he had been 'deranged by his misfortunes', but on balance thought not, for she could detect 'no phrenzy in his eyes'. Richard had noticed some 'ugly fellows' lurking on the street corner as he was arriving, and he went home just before midnight, wearing Fordyce's clothes to act as a decoy.[28] Fordyce himself departed several hours later, after arguing violently with his wife. Later that morning all were relieved to hear that he had left for Dover, taking £100 advanced by Richard to cover his expenses.

The crisis came to a head in London on 22 June. 'It is beyond the power of words to describe the general consternation of the metropolis at this instant,' reported the *Gentleman's Magazine*. 'The whole city was in an uproar; many of the first families in tears.'[29] The day started with the news that one of the City's greatest banks had stopped payment, having rashly accepted £100,000 worth of Scottish bills, and a false rumour was circulating that the Bank of England would soon follow suit. At the Adam brothers' ambitious Adelphi housing development near Charing Cross, where the largely Scots workforce were entertained by perambulating bagpipers, two thousand men were laid off.

Horace Walpole, the wittiest commentator of his day, offered a characteristically lively appraisal. 'Will you believe,' he wrote, 'that one rascally and extravagant banker had brought Britannia, Queen of the Indies, to the precipice of bankruptcy!' A story, repeated by Walpole, did the rounds that Fordyce had visited a Quaker banker, begging for a loan. 'I have known several persons ruined by *two dice*,' the old man was said to have replied, 'but I will not be ruined by *Four dice*.'[30]

Relative calm only returned to the London markets later in the week, after the Bank of England stepped in to offer credit to some of the City's most reputable merchants and financiers. But it would not prop up the Ayr Bank, a splashy new operation underwritten by two dukes – Queensberry and Buccleuch – which had over the

Alexander Fordyce, clutching a purse full of gold and a 'Scotch Bill' for £10,000.

previous three years pumped out some £200,000 in paper notes. The Ayr Bank stopped payments of coin for their notes on 25 June. 'We are here in a very melancholy Situation,' wrote David Hume, in Edinburgh, to Adam Smith, who was hard at work on *The Wealth of Nations*. 'The Carron Company is reeling, which is one of the greatest Calamities of the whole, as they gave Employment to near 10,000 People. Do these Events any-wise affect your Theory? Or will it occasion the revisal of any chapters?'[31]

LADY ERSKINE, a young widow with a highly developed sense of social decorum, took pity on the Lindsay sisters in the last week of June, and invited them to stay with her in Hanover Square. After breakfast on their first morning there, a 'visitor of considerable fashion' called on their hostess; a few minutes later, Richard's arrival was announced. The sisters squirmed with embarrassment. He clearly had no idea that an invitation from Lady Erskine might be necessary, or that he should at least have asked them to pave the way for his call by mentioning that he might wish to see them – such delicacies as these 'his heart would have scouted as the frippery of politeness'. As he strode across the drawing room to greet them, Anne noticed the reaction of their hostess. 'The chill of Lady Erskine's regard, I might say the contempt,' she recalled, 'might have driven all the warm blood of Atkinson's body into his heart, like the drop of brandy which is above all proof, had he perceived it; but he was not thinking about her, and was blind as a beetle.'[32]

Richard had come with the latest news from the City. Now that the worst was over, he said, it was time 'to bury the dead, and support those who have survived it'. Soon the first visitor left, and since Lady Erskine's frostiness had been 'only to mark to the other that he was not one of *her set*, being a citizen, and one of the people employed to stop if possible the fall of the Stocks', she was now perfectly civil towards him. 'Your Mr. Atkinson,' she remarked to the sisters after he had taken his leave, 'I really take to be a good creature.' Her loftiness vexed them; as Anne later wrote:

To have been angry would have placed us in the wrong; was he not a good creature? And the best of all good creatures? He was not a man of fashion. Why then be angry at Lady Erskine for calling him what he was? Because we wished her to respect him both on our account and his own, and she would not give a particle more than was barely due to him whom she esteemed *mauvais ton*, which was with her the greatest nuisance it was possible to bring into society. His smile, his bow, his method of walking straight down the throat of the person he talked to, all put her more out of temper than I thought her collected manner would have condescended to be.[33]

Soon afterwards, the Countess of Balcarres arrived to take her daughters home to Scotland. 'It was the kind Atkinson who had our last sorrowful look on departing,' Anne recalled. 'He stood at the door of the carriage as if he was losing his all for the first time.'[34] Before heading north, the sisters spent a month with their uncle in Hertfordshire. The summer had been hot and dry, and a haze of dust lingered over the fields. One day, as her stay was drawing to a close, Anne was taking a 'little melancholy walk' in a shrubbery that opened on to the road, when a carriage stopped and Richard jumped out: 'I screamed for joy, and ran up to him as to our good Angel, could one be supposed stepping out of a Post-chaise.' So busy had Richard been salvaging his own affairs that he had barely left his desk during the intervening weeks. Anne asked him how much the partnership of Mure, Son & Atkinson had lost. 'By everything I can guess,' he replied, 'the sum will be above two & forty thousand pounds.' When she wondered what proportion of this amount he was personally liable for, he grasped her hand. 'Such a part,' he said, 'as sweeps bare every foundation on which presumption might have dared to build her castle.'[35]

AFTER A SUMMER of speculation about the whereabouts of the rogue banker – 'Mr. Fordyce must be a most compleat Ubiquarian,' observed one newspaper, 'since he possesses the strange power, if we credit what the public prints assert, of his being almost at the same instant in Holland, Italy, France and England' – he returned on 6 September.[36] He was lucky to be alive. A mile off the coast at Rye, the cutter on which Fordyce was crossing had snagged a wreck, gouging a hole in its bottom; the leak was temporarily plugged by a barrel of salt beef, and he and his fellow passengers had been rescued by a passing boat.

At midday on 12 September, passing with difficulty through the crowd gathered to jeer at him, Fordyce entered Guildhall. For the first two hours of his bankruptcy hearing, a succession of debts were proved before the commissioners, including £16,000 to the Bank of England and £35,000 to Mure, Son & Atkinson. Then the creditors began to interrogate Fordyce, first wishing to know how much of their money he had absconded with – to which Fordyce tearfully responded that, far from this being true, he had been obliged 'to borrow a small trifle from a friend, to pay for a few pair of stockings which he had occasion for on his journey'.[37] Some of the creditors were suspicious of Richard's role, observing that Fordyce had transferred large sums of money into his account during the week leading up to 9 June; but Fordyce accounted for this, explaining that Richard was a 'particular friend' who had 'on emergencies, given him bills on the Bank, which he gave in payment to the Bank Clerks in the morning and refunded the money to Mr. Atkinson in the afternoon'.[38]

The commissioners proved compassionate; they even returned Fordyce's pocket watch and Margaret's jewellery. 'The benevolent temper of the English nation never appeared more strongly than at Mr. Fordyce's examination last Saturday,' reported the *London Chronicle*. 'Calumniated as he had been in all the public prints, the moment he shewed himself only intentionally upright, resentment gave way to commiseration; his misfortunes even added dignity to his character, and the very rabble grumbled pity.'[39]

After the trial, the contents of the Fordyce residences were sold off at auction. Richard purchased a pair of horses, which he presented to Margaret; another kind creditor bought back her carriage. The playwright Samuel Foote acquired a single pillow; on being asked what possible use he could have for such an item, he was said to have answered: 'Why, to tell you the truth, I do not sleep very well at night, and I am sure this must give me many a good nap, when the proprietor of it (though he *owed so much*) could sleep upon it.'[40] Foote's next production, a satire called *The Bankrupt*, would draw heavily on Fordyce's woes.

THE BANKING CRISIS of 1772 was short-lived, but its ill effects would soon ripple around the empire, bringing a spell of optimism in the Atlantic economy to a close. Many American merchants found themselves with warehouses full of goods imported from Britain, and debts they could no longer discharge. This, in turn, ruined many businesses in the mother country. One British politician would later observe that the long credit terms allowed to merchants in the colonies, and the difficulty of recovering debts from them, had 'made bankrupts of almost three-fourths of the merchants of London trading to America'.[41]

Despite Robert Erskine's best efforts, the ironworks at Ringwood continued to test Richard and his fellow trustees' patience, and they finally resolved to put it up for sale. Advertisements appeared in the *New-York Gazette* in September 1772, but there were no takers. Meanwhile they instructed their American agents to sell off their pig iron warehoused in New York 'as fast & as far' as possible, only to find that Reade & Yates, themselves in deep financial trouble, had been stockpiling it for use as a currency with which to settle their own bills. 'Had your object been to destroy us as a Company,' the trustees wrote in December 1772, 'you could not have held a Conduct more likely to effect your Purpose.'[42]

Richard would with hindsight look back on 1772 as a year of 'horrors'. On a personal level, he had been working towards a larger share of the partnership, which he had hoped might assist a cause as yet unarticulated, but extremely close to his heart. Alexander Fordyce's bankruptcy not only demolished Richard's 'castles in the air'. It also had consequences that would ultimately lead to a great diminution of the Atlantic empire.

FIVE

All the Tea in Boston

TWICE A YEAR, great auctions of tea and other luxurious goods took place at the headquarters of the East India Company in London. The Bank of England invariably granted the Company a short-term loan before each sale, to ease its cash flow as it waited for accounts to be settled – £300,000 was the sum advanced in the spring of 1772. But with many merchants unexpectedly strapped for funds that summer and unable to pay their bills, even the almighty East India Company was snared in the financial crisis. When the Company defaulted on a payment to the Treasury in August, its wobbling finances became public knowledge and its stock price started to slide; within weeks it had tumbled from £225 to £140. The collapse, of course, came too late for Alexander Fordyce; had he been able to hold out till then, as one journalist pointed out in late September, he would have made as much money 'as not only would have settled all his affairs, but have left an handsome fortune for life'.[1]

The East India Company's problems stemmed partly from the American public's widespread reluctance to consume its tea. Back in 1767, after the repeal of the Stamp Act, parliament had introduced taxes on various items – glass, paint, lead, paper and tea – imported into the colonies. While bearing a superficial resemblance to the taxes used to regulate the flow of trade throughout the British empire, the purpose of these so-called 'Townshend duties' (named after Chancellor of the Exchequer Charles Townshend, their originator) was to raise money for the Treasury, which made them quite as unpalatable to many colonists as the Stamp Act.

The Americans had retaliated against the duties with the powerful weapon of non-importation, which kept out around 40 per cent of British imports. Their tactic worked. In April 1770, shortly after Lord North became prime minister, all the duties were repealed, apart from the one on tea – which was kept in order to assert parliament's authority to raise tax from the colonies. After the subsequent collapse of the non-importation movement, goods from the mother country flooded the colonies. Even so, contraband Dutch tea continued to dominate the American market; less than a quarter of the tea consumed there came through legal British channels. By the end of 1772, there were said to be seventeen million pounds of surplus leaves rotting in the East India Company's warehouses around the City of London.

The British government had for some time wished to rein in the overbearing East India Company, and its financial woes provided Lord North with vital leverage. Through the Regulating Act, passed in June 1773, ministers gained some control over the management of India; in return, the Company was granted a loan of £1,400,000, as well as concessions to help reduce its tea mountain. Under the Tea Act, all duties previously charged on leaves imported to Britain and then re-exported to America were cancelled; the saving could be passed on to consumers. Suddenly, a pound of the Company's fully taxed tea cost Americans a penny less than the smuggled variety. Ministers were confident that the lower prices would persuade American consumers to swallow their pride, but they were quite wrong; the colonists saw the Tea Act for what it was, a clumsy attempt to trick them into accepting the Townshend duty and thus the principle of parliamentary taxation.

On 20 August 1773, Lord North and his Treasury Board issued a licence for the export of 600,000 pounds of tea to the ports of Boston, New York, Philadelphia and Charleston. The *Dartmouth*, laden with 114 chests of tea, entered Boston harbour on 28 November; from then its captain had twenty days to pay the duty on his

The 'Mohawks' empty the tea chests into Boston harbour.

cargo, or else the vessel would be impounded. Leading merchants of the town, insisting that the tea must be rejected, requested a special clearance to allow the ship to leave port without unloading its cargo – but the governor of Massachusetts, Thomas Hutchinson, declined to grant permission. Soon two more vessels filled with tea arrived from London and moored alongside the *Dartmouth*.

On 16 December, the day before the *Dartmouth*'s customs payment was due, a crowd of several thousand gathered to hear the ship's owner, a local merchant, reveal that Governor Hutchinson remained adamant in his refusal to let it depart. As the meeting broke up in the late afternoon, a number of men dressed as 'Aboriginal Natives', their faces blackened with coal dust, 'gave the War-Whoop', a pre-arranged signal to hurry to the three vessels.[2] Over several hours, by the light of lanterns, these self-styled 'Mohawks' smashed open 342 chests of tea and threw them overboard. Next morning, at high tide, the broken-up tea chests could be seen bobbing above a vast slick of briny sludge that stretched across the bay.

BRITISH PARLIAMENTARY ELECTIONS during the eighteenth century were notorious for their bribery, bullying and other skulduggery – sins which could undoubtedly be laid at the door of Sir James Lowther, who owned great tracts of Cumberland and Westmorland, and whose sense of entitlement was so inflated that he saw the parliamentary seats returned by those counties, and all the boroughs within, as his personal property.

Much more importantly – at least for the purposes of this story – John Robinson was Lowther's law agent, land steward and chief stooge. Born in 1727 the son of an Appleby draper, Robinson had been articled to his uncle Richard Wordsworth, attorney-at-law to the Lowther family, at the age of seventeen. Over the years he had upset numerous people while executing his employer's orders, and many blamed the 'dirty attorney of Appleby' for the baronet's obnoxious behaviour in general.[3]

Lackey though he may have been, John Robinson did not lack political ambitions of his own. In January 1764, he was returned through Lowther's influence as MP for the county of Westmorland. He would (at least in the beginning) faithfully support his patron's interests, while forging a close friendship with another of Lowther's men, Charles Jenkinson, the MP for Cockermouth, who was at that time Secretary to the Treasury. In 1765 Robinson acquired a long lease on the White House in Appleby, which he remodelled in Venetian style; its ogee-arched windows remain to this day an incongruously exotic feature of the town's handsome main street.

George Atkinson was only three years younger than Robinson, and they must have moved in overlapping local circles; so it seems likely that they were already well acquainted when, in 1769, George applied to Robinson to sponsor a parliamentary bill permitting the enclosure of the common at Temple Sowerby. Indeed, Robinson may have urged George to make the application – for the enclosure of common land was a well-worn method of forging political allegiances, through the creation of freeholders who would gain the franchise. George had hitherto been ineligible to vote, for what land he owned was held under a thousand-year lease from the lord of the manor, Sir William Dalston. It certainly served Sir James Lowther's interest to facilitate the enclosure at Temple Sowerby, for he was at the time tussling with the Duke of Portland for political supremacy in the area. Dalston, for one, detected mischief in the scheme. 'The Lowtherians Resentment is so great,' he told the duke, 'as to spirit up my Lease-hold Tenants of Temple Sowerby to the Honourable House of Commons against me, for liberty to take up a large Quantity of waiste Ground where I am Lord, without consulting or acquainting me with it, and directly against my Opinion.'[4]

John Robinson's focus shifted from Westmorland to Westminster in 1770, on his appointment as Secretary to the Treasury under Lord North. The new prime minister – whose courtesy title, as the heir to an earldom, meant that he sat in the Commons, not the Lords – was one of the warmest men in politics, with a quick wit and a nice line in self-deprecation. In his appearance, North cut a clumsy figure, of which Horace Walpole offered this uncharitable description: 'Two large prominent eyes that rolled about to no purpose (for he was utterly short-sighted), a wide mouth, thick lips, and inflated visage, gave him the air of a blind trumpeter.'[5]

Robinson had been warned that his post at the Treasury would involve 'a Sea of Troubles', and it certainly required the mastery of several briefs.[6] There was the nation's financial administration, which tied him up in correspondence with officials throughout the land; there were twice- or thrice-weekly Treasury Board meetings, chaired by Lord North, after which Robinson was responsible for issuing all the necessary orders, contracts and payments of money; and there was the role of chief whip in all but name, through which he managed the prime minister's parliamentary business. Although the Secretary to the Treasury operated behind the scenes, he wielded great influence.

In the spring of 1773, four years after George Atkinson's application, Robinson at last placed his private bill to enclose 'Temple Sowerby Moor' before parliament; royal assent was granted on 28 May.[7] Now the commissioners appointed to oversee the division of the common could get to work. The 360 acres were distributed between the heads of twenty-four households in Temple Sowerby, and the resulting fields demarcated with hawthorn saplings; the area was then mapped out on parchment and executed as a legal document. George, who bankrolled the process, was allotted fifteen acres in lieu of his expenses, taking his overall share of the land to fifty-one acres.

GEORGE III OPENED PARLIAMENT on 13 January 1774 with a 'gracious speech' outlining his government's priorities for the coming session.[8] News of the Boston 'tea party' arrived a week later, however, and the unruly state of the American colonies suddenly trumped all other concerns. On 29 January, the cabinet agreed that strong measures would be needed to bring the colonies back into line; as a result, the passing of a series of 'coercive' acts would occupy parliament over the coming months.

Lord North announced the measures that would be contained within the Boston Port Act on 14 March; the town's harbour would be shut up for business until its people had made 'full satisfaction' to the East India Company for the destruction of the tea.[9] The House of Commons almost unanimously welcomed the legislation; even Colonel Barré, a hero to the Sons of Liberty, gave it 'his hearty affirmative'.[10] Three more coercive acts were nodded through before the summer recess, one of which revoked Massachusetts' 1691 charter and restricted the people's right of assembly; another allowed the governor to move a trial to Britain if he believed a fair hearing was unlikely in the colony; and a third permitted uninhabited houses, outhouses and barns to be requisitioned as accommodation for British soldiers. Meanwhile a law extending the boundaries of Canada, and guaranteeing the free practice of Catholicism there, angered many Americans, who saw it as an assault on their territory and their faith.

The 'intolerable acts', as they soon became known throughout the thirteen colonies, turned hordes of wavering loyalists against the mother country. In New Jersey, Robert Erskine continued to enjoy a frank correspondence with Richard Atkinson – 'I write to you as a brother & as a friend, and it is a relief to give you my sentiments naked open & undisguised,' he wrote on one occasion – but from this time onwards, his tone is one of noticeable disaffection.[11] 'I have had a great deal too much business on my own hands to think of, much less to write on politicks till now,' he wrote in June 1774, 'but things draw fast to a Crisis if the news be Confirmed that an obsolete Act of Henry the VIII is to be extended to this Country whereby people obnoxious to the Governor here or Government at home may be transported for trial to Britain. I have no doubt that a total suspension of Commerse to and from Great Britain and the West Indies will Certainly take place.'[12]

THESE ILL WINDS from America did not entirely blow the domestic agenda off course during the parliamentary session of 1774. As the king had heralded back in January, his government introduced bold measures to improve the 'state of the gold coin', and not before time, because guinea, half-guinea and quarter-guinea coins had become so debased – through 'clipping' (filing metal from a coin's circumference) and 'sweating' (collecting metallic dust from coins shaken in a bag) – that they were on average one-tenth lighter than their legal weight.[13] The Recoinage Act passed on 10 May 1774; by a Royal Proclamation pinned to the door of every church in the land, the order went out that all 'light' gold should be passed over to the official collectors for the district. They would take it at face value, cut and deface it, and transport it to the Bank of England in London, returning with pristine coin of the correct weight. Over the following four years, gold coins worth £16,500,000 would be renewed by this process.

John Robinson ran the operation out of the Treasury in Whitehall, commissioning 130 local money changers and settling terms with them. It was necessary that they should be men of substance, since the payments they would make to those handing in defective coins would need to come out of their own coffers – they would be reimbursed for their services later. 'The Allowances are from a third to one per cent in lieu of all risque, trouble, loss of Interest and Expences,' Robinson told prospective changers.[14] He appointed

George and Matthew Atkinson to oversee the recoinage in West-morland; the county was so remote from the capital that he allowed them a special commission of 1¼ per cent on all the money they exchanged.[15]

Robinson's choice of the Atkinson brothers for his home county may have been rooted in old acquaintance, but they were also eminently qualified for the task, for banking had overtaken tanning to become their primary line of business. The difference between the two occupations was not so great as it might sound, for tanning was a capital-intensive trade, and large sums of money passed through the brothers' books. Moreover, they permitted their customers what would these days be considered excessively long payment terms – often a year or more – and it was a relatively small leap from providing credit to offering bank accounts.

During the early stages of the industrial revolution, when coin was often scarce, manufacturers regularly relied on brokers to convert the bills of exchange that they received for their goods into gold and silver with which they could pay their workers. Since the 1750s, George and Matthew Atkinson had been performing this service for the proprietors of Backbarrow ironworks, at the southern tip of Lake Windermere, where it was the custom to hold a grand payday at the feast of Candlemas. Every year, in January, the partners of the iron-works would make the eighty-mile round trip to Temple Sowerby to exchange paper bills for coin; the delegation generally consisted of at least half a dozen armed men, passing as it did through some truly desolate terrain. Towards the end of 1774, however, gold was in such universally short supply – £4,500,000 had been withdrawn from public circulation over the summer – that the Atkinson brothers' usual banking contacts in Newcastle and Glasgow could not provide the £14,000 in coin needed for the Backbarrow payday.

Over the autumn, George had conveyed several loads of 'light' gold – on two occasions, more than £20,000 – down to London to be recoined, and he now proposed to his friends at Backbarrow a scheme that would have to be kept secret. He wrote from Temple Sowerby:

The only method that we can think of to be on a certainty is to fetch about £8000 from London in this way – that two of your people must come here the 29th day of January with all the bills that have come to your hands then, and they shall have £4000 home with them next day. And I will go off in that night, fly to London, get there on Wednesday night, stay Thursday and Friday to get the bills discounted, and set out on Saturday or Sunday morning and be here on the 8th or 9th with as much as will make your payments easy. The only objection to this plan is the short days and dark moon, and to balance that we will take 4 days to come down instead of 3 which was our limited time last August, and after one is 60 or 80 miles from London the danger of robbery is over.[16]

Such a mission entailed a good deal of risk, for the lonely roads surrounding the capital were haunted by highwaymen legendary for their brazenness; only two months earlier the prime minister had himself been held up at gunpoint and relieved of his pocket watch and a few guineas.

LORD NORTH CALLED a general election in September 1774, six months sooner than strictly necessary, for it made sense to get this business out of the way – a 'Continental Congress' had recently assembled at Philadelphia to debate the colonies' collective response to the 'intolerable acts', and trouble was looming. John Robinson assisted the prime minister with the purchase of seats for those men whose presence in the House of Commons the ministry deemed necessary. (With patrons of 'pocket boroughs' demanding around £3,000 per seat, the Treasury spent nearly £50,000.) Sir James Lowther, having quarrelled with Robinson, chose to represent Westmorland himself – George Atkinson, as a newly minted free-holder of the county, dutifully awarded Lowther his vote.[17] Robinson secured a Treasury-sponsored seat at Harwich in Essex.

Twelve of the thirteen American colonies, all apart from Geor-gia, sent delegates to the First Continental Congress; the sibling territories had not always agreed, but their anger towards the mother country now bound them together. 'The Oliverian spirit in New England is effectually roused and diffuses over the whole Continent,' Robert Erskine wrote to Richard Atkinson on 5 October. 'The rulers at home have gone too too too far: the Boston Port Bill would have been very deficient of digestion, but Altering Charters, the due course of justice & the Canada Bill are emitents which cannot possibly be swallowed and must be thrown up again.'[18]

Congress published its resolutions on 20 October. The import of any goods from Britain, and sugar, coffee or pimento from the British West Indies, would be banned almost immediately, and no American goods would be sent to Britain or the West Indies after 10 September 1775 unless the coercive acts were repealed. On its final day, Congress issued a 'loyal address' to the king, listing its grievances in carefully deferential language; but since His Majesty viewed Congress as an illegal body and the imperial relationship as non-negotiable, he did not see fit to dignify the petition with a response.

The West India lobby took particular fright at the resolutions of Congress, since sugar planters looked to the American colonies for much of the basic food on which their enslaved workforce subsisted. On 18 January 1775, more than two hundred men gathered at the London Tavern to discuss what to do next; Richard was present, and he argued firmly (but with little effect) against a proposal to send parliament a petition warning of the calamity threatened by the resolutions, pointing out that since it 'was only meant to recommend to the consideration of Parliament, what Parliament would certainly consider of themselves, it was a futile measure'.[19] His assertion would be proved correct. The government, inundated with merchants' entreaties on the subject, set up a special panel for their assessment, which was dubbed the 'Committee of Oblivion'. It was two months before the West Indians' petition reached the top of the pile; by this time the ministers had already made the policy decisions that the petitioners had been hoping to influence.

It was alarming that West Indian planters should rely so much upon American grain and rice, and crucial that a substitute for these starchy crops was found – one that would grow on the islands. Thus, in March 1775, the Society of West India Merchants announced the reward of £100 for anyone who brought 'from any part of the World, a plant of the true Bread Fruit Tree, in a thriving Vegetation, properly certified to be of the best sort of that Fruit'.[20] Captain Cook had enthused about this plant after visiting Tahiti five years earlier. 'The fruit is about the size and shape of a child's head,' he had written, a rather unsettling description. 'It must be roasted before it is eaten, being first divided into three or four parts: its taste is insipid, with a slight sweetness somewhat resembling that of the crumb of wheaten-bread mixed with a Jerusalem artichoke.'[21]

BOSTON, THE HUB OF colonial discontent, remained calm for the time being. 'The winter has passed over without any great Bickerings between the Inhabitants of this town and His Majesty's Troops,' General Thomas Gage reported to Lord Dartmouth, the Colonial Secretary, on 28 March 1775.[22] Two weeks later, though, Gage received orders from Dartmouth to use force in disarming any rebels. Before dawn on 19 April, seven hundred soldiers marched from Boston to seize a stockpile of weapons from the village of Concord, some seventeen miles away. The mission was meant to be secret, but everyone living along the route had somehow been alerted. At Lexington, a skirmish blew up between redcoats and rebel militia that left eight local men dead. By the time the British reached Concord, the colonists' stash was no longer in evidence; and as they withdrew, a running battle started that continued all the way back to Boston. Harassed by crossfire, about 250 redcoats were either killed or wounded, versus ninety rebel casualties.

These clashes signalled a new escalation of the conflict. Within days, an army of fifteen thousand rebel volunteers had mustered to block access to the peninsula on which Boston was built, and where the British were garrisoned. On 3 May, Robert Erskine informed his employers in London that he had received an application for gunpowder from the 'principal people of the County of Borgen in the Jerseys, in which your Iron Works are situated', and that these men were forming a militia to defend themselves against the British. He no longer believed that a reconciliation between America and the mother country was possible – unless, that is, 'Blood seals the Contract'.[23]

Congress convened again at Philadelphia on 10 May; among the delegates was Benjamin Franklin, recently returned from London. On 14 June Congress voted to establish its own fighting force – the 'American Continental Army' – and appointed George Washington, a wealthy Virginia planter, as its commander-in-chief. Meanwhile at Boston, on 17 June, a British force led by General William Howe attacked the Charlestown peninsula – the closest promontory across the water from the town – and captured it from rebels occupying Bunker Hill. This was a tactical victory for the British, for it secured control of Boston harbour, but a Pyrrhic one, too, with more than a thousand redcoats dead or wounded – twice the casualties of their opponents. Only recently, ministers had sneered at the 'raw, undisciplined, cowardly' colonists, but General Gage advised them to think again: 'The Tryals we have had shew that the Rebels are not the despicable Rabble too many have supposed them to be.'[24]

BY NOW, GAGE was finding it near impossible to obtain food for the eight thousand men under his command. 'All the ports from whence our supplies usually came,' he wrote to the Treasury on 19 May, 'have refused suffering any provision or necessary whatever to be shipped for the king's use.'[25] The Treasury was the Whitehall department with responsibility for army provisions; which is why Lord North, as First Lord of the Treasury (and therefore, according to convention, prime minister), needed to attend to the minutiae of feeding a garrison more than three thousand miles away. On 13 June the Treasury Board ordered their usual contractors to ship 4,000 barrels of salt pork, 6,000 barrels of flour and 1,000 firkins of butter to Boston.

News of the Battle of Bunker Hill reached London on 25 July; the following day, Lord North solemnly informed the king that the conflict had now grown 'to such a height, that it must be treated as a foreign war'.[26] At some point it must have dawned on the prime minister and his colleagues at the Treasury that if the soldiers cooped up at Boston were to remain healthy over the winter, they would need better than salt rations to sustain them; and yet, given the onset of the hurricane season, it was perilously late in the year to start planning the dispatch of fresh food supplies. At the Treasury, it fell to John Robinson to procure the shipping that would be needed for such an operation. He soon discovered that the army's most robust transport vessels had already left for America; meanwhile his next port of call, the London merchants who specialized in the America trade, refused to charter their ships to the Treasury, fearing the consequences for their colonial property if they were seen to be aiding the authorities. Sometime during August, it seems that Robinson sought Richard Atkinson's advice on this knotty problem. The partnership of Mure, Son & Atkinson had never undertaken government business before, but Richard readily offered his assistance.

On 8 September, Robinson confirmed that the Treasury wished to send large quantities of food and fuel to Boston before the arrival of winter; later that day, Richard attended Lord North at Downing Street, and offered to obtain and ship the necessary items. The prime minister agreed to his terms – a commission of 2½ per cent, as was the mercantile norm – with one notable exception. Given that the price of rum was almost as volatile as the spirit itself, Lord North preferred to fix its cost beforehand; so the two men agreed to use the price quoted in the standing contract for supplying the navy with rum in Jamaica, adding on the 'usual freight of 6 pence per gallon', and allowances of 4 per cent for insurance and 10 per cent for leakage.[27]

The rushed manner in which Lord North engaged Richard's services reflected the emergency. No contract was drawn up; no record of the agreement made it into the Treasury Board minutes.

Richard at once committed four of Mure, Son & Atkinson's vessels to the expedition, swaying fellow merchants to volunteer ships. These were the items on the prime minister's 'shopping list':

4375 Chaldron of Coals
468,750 Galls of Porter
2,000 Sheep
2,000 Hogs
Potatoes
Carrots
Sour Crout
Onions
Sallad Seed
Malt – a small Quantity for the Hospitall
Vinegar – a reasonable Quantity for six Months Consumption
20 Boxes of Tin Plates
33,320 Pounds Wt of Candles to be shipt from Cork
100,000 Gallons of Rum – to be sent from Jamaica next Spring
400 Hogsheads of Melasses – ditto[28]

The list was largely compiled through guesswork. 'We are busy sending out every Comfort & Conveniency for the Troops,' Robinson wrote to Charles Jenkinson on 19 September, 'but since Gen. Gage does not tell us anything they want or may be useful, we are obliged I may say to grope for it.'[29] The *Thames* set sail for Boston at the end of September, the first of thirty-six ships that would depart over the following two months as soon as their holds were packed and winds permitted. The captain of the *Thames*, David Laird, was not only one of Mure, Son & Atkinson's longest-serving employees – it was he who had eight years earlier been involved in the altercation over Jonathan Strong's fate – but was also known to General Howe, the new commander-in-chief of the British forces in America, both men having fought at the Battle of Havana back in 1762.

As is clear from his correspondence with General Howe, Richard took great pains to make sure the supplies arrived in optimum condition. Five hundred tons of potatoes were loaded gently into the ships 'so as not to bruise them', and onions were stored in hampers for the same reason. To guarantee the safe passage of livestock, Richard ordered generous pens to be built in the ships' tween decks. The Lincolnshire breed of sheep was chosen as fittest to undergo the voyage, in preparation for which the animals were kept on dry food for ten days before being taken on board; the pigs were the 'half fed kind from the Country & of a large Size, such as will pretty certainly get fat upon the Voyage, a Plentiful Stock of Beans & Water being provided for their Consumption'.[30] As a further incentive to take care of the animals, Richard offered the ships' captains a bonus of 2s 6d for each one they landed alive.

Scurvy, which we now know to be caused by a lack of vitamin C, was by no means limited to seafaring men; it often afflicted those subsisting on salt rations. Sauerkraut, or 'sour crout', was widely believed to be effective against the disease, and its main ingredient, cabbage, was just then coming into season. Richard planned to send up to 300 tons of the stuff out to America. 'We are informed that in general the Sailors have disliked it at first & afterwards grown extremely fond of it,' he told General Howe. 'This first dislike may we hope be lessened by our having left Juniper berries & Spices out of the composition which appear to contribute nothing to its Preservation.' Normally, it would be unwise to seal and ship casks of sauerkraut during its six-week fermentation period, as they were likely to rupture – but such obstacles did not faze Richard. 'We have caused Valves to be made (which cost a mere Trifle) to fix in the Bungs of the Casks which Valves being kept down by a Spiral Spring strong enough to resist any thing that can happen in rolling the Cask, will at the same time give way to a Pressure far less than sufficient to burst it & so let out the expanded air,' he explained to Howe. 'By this means we shall be able to ship the Sour Krout within a week or ten days of gathering the Cabbage.'[31]

John Robinson kept the king updated on the progress of the Boston expedition. 'Mr. Robinson,' starts one of his memoranda, 'has the Honour to send, by Lord North's Directions, for His

Majesty's Inspection, two Casks of Sour Crout, put up with Valves, in the same Manner as the Casks shipped for America; and also one of the Valves – The Cask marked No. 1 has been sometime made and may be nearly fit for use, that marked No. 2 is at present in a state of Strong Fermentation.'[32] No detail affecting the comfort of His Majesty's troops was beneath royal scrutiny.

All the while, the press provided a sardonic commentary on these goings-on. 'One person has contracted for several thousand cabbages at 3d. each, which, were they brought to market at home, would barely fetch half that price,' reported the *Evening Advertiser* on 5 October. 'It is computed, that, by the time the above sheep and hogs arrive at the places of their destination, they will stand the government (or rather the public) in no less than *two shillings* per pound, bones included, which occasioned a Wag to remark, that the Ministry have brought their pigs to a *fine market*.'[33]

DURING THE SUMMER of 1775, Congress ordered all able-bodied men to form into companies of militia – an edict that presented Robert Erskine with a headache, for he knew that were his forgemen, carpenters and blacksmiths to enlist in different units from each other, production at the ironworks would soon seize up. He therefore applied to the New Jersey Congress for permission to raise his own company of foot soldiers, and gained his captain's commission in mid-August.

Erskine explained the situation in his next letter to Richard, neglecting to mention that the owners of the ironworks would bear the cost of the muskets, bayonets, flints, powder and shot with which their employees would, if necessary, fight the British. He also expressed his disappointment at not having received a personal letter from Richard for the best part of a year: 'You would add greatly to my satisfaction were you to favour me oftener with a few lines directly from yourself – I know, my Dear Sir, the multiplicity of your engagements and that you have no time to throw away in letters of mere Compliments – but I cannot help wishing to hear from you were it ever so short, especially since I heard of your bad state of health.'[34] (This is the earliest mention I have found of Richard's fragile constitution.)

It was not long before Erskine faced a crisis at the ironworks, after the London-based proprietors decided they would no longer honour his bills drawn on them. With little coin circulating in New Jersey, Erskine started dipping into his stock of iron – 'a commodity which neither fire nor vermin can destroy' – to settle with tradesmen.[35] As he informed Richard on 6 December:

> I have between 6 & 700 Ton of pig & 20 & 30 Tons Bar at the Works and expect to make 50 more before the frost sets in. I have no reason to despair, it gives me some satisfaction to tell you so, because I have no doubt it will give you pleasure. I know it would pain you to see anyone in distress, much more one who has had so many proofs of your regard – Distress did I say? Oh my country! To what art thou Driving – this gives me poignant distress indeed. How long will madness and infatuation Continue?[36]

The first four ships of Richard's provisioning fleet limped into Boston harbour on 19 December, with the *Thames* at their head, having experienced atrocious storms during the twelve-week crossing. On 31 December, General Howe wrote to John Robinson with a description of the cargoes of the nine ships so far arrived. The supplies of porter, malt, vinegar, salad seed and sauerkraut had held up well, but most of the potatoes had putrefied in the heat of the hold. Only forty out of 550 sheep and seventy-four out of 290 pigs had landed alive; their pens had proved too spacious, and they had repeatedly been 'thrown upon one another by the Violent motion of the Ship'.[37] Most of the carcasses were too badly crushed to be fit for consumption and had been thrown overboard.

The expedition's goal had been to bring home comforts to the besieged garrison over the winter, but it proved an abject failure. A foot of snow had fallen in Boston on Christmas Eve, and fuel was in such short supply that Howe authorized the scrapping of old wharves, houses and ships for firewood. The general would be forced to place his troops on short rations in mid-January 1776. In the end, just twenty-four of the thirty-six provisioning ships made it to Boston, including seven stragglers that arrived too late for their rotting cargoes to be unloaded, since by then the garrison was on the point of departure. (The remaining twelve ships were forced 'by Stress of Weather' to put into Antigua for essential repairs.)[38]

On the morning of 5 March, Howe discovered that Washington's Continental Army had, overnight, occupied the Dorchester Heights, a lofty no-man's-land across the water. Twenty American cannons now pointed towards Boston. The next ten days saw the packing up of the British garrison. Any ordnance that could not be carried away was destroyed or dumped in the sea; seventy-nine horses and 358 tons of hay were also left behind.[39] On 17 March, with the arrival of a fair wind, 120 ships carrying more than ten thousand troops and loyalists set sail for Halifax, Nova Scotia.

SIX

The Rum Contracts

AN ARMY THAT LACKS a strong supply of food, clothing and shelter will be fatally weakened; and yet military historians have often ignored the behind-the-scenes contribution of those working to provide these necessities. As Professor Arthur Bowler, one of the few academics to have studied the logistical minutiae of the American conflict, has written: 'Since human society began, minstrels and historians have told over and again the exploits of men on the field of battle while condemning to limbo by the process of neglect the more prosaic activities of contractors, commissaries, quartermasters, subtlers, and administrators generally.'[1] Presumably these story-tellers have considered the deeds of such people to be too boringly deficient in that stirring narrative quality, jeopardy, to merit their attention – but what greater jeopardy could there be than knowing that a vast army, struggling to save an empire on the other side of a wide ocean, looks to you for its every need? This was the burden that Richard Atkinson would bear for the next six years.

By the start of 1776, it was clear that the redcoat army fighting the American rebels would have to be almost entirely provisioned from home. The shortcomings of the system by which the Admiralty was the government department with responsibility for shipping the troops out to America, while it fell to the Treasury to organize the delivery of their supplies, were perfectly obvious – but the Navy Board categorically refused to offer assistance.

Custom dictated that each British soldier in the field received the same basic ration: one pound of bread and either one pound of salted beef or nine ounces of salted pork every day, plus items issued on a weekly basis, typically eight ounces of rice or oatmeal, six ounces of butter or cheese and three pints of pease. On 9 February, the Treasury Board settled terms with six merchant syndicates who would between them, over the following year, supply provisions for 36,000 men in America and 12,000 men in Canada, at a cost of 5¼d for each daily ration. Richard was the managing partner of the group that won the contract to feed the army in Canada.

Two weeks later, the Treasury agreed to engage Mure, Son & Atkinson to 'take up a sufficient Quantity of Shipping to carry the Provisions ordered from Time to Time by this Board for the Supply of the Forces in America'.[2] The individual contractors would arrange for supplies to be taken to Cork, on Ireland's south coast, where under the direction of a Treasury commissary they would be loaded into ships chartered by Mure, Son & Atkinson. The provisions would be sent to America in quarterly batches, with ships making two return crossings every year; that, anyhow, was the theory.

During the spring of 1776, the Treasury Board and the Navy Board – which was preparing to take 27,000 infantry, plus a cavalry regiment and 950 horses, out to America – were in fierce competition for the limited pool of merchant shipping that was available to hire. By the end of April, Richard had succeeded in chartering fifty-two ships on the Treasury's behalf; but then the Navy Board, urgently needing vessels to carry horses, unilaterally hiked the previously fixed hire rate of 11s to 12s 6d per ton per day. This placed Richard, who was still obliged to offer the lower rate, at a serious disadvantage, and over the next six weeks he managed to charter only nine more ships. On 12 June Richard expressed his concerns at a meeting between Lord North and Lord Sandwich, First Lord of the Admiralty; afterwards the Treasury Board put up its rate to 12s 6d, while the Navy Board dropped its rate back down to 11s. The manoeuvre enabled Richard to hire seventy-six more vessels over the next seven weeks, although merchant shipping was so scarce by then that he was forced to cast around in ports as distant as Amsterdam and Hamburg.

Once chartered, the Treasury required Mure, Son & Atkinson to have the merchant ships armed 'in due Proportion to their Burthen', meaning that a large number of cannons in a variety of sizes had to be found at short notice.[3] Thus (to give two examples) the *Locke*, an ex-East Indiaman of 685 tons' capacity, was furnished with twenty nine-pounder and six four-pounder cannons, while the *Lyon*, a vessel of 170 tons from the port of Leith, was fitted with ten two-pounders and eight swivel guns. 'You are already, Sir, apprized of the Disappointment we have met with in Guns,' Richard wrote to John Robinson at the Treasury. 'This has driven us to ransack this Town and its Environs for light six Pounders.'[4]

Although rum did not fall within the standard army ration, it was still considered essential. It provided warmth on cold nights; it made bad water drinkable; it offered relief from pain; and it prevented wounds from turning septic. On 2 May, the Treasury Board settled terms with five West India merchants, each of whom was to supply 100,000 gallons of rum from the sugar island with which he was closely connected. Richard's tender for Jamaican rum was the winning bid for that colony. Each island distilled its rum to a different strength, and Jamaican rum was most potent of all – a distinction which did not, however, quite account for the discrepancy between the 5s 3d per gallon that the Treasury agreed to pay Richard, and the 3s secured by a Barbados merchant. The suspicion that Richard had negotiated an outrageously good deal for himself by underhand means would follow him around like a bad smell for the rest of his days.

THE ABSENCE OF any surviving letters between Richard and his siblings at Temple Sowerby has left a glaring gap in the family correspondence, and I have little sense of the dynamic that existed between them. But they were by no means estranged. George Atkinson saw his youngest brother quite often during the mid-1770s, when his duties as the Treasury's money changer in Westmorland regularly took him to the capital; the task of replacing the nation's defective gold coinage would take four years to complete.

As for Bridget, who we last met in 1762 – it's fair to say she had been far from idle, not only having given birth to ten children (two of whom died in infancy), but also running the family house and farm. During the late 1760s, Bridget and George had taken the lease on one of Lord Thanet's new farms across the river at Whinfell; it was just as well that she did not mind getting her hands dirty, for it was a condition of the tenancy that the land should be cleared, and she often came home reeking of gorse smoke.[5] (One lucky day, while turning over an old rabbit warren, Bridget's plough unearthed a gold 'fede-ring' brooch – two pairs of arms joined together with clasped hands, with a devout message in raised letters on the sleeves – that dated back to the fourteenth century, when Whinfell had been a deer park belonging to the great Clifford family.) Bridget abhorred waste of any kind, and made a point of planting apple trees in the corners of her fields where the plough could not reach – it became a kind of signature of her occupancy. The topographer William Hutchinson, who toured the northern counties in 1774, observed the Atkinsons' farm approvingly. 'We then passed Whinfield Park,' he wrote, 'where we had the pleasure of viewing a large tract of ground, lately enclosed from the park, and growing corn. There is not any thing can give greater satisfaction to the eye of the traveller,

The gold brooch that was ploughed up on Bridget's farm.

than to behold cultivation and industry stretching their paces over the heath and waste, the forest and the chase – population must follow, and riches ensue.'[6]

So far as I know, Bridget only visited London twice – and her second visit, as an old woman, would be a miserable business. The first time, in May 1776, when she was forty-three, George brought her down with him after the weaning of their final child. George returned to Westmorland a week later; Bridget, on the other hand, decided to stay put until her husband came back with another consignment of 'light' gold. It was, in fact, her brother-in-law Richard who urged her to remain in the capital, as Bridget explained in a letter to her eldest child, fifteen-year-old Dorothy:

> Your Uncle was not willing I should return with your Father.
> He purposed my seeing the King go to the House of Lords and
> two or three Little jaunts into the country. I have been foolish
> enough my Dear Dolly in buying you a peice of Checked
> Muslin for a Gown and also a peice of striped Lutestring for
> another it is not very fashionable but I got it cheap. I durst not
> sent your Hatt and cloak by your Father I am sure they would
> have been quite spoiled. I have almost spent all my Monny,
> many Temptations are here.[7]

Bridget must have spent a good deal of her 'Monny' on shells, for a cart would soon arrive at Temple Sowerby, delivering a box that contained, among other things, '54 pretty shells in a Bag & 4 mighty ugly ones loose'.[8] Her collection was acquiring a global dimension; her latest coup had been to persuade George Dixon, a Kirkoswald man who was appointed armourer of the *Discovery* on Captain Cook's third voyage, to keep an eye out for specimens. 'Hear is sum smal Qurosetes such as large Locusts, small spotted snakes, but no shells of any account,' Dixon would report from Cape Town on 24 November 1776. 'What is qureas I shall get, if our stay will Permit (but ounderstand we must sail on Wednesday first from this for New Zealand, in the South Sees).'[9]

Shortly after returning from London, Bridget would oversee the 'inocolation' of her four youngest children against the smallpox.[10] This nerve-racking procedure involved scratching the skin with a needle, then rubbing the contents of a smallpox pustule into the wound. Within days, symptoms including a high fever, a painful rash and pustules might start to appear, and the danger period could last a fortnight; the possible side effects of this treatment ranged from disfigurement to death.

This, of course, was some twenty years before Edward Jenner's famous experiments of the 1790s, which confirmed the common rural belief that an infection from cowpox conferred immunity to smallpox, and explained why milkmaids were possessed of such flawless complexions. As a young man, in 1772, Jenner had attended George Fordyce's courses on the 'practice of Physick', the 'Materia Medica' and chemistry.[11] A brief sentence in a letter written by Bridget to her husband George around this time (she neglected to give the date) offers an obscure hint, tucked among chit-chat about prison visits and church pews, that she knew about the connection between cowpox and smallpox, and might even have discussed it with George Fordyce. 'I shall go to the Gaol to see poor Mr. Bird,' she wrote. 'I was sure Dr. Fordice would be of my Opinion in regard to Matts Cow but all the World could not convince my Sister. I am glad you have got the Seats in the Church made up I hope our Rector and you are sitting in it today it is a great acquisision and a good thing as I saw no use that piece of Space was to any one and now we shall have room enough for all our Family.'[12]

I LIKE TO IMAGINE Bridget and Richard, the two pivotal characters in this story, standing side-by-side in the crowd that watched George III travel in his golden coach to the House of Lords to close parliament on 23 May 1776. (I cycle along the processional route, past St James's Park, on my way into work every day.) The king addressed his subjects solemnly on that occasion, expressing regret that he had recently found it necessary to ask his 'faithful Commons' for extra money to pay for the American conflict, and still holding out hopes that his 'rebellious subjects' would yet be 'awakened to a sense of their errors'.[13]

But it was too late for that. In Philadelphia, on 4 July, Congress ratified the final text of the 'unanimous declaration of the Thirteen United States of America'. The document, which started by stating the 'self-evident' truth that all men were 'created equal', went on to list the 'Injuries and Usurpations' to which the colonists had been subjected, before drawing the following conclusion: 'A Prince, whose Character is thus marked by every Act which may define a Tyrant, is unfit to be the Ruler of a free People.'[14] The text was in large part drafted by the Virginia planter Thomas Jefferson, and its pretensions to moral authority did not go unchallenged. 'If slavery be thus fatally contagious,' pondered Samuel Johnson, 'how is it that we hear the loudest yelps for liberty among the drivers of negroes?'[15]

The withdrawal of British forces from Boston in March 1776 had left them without access to a port between Nova Scotia and Florida. Now the British high command aspired to make New York their headquarters, since it held the key to the American interior, as the gateway to the mighty Hudson River; for the time being, though, the Continental Army controlled the island of Manhattan. General Howe sailed from Nova Scotia with nine thousand men, seizing Staten Island – five miles south of Manhattan – at the end of June. Two weeks later Admiral Howe, the general's brother, arrived at the head of a fleet carrying eleven thousand troops. Thirteen thousand more would soon follow, including a large contingent of Hessians – German mercenaries hired to serve alongside the redcoats.

When Robert Erskine learnt, on 12 July, that five British warships had outrun rebel batteries defending the mouth of the Hudson, and were now anchored only twenty miles from Ringwood, he set to work on a contrivance to prevent further incursions. Erskine's 'Marine Chevaux de Frise' – along the same lines as the wooden frames with spikes that were used to head off cavalry charges – was a tetrahedron made of oak beams tipped with iron points that would pierce the hull of any ship passing over it. Eight days later, he presented a scale model for General Washington's inspection; he also

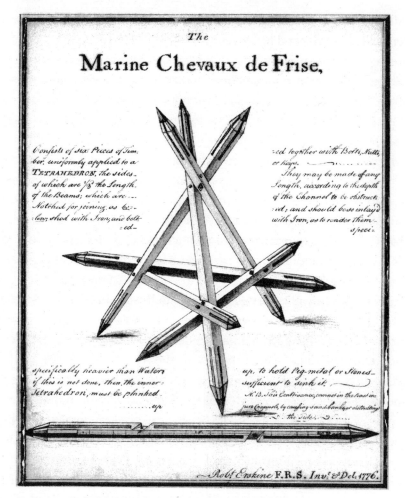

Robert Erskine's device to prevent the British from penetrating the Hudson River.

wrote to Benjamin Franklin in Philadelphia, offering it for use on the Delaware River. In the end, similar devices of a rival design were used to defend the Hudson, although it appears that the ironworks at Ringwood provided the spikes – Erskine's cash book records a debit of £1,022 against 'the United States' for eleven tons supplied to make 'Chevaux-de-frise'.[16]

During the autumn of 1776, the British advance seemed almost unstoppable. Four thousand redcoats landed at Kip's Bay, on the east side of Manhattan, on 15 September; within hours they had taken New York. By the end of November, General Howe was confidently predicting the expulsion of the Continental Army from New Jersey; this territory, with its abundance of 'covering, forage, and supplies of fresh provisions', would make fine winter quarters for his troops.[17] '*I think the game is pretty near up,*' General Washington told his brother on 18 December. 'No Man, I believe, ever had a greater choice of difficulties and less means to extricate himself from them.'[18]

A week after writing these words, on Christmas night, Washington led a straggling column across the icy Delaware River. The next morning, after a short battle, they captured two-thirds of the Hessian brigade garrisoning the small town of Trenton, New Jersey. This modest victory marked a turnaround for the rebels; another morale-boosting win followed ten days later at Princeton. Howe's hopes that his army might achieve self-sufficiency were dashed; from now on, he told the Treasury Board, all provisions must come from Britain – since America could be relied upon for nothing.

'WE ARE IN FORCE sufficient to enter upon offensive Operations,' General Howe had written to ministers in London on 6 August 1776, 'but I am detained by the Want of Camp Equipage, particularly Kettles and Cantines, so essential in the Field, and without which too much is to be apprehended on the Score of Health.'[19] Consequently, on 14 September, the Treasury ordered Richard Atkinson to supply 'barrack furniture' for 25,000 men, uniforms for 5,000 loyalist militia, and a pair of 'thick milled woollen mittens for every man', as well as to 'take up & arm shipping sufficient to carry the whole together with the Camp Equipage Shoes Stocking & Linnen for the next Campaign'.

Richard's clerks immediately set about sourcing thousands of beds, bolsters, blankets, candles, candlesticks, rugs, pokers and tongs. 'We are obliged to obtain goods of all Sorts from the Makers as matter of favor & preference,' he commented, 'whilst their workmen are universally Engaged in Combinations & all the Licentiousness arising from a Superabundance of employment.'[20] (A collective demand for improvements in pay or conditions was known as a 'combination'.) With winter coming, shortcuts were needed, and Richard warned General Guy Carleton, commander-in-chief in Canada, that he had ordered 30,000 yards of 'legging dyed at Leeds to be sent unpressed'; the material might seem coarser than usual, but it would not be any 'less durable or less warm'.[21]

The sheer unpredictability of the business of provisioning the army in America was already abundantly clear. The idea that each of the Treasury's ships would make two return crossings a year had proved hopelessly optimistic. In August 1776, a westerly wind confined several Canada-bound ships to the English Channel for three weeks, giving rise to fears that they would fail to reach Quebec before the annual freezing of the St Lawrence River. Such setbacks were intensely stressful for all concerned. 'I am sorry to find Lord North by his letter so uneasy at all the Victualling ships being not yet sailed for Canada,' the king wrote to John Robinson, 'as I attribute part of it to his not being in good spirits.'[22] By 26 September, when the last of the twenty-nine ships destined for Quebec that year sailed from Cork, Richard and his partners in the Canada contract had supplied 591,500 pounds of salt beef, 2,366,000 pounds of salt pork, 3,458,000 pounds of flour, 1,274,000 pounds of bread, 253,496 pounds of butter, 610,985 pounds of oatmeal, and 27,420 bushels of peas for the consumption of the troops.

The mounting cost of feeding the army soon began to attract scrutiny. Richard's name was not mentioned during a robust parliamentary debate about the subject on 21 February 1777 – surprisingly, perhaps, given that more than one-third of the Treasury's expenditure on the war over the previous year had passed through his books and those of his various partners. Colonel Barré did, however, observe that 5s 3d per gallon for the 100,000 gallons of Jamaican rum supplied by Richard was a 'most unheard of and exorbitant price' – but Lord North insisted it had 'left little or no profit for the contractor'.[23]

The prime minister's annual budget, delivered on 14 May, revealed a shortfall of £5 million that would have to be met with a public loan. When, by way of response, the opposition launched a stinging attack on the cost of the war, Colonel Barré returned to the cost of the rum; the contractor, he suggested, must be a 'very good friend of the treasury indeed'. Not so, said Lord North: 'The contract with Mr. Atkinson was for rum of the very best proof, the finest that could be had in Jamaica.' Indeed, he continued, once freight, leakage, insurance and commission were taken into account, the 5s 3d agreed by the Treasury Board, 'so far from being a bad bargain, was evidently a very favourable one'. Barré replied sarcastically that on such terms the poor contractor 'must be ruined', and it was cruel of the Treasury to treat him so unfairly: 'He now plainly saw the reason why people of all sorts were so shy of taking government contracts. But this Mr. Atkinson must be the greatest idiot in the whole contracting world: did he make his contracts for sour crout and porter upon the same principles?'[24]

At one point during these proceedings Lord North tripped over his numbers and confessed that he was not certain whether the values he was quoting were in pounds sterling or Jamaica's local currency – a hugely embarrassing slip-up. Afterwards the *Morning Post* gossiped that Sir Grey Cooper – John Robinson's fellow Secretary to the Treasury, who sat beside the prime minister during debates and was meant to feed him with facts and figures – had received a 'private whipping' for the blunder.[25]

Decisive action was clearly needed to head off a brewing political scandal. The next time Richard was summoned before Lord North and his Treasury Board, on 3 June, it was agreed that some independent merchants should be asked to evaluate whether the rum might reasonably have been cheaper and, if so, how much it ought to have cost. Beeston Long, the chairman of the Society of West India Merchants, and two other City of London grandees, were appointed referees.

THE TREASURY BOARD had already given General Howe the go-ahead to order more rum direct from the merchants who had shipped such large amounts of it to New York during the summer of 1776. It was typical that Richard should have been the only one of the five original suppliers who was far-sighted enough to appoint an American agent. He wrote to Howe on 14 January 1777 offering to furnish as much rum as necessary: 'We have by various Conveyances ordered our Agents in Jamaica to secure a sufficient Quantity to enable them to execute your Excellency's Commands to what extent soever they may receive them.'[26] The same day he informed Joshua Loring, the merchant acting as his agent in New York: 'Doubting as we do whether any of the other Contractors have made proper dispositions for a supply in the West Indies, we think it probable that the General may call upon us for more than one fourth part of his whole supply.'[27]

In the event, this would prove quite an underestimate. On 1 April, Howe and Loring concluded an agreement for Mure, Son & Atkinson to provide 350,000 gallons of rum. This colossal order – equivalent to one-sixth of the volume that would be exported from the West Indies to Britain that year – was the entire quantity required by the army for the year ahead.[28] (General Howe told John Robinson that he had thought it advisable to confine the order to Mure, Son & Atkinson, rather than divide it between several contractors, so that 'there might be no disappointment in the main Object'.)[29] Unfortunately Howe and Loring chose not to specify the cost. Instead they declared: 'Whereas the price of Rum is very fluctuating and it is impossible to obtain sufficient Information on that Head, it is agreed by & between the Partys that the same be referred as a Point hereafter to be settled upon the most reasonable Terms between the right Honourable the Lords Commissioners of his Majesty's Treasury and the said Messrs Mure Son & Atkinson.'[30]

The Lords of the Treasury heard about the new contract in early June, shortly after Lord North's humiliating budget speech, and they soon told Howe that they were unable to 'ascertain here the price to be paid for Rum', instead ordering him to settle the matter from New York.[31] Unsurprisingly, Richard saw things differently; he believed a clear understanding had existed that any top-up order from America needed only to specify the quantity of rum, since the price had already been fixed at the time of the previous contract in May 1776.

The Lords of the Treasury would spend many hours considering the rum contracts over the summer of 1777, and Richard would be repeatedly summoned to appear before them. On 10 July they ordered him to cut his agency rate from 2½ to 1½ per cent, an indignity to which he 'chearfully' submitted, while voicing concerns that his rival merchants might see this as a scheme of his own devising to undercut them. 'These things are not reckoned reputable in the City,' he told John Robinson.[32]

Sometime in mid-July, Beeston Long and the other referees filed their report on Richard's previous rum contract, the one from May 1776. They concluded that the spirit had been too expensive at 5s 3d per gallon, and proposed it should be priced at 4s ¾d – a reduction of nearly a quarter. Richard disputed this figure on grounds that they had incorrectly estimated the cost of the insurance premium at 13½ per cent – despite having seen the *actual* policies, which showed that of the 1,126 puncheons of rum which Mure, Son & Atkinson had arranged to be shipped to America, the premium paid on 826 barrels had been 15 per cent of their value, and on 100 barrels it had been 25 per cent. On 200 barrels Richard had been unable to secure cover – too bad that this last consignment had been seized by privateers. According to Richard's calculations, these costs and uninsured losses were equivalent to an insurance premium of 31½ per cent – which proved that, far from having profited by the contract, as was claimed, he had lost by it.

After the referees refused to concede that he might have a point, Richard's tone turned combative. On 23 July he wrote to the Treasury Board, hoping they would 'consider the increased price of 5s. 6d. as the very lowest' fair price for the rum.[33] By mid-August his patience was all but exhausted, and he wrote an exasperated letter to the Treasury, reeling off some of the unforeseeable events that 'every Contractor not meaning to ruin himself' was obliged to factor into his prices:

Short Crops in Jamaica. Combinations against him. Negligence
of Agents. Misconduct of Masters of Ships. Want of supply of
Lumber. Long Detention & consequent Leakage and Expences
in following the army from Port to Port in America; but *above
all* that imminent Danger inseparable from the nature of the
Undertaking, by which so heavy a Loss has been actually
sustained, *the Danger of uninsurable Risques*.[34]

It was a howl of frustration from a man whose considerable
powers of persuasion seemed for once to have deserted him.

LIKE ALL CIVIL WARS, the conflict in America created fault
lines that severed families and friendships; such was the rift between
Benjamin Franklin and his loyalist son William, the last colonial
governor of New Jersey, that they never made their peace. Suffice to
say, Robert Erskine could not have foreseen that within five years of
his arrival in New Jersey he would find himself on the opposite side
of a full-blown war from his friend Richard Atkinson.

Before his move to the colonies, Erskine had been a surveyor of
some repute. The first map he drew for George Washington, which
charted adjoining districts of New Jersey and New York, was small
enough to be folded in a pocket; Erskine handed it to the general
himself. Shortly afterwards, on 19 July 1777, Washington wrote to
Congress: 'A good Geographer to Survey the roads and take sketches
of the Country where the Army is to Act would be extremely useful
and might be attended with exceeding valuable consequences.'[35]
Which is how Erskine came to be appointed Surveyor General to
the Continental Army, with the rank of colonel. However, his sense
of obligation towards Richard and the other owners of the ironworks prevented him from taking up the position until he had made
arrangements for his absence. 'The great Confidence my employers
have all along placed in my integrity and honour, has demanded
my best endeavours on their behalf,' Erskine explained to Washington. 'What ever feuds and differences take place between States and
nations yet these cannot alter the nature of justice between man &

man; or cancel the duty, one individual owes to another.'[36] Despite the political chasm dividing him from the men who had sent him to America in the first place, his loyalty towards them did not falter.

During the next three years, Erskine and his team of assistant surveyors, draughtsmen and chain-bearers traversed New Jersey, New York, Connecticut and Pennsylvania, creating more than 250 maps that would prove of inestimable value to the revolutionary cause. He would never meet Richard Atkinson again; for a heavy cold contracted in the field soon turned into a fever, and he died at Ringwood on 2 October 1780. Less than two years later, the New Jersey legislature would pass an act confiscating the ironworks from its British proprietors and vesting control in Erskine's widow and her second husband.[37]

ALTHOUGH THE FRENCH loudly protested their neutrality, it was an open secret that they were providing all manner of supplies to the American rebels – cannons, rifles, gunpowder, clothes, leather, salt, brandy and wine. American privateers, meanwhile, were welcomed at French ports. 'I trust the different Vessels that hover round the Island will be put on their guard particularly to protect Liverpool, Whitehaven, the Clyde and even Bristol,' the king wrote to John Robinson in May 1777, 'for I do suspect that the Rebel vessels which have been assembling at Nantes and Bordeaux mean some stroke of that kind which will undoubtedly occasion much discontent among the Merchants.'[38]

Sure enough, in August, at the mouth of the English Channel, American privateers managed to pick off two ships from a 160-strong merchant convoy returning from Jamaica, and sailed them to Nantes, where they were plundered, stripped of their rigging and abandoned on mud flats. One of the vessels, the *Hanover Planter*, which belonged to Mure, Son & Atkinson, had 360 hogsheads of sugar and eighty-seven puncheons of rum on board. Lord Stormont, the British ambassador to France, personally negotiated the return of the ships and their valuable cargoes, an outcome which prompted Lord North to write, on 25 September, that he was 'more sanguine' than he had been for a while in his 'expectations of the continuance of peace'.[39]

The main thrust of the British campaign in America for 1777 was to isolate the rebellious New England colonies from the more loyalist middle colonies by securing the Hudson River; General Burgoyne would lead a southbound expedition from Montreal, with General Howe leading a northbound one from New York, and the two forces would converge on Albany. 'Gentleman Johnny' Burgoyne's push started well, with the capture of Fort Ticonderoga on 6 July. Howe changed his mind, however, and instead sent his army south to take Philadelphia. An inveterate gambler, Burgoyne chose to press ahead, but his luck ran out at Saratoga on 17 October; surrounded by the Continental Army, he was forced to surrender with nearly six thousand men. The defeat would prove a turning point of the war, for it persuaded the French that it might be worth openly backing the American cause. 'This unhappy Event,' Lord Stormont reported from Paris, 'has greatly elevated all our secret Enemies here, and they break out, tho' not in my Presence into the most intemperate Joy.'[40]

RICHARD'S RUM CONTRACTS would go down as a footnote in the history of the American war, yet they consumed an undue quantity of ministerial time, and generated a mind-numbing amount of paperwork. I could well imagine how all those beleaguered clerks must have felt; after weeks spent sifting through hundreds of Treasury and Colonial Office box files and letterbook volumes in the bunker-like confines of the National Archives at Kew, I myself felt heartily sick of the business.

A letter in which General Howe refused to suggest a price for the rum reached Whitehall from Philadelphia in January 1778; he merely expressed his regret that the affairs of Mure, Son & Atkinson, who had 'exerted themselves so manifestly upon every occasion which has fallen under my Observation', should have been left undetermined for so long 'from a Chain of Difficultys they could not foresee'.[41] Richard continued to press the Treasury Board for a decision. The 'unexampled Hardship' of his case, he argued on 12 January, had only worsened in recent months – of the 4,032 puncheons of rum shipped by Mure, Son & Atkinson in fulfilment of the April 1777 agreement, 1,490 barrels had been lost to American privateers.[42]

The Lords of the Treasury again summoned Richard before them on 22 January, and informed him that they wished to turn the last rum contract retrospectively into an agency agreement, and for Mure, Son & Atkinson to bill them for the various costs of fulfilling it, plus the usual 1½ per cent commission. However, Richard rejected their proposal as completely unworkable:

> Your Lordships know that we offered originally to transact this branch of business on a commission if it had been thought fit. But when your Lordships very properly determined that so distant a service was not fit to be carried on otherwise than upon contract, we considered ourselves as accountable to no body for our proceedings & executed what we had undertaken in a way so entirely interwoven with our other affairs in Jamaica & concerns of shipping: that they cannot now be separated.[43]

When Richard learnt, two days later, that the Treasury Board still planned to convert this contract into an agency, despite his objections, he wrote again: 'I have already in so many ways submitted to you the Impossibility of stating the Expences *as an Account*, that I am at a Loss how to assert that Impossibility in Terms more decisive.' So sure did he remain of his position that he offered to hand over the arbitration of the rum contracts to another 'indifferently chosen' referee, and the decision was soon entrusted to Stephen Fuller, the Jamaican Assembly's agent in Britain.[44]

By now, Richard's role as the government's shipping agent had started to attract hostile attention. A letter in the *Public Ledger*, published on 17 December 1777, made the scandalous claim that Richard paid a £5,000 salary to his friend John Robinson, Secretary to the

Treasury, which he funded by overcharging for the shipping that he chartered on the Treasury's behalf. This could not go unchallenged, and a jury found in Richard's favour, judging the article to be 'grossly libellous', since it falsely accused him of 'imposing on his employer, and bribing a person to avoid detection'.[45]

Some mud must have stuck, nonetheless, since shortly afterwards, in the House of Lords, the Earl of Effingham tabled motions to obtain 'more *accurate* accounts from the Treasury of the ships taken up by them for the service of America'.[46] On 12 March 1778, before a committee of the House, Richard endured lengthy interrogation about the transport service. When the Duke of Richmond enquired what he charged for his agency, Richard explained that he had originally received the standard merchant's commission of 2½ per cent, until the Treasury Board docked it by a point. Lord Shelburne wondered whether Richard thought the Treasury 'had been too hard upon him', to which he replied that 'he must say he seriously did' (a response which apparently 'set the House a laughing heartily'). Lord Effingham invoked parliamentary privilege, which protected him against defamation charges, for what he had to say on the subject: 'These premises fully authorised him to brand this transaction with its true name, a job; and that of the most disgraceful nature. It carried about it all its proper marks; it was a most beneficial contract, made in the dark, with a favourite contractor.'[47] The word 'job' was often used during the eighteenth century in connection with grasping corruption – Dr Johnson's dictionary definition was 'a low mean lucrative busy affair'.[48]

This discussion was merely the curtain-raiser for a heated debate in the lower house, on 23 March, in which Colonel Barré tabled a motion for a select committee to investigate the money squandered on the 'disgraceful, ruinous, and inglorious' war.[49] The motion was passed, whereupon the committee of twenty-one MPs decided to focus on the rum business – and specifically on Richard's first contract, whose terms had been so hastily agreed with Lord North back in September 1775. This particular transaction had not come under the referees' scrutiny, but now, over the following weeks, more than two dozen witnesses – under-secretaries, chief clerks, insurance brokers, sugar brokers, planters and merchants among them – were called upon to analyse its every last detail.

It was soon revealed that Richard had managed, almost by accident, to make an excellent bargain for himself. As it turned out, the price paid by the Royal Navy for its rum in Jamaica, which was the basis for his deal with the prime minister, was surprisingly high. John Robinson had only later worked out why this should be so, when he discovered that rum was just one component of a much more extensive naval provisioning contract. Whereas the Treasury Board treated rum as a separate item, in the navy 'grog' was part of the standard daily ration. Three merchants in Jamaica had bid for the navy's provisioning contract, quoting individual prices for each item – bread, beef, pork, pease, oatmeal, butter, vinegar, rum – from which a total cost per man, per day had been calculated. While the winning tender had been the cheapest overall, for rum it had been on the high side.

THE LONG-DREADED ALLIANCE between America and France finally materialized in a treaty signed on 6 February 1778. No longer was the war at arm's length, on the other side of a wide ocean; now it threatened British shores. On the night of 23 April, Captain John Paul Jones of the *Ranger*, an American naval vessel sailing out of Brest, raided Whitehaven, the Cumberland port where he had once served his apprenticeship, disembarking thirty men who spiked the town's cannons and set fire to ships in its harbour. Meanwhile, down south, where the threat of invasion was all too real – French troops were reportedly massing in Brittany and Normandy – a series of tented cities sprang up to accommodate the newly mobilized county militia.

The Treasury Board invited tenders for supplying the camps with bread, wood, forage and straw; the winning bid came from Simon Fraser, one of Richard's close friends. In its contract with Fraser, the Treasury specified that the army's 'ammunition bread' should be baked from whole wheat into loaves of six pounds. But many of the soldiers refused to eat this coarse bread; Colonel Henry Herbert of the Wiltshire Regiment, camped at Winchester, complained to John Robinson that it contained 'Bran capable of purging a Horse'.[50]

When the tradesman sub-contracted to supply the bread unilaterally took it upon himself to provide bran-free loaves for the troops, Richard, who was Fraser's hitherto silent partner in the contract, reluctantly intervened. He wrote to the baker:

> I understand that you have agreed to deliver Bread of Better
> Quality than the Contract specifies without increase of Price
> or diminution of Weight. This I am confident Mr. Fraser will
> have put a stop to, but lest he should have missed you, or by
> any other accident this letter should find you still undecided,
> I am to desire, and Expressly to direct that on no account
> whatsoever you deliver any other Bread than is described in
> the Contract.[51]

A few days later Richard visited Coxheath camp, near Maidstone, to smooth over the matter with its commander, General William Keppel. 'I have this morning seen Mr. Atkinson, and If he is as Honest as he *appears* Sensible; & *is* Clear – The Camps will be very well furnished with Every Article he is Contractor for,' Keppel told General Amherst, the British commander-in-chief, on 18 June. 'We parted very Good friends as he may tell you; and perfectly satisfied with each other.'[52] But Keppel, after going without bread for two days, soon downgraded his opinion of Richard and his ilk. 'The Contractors deserve to be hanged,' he wrote to Amherst on 23 June. 'It is Mr. Atkinson or Mr. Frazar that is to supply Bread, and good Bread, every delivery in Camp, and they must be made answerable notwithstanding they are under the Protection of Mr. Robinson altho' he perhaps deserves hanging as much as either of them.' Keppel, whose political allegiances lay with his cousin, the Duke of Richmond, added a telling postscript: 'I beg this Letter may be considered as a publick one.'[53]

As was bound to happen, the press picked up the story and mangled the facts. 'The contracts for serving all the camps with *bread*,' reported the *Evening Post*, 'are executed by Mr. Atkinson, partner with Lord Bute's agent, and brother-in-law to Mr. Robinson, of the Treasury. The bread has been scandalously bad, but how should it be otherwise. Every thing is now an arrant *job*. Mr. Atkinson is a Scotchman.'[54]

All this time, of course, Richard was making a fortune. Of the £1,406,923 expended by the Paymaster of the Forces for the twelve months up to February 1778, some £495,020 had been billed by Mure, Son & Atkinson, and £133,772 by Richard on behalf of the Canada contractors – although how much of this was profit is impossible to say.[55] But he was also under constant pressure; in particular, the burden of managing the transport fleet that shipped the army's supplies across the ocean lay heavy upon his shoulders. His partners, the Mures, offered negligible support, for they rarely came to town. Clearly Richard was unable, or unwilling, to delegate the fine details of the government contracts to his clerks, for the hundreds of letters, reports and bills from Mure, Son & Atkinson which are scattered throughout the public archives are mostly in his handwriting. He made himself so indispensable to Lord North and the Treasury Board that he became their first port of call for any business requiring special speed or discretion. He had a heroic capacity for work, often writing, writing, writing late into the night, and his letters generally convey boundless energy and optimism. The issue of the rum contracts, still unresolved, enveloped his activities in a cloud of opprobrium – and yet here he was, pulling off astonishing logistical feats in the service of king and empire. At times he must have felt close to buckling beneath the intolerable weight of it all.

SEVEN

Jamaica Imperilled

FRANCE'S ENTRY INTO the war forced a rethink of Britain's military strategy. Suddenly, due to the produce of the mainland contributing so much less to the national purse than that of the sugar islands, saving the American colonies was a lower priority than defending the West Indian ones. Lord North and his cabinet immediately ordered the evacuation of Philadelphia, to free up a large force for redeployment in the West Indies. On 18 June 1778, after nine months' occupation, General Sir Henry Clinton – Howe's successor as commander-in-chief in America – led his army out of the city, marching overland to New York to avoid a confrontation with the French fleet.

One of the most serious provisioning crises of the war would unfold over the following months. The efficiency of the transport fleet that Richard ran on behalf of the Treasury was greatly dependent on its ships being swiftly unloaded in America, then released immediately to return to the main depot at Cork, to pick up another batch of supplies. But the process had been hindered right from the start by difficulties at New York. During the first year of the war, after a fire destroyed much of the town, thirty-nine vessels chartered by Mure, Son & Atkinson were pressed into service as floating warehouses. Following this episode, General Howe had recruited David Laird, erstwhile captain of the *Thames*, to act as agent and supervisor for the transport ships arriving in America;

but their slow turnaround was a problem Richard continued to grapple with.

A few weeks after the British withdrawal from Philadelphia, a French naval squadron appeared on the horizon outside New York harbour. 'Captain Laird is now and has been so bussie since his return from Philadelphia that he has no time to write,' Thomas Skelton, Laird's deputy, wrote to Richard on 14 July. 'The Count De Estaing has been these three days past at Anchor off Sandy Hook with 15 Sail of men of war, 11 of them line of battle Ships.' Now that New York was under blockade, Skelton cautioned, there was 'no saying' when ships might be able to depart for Ireland.[1]

The panic presently subsided, for the French fleet sailed away after eleven days. Already that summer, however, with so many vessels having failed to return, the Treasury Board had directed Mure, Son & Atkinson to take up '3,000 Tons of the stoutest & strongest ships they can meet with, & send them to Cork, & arm them immediately'.[2] When Richard received Skelton's letter, on 24 August, he passed it to John Robinson; the Lords of the Treasury were sufficiently rattled to order a further 5,000 tons of shipping. Six weeks later, Richard had managed to charter the ships, although finding crews for them was proving more of a challenge. 'The difficulty of this part of the Service increases with the Scarcity of Seamen,' he told Robinson, 'and we fear admits of no remedy, as the Men cannot be kept on board against their Consent.'[3] By the end of October, however, twenty-two vessels with a capacity of 7,965 tons, crewed by 1,608 sailors, were ready for loading at Cork.

General Clinton, meanwhile, warned that stores in New York were running low. The hold-up of ships in America was undoubtedly the nub of the problem; yet poor communications were also to blame, for the baffling reports of the commissary in New York meant that John Robinson could barely work out whether the troops were eating 46,000 rations a day, as allowed for, or considerably more than that. (Somehow, in seven months, they had managed to consume an extra three and a half million pounds of bread and flour, and an extra two million pounds of meat.) In November,

Robinson penned a blistering eleven-page reprimand to the commissary – such was the gravity of the situation that he ran the letter past George III himself. 'The Drafts seem highly proper but oblige me again to repeat that the inaccuracy in stating the Rations in N. America is most extraordinary and encourages the opinion of fraud or great negligence,' wrote the king. 'Nothing can be more proper than the part taken by Mr. Robinson in the whole of this transaction.'[4]

By mid-December, the warehouses in New York were near empty. Clinton told the Colonial Secretary, Lord George Germain:

> Your Lordship will be startled when I inform you that this Army has now but a fortnight's Flour left. I hear no accounts that can give me hopes that Supplies are on the Coasts, and the North West Winds which blow violently and almost invariably at this Season make the arrival of any Fleet in this Port very precarious indeed. Our Meat with the assistance of Cattle purchased here will last about forty days beyond Xmas, and a Bread composed of Pease, Indian Corn and Oatmeal can be furnished for about the same time. After that I know not how We shall Subsist.[5]

This episode was a striking reminder of the extent to which the redcoat army relied upon the exertions of the Treasury Board, and Mure, Son & Atkinson, and many more links in the extended supply chain. Fortunately for General Clinton, the first of the previous autumn's intake of shipping sailed into New York harbour on 4 January 1779, and the crisis was averted.

Now, more than ever, John Robinson wished that the Treasury could be shot of its responsibility for shipping the army's supplies to America, and he reopened talks on the subject with the Admiralty; in February, the Navy Board agreed to take on the role. It was settled that the Navy Board would start shipping the army's provisions from May 1779, and would replace the Treasury Board's policy of sending individual armed vessels with their own system of dispatching large convoys of merchant ships under naval protection. Richard received instructions to discharge from service the 130-odd ships under his management; these new arrangements terminated a large portion of his government business, and he was clearly annoyed to be presented with a *fait accompli*. 'Having heard of no Imputation of Misconduct on our part or dissatisfaction on that of the Board,' he wrote to Robinson, 'it was not without some Degree of surprize that we thus received Information of a treaty so far advanced.'[6]

Meanwhile the fog surrounding Richard's rum contracts was no closer to lifting. Stephen Fuller, the agent of the Jamaican Assembly in London, had failed to come up with a formula for pricing the additional 350,000 gallons ordered by General Howe back in April 1777; now the Lords of the Treasury proposed passing the matter to two new referees, who would themselves have the power 'to name an umpire, If they shall see occasion'.[7] Richard consented to the plan, choosing his old friend Francis Baring to act on his behalf; the Treasury Board nominated the merchant John Purrier. But the arbitration process once again stalled in May 1779, when Baring and Purrier wrote to the Treasury stating 'their Inability to proceed to the award', and requesting further directions.[8]

On 20 July, Lord North chaired a special meeting about the rum contracts; it was attended by all five Lords of the Treasury, as well as the Attorney General, Alexander Wedderburn, a notorious bully. The terse language of the minutes – 'Mr. Atkinson is called in & heard and Mr. Attorney General states to him some Ideas for the settling of this Business for his Consideration' – masks what Richard would later recall as one of the most bruising encounters of his life.[9] As for the Treasury Board's proposed solution, which was to lump all three of his rum contracts together and judge them on criteria that he regarded as 'feigned' – it offended his sense of justice. The following day, Richard reiterated his position: 'I beg leave to repeat that I consider the three Contracts as things perfectly distinct and unconnected with each other.' He could hardly believe, having 'invested his Fortune in a most arduous & essential Service to the Army', that the Treasury was now attempting to browbeat him into submission.[10]

DURING HIS PREMIERSHIP, Lord North suffered from debilitating bouts of what would nowadays be diagnosed as depression, and he made repeated failed attempts to quit his office. 'Lord North cannot conceive what can induce his Majesty, after so many proofs of Lord North's unfitness for his situation, to determine at all events to keep him at the head of the Administration,' the prime minister had written in March 1778, in the third person as was customary for letters to the monarch.[11] He again tried to break free in June 1779, but Spain was by now on the point of entering the war, and the king responded that his resignation 'would be highly unbecoming at this hour'.[12]

The French and Spanish allies planned a naval assault on the British Isles that summer, to be followed up with a land invasion by an army of more than thirty thousand men. In the event, the Spanish navy arrived six weeks late at the agreed rendezvous off the coast of north-west Spain, and as the French fleet sweltered in the heat, many sailors fell sick. The Bourbon allies at last headed north on 25 July, but their bad luck continued; as adverse winds slowed their progress, they missed out on the plunder from two British merchant convoys returning from the Leeward Islands and Jamaica. On 16 August the combined fleet, numbering sixty-six ships of the line, was spotted off Plymouth; two days later a great easterly gale scattered them into the Atlantic. Like its predecessor of 1588, the Armada of 1779 ended in failure.

Still, the mood in Britain remained sombre. 'Never did a deeper political Gloom over-spread England, than in the Autumn of 1779,' Nathaniel Wraxall would later recall in his *Historical Memoirs*.[13] And few men were gloomier than Lord North. In November, John Robinson told Charles Jenkinson about a harrowing conversation in which the prime minister had confessed that he could not bear to be thought 'the Cause of the destruction of His Majesty's Power' and perhaps the collapse of his country: 'He then My Dear Sir fell into such a Scene of Distress, I assure you as made my Heart bleed for him, & drew Tears from my Eyes.'[14]

Even as Britain's own shores were threatened, its gravest concern remained the West Indies. 'Our Islands must be defended even at the risk of an invasion of this Island,' the king wrote in September 1779. 'If we lose our Sugar Islands it will be impossible to raise Money to continue the War.'[15] These colonies, unfortunately, were highly vulnerable to attack; most of them were dotted among the Lesser Antilles, a chain of islands enclosing the Caribbean Sea, and surrounded by enemy possessions, while Jamaica, the largest and most valuable, lay a thousand miles to the west.

Dominica had been the first island to fall prey to the French, and its capture horrified all those who held an interest in the West Indies. On 3 December 1778, at a packed meeting of merchants and planters held at the London Tavern, a vote was carried to petition the king to cease the 'predatory war' in America. Richard led the minority who opposed the petition, claiming that many of its assertions were 'absolutely false'.[16] The news soon afterwards that Saint Lucia had been wrested away from the French temporarily calmed the merchants' nerves. In June 1779, however, Admiral d'Estaing took Saint Vincent without a shot being fired, followed days later by Grenada, and reportedly swore that by the time he was finished, the King of England would not have enough sugar 'to sweeten his tea'.[17]

On 25 September, word reached London that d'Estaing had sailed his fleet to Saint Domingue, the French colony to the east of Jamaica. Four days later, twelve of Jamaica's most prominent merchants and planters – including Richard – met to prepare a statement to be placed before Lord George Germain. They reminded the minister that there were fewer than two thousand regular soldiers stationed in Jamaica, and suggested that its militia, a corps made up of all able-bodied white males, was quite unequal to the task of its defence. Not only were these men 'unused to discipline' and 'unfit to undergo fatigue', but their absence from the workplace left 'all the Women & Children, all the boiling Houses, & Distillerys, and all the Plantations desolate, & abandoned to the Mercy of the Slaves;

a grievance in some respects but little inferior to that of being left to the Mercy of the Enemy'.[18]

Ten days later came news that six thousand French troops were headed for the Caribbean. While ministers vacillated, the merchants took command of the situation. On 15 October, a fund was established to provide a bounty of five guineas to each man enlisting for a new Jamaican regiment, payable on 'his being approved by the commanding officer'.[19] Richard subscribed £100, as did each of his partners, and donations soon flooded in from many prominent Jamaican proprietors.

As it happened, a regiment of eight hundred infantry, the 88th Foot, had been ready to embark for Jamaica since the summer, but the Navy Board had not yet found vessels to carry them in. On Saturday 23 October, Richard and his fellow merchant Samuel Long called upon Germain and offered to provide transport ships for the regiment. They found a sympathetic audience in the Colonial Secretary – indeed, he had personal reason to be concerned for Jamaica's safety, having three years earlier appointed his six-year-old son to the lucrative office of Receiver General of the island. Germain agreed to find an extra 750 recruits, and informed the Admiralty that transport would be required; the Admiralty ordered the Navy Board to provide the necessary vessels; the Navy Board found merchants willing to undertake the service; and the merchants told the captains to cease loading commercial goods and instead take on board provisions for the troops.

All was in hand, it seemed, until the commander-in-chief, General Amherst, declared himself unwilling to commit so many men to the defence of Jamaica. 'What think you of Lord Amherst disavowing the directions given last Saturday concerning the recruits,' Richard asked his friend William Knox, who was Germain's deputy at the colonial office. 'The ships are all engaged, the provisions laid in, and the whole expence incurred; nothing will move him.' As Richard was finishing his letter to Knox, another arrived, prompting the following postscript: 'Since writing what precedes I have (near midnight) received Lord Amherst's letter in answer to one we

123

wrote him to-day as a last effort, in which he maintains his character, and all the recruits we are to get are a hundred and twenty-five.
A thought strikes me by which I think the shame of this transaction
may be hid. I will see Lord North upon it in the morning if he is not
gone (as Lord George is) into the country.'[20]

In the end, through determined lobbying, Richard managed to
have the number of recruits raised to 350 – two hundred of whom
were immediately press-ganged at Chatham. Samuel Long, Richard's collaborator during these operations, rode down to Gravesend
on 5 November to see them all embarked.

The merchants' forwardness soon became public knowledge.
'The following extraordinary notice of the sailing of the Jamaica
fleet, was stuck up at Lloyd's coffee house yesterday evening,' the
Evening Post reported, in droll mode:

> *Admiralty, Nov. 12, twelve o'clock.* Mr. Atkinson presents
> compliments to Mr. Long, and acquaints him, that the fleet
> will sail from Portsmouth in the first fair wind after Sir Geo.
> Rodney's ship is ready, without waiting for any thing that is
> not then got round; Sir George goes down tomorrow. Mr. A.
> submits to Mr. Long, whether notice should not be sent to both
> coffee houses.[21]

The threat to Jamaica appeared to lift when the news came soon
afterwards that the French fleet had been sighted off Georgia. Even
so, on 8 December 1779, the Jamaica agent Stephen Fuller presented
a petition to Lord George Germain, complaining that too little
was being done for the island's defence. The Colonial Secretary
replied that although the king and his ministers appreciated the
'very great value & importance of Jamaica', they were not prepared
to disclose the 'amount or the nature' of measures adopted for its
safety.[22] Germain's lofty response caused a rift in the Jamaica lobby
between those inclined to condemn the ministry and those who
favoured a more collaborative approach. On 17 December, at a meeting from which Richard was conspicuously absent, the planters and

merchants appointed a sub-committee to campaign for greater naval and military protection for their island. 'I see the Proprietors of Jamaica after all the attention shewn to them shew still a disposition to give trouble,' the king observed to John Robinson.[23]

Before Christmas, news came of a great victory at Savannah, the capital of Georgia, where the occupying British had repelled a much larger besieging force supported by the French navy; subsequently Admiral d'Estaing had limped back to France with his fleet. On Christmas Eve, the cabinet resolved to send three thousand more troops to Jamaica, in addition to five thousand men who were about to embark for the Leeward Islands. Only Lord Amherst objected, maintaining that the loss of men would leave the kingdom 'in too defenceless a State' – but the king overruled his commander-in-chief, and four regiments were ordered to ready themselves.[24]

Although more troops would be dispatched to the West Indies over the winter of 1779–80 than had been sent to America since 1776, many of the Jamaica lobby continued to harp on about the previous autumn's invasion scare. 'The safety of such a possession as Jamaica ought not to have been left to chance,' they moaned in a petition placed before the Commons on 10 February. During the parliamentary debate that followed, the absentee planter Richard Pennant accused the prime minister of caring so little about Jamaica that he never bothered to read its governor's reports, an act of negligence for which he 'deserved to be impeached'. (At which point North was said to have bellowed across the chamber: 'Impeach me – impeach me now.') Germain questioned the legitimacy of the lobbyists' petition, given that the 'meeting at which it had been resolved upon, had never been advertised' – a claim denied by Pennant, who said he 'had the advertisements in his pocket, and he was very sure, that Mr. Atkinson was the only one present, who had any objection at all'.[25] (This was a lie, for the minutes of the meeting on 17 December prove that Richard was not there.)[26] Thomas Townshend, a vocal opponent of the war, suggested that Richard's censure of the petition was quite meaningless, given his manifold connections with the ministry: 'He held the greatest number of contracts, and was to be heard of at the Admiralty Office, the Navy Office, the Victualling Office, the War Office, and, in short, at every place where money was to be gotten. In fact, he appeared to be the principal Minister, and perhaps he was the most *active* Minister we had.'[27]

THE POLITICAL CAMPAIGNER John Horne Tooke, released from prison after serving a short sentence for seditious libel, chose to channel his anger into a polemical investigation of the public finances. *Facts Addressed to the Landholders*, which Horne Tooke co-wrote with the radical economist Dr Richard Price, came out in January 1780; it soon ran to eight editions. The activities of Mure, Son & Atkinson had come to epitomize the profligacy of the ministry, and Richard's rum contracts received the dubious honour of their own chapter. They were an easy target, a throwaway line – 'as cheap as Mr. Atkinson's rum', Horace Walpole would write, describing something that wasn't cheap at all.[28] On 8 February, the freeholders of Yorkshire, hobbled by heavy taxes and the low value of grain, presented parliament with a petition demanding 'economical' reforms – this would soon be followed by similar petitions from twenty-eight counties and eleven boroughs. Three days later, in an epic speech that Lord North admitted was 'one of the most able he had ever heard', the Irish statesman Edmund Burke demanded a root-and-branch reform of every category of national expenditure.[29]

The press, as ever, greatly enjoyed the prime minister's discomfiture. The *London Courant* waggishly proposed that he should set up a 'new Board' to restore parliament 'to its proper purity', whose first task would be to dispose of the largest vermin. 'The Duke of Richmond and Lord Shelburne,' the journalist suggested, 'will take a great deal of killing; so will Barré and Fox (the latter already judged, like Shelburne, pistol-proof). As for the inferior class, including all the apostate country gentlemen, they had better be executed by contract. Mure and Atkinson will of course offer proposals to the Board; and as in their extensive undertakings they must necessarily have many expert cut-throats under them, they will probably do the business per head as reasonably as they do any other.'[30]

*Fenchurch Street, looking west. The Ironmongers' Hall dominates the foreground;
Richard's house was set back behind gates on the left-hand side.*

The mood of pent-up public fury spilled over in London on
2 June 1780, when a march against Catholic emancipation led by
Lord George Gordon disintegrated into a five-day orgy of looting
and arson. Richard had recently moved to 32 Fenchurch Street, a
mansion set back behind a gateway and courtyard on one of the
City's main thoroughfares – as was usual at this time, it acted as both
his home and place of business. Its location was midway between
flashpoints at the Bank of England and the Tower of London, and
I wondered whether he was caught up in the violence. I was excited
to find a report in the *Morning Chronicle* of a bishop whose carriage
had been surrounded and had its wheels taken off; this prelate had
found refuge in 'Mr. Atkinson's house', but thirty men had subsequently broken down the door, forcing him to escape from a rear
window.[31] Disappointingly, after further digging, I learnt that the
'Mr. Atkinson' in this story was not Richard, but a lawyer in Westminster – such are the minor hiccups of historical research.

On 15 June, as the capital was clearing up after the riots – some
put the number of dead and wounded at seven hundred – a measure of good news arrived from South Carolina. After a siege lasting

six weeks, the American garrison at Charleston had surrendered to General Clinton, who had taken five thousand prisoners. Reports from the West Indies, however, were less cheering. An outbreak of fever in Saint Lucia had killed hundreds of soldiers and left many too feeble for duty. The best medicine was believed to be claret – but dispensing it to the men would involve a thicket of red tape. William Knox, under-secretary at the colonial office, asked Richard for his ideas about the best way to supply it. 'By the Act of Navigation, no Wine can be imported into our Colonies from Europe, unless from Great Britain, Madeira or the Azores,' Richard advised. 'Guernsey, Jersey & Ireland are equally prohibited to send Wines directly to the Colonies. A neutral Ship might be sent to Bourdeaux or any other Port in France, to clear out for Holland & stop in Great Britain, & might tranship the Wine by License as abovementioned.'[32]

On 9 August, in a major setback for the merchant community, the Spanish fleet intercepted a convoy recently departed from Portsmouth, seizing fifty-five ships mostly headed for the West Indies; their cargo was valued at £1,500,000. The plunder also included five East Indiaman ships – a loss from which Richard managed, in a letter to Knox dated 12 September, to spin a silver lining of sorts:

> You desired Information some time ago about the means of supplying Wine to the Army in the West Indies, which leads me to communicate to you an Offer that has just been made me of the Refusal of about four thousand Dozen of Claret in Bottles at Madeira which had been sent thither to meet the outward bound India Ships which are taken. The only Objection there can be to the Quality is that it is too good, but I am confident that no such speedy Supply can be sent by any other Mode.[33]

When the Treasury Board next met, Mure, Son & Atkinson were ordered to send a ship to Madeira to pick up the claret and 'proceed with it to Saint Lucia with the utmost expedition'.[34]

*

SPAIN HAD PLACED the Rock of Gibraltar under siege from both land and sea within a week of declaring war on Britain in June 1779. The following spring, Admiral Sir George Rodney had managed to sidestep the blockade to deliver provisions to the eight thousand men trapped there; but letters since smuggled from Gibraltar reported dwindling stores of beef, butter, oats, pease and wheat, as well as coal, candles, lamp oil, rum and vinegar. In September 1780 John Robinson received instructions from Lord George Germain to procure two years' worth of every necessity while maintaining the strictest secrecy, to prevent whispers of the mission from reaching Spain. Naturally, the Treasury Board awarded the contract to Mure, Son & Atkinson.

But a complication with the coal supply threatened to expose the operation. At the start of the siege, the Treasury had cancelled various standing contracts for the supply of the garrison; it had not, however, revoked the contract held by the powerful Fox family to provide coal, since this fell within the remit of Charles Jenkinson, the Secretary at War. The Foxes' agent, anticipating an expedition to Gibraltar, had already filled a number of collier vessels which were now ready to leave. Robinson asked Jenkinson to lay them off immediately. 'To put in Motion the Ships avowedly taken up by your Contractor for carrying Coals to Gibraltar,' he explained, 'loaden as such, & known to be so by every Man on board – would I fear at once make the discovery.'[35] It was Richard who came up with a solution; so as to 'preserve the secret, and avoid giving offence to the contractors', he offered to procure the coals himself, while passing on the benefit of any mark-up and commission to 'the Mr. Foxes'. (William Knox would tell this story years later, in his memoirs, 'in justice to the memory of a man who possessed the best talents for executive business that I ever was acquainted with'.)[36]

Admiral George Darby received orders to sail for Gibraltar on 1 January 1781, but repairs prevented his fleet from leaving until mid-March. Fortunately, as Darby rounded Cape St Vincent with twenty-nine ships of the line and almost a hundred store ships, the Spanish navy was nowhere to be seen. The British fleet swept into the Bay of Gibraltar on 12 April, swiftly unloaded its cargo, and departed nine days later.

Because the expedition was so hush-hush, the paper trail was minimal, which is why it barely appears in the official records; but it was clearly a mammoth undertaking. Mure, Son & Atkinson billed the Treasury £266,858, which John Robinson tucked away in the public accounts under the heading 'Provisions and Stores shipped for Special Service'.[37] By way of comparison, Richard had invoiced £108,487 for the supplies sent out to Boston in the autumn of 1775.[38] Unlike the earlier mission, however, the relief of Gibraltar was a resounding success – not least because it provided the fuel for a conflagration, eighteen months later, that would help bring the war to a close.

GENERAL WASHINGTON'S MOOD was sombre during the latter months of 1780; with the Continental dollar almost worthless, deemed 'fit for nothing But Bum Fodder', his troops were restless.[39] 'We have been half our time without provision & are likely to remain so,' he wrote on 5 October. 'We have no Magazines, nor money to form them. And in a little time we shall have no men, if we had money to pay them.'[40] The national finances of the French were also fast unravelling; from a British perspective, a strategy of attrition offered the best odds of winning the war.

In December, Richard and his fellow contractors agreed terms with the Treasury to provision the army in America over the following year; they would supply rations for a total of 86,000 soldiers at $5^{27}/_{32}$d per day. Richard's Canada syndicate would feed fifteen thousand men.[41] But beasts even more voracious than humans also relied upon the Treasury for their rations – the army's four thousand-odd horses, each of which daily chomped through about nine pounds of oats or twenty pounds of hay. During the war, Mure, Son & Atkinson would invoice £219,271 for oats alone. This species of grass grows best in a cool, damp climate; so it was fitting that Richard should turn to sub-contractors from such a region – namely, his brothers at Temple Sowerby.

Evidence of George and Matthew Atkinson's involvement in the enterprise lies in a scuffed leatherbound book that I inherited, which appears to be their main business ledger, under an account headed 'Oats, Meal, Sacks, Casks'. No letters exist on the subject, or at least none that I have seen, so it is left to the numbers to do the talking – and they are large numbers. In March 1781, for example, the Treasury ordered Mure, Son & Atkinson to supply General Clinton with 50,000 quarters of oats. The Navy Board was unable to provide transport on this occasion, so Mure, Son & Atkinson also chartered 10,000 tons of shipping (around thirty vessels) to carry the load to New York. Richard invoiced the Treasury £36,956 for the oats and £43,181 for the shipping; his brothers, meanwhile, having settled with the suppliers of the grain, made a profit of £9,800, as is revealed by the transfer of this sum from the 'Oats, Meal, Sacks, Casks' account into their profit and loss account.[42]

The high price of the oats did not go unremarked. In the House of Commons, Sir Philip Jennings Clerke – a sworn scourge of contractors – commented that an 'ingenious gentleman had calculated what the real cost of oats was to government on their arrival in America, and it had been found to be exactly three oats for a halfpenny'.[43] Edmund Burke 'shuddered' at the expense, pointing out that the money spent on buying and shipping the oats would have purchased two new frigates for the navy.[44]

I was exhilarated to uncover the Temple Sowerby connection to the oat supply – even if it looked suspiciously like profiteering. When I started writing the story of the Atkinson family, I had hoped to connect them to the big events of the time. Here, in miniature, was exactly what I'd wanted to achieve, for in tracing a route through the various documents – from General Clinton's letter from New York to the colonial office in London, via the Treasury Board minutes and Mure, Son & Atkinson's invoices, finally to the handwritten ledger on the desk in front of me – I was able to follow the trail from the British headquarters in America, via Westminster, all the way back to Westmorland. And I knew exactly where nearly £10,000 of public money had gone – straight into my ancestors' pockets.

EIGHT

A Heartbreaking Letter

LADY ANNE LINDSAY'S self-imposed exile in Scotland, follow-ing her brother-in-law Fordyce's bankruptcy, would last four years. In Edinburgh, that great city of the Enlightenment, she would shine in the company of some brilliant older men, notably the philoso-phers David Hume and Lord Monboddo. At one memorable dinner, hosted by the physician Sir Alexander Dick in 1773, she even man-aged to impress Samuel Johnson.

The famous doctor of letters, then sixty-three, was touring Scotland at the time with the 'faithful Bozzy, his friend, adorer and biographer'. The old Countess of Eglinton, Johnson told the spell-bound company, always called him 'Son', since he had been born the year after she was married. James Boswell interrupted to correct the great man – no, he said, it was the year *before* she was married. 'Had that been the case,' Johnson retorted, 'she would have had little to boast of.' At this point Anne piped up: 'Would not the *Son* have excused the *Sin?*' Prior to her interjection, Anne noticed, Johnson had been 'disposed to be sulky', but afterwards he became 'exces-sively agreeable & entertaining'. Most pleasingly, she had later watched Boswell 'steal to the window to put down the *Jeu de mot* in his commonplace book'.[1]

It was during these years that Anne would make the acquaint-ance of Henry Dundas, an ambitious young lawyer who had lost much of his fortune in the banking crash of 1772, and had recently been elected to parliament for the first time. Anne's friendship with Dundas was never quite straightforward; the 'partiality' he formed for her 'had for its basis *nothing at all*', as she recalled it. 'It was a hearty, serviceable, admiring, gallant good-will, such as was in his nature for all womankind, old and young, tho' more particularly for the young.'[2]

Lady Margaret Fordyce's time in Scotland had been curtailed by the unwelcome discovery that the £500 a year settled on her by her husband before their marriage, while safe from the grasp of his creditors, was dependent on their living together. She returned to London, and they set up home at Harley Street in Marylebone, on the unfashionable north side of Oxford Street. Their reconciliation proved merely perfunctory, but luckily he was often away. In a typically outlandish bid to make a new fortune, Alexander Fordyce was busy setting up a chemical works at South Shields, near Newcastle, to harness a method of manufacturing 'fossil alkali' (sodium carbonate) and 'marine acid' (hydrochloric acid) which had recently been discovered by his chemist nephew George.

It was only in 1777, when she was twenty-six, that Anne decided to move back to London, after a modest legacy from her grandmother endowed her with some financial independence. Despite their connection to the notorious bankrupt Fordyce, the sisters still had an entrée into the smartest salons, where as Anne would recall they were 'prized by many and welcomed like little holidays into society'.[3] Often they were asked to sing, at which they were both extremely accomplished. 'Lady Margaret Fordyce is at this time confessedly the first voice in the list of *fashionable amateurs*; she is a pupil of the *Italian school*, and executes the most difficult passages in the most finished manner,' reported one newspaper. 'Lady Anne Lindsay has likewise a charming pipe, but her style is quite the reverse of her sister's being entirely confined to the plaintive melody of *Scotch ballads!*'[4] The novelist Fanny Burney described the sisters' late arrival one evening at a lavish party at Lady Gideon's: 'I had hopes they would have sung, but I was disappointed, for they only looked handsome.'[5] It goes without saying that Richard was delighted to have them both back in the capital – Anne remembered him welcoming them 'like boons sent from Heaven'.[6]

Anne's male admirers tended to follow a pattern – as she herself described it, 'starting up with zeal . . . vanishing like meteors'. She attributed this to her relative poverty: 'I had nothing for my lovers to pay their debts with, or to appropriate to younger children.'[7] Viscount Wentworth was one of the few who stuck around. They first met at a musical soirée in 1778, where he was charmed by her singing, while she was taken with his flute-playing, not to mention his fine figure, which 'spoke him more decidedly the man of rank' than most of his sex.[8] But Anne would soon learn that Wentworth was less available than he appeared. For more than a decade, he had been living with a mistress, Catharine Vanloo; she had come over from Flanders as the governess to his younger sisters, seducing him when he was virtually a boy, and had since borne him two children. He was also in regular attendance at the gaming tables of St James's, where he was diligently squandering his inheritance. The on-off relationship between Anne and Lord Wentworth would cause them both considerable anguish over the coming years.

One day in 1779, Richard overheard the Lindsay sisters discussing the pension for which their mother, Lady Balcarres, had unsuccessfully applied to the king, and he discreetly asked Anne ('pardon me the presumption of the question') where she kept her money. 'In the Moon! We are all as poor as Church mice,' she answered. 'I am the only person of fortune in the family as I had a legacy left me in money, of £300, not long ago, by my Grandmother.' Richard went on to explain that there were many ways in which such a sum might be put to work, and he begged Anne to entrust it to his care. ''Tis so little, my good friend, that it is scarce worthy your troubling yourself about it,' she said. 'We must teach it then to become bigger,' he replied with a smile.[9]

The worst hurricane in memory tore through the West Indies in October 1780; the western parishes of Jamaica took a particular pounding. This was yet more dire news for Richard's partner Hutchison Mure, whose Suffolk residence, Great Saxham Hall, had burnt down the previous year. Financial troubles now forced Mure into the confession of an 'alarming and disgraceful secret', hidden for fifteen years. Back in 1766, when Richard joined the partnership, Mure had neglected to mention private debts of £30,000 for which they would be jointly liable, an omission which had caused the old man so much stress during the intervening years that 'he had sometimes feared for his reason'.[10] His creditors were closing in; unless he could quickly sell off a couple of his sugar estates, he would be undone.

Although the revelation came as a profound shock to Richard, it also presented him with the opportunity to acquire Jamaican property of his own for a good price. In raising the capital to buy Dean's Valley Dry Works in Westmoreland Parish, he was assisted by a loan of half its value from his friend Captain David Laird; while he purchased the Bogue estate in St James Parish as a joint venture with a slippery financier named Paul Benfield.[11] Through these transactions, Richard became the co-owner of some five hundred enslaved men, women and children. A few months later, in April 1781, Hutchison Mure folded his Suffolk landholdings into the assets of the partnership, paving the way for another of his sons – William, who had previously been living in Jamaica – to join the firm.[12] Thus Mure, Son & Atkinson became Mures, Atkinson & Mure.

THE TREASURY WAS FORCED to borrow vast sums of money during the American war, the national debt nearly doubling in seven years. Doom-mongers predicted economic collapse; but the enormity of these sovereign debts paradoxically confirmed the strength of the British financial system. It was the Treasury's practice to pay a low interest rate on government loan stock, but to sell it to investors at a generous discount on its nominal value – this, in time, guaranteed a handsome return on their initial outlay. The close-knit relationship between the Treasury and the most powerful men of the City of London ensured the ministry's access to funds for pursuing the war. A slice of the national debt was the most secure possible investment, and financiers selected by the Treasury to partake of the loan stock gained the power to bestow considerable largesse on family, friends and associates.

When Lord North announced to the House of Commons, on 7 March 1781, that he would need a £12 million loan for the following year, he neither expected an easy ride, nor did he receive one. Charles James Fox, who took an opposing view to the prime minister on almost all matters, sourly accused him of raiding the public purse in order to prop up his parliamentary majority through bribes for supporters. Sir Philip Jennings Clerke suggested that North had parcelled out the loan to his private friends as a reward for past services: 'In particular, he was well informed that Mr. Atkinson the contractor, and partner with Mr. Mure, had no less than £3,300,000 to his own share.'[13] The prime minister rubbished the 'very idea' of such a sum being allocated to one man: 'Great bankers, the House well knew, applied for many other persons, as well as on their own account, but no person would have such a proportion as the hon. gentleman had mentioned.'[14]

This was far from the end of the matter. In a fierce debate the following week, the opposition let rip about the mishandling of the loan, and the role of a certain notorious rum contractor. George Byng, MP for Middlesex, complained that the list of individual subscribers and their allocations had not been sent to the Bank of England, as was customary, before the loan was presented to parliament; instead, he claimed, it had been held back at the Treasury for three days, where it had 'undergone many garblings, and many corrections'. Moreover, he knew of 'very suspicious' circumstances relating to the part played by Richard in the distribution of the loan: 'It was pretty certain that he was in a room at the Treasury by himself, with the list, while many respectable and responsible men had it not in their power to converse with the noble lord on the subject.'

John Robinson, in a rare speech, admitted that Richard had been consulted about small-scale applicants from the City whose names were unknown to the Treasury – lottery-office keepers, tailors and suchlike – but 'as to Mr. Atkinson having the list in a room by himself, the fact had never happened, he had neither settled the list, nor had he the list to interfere with at all'.[15]

When the full list of subscribers was published, Mures, Atkinson & Mure's official portion was found to be £200,000 – a sizeable chunk, but by no means unprecedented. Richard had also quietly set aside loan stock worth £30,000 for Anne Lindsay's personal benefit. The financial markets were buoyant. 'The stock has risen greatly already,' he told her shortly afterwards, 'but a week hence it will overtop expectation: *have you nerves to stand it?*'[16] On 13 March, the noise of cannon fire at the Tower of London reverberated around the City. Admiral Rodney had captured the Dutch island of Saint Eustatius in the West Indies, cutting off a crucial source of supplies for the Continental Army; almost half the ships entering Philadelphia and Baltimore over the previous year had come from this supposedly neutral port. 'What an unlooked-for piece of good fortune,' wrote Richard to Anne.

A few days passed, and the markets climbed even higher: 'All remains steady.' Then came news of failed peace negotiations with France and Spain, and the stock tumbled. When Anne heard what had happened, she put on her 'oldest bonnet', strolled up to the open fields at the top of Harley Street, and 'walked and reasoned and fatigued' herself into accepting her diminished expectations: 'I have not lost all (thought I) if I can feel in this manner, and if I still possess the friendship of Atkinson.'[17]

Richard called at Harley Street early the next day. Fordyce was away, and Margaret indisposed; as he had hoped, he had Anne all to himself. 'You are a philosopher indeed,' he smiled as he entered the room. 'I had fortunately reason, from a friend of mine who crossed with the messenger, to suspect how this was likely to be.' He had cashed in her loan stock, if not at the very top of the market, then not far off it. 'Here is your little gain,' he said, handing her a printed certificate for 'long Annuities' worth £3,475, which promised her £200 a year.

It was the first time she had ever felt herself to be 'decidedly rich', and she reacted by bursting into tears.[18] 'The more I reflect on the generous proof you gave me this morning of your friendship & zeal for the interests of one who is so destitute of every means of shewing her gratitude but by her words,' she would write to him later that day, 'the more vexed I am with this vile tongue that did not do my feelings Justice.'[19]

The City of London was abuzz with rumours of staggering gains. 'It is reported upon 'Change,' said the *Gazetteer*, 'that the *celebrated* Mr. Atkinson's *clerks* are complimented with upwards of £150,000 of the new loan.'[20] Meanwhile, at Westminster, Sir George Savile introduced a parliamentary motion for a committee to look into the allocation of the loan, on grounds that a 'certain gentleman' had been allowed to doctor the lists 'in what manner best suited his own interest'.[21] George Byng, seconding the motion, pedantically read out to the chamber the names of the loan's 1,147 subscribers; among those that caught his eye were Messrs. Smith & Sill, who were well known as Richard's lawyers, and David Laird, whose £10,000 allocation was most surprising, since he had only arrived from America 'a few days before the noble lord opened his budget; but Captain Laird is the friend of Mr. Atkinson'.[22]

To avoid the scrutiny of her peers and – worse still – the clutches of her brother-in-law, Anne kept her newly acquired fortune a secret. Alexander Fordyce bragged endlessly about the riches that would soon spew forth from his soap-making factory in County Durham; but he was up to his old tricks again, bullying associates into lending him money, and flying into a rage if anyone had the temerity to question his dealings. 'He has drained the best powers of every friend he has,' Richard told Anne. 'Our House has suffered (if a mercantile interest is included) above a Hundred thousand pounds by him, he holds it as his worst enemy because it will go no further. Apart from this I have lent him (which I consider as gone) £13,000, and by what shifts and duplicities has it been obtained!'[23]

Once more, during a tearful two-hour tête-à-tête that dredged up unwelcome memories of that fateful day, nine years earlier, when he had brought word of her husband's impending bankruptcy, it fell to Richard to break to Margaret the unwelcome news of these debts.

The following morning, as the sisters were eating breakfast, bailiffs turned up at Harley Street to seize the contents of the house; but Richard was already on the spot, waiting to intercept them, and immediately took charge of the situation, paying off the sum for which Fordyce was being pursued. As Anne would recall: 'When he returned to us (gentle and unostentatious in all his modes), he sat down on his chair as if he thanked the friendship of those who allowed him to occupy it. This painful business over for the present, he departed, leaving a letter which he said he had forgot to deliver to Margaret, containing Two hundred pounds to discharge her own immediate bills.'[24]

GIVEN THE RUMPUS surrounding Richard's rum contracts, their settlement was a surprisingly low-key business. What ought to have been the routine matter of agreeing a fair price for this most ordinary of commodities had mutated into a full-blown political scandal, the subject of at least twenty-seven Treasury Board meetings. But on 31 May 1781, after a hiatus of almost two years while waiting for the Attorney General to determine the principles by which they should be guided, the referees Francis Baring and John Purrier were ready to deliver their verdict.

They marked down both Richard's first contract (100,000 gallons at the price paid by the navy in Jamaica, plus freight, leakage and insurance, agreed with the prime minister in September 1775) and his second (100,000 gallons at 5s 3d, agreed with the Treasury in May 1776), compelling him to refund £9,171 of the £61,608 that he had already received. (Even so, the judgement offered Richard vindication of sorts, for during the first failed attempt at arbitration, four years earlier, Beeston Long had refused to take the soaring cost of insurance into consideration; Baring and Purrier, on the other hand, factored it into their calculations.) With the referees' ruling on his third contract (350,000 gallons at a price to be determined by the Treasury, agreed with General Howe in April 1777), Richard had cause for satisfaction, for they set the price at 5s 2d per gallon – only a penny less than the much-criticized second contract.

Furthermore, Captain Laird certified that 499,738 gallons had been delivered to New York in fulfilment of the third contract, in nineteen ships unloaded under his supervision – a colossal over-delivery which valued the rum at £129,099.[25] Mures, Atkinson & Mure had already been paid most of this amount; the remaining £24,767 was authorized by royal warrant on 26 July, in the dead of the summer recess, when anyone who might have kicked up a fuss was out of town.[26] The final settlement of the rum business marked the end of one difficult chapter of Richard's life, and the start of another, more emotional one.

IT WAS SOON after my discovery of Bridget Atkinson's 'receipt book' – at a time when it was first dawning on me that I had somehow unearthed an astonishing family story, but as yet had little sense of where it might lead me – that I learnt about Richard's correspondence with Lady Anne Lindsay, in an old volume which I came across online. How many such letters existed, the book did not divulge; to find out more, I would need to visit the National Library of Scotland.

One Thursday evening, just before midnight, I boarded the sleeper train at Euston; seven hours later it trundled into Edinburgh Waverley station, on a gleaming spring morning. I arrived at the library as it opened – I had already been warned by the curator of manuscripts that the reading room would close at lunchtime, and there was a great deal for me to get through. I started with the printed catalogue of the Lindsay family archive, and was amazed to learn that the collection included hundreds of letters written by members of the Atkinson family over three generations – Richard had merely initiated a correspondence which had continued into the 1830s. I had an inkling that these later letters might relate to Jamaican property, but this would need investigation another time – the twenty-six letters written by Richard to Anne would keep me busy for one morning. Three hours later, I emerged on to the cobbles of Edinburgh's Old Town, into bright sunshine, feeling giddy, elated, and just a little besotted with my namesake.

Until this moment in the story, Richard's most heartfelt sentiments have remained under wraps – which might, perhaps, have
caused you to draw the conclusion that he was not the marrying
type. You would be mistaken, though, for Richard had fallen in love
with Anne Lindsay the moment he first laid eyes on her, and had
ever since been working towards a day when he might have sufficient wealth to transcend the social gulf that separated them.

One Sunday in July 1781, when he was forty-two, Richard sat
down to write the letter on which his future happiness would hinge.
He had already primed Anne to expect a note about a 'matter more
interesting' to him than any other, hoping that she might be able
to offer him 'very salutary counsel' on a point where he confessed
himself 'at a loss how to decide'.[27] That evening Anne was alone
at Harley Street, and expecting a visit from her fickle suitor Lord
Wentworth, when Richard's letter was delivered – her first impression was that 'it was a thick one'.[28]

When Anne (much, much later) wrote her life story, she cherry-
picked quotes from hundreds of old letters so that they slotted
neatly into her narrative – rather as I have tried to do. When the
time came to recount the circumstances surrounding this particular
letter, however, her powers of précis deserted her; instead she chose
to present Richard's words unabridged. As she would explain to her
readers: 'It is so much my duty to do justice to that excellent man,
that you must forgive me if on this occasion I sacrifice your patience
to him.'[29] Two hundred years on, I find myself facing a similar predicament – the main difference being that I am not quite so willing
to test my readers' patience. So I will only say that Richard's letter,
as an account of how he had reached this pivotal moment, is as
revealing a self-portrait of the man as exists, and can be found in its
entirety on page 419. But here is its tremulous final paragraph:

And now, by what *tenderest* Epithet, shall I adjure *My Counsellor*
to tell me whether my Desires ought to be laid at my fair
Friend's Feet or not! I tremble from the fear of diminishing
the Share I at present hold in her Esteem, but the Knowledge

I have of the Generosity of her Heart supports me in the Hope that she will not put an unkind Construction upon any part of my Conduct. And altho' I suspect her in one particular to be *an Economist* yet I am sure she is *no Niggard*, but that her Heart will feel the *inestimable* Value of a frank Avowal – and that if *your happy* Counsel at eleven tomorrow (if not forbid) is to embolden me to submit my Passion – *she* will with *one* Look of Kindness at our *first* Interview extend to me the Golden Sceptre and tranquilize my Spirits by *that* assurance that there exists no absolute & insurmountable Bar to my Happiness; beyond which meaning I will not attempt to interpret her Goodness till she gives me leave. How many Blessings does my Heart wish to pour upon her![30]

Anne had not quite finished reading this 'heart-breaking letter' when she heard Margaret come in through the front door, and she hastily retreated to her bedchamber, for she did not want her sister to know that she had been sobbing. Anne realized, from the 'delusion of hope' which pervaded Richard's letter, that 'no report respecting Lord Wentworth' had reached his ears; and it was with deep sadness that she sat down at her desk and revealed her attachment to another man. 'Never did I find a letter so difficult to write, every feeling in my nature was at jar,' she recalled. 'Loaded with obligations, in my own person and in Margaret's, yet returning nothing, disappointing the constant heart that had been so long devoted to me . . . The Watchman called one . . . and two . . . and three . . . and four; and five found me with the pen still in my hand, & my letter unfinished.'[31]

At eight on Monday morning, a messenger delivered Anne's letter to Fenchurch Street. 'Could I only find words, gentle without conveying Illusion, unreserved yet consoling how eagerly would I not use them,' she had written,

But there I must stop – if you will permit to make him who calls himself my client my confidant perhaps I may in the course of a day or two find courage to paint the situation of

a heart which has long strayed from home into the possession
of one who I hope has by degrees learnt to value it – there it
rests and ever will remain. I would not have hurried this point
to my friend had I not learnt at one time from a painfull
experience how severe a moment that of uncertainty is. God
bless you, I pray for your happiness.[32]

Richard called at Harley Street on Wednesday, at Anne's invitation, and was shown up to the drawing room. 'Ten years seemed
added to his appearance, which made me start, and filled my heart
with something like remorse,' she remembered.[33] The conversation
was general, for he was one of several callers that morning, and was
thus unable to say what he had wished to be able to say. That evening he wrote to Anne:

Escaped at length from the tiresome Task of talking about one
thing whilst my mind is wholly intent upon another, I fly to the
Relief which an undisguised communication with my Friend
alone can give me. I hope I did not betray myself today to
Lady M, altho' I am not sure of it. I do not misinterpret your
Intention in not seeing me alone, but you had very near taxed
my Fortitude too high. The Wind & the Dust for these two
days (of which from the Impossibility of excusing myself from
seeing multitudes if I staid at home I have spent a great part in
the Streets) have been my very good Auxiliaries in preventing
observation.[34]

Richard's great dread, having revealed his innermost feelings to
Anne, was that she might henceforth shun his company, to avoid
'adding fresh Fuel to a hopeless Flame'; so he set out to prove that
any such qualms were unnecessary. 'For the Inquietude I have given
you I will not attempt a *common* Apology which you would despise,'
he wrote to her the following week. 'I rather dare flatter myself with
your approbation of my having *disclosed* my Sentiments under the
circumstances in which I did it; and that *bearing* Adversity like a

Man, my Friend will not think hardly of me for having *felt* it as a Man.' Now, as he explained, he hoped to foster a relationship of a fraternal kind:

> My *Hopes* are *dead*. I know too well the force of a true
> attachment in a strong and virtuous Mind to expect a change
> whilst any thing like a proper conduct is reciprocally held.
> I solemnly repeat therefore that all my *Hopes* are at an end.
> That I feel I can rejoice in your happiness with another, and
> when the proper time arrives can *cordially* court his Friendship.
> I entertain not a Sentiment at this Moment that ought to alarm
> or offend him. *Let* me not then upon mistaken Ground *be held*
> *distant!* Let me have leave to cultivate the Affection of a Brother,
> and to watch over your Welfare as far as my Knowledge
> extends, with a kind Brother's Care![35]

NINE

Mortal Thoughts

THE RELENTLESS WORKLOAD of the war years, as well as the recent blow of his failed marriage proposal, had taken their toll on Richard's health. He would spend much of the autumn of 1781 at Brighthelmstone, a resort in vogue ever since the publication of *A Dissertation on the Use of Sea-Water in the Diseases of the Glands* by Richard Russell, a local physician, nearly thirty years earlier. (The town's altered status – from sleepy fishing village to princely destination – would be accompanied by a change of name, with 'Brighton' soon replacing its more cumbersome precursor.) Richard had managed to secure a good house at the bottom of West Street, overlooking the steep shingle beach. 'The Place as full as can be conceived,' he told Anne on 22 August. 'All the World now resorting to the Rooms since the D & Ds of Cumberland have led the way.'[1] (The duke was a younger brother of the king, who had caused a great scandal by marrying a commoner.)

The Lindsay sisters stayed several weeks with Richard at Brighton during the season, and they made it their mission to launch him into the best society. As Anne afterwards recalled: 'I now saw that the only way in which I could be of present use to Atkinson was by impressing on Margaret that we owed it to his friendship to give him every aid on entering more into company than his habits had hitherto led him to do.' Music and dancing were the principal diversions at Brighton. Richard himself laid on entertainments, engaging some 'choice Catch-singers' from London to stay a few days of every week down in the resort; meanwhile the sisters sang at the soirées of their royal friends, the Cumberlands.[2] Anne watched Richard moving uneasily among the fashionable set, showing his discomfort in their society: 'The manners of the excellent Atkinson were so unlike those of the day that while his heart was glowing with benevolence, ten to one his manner was astonishing all around, and creating a sensation of pain from its familiarity to the persons in the world he felt most respectfully towards.'[3]

Richard's melancholia increased after the deaths, in quick succession, of his two eldest siblings. Jane, who had never married, died at Temple Sowerby on 26 August, aged fifty-three. Six weeks later George, suffering from a 'large tumour on his neck', came down to London to submit to the knife of John Hunter, the king's surgeon; he died two days later in 'excruciating pain', aged fifty-one, and was buried in the little church at Rood Lane, a stone's throw from Fenchurch Street.[4] Sadly, I have no way of finding out whether Bridget was there to hold George's hand during his final hours, nor whether Richard was at his brother's bedside – this event is not recorded by any family letters, only in a brief newspaper report.

Thus mortal thoughts were uppermost in Richard's mind, and he now set about writing his will. 'If ever Man was entitled to dispose of his fortune according to his own sentiments, it is myself,' he would tell Anne, declaring it his intention not only to make ample provision for her in the event of his death, but also to remove any financial obstacles to her marriage to Lord Wentworth:

> I am clearly convinced that the probability of enjoyment in Life is *with me* at an end. All my Hopes are therefore centred in standing as high as I can in your Esteem, and promoting your Happiness in the way it can be pursued; and strange as it would sound to the multitude, yet I trust my Friend will find nothing *to reprove* in the strong Wish I express that her Happiness were in its own way completed, and even that *I* could be made instrumental in accelerating it.[5]

ON 25 NOVEMBER 1781, a messenger drew up outside the house of Colonial Secretary Lord George Germain in Pall Mall, conveying a report that a Franco-American army had encircled a British force of nine thousand men at Yorktown in Virginia, and on 17 October, following ten days' bombardment, General Cornwallis had capitulated. Germain immediately went to see Lord North at Downing Street, who received the news 'as he would have taken a Ball in his Breast', repeatedly exclaiming 'Oh, God! it is all over!' as he paced up and down the room.[6]

The Battle of Yorktown ended British hopes of holding on to the American colonies, and unleashed a tide of recriminations back home. Of all the events which had contributed to the catastrophe, a consensus formed that Sir George Rodney's deeds on the island of Saint Eustatius had been among the most discreditable. Britain had declared war on the Dutch Republic in December 1780, infuriated by the partiality shown by this supposedly neutral nation towards its enemies. Admiral Rodney had seized the Dutch freeport of Saint Eustatius in February 1781; according to prize protocol, he was due a one-sixteenth share of all captured goods, and he chose to spend the next three months auctioning off the contents of the Dutch warehouses, rather than giving chase to his French adversary, Admiral de Grasse. In July, as the hurricane season approached, naval operations in the West Indies were suspended as usual, and Rodney decided to return to England, leaving behind a reduced fleet to follow the French towards the American mainland.

Admiral Graves had arrived at the mouth of Chesapeake Bay on 5 September, hoping to bring relief to Cornwallis's besieged army, only to find its entrance blocked by Admiral de Grasse. The two squadrons traded fire throughout the afternoon, causing heavy damage on both sides, and Graves subsequently retreated to New York. It was the correct decision, even if it did seal the fate of the American colonies; for the destruction of the fleet would have led to the obliteration of Britain's interests in the West Indies.

Meanwhile, in London, Sir George Rodney set about defending himself against accusations of avarice. His claims of ill health won him scant sympathy. 'Spending so much Time in the damp Vaults of St Eustatia, in taking a minute Cognisance of their Contents, even to a single Pound of Tub Butter and Stockfish, must have affected a Constitution much more athletic than that of the *gallant* Admiral,' scoffed the *Public Advertiser*.[7] During the autumn, Rodney admitted a stream of visitors to his house in Hertford Street; Richard's name appears twice in the visitors' book, on 16 and 30 November, but we can only guess at what they discussed.[8]

Lord North's ministry quickly unravelled following the disaster at Yorktown. The prime minister could no longer hide his ambivalent feelings about the war, long suppressed out of duty to his monarch. On 12 December, Sir James Lowther placed a motion to end the conflict before the House of Commons. North objected to the wording of Lowther's motion, claiming that it would undermine the country's ability to forge an advantageous peace; while Germain, as Colonial Secretary, vowed he would never sign any document recognizing America's independence. Two days later, in a mute display of ministerial disagreement, halfway through a heated debate on the subject, North stood up from the front bench and sat down behind it, 'leaving Lord George Germain alone in that conspicuous Situation, exposed to the Attacks of the Opposition'.[9]

The Christmas recess ought to have offered Lord North respite from his political foes; instead he found himself a hostage to his so-called friends. Henry Dundas, now Lord Advocate of Scotland, was a powerful debater who also commanded a sizeable contingent of Scottish MPs. So long as Lord George Germain continued to hold office, Dundas told the prime minister, he and his supporters would stay away from the House. At a time when the ministry's majority was ebbing away, this ultimatum could not be ignored – and soon Germain was gone.

On 25 February 1782, Lord North announced a new loan to plug the hole in the national finances; this time £13,500,000 would be needed. To avoid a repetition of the previous year's controversy – when Richard was alleged to have sat in a room at the Treasury where he apportioned the loan to subscribers of his choosing – the prime minister invited tenders from two groups of City men. The *General Advertiser* announced the winning team:

> The conductors of this grand operation are no other (take them as they are) than Edward Payne, Esq., a wealthy linen-draper; the Right Honourable Thomas Harley, contractor for cloathing and remittances; the Scotch banker, Mr. Drummond, contract-copartner with Mr. Harley, and the renowned, immaculate, and undaunted Richard Atkinson, the famous rum-contractor. On the three first there needs no comment; but surely the Minister must have been drunk with contract rum, who could presume to bring the last personage forward again to public inspection . . . Atkinson, the former disciple, and now the fair representative of Samuel Touchet! Atkinson! of whom a late Alderman emphatically said, *Samuel Touchet will never die while that fellow lives.*[10]

This last was a cruel jibe – for Touchet, who was Richard's earliest mentor, had some years before hanged himself from his bedpost, a despised and broken man.

'We have agreed for the Loan on the same Terms we should have offered had there been no opposition,' Richard told Anne, at the end of a long day of negotiations at Downing Street. '*Low,* but in my opinion *safe.*'[11] Although Mures, Atkinson & Mure this time took a £2 million share of the loan, Hutchison Mure wished to hold on to just £200,000 for the direct benefit of the partnership. Richard was free to distribute the remainder of the loan stock as he saw fit, and he chose to place much of it under his friends' names without telling them – planning only to reveal what he had done once he could pass on 'the gain with the intelligence'.[12] He showed this list of secret beneficiaries to Anne; her own name, naturally, came at the very top.

LORD NORTH'S MINISTRY suffered its first outright parliamentary defeat on 27 February. The following week, news came of the surrender to the Spanish of the Mediterranean island of Minorca. This event was not unexpected, for the fortress of St Philip was riddled with scurvy, and Mures, Atkinson & Mure had recently been ordered to dispatch emergency supplies of lemons, rice, molasses, essence of spruce, 'portable soup', salt, sugar, tea leaves and strong red wine; but still, it harked back to a dark moment in 1756 when, as Charles James Fox taunted the prime minister, the 'loss of Minorca alone' had been considered 'sufficient grounds for the removal of an administration'.[13]

Shortly afterwards, what seemed like better news arrived from the West Indies – Admiral Hood had apparently trounced Admiral de Grasse's squadron and rescued Saint Kitts from invasion. Richard obtained this information on 8 March, via a ship returning from Jamaica, and immediately passed it to Philip Stephens, the first secretary of the Admiralty. The opposition were sceptical, however, suspecting the story to be a fabrication 'coined on purpose' to provide relief to the failing ministry.[14] 'That Messrs. Muir and Atkinson should fly with alacrity to Government with any thing in the shape of good news, will not be wondered at, when it is considered how deeply they are interested in it,' commented the *London Courant*.[15] When official word reached the Admiralty on 12 March, it was clear that the earlier report had been an exaggeration. Hood had indeed outmanoeuvred de Grasse's superior fleet, but still the French had managed to capture Saint Kitts.

On 15 March the ministry scraped through a motion of no confidence by just nine votes. 'The rats were very bad,' complained John Robinson, whose job it was as chief whip to keep the sinking ship afloat.[16] To everyone except the monarch a change of ministry seemed inevitable. For a few days the king bleakly pondered his own abdication, before reluctantly granting Lord North permission to resign.

Late on the afternoon of 20 March, Lord Surrey, from the opposition benches, stood up in the packed chamber of the House of Commons to propose a motion for the removal of the ministers; at the same time Lord North rose to make a short statement of his own. After an hour's wrangling over which noble lord should take the floor first, North prevailed and announced the end of his ministry. Parliament adjourned immediately. Outside snow was falling, and MPs impatiently thronged Old Palace Yard while their carriages were summoned from afar. Lord North, on the other hand, had told his coachman to wait outside, so his was the first carriage to roll up. 'Good night, Gentlemen,' he said as he climbed in, 'you see what it is to be in the Secret.'[17]

The following week was marked by the customary scramble to reward the loyal supporters of the outgoing ministry. One of these, James Macpherson, was a Scotsman notorious for his 'discovery' of an epic poem by the third-century bard Ossian, which he had 'translated' from the Gaelic. Published to great fanfare in 1761, *Fingal* had soon been exposed as a literary hoax – Samuel Johnson denounced its author as a 'mountebank, a liar, and a fraud'. Macpherson had served the Treasury first as a pamphleteer (a role for which he was eminently qualified, given his proven ability to make things up), and latterly from the back benches of the House of Commons. Lord North wished to award Macpherson a pension, but was unable to do so unless he vacated his parliamentary seat; Richard provided a solution to this predicament, at the same time turning it to the Lindsay sisters' advantage, by offering to pay Macpherson a lump sum of £4,200 from his own money, in return for pensions of £150 a year for each of them, to come out of a special fund set aside for 'indigent young women of quality'.[18]

Lord North's handwriting was dreadful at the best of times, but the letters from his final day in office betray the sheer intensity of his haste. Among the warrants sent over to St James's Palace for royal signature on 26 March were those for the Lindsays' pensions, and also for John Robinson's pension of £1,000 a year. 'In order to produce £1,000 nett, the Pension must be of £1,500,' observed North in a scrawled postscript.[19] At nine the next morning the king wrote: 'I can by no means think Mr. Robinson should have the fees paid out of his Pension of £1,000 per annum; I therefore return it unsigned that it may be altered, but it must be here before eleven this day and antedated some days.'[20] And two hours later: 'Where is Robinson's Warrant?'[21] By the afternoon, the Marquess of Rockingham had kissed hands and was again prime minister, some sixteen years since last holding the office.

Entirely unmerited though they were, no one thought to pass comment on the pensions awarded to the Lindsay sisters. John Robinson's pension, on the other hand, generated a barrage of abuse. John Sawbridge, an MP for the City of London with a republican reputation, launched a vindictive attack on Robinson in the Commons. Why did Robinson need this lavish sum, when he already owned a 'very fine house' in St James's Square and a 'most superb villa' just outside the metropolis? And how had he been able to buy these valuable properties in the first place? In response, Robinson disclosed that he had sold his 'paternal estate' in Westmorland for £23,000, and had given the proceeds to his daughter on her recent marriage; that he had borrowed £12,800 to buy his 'small house in the country'; that he did not own the house in St James's Square, but had taken it on a repairing lease for the annual rent of £150; and that he had a backlog of bills and two families to support.[22]

Sawbridge's insinuation was that Robinson had derived financial benefit from his connection to his favourite contractor – but whether Richard ever paid backhanders to the Secretary to the Treasury, we'll never know. Certainly, though, Richard had recently assisted his friend with a delicate money problem. In August 1781, Robinson's only child Mary had become engaged to Henry Nevill, the heir to Lord Abergavenny. Much to the future father-in-law's disappointment, however, the young blood had turned out to be a gamester. Robinson, having already settled a dowry of £25,000 on his daughter, agreed to bail Nevill out, but insisted on a full reckoning of his debts. Richard had gone down with Robinson to Sussex, and then to Monmouthshire, to perform the due diligence that preceded the marriage. When Nevill, having sworn he owed no more than £18,000, discovered the true figure to be £26,000, he persuaded his attorney to present a false account to Robinson, and agreed to repay the secret balance from his wife-to-be's marriage settlement. After the wedding, Robinson cleared all the debts admitted by Nevill, and Richard paid off tradesmen's bills worth more than £400. All this expense would almost ruin Robinson; he gave up the house in St James's Square, and sold his coach-horses. Unsurprisingly, he chose not to divulge these details in the House of Commons.

WHILE LORD NORTH'S ministry was fading away, France plotted its annexation of Britain's sugar islands. Faced with such a clear danger, the West India lobby put aside their political differences and on 2 January 1782 presented a grand petition to George III in which they begged for 'reinforcements, naval and military' to be sent without delay. The king, it was reported, received the petition with a respect that had not always been 'shewn to his people' when they had 'presumed to approach him on the subject of public grievances'.[23] Unusually for a document that implied criticism of the ministry, Richard was one of the signatories.

Violent winds in the English Channel prevented Admiral Rodney's fleet from setting out for the West Indies until mid-January 1782. All this time, the French navy under Admiral de Grasse continued to pick off the Leeward Islands; the fall of Saint Kitts was swiftly followed by the surrender of Nevis and Montserrat. On 25 February, Rodney finally joined up with Admiral Hood, and the combined fleet anchored at Saint Lucia, where it was well positioned to keep watch over the enemy at neighbouring Martinique. By 8 April the French were on the move, and believed to be planning a rendezvous with the Spanish at Santo Domingo before heading west to Jamaica; the French flagship, the *Ville de Paris*, was rumoured to have fifty thousand manacles on board, to be used for restraining the island's enslaved population.

Early on 12 April, the British caught up with the French off the coast of Dominica, near the rocky islets known as Les Saintes. The engagement started in the time-honoured manner, with the warships of the two nations – thirty-six British, thirty French – sailing in parallel lines in opposite directions while blasting away at each other. But after several hours' battle, when the smoke was at its

Admiral de Grasse relinquishes his sword to 'the Gallant Admiral Rodney'.

thickest, the wind changed, which suddenly divided the French line. A number of British vessels were able to glide through the gap, and proceeded to bombard the enemy at close range from both sides. By evening, five French ships had been captured, including the *Ville de Paris*, with Admiral de Grasse on board. The fatalities ran into thousands; the sharks fed well that night.

The story of this great British victory, by which Jamaica was rescued from the clutches of the French, electrified the nation. The Battle of the Saintes was the first time that 'breaking the line' was recognized as a naval tactic, and in its aftermath the theoreticians squabbled over whose idea it had been. It's possible that Richard played a small role in its conception.

John Clerk of Eldin, the Scottish author of an influential textbook about naval tactics despite never having been to sea, was the first to take credit; he claimed to have attended a meeting with 'Richard Atkinson, the particular friend of Sir George Rodney' in January 1780, at which he had communicated his 'theories of attack from both the windward and leeward', in particular his 'doctrine of cutting the enemy's line', all of which Richard had promised to tell the admiral.[24] The playwright Richard Cumberland, on the other hand, believed the idea had occurred to Rodney while they were both the guests of Lord George Germain during the autumn of 1781; Cumberland recalled the admiral rounding up a heap of cherry stones at the dinner table and arranging them 'as two fleets drawn up in line and opposed to each other', before animatedly steering the pips representing his warships among those of his enemy.[25] Both accounts were later disputed by Sir Howard Douglas, who insisted that his father, Rodney's Captain of the Fleet, had been the 'original suggester' of the manoeuvre.[26] In any case, through his brilliant deployment of this tactic at the Battle of the Saintes, Admiral Rodney was reinvented as the great saviour of the empire, a silhouette to be found gracing countless commemorative medals, tankards and punchbowls.

DESPITE HIS FAILURE to unite the Atkinson and Lindsay lines through marriage, Richard continued to promote the interests of both families. Through the patronage of Sir William James, one of his partners in the contract to provision the army in Canada and chairman of the East India Company in 1779, Richard had obtained a coveted Bengal writership – a junior clerical position – for his nephew Michael Atkinson, George and Bridget's eldest son.[27] Richard's next nephew, George, had meanwhile joined Mures, Atkinson & Mure's counting house at Fenchurch Street in order to learn the rudiments of the West India trade, with a view to joining the partnership at some future date.

As for the Lindsay family – Richard's devotion to their cause was almost limitless. Anne was by now the mistress of a £30,000 fortune after he managed to sell her 'secret share' of the 1782 loan for a 'princely gain'.[28] Richard also loyally served the interests of Anne's brothers, in particular guiding the older ones through the complex negotiations for army commissions – the going rate for a lieutenant-colonelcy being at that time around £5,000. Alexander, sixth Earl of Balcarres, who was Anne's junior by thirteen months, had served under General Burgoyne in America, proving his mettle (and good fortune) during fierce fighting near Ticonderoga, where 'thirteen balls passed through a jacket, waistcoat, and breeches' without inflicting so much as a scratch.[29] Soon afterwards, at Saratoga, Balcarres had been captured and paroled to New York in exchange for a Continental Army officer of the same rank.

Colin Lindsay, Anne's third brother, had also served in America before landing at Gibraltar with Rodney's expedition in the spring of 1780. Two years later he was still cooped up there, and the garrison's supplies were once again running low. So impregnable was the Rock that the French and Spanish allies could find no way of taking it by land; instead they planned a grand assault from the sea. A French engineer devised a system of floating batteries, built from the hulls of old vessels; ten of these monsters, each armed with fifteen cannons, were anchored in a line five hundred yards from the shore. The offensive started on the morning of 13 September 1782, and the batteries went to work blasting away at the fortress.

But one commodity of which Gibraltar did have plenty was coal, left over from Richard's supply eighteen months earlier. By late afternoon the garrison's forges had built up a blistering heat, and it was time to unleash the British secret weapon – more than a hundred cannons which rained down red-hot shot on the floating batteries. Within hours they were destroyed, and nine enemy warships had also been consumed by fire. The following month, Admiral Howe sailed unchallenged into the bay with thirty-four warships and thirty-one transport ships, bringing relief to Gibraltar for the third and final time. Richard played no role in this mission; for the new Treasury Board showed no desire to engage his services.

THE YOUNGEST OF the Lindsay sisters, nineteen-year-old Elizabeth, married Philip Yorke, heir to the Earl of Hardwicke, in July 1782; Richard helped draw up her marriage settlement.[30] Announcing the nuptials in its gossip column, the *Morning Herald* also suggested that another marriage was imminent, though 'not with quite so much advanced certainty', between Lady Anne Lindsay and Viscount Wentworth.[31] But this was no longer true; for the death of Catharine Vanloo several months earlier had dealt their engagement a fatal blow. Anne now felt that were she to marry Wentworth, it would be merely to fill the vacancy left by his late mistress.

Nor had he curbed his gambling. Late one evening that summer, Wentworth turned up at Harley Street in great distress and confessed to Anne that he had spent the previous three days and nights at his club, where he had squandered such a vast sum that he had been forced to borrow from moneylenders on terms 'usurious beyond the common pitch of usury'. Anne's decision to free him from the grip of these men derived more from pity than love; and he could never know that it was she who had saved him. With some reluctance, for it would not be easy to explain her motives 'without opening ill-healed wounds', she asked Richard to carry out the business on her behalf.[32] Wentworth accepted Richard's offer of a loan with complacent civility, and unwittingly borrowed £4,500 of Anne's fortune. 'I have been very busyly employed in *paying money* lately, & this morning have washed my hands of all Israelitish connections,' he told his sister on 20 August. 'I am now as poor as a Rat, tho' hope I have laid in a fresh stock of credit, which I shall use sparingly.'[33]

A few months later, Richard rescued Anne from another unpleasant situation. 'Leon', a blackmailer who appeared to have inside knowledge of Wentworth's rackety private life, perhaps through a connection with the late Mrs Vanloo, threatened to publish all the love letters Anne had ever written to him, and thus reveal to the world the 'Villanous art' that she had practised against his dead mistress: 'how you endeavourd by every means in your power to push her away from his house from his Children to send her abroad – in short what did you not do to make her miserable that you might triumph as Lady W – a title his Lordship never meant to bestow upon you'.[34] Richard drafted a sharp reply, which was duly left at Seagoes Coffee House in Holborn. 'Your threatening Letter has been laid before Counsel,' he wrote, 'and it appears that by Act of Parliament the punishment for *sending it* is *Death*. From circumstances known to one of the Persons mentioned you are already in part traced, and to push the Enquiry to your compleat Detection and punishment is far from difficult. The smallest publick Impertinence will at once fix that purpose and facilitate its execution.'[35]

Although Richard always insisted that Anne's fortune was hers to treat entirely as she pleased, and pressed her to spend more, she had mixed feelings about doing so. She appreciated the luxuries it bought, such as the well-appointed box at the King's Theatre in the Haymarket, within nodding distance of the Duke of Cumberland and Prince of Wales's boxes – her subscription was in Richard's name, but she had all the benefit.[36] She did not, however, enjoy the secrecy surrounding her money; and nor could she shake the feeling that it was slightly ill-gotten. 'I often wished,' she later wrote, 'I could have possessed my pension and a quiet £5,000 only, rather than be subjected to the censure of people who might blame me for deriving any advantage from the Funds, thro' the means of a rejected lover.'[37]

For various reasons, Richard was short of ready money during the latter months of 1782, and Anne was happy to tie up half of her capital, some £15,000, to relieve him of the burden of a loan to the estate of the late Captain John Bentinck. But when Richard tried to persuade her to accept documents that would identify her as a mortgagee on the Bentinck estate in Norfolk, she refused, feebly protesting that she did not have a writing desk to lock them in. When he offered to buy her such an item, a fear that he would make an expensive present of it tyrannized over her better judgement. 'I promised I would procure myself a bureau,' she recalled, 'but without intending to do it.'[38]

The will that Richard began planning in the wake of his siblings' deaths had meanwhile swollen into an ambitious document; it had taken him and his lawyers more than a year to prepare. On 22 December 1782, the day before he signed it, Richard sent the final draft over to Anne, along with a covering letter, to make sure he had her concurrence 'in the propriety' of every part of it:

I cannot say that I am sorry to find a necessity for changing the Plan we before talked of and tying up the Estates for the

present Generation. I think it will be the means of their doing
the more good. I have no Wish that any Nephew of mine should
be put above being the Builder of his own fortunes, for I do not
think it would contribute to his happiness. Assistance therein
I would afford him, but not enough to make him dream that he
was to plant himself there, and live a vegetable Life upon the
Income. As the matter now stands arranged, I solemnly declare
I think I have left as much to my own family as will do them
any good, and that my own Sentiments are somewhat wounded
by leaving so little in your power, and I sincerely ask it of your
friendship to tell me truly your thoughts thereon.

At this point, Richard enters into a rather tortuous declaration
of the 'ardor' with which his soul rushes 'to a communication' with
hers 'in points where I feel they are made to embrace each other in
spite of all the empty formalities of Life' – before acknowledging
that he is 'wandering' from his purpose, and continuing:

Let us my dear Friend talk all this fully over & put it into such
form as may be most to the purpose if the Event of my Death
should happen – and forgive this ill connected Letter – when I
took the Pen I meant only to write half a dozen Lines . . . but
I am some way got into a way of writing straight forward to
you, without forethought or attempt at Correction of what I
have wrote, that *indeed* is not a careless contempt of my Friend
– but (as I think) a part of that extreme desire which possesses
me to throw my whole Heart open to her, to throw its most
secret Sensations unveiled before her. The Consciousness that
her Eye must review it would be sufficient to keep out all the
black Family, & as to human Frailties, the Heart knows much
less than mine that does not know that under the Influence of a
generous confidence they would become the very Cement of its
best Happiness. But there's no end of Dissertation. And so – it
being near two in the morning, I say – *Fingers* be at rest – &
Mind take thy chance of being so to.[39]

TEN

A Royal Coup

SHELVES EITHER SIDE of my sitting room fireplace display blue and white Chinese porcelain of a pattern representing flowers and butterflies – plates, bowls, sauceboats and soup tureens – the remnants of a much larger dinner set which evidently saw plenty of active service in its day. I had always wondered how this china might have come into my family, but it was only when I found out about Richard Atkinson's ship, the *Bessborough*, that its provenance began to emerge.

Launched at Rotherhithe on 27 November 1772, the *Bessborough* held one of the East India Company's valuable licences to carry porcelain, silk and tea back from China. Such ships were the super-tankers of their day – the *Bessborough* was 144 feet long and 39 feet broad, with three decks and 907 tons' capacity. Richard commissioned the building of the vessel and acted as its managing owner, a role known as 'ship's husband'. Shipping on such a scale and over such epic distances carried grave risks, too great for an individual to bear, and East Indiaman vessels were typically owned by syndicates, their holdings divided up into one-sixteenth shares.

When the *Bessborough* returned from its second voyage, in October 1781, it was in need of a total overhaul. (It had been caught up in conflict on the Indian subcontinent during the four years it was away, having assisted in the blockade of the French enclave of Pondicherry in August 1778.)[1] Some prickly correspondence about

163

the repairs reveals tensions between Richard and another of the *Bessborough*'s owners, the globetrotting botanist Sir Joseph Banks. On one occasion, when Banks sent a note complaining how long it was taking to put the ship into dry dock at Deptford, Richard's reply conveyed a clear flash of irritation. 'I very frankly confess to you,' he shot back, 'that I think the Distrust expressed by your Letter of this Date might have been spared till you had better foundation for it than the Suggestions to which you seem lately to have paid attention. I know of no reason but the want of Water for the Bessborough's not getting into Dock, and believe that no other exists.'[2] By December 1782, the newly copper-bottomed *Bessborough* was once again seaworthy and ready to embark upon its third voyage to China.

One afternoon at the British Library I was scrutinizing a hefty tome called *Chinese Armorial Porcelain*, hunting through thousands of pictures for a match with my own china. I turned a page, and there it was – a plate exactly like mine, apart from the coat of arms painted in its middle. (The Atkinson version has a humble monogram.) '*Montgomerie* quartering *Eglinton*,' read the caption. 'This service was undoubtedly made for Captain Alexander Montgomerie of the Hon. East India Company who commanded the East Indiaman *Bessborough* at Canton in 1780.'[3] It was a eureka moment – I could only imagine that Montgomerie must have purchased my porcelain at the same time as his own.

This explanation, already plausible, was later reinforced when I found Captain Montgomerie's papers relating to the *Bessborough*'s second voyage in the library of the National Maritime Museum at Greenwich. The East India Company allowed its ships' officers generous personal trading allowances – eighty tons going out, sixty tons coming home – and the first of Montgomerie's invoice books records that his outward cargo included beads, buttons, gold thread, ribbons, canvas, cordage, saddlery, claret, port, Jamaica rum, glassware, hats, linseed oil, tar, ironware, sheet copper, knives, sword blades, pianofortes, sheet music, stationery, prints, periodicals and books. It also shows that he bought 262 chests of opium in India,

A soup tureen, brought back from China on board the Bessborough.

to be exchanged for tea in China.⁴ A second invoice book records that on the return passage, Montgomerie's personal goods included hyson tea, cassia bark, rhubarb, wallpaper, silks, nankeen (a kind of cotton cloth), 'Gambouge' (a deep yellow pigment) and porcelain. More specifically, listed among his buys at Canton in November 1780, from a merchant called Synchong, are '3 Table Setts of the Best Blue & White Stone China, scolloped border, Gold Edge, & Landscape pattern consisting of 170 Pieces', as well as another set of the same pattern bearing 'Captn. Montgomerie's Arms'.⁵ This, I am certain, is the record of my china's purchase.

THE HEADQUARTERS OF the Honourable East India Company – to use the official title of this most morally dubious of corporations – were on Leadenhall Street, two minutes' walk from Richard's premises in Fenchurch Street. Behind a deceptively narrow façade, East India House stretched back some three hundred feet, and included rooms for the twenty-four directors and their clerks, a garden and courtyard, warehouses, and a General Court Room for the meetings of stockholders, known as 'proprietors'. The East India Company's politics had grown ever more rancorous over the previous decade, despite the supposed restraining influence of Lord North's Regulating Act of 1773. This legislation had subsumed the presidencies of Madras and Bombay under Bengal's control; but Warren Hastings, promoted to Governor General of Bengal, had proved a divisive figure, and Lord North's attempts to dismiss him had been thwarted by the proprietors. Meanwhile, John Robinson had set about building a government power base within the Company by actively encouraging the ministry's supporters to purchase stock, holding out the possibility of rewards for those who made themselves useful in the General Court of Proprietors. Richard had owned stock nominally worth £1,000, enough to qualify him to vote, since October 1773.[6]

It was inevitable, given the extent of his commercial interests, that Richard should cross paths with some shady characters, and the aforementioned Paul Benfield, co-purchaser of the Bogue estate in Jamaica, was perhaps the shadiest of the lot. How Richard first got mixed up in his affairs is not entirely clear, but the two men likely met in late 1779 or early 1780; it would be an exaggeration to call them friends, but they must have seemed useful to one another. Benfield – nicknamed 'Count Rupee' – was a key player in one of the East India Company's most toxic scandals, which had originated in Madras during the 1760s. The business centred on the spiralling debts of the Nawab of Arcot, ruler of southern India's Carnatic region, who had borrowed vast sums at exorbitant rates of interest from many local Company officials.

Benfield, who was foremost of the old man's creditors, was among a handful of Company servants recalled to England to account for their disruptive activities. John Macpherson was another; he arrived in London in July 1777, joining forces with his cousin, James 'Ossian' Macpherson, on a press campaign to justify his actions. (It was James Macpherson whose pro-ministry pamphleteering would later be rewarded with a lump sum paid by Richard on Lord North's behalf.) Benfield purchased a Wiltshire estate that included an electoral interest in Cricklade, a borough with notoriously bribable voters; at the general election of September 1780, he and John Macpherson were returned as the town's two MPs. Three months later, the directors of the East India Company cleared Benfield of wrongdoing and granted him leave to return to Madras. However, a group of irate proprietors led by Edmund Burke pressed for a hearing of their own. At the subsequent inquiry, on 17 January 1781, the motion was carried in Benfield's favour by a narrow margin; a week later he set off for India.

It was in the midst of all this clamour, on 31 December 1780, that Richard and Benfield had each signed the legal instrument with which Hutchison Mure vested in them the joint ownership of the Bogue estate.[7] Benfield had no wish to become a sugar baron; his share of the investment was simply a vehicle for his East Indian loot. He would gradually pay for his half of the Jamaican property with bills, gold and diamonds remitted from Madras.

In March 1781, eighteen-year-old Michael Atkinson – George and Bridget's eldest son – sailed to Calcutta to take up his East India Company writership, travelling on the same ship as John Macpherson, recently appointed by Lord North to the Supreme Council of Bengal. Michael's family connections would prove of great value on the subcontinent. 'Our friend, Mr. John Macpherson, will explain to you how much we all owe in these disagreeable times to the ability, friendship and exertions of Mr. Atkinson,' James Macpherson wrote to Governor General Hastings on 22 April 1782. 'Mr. Atkinson has a nephew, under your government, who went out last year under the protection of Mr. Macpherson. In policy, as well as gratitude, decided support and a marked attention are due to that young gentleman on account of his Uncle.'[8]

TIME AND AGAIN I would marvel at Richard's uncanny knack of positioning himself, if not at the epicentre of major events, then extraordinarily close by. Often it feels as though he is just offstage, pulling strings – something that James Gillray suggests in an early engraving, *Banco to the Knave*, which was published on 12 April 1782, just after the fall of the North ministry. Lord North is depicted presiding over a large card table, looking down dolefully as he acknowledges that it is all over; Charles James Fox has a huge pile of gold guineas in front of him, Lord Rockingham a smaller one. A cheering crowd of supporters throngs round them; and at one end of the table sits a croupier, representing (though looking nothing like) John Robinson, who

*Banco to the Knave, in which the change of
ministry is likened to a game of cards.*

says simply: 'Atkinson cut the cards.'
Richard's political skills would come
into their own during the two years
of intense turbulence that followed the
demise of Lord North's government.

Lord Rockingham's ministry was short-lived, for he died from
influenza in July 1782. The most pressing business of his successor,
the Earl of Shelburne, was to end the war; the provisional terms
of an Anglo-American peace treaty were signed in Paris on 30
November. The new land boundaries between the British territory
of Canada and the fledgling United States of America were drawn
on terms that were noticeably generous to the latter. 'The English
buy peace rather than make it,' the French foreign minister sniped
from the sidelines.[9]

Many MPs agreed with this assessment – the prime minister
had given too much away. John Robinson was troubled to learn that

Lord North was planning to vote against Shelburne's peace treaty, and drafted a memorandum to his old master, warning that such an action might 'shake the Government and the Constitution of this Country to its Foundation'.[10] He asked Richard for his thoughts on the document. 'Upon the best consideration I can give the matter, I cannot help feeling an Indelicacy towards an *old* Friend, in the communication,' Richard replied on 6 February 1783.[11]

As Shelburne's grip on power weakened, it was clear that he would need to join forces with one of the other main parliamentary factions, but he failed to form a coalition with either Lord North or Charles James Fox. Instead something unthinkable happened. Fox sent a 'civil' message to North, and these once-mortal enemies met to coordinate tactics for a forthcoming debate. Only recently, Fox had declared that he would not 'for an instant' consider working with Lord North or his allies – men who 'in every public and private transaction' had shown themselves 'void of every principle of honour'.[12] Now MPs were flabbergasted by the spectacle of Fox and North sitting side-by-side on the opposition front bench. On 24 February, the weight of adverse parliamentary numbers bearing down upon him, Lord Shelburne tendered his resignation.

At this time, broadly speaking, there were two political parties – Whig and Tory – but they were not monoliths in the sense that we know today, instead loose social alliances sharing a general outlook, clustered around strong individuals. Aristocratic Whigs had engineered the Glorious Revolution, and they saw political power as emanating from the people through a 'contract' existing with their monarch, who was to be opposed if he overrode their interests. Lord North was, if anything, a moderate Tory – a grouping associated with the landed gentry – but would not have been fenced in by this label. By the 1780s, however, the political parties were starting to become more clearly defined, with economic reform and the reduction of royal power at the heart of the revitalized Whigs' ideology.

Charles James Fox, their leader, was a colossus of the House of Commons – the subject of more political cartoons than any other man of his time. A hostility existed between Fox and the king that was more deep-seated than mere partisan difference, for they were also polar opposites in temperament – while the monarch was a man of markedly moderate habits, Fox was the 'hero in Parliament, at the gaming-table, at Newmarket'.[13] According to the king, Fox was someone 'who every honest Man' would wish 'to keep out of Power'; which is why the prospect of such an individual leading his government was almost too painful to contemplate.[14]

It was Henry Dundas, the Lord Advocate, who first proposed William Pitt, the Chancellor of the Exchequer, as a candidate to replace Shelburne. As the second son of the late Earl of Chatham – Pitt the Elder – the younger Pitt certainly had pedigree, even if he lacked experience. He had entered parliament only two years earlier, aged twenty-one, as a protégé of Sir James Lowther. ('Appleby is the Place I am to represent,' he had written to his mother, 'and the Election will be made (probably in a week or Ten days) without my having any Trouble, or even visiting my Constituents.')[15] Shelburne, while resigning from office, suggested to the king that he might consider inviting Pitt to form a ministry. After putting this idea to the young man, the king reported that he had responded with a 'spirit and inclination that makes me think he will not decline'.[16] Pitt spent the evening of 24 February with Dundas, trying to work out whether a working majority in the Commons was within his grasp. 'I feel all the difficulties of the Undertaking and am by no means in Love with the Object,' Pitt told his mother the following day. 'The great Article to decide by, seems that of numbers.'[17]

Dundas next asked John Robinson, whose knowledge of the shifting sands of parliamentary loyalties was unrivalled, to compile a breakdown of those MPs who were likely to support Pitt, and those who would likely oppose him. The plot to bring Pitt into power was a profound secret. To avoid raising suspicions, Robinson asked Richard, as a mutual friend – for Richard knew Dundas fairly well, not least as another of Anne Lindsay's admirers – to carry the completed document from his house at Sion Hill, near Brentford, to Dundas's residence in Leicester Square, so that he himself 'might have no communication with the Advocate'.[18]

If Anne Lindsay's account of 27 February is to be believed, the day might have ended quite differently. She would describe the following story as a 'whimsical little instance to prove on what trifling circumstances important matters in the line of politicks often hinge'. That morning Richard, on his way from John Robinson's house into town, had unexpectedly dropped in at Harley Street while she was getting dressed, and sent up a note asking her to come down immediately, since he had something important to tell her:

> One pin was necessary to tuck up my hair, and to change a
> gown all over with powder for a clean one. I hurried below, and
> found him with his watch in his hand, departing. 'O! what may
> not these five minutes delay have cost,' said he. 'Pitt has not
> seen this canvass . . . I have this instant got it, it is triumphant!
> He promised to be with the King as 11 o'clock struck, it wants
> but three minutes of it; if he is not gone, he is our Minister . . .
> God bless you!' And off he rushed. Half an hour brought him
> back with a dejected air. 'Alas!' said he, 'I was too late. He had
> set off five minutes before I reached his house, leaving this
> note: *Had the canvass been favourable you would have been here.*
> *I must decline; perhaps 'tis best.'*[19]

Far-fetched though this tale might sound, it seems likely that some version of it took place. John Robinson himself, in a letter to Charles Jenkinson, alluded to a last-minute setback when he described how a 'ray of Light' which might have persuaded Pitt to form a ministry 'came forward a *few* Hours too late'.[20] George III now approached Lord North, who refused to lead, but agreed to serve in a coalition cabinet; all of which is how, on 3 March, the king came to offer the reins of government to his arch-enemy Fox, on condition that an independent peer nominally headed the ministry. But Fox would not serve under any prime minister except the Duke of Portland, who was unacceptable to the monarch.

During this nail-biting time, Robinson was confined to his country residence by gout. (Anyone wondering how gout might justify

The gout, which tormented many eighteenth-century gentlemen
of a certain age.

his absence from Westminster at such a critical moment need only examine Gillray's depiction of the illness, in which some infernal creature sinks its fangs and talons into the swollen foot of a sufferer.) On 14 March, after the nation had been without a prime minister for three weeks, Robinson wrote to Jenkinson, who was in close contact with the king, suggesting that he make one last attempt to 'set the Wheel a-going thro' Atkinson, with the Advocate & Pitt'.[21]

Two days later, the king reluctantly agreed to let the Duke of Portland form a ministry, but refused to deal directly with him, only through Lord North. Portland was at last granted an audience on 20 March, but admitted he could not yet name his cabinet; George III, sensing an opportunity, dispatched a one-line letter: 'Mr. Pitt, I desire you will come here immediately.'[22] The next day, Portland again waited on the monarch, who refused even to glance at a partial list of the cabinet, insisting on every post being filled before he would look at it. 'The D. of P. has been with the King & they have parted angrily,' Richard told Robinson that night. 'Demands, no less than Honours & Power *unlimited*! If the Parties quarrel *clearly* between themselves, the thing *will do*. If the King quarrels *with them*, it will *not* do.'[23] Pitt, meanwhile, was hoping for signs of support in the Commons, but none were forthcoming, and he again turned down the premiership. Richard wrote on 25 March:

> The blossoms of yesterday are finally *blasted*. Upon a very
> recent conversation between Mr. Pitt and the Advocate,
> the latter gives the business up as wholly at an end. All that
> can remain will be to give such support as one can to the
> Government, for by Heaven I am convinced there are not
> materials in the country to form another. This young man's
> mind is not large enough to embrace so great an object, and
> his notions of the purity and steadiness of political principle
> absolutely incompatible with the morals, manners, and grounds
> of attachment of those by whose means alone the Government
> of this country can be carried on.[24]

The king held out for another week as he pondered the 'cruel dilemma' of being forced to appoint a ministry made up of men 'who will not accept office without making me a kind of slave'.[25] Not for the first time, he contemplated abdication. On 1 April, after five weeks of political deadlock, George III signalled that the new cabinet would be expected at St James's the following day to kiss hands. John Robinson commented: 'Poor King, how very very much does His Situation deserve pity.'[26]

BEFORE THIS DISRUPTION, Henry Dundas had been working on a bill to place the East India Company and its territories under tighter government control. It would be hard to overstate the importance of the Company to the commercial life of Britain at this time. Some historians have characterized it as the first multinational corporation, but it was so much more powerful than even this description might suggest, possessed of a vast private army with which it had subjugated emperors and princes; and thus huge swathes of the Indian subcontinent were effectively ruled from nondescript offices in the City of London.

Dundas had been taking an interest in Indian affairs since 1781, when he was appointed chairman of a secret committee set up to investigate the war against Hyder Ali, the great Sultan of Mysore; before long his scrutiny would extend to every aspect of the Company's activities. But when he finally placed his India Bill before parliament, on 14 April 1783, the new ministers made it clear that they would not give it their support, and thus it was still-born.

Although the Duke of Portland was officially prime minister, his 'indolent habits and moderate capacity led him to relish power rather than to seek it' – this was Anne Lindsay's pithy analysis – which meant that Charles James Fox was leader in all but name.[27] In those days, before the existence of a professional civil service, or salaries for MPs, ministers relied upon royal patronage to reward those who laboured on the government's behalf. The king so hated this particular ministry, however, that he simply shut down the supply of offices, sinecures, titles and pensions that were needed to keep the cogs of administration well greased. 'I do not mean to grant a single Peerage or other Mark of Favour,' he told Lord Shelburne.[28]

It would turn out there was good reason why Fox had given Dundas's India Bill such short shrift in the spring, as he harboured plans for legislation of his own. Fox placed his India Bill before the House of Commons on 18 November. One measure alone contained enough powder to touch off a massive blast in the cellars of East India House; this was the plan to establish a board of seven commissioners, nominated by parliament, who would have the 'power to appoint and displace officers in India'.[29] To those who detested Fox, or owned East India Company stock, the bill seemed like the 'boldest and most unconstitutional measure ever attempted', a brazen scheme to steal the patronage of the Company and put it to work for his personal political ends.[30] The bill's first reading was on 20 November, and Fox made it clear that he intended 'to take the House, not only by force but by violence'.[31]

Richard led the East India Company's resistance to Fox's India Bill from the start. On 21 November, at a Grand Court held at the Company's headquarters on Leadenhall Street, he was appointed to

*A Transfer of East India Stock, in which Fox makes off
with East India House.*

a committee of nine proprietors tasked with defending its rights and privileges; but the chairman of the group immediately fell ill, leaving Richard to step into his shoes. The committee's first undertaking was to compose a strongly worded petition, objecting to the seizure of 'lands, tenements, houses, warehouses, and other buildings; books, records, charters, letters, and other papers; ships, vessels, goods, wares, merchandizes, money, securities for money, and other effects' that was threatened by Fox's bill.[32] This document was placed before the Commons three days later.

The committee's next task was to disprove Fox's claim that the Company was £8 million in debt – an assertion which had caused the price of its stock to slide from £138 to £115 in just three days.

By the time of the bill's second reading, on 27 November, Richard had compiled a detailed report on the Company's finances – by *his* reckoning, it was almost £4 million in credit. At the start of the debate, two lawyers presented Richard's conclusions from the bar of the House of Commons. Fox then stood up to give his response. The report, with 'many things inserted, which ought to have been omitted, and many things omitted, which ought to have been inserted', was a staggering distortion of the Company's affairs, he asserted, and he condemned the men who had dared to produce 'an account so full of imposition and absurdity'.[33] Fox's display of righteous indignation dazzled his enemies; William Pitt, leading the opposition, complained that he had 'run through the account with a volubility that rendered comprehension difficult, and detection almost impossible'.[34] When the House divided, at 4.30 a.m., the ministry prevailed by a decisive 229 votes to 120. 'The shameful impositions of the Company, in the printed state of their affairs, were completely detected and exposed,' said one newspaper. 'Opposition seemed planet-struck.'[35]

I find this incident fascinating because it shines light on a critical flaw in Richard's character, one that might be considered the source of many of the Atkinson family's future troubles. Francis Baring, writing to Lord Shelburne two days later, pinpointed Richard's role in the drubbing:

> Atkinson has brought Mr. Pitt into a scrape by endeavouring
> to prove *too much*, & of which he was warned at the outset; but
> it ever was the case with him, his talents & imagination are
> so rapid that they always run away with judgment; & at this
> moment instead of taking ground which is sound, defensible
> against every attack, & sufficient for the purpose; he is
> endeavouring to elucidate & support, various articles which
> he must know himself to be moonshine.[36]

On 3 December, as Fox named his board of seven commissioners – all of whom, it was muttered, were better known at Brooks's Club

Richard 'Rum' Atkinson, whose tangled legacy
is at the heart of this story. This miniature – here
much enlarged   was painted by Richard Cosway
in 1783, and belonged to Lady Anne Lindsay.
Do I detect a certain sadness in its subject's eyes?

Temple Sowerby House in 1930. The original farmhouse squats behind the Georgian extension; the bay window and porch are clumsy Victorian add-ons.

The legal document, inscribed on vellum and dated 1577, that granted my nine-times great-grandfather William Atkinson a thousand-year lease on the land he occupied at Temple Sowerby.

My grandparents, my father and me in the walled garden at Temple Sowerby in 1968; and me again, this time on my own two feet, outside the house three years later.

Two views of the gallery at Temple Sowerby in
about 1915. This light-filled corridor no longer
exists, having been subdivided into hotel bedrooms.
Eagle-eyed viewers will spot John Robinson's
portrait above the chair in the top picture.

George Atkinson, probably painted in London in the 1770s while he was down on Treasury business. Close inspection reveals George, who was a tanner by trade, to be holding a volume of poetry. This portrait hung in the dining room at Chesters until the great sale of 1930 – I have no idea where it is now.

Bridget Atkinson's 'receipt book', and her cure for insanity. Approach with extreme caution.

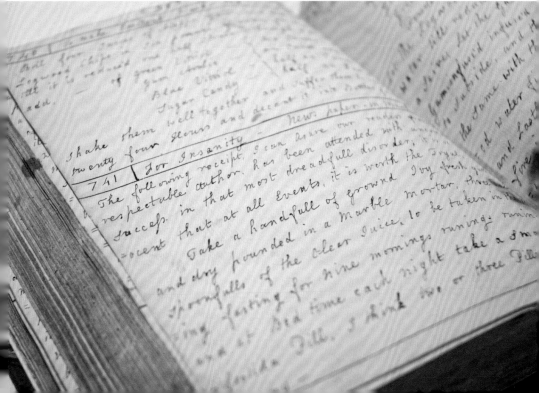

Lady Anne Lindsay, the love of Richard Atkinson's life.
Not only was she a great beauty, but also a gifted writer,
singer, painter and conversationalist.

The *Bessborough*, of which Richard was 'ship's husband', depicted
in three positions in the English Channel, its decks crowded with
people. Launched in 1772, this East Indiaman undertook four
voyages to China before being sold as a hulk in 1788.

John Robinson in later life, portrayed in his capacity as Surveyor General of Woods, holding a letter addressed to the king. Between 1788 and 1802, Robinson oversaw the planting of more than eleven million acorns in Windsor Great Park.

A crowd outside a print shop jostling for a glimpse of its latest wares. Political and social visual satire flourished in the late eighteenth century; James Gillray (1756–1815) and Thomas Rowlandson (1756–1827) were the masters of the genre.

Gillray's *Westminster School*. Pitt the Younger is birched by Fox.
Richard Atkinson (whose 'Rum Contract' pokes out of his pocket)
awaits punishment, clinging to the bespectacled Edmund Burke;
as does John Robinson (identified by the rats fleeing his garments),
piggy-backing the corpulent figure of Lord North.

than in Bengal – Pitt conspicuously stayed away from Westminster. At its final reading in the lower chamber, on 8 December, the India Bill passed by a majority of more than two to one, and Fox was able to carry it up triumphantly to the House of Lords.

JOHN ROBINSON HAD stayed away from Westminster while the India Bill passed through the Commons, conveniently blaming his absence on a further attack of gout, in part to avoid the very public treachery of being seen to vote against Lord North. Once again, Richard acted as Robinson's go-between with Henry Dundas and others; this explains why much of the tiny amount of correspondence to have survived from this deepest of political intrigues is in Richard's handwriting.

The India Bill's passage through the Lords, it would seem, was a foregone conclusion. 'We are informed that Ministers have an ascertained majority of two or three and thirty Peers,' reported the *London Chronicle*.[37] However the king, and many others, saw Charles James Fox as a dangerous man who had to be stopped; and so the battle lines were drawn for the greatest test of the respective powers of the monarch and parliament since the Glorious Revolution. On 1 December, Lord Chancellor Thurlow – who strongly opposed the bill – placed a memorandum before the king which professed 'to wish to know' whether the legislation appeared to 'His Majesty in this light: a plan to take more than half the royal power'. Thurlow's message also suggested that were the king to take the highly unusual step of revealing his feelings on this matter, 'in a manner which would make it impossible to pretend a doubt', the bill would face defeat in the House of Lords.[38] Two days later, Richard learnt that the Chancellor's communication with the king had produced the desired effect. 'As far as I can learn or judge,' he told Robinson, 'every thing stands prepared for the blow if a certain Person has Courage to strike it.'[39]

That 'certain Person' was, of course, George III. But he would not strike the 'blow' until William Pitt had indicated his readiness to take office; and first Pitt needed to be sure that a parliamentary majority lay within his reach. On the evening of 5 December, Robinson received a message from Dundas, urgently requesting an analysis of the House of Commons. 'That Night I worked until past 2 & the last Night until towards 3 this Morning, & both Days, except some little Interruptions, until this Moment that it is finished as well as may be in such a Hurry for my Pen has been constantly driving all the above mentioned space of time,' Robinson wrote to Jenkinson, in evident haste, two days later.[40]

What Robinson omitted to say was that Richard was also present at Sion Hill, his pen likewise 'driving' round the clock to compile the document. We know as much because a rough version of this highly speculative survey, in Richard's handwriting – one page is splashed with what looks like strong black coffee – exists in the family archive of John Robinson's descendant, the Marquess of Abergavenny. The two men drew up a list of all 558 parliamentary seats, dividing them into four columns headed P, H, D and C, for 'Pro', 'Hopeful', 'Doubtful' and 'Contra', according to the sitting member's likely stance towards a Pitt ministry.[41]

Richard carried the finished document across town to Dundas on the evening of 7 December. 'I found our Friend last night & looked over the Paper with him,' he reported back to Robinson, in deliberately veiled language. 'Although at the first Blush it had not appeared quite so favorable as had been expected, yet on fuller consideration and going through the whole it was admitted that the turn was throughout strongly given to the unfavorable Side & that there was no *manly* ground of apprehension.'[42]

THE INDIA BILL received its first reading in the House of Lords on 9 December. Richard, who had prepared a petition from the East India Company for presentation during the debate – another 'Bomb from the India House', as John Robinson put it – briefed Lord Thurlow first at his house in Great Ormond Street.[43] The following day, after learning that Pitt was ready to 'receive the burthen' of office, George III instructed Lord Temple to make peers aware of his strong aversion to the India Bill. Richard summarized these manoeuvres for Robinson, ending with the royal trump card: 'He has given authority to say (when it shall be necessary) that whoever votes in the House of Lords for the India Bill is not *his* friend.'[44]

The king's intervention had an electrifying effect. On 15 December, the East India Company's lawyers gave evidence in the upper house for eleven hours before seeking permission, as it neared midnight, to continue the next day; somehow the opposition managed to muster a majority of eight votes on a motion to adjourn the debate, in effect postponing the decisive division on the second reading. Around thirty peers, it seemed, had switched sides.

That same evening, four conspirators – William Pitt, Henry Dundas, John Robinson and Richard Atkinson – discussed tactics over a secret dinner hosted by Dundas at Leicester Square. In a note calling Robinson into town, Richard explained that the covert nature of the gathering was 'lest the measure in agitation should be guessed at'.[45] This 'measure' was a general election, and their objective was to identify the means by which a majority in the House of Commons might in due course be obtained.

It is at moments such as this that the gulf between parliamentary democracy then and now seems at its most unbridgeable. The minutes of this and subsequent meetings, which are in Richard's handwriting, identify thirteen landowners who between them controlled forty-one seats that might be purchased with royal patronage; sixty-nine seats that might be bought using a combination of money, offices and honours; and sixty-five seats for which money alone would suffice. Even Robinson, no wide-eyed innocent, was horrified by the projected expenditure – £193,500 for 134 seats to ensure a majority – and he would distance himself from the figures. 'Parliamentary State of Boroughs and their Situations with Remarks, preparatory to a New Parliament in 178- on a Change of Administration and Mr. Pitt's coming in,' he noted on the minutes. 'Sketch out at several Meetings at Lord Advocate Dundas's in Leicester Square and a wild wide Calculate of the money wanted for Seats but which I always disapproved and thought very wrong.'[46]

For Communication

These are supposed to be partly accessible in one way & part in other ways which till communication cannot be well judged of.

D. Northumb. — 7 — Launceston — 2
Newport — 2
Beeralston — 2
Northumberland — 1

Mr Elliot — 7 — Liskeard — 2
St Germans — 2 — Suppose 10,000
Grampound — 2
Cornwall — 1

Lord Falmouth — 3 — Tregony — 2
Mitchell — 1 — 9,000

Sir F. Bassett — 5 — Mitchell — 1
Truro Quere — 2 — 12,000
Penryn Quere — 2

Lord Orford — 4 — Ashburton — 1
Callington Quere — 2
Castle rising — 1

D. of Newcastle — 6 — Aldborough — 2
Boroughbridge — 2
Retford — 1
Newark — 1

Lord Sandwich — 3 — Huntingdon — 2
Huntingdonsh. — 1 — Suppose Office

Mr Howard (Bagot) — Castlerising — 1
Mr Hooper — Christchurch — 2
Lord Hertford — 3 — Orford — 2 — Suppose Office
Coventry — 1
Lord Sackville — 2 — East Grinstead — 2
Sir Jno Honeywood — 2 — Steyning — 1
Himself — 1
Lord Aylesbury — 4 — Marlbro — 2 — Suppose 1 Seat 3000
Great Bedwen — 2
Mr Selwin — 2 — Luggershall — 1 — Do — 3,500
Himself — 1
Mr Shaftoe — 2 — Downton — 1 — Do — 3,500
Lord Lisburne — 2 — Himself
Government Influence
Portsmouth
Dartmouth
Harwich
Plymouth — Arrangement rather than 6 pence
Aldborough Suffolk — 2
XX Lord Powis — 2 — Montgomery
Ludlow
Lord Galway — 2 — Pontefract — 2
Mr Walsh — Winchester — 1 — XX

Sixty-nine parliamentary seats and their proprietors, in Richard's handwriting.

The struggle reached its climax on 17 December. Fox had tabled an emergency resolution to protest against the king's flagrant violation of the rule that he could only operate through his ministers, and this business in the lower chamber would coincide with the crucial vote on the India Bill along the corridor in the House of Lords. At midnight, while both houses were still in the throes of debate, Richard dashed off a note to Robinson with some unexpected news. 'My dear Sir,' he wrote, 'I am dragged into the India Direction.' Earlier that day, during a meeting of the proprietors at East India House, while Richard was in a side room dealing with an urgent query from Lord Thurlow, he had without warning been nominated to fill one of two vacancies caused by the resignation of Foxite directors. 'Tomorrow I will breakfast in Leicester Square & take a Servant with me to send out to you. You stand high with Mr. Pitt about which I have more to tell you than I can well write,' he concluded.[47]

At noon the following day, Richard sent Robinson a high-spirited message to say that the India Bill was demolished, defeated in the Lords by a majority of nineteen: 'What a constitution of Character this is!'[48] That evening, as Portland, Fox and North were in conference, a messenger brought a letter from George III demanding the surrender of their seals of office. 'I choose this method,' explained the king, 'as Audiences on such occasions must be unpleasant.'[49]

ELEVEN

Secret Influence

LADY ANNE LINDSAY was firmly of the opinion that Richard received insufficient recognition for his role in the slaying of Fox's India Bill. 'Abilities in a certain rank of life have not always fair play granted them,' she would later comment:

> On several occasions when he showed me able statements prepared for Mr. Dundas and for Lord Thurlow to convey to the King, I could discover that they would be transcribed over by themselves before they reached the Royal eye. I expressed an idea of this kind to Atkinson. He smiled, and said it might be so . . . Men were men; providing he could do good, it was the same thing to him who had the credit of it.[1]

To this day, Richard's part in the 'coup' that would usher William Pitt the Younger into power – a watershed event in British political history – has not been fully acknowledged by historians. John Robinson's survey of the House of Commons, and the papers estimating the cost of parliamentary seats, are among the most revealing documents dating back to this drama – and yet, so far as I am aware, no researcher has detected Richard's hand in them, either because they have not identified the handwriting as his or, more likely, because they have seen them in transcript only. The papers are held by Lord Abergavenny at his family archive in Sussex; another way to access them is through a book, the *Parliamentary Papers of John Robinson*, compiled by Professor W.T. Laprade in 1922. But he was working from transcripts made in the 1890s: 'The task of preparing these papers for publication has been the more difficult in that the editor has never seen the originals.'[2] Since then, biographers of Pitt the Younger have relied upon Laprade as their primary source, which meant that I was maybe the first researcher to recognize Richard as the actual *author* of the documents – a genuinely thrilling discovery for an amateur historian.

WILLIAM PITT took office on 19 December 1783, aged twenty-four, and set about cobbling together a cabinet. He had few heavyweight candidates at his disposal, especially since he chose to forgo the services of Lord Shelburne, under whom he had served as Chancellor of the Exchequer. He also purposely distanced himself from those who had cleared his path to power; Henry Dundas was appointed to the relatively junior post of Treasurer of the Navy.

The newly deposed coalition greeted Pitt's premiership with barely disguised mirth. 'We are so strong,' wrote Fox, 'that nobody else can undertake without madness, and if they do I think we shall destroy them almost as soon as they are formed.'[3] As yet, Pitt plainly lacked the parliamentary majority that he needed; but there was no greater practitioner of the dark art of luring MPs across the floor than John Robinson. 'No Man in the House of Commons knew so much of its original Composition; the Means by which every Individual attained his Seat; and in many Instances, how far, and through what Channels, he might prove accessible,' Nathaniel Wraxall would observe.[4] With the king's blessing, the vaults of royal patronage were thrown wide open. The sparkle of honours, offices and pensions was too much for most men to resist, and Robinson now set about deploying these baubles to devastating effect.

Over the Christmas holidays, Robinson had so many letters to write, and the weather was in any case so bitterly cold, that he did not leave home once in nine days. He first set about securing the great political proprietors – an earldom was promised to his old patron Sir

James Lowther in return for the nine seats under his control. Word soon got around. The *Morning Chronicle* portrayed 'Jack' Robinson as a kind of magician of the gutter: 'Jack can shew wonderful tricks with Rats, he can turn their skins and fur into ermine, and make them appear outwardly much nobler creatures than common Rats.'[5] The *Public Advertiser* printed an 'IMPORTANT WARNING!!!' that one Robinson, 'Secretary to the Secret Influence', was grubbing around for seats, and that gentlemen should be 'on their Guard against the Grand Corruptor or his Agents'.[6] Soon afterwards the same newspaper hinted at the identity of Robinson's chief accomplice: 'To my certain Knowledge there are TWO *Rats*, one of whom has for twelve Years burrowed in the Treasury; the other in a dirtier Place, yet shall be nameless. These have been seen lately gnawing some valuable Parchments in Leadenhall Street, and are supposed to have committed many daring Depredations on the Public.'[7] I think we can guess the name of that second rat.

Already Richard was liaising with Dundas about the fine detail of a new India Bill, with a view to smoothing out any potential objections beforehand. 'I saw Mr. D today who is confined with a complaint in his head, whether Rheumatick or Tooth Ach is not quite clear,' Richard told Robinson on 31 December. 'His Bill does not go to all the Objects we had in view; but in as far as it goes to them, it does not materially differ from ours.'[8] Pitt revealed these plans to a secret committee of the directors of the East India Company on 5 January 1784; broadly speaking, political control over the Company's affairs would pass to the Crown, while its commercial business and patronage would remain intact.

Parliament assembled to debate the 'state of the nation' on 12 January. It promised to be a historic occasion, and as many people 'as ever were wedged together in the same place' crowded into the public gallery of the Commons.[9] '*The Battle is at this moment joined*, and the Debate of the night determines King George or King Charles,' Richard declared. 'My opinion of the Result is, a small majority for the present ministry tonight, a Dissolution this Week & *King George for ever*.'[10] For sixteen hours, the prime minister faced down intense abuse from the benches before him about the underhand method of his installation. When the House rose, past six in the morning, the false optimism of Richard's prediction was revealed; the opposition carried the vote by 232 to 193. 'King Charles' reigned – for the time being.

Richard was formally elected a director of the East India Company on 14 January. Pitt placed his India Bill before parliament that same day, at pains to stress that the legislation had been 'chiefly founded on the resolutions of proprietors of India-stock'.[11] After its second reading, the bill was defeated on 23 January by eight votes – an event that terminated John Robinson's long friendship with Lord North. Robinson had been secretly plotting against his former master for the best part of a year, but had hitherto refrained from openly voting against him. The next day, Robinson called upon North at his Grosvenor Square residence, but was refused entry. 'I do not desire any explanation of your conduct,' North wrote afterwards. 'You are so good as to say that you felt some difficulty in making the option between being my friend & my enemy; you have chosen the latter, & your choice has put it out of my power to make any: your option has necessarily determined mine.'[12]

The Infant Hercules, in which Pitt strangles two snakes representing Fox and North.

After the defeat of Pitt's India Bill, the confidence of some of his closest supporters started to falter. 'Whilst the King, Mr. Pitt, & Mr. Dundas are I really believe untainted with Timidity,' observed Richard on 27 January, 'I fear there may lurk some Sparks of it in other members of the Cabinet.'[13] Beyond Westminster, however, the populace began voicing their support for George III and his new minister. The first stirrings were on 16 January, in the City of London, when a cavalcade of dignitaries – the Lord Mayor, aldermen, sheriffs and other bigwigs – waited upon the king to congratulate him for exerting his prerogative 'in a manner so salutary and consti-tutional'.[14] Soon, similarly approving addresses started trickling in from places as far-flung as Penzance and the Orkneys, turning into a torrent over the following weeks.

IF ANY OF THESE events were of the least interest to Dorothy Atkinson, she did not think to mention them in her correspondence. Richard's eldest niece, now twenty-two, had earlier that winter come to live with her uncle at Fenchurch Street, joining her younger brothers George and Dick, who were both learning to be merchants. It was Anne Lindsay who, for reasons not entirely selfless, had urged Richard to invite Dorothy down from Temple Sowerby. She would later explain:

> To marry Lord Wentworth was no longer in my intention.
> To marry any other person and break the heart of my best of
> Friends by a new attachment, I felt impossible. To remain
> single, or to marry himself (which I could not bring myself to
> do) was my sole alternative, and in Truth it contained so little
> Happiness to me either way, that I sometimes wished I had five
> thousand pounds only and the liberty I had lost. By one means
> only I saw I might regain it & of this there was but a poor
> chance – if I could get the Happiness of Atkinson made up
> from some other quarter by some amiable woman then I saw
> I should be my own mistress again.[15]

Dorothy made a favourable impression on the Lindsay sisters. 'She was a tall fine girl,' Anne recalled, 'of a sweet and ingenuous countenance, and resembled himself in a manner that rendered her the more interesting to us.' She would need schooling in the ways of society, for 'she was awkward, being from the wilds of Westmoreland', but there were few instructors more qualified than the Lindsay sisters.[16] Dorothy kept up a delightfully artless correspondence with her mother, Bridget, about her new life in the capital. Here is a letter dated 2 March 1784:

> I think I left off my dear mother with telling you that we were to dine at Mr. Mure's on Sunday. My uncle and I accordingly went in the coach about two to Lady Balcarres' where I was received by her, Lady Margaret and Lady Ann with that politeness which always distinguishes people of real fashion – and with particular kindness upon my uncle's account. We stayed till four and made an appointment for me to go to the opera with the Ladies on Tuesday – we then went to Mr. Mure's where George and Dick joined us there was none but ourselves and a very pleasant day we spent *no cards introduced.*
>
> On Monday morning I went out in the carriage to call upon Lady Ann who by my uncle's desire went a shopping with me. I was to get whatever she thought proper for me – and so in the first place we bought of Mr. Alanson one & twenty yards of white satin at 10d. per yard for a night gown & petticoat, bespoke a pair of stays of rose colloured tabby – next we got a piece of fine Linnen for a morning gown, also bespoke an hoop and last of all a balloon hat for the opera.
>
> On Tuesday I went to Miss Williams and fixed upon two Vallancine edgings for the plain muslin. I have also had from her a long white sattin cloak & muff the cloak trimmed with white skin a black hat and two caps. I will send you patterns of the Gowns when they come home. I went from Miss Williams to Lady Balcarras's where I had my hair dressed and the Lady's

equipped me in my Balloon & for the opera. I dined with them
and my uncle joined us at the opera house. It was very
agreeable indeed – the Ladies have the Duke of Cumberland's
box during his absence it is adjoining to that of the Prince of
Wales (who was there) and is the next best to his – Vestris is
still here and performed wonders. Lord Wentworth, my uncle
and I supped at Lady B's. We set his Lordship down and then
came home.

There is one thing which will confine me a little. My uncle
does not chuse that I should go out at all but in the coach –
and one of the Footmen always attends me – but when I go
to buy my aunt's gown and to execute my other commissions
I mean to take a hackney coach least I should make bad
bargains. I forgot to tell you that Miss Fordyce came of Sunday
morning and breakfasted with us. She says she is quite weary
of the pursuit of shells not having got any new ones these
twelve months. I must I think keep this letter till the house
sends a frank as all this scribble is scarcely worth paying
postage for.[17]

THROUGHOUT THE WINTER, John Robinson continued
to chip away at Fox's parliamentary majority through the sustained deployment of royal patronage. Meanwhile, preparations
were under way for the general election that might be called at any
time. On 29 February, Pitt's election committee met at Dundas's
house in Leicester Square. Some papers from this gathering still
exist; they are mostly in Richard's handwriting. One document lists
seventy boroughs whose seats were likely to be actively contested,
and a 'measures to be taken' column records what was agreed about
each place: '*Callington* – Mr. Pitt to learn of Lord Orford whether
he sets up one or two members . . . *Chippenham* – Lord Weymouth
to be spoke to by Mr. Dundas about Sir Edwd Bayntun's Interest
. . . *Northampton* – Mr. Robinson to consult H. Drummond about
opposing Lord Lucan . . . *Poole* – Mr. Atkinson to converse with
F. Baring on this Subject.' Another paper sets out forty-two seats

John Robinson, portrayed as a rat catcher, snaring MPs
with money and honours.

reckoned 'certain for Money', and the names of thirty-four potential candidates – Francis Baring and Nathaniel Wraxall are among
eleven men listed as Richard's nominees. Yet another document, this
time written by Robinson, suggests 'Persons who will pay £1,500 or
perhaps somewhat more' for seats, and those who will pay '£2,000
or £2,500 or perhaps £3,000'.[18] Here is the first clue that Richard was considering a political career – for his name is to be found
within this last category of men with very deep pockets indeed.

On 1 March, in the House of Commons, Fox tabled a motion
urging the king to dismiss his ministers; it passed by just twelve
votes. A week later, Fox moved to communicate to the monarch
that 'no administration, however legally appointed, can serve his
Majesty and the public with effect, which does not enjoy the confidence of this House'.[19] When this motion passed by a single vote,
Fox must have known his time was up, for the next day he permitted
the Mutiny Act – a law to prevent the existence of a standing army
without parliament's consent, renewed annually and about to expire
– to pass without opposition, thus removing the final impediment to
a general election. On 22 March, the king borrowed £24,000 from

the banker Henry Drummond to fund the purchase of parliamentary seats by the Treasury; two days later, he dissolved parliament.

Richard agreed to stand for the City of London – how much coaxing he needed is not clear, but Anne Lindsay recalled a certain reticence on his part: 'It gave him eminence, but to be its Member he thought would interfere too much with his private business.'[20] As a necessary preliminary to his candidacy, on 24 March, Richard was admitted to the freedom of the Goldsmiths' Company. Two days later a group of supporters, led by Edward Payne, a former governor of the Bank of England, met at the London Tavern, where they passed a resolution to recommend him to the electorate. Of the City's four sitting MPs, John Sawbridge was most vulnerable to challenge, and it was his seat that Richard hoped to snatch – for it was Sawbridge who had two years earlier shown such malice on the subject of Robinson's pension.

Nowadays, a general election campaign usually lasts about five weeks, while the polls remain open for just fifteen hours, but during the eighteenth century, almost the reverse was the case – a short canvassing period was followed by an extended poll. Also unlike today, votes were cast publicly – which meant that numbers could be totted up along the way.

The moment Richard's candidacy was announced, personal attacks upon him started appearing in the press. First came the story of two merchant ships, the *Venus* and the *Monarch*, both of which he had chartered in 1780 to bring sugar from Jamaica, but which had subsequently been requisitioned to serve as army transports. After all but one of its crew perished through sickness, the *Venus* had been abandoned and burnt by order of its commanding officer, and Mure, Son & Atkinson had received damages of £3,500 from the governor of Jamaica. The ship's owner, however, had successfully prosecuted a claim against Richard for this compensation money. ('A more gross violation of justice never was attempted,' thundered the *Gazetteer*.)[21] A similar action regarding the *Monarch*, which foundered in the disastrous hurricane of October 1780, had been settled out of court. 'They have attacked me on the Rum, & on the Story of two Ships lost on the Spanish Main,' Richard complained to Robinson. 'On Rum, henceforward *Silence!'*

Francis Baring and John Purrier, the ultimate referees of the rum contracts, offered their support through a handbill in which they declared that they had been fully satisfied by 'the Uprightness of Mr. Atkinson's conduct' – not that Richard expected this message to be treated with any great respect by the citizenry of London. 'You will believe that the pissing Posts will not be uncloathed with it,' he told Robinson.[22]

The twenty thousand-strong electorate of the City of London, comprising the membership of the ancient livery companies, had one week in which to cast their votes. Richard's appearance on the hustings at Guildhall, as polling opened on 30 March, was greeted by 'hisses and groans' from the crowd.[23] That same day, the *Gazetteer* published a vicious denunciation:

> Is it possible that the Livery of London can be so utterly
> destitute of common sense, common honour, and common
> spirit – so drunk with ignorance of their real interests, so dead
> to every thing that renders a public body respectable, as to
> elect Richard Atkinson in preference to John Sawbridge?
> What is Atkinson? A man hackneyed in whatever renders a
> public man infamous, a private man contemptible. In this
> man's dealings with the public, he has perpetuated an act of
> such an extraordinary nature, that the base trick is grown
> into a proverb; his original obscure name is forgotten; and he
> is elevated into the notorious distinction of '*The Rum Contractor*'
> – added to this you find him high upon all lists of *loans,*
> *contractors*, &c. and never known but in some of those numerous
> *jobs* by which, in a time of public calamity, he has made a
> considerable fortune from the distresses of the nation. In
> private life what is he? A being who has progressed from the
> very lowest and meanest sphere, through all the gradations of
> a various life, to the accession of great wealth; steady to the
> object of *making money* . . .[24]

At the end of the second day of polling, Richard was running fifth, having received 419 votes, with Sawbridge eighty-nine votes ahead; but still he remained upbeat. 'In spite of News Papers & Reports depend upon it I am safe for the City,' he assured Robinson that evening.[25]

The following morning, a handbill pinned up throughout the City smeared Richard's name still further. Its author was one John Berens, who identified himself as an assignee of the estate of Peter Hasenclever, founder of the ironworks of which Richard had been a proprietor before the American war. Without offering a shred of evidence, Berens linked Richard to a forged bill of exchange, accused him of perjury, and claimed he had deceived Hasenclever's creditors. Next morning, in an open letter to the 'worthy Liverymen', Richard offered a concise explanation of the Hasenclever business. 'Gentlemen and fellow-citizens,' he concluded, 'you can be at no loss to judge of the purpose for which these repeated attacks are made upon me, and I most cheerfully commit myself to your generosity and spirit to turn them on the heads of their fabricators.'[26] On the fourth day of polling, for the first time, Richard received more votes than Sawbridge.[27]

At the start of the seventh and final day, the first three candidates – Brook Watson, Sir Watkin Lewes and Nathaniel Newnham – were safely ahead, but the fourth seat hung in the balance. On this day Richard received 434 votes and Sawbridge 357 – which overall left Richard short by just seven votes. Indeed, he almost pipped Sawbridge, since soon after 3 p.m., when poll books closed, 'three postchaises, each containing three voters, who had been brought up from distant parts of England by Atkinson, arrived at the hustings'.[28] The *Morning Herald* gleefully imagined Pitt receiving the news of Sawbridge's victory during dinner at Downing Street, and the ensuing rumpus causing the contents of the soup tureen to end up 'in the Rat-catcher's breeches'.[29]

But Richard and his supporters, after such a dirty campaign, were in no mood to concede; at a crowded meeting on 9 April, they demanded a scrutiny of the votes. (An unusual step – the last time a

scrutiny had taken place in the City of London was fifty years earlier.)
The Lord Mayor ordered the livery companies to provide lists of their
membership, and the two rival camps set up headquarters to gather
information about the electorate; Richard's followers sat daily at the
King's Head Tavern in the Poultry, while Sawbridge's supporters
took up residence at the Guildhall Coffee-house on Cheapside. Had
any liveryman been impersonated? Had any liveryman voted twice?
Were all liverymen up to date with their company fees? The *Morning
Post* reported: 'Bets run much against Mr. Sawbridge in the city.'[30]

WHILE THESE ENQUIRIES were in progress, Richard was
taken up with the annual elections at East India House, working
closely with Francis Baring, who had been a director of the Company since 1779. The careers of the two men, friends for almost
thirty years, had run along parallel tracks since they left Samuel
Touchet's employment in the early 1760s. Richard had been the
first to achieve prominence through his services to Lord North's
ministry; but Baring had been later favoured by Lord Shelburne's
ministry with contracts to provision the army at the tail end of the
American war, more or less picking up where Richard had left off.

The East India Company elections of 1784 would prove unusually
contentious. Under rules set by the Regulating Act, directors held
office on a revolving four-year basis, which meant that each year
six of the twenty-four stood down, to spend a year 'out by rota-
tion'. John Robinson wrote to 220 proprietors soliciting votes for
Pitt's favoured candidates. Richard, meanwhile, was plotting to oust
the 'slow & languid' chairman, Nathaniel Smith; he and Baring had
already agreed with Laurence Sulivan, an influential director, that
they would have free rein to 'settle the Chairs' if Pitt's candidates
prevailed in the election on 14 April.[31]

Richard envisaged Baring as chairman, and taking the deputy
chair for himself. Sulivan changed his mind, however, and decided
to put himself forward. While Richard considered Sulivan not only
an ally, but 'by far the fittest Man for the Office', Pitt and Dundas
refused to countenance his election as chairman so long as his friend

Warren Hastings held power in Bengal.[32] Robinson tried to dis-suade Sulivan from standing, claiming that Fox would table a hostile motion against him, and Pitt could not prevent such a measure 'lest he should be suspected of screening any Man improperly'; but then Sulivan arranged a meeting with the prime minister, who falsely denied objecting to his candidacy. Sulivan would write, somewhat bitterly, after losing by a single vote to Smith, the incumbent medi-ocrity: 'Atkinson and Baring have been smothered in their own Pit – and instead of sharing Power with me which they might have done they are now of no consequence whatever.'[33]

RICHARD'S ELECTORAL SCRUTINY, before the Sheriffs of the City of London in the domed Council Room at Guildhall, began on 26 April. With little precedent to follow, the opposing teams agreed that they would examine doubtful votes from each of the eighty-odd livery companies in alphabetical order – from Apothe-caries to Wheelwrights. Sawbridge had hired an expensive legal team; Richard preferred to represent himself, believing lawyers 'were unnecessary, tending to create delays'.[34]

On the first day the tally was even, with three invalid votes struck off each candidate's score. 'Mr. Atkinson had of himself singly to contend against the Quirks and Quibbles of experienced Lawyers,' reported the *St James's Chronicle*, 'and in some Instances appeared an Over-Match for them.'[35] After the second day, when Richard queried the votes of a cooper, a dyer, a painter-stainer and two innholders, and Sawbridge's legal team those of a joiner, a wine-drawer, a gun-smith, a grocer, a blacksmith and a girdler, the tally stood at five bad votes for Richard and three for Sawbridge. The scrutiny inched for-ward in this pettifogging mode until 3 May, by which time Richard had been docked thirteen votes and Sawbridge eleven, and Rich-ard's supporters gave notice that they would take part no further. 'In six days you have decided upon 33 or 34 votes only,' they told the Sheriffs. 'To continue a proceeding at once troublesome, expensive, inadequate, inconclusive and dangerous, appears very improper.'[36] On 4 May, John Sawbridge was declared MP for London.

As it happened, a still more rancorous contest was under way in Westminster, where one of the two sitting members, Charles James Fox, was in danger of losing his seat. (An idiosyncrasy of this constituency was that polling lasted forty days.) In this frenzied atmosphere, even members of the 'gentle sex' turned into violent partisans. One night in the coffee room of the opera house on the Haymarket, Lady Margaret Fordyce, with a 'ferocity truly *clannish*', reportedly snatched the laurel sprig denoting Foxite allegiance from another woman's bosom. 'Has *secret influence* entirely subdued her Ladyship,' wondered the *Morning Herald*, 'that decency and good manners is no longer to be attended to?'[37]

Fox would hold on to his seat, by a whisker, but dozens of his acolytes were not so lucky – they came to be known as 'Fox's Martyrs'. When, on 24 May, the Commons divided for the first time after the election, Pitt was able to savour the sweet sensation of a three-figure majority. It was a triumph for which John Robinson, in particular, reaped his reward. The *London Gazette* announced the creation of ten new peerages, the most senior of which was the earldom of Abergavenny, to be conferred upon Robinson's daughter's ailing father-in-law – meaning that she would soon become a countess. Lowther's earldom of Lonsdale came lower down the list, and he felt the affront keenly, for Robinson had once been his servant. 'I am told that Sir James Lowther is very much discontented & violent about his peerage, on account of the precedence which John Robinson's grandson will have over the Lowthers,' Francis Baring gossiped to Lord Shelburne. 'They even apprehend that he may join opposition upon that account.'[38]

The corrupt nature of eighteenth-century politics meant that Richard did not have to wait long for a parliamentary seat. When it seemed that he might not succeed in London, Pitt asked Sir Edward Dering – described by Horace Walpole as 'a foolish Kentish Knight' – to put a seat aside for him.[39] Richard's lawyer John Smith was duly returned as MP for the tiny Cinque Port of New Romney in *locum tenens*, before vacating for his client in mid-June. (Years later, Dering would write to Pitt citing his consent to this arrangement, 'though much against Sir Edward's inclination as not liking Mr. Atkinson's Character', as a reason why he deserved a peerage.)[40] It seems that Pitt placed a high value on Richard's expertise – many thought too high a value. As the *Morning Herald* bellowed: 'The *Rum* Mr. Atkinson – strange as it may sound to the ears of the world – is at this moment *Minister of finance* for this insulted empire! – not a single measure is adopted without his approbation.'[41]

TWELVE

A Dose of Vitriol

WILLIAM PITT THE YOUNGER'S sheer youthfulness when he came to power was a gift to satirists; many portrayed him as a callow schoolboy, running the country under the watchful eye of his Cambridge tutor George Pretyman. One 'anecdote' from the *Rolliad*, a collection of squibs first published in the *Morning Herald*, describes a typical day at Downing Street in June 1784:

> Mr. Pitt rises about *nine*, when the weather is clear, but if it should rain, Dr. Prettyman advises him to lie about an hour longer. About *ten* he generally blows his nose and cuts his toe nails, and while he takes the exercise of his *Bidet*, Dr. Prettyman reads to him the different petitions and memorials that have been presented to him. About *eleven* his valet brings in Mr. Atkinson and a *warm shirt*, and they talk over *new scrip*, and other matters of finance. Mr. Atkinson has said to *his* confidential friends round change, that Mr. Pitt always speaks to him with great *affability*. At *twelve* Mr. Pitt retires to the water closet, adjoining to which is a small cabinet from whence Mr. Jenkinson confers with him on the *secret instructions* from Buckingham House . . .[1]

Now the House of Commons lay at his command, Pitt wasted no time in placing a new India Bill before parliament. As a prelude, a select committee conducted an investigation into the East India Company's accounts; its report, which came out on 22 June, cast doubt on some numbers submitted by Richard on behalf of the directors.[2] Two days later, Charles James Fox warned MPs not to be 'led by Forgeries and false Calculations' into forming a positive impression of the Company's financial health – causing Richard, in what appears to have been his maiden speech, to defend himself against 'so foul an imputation'.[3] By the time of the next debate on the Company's affairs, a week later, Richard had presented the prime minister with a paper rebutting seventy-three negative assertions made by the select committee.[4] 'I am really almost knocked up with the matters which are & have been in hand,' he told Robinson.[5]

On 6 July, during a stifling heatwave, Pitt introduced his India legislation to a listless House. A Board of Control would be appointed by the Crown, and vested with powers to supervise all aspects of the East India Company's civil and military governance at home and in India. The proprietors would lose much of their clout, since they would hold no veto over joint decisions of the Court of Directors and Board of Control. The directors would keep their valuable patronage, which included the appointment of 'writers' to the Company's administration in India, and cadets and assistant surgeons to its armies. The bill passed its second reading, without division, a week later.

ANNE LINDSAY SPENT much of the early summer of 1784 making arrangements for an expedition to the continent. The Lindsay sisters' circle of friends included the 'lovely, soft' Maria Fitzherbert, who had experienced the misfortune of being widowed twice before she was twenty-five. It was in Anne's box at the opera house that the Prince of Wales was said to have 'first beheld' Mrs Fitzherbert. 'He soon took me aside,' Anne recalled, 'to ask me what Angel was it that sat beside me in a white hood? I told him, and from that moment he appeared to live but in the hope of meeting her again and again, and of drowning himself like the poor fly in the sweets he should have shunned.'[6]

The match was ill-starred from the start. Mrs Fitzherbert was certainly gratified by the attentions of the prince, who was six years her junior, but too proper to consent to be his mistress, and her status as both a commoner and a Catholic made it unthinkable they could marry. Such hindrances did not deter the 21-year-old prince, though, and his assault upon the virtue of *La Belle Veuve* was soon tittle-tattle everywhere.

Anne's decision to go abroad was in part motivated by the fact that she could now afford to do so; for it was two years since, 'through Atkinson's kindness', she had been 'blessed with independence enough to venture to form a wish of amusements beyond the common habits' of her past life. She also felt an urge to cut loose from her benefactor. As she later explained: 'There was a set of invisible ties of restraint . . . which I wished to relax, not to break. I thought Atkinson might profit by my absence.'[7] She started casting around for travel companions; one day in June, Mrs Fitzherbert called upon her and proposed they set off as soon as possible.

Richard had grave doubts about the propriety of such a trip. 'I do not reason upon the measure itself in which there can be nothing wrong but upon the opinions of the World,' he told Anne on 2 July. 'Whatever may be *our* Conviction that a desire *to avoid* the pursuer is your friend's Motive, the general opinion will I fear remain fixed that if that purpose had been very sincere the means of carrying it into effect might long since have been found & might still be found without going abroad for two or three Months. Were there any Gentleman of your own family or connection of the Party, I should think nothing of it, but in truth I fear that the fair young Widow so circumstanced makes no Chaperon at all.'[8]

Prince George, for his part, tried to dissuade his *inamorata* from leaving by means of an absurd display of histrionics, which included swallowing physic – a purgative – to make himself look pale and drawn, and other tactics that Anne considered unworthy of 'any honest man'. Finally, the evening before Mrs Fitzherbert was due to depart, the prince stabbed himself with a sword. Although he did himself no serious harm, he 'bled like a calf', and subsequently threatened to rip off his bandages unless she solemnly promised to marry him when she returned from France. The next morning Mrs Fitzherbert fled for the port of Dover. Anne followed two days later in her newly purchased dark chocolate post-chaise, having 'bade adieu' the previous night to the 'excellent friend' who had made her adventure possible.[9]

ON 12 JULY, while Anne's carriage bounced along the turnpike to Dover, Richard was speaking in a parliamentary debate about a bill to suppress smuggling that would – in his view unfairly – make the owner of a ship answerable for an attempt by one of its crew to import even the smallest amount of contraband spirits or tea. Afterwards a writer in the *Morning Chronicle*, who confessed he had hitherto not been 'in the habit of admiring Mr. Atkinson's political character', commented that Richard's speech on the subject had been 'replete with sound reasoning, unanswerable argument, great commercial knowledge, and above all, the present principles of the constitutional laws of the land'.[10]

Certainly, smuggling had reached epidemic levels. In coastal areas, large bands of armed men operated in plain sight; even in London it was 'no unusual thing to see Gangs of 10, and 15, and 20 Horsemen riding even in the Day time with Impunity'.[11] Law enforcement was too blunt an instrument with which to combat criminality on such a scale. Instead Pitt and his advisors hit upon the tool of tax reduction – for if, they reasoned, the duties on contraband items were lowered so as 'to make the temptation no longer adequate to the risk', then smugglers would go out of business.[12] Tea, taxed at an eye-watering 119 per cent, was the obvious commodity on which to test this theory.

Pitt's proposal was to cut the duty on common Bohea tea to 12½ per cent, and on finer varieties to between 15 and 30 per cent; at the same time, the reduced tea duties would be offset by a marked increase in the window tax. Richard's fingerprints can be found all over this initiative; several documents in his handwriting crop up among Pitt's papers, now in the National Archives, with titles such as a 'Computation of the Average Price of each Species of the Tea now laying in the Company Warehouses uncleared by the Buyers – when the old Duties shall all be deducted & a new one of 12½ per Cent imposed' and a 'State of the actual Cost of the Tea to be imported by the India Company this present Summer 1784, with the new Duties payable thereon'.[13]

The measure worked. At a stroke, demand for the East India Company's legally imported leaves doubled, and its stock soon ran low. While the directors waited for new shipments of tea to arrive from China, they set up a committee – Richard was one of three active members, Francis Baring another – to plug the gap through purchases from European merchants. The smugglers attempted to sabotage the first of the Company's tea sales in the autumn; a number of strange men with 'Silk-Handkerchiefs round their Necks, and Weather beaten Countenances' descended on Leadenhall Street and forced up the auction prices to levels that threatened, but ultimately failed, to wreck the scheme.[14]

Richard had been far from happy with the state in which Pitt placed his India Bill before parliament. 'I cannot my dearest friend describe to you to how great a degree the publick business has incommoded me since you left us,' he would write to Anne on 21 July, as the legislation underwent line-by-line scrutiny during the committee stage. 'The India Bill was brought in *without communication* and full of Errors & Infirmities. I induced the Directors as a body to make private Representations setting them to rights & prepared all the Remarks & Amendments. They are every one in the course of being adopted & we shall make the Bill a good Bill at last & consistent in its Principle.'[15] The bill passed through the Commons without division on its third reading; apart from some choice invective from Edmund Burke, who had been the chief architect of Fox's India Bill, it was all quite unremarkable. The king wrote to Pitt the following morning to express his relief: 'I trust now little more trouble will be given in finishing the business of this Session, as Mr. Fox's Speech yesterday was I suppose his last Words on the Occasion and that He will retire to his new purchased Villa.'[16]

Pitt's India Act of 1784 would settle the constitution of British rule in India for more than seventy years – until the demise of the East India Company.

WHILE THE SUMMER reached its dog days, and the ranks of 'country gentlemen' thinned out as they left town for the shires, Richard remained dutifully at Westminster. Following the smooth passage of the India Act, the opposition were gripped by the conviction that Pitt's parliamentary majority had been purchased with East India Company money. During a lengthy monologue on 30 July, Edmund Burke pointed to the seats directly behind the ministerial front bench, where Richard and other MPs with Company connections were seated. 'The India bench,' Burke proclaimed, 'was very properly placed *above* the Treasury Bench, because the latter was subordinate to the former, and ruled by it.'[17] Richard wrote to Robinson late that evening. 'I think the fates have set a Spell upon me to prevent my getting to Sion Hill,' he sighed. 'I cannot describe to you how the India business at both ends of the Town has harassed me. We have fixed the Dividend in the Committee tonight at 8 per Cent without either Fox or Eden making their appearance. *They have unchained Burke who raved like a Bedlamite for two hours & I consider this as a proof that the sober Men of the Party mean to absent themselves.*'[18]

Early on Sunday 1 August, Richard set out with his niece Dorothy for Hamels Park, the Hertfordshire home of Lady Elizabeth Yorke, the youngest of the Lindsay sisters. He returned to Fenchurch Street that night on his own, carrying a bundle of correspondence addressed to Anne, who had recently arrived at the fashionable resort of Spa. Before forwarding her family's letters on to Anne, he added one of his own, which serves as an expression of his general world-weariness at this point in his life:

> I have since been almost worn out with a new point that has
> arisen in East India matters which will be managed right,
> and will I hope in a very few days close our Campaign on India
> Affairs in Parliament. I cannot attempt to give you in any

compass of a Letter the least Idea of the particulars, & shall
therefore only say that whilst I am conscious of having done
essential Service both to the Company & the Publick, I am
equally certain that nobody will thank me in either department.
Such is the vile nature of publick business! This my dearest
friend I say to *yourself.* I become every day more & more
convinced of the justice of an opinion I long ago gave you that
publick business may serve for an amusement, where the Grasp
at happiness has failed, but contains nothing in it that comes
home to the Heart.[19]

On 18 August, John Robinson hosted a grand party to celebrate the end of the parliamentary session. As Richard told Anne:
'We all dine tomorrow at Sion Hill viz. Mr. Pitt, Dundas, & the
Chancellor.'[20] It was, in fact, Richard who provided the centrepiece
of the politicians' feast that evening, but its carriage across town
presented a distinct challenge, as his letter to Robinson suggests:
'I am lucky enough to have a Turtle under my Command – about
lb 60, or 70 – & if I had the means of sending it out to you, should
be glad to spare you the trouble of sending for it, but I know not of
any Conveyance by which it can be sent with safety therefore shall
trust to your sending for it in the course of tomorrow and whether
I am at home or not my servants will have instructions where to
find it.'[21]

The preparation of a 'turtle dinner' was one of the most daunting
challenges of the eighteenth-century culinary repertoire. Hannah
Glasse opens her recipe for turtle prepared 'the West India Way'
with the following instructions: 'Take the turtle out of the water the
night before you dress it, and lay it on its back, in the morning cut
its head off, and hang it by its hind fins for it to bleed till the blood
is all out, then cut the callapee, which is the belly, round, and raise
it up; cut as much meat to it as you can, throw it into spring-water
with a little salt, cut the fins off, and scald them with the head . . .'[22]
The custom was to serve the turtle in five dishes that showed off
its fleshy charms to the greatest effect – the 'calipash' (baked back

meat), the 'calipee' (boiled belly meat), the guts (stewed in a creamy sauce), the fins (served in a clear broth) and, the climax, a tureen of luxurious turtle soup. Oh to have been a fly on the wall – or in the soup – at that particular dinner.

THE PASSING OF THE INDIA ACT by no means restored harmony to Leadenhall Street, for bitter differences would arise that autumn among the directors of the Company and the newly established Board of Control over an issue which had poisoned Indian politics for twenty years – namely, the Nawab of Arcot's debts. As Paul Benfield's agent, Richard supported the claims of the men, including several of his fellow directors, who had lent the prince vast sums at what many considered usurious rates of interest; but the chairman of the Company, Nathaniel Smith, took an opposing view. At a meeting of the directors on 23 September, Smith pushed through a draft dispatch to Madras which contained 'some very extraordinary Complimentary Paragraphs' about its governor, Lord Macartney, an enemy of the Arcot creditors, as well as drafting a 'most cruel and insulting Letter' to the nawab that was highly critical of Benfield.[23]

Richard was one of seven directors who signed a strongly worded dissent from this correspondence on 6 October, absolving themselves from 'all Responsibility for the Consequences to ensue therefrom'.[24] Two days later the Board of Control, headed by Henry Dundas, decided to radically rewrite Smith's dispatch to Madras so that it recognized the validity of all the nawab's debts, and established a sinking fund to settle them with his territorial revenues. To those who believed, like Edmund Burke, that the so-called 'Arcot Squad' had exerted undue influence during the general election – here, in the form of payment for services rendered to the ministry, was corroboration.

In the midst of this scheming, on 2 October, Richard was elected an alderman of the City of London. Although a tremendous honour, he felt rather pressed into service – 'the Devil has at length directed these Aldermen to resign,' he wrote about the two vacancies which had arisen – but his refusal to stand would have generated too much censure.[25] Following the election, Richard threw an entertainment for his Tower Ward voters at the Ship Tavern. Newspaper accounts suggest there was no shortage of refreshments: 'One gentleman was picked up and placed in a baker's basket; he was then carried in state to his own door, preceded by a choice band of choristers smoaking their pipes, and chaunting, *"he was drunk, he was drunk, he was drunk when he died!"* Another tippling rogue was *served up to his wife and family* on a window shutter, covered over with tobacco pipes arranged in beautiful order.'[26]

Richard wrote to Anne in the Netherlands on 12 October; he had not heard from her in a while. 'Still is the Oracle of Brussels silent although Devotions are performed,' he declared, his heartfelt words suggesting that he was still deeply in love with her:

Keeping within my *Heathen* Creed, I must say that Destiny has hitherto directed the Views of my Life to *Hope*. To her therefore I will still burn Incense; alas *without hope* that a superior Deity will ever assume her rightful Throne. News of our Friends I have none. For the private reason you know of (*and for no other*) I went to Brighthelmstone on Saturday – returned last night at Midnight. Was *sworn in* as Alderman today. Dined with the Lord Mayor, in a Company so stupid that Wilkes (who honestly tried) could not enliven it, *et me voici*, at nine o'Clock waiting for an Interview on India matters which grow infinitely entangled and intending again to take the Command of my Battery as much before the end of the Week as I can.[27]

The 'private reason' for Richard's visit to Brighton was to lobby Pitt, who had taken a house there. Dundas was pressing for Sir Archibald Campbell, recently governor of Jamaica, to be appointed commander-in-chief in India; Richard meanwhile hoped to man-oeuvre Anne's brother, Lord Balcarres, into the colonelcy of the 78th Highlanders, which would make him Campbell's second-in-command. But his tête-à-tête with the prime minister failed to bear the intended fruit. A member of the Board of Control, Lord Sydney (the recently ennobled Thomas Townshend), an arch-critic of Richard's contracts during the American war, had warned Pitt to distance himself from Campbell's nomination: 'You will find a Combination of the most insatiable Ambition & the most sordid Avarice & Villany at the bottom of this base Work.'[28]

Richard broke the news to Lord Balcarres in a letter dated 29 October:

> I am sorry to acquaint you that our India Politicks have
> gone very perversely, and that by means of Lord Sydney's
> persevering in a ministerial recommendation, whilst Mr. Pitt
> disavowed all interference on the part of the Ministry, the
> Court of Directors was ensnared & in vindication of what the
> majority of them thought their own honour, have appointed
> General Sloper Commander in Chief in India. Your Lordship
> will have seen some impertinences in the News papers about
> your being appointed second in command. It is impossible for
> me to guess how that Report got about for I assure you I never
> opened my Lips on the subject to any body out of the small
> Circle that was originally in the knowledge of our Castle
> building on that subject.[29]

According to rumours in the press, Richard would soon be made a baronet. The *Gazetteer* reported on 17 November that John Robinson, as a reward for 'rendering the House of Commons a cypher in the constitution', had been offered the honour for any friend he cared to name, and had nominated 'one Atkinson, distinguished for his sagacity in making the rum contract'.[30] Whether this was true or not, the two men hardly saw each other during the autumn of 1784. 'I think it an age since we met & wish most ardently for an opportunity, though no particularly pressing matter occurs,' Richard wrote on 2 December. 'I have been since Sunday confined (mostly in bed) with a Fever, taken I believe just in time to prevent its becoming rather a serious one. It is almost gone but not quite; and I am today for the first time able to sit up the whole day, and hope there is little doubt of my getting clear of it very soon.'[31] Richard's own assessment of his illness was characteristically sanguine. East India Company minutes hint at its gravity, however, for he was absent from all but two of the fourteen meetings of the directors held in December.

Richard spent January 1785 in Brighton, convalescing beside the wintry sea; by the end of the month, he felt sufficiently recovered to write Dundas a lengthy private memorandum about 'necessary reforms' in the Court of Directors.[32] Soon he was back in London.

He next attended East India House on 16 February, where a critical decision – the choice of the next Governor General of Bengal, a successor to Warren Hastings – was scheduled for the following day. According to a report in the *Gazetteer*, the prime minister summoned Richard, along with Laurence Sulivan, to Downing Street on the eve of the vote, and declared that he wished them to nominate Lord Macartney for the post. Both directors were said to have been dumbfounded at this intervention; Richard apparently replied that the 'proposition was so contrary to his feelings, and so contradictory to the principles on which his friends had hitherto embraced the interests of Mr. Pitt, that he should exert himself in the Court of Directors, and elsewhere, to oppose the appointment of Lord Macartney'.[33] Whether or not this exchange took place (for it was later denied) would in any case prove immaterial, since Richard was prevented from casting his vote by the 'most extraordinary accident in the World'.[34]

Next morning, his servant mistakenly gave him the wrong medicine – oil of vitriol, known today as sulphuric acid, instead of the physic that was intended. Without George Fordyce's swift intervention, the blunder would have killed Richard, and it certainly left him too weak to attend the Court of Directors.

All but two of the twenty-four directors showed up at East India House that day, and when the motion was put 'that Lord Macartney succeed to Bengal on the Resignation or Removal of Mr. Hastings', they divided eleven against eleven.[35] It fell to the Secretary to draw a deciding lot from the ballot glass – he pulled out Macartney's name. 'What a singular constitution is that of Leadenhall House,' commented the *Gazetteer*, 'that thus the fate of India should depend on a *toss-up*.'[36] Two weeks later those jesters at the same newspaper came up with an idea for a cartoon: 'A Contractor Refunding His Ill-gotten Wealth,' its caption would read. 'When a certain rum contractor had about a fortnight ago swallowed a dose of *vitriol* instead of a gentle purgative – Dr. Fordyce *hung him up by the heels*; a good hint for a caricature!'[37]

Richard next visited East India House on 28 February, in advance of a parliamentary debate about the Nawab of Arcot's debts and the ministry's recent recognition of their validity. That evening, in the House of Commons, Charles James Fox moved that correspondence on the subject from the Court of Directors be handed over for inspection; Philip Francis, seconding the motion, warned Pitt and Dundas that 'their personal characters were more endangered than they perhaps imagined' by rumours of a 'collusion between the board of control and the creditors of the nabob' – a declaration which Dundas, who spoke next, treated 'with some degree of ridicule'.[38] Just as the debate seemed to have run its natural course, Edmund Burke rose to his feet, showing signs of emotion; what followed would go down as one of this prodigious orator's most epic speeches.

If Burke's overarching theme that night was the damage caused by the greed of the East India Company, the chief villain of the piece was Paul Benfield – 'a criminal, who long since ought to have fattened the region's kites with his offal'.[39] Richard, as Benfield's 'agent and attorney', fared little better. 'Every one who hears me, is well acquainted with the sacred friendship, and the steady mutual attachment that subsists between him and the present minister,' Burke declared, before protesting at the manner in which Richard had been permitted to make Pitt's India Bill 'his own', and the 'authority with which he brought up clause after clause, to stuff and fatten the rankness of that corrupt Act'. Next, Burke turned his attention to the previous year's general election, observing that Richard had kept a 'sort of public office or counting-house' from which the business of securing Pitt's majority had been conducted:

It was managed upon India principles, and for an Indian interest. This was the golden cup of abominations; this the chalice of the fornications of rapine, usury, and oppression, which was held out by the gorgeous eastern harlot; which so many of the people, so many of the nobles of this land had drained to the very dregs. Do you think that no reckoning was to follow this lewd debauch? That no payment was to be demanded for this riot of public drunkenness and national prostitution?[40]

The speech, brimming with high-flown imagery, was vintage Burke. He finally sat down at one in the morning, having hectored the chamber for five hours. 'So absurd, as well as unfounded, did the accusations appear,' recalled Nathaniel Wraxall, 'that the treasury bench remained silent' – but, then, he would say that, for he too was in Paul Benfield's pocket.[41]

LADY ANNE LINDSAY and Mrs Fitzherbert had arrived at Paris in December 1784. Lady Margaret Fordyce joined them there; the plan was that they would all take a tour of the Swiss glaciers, before returning to England in the summer. But Margaret brought worrying news of Richard's health; shortly before her departure he had suffered 'something resembling a paralytic attack', and his condition remained precarious. 'My heart,' wrote Anne, 'trembled at the sound of the Palsy.'[42] The sisters decided to stay in Paris to await further bulletins.

Richard returned to Brighton in early March, accompanied by his niece Dorothy. His letters to Paris were deceptively cheerful. 'All you have to do,' he told Anne, 'is to double the number of your letters while I am an invalid, as they will be my best medicine; amuse yourself well, and let me partake of it.'[43] And he expressly forbade the sisters from coming home on his account, insisting that their proximity to him would create a wish for more of their society 'than he ought to be indulged in'.[44]

With the arrival of spring, Richard seemed to rally. Bridget wrote to Dorothy on 19 April:

> I am glad your Uncle is better tho' ever so Little. Some people
> are even in this country very Long in recovering from a fever
> and yet Lives many many years which I hope in God may be
> the case with my good Brother and Freind, if I think ever so
> Little on the contrary I find it is one of the things I cannot bear
> to think on. I hope you will be gone to Brighthelmstone if you
> can be of Service to your Uncle do not mind forms but ask your
> Uncle and do not waite his asking you is he not in place of a
> Father and what is there out of Character in atending a Sick
> relation at any time or any place?[45]

Three days later, Richard felt well enough to sit up in bed and dictate a message for Francis Baring to deliver at East India House 'concerning the necessity of considerable and immediate Tea Purchases which opinion Mr. B is at liberty to make any use of he pleases'.[46]

But Richard's improvement turned out to be illusory, and his end was sudden. On 26 May a physician came from Lewes, who 'found his pulse to be that of a dying man'. At eleven that evening, Richard asked Dorothy to bring him a calf's foot jelly. While she was out of the room, and his servant was tidying up the bedclothes, he whispered *I shall faint*, and died 'without a groan or struggle'.[47]

PART II

The Torrid Zone

THIRTEEN

The Newcastle Attorney

I WISH I COULD describe Richard's final months in greater detail. Dorothy nursed him during this time, and she must have written to Bridget at Temple Sowerby with news of his decline – but no such letters have survived. As for what caused Richard's death, we cannot know for sure, but it seems likely to have been tuberculosis. (An explanation supported by Nathaniel Wraxall, whose memoirs – one of the livelier commentaries on the events of the period – refer to Richard being carried off 'in the vigour of his age' by a 'feverish and consumptive complaint'.)[1]

I was on the point of accepting that there was no more to know on the subject when I came upon the brief description of Richard's dying moments, including his last words, in a letter from Lady Elizabeth Yorke to her sisters in Paris. It was a wonderful archival discovery, as well as a vexing one; for while the first sheet of the letter had been preserved, the rest had gone astray. Elizabeth told how, on hearing news of Richard's death, and feeling it her 'duty to do all to *his* niece that I could have done for a *sister*', she had rushed to Dorothy at Fenchurch Street: 'Oh my dearest Sisters may you never enter that house again! for if I found it so melancholy, so chearless, what must it appear to you! I found her in the greatest affliction, the gloomy appearance of the House & the want of air, made me immediately consider that the best thing I could do would be to carry her' – and here the page ends . . .[2]

Many years later, Anne would recount the rest of this sad episode in her memoirs. Elizabeth had postponed a ball that she was about to give in London; instead she bundled Dorothy away to Hertfordshire in a well-intentioned attempt to 'restore her spirits', recruiting another guest to 'read Shakespeare to her from morning to night'. Evidently this treatment failed, however, for Dorothy had left the Yorkes earlier than planned, and hurried home to her mother in Westmorland – conduct which made her guilty, in Anne's opinion, of 'unpardonable' ingratitude.[3]

RICHARD'S DEATH left me bereft. He was such a dynamic personality, such an incurable optimist, and it seemed unthinkable that he would no longer be present in this story. (Although, as we shall see, his influence would reverberate down subsequent generations of the Atkinson family as they grappled with his complex legacy.) By chance he was the same age as me, almost to the month, when I came to write about his death – a coincidence that added a frisson to my emotional response. I certainly felt humbled by how much he had packed into his forty-six years.

Richard's character had embodied some startling contradictions. Indeed, the gulf between his private and public identities could hardly have seemed wider; on the one hand there was the rejected lover and saintly benefactor, as recalled by Lady Anne Lindsay, and on the other there was the shrewd businessman and political fixer, as portrayed by his critics. (He was also, lest we forget, a slave owner.) The more time I spent in the company of these multiple Richard Atkinsons, however, the easier I found it to see them as facets of the same man. I came to realize, too, that Anne's memoirs had been written with the rose-tinted nostalgia of thirty years' hindsight – but, equally, that the *ad hominem* attacks of the journalists often bore little relation to the target of their derision.

So now we reach what is, for me, the greatest mystery of this story – the discovery of a record so unsettling that it made me wonder whether I would ever know Richard at all. It consists of the copy of a legal deed, which I found within a crumbling volume in the archive of the Registrar-General's Office at Spanish Town, the old colonial capital of Jamaica. This document states that on 1 May 1785, Samuel Mure agreed to 'Grant Bargain Sell Transfer Assign and Deliver over unto the said Richard Atkinson his heirs and assigns the following Negro Slaves viz. Betty and her Three Children with the future Issue Offspring and Increase of the said Slaves', in exchange for £120 of the island's currency.[4] Betty's vendor, Samuel Mure, was one of Hutchison Mure's sons, and managed several of his family's sugar estates in Jamaica.

For what earthly reason could Richard have felt the need to purchase four 'Negro Slaves' less than a month before his death? I turned the question over and over in my mind, trying to imagine scenarios that might have led to so singular a transaction – but ultimately it seemed so domestic, so *private*, that I could only suppose Betty was Richard's mistress, and the three children were *his* children. Then I remembered the letter written by Richard in December 1782, sent to Anne along with the final draft of his will, in which he had expressed a desire to throw his 'whole Heart open to her' and to reveal 'its most secret Sensations'. As attentive readers may recall, he had continued in the same intimate vein: 'The Consciousness that her Eye must review it would be sufficient to keep out all the *black* Family, & as to human Frailties, the Heart knows much less than mine that does not know that under the Influence of a generous confidence they would become the very Cement of its best Happiness.'[5]

The first time I read that passage, I must confess, my eyes slid over it – I suppose I thought Richard's reference to 'the *black* Family' was an obscure figure of speech. It had not crossed my mind that he might mean a black family of his own, for I knew he had never visited Jamaica – the dense paper trail of his letters in all the archives left no gap long enough to allow for such an absence. But black servants could be found in many wealthy London households at this time, and it seems likely that the Mures brought Betty over to work for them; she must at some point have entered into a relationship with Richard. According to the laws of slavery, the offspring of an enslaved female automatically belonged to her owner; so presumably, through his deathbed purchase, Richard hoped to spare Betty and the children the fate of being returned to the West Indies. (If he had wished unambiguously to guarantee their liberty, he could have freed them in a codicil to his will – which would, however, have carried the drawback of declaring their existence to the world.)

The whole subject is deeply uncomfortable, especially as the scarcity of information has driven me so much further down the path of conjecture than I would like. The story of Betty and her family raises so many questions, none of which, I suspect, will ever be answered – there is too little information to go on. Where was she born? Where did she grow up? How did Richard treat her? What were the children called? Did Richard make provision for them after his death? Did they go on to have families? *Might any of their descendants be alive today?*

RICHARD'S BODY WAS INTERRED beneath the middle aisle of Brighton's ancient parish church of St Nicholas of Myra, patron saint of merchants, on a grassy hill high above the English Channel. His death automatically triggered several elections – within weeks a new MP for New Romney, a new alderman for Tower Ward and a new director of the East India Company had replaced him. As the economist Dr Richard Price wrote to the former Lord Shelburne, now Marquess of Lansdowne: 'Your Lordship has seen in the Newspapers that Alderman Atkinson is dead. He has made a great noise and bustle, and rose from a mean station to wealth and honours. But what does it all signify?'[6]

The *Morning Chronicle* ran an admiring obituary on 9 June, observing that Richard had arrived in London a 'mere adventurer, unsustained by any inheritance, by few family friends of any power, and by no acquisitions, which education imparts, but common penmanship and arithmetick', and had managed through 'good sense and persevering industry' to rise from the 'bottom of society to the summit of affluence'.[7] Other newspapers ran less respectful pieces,

Near this Place
in the Middle Iſle
Lies depoſited the
Remains of
RICHARD ATKINSON *Eſq?*
Member of Parliament for
New ROMNEY and
ALDERMAN of the
City of LONDON
Ob! 26!ʰ May 1785
Ætatis 47

Richard Atkinson's tombstone in Brighton parish church.

which caused a few readers to leap to his defence. 'The fidelity with which the Alderman executed all his contracts with government is worthy of notice,' observed one correspondent to the *Public Adver-tiser.* 'Whatever mistakes or misconduct may be attributed to the commanders by sea or land employed by our then Ministry, no part of their ill success was ever attributed by them to any neglect of the late Alderman not fulfilling his contracts with punctuality.'[8]

Richard had planned his will to be the mechanism by which he would enrich his closest friends and elevate the next generation of the Atkinson family. As you might expect, it was highly detailed; it was also full of the windy repetitions and circumlocutions with which such documents abound. In essence, though, Richard expected the produce of his two Jamaican estates to fund annuities worth more than £5,000 a year. Lady Anne Lindsay, Lady Margaret Fordyce and John Robinson would each receive £700 a year; his brother Matthew Atkinson, sister Margaret Taylor and sister-in-law Bridget Atkinson would each receive £200 a year, as would Captain John Bentinck's son William; while his nine nieces and George Fordyce's two daughters would each receive £200 a year as soon as they came of age. Richard also anticipated the estates generating surplus income, above what was needed to pay the annuities, which would accumulate into a substantial fund; lump sums of £3,000 would be paid from this fund to each of his eight nephews when they came of age, and any remaining money would be divided equally between his nine nieces and any daughters Lady Anne Lindsay might end up having. The Bogue estate would eventually pass to the sons of his brother George, while the Dean's Valley estate would go to the sons of his brother Matthew. It was soon to become all too clear that in attempting to spread his wealth so widely, Richard had disastrously overreached himself.

Anne and Margaret returned to London three weeks after Richard's death, filled with remorse at their failure to visit him before it was too late. Their family attempted to absolve them of their guilt. 'Do not, do not repine my dearest sisters that you were not at Brighthelmstone during the last moments of our much loved, much regretted Friend,' wrote Elizabeth. 'I feel your distresses & know how poignant your grief must be.'[9] Their brother, Lord Balcarres, insisted that their conduct had been perfectly correct: 'Whatever Regret you may have for not being present at his Dissolution, you have certainly no Room for reproach, and if you had come over I am certain it would have fretted him.'[10]

The size of Richard's fortune would be the cause of much gossip over the following weeks – £300,000 was a figure bandied about in the press – and the wax seal on his will had barely been broken before scurrilous rumours started circulating about the nature of his friendship with Anne, especially given the provision made for her non-existent daughters. '*The* WILL – *and the* AFFAIRS. What mistakes and pleasantry have Lady Anne Lindsay's *children* and Atkinson's *will* occasioned!' exclaimed the *Public Advertiser*.[11] As she would herself observe: 'Such generous conduct as Mr. Atkinson's is not made for the comprehension of the world.'[12]

Everywhere Anne went, people congratulated her on her inheritance – yet she felt 'bent down to the ground by private sorrow'.[13] Her memories of this time would remain raw for the rest of her life. 'Do I pretend to have a heart?' she would write years later. 'Am I not a stone that I should have hesitated and postponed my return when his health became a question? Would he not have gone to the end of the world to do good to mine? O! my kind friend! why had not you the shoulder of the person you loved to lay your poor head on?'[14]

FOR THE MURE FAMILY, Richard's death was a catastrophe. While their late partner had been building the reputation of their firm as one of the foremost merchant houses in the City of London, the younger Mures – Robert and William – led a bone-idle existence, shooting and fishing on their elderly father's estate in Suffolk. After the mansion at Great Saxham burnt down, in 1779, the family had moved into the stable block, on to which two wings had been added, giving it the air of an Italian villa. Apparently it was a dull household. 'Mr. Mure's daughter and sons didn't seem to me to be very fond of laughing,' recalled the Comte de La Rochefoucauld, who stayed at Great Saxham during the summer of 1784. 'The worst drawback there in going to dinner with Mr. Mure is the great length of time he stays at table, generally three and a half hours. I once sat there five hours, without leaving the table, just eating and drinking.'[15]

In Richard's absence, the Mures soon fell into financial difficulties, and they immediately set about talking down the size of his estate, a good deal of which would have to come out of the assets of the partnership. 'As very much depends upon the state of Mr. Atkinson's Personal Property we are busy in making up his accounts,' Robert Mure wrote to Lord Balcarres, a trustee of Richard's will, barely a week after his death. 'I have to observe that from the very large sums he had expended upon the Improvement of his Estates in Jamaica they will be very much increased in Value, his Personalty proportionately diminished.'[16] Two months later, the Mures would attribute their cash-flow problems to Richard having taken sums 'amounting to £78,000' out of the house between the time of writing his will and his death.[17] This was a foretaste of the wrangling that would consume the energies of an entire generation, and ultimately serve the interests of no one – save the lawyers.

*

BRIDGET ATKINSON had spent little time in her brother-in-law's company – the last occasion on which I can say they certainly met was in 1776 – yet his demise came as a heavy blow. Following the death of her husband, George, she had gratefully accepted Richard's offer to act as protector to her eight children: Dorothy, Michael, George, Richard, Matthew, John, Bridget and Jane. Already her two eldest sons had departed for the colonies. Michael had sailed for India in 1781; George, meanwhile, had gone out to Jamaica in the summer of 1784, and was now employed at the merchant house of Mures & Dunlop in Kingston, from where he could also keep an eye on his uncle's estates. (He took his hound out with him; Bridget's pocket account book records the purchase of a dog collar, engraved 'Jock – G. Atkinson – Deans Valley'.)[18] For the younger Atkinson boys, lacking their uncle's patronage, their futures were suddenly filled with uncertainty.

Bridget and her brother-in-law Matthew were both appalled when they learnt how much Lady Anne Lindsay stood to gain from Richard's will; they saw her as an undeserving heiress, and set out to frustrate her claim. Anne, not surprisingly, saw the matter in a different light: 'The family of Atkinson having seen their brother but once in the course of twenty years, were not in the habit of forming expectations from him, till his invitation of Dolly awakened them. They now affected to be mortified at the destination of his property.'[19]

The Mures started putting about rumours that their late partner's estate was too insubstantial to support his legacies. Matthew Atkinson and his brother-in-law George Taylor – who were both executors of Richard's will – travelled south for a potentially tense meeting at Fenchurch Street in March 1786. 'I am anxious to know upon what terms Messrs. Mures & my uncles parted I fear not well,' Dorothy wrote to Bridget, from Newcastle, on 31 March.[20] But the Mures evidently smoothed over the Atkinsons' concerns, for Dorothy wrote joyfully to her mother a few days later:

> I cannot let you remain a moment in ignorance of what I have
> learnt from my uncle. There is not the smallest doubt but every

annuity and every legacy will be paid to a farthing – there are no chancery suits but *imaginary ones* – no difficulties but the *like* – and Mr. Taylor says that every one of the Mr. Mures have behaved with more kindness, attention and patience than he can describe. You may set your heart quite at rest – what needless vexation have we suffered.[21]

The Lindsay sisters would also soon experience the Mures' double dealings. In the eyes of the world, Anne was a wealthy heiress; wherever she went, she sensed once-indifferent bachelors sizing her up anew. (The *Morning Herald* commented with cheerful malice on her 'ostentatious' coach: 'It surely is a splendid compliment to Mr. Atkinson's *hearse!*')[22] But her true situation was far from clear, for she was yet to receive a penny of her legacy; and so she was aghast when John Smith, Richard's lawyer, informed her that the Mures were planning a raid on their late partner's estate to pay off 'old debts' of more than thirty years' standing. It might be necessary, Smith warned, for her to make 'some concessions'.[23]

Soon afterwards, Anne and Margaret had a bizarre meeting with Robert Mure. Anne later wrote:

Never did I see so strange a wrestle amongst the good and bad qualities as appeared in his countenance. He entered covered with purple blushes, and a few tears, which the recollection of the benefactor of his House forced from his heart to his eyes, giving him the aspect of a red cabbage throwing off the dews of the morning; but the good emotion departed with the tears, and he became hard and collected like the said cabbage.[24]

Mure stammered that he and his brother William were planning, through the courts if necessary, to challenge Richard's estate for the stock he had acquired through floating the government loan of 1782, of which he had set aside £30,000 for Anne's benefit. The Mure brothers did concede that their father Hutchison, as senior partner, had told Richard that he could dispose of the stock as he pleased, but the permission had been granted verbally, not in writing, and therefore they considered it the property of the house.

AT TEMPLE SOWERBY, on 10 August 1786, Bridget locked and bolted her bedchamber door as usual before turning in for the night. She woke at about two in the morning to feel her bed shaking, 'as if somebody had got from under it', and the floorboards cracking, 'as if somebody was walking on them'. Were she to live in a land where earthquakes occurred, she wrote in her diary, she would suppose this to have been one – but instead she put it down to a 'nervous Simptom'.[25] The shock would be felt across the northern counties of England, but it is hardly surprising that Bridget blamed it on her nerves, for they were in an unusually jangled state.

A few months earlier, the Atkinson family had hired an ambitious young attorney-at-law, Nathaniel Clayton, to defend their interests against the Mures. Clayton came from a line of Newcastle upon Tyne worthies – his grandfather and uncle had both been mayor – and had started his legal practice in the Bigg Market back in 1778, when he was twenty-two. He was also town clerk of Newcastle, having paid £2,100 for the lease on that office in June 1785. The fees earned by the incumbent were quite nominal; its main advantage lay in the valuable inside knowledge to which the town clerk was privy through his dealings with the council.

Shortly after accepting the Atkinsons' brief, Clayton had fallen in love with Dorothy, who was staying with friends in Newcastle. His earliest letters to her still exist. The first starts: 'Madam, I cannot reconcile it to myself to delay a Declaration of my unalterable Regard, and that it has become absolutely essential to my Happiness to obtain your Confidence & good Opinion . . .'[26]

Dorothy's reply has not survived, but it seems to have caused him pain. 'Dear Madam,' began his second letter:

The Rapidity with which my favourable Opinion of you grew into Esteem, and that Esteem into Love, I have felt but cannot describe. I have urged on the Decision of my Fate with

inconsiderate Rashness, & have now only to deplore how vain
they are who teach that cruel Certainty is more tolerable than
a state of anxious Doubt. *My* Heart has also undergone a
solemn & a strict Examination. I find it unchangeably yours,
and that it cannot be estranged, til it shall cease to beat.[27]

This time Dorothy must have given her admirer cause for hope,
for his next letter is much more playful:

My most amiable Girl, I am much at a Loss to justify my
giving you the Trouble of receiving my Letters, otherwise than
by imputing it to that Propensity which Lovers have to *write* as
well as *talk Nonsense* to their Mistresses, & to the hope that, as
I have been pardoned for teazing my Angel with Declarations
of my Love for her, I shall also experience her Lenity, when
I more solemnly, in black & white, assure her that she is the
dearest Creature upon Earth & that I am the most enamoured
Swain.[28]

Bridget reacted badly to the news of her daughter's attachment
– perhaps forgetting her own mother's opposition to her engagement nearly thirty years earlier – which in turn caused Dorothy to
hesitate. 'I begin to think I have been too hasty with regard to Mr.
Clayton,' she wrote to Bridget. 'I perceive an impropriety in marrying whilst our family affairs are in such an unsettled state. I shall
be guided by your opinion, for I can with truth assure you my dear
mother that I never will marry without your intire approbation.'[29]
But Bridget did not stand in the way for long, offering Dorothy her
acquiescence at the end of October 1786:

I have nothing to disapprove in Mr. Claytons conduct to you
or to myself only I am very Sorry he ever distinguished you by
his regard. If you continue in the same mind and wish for my
consent you shall have it most certainly only pray do not Let
Mr. Clayton write me any more it affects my Spirits more than

you can imagen indeed the Loss of a companion and one I could
at times consult upon every Occasion is hard to bear but – to
part with a child is scarce supportable and yet a Match which
all your Freinds think a very good one a man rising in the
World I should not be able to bear my own reflections if
I prevent it so God direct you for the best.[30]

Nathaniel Clayton rode over to Temple Sowerby on 22 November,
a pouch full of gold rings in his pocket. 'The Goldsmith appearing
to have but little faith in the Measure of thy *fourth* Finger you gave
me I was much alarmed lest that mystical Instrument, which I am
to give as an earnest of Happiness & Love, should prove a perpetual
Source of Uneasiness by its not being of a proper Size,' he had written to Dorothy beforehand. 'From this Dilemma I have however
been happily relieved by obtaining a Number of Rings of different
Shapes & Sizes for thy Choice, & it will not be an unpleasant Duty
on Wednesday Afternoon to try them all.'[31] The following day, they
were married in the village church.

The newlyweds immediately set off for London, their purpose
being to meet the various beneficiaries of the Atkinson estate and to
prevent it from ending up in the Court of Chancery – for chancery
suits, often involving matters of inheritance, were liable to drag on
for generations, bleeding families dry in the process. One night the
Claytons dined with Anne Lindsay; Francis Baring was the only
other guest. After they had finished eating, and Baring had left,
Anne launched into a tirade about Robert Mure's 'iniquitous claims'
upon Richard's estate, which she believed would prove 'equally ruinous' to the Atkinson family's interests as to her own.[32]

Back at Temple Sowerby, Bridget was furious when she found
out who the Claytons had been fraternizing with. Dorothy wrote
from lodgings in Charlotte Street:

You tell me you are 'angry very angry' that I should listen
to what Lady Anne had to say against Mr. Mure. Let me ask
you my dear mother how it is possible for me to judge of a

cause, without first hearing both sides, the truth of which maxim cannot be more clearly evinced than by your violent prepossession on behalf of Mr. Mure who is making claims upon the fortune and casting reflections upon the memory of my dear uncle, that are neither conscientious nor justifiable – those are not the suggestions of Lady Anne but incontestible facts.[33]

Dorothy and Nathaniel did not enjoy much of a honeymoon. It rained almost the entire month they were in the capital, and their business and social commitments left little time for shopping or other gaieties. After Christmas in Westmorland, they returned to Newcastle to take up residence at Nathaniel's house on Westgate Street, next door to the Assembly Rooms. 'The business of today is receiving cards of congratulation,' Dorothy wrote to her mother on 8 January 1787. 'Happily it is not the fashion to answer them.'[34] (She was always a reluctant correspondent.) Within weeks, Dorothy had fallen pregnant – a condition in which she would spend a large part of the following two decades.

Nathaniel was called down to London in the late spring on Atkinson family business. George Atkinson – Bridget's second son – returned from Jamaica in early June, after three years away, and struck up an immediate rapport with his new brother-in-law. Together, Nathaniel and George tackled the legal representatives of Paul Benfield – who of course owned half the Bogue estate in Jamaica. They also dined with John Robinson at Sion Hill. During his stay in the capital, Nathaniel found time to sit for a portrait. 'My Picture is finished,' he wrote to Dorothy on 30 June, 'and looks so smart that I am in hopes beholders will cease to wonder how I obtained the best woman upon Earth for my Wife.'[35]

By August, Dorothy had started to grow cumbersome in her pregnancy. 'My Dorothy is vastly well,' Nathaniel told Bridget, 'but does not move up & down Stairs quite so expeditiously as she has wont.'[36] A 'sweet little Boy' arrived in November, and was named after his father.[37] In the spring of 1788, after 'little Nat' had safely recovered from his smallpox inoculation, Nathaniel was yet again needed in London.[38] 'I confess I am not yet so fashionable a husband as to relish these unreasonable absences,' he told his mother-in-law. 'I have therefore endeavoured to prevail on Dorothy to accompany me on my next Trip which She has consented to do on Condition that you will take the Boy and be engaged under the penalty of forfeiting your whole Cabinet of Shells to return him on Demand.'[39]

THREE YEARS AFTER his death, Richard Atkinson's tangled affairs still attracted much prurient interest. In March 1788, James Boswell attended a dinner given by the Earl of Lonsdale at which 'much good wine' was taken.[40] One of the guests, Sir James Johnstone, insisted that 'Alderman Atkinson' had explicitly mentioned in his will a love correspondence between himself and Lady Anne Lindsay, 'his own letter consisting of twenty four pages and hers of twelve', and had left money to her three children, including one with whom she was secretly pregnant while in France.[41] Another guest, Sir Michael Le Fleming, disputed this account. The baronets made a wager, the forfeit being dinner at the London Tavern. Boswell, acting as referee, duly inspected Richard's will at Doctors' Commons the following Saturday; but his journal fails to record whether Johnstone was ever required to pay up.

By the summer of 1788, the negotiations around Richard's estate had stalled. What the various parties did agree was that he had owed his partners about £35,000 at the time of his death – a figure which had since risen to £50,000, including interest and bad debts. Richard had also owed Captain David Laird £16,500, secured as a mortgage on the Dean's Valley estate – this money was due for repayment in 1792. On the other hand, Richard's personal effects, including East India stock, his wharf and warehouses at Rotherhithe, and sizeable loans to the Nevill and North families, were valued at £22,000; additional holdings, including shares in the *Bessborough* and loans to Lord Wentworth and the family of the late Captain John Bentinck, were worth £38,000. With the liabilities of Richard's estate greatly exceeding its liquid assets, the forced sale of the Jamaican plantations seemed inevitable. For his heirs, this would be the worst possible outcome, since the payment of their annuities depended upon the produce of those estates.

Richard had clearly stated in his will that he managed the business affairs of Lady Anne Lindsay, that he had borrowed almost £20,000 from her funds, and that this money remained hers. It was partly through Anne's own carelessness that her grip on the funds was less tight than it should have been, for Richard had repeatedly offered to buy her a bureau in which to lock up her financial certificates, reminding her that 'possession is eleven points of the law'.[42] But she had preferred him to look after them for her; she had also refused to let him reveal her identity when he used her money to fund loans to Lord Wentworth and the Bentinck family. Now she lacked the documentary evidence with which to stake her claims.

Anne was treated shabbily by almost all her fellow heirs; when John Robinson warned her against 'some intemperance' such as 'forcing the sale of the estates' in order to release the money that was owed to her, she described it as the 'speech of the Wolf to the Lamb whom he accuses of puddling the stream above, though she drinks below'.[43] Her own brothers offered little support against the bullies. Lord Balcarres, much of whose money was tied up in the Fenchurch Street house, was pressed by creditors from all sides. The next Lindsay brother, Robert, recently returned from India with a substantial fortune, was forced to choose between propping up his sister and his brother; he chose the latter. 'Whatever my intentions were formerly in your favor in case of a Law Suit I must now *retract them,*' he explained to Anne, 'for unless I step forward to assist Bal – with *my whole* he is ruined past redemption!'[44] The Atkinson family rejected a proposal devised by Anne's lawyer, which would have entailed 'considerable sacrifice' on her part but prevented the sale of the Jamaican estates.[45] Thus finding herself without a single 'friend to lean on', Anne felt she had no choice but to agree a 'miserable *Compromise*' with Richard's executors.[46] By a deed dated 10 June 1790, she signed away 'realities, claims, and expectations' worth by her reckoning around £48,000, so as to secure for herself and Margaret the £700 annuities left them by Richard.

Even once this distasteful business was concluded, Anne failed to find the serenity she craved. 'I had hoped to have been able to tell you that all our pecuniary plagues were settled,' she wrote to the politician William Windham, with whom she was in the throes of an intense but ultimately doomed romance. 'The Partners & Executors of my friend Atkinson, after beating me out of everything, are now quarrelling about the division of the spoils, and will not adhere to their own offers, or submit to arbitration. On this account I find myself most unwillingly obliged to pursue these gentlemen by law for redress. My hopes of ease are at an end, my prospects closed, and life will probably be consumed in the conflict.'[47] These words were more far-sighted than she could ever have imagined.

FOURTEEN

Taking Possession

TWELVE GENTLEMEN, united by their loathing of slavery, gathered for the first time at the offices of the publisher James Phillips at George Yard, in the City of London, on 22 May 1787. One of them was the civil servant-turned-campaigner Granville Sharp, who had been battling against the institution since 1767, when he managed to prevent Jonathan Strong from being bundled off to Jamaica on board one of Mure, Son & Atkinson's ships. Sharp had played an advisory role in the important Somerset case of 1772, when, the same week as the Fordyce financial scandal was unfolding, the Lord Chief Justice, Lord Mansfield, had ruled that slavery was unsupported by the common law in England and Wales. But Sharp's anti-slavery campaign remained a fringe cause, since so much of Britain's wealth derived from the West Indies.

Olaudah Equiano first visited Granville Sharp in March 1783. Equiano was a former slave who, as a boy, had been sent by his master to be educated in England; later, after returning to America, he had worked to buy his freedom. He had settled in London in about 1768, considering it safer than the colonies, where the danger of being kidnapped and returned to slavery was ever present. Equiano was moved to call on Sharp after spotting a newspaper report about a legal case then being heard at Guildhall, relating to some events during a transatlantic slave voyage, the facts of which 'seemed to make every person present shudder'.[1]

Originating in Liverpool, the *Zong* had set sail from the Gold Coast on 6 September 1781, headed for Jamaica with 440 enslaved Africans on board. The ocean crossing was beset by headwinds, contrary currents and navigational errors, and sixty of the captives had died from fever by the last week of November. As Captain Luke Collingwood observed his ship's supply of drinking water dwindling, and his valuable cargo perishing, he knew that the insurance policy taken out for the voyage contained a loophole; although those Africans who died from sickness counted as a 'dead loss', and were uninsured, compensation would be paid for any who succumbed to what was loosely termed the 'perils of the seas'. On 29 November, Collingwood ordered his crew to start throwing sick Africans overboard – 132 drowned over the following three days. On 28 December, the *Zong* anchored at Black River, Jamaica, disembarking just 208 slaves.[2] Back in London, when the underwriters refused to pay the £3,960 compensation that was claimed for the drowned Africans – £30 for each man, woman and child – the *Zong*'s owners took the dispute to court, arguing that rough seas had 'retarded' their ship and 'obliged' the crew to jettison its human cargo.[3] From a legal perspective, the case of *Gregson v Gilbert* was clear-cut – Lord Mansfield admitted that it was the 'same as if horses had been thrown overboard' – and the jury found for the shipowners.[4] Granville Sharp later unsuccessfully tried to have the crew prosecuted for murder.

The story of the *Zong* inspired many people to query the moral basis of slavery for the first time. Thomas Clarkson was a divinity student whose response to the question 'Is it lawful to enslave the unconsenting?' won the prestigious Latin essay prize at Cambridge University in 1785. His dissertation was published the following year as *An Essay on the Slavery and Commerce of the Human Species, particularly the African*. Clarkson's tract would prove highly influential – it was said that William Wilberforce, the earnest young MP for the county of Yorkshire, turned his attention 'seriously to the subject' after reading it.[5] Wilberforce's political stirring, however, would occur following a conversation that was said to have taken place under an ancient oak tree at William Pitt's estate in Kent.

The prime minister, witnessing the eloquence with which his friend spoke against the slave trade, urged him to take up the cause in the House of Commons.

Two weeks after first meeting, the twelve abolitionists gathered again, this time to decide what exactly they would be campaigning to abolish – the slave trade or, more all-embracingly, the institution of slavery. They soon agreed that the sheer weight of West Indian interests made the abolition of slavery too ambitious a goal. They also suspected they did not need to aim so high, for the enslaved population was in constant decline across the West Indies, with deaths outstripping births, and planters relied upon new arrivals to keep up their workforces; so were they to succeed in ending the slave trade, the abolitionists realized, they would be 'laying the axe at the very root' of slavery itself.[6] Thus the Committee for the Abolition of the Slave Trade was formed, with Granville Sharp in its chair, and William Wilberforce its parliamentary representative.

Thomas Clarkson would soon distinguish himself as the committee's most tireless campaigner. He immediately set out on a five-month investigation of the slave trade, with a focus on the ports of Bristol and Liverpool, where he interviewed hundreds of slave ship captains and sailors. In Liverpool, he spotted a sinister display of iron instruments in a shop window – handcuffs, shackles, thumb screws and a 'speculum oris', a surgical device used to force open the mouths of those on hunger strike – and purchased them as props for his public talks. While Clarkson was on the road, the committee launched the anti-slavery movement, sending out circular letters to a largely Quaker list of sympathizers. The pottery manufacturer Josiah Wedgwood was an influential early recruit to the cause; his jasperware cameos of a chained African, imploring 'Am I not a man and a brother?', which went into mass production during the autumn of 1787, proved wildly popular, and the 'kneeling slave' motif soon adorned bracelets, brooches, buckles, pendants and snuffboxes across the land.

Clarkson had experienced much hostility in Liverpool, so he was amazed by the warmth of his reception in Manchester; while

*The iconic image of the 'kneeling slave', believed to be
by the engraver Thomas Bewick.*

preaching a sermon to the packed collegiate church of this mill
town, he was startled to find a 'great crowd of black people standing round the pulpit'.[7] It was late October, and Clarkson had not
seen a newspaper in weeks – otherwise he would have known that
anti-slavery petitions were spontaneously breaking out around the
country. When Manchester's petition was delivered to the House of
Commons, on 11 February 1788, it was the heftiest yet, containing
the signatures of two-thirds of the town's adult male population. On
the same day, William Pitt ordered a committee of the Privy Council
headed by Lord Hawkesbury (as Charles Jenkinson was now known)
to carry out a thorough investigation of the slave trade.

Wilberforce was unwell for several months in early 1788, and
unable to put forward a parliamentary motion to abolish the slave
trade that year. But his friend Sir William Dolben, who was horrified by the cramped dimensions of a slave ship that he had visited on
the Thames, succeeded in pushing through legislation that limited
a vessel's human cargo to five heads for every three tons' capacity
up to 207 tons, then one head per ton. Some abolitionists felt that
Dolben's Act legitimized the viewpoint that the slave trade was not
fundamentally wrong, merely in need of tighter regulation; but to
those in the West Indies who depended upon a constant drip-feed

of slave labour, the measure signalled calamity. 'God knows what will be the consequence if the present Bill is passed,' wrote Stephen Fuller, the island agent and chief lobbyist for Jamaican interests. 'It may end in destruction of all the Whites in Jamaica.'[8]

Through the medium of Lord Hawkesbury's committee, the abolitionists could for the first time place on public record a mass of damning evidence against the slave trade. Clarkson rounded up witnesses, but found that many of those who had been happy to speak out in private were suddenly overcome by reserve, such as one previously garrulous man who explained that as the 'nearest relation of a rich person concerned in the traffic', he would 'ruin all his expectations from that quarter' if he testified.[9] Among those who did provide powerful statements were the slave captain-turned-clergyman John Newton, whose hymn about moral redemption, 'Amazing Grace', was little known at this point; and the ship's surgeon Alexander Falconbridge, whose *Account of the Slave Trade on the Coast of Africa* offered a first-hand report of its brutalities.

Stephen Fuller, meanwhile, assembled a heavyweight line-up to defend slavery, including five 'totally disinterested' admirals who had served in the West Indies.[10] Admiral Rodney claimed there was 'not a Slave but lives better than any poor honest day labourer in England', and especially so in Jamaica, where he had never known any planter 'using Cruelty to their Slaves'.[11] A Liverpool merchant, Robert Norris, likened the middle passage almost to a pleasure cruise, during which the African passengers were treated to delicious meals, entertained with music, dancing and games before dinner, and accommodated in pleasant quarters 'perfumed with frankincense and lime-juice'.[12] Clarkson and his allies exposed this particular lie by circulating a scale drawing of a Liverpool ship, the *Brookes*, tight-packed with captives laid out on bare boards. The cargo of 454 enslaved Africans depicted by the plan was in line with the new limit imposed by Sir William Dolben's recent legislation – but a caption revealed that the *Brookes* had at one time carried as many as 609 Africans, cramming them in by making them sit in lines between each other's knees, and lie on their sides instead of their backs.[13]

Hawkesbury's committee published its report on the slave trade in the spring of 1789. Pitt presented the weighty volume to the Commons on 25 April, which gave MPs less than three weeks to digest its contents before debating the subject. On 12 May, Wilberforce rose to address parliament on the subject of slavery for the first time. From the start, he maintained that questions of personal culpability were irrelevant. 'We are all guilty – we ought all to plead guilty, and not to exculpate ourselves by throwing the blame on others,' he advised his fellow members.[14] For the next three and a half hours, in his disarmingly melodious voice, he proceeded to discredit every aspect of the slave trade, ending his speech with twelve propositions in favour of its abolition. It was a mesmerizing performance, which achieved the rare feat of uniting both William Pitt and Charles James Fox in its praise.

Those speaking up for the slave trade based their arguments on cold, commercial logic. Lord Penrhyn, a prominent Jamaican absentee, claimed that £70 million of mortgages on West Indian property would become worthless if the trade were abolished. Alderman Nathaniel Newnham, a member for the City of London, said he could not consent to propositions 'which, if carried, would fill the city with men suffering as much as the poor Africans'.[15] Over the following weeks, the pro-slavery lobby worked on indecisive MPs, reasoning that the Hawkesbury report was too flimsy a body of evidence to inform so momentous a decision, and convincing them to place the issue before a select committee of the House of Commons. Through the use of such stalling tactics, the abolitionists would time and again be thwarted.

ELSEWHERE IN LONDON that summer, in the studio of the painter Lemuel Abbott just off Bedford Square, a young man sat for his picture. Curiously, Bridget Atkinson's third son was the first member of my eighteenth-century family of whom I was ever aware. In 1981, when I was thirteen, the portrait of a Richard Atkinson 'who lived at Temple Sowerby' came up for sale through Sotheby's. The black-and-white reproduction in the auction catalogue showed a handsome, serious young man wearing a powdered wig, plain cutaway coat and white shirt with a frilled stock; the vendor was identified as 'Mrs. Dixon Scott', who I now know to have been my dad's third cousin.[16] Although my mother gamely placed a bid, at a time when she could ill afford it, the price rose way beyond the estimate. I can still recall my disappointment on being told that my namesake's picture had been bought by a nameless collector.

Shortly after his portrait was finished, Dick sailed to Madeira to take up a position working for a British wine merchant. Four hundred miles off the coast of Africa, this Portuguese island was less remote than it might sound, for it was an important stopover on the shipping routes to both the East and West Indies. Bridget packed Dick off with various home comforts, including some cured meats. 'Your Hams were presented to Mr. Murdoch the only Partner at present resident in the Island & with whom I live,' he wrote on 6 September 1789, shortly after his arrival. 'I have a couple of rooms at a small distance from & on the opposite side of the street from the House; the one fronts to the street down which there is a fine cooling streem of water always runing, the other which is my bedroom looks into a small garden in which I employ some leisure moments.' Renowned though Madeira may have been for its grapes, Dick was less than impressed by its melons: 'Either from the little care that is taken in the raising them or from being chiefly of the large watery sorts, they are by no means superior nor indeed do I think them equal to many I have eat at T. Sowerby. I shall however send you some seed, especially of the Water Melon, which we have of an astonishing size.'[17]

On 4 November, the Atkinson family would be rocked by the death of Matthew, middle brother of George and Richard, the last male of the older generation. Bridget's diary entry for this day reads simply: 'My brother Matthew died at twelve minutes before nine in the morning.'[18] He left a widow and eight children, the eldest of whom was sixteen, the youngest less than a year old. Matthew's demise cut both his and Bridget's branches of the family adrift, for he had kept the Temple Sowerby banking business going since George's death eight years earlier.

Matthew's death was especially unsettling news for one of his nephews. Bridget had been nurturing hopes that her fourth son, Matt, would enter the family trade, which since 1778 had included responsibility for the collection of the land and excise taxes throughout Cumberland and Westmorland. But one of George and Matthew's former associates, John Jackson, had recently started 'Creeping into the Business', having applied for the 'Excise Money', and was openly boasting of his determination to unseat the Atkinson family.[19] Matt, who was an affable but directionless young man of twenty, stood no chance in the face of such blatant ambition.

Bridget laid bare her distress in an anguished letter that she wrote to her son-in-law, Nathaniel Clayton, a few days before Matthew's death. 'All is I fear lost to my poor Boys,' she lamented. 'George says there is an opening for them at Jamaica I do not Look upon the West Indies to be a place at present to make a fortune or Mend the Morals of a young man it kills me to think of all my Boys going to Jamaica and where else can they go.' Matt's health was a particular cause for concern: 'He has had a complaint in his Bowells for a Month past he is troubled with a Head ach which is at times very Bad and would render Jamaica dangerous and I think where he gos I will go for what comfort can I have when all my Sons are gone from me none here I am Sure my Heart is near Broke.'[20]

AS THE MURES' financial problems deepened, their relations with the Atkinson family deteriorated. By their reckoning, Paul Benfield and their late partner's estate jointly owed them at least £60,000 for the purchase of the Bogue estate – even though the property was worth £40,000 at most, as Robert Mure candidly admitted. During the autumn of 1789, the Mures spread the rumour that Benfield was on his way back from Madras to settle his debt with them, raising credit for their ailing house on the strength of this report; at the same time they threatened to have Benfield arrested for debt the moment he set foot on English soil.

By now, Benfield's legal team were starting to wonder whether the Bogue purchase had been deliberately dreamt up as a scheme to defraud their client. Robert Mure's multiple roles only thickened the fog that surrounded this 'entangled, perplexed, & complicated' business.[21] 'He is *one of the Persons who sold* the Bogue to you & Atkinson,' wrote Benfield's advisor, Nathaniel Wraxall. 'He is a *Partner* with Atkinson. He is an *Executor* to Atkinson's Will. He is a *Trustee* to Atkinson's Will; and He is, lastly, a *Demandant* for the Purchase Money due for the Bogue. How are we to negotiate with a Man in all these various, & discordant Capacities?'[22]

In March 1790, Benfield's lawyers applied for an injunction that would prevent the Mures from harassing their client. Although not granted – on a technicality, for Benfield's team were unable to subpoena Hutchison Mure, aged seventy-nine, on his sickbed in Suffolk – it was clear that the Mures could not afford to litigate, and would 'sooner or later' need to reach a compromise.[23] Now Benfield's lawyers went on the offensive against the Atkinson estate. Clutching a letter in which Richard had once offered their client the option of relinquishing his share of the Bogue, they threatened the estate with a lawsuit to force the payment of £36,000 – half the sale price, plus accumulated costs – to take Benfield's interest in the Jamaican property off his hands.

It was at this miserable juncture that Francis Baring, motivated by strong feelings of 'friendship & regard' for the Atkinson family, came to the rescue – negotiating with the Mures to buy out Benfield's half share of the Bogue estate for £22,000.[24] Baring advanced them £6,000 of the money and Nathaniel Clayton the rest, which is how both men came to be creditors to Richard Atkinson's estate.

THE SELECT COMMITTEE which had been set up after the first debates about the slave trade published its findings in early 1791, in three fat printed volumes. William Wilberforce planned to bring in a bill to 'prevent the farther importation of Slaves into the British West Indies' during the next session of parliament, but he realized that few MPs would care to wade through all 1,700 pages of the report, so he worked at full tilt to produce an abridged version that was ready just a few days ahead of the debate.[25]

Wilberforce opened the proceedings on 18 April, and spoke with supreme moral authority; the cross-party trinity of Pitt, Fox and Burke added their support. On the other hand, 'tun-bellied Tommy' Grosvenor, MP for Chester, conceded that the traffic in slaves 'was not an amiable trade', but pointed out that 'neither was the trade of a butcher an amiable trade, and yet a mutton chop was, neverthe-less, a very good thing'.[26] Alderman Brook Watson, representing the City of London, argued that ending the slave trade would not only 'ruin the West Indies', it would also destroy the nation's New-foundland fishery, 'which the slaves in the West Indies supported, by consuming that part of the fish that was fit for no other consump-tion'.[27] Past three in the morning, after two long nights of debate, the House divided. The abolitionists suspected they would lose, but were unprepared for the scale of their defeat – 163 votes to 88.

Vested interests had killed the slave trade bill. 'Commerce chinked its purse,' commented Horace Walpole, 'and that sound is generally prevalent with the majority.'[28] But other factors had con-tributed to its trouncing – most specifically, violent uprisings in France and the West Indies. On 14 July 1789, a mob had stormed the Bastille fortress, a symbol of royal authority in the middle of Paris. That autumn, Thomas Clarkson had travelled to the French capital in order to forge links with abolitionists; by the time he returned to London, six months later, the intoxicated mood of *liberté* had fermented into something more frightening. The revolutionary fer-vour soon spread to the West Indies. In October 1790, Vincent Ogé, a mixed-race coffee merchant who Clarkson had met in Paris, led a rebellion in the French colony of Saint Domingue, demanding civil rights for his fellow 'mulattoes' – it would end with his execution on the breaking wheel in the square at Cap-Français. Then, in February 1791, news arrived in London of a slave insurrection on the British sugar island of Dominica; although quickly suppressed, it gravely injured Wilberforce's embryonic bill.

The Comte de Mirabeau had memorably described the white population of Saint Domingue as sleeping 'at the foot of Vesuvius', and in August 1791 the volcano finally blew its top, as enslaved

Racial violence erupts in Saint Domingue in August 1791.

blacks from the Northern Province rose up in an orgy of arson and bloodshed. Soon, most of the plantations within fifty miles of Cap-Français had been reduced to ashes. Many of the *grands blancs* fled to nearby Jamaica, taking with them their most valued slaves and, as many British planters feared, the contagion of unrest. On 10 December, as rumours swirled round Jamaica of a secret society called 'the Cat Club', where enslaved men met to drink 'King Wilberforce's health out of a Cat's skull by way of a cup', General Williamson, the island's governor, declared martial law.[29]

Following the defeat of the 1791 bill, abolitionists hit upon a novel way to show their disapproval. William Fox's *Address to the People of Great Britain, on the Propriety of Abstaining from West India Sugar and Rum* suggested that all consumers of West Indian sugar had blood on their hands: 'A family that uses only 5lb. of sugar per week, with the proportion of rum, will, by abstaining from the consumption 21 months, prevent the slavery or murder of one fellow-creature.'[30] Fox's pamphlet ran to twenty-five editions, convincing thousands of 'anti-saccharite' families to boycott slave-produced sugar.

Ahead of the 1792 parliamentary session, the Committee for the Abolition of the Slave Trade set another petition campaign going. This time, unlike the spontaneous outbreak four years earlier, it would be a highly disciplined affair, with local committees receiving strict instructions to hold off from submitting their petitions until told to do so. ('By no means let the People of Brough add their Names to those of Appleby,' Clarkson cautioned his Penrith contact. 'The two Petitions must be perfectly distinct. It is on the number of Petitions that the H. of Commons will count.')[31] More than five hundred anti-slavery petitions, bearing half a million signatures, would arrive at Westminster that spring – at a time when the nation's population was about eight million, and perhaps half the adults were illiterate, this was an incontrovertible expression of public feeling.

Even so, with lurid tales circulating of the slaughter of French planters in their beds, and the rape of their wives, the insurgency in Saint Domingue greatly damaged the abolitionist cause. Many sympathizers urged Wilberforce to pause for a while, but he chose to plough on regardless. On 2 April 1792, after a passionate speech to a packed Commons, Wilberforce moved that the slave trade should be abolished, and the debate was opened up to the floor. Late in the evening Henry Dundas, now Home Secretary, rose to speak. He had long shared Wilberforce's views about the necessity of ending the slave trade, he declared – but he challenged the 'prudence' of an immediate abolition, instead proposing a 'middle way of proceeding' whereby the trade would be eliminated over the course of an unspecified number of years.[32] He then successfully moved for the word 'gradually' to be added to the original motion. At dawn the House of Commons overwhelmingly, by a margin of almost three to one, voted to 'gradually' abolish the slave trade.

This outcome left neither side satisfied. Wilberforce and his followers felt betrayed by Dundas. The pro-slavery lobby, suspecting that the motion would never have passed under its original wording, felt robbed of the chance to settle the question decisively. They need not have worried. The following month, the House of Lords rejected the bill, thereby stalling the abolitionist movement for fifteen years.

*The Gradual Abolition of the Slave Trade, in which the royal family
attempts to reduce its consumption of sugar 'by Degrees'.*

AFTER BUYING OUT Benfield's interest in the Bogue estate,
Francis Baring and Nathaniel Clayton settled with the Mures that
Bridget's sons George and Dick would take possession of both their
late uncle's West Indian properties; at least now they would be able
to prevent their inheritance from falling into ruin. George sailed to
Jamaica in the autumn of 1791, landing at the bustling port of Lucea
shortly before Christmas; twelve miles along a winding, dusty road,
he was reunited with Dick, who had been learning how to be a
sugar planter at the Mures' Saxham estate. Samuel Mure (brother
of Robert and William) relinquished his power of attorney over the
Bogue and Dean's Valley estates without fuss. A few days later,
the Atkinson brothers rode thirty miles along the north coast of the
island to the Bogue, where Dick would remain.

Two miles south of Montego Bay, the Bogue estate encompassed
1,300 acres bordering the emerald lagoon from which it took its
name; this was the deceptively Arcadian setting for a factory complex
operated by about two hundred enslaved Africans. Its infrastructure
comprised a sugar works, including a cattle-powered mill, boiling
and curing houses, distillery, stores and trash houses; offices for

243

the (white) overseer and his deputies; workshops for the (enslaved) blacksmiths, carpenters, coopers, stonemasons and wheelwrights; a hospital for the sick and injured; a 'great house' for the proprietor; and a village of palm-thatched huts. The enslaved families also had access to plots where they grew the beans, cassava, maize, pumpkins and yams, and raised the poultry, goats and pigs, with which they supplemented the basic salt provisions supplied by the estate.

Sugar estates ran according to the principle of divide and rule, with rivalries among the enslaved population actively promoted by their white overlords. Members of the same family were separated; and a class hierarchy was imposed, whereby workers with white fathers or lighter skin were privileged over those with darker skin, and domestic servants, artisans and drivers had higher status than field workers. One of the first 'skills' that Dick would be expected to acquire, as a newly arrived sugar planter, was that of asserting his authority. 'Men, from their first entrance into the West Indies, are taught to practice severities to the slaves,' wrote an old Jamaica hand, 'so that in time their hearts become callous to all tender feelings which soften and dignify our nature.'[33]

Grotesque evidence of this callousness is provided by Thomas Thistlewood's diary. Born in Lincolnshire in 1721, Thistlewood was for many years the overseer on the Egypt estate in Westmoreland Parish. A keen botanist who exchanged tree and shrub specimens with the Mures at Saxham, he was also a sexual predator who logged 3,852 acts of congress with 138 women, and a sadist who enacted the cruellest of penalties for the pettiest of crimes. Notoriously, he devised 'Derby's dose' to punish an enslaved boy who was caught eating sugar cane stalks; first the lad was flogged, then salt pickle, lime juice and chilli pepper were rubbed into his wounds, and finally another slave defecated into his mouth before he was gagged for several hours. Not surprisingly, the enslaved population continually showed signs of resistance, most frequently through minor acts of disobedience or running away, less often through assassination and violent rebellion; it was their fear of the latter, coupled with absolute impunity, that turned white men into despots.

At the end of each day, the tropical sun plunged into the sea on the horizon, and darkness fell within a few short minutes. While the fragrance of orange blossom drifted in the air, the tree frogs resumed their otherworldly nocturnal song and the fireflies shot 'electric meteors from their eyes', the white men amused themselves by drinking rum, playing cards, smoking cigars and raping the enslaved women.[34]

DICK'S ARRIVAL AT the Bogue coincided with the start of the harvest, or 'crop', as it was known. This was a noisy time of year, characterized by the 'beating of the coppers, the clanking of the iron, the driving of the cogs, the wedging of the gudgeons, the repetition of the hammers, and the hooping of the casks', as preparations were made for the intensive bout of sugar production ahead.[35] The cutting of the cane started after the Christmas holidays, when the enslaved workers were given three days off, and continued until the coming of the rains in April or May; for four months or so, the sugar works operated round the clock.

Cutting the cane – a tall reed with sharp, serrated leaves – was brutal work carried out by the physically toughest individuals, motivated by a driver cracking a whip. The moment the cane was cut, its juices started to ferment, and there was little time to lose; it was rapidly bundled on to waggons to be carted to the mill, which was positioned on a knoll above the rest of the sugar works. Here women pushed the canes, six or seven at a time, through three large hardwood rollers – forwards through the first and second, back through the second and third – to extract the cloudy, sweet liquor, which was channelled via a lead-lined gutter to the boiling house below. (A hatchet was kept close at hand, ready to amputate fingers caught in the rollers.) The cane trash was meanwhile collected up and kept as fuel. The women often sang while they worked. 'It appears somewhat singular,' observed one planter, 'that all their tunes, if tunes they can be called, are of a plaintive cast.'[36]

In the boiling house, the cane juice was funnelled into an enormous cauldron, a small amount of lime added, and a fierce fire lit beneath. As the liquid heated, a raft of scum rose up; the flames were then doused, and the cauldron was left for an hour or so to let further impurities float to the surface. The clarified juice was next siphoned into the largest of a tapering sequence of about six copper pans; once boiled to nearly the 'colour of Madeira wine', the liquor was transferred to a slightly smaller copper set over a slightly hotter fire.[37] The cycle was repeated through to the final, smallest copper. When the liquor was thick and tacky, it was conveyed to a shallow wooden container about a foot deep and six feet square – the same volume as a hogshead barrel – to cool into an oozing mass of coarse crystals. Workers assigned to the boiling house had to remain on their mettle for the duration of their twelve-hour shifts – the slightest lapse of concentration might cause, at the very least, a disfiguring burn.

Afterwards the treacly sludge was carried in pails to the curing house, a large, airy building next to the boiling house, and poured

A highly simplified illustration of the process of making sugar.

into upright hogsheads balanced on joists above a large cistern. Over about three weeks, the molasses dripped through holes bored in the bottom of the barrels into the cistern below, leaving behind dark muscovado sugar in the barrel. The molasses were then taken to the distillery, where they were mixed with water, the juice of tainted canes, the skimmings from the boiling house coppers and the yeasty sediment from previous batches known as dunder; once fermented, the liquor was drawn off to be twice distilled, ending up as puncheons of potent Jamaica rum.

AFTER DICK HAD SETTLED at the Bogue, George crossed the island to inspect their late uncle's other property, fifteen miles to the south in Westmoreland Parish. Located on a wide flood plain, and sheltered by densely wooded hills, the Dean's Valley Dry Works (to give the estate its full designation) was so called because it lacked access to the gushing spring that delivered power to the neighbouring Dean's Valley Water Works, instead relying on 'dry' cattle to drive its cane mill.

George was pleased to see the sugar crop at Dean's Valley looking 'very promising', but dismayed to learn that ten enslaved Africans had recently died there from fever; it seemed that the low-lying position of the estate hospital might be partly to blame. The great house, too, was so unhealthily situated, and in such a poor state of repair, that George wondered whether pulling it down and rebuilding it on the side of the hill might not be the best plan – for only then would he and Dick be able to stay for 'two or three weeks at a time, which at present it would be madness to venture'. It was necessary, George told Francis Baring, that these visits should be regular: 'The Negroes on both Estates are very deficient in that confidence and attachment which the residence of a Master alone inspires and which it will be our particular study to supply.'[38]

By February 1792, George was in Kingston, the commercial hub of the island. Worldly visitors, sailing into the town's magnificent harbour and viewing the 'sapphire haze' of the Blue Mountains for the first time, sometimes fancied a resemblance to the Bay of

Kingston harbour, with Port Royal in the foreground,
the Blue Mountains behind.

Naples.[39] But the spell was broken the moment they stepped ashore; for Kingston's charms were notoriously coarse, and centred around brothels, taverns and grog shops. In contrast the parish church, which lay a few blocks back from the wharves, was conspicuously neglected, moving one writer to comment: 'It is a pity that the morals of the people are not corrected, so as to have it as much frequented by the living as the dead.'[40]

Kingston's merchants mostly lived on the outskirts of town, on higher ground, in residences with broad verandahs and shady balconies; driving downtown to their offices at about seven in the morning, they generally paused for a 'second breakfast' at noon, shutting up shop in time for dinner at four. The Jamaican merchant house of which Samuel Mure was a partner, Mures & Dunlop, was by now so caught up in the disorderly finances of the Fenchurch Street firm that George, sensing a trap, had wisely resisted the Mures' attempts to have him join it; instead he would spend the next few months sounding out potential business partners on the island.

248

George was a restless young man, with a volatile temper and a burning desire to make some money of his own; without his own establishment, however, his hands were tied. 'Opportunities have occurred since my arrival here by which had I been at liberty to have acted an ample fortune might have been realized without anything like comparative Risk,' he told Baring on 11 June.[41] So he boarded a ship home in July, somewhat reluctantly leaving Dick (who had not taken to the sugar planter's life) in charge of the family estates. 'He one day talks of taking a trip to America, the next he means to return to England,' George wrote about his brother. 'One day he is to go home to marry Miss Howard, another that she is to come out to him next year, in short I don't know what to make of him.'[42] As it happened, fate (arriving in a winged form) would soon swoop down and pluck the decision out of Dick's hands.

FIFTEEN

Fevered Isle

ON 1 FEBRUARY 1793, ten days after dispatching Louis XVI at the guillotine, the French Republic declared war upon Britain and the Netherlands. The Royal Navy immediately mobilized its press gangs – this being the only sure method of recruiting thousands of sailors at short notice. Locals often banded together to resist the navy's thugs; on 19 February the men of North Shields, a port at the mouth of the River Tyne in Northumberland, confronted a gang with 'their jackets reversed' (a mark of deep contempt), threatening to tear them 'limb from limb'.[1]

The following month, five hundred men marched on Newcastle to protest against another round of impressments, only turning round when they learnt that the army was preparing to use force against them. 'We had a little allarm in the afternoon yesterday, the Drums beat to arms, the Sailors at Shields are again in a state of Riot and confusion,' Dorothy Clayton wrote to her mother, Bridget, on 20 March. At the time Nathaniel was in London on business, leaving her at home with the children in Westgate Street: 'The three Boys are scampering round me little John is just as riotous and as entertaining as any of them he is surprizingly good humoured and at the same time extremely lively.'[2] After six years of marriage, Dorothy was in the early stages of her fifth pregnancy.

The war had an instantly stifling effect on the nation's trade. One day in early April, after a run of unexpected withdrawals, the

Commercial Bank of Newcastle stopped payment, and the rest of the town's banks soon followed. 'Mr. Clayton did not come home 'til four oClock this morning from a Committee of the principal Inhabitants of this Town,' Dorothy wrote to Bridget at Temple Sowerby. 'He bids me tell you that they have arranged a plan which will in a few days restore the public credit – I give you a *hint* at the begining of my Letter.' At the top of the first page, she had scribbled this urgent instruction: 'If you have any *Scotch Notes* get rid of them as fast as you can you may take any Newcastle ones with the greatest of Safety – *not a word* of this to any body for ye world.'³ But the panic proved contagious; by mid-April more than a hundred small banks had failed. Meanwhile inflation was running rampant, and Bridget and Dorothy started comparing the cost of provisions in their respective neighbourhoods – '1 Bushel of Peas 12d., Cayenne Bottle 5d.', wrote the daughter in a letter dated 5 May.⁴

FOLLOWING HIS FRUSTRATINGLY brief stay in Jamaica, George Atkinson returned to London in September 1792, settling into lodgings at Gray's Inn. Over the winter, as one of his uncle's executors, he was obliged to attend regular meetings with the grasping Mures at Fenchurch Street. These were dispiriting affairs, for George realized not only that Robert and William Mure were utterly disinclined to promote his interests in Jamaica, but also that they had falsified their accounts in an attempt to cheat the Atkinson estate. As Nathaniel Clayton observed: 'There is something so bare-faced in the object, and the Measures to effect it are taken with such unblushing Effrontery that I am appalled at the Reflection that We have to do with such Men.'⁵ For George, who had run up consider-able personal debt and could see no prospect of discharging it, this was a dark time – so much so that his sister Dorothy would later admit that his 'dispondency' had caused her to 'dread the worst of consequences'.⁶

One day in March 1793, Samuel Mure and William Dunlop, part-ners in the Jamaican merchant house, called on George to inform him that they planned to dissolve their concern and set up a new house to unite the London and Kingston branches of the Mures' affairs. They hoped he might agree to run the Kingston office; as the partner resident in Jamaica he would be entitled to one-third of the general profits. Moreover, William Dunlop had long held the post of Agent General of Jamaica, executing business on the governor's behalf – the position had netted him £10,000 a year during the American war – and he now promised to help George secure the office. This proposal must have been extremely tempting, for it was certain that the conflict with France would soon reach Jamaica. As the historian Bryan Edwards would explain in a book published that same year: 'Never were the West Indian colonies the cause of war; but whenever the two nations of France and England are engaged in any quarrel, from whatever cause it may arise, thither they repair to decide their differences.'[7]

But Nathaniel Clayton and Sir Francis Baring (who had recently been made a baronet) were both sceptical of the Mures' motives. 'I conceive the Mures to want Merchantile Credit, and the necessary energy to avail themselves of it if they possessed it,' wrote Nathaniel. 'I look at their Proposition as flowing from no wish to serve you, but founded on the Sole Views of securing a continuance of that prop to the declining Credit of the House, which the Funds of your Uncle, and the aid of your Friends afford.'[8] George replied: 'The Question appears to be whether something advantageous to myself and Family may not be made out of the proposal, at the same time steering clear of those dangers which threaten to accompany it.'[9]

His negotiations were a success. The Mures abandoned their plan that George should become a partner in the merged business, and George in turn persuaded Samuel Mure to return with him to Jamaica to form a different partnership – the two of them, plus George Bogle, formerly a clerk at Mures & Dunlop. (The Bogles were a prominent Glasgow merchant dynasty.) Although the new partnership – to be known as Atkinson, Mure & Bogle – would draw on the resources of the failing Fenchurch Street house, the Kingston partners were shielded from its liabilities. One early June morning,

George departed with Samuel Mure for Falmouth, where they boarded the packet boat to Jamaica. Nathaniel, who saw them leave Gray's Inn, afterwards sent his mother-in-law a comforting note: 'They both set off in high Spirits and I trust with very good reason. The Prospect is very comfortable, particularly to poor George, whose Time has hitherto been wasted with little advantage to himself or others. He has left some Things for you in my Charge which I will convey safe & soon – I will not say how valuable a Present the shells are that you may be the more delighted when they arrive.'[10]

Bridget was in need of some consolation, for the welfare of her boys had lately been causing her much anxiety. One event she had long dreaded had recently come to pass – her gentle fourth son, Matt, had gone out to Jamaica. He had left Temple Sowerby on 13 January 1793, boarding the *Hope* at Whitehaven; the ship had set sail, then put straight back into port. Rough seas had detained it there for three weeks, and during this time Matt had met Ann Littledale. The Littledales were a Whitehaven merchant family of considerable local standing; Ann's late father, Isaac, had captained his own ship, the *Hero*, which transported convicts out to the American colonies (this was before the revolution) and brought back Virginia tobacco. George Washington dealt with the partnership of Dixon & Littledale; the future first president hosted Isaac at Mount Vernon in February 1760, and attended the launch of the *Hero* in nearby Alexandria, an event that Washington recorded in his diary as going off 'extreamely well'.[11] Anyway – by the time of the *Hope*'s departure, on 7 February 1793, Britain was at war with France, and Matt and Ann were engaged to be married.

The rest of Matt's voyage was scarcely less eventful. The following week the *Hope* was caught in a storm, and nearly wrecked on rocks known as the Bishops and Clerks off the Pembrokeshire coast. On 16 February it put into Milford Haven, where its crew was pressed into the service of the navy. It sailed again for Cork on 24 March, pausing there another five weeks while waiting to join an armed convoy, as the seas were now swarming with French privateers. Matt disembarked at Jamaica on 24 June, and George arrived just a few weeks later. Wretched news awaited – their brother Dick had died at Saxham on 15 May.

Dick's death, at the age of twenty-five, was a reminder of the risks undertaken by young men who hoped to make a fortune in the 'torrid zone' – for one-third of them would be dead within three years of first landing in the West Indies. Malaria and yellow fever were the chief assassins. Malaria, spread by the *Anopheles* mosquito, was characterized by chills, fever and sweating, accompanied by nausea, vomiting and headaches. The most effective medicine was powdered 'Peruvian bark', or quinine, from the cinchona tree in the Andes, with which the patient was dosed in 'as great quantity, as his stomach will bear'; another common treatment was mercury 'rubbed on the legs and thighs'.[12] Yellow fever was carried by the *Aedes* mosquito, which had migrated from Africa on board slave ships. While most patients recovered from its early symptoms, a doomed minority entered a second phase. As their liver and kidneys disintegrated, they turned 'as deep a colour as the skin of an American savage' and began vomiting a 'matter resembling the grounds of coffee' – this was digested blood.[13] Their suffering was beyond endurance, and death came as a blessing.

BRIDGET ATKINSON had not seen her eldest son, Michael, in twelve years; the six-month voyage from India to England, and then back again, somewhat ruled out home leave. Since 1791, Michael had been based at Jangipur, an isolated spot a few days upriver from Calcutta, where he ran the 'greatest station for manufacturing silk in possession of the India company', employing three thousand people.[14] He had made it his purpose to improve the silk thread produced by the factory, finding the locally reared cocoons to be of inferior quality; it was through his vigorous lobbying that the directors at Leadenhall Street would order their servants at Canton to supply Chinese silkworms and mulberry saplings with which he initiated a breeding programme.

Only John, the youngest of Bridget's five sons, remained in England by the summer of 1793, and even he was two hundred miles away, at Cambridge University. John had been admitted to St John's College in June 1790, where he was lucky enough to secure some of the most desirable rooms in college: 'I have four of them, a *Gip* or Servants Room, a sitting Room, an excellent Bed room and a Study: my sitting Room measures 22 Feet by 24 and has *allowedly* the best *looks out*, and I am inclined to think the only pleasant one in Cambridge, it commands the Gardens of Trinity and the Library, the River Cam, and the Walks and Pleasure Grounds of both Trinity and St Johns, so far as the Trees in them will permit.'[15]

John was an affectionate son who always kept an eye out for fossilized shells for his mother during rambles through the chalky fields near Cambridge. 'I shall send some Auricula Plants,' he would write in a note that heralded a delivery to Temple Sowerby. 'I won't tell you what they cost me lest you should think me expensive. In the Box you'll also find the Seed of the Blue Flower which I gathered from different Stems, wherever I thought I saw a Difference of Shade & if I am not mistaken you'll find several Shades of Blue amongst them. I shall put in a Fossil or two rather to convince you of the Firmness of the Marl in which I found them – than for their own Value.'[16] John was also attentive to his younger sisters, Bridget and Jane, and took great pleasure in sending them parcels of books, along with advice on how to develop their literary tastes: 'I hope you will not think it is from giving you Books that I think myself entitled to dictate to you, but from a very different Reason, a Desire to see you possessed of what few Ladies are, a Capacity to write and judge of writing.' They might refine their handwriting, he suggested, by copying out articles from the *Spectator*: 'It has a wonderful Effect in making writing easy and elegant. I would not have you give more than half an Hour a Day to this Exercise; don't think it a *childish Exercise* for I assure you some of the most sensible Men I know do it.'[17]

Following his examinations at the end of May 1793, John travelled up to Temple Sowerby with a Cambridge friend, Christopher Wordsworth; they clubbed together with another local fellow to hire a post-chaise, which was 'very nearly as cheap' as the stage

coach, and 'much more agreeable'.[18] John's plans for the long vacation encompassed reading, shooting, fishing and haymaking. 'We
on Friday put 24 Cartloads of the Long Croft into the Stack and
11 out of the Moss field and intend today putting the Remainder of
those Fields there, which will yield from 30 to 40 Load each,' John
wrote to his mother on 29 July. (Bridget was holidaying with the
Claytons at Newbiggin-by-the-Sea, in Northumberland.) 'There is
a letter here from George Dixon who has arrived again in London,
begging your Acceptance of some Shells which accompanied it they
appear to be and he says they are very rare ones.'[19] I imagine Bridget
finding this gift very acceptable indeed – since serving on Captain
Cook's third voyage, Dixon had become famous as a circumnavi-
gator, and in 1789 he had published *A Voyage Round the World; but
More Particularly to the North-West Coast of America*, which included
descriptions of wondrous shells he had found in the Sandwich and
Falkland Islands.

Dorothy gave birth to her fifth child, yet another boy, on
10 October. 'He has shewn considerable Talents in sucking & sleeping,' Nathaniel wrote to Bridget two days later, 'and promises to
be as strong & rompy as any of the rest.'[20] The first four Clayton
offspring were said to be thrilled by the addition to their number: 'It
has puzzled Nat much to find whence, how & when he came. Little
John calls him "diddle" by which Name he goes til we have found
out one for him, about which we are at a Loss. Can you help us to
one?'[21] In the end, 'Michael' won the day, for reasons that Nathaniel
would explain thus: 'Shawls – China – Pictures & everything desirable have corrupted Dorothy & nothing will serve her but that the
Brat shall bear the Name of her Benefactor in the East Indies.'[22]

DURING THE SUMMER of 1793, while Matt was adjusting
to his new life as a sugar planter, George was in Kingston, eyeing
up business opportunities in the troubled French colony of Saint
Domingue. The lawyer Léger Félicité Sonthonax had landed there
the previous September, bearing orders from the republican government to implement equal rights for all free citizens, regardless of the

colour of their skin. Meanwhile, in London, a delegation of royalist planters from Saint Domingue, terrified by the turn of events in their mother country, had initiated talks to transfer their colony's allegiances to George III.

Sonthonax realized that his best chance of preventing the British annexation of the 'Pearl of the Antilles' lay in a military alliance with the black population; therefore, on 29 August 1793, he proclaimed the abolition of slavery in the north of the colony. Ten days later the governor of Jamaica, General Adam Williamson, dispatched a small force to the coffee-growing region of the Grand'Anse, on Saint Domingue's southern peninsula; when the redcoats disembarked at Jérémie, the local planters were ready and waiting, welcoming the men with cheers of *'Vivent les Anglais!'* The Môle Saint Nicolas, a naval bastion commanding the strait between Saint Domingue and Cuba at the tip of the colony's northern peninsula, surrendered to another British force on 22 September.

The invasion of Saint Domingue could hardly have been better timed for the fledgling partnership of Atkinson, Mure & Bogle. General Williamson had already confirmed George Atkinson's appointment as his Agent General in Jamaica, and now George Bogle was invited to join the expeditionary force as Agent General in Saint Domingue, on the same package as his partner in Jamaica – a salary of a guinea per day, plus 5 per cent commission on all transactions passing through his books. Hugely to the partnership's advantage, the cost of occupying Saint Domingue would prove 'unavoidably great' right from the start.[23] Major engineering works were needed to restore the Môle Saint Nicolas to a 'proper state of defence'. Two camps of whites displaced by the turbulence in the north, each sheltering about eight hundred refugees, not only required basic provisions but also wine, candles, soap and clothes. The house of Atkinson, Mure & Bogle shipped everything over from Kingston, while increasing scarcity obliged George to pay ever more 'extravagant prices' for barrels of salt pork and beef, until there was 'none to be procured in Jamaica'. Soldiers, ships, weapons, fortifications, hospitals, prisons – with the expenditure on all these heads mounting uncontrollably, Bogle was hard pressed to show William-son accounts that were even 'tolerably accurate'.[24] Meanwhile, George felt rising panic about the solvency of the partnership, since many of its payments for the supplies were made with bills drawn upon the house at Fenchurch Street – and it was no secret that the Mures' finances were less well founded than they had once been.

Sir Francis Baring wrote to George in November, warning that the Mures were on the verge of bankruptcy; he also related a recent incident that summed up their incompetence. William Mure had written to Henry Dundas, Pitt's right-hand man, requesting the vacant Postmaster's office in Jamaica on behalf of the Kingston partnership: 'We think it not improper to state at the same time to Mr. Dundas that Mr. Atkinson, one of the Persons to be benefited by this appointment, is the Nephew of the late Mr. Richard Atkinson and as such we trust may be considered as having some claim upon Mr. Pitt & Mr. Dundas's generosity from his Uncle's attachment & Services.'[25] Dundas had forwarded Mure's note to Baring: 'You may read it, put it on the fire, and tell your friends that if I had showed such a letter and made such a Proposition to Mr. Pitt, any further conversation on the subject would have been cut very short.'[26] George was livid when he heard about William Mure's bungling behaviour. 'This Man,' he fumed, 'seems born to perplex & ruin every Thing in which he is engaged.'[27]

The Fenchurch Street house finally stopped payments on 29 December, defeated by a court order to honour a debt of nearly £52,000 due to Mures & Dunlop. Hutchison Mure and two of his sons – Robert and William – were named bankrupts. Baring immediately communicated the news to Nathaniel Clayton in Newcastle, who replied: 'I cannot look on any Event with much regret that will separate us from the house of Mures.'[28] On the same day, Nathaniel wrote to Bridget: 'I confess, my dear Mother, I am not surprised at what has happened. Their neglect of Business & enormous expences threatened the Storm which is now burst on the Mures. Though we may be Losers to a small Extent We shall get rid of them – an advantage more than overbalancing the Mischief.'[29]

Richard Atkinson's former residence at 32 Fenchurch Street, and its contents, were sold off in March 1794, in hundreds of lots including 'Window Curtains, Mahogany and Japaned Chairs, Pier Glasses, Turkey and Wilton Carpets, capital large Dining and Counting-house Tables of fine Mahogany, Wardrobes, Drawers, Bureaus and Bookcases, Sideboards, Kitchen Utensils, &c. &c.'.[30] Nathaniel, who attended the first day of the auction, sent Bridget a copy of the catalogue. 'There is no such Thing to be found there as the Collection of Hogarth's Prints,' he wrote. 'As soon as the Bustle which the Sale must occasion is over I will endeavour to learn what has become of it.'[31] Hutchison Mure would die a few months later, aged eighty-three, reportedly from a 'broken heart, in consequence of the unfortunate state of his affairs'.[32]

The Mures' bankruptcy might easily have brought down the house of Atkinson, Mure & Bogle – but Sir Francis Baring saved the day, and agreed to honour all the Jamaican firm's outstanding bills drawn on the Fenchurch Street house, worth some £36,000. Through his intervention, the partners emerged from the crisis with creditworthiness that was not only unimpaired, but improved; from this time onwards, they enjoyed the privilege of drawing on Barings in London, and they could not have wished for a more prestigious connection. As Baring himself would later write: 'By these means the house at Kingston was saved, secured, & when it was found that our support could be relied on, their credit rose in such a manner, that the premium on their bills which was only 5 per cent at the commencement was soon 10, 12 & finally 15 per Cent.'[33]

I WOULD NEVER have found out the half of my family's business dealings in Jamaica had it not been for a stroke of tremendous luck. I discovered early on in my research that Richard Atkinson and Francis Baring were friends, for family papers mentioned the connection between the two men. Later, when I started looking into Richard's rum contracts, and then his role at the East India Company, I learnt that Baring had also been involved. Even so, a certain mystery surrounded their friendship, for no correspondence between them seemed to exist. I suspected that since they were neighbours – Baring lived at Mincing Lane, just round the corner from Fenchurch Street – there was little need to write down what could quite as easily be spoken.

By the mid-1790s, Baring had established one of the most revered merchant banks in the City of London – a status it would retain for two centuries, until catastrophic losses caused by a Singapore-based derivatives broker called Nick Leeson brought the house down in spectacular style. On 26 February 1995, the Dutch bank ING purchased Barings for the nominal sum of £1; among the assets it acquired was a collection of papers spanning the firm's 230-year global history, including thousands of letterbooks, deal prospectuses, ledgers and maps. The Baring Archive is now kept at ING's Moorgate offices.

Archival research can feel a bit like old-fashioned mineral prospecting – it is a highly speculative business, where you turn up for work motivated by the possibility that you might unearth a seam of documentary ore, suitable for conversion into polished narrative. Before I visited the Baring Archive for the first time, in April 2011, I had told the librarian that I wished to see anything connected with the Atkinson family's activities in London or Jamaica – not the most focused of requests, I must admit. On arrival, I was ushered into a small, windowless reading room and shown a pile of folders containing papers mostly dating from the 1820s onwards. They all had an Atkinson connection – but they were too tangential and impersonal to add much to the story I was researching.

Four years later, my family research hobby had evolved into a full-blown book project. I was halfway through a draft manuscript, and had started fretting about how I would account for the great gaps in my knowledge about the Atkinsons' business affairs in Jamaica – a subject on which the family correspondence had proved remarkably unforthcoming. One day, I was exploring the Baring Archive's website, reading a guide to the earliest part of the collection, when a sentence leapt out from the screen: 'Of particular note are some boxes of papers relating to the business of Atkinson,

Mure & Bogle of Jamaica and elsewhere, following the failure of their London agent in 1793.'[34]

This threw me off balance, for I was convinced I'd never seen any material that matched this description. I made another appointment to visit the archive. A few days later, to my utter astonishment, the librarian produced five volumes containing twenty years of correspondence between the houses of Atkinson and Baring in both directions of travel – more than a thousand pages. This was the motherlode I had been dreaming of.

DURING THE EIGHTEENTH CENTURY, most of the senior administrative positions in the West Indies were 'patent offices', granted to their holders as marks of favour by the Crown. These sinecurists almost invariably lived in Britain, delegating their official obligations to deputies on the spot. The system was every bit as rotten as it sounds; quite how much so can be shown through one example. During the dying hours of Lord Bute's ministry in 1763, Charles Wyndham, the three-year-old third son of the Earl of Egremont, a crony of the outgoing prime minister, was granted the office of Island Secretary of Jamaica for the duration of his lifetime. When, in 1781, Wyndham reached his majority, he leased the office to Hutchison Mure and Richard Atkinson for twenty-one years, in exchange for £2,500 a year – useful pocket money for a young libertine about town.[35] Since William Dunlop's retirement, George Atkinson had been acting as Island Secretary, performing its duties and raking in the appropriate fees.

The Island Secretariat occupied a large brick building on Spanish Town's main square, close by the King's House, the residence of the governor. This was the colony's bureaucratic hub; it was here that Jamaica's laws and proclamations were published, its property titles registered and its business transactions recorded. (It was in one of its volumes that I found the deed relating to Richard Atkinson's purchase of Betty and the three children.) Edward Long, the eighteenth-century historian of Jamaica, described the Island Secretary as a 'great pluralist', listing nine posts that fell within his compass: 'He is secretary of the island, clerk of the enrollments and records, clerk of the council, clerk of the court of errors, clerk of the court of ordinary, clerk of the committee of correspondence, associate-judge on trials *per* commission for piracy, commissary-general of the island, and notary-public, besides some other duties relative to trade, persons leaving the island, &c.'[36] In peacetime, only the governorship of Jamaica was considered more valuable than the Island Secretary's office. 'The fees attached to it are very considerable,' observed one critic. 'Every patent commission, and other instrument, has its stated price, and even the records of office can only be opened with a *golden key*.'[37] In time of war, however, its greatest value lay in the overlap with the duties of the Agent General (a far more potentially lucrative post in the gift of the governor), which made it practical that the two offices should be held by the same person.

One of Sir Francis Baring's first actions on behalf of Atkinson, Mure & Bogle, following the collapse of the Fenchurch Street house, was to secure the Island Secretary's office for them. In February 1794, when Charles Wyndham's rent for the lease fell due, the Mures' assignees in bankruptcy (the court officials with responsibility for distributing their assets to their creditors) refused to pay up. Instead Baring shouldered the expense, and subsequently renewed the lease on George Atkinson's behalf for the same annual rent, plus a lump sum of £6,000. Nathaniel passed on the news: 'With such a Friend all must go well.'[38]

OVER THE SUMMER of 1793, William Pitt and Henry Dundas were planning a major campaign to dislodge the French from their most prized West Indian possessions. 'Success in those quarters I consider of infinite moment,' Dundas wrote, 'both in the view of humbling the power of France, and with the view of enlarging our national wealth and security.'[39] General Sir Charles Grey accepted the military command, and Admiral Sir John Jervis that of the navy. The original scheme was for the fleet to leave Portsmouth on 20 September, reaching the Caribbean at the end of the rainy season;

this would allow six relatively disease-free months for the conquest of Martinique, Guadeloupe and Saint Lucia. In fact, the expedition sailed two months late and at half its planned strength.

Before its departure, Sir Francis Baring wrote to his friend Admiral Jervis, warmly recommending the services of Atkinson, Mure & Bogle should mercantile assistance be required. In Jamaica, towards the end of January 1794, George received the 'kindest possible Letter' from the admiral, whose fleet was then at anchor off Barbados, with an invitation to act as agent to the expeditionary force; the commanders would consider no other candidate until they had heard back from him. 'I am using every Exertion to be able to embrace the earliest Opportunity of joining Sir John Jervis & Sir Charles Grey,' George wrote to Baring on 8 February. 'Whatever Commercial Business occurs whilst I am there, of course will be thrown into the Channel of your House; and in Case the Exped-ition against Martinique is attended with success I am inclined to think it may prove considerable.'[40] George wrote in a similarly buoyant mood to Nathaniel, who offered this prediction to Bridget: 'The Continuance of the war even a year will make his Fortune unquestionably.'[41]

As George boarded the schooner *Berbice* to make his rendez-vous with the fleet, the British forces started picking off the French sugar islands one by one. Martinique, where the most important French naval base in the region was located, fell on 25 March, after a siege lasting forty-seven days. Grey immediately appointed the officials necessary for the 'purpose of carrying on some regu-lation & collecting the Port duties, &ca at Martinico'.[42] George missed out on these spoils, however, for he was still five hundred miles away. After a rough passage from Jamaica, the *Berbice* had put in 'for the second time in great Distress' at Puerto Rico, where-upon its captain had dropped dead from a fever, leaving insufficient hands to sail the ship. 'The unforeseen Delays I have met with in this Voyage have been peculiarly irksome,' George wrote from San Juan on 4 April. 'My Stay with Sir John Jervis must now necessarily be very short.'[43]

Saint Lucia fell without the loss of a single man on 4 April, and Guadeloupe gave way soon afterwards. On 28 April, five days after General Grey declared the campaign 'successfully closed', George caught up with the fleet.[44] The last three months had been a complete waste of his time, as he wrote to tell Baring from a cabin on board Jervis's 98-gun flagship, the *Boyne*:

> I now am only anxious to get down by the quickest possible
> Conveyance to Jamaica. If the Jamaica Packet does not put in
> here in a Day or two, Sir John is so obliging as to promise to
> dispatch a 74 the Instant we get to Martinique for which place
> we expect to sail in a day or two. Sir Chas & he are as you
> readily will believe in high Spirits at the Termination of so
> glorious a Campaign – I could for more Reasons than one
> regret my not having been a Witness & Companion through it,
> but having escaped my late Dangers with Life I think I should
> be culpable of complaining.[45]

SIXTEEN

Maroon War

RETURNING TO JAMAICA on 12 May 1794, George Atkinson had barely been on dry land an hour before being served with a writ, arising from one of the Mures' creditors, which threatened the seizure of the Dean's Valley estate. The following week, having worked his way through a great stack of correspondence, George wrote to Sir Francis Baring: 'No Words can express the Sense I entertain of your Friendship in rescuing our Establishment from the Ruin which threatened to overwhelm it.'[1] A month later, as he was preparing to go to court over the estate, George learnt that his patron Baring and brother-in-law Nathaniel Clayton had jointly paid off Captain Laird's mortgage on the property, thereby forestalling the legal proceedings.

The British occupation of Saint Domingue had hitherto remained confined to Jérémie and the Môle Saint Nicolas, pending the arrival of reinforcements; but at last, on 30 May, a naval squadron dropped anchor near the colony's capital, Port-au-Prince. Two nights later, under cover of a thunderstorm that muffled the noise of their approach, sixty bayonet-wielding redcoats captured Fort Bizoton, which commanded the harbour; and on 4 June the British took control of the town, having sustained just thirteen fatalities.

The French royalist inhabitants of Port-au-Prince offered the invaders a guarded welcome. The British commander, Brigadier John Whyte, responded by seizing forty-five merchant vessels, many of them heavily laden with sugar, coffee, cotton and indigo destined for France – an undiplomatic way to start the occupation. The house of Atkinson, Mure & Bogle was well placed to handle the sale of the ships and their cargoes, conservatively valued at £400,000. 'Mr. Bogle is at Port au Prince as Commissary and is appointed one of the three Prize Agents for the Army; which as the Booty taken is considerable will throw some Emolument in the way of our House,' George told Baring on 15 June. 'The Competition in Purchases will I imagine be considerable and Speculators will crowd from this & other Islands.'[2]

George married Susan Dunkley, the seventeen-year-old heiress to sugar estates in Clarendon Parish, on 30 July. (The previous year, in London, he had proposed to Dorothy Baring, Sir Francis' second daughter – it would have been a shrewd alliance – but she had 'positively refused to go out with him to Jamaica'.)[3] Due to the vagaries of the postal service, it was several months before the rest of the Atkinson family, back in England, heard George's scintillating news. 'A letter from George talks of his Wife but evidently refers to a former Letter announcing his Marriage which has not yet come to hand,' Nathaniel told Bridget on 18 November.[4] John, who was then studying law in London, managed to obtain a little more information about this mysterious new sister-in-law: 'I have been enquiring of different West India People and find that she is a very beautiful young Lady of the first connections, was educated at Queen Square but not remarkable for the Largeness of her Fortune which on the whole I was rather glad to find for I was apprehensive he might have married to free himself from his account with the Mures &c. but I now see clearly that he has shot ahead of all his Difficulties.'[5]

WHILE THE REDCOATS garrisoned at Port-au-Prince dug fortifications against the French republican forces camped in the nearby mountains, the harsh tropical sun and rain beat down upon them, and yellow fever scythed through them. By November 1794, more than a thousand British soldiers were dead from the disease.

'They dropt,' wrote the historian Bryan Edwards, 'like the leaves in autumn.'[6] In neighbouring Jamaica, too, this would prove a sickly year. George wrote to Baring on 17 November apologizing for the lateness of the partnership's quarterly accounts, due to the recent deaths of two of his clerks; soon afterwards he suffered a 'violent attack' of his own, which he was lucky to survive.[7] George would remain too feeble to tackle anything but the simplest correspondence for several months.

The cost of occupying Saint Domingue escalated rapidly following the capture of Port-au-Prince. For the three months ending 30 September 1794, George's account with General Williamson of 'money paid and advanced by him for carrying on His Majesty's Service' totalled £124,216 – about the same amount as for the first nine months of the occupation.[8] George Bogle and George Atkinson, as the agents for Saint Domingue and Jamaica respectively, were each entitled to charge a 5 per cent commission on their official transactions; and since the whole of this expenditure passed first through Bogle's books, and then through George's, the partnership benefited twice over.

A few months later, after General Williamson warned the Treasury Board that he had drawn bills totalling £152,324 for the final quarter of 1794, Henry Dundas demanded the 'most regular and minute Investigation' into the accounts.[9] 'The Rate of the Commission to the Agent General, for Business done by him, a Part of which is merely the negociating Bills, appears to be much too high,' reported George Rose, Secretary to the Treasury, 'but the double Commission to one Agent in St. Domingo, and another in Jamaica, for the same Sums, is utterly inadmissible.'[10]

Williamson would draw more than £230,000 during the first quarter of 1795, and the Treasury's foot-dragging over the payment of these sums only added to George's worries. 'I am very sincerely sorry for the Difficulties you have met with,' he wrote to Baring in July 1795. 'My Mind is the more harrassed from the Rapid Increase of Expenditure on account of the new Corps raising in St. Domingo, all of whom we must pay & feed; and the least Hesitation or Check on our part would occasion the immediate Loss of that Island.'" The Lords of the Treasury did eventually agree to honour Williamson's bills in full, even as they registered their distaste at the 'exorbitancy' of the commission paid to Atkinson, Mure & Bogle.[12]

After a strong start for Britain and her allies, the momentum of the war had soon switched. In the West Indies, the French took back Guadeloupe in October 1794 and Saint Lucia four months later. In northern Europe, where a coalition of British, Hanoverian, Dutch, Austrian and Prussian forces had been struggling to hold back a massive French army, the following winter would prove one of the bleakest ever recorded. In December the great rivers froze over, enabling French troops to advance deep into Dutch territory; the following month, a revolutionary committee in Amsterdam pro-claimed the birth of the Batavian Republic, and welcomed the French into their city. The ragtag remnants of the British army were forced to beat an urgent retreat. Thousands of men perished in the cold; a hardy minority reached the port of Bremen, from where they were shipped home.

One day in April 1795, while John Atkinson was on his way to a trial at Westminster Hall, he met some survivors of the Flanders campaign who had only that morning disembarked at Greenwich. He was deeply moved by their stories, and the same evening described the encounter in a letter to his mother:

> I addressed myself to one of them who assured me that he was the only one remaining of his Company and that 14 were all that remained of the first Detachment, which originally amounted to upwards of 3000 Men. The Hardships they endured were he said inconceivable, that he himself in their Retreat from Holland counted one afternoon on a Common 86 Men frozen to death and that the whole Loss in that Retreat amounted at least to 5000 Men. Whilst I was talking with him a Man came up to inquire for a Friend of the Grenadiers Company of the same Detachment, his answer was 'I did not know him, but I believe I saw the last of them lay down in a

field one Day'. To 8 or 10 other Inquiries he was more clear in his answers but they were invariably the same, that *they were dead.* Upon the whole I cannot say that I ever have been more affected with what so little concerned myself.[13]

THE EARL OF BALCARRES – Lady Anne Lindsay's brother – landed at Jamaica on 21 April 1795 to replace General Williamson. He had long sought a lucrative military posting overseas, and the Jamaican governorship – said to be worth some £9,000 a year – was the plum for which he had been waiting. George welcomed Lord Balcarres' arrival, in spite of tensions between the Atkinson and Lindsay families. 'I cannot think he would act hostilely towards me,' he told Sir Francis Baring. 'By making himself thoroughly Master of the real Situation of my late Uncle's Estates here, he may be enabled effectually to remove all Expectation still existing in the Minds of his Sisters that they are to receive Emolument therefrom.'[14]

The new governor found Jamaica in a tense state; within weeks of his arrival, a mysterious fire consumed much of Montego Bay. Balcarres was convinced that the French government – the National Convention – lay behind this mischief. 'Although there is every

Alexander Lindsay, sixth Earl of Balcarres.

appearance of Happiness & Contentment among the slaves in Jamaica that has not deterred the Agents of the Convention from introducing persons of various descriptions into the interior of the Country, & particularly Mullatoes & Negroes from St. Domingo,' he told the Duke of Portland, the cabinet minister to whom he reported. 'I think the Gentlemen of the Country shew a Supineness & a Care-lessness upon this Point.'[15]

Perhaps this was true – but threats from within were a fact of life to which the planters were wearily habituated. Surprisingly, given their occupation of the island since 1655, the British had never fully completed the conquest of Jamaica; the descendants of Africans enslaved by the original Spanish colonists continued to live free in its rugged interior. During the early decades of British rule, these 'Maroons' had regularly plundered and burned plantations that they perceived to be encroaching on their territory. By a peace treaty signed in 1739, the colonists had acknowledged the existence of five Maroon strongholds dotted along the island's mountainous spine, and had permitted the inhabitants to exist on their own terms, albeit under the supervision of a resident British officer. The Maroons, in return, had agreed to hunt down and hand back runaway slaves.

The treaty had held for more than fifty years – during which time large expanses of Jamaica's western parishes had been cleared and planted with sugar cane – but on increasingly frayed terms. At Mon-tego Bay, shortly after the fire, a couple of Maroon lads were caught stealing pigs and sentenced to be flogged; a runaway slave who had recently been returned to his owner by the Maroons was assigned to administer the punishment. The Maroons retaliated against this unforgiveable affront with the expulsion of Captain Craskell, the British superintendent of Trelawny Town, the most populous of their settlements. On 18 July the magistrates at Montego Bay wrote to Lord Balcarres, warning that a 'very serious disturbance' was imminent at Trelawny Town: 'All the people belonging to the town have been called in; the women are sent into the woods; and, between this and Monday, they propose to kill their cattle and their children, who may be an incumbrance.'[16]

The Maroon settlement at Trelawny Town.

In Spanish Town, on 2 August, Lord Balcarres called a council of war. 'My opinion is, strike at the Maroons of Trelawney Town,' he argued. 'Strike at that source of rebellion, and its fibres will be cut off.'[17] The council voted unanimously for martial law to be imposed and the island militia to be mobilized. Balcarres appointed George Atkinson to serve as one of his aides-de-camp, conferring upon him the militia rank of lieutenant-colonel. (This explains why several of the governor's private dispatches to his superiors in London, now held at the National Archives, are in George's handwriting.) It is hard not to form the impression that Lord Balcarres and his advisors were spoiling for a fight.

Two weeks earlier, due to a mix-up at the War Office in London, a convoy of merchant ships transporting the 83rd Regiment of Foot to Saint Domingue had landed by mistake in Jamaica, which caused their charter-parties to expire; it had fallen to George, as Agent General, to hire new vessels to carry the troops onwards. Now Lord Balcarres ordered the regiment back to Jamaica; the men

disembarked at Montego Bay on 4 August to join the light dragoons already mustered there, as well as the massed ranks of the
militia. Matt Atkinson, an ensign in the St James Parish corps, must
have been among them; but I know nothing more about his military
exploits than this. (The only reference I have found to Matt from
around this time is in a letter written by one of his mother's neighbours at Temple Sowerby, which refers to him having been 'called
off to carry a musket' due to the 'insurrection of the Maroons', and
thus failing to send home some cinnamon trees with the last sugar
fleet of the year.)[18]

The opposing forces were ludicrously mismatched. On the one
side were the Maroons, few in number but skilled in disguise, light
on their feet and familiar with the complex terrain. On the other
side were the British, ten times more numerous, but stupidly conspicuous in their bright woollen uniforms and hopelessly attired for
scrambling through bush.

Lord Balcarres arrived at Montego Bay on 8 August and at once
issued a stern proclamation. The Trelawny Maroons had four days
to submit to 'his Majesty's Mercy', or they would bear the consequences. 'You have entered into a most unprovoked, ungrateful,
and a most dangerous Rebellion,' he thundered. 'You have forced the
Country which has long cherished and fostered you as its Children
to consider you as an Enemy.'[19] The Maroons marked the passing of
the governor's deadline, on 12 August, by burning Trelawny Town
and retreating into the hills; they also ambushed and shot dead the
colonel of the light dragoons, along with fourteen of his regiment
and thirteen militiamen. At headquarters that evening, Lord Balcarres slipped on a wet plank and banged his head; but George was
on hand to provide 'able assistance' while he recovered from his con-
cussion.[20] The next day, a sizeable bounty was announced for each
Maroon brought in as prisoner – £20 for men capable of bearing
arms, £10 for women or children.

The British soon learnt that ousting the Maroons from the densely
wooded limestone terrain of the 'cockpit' country would be harder
than they had anticipated. In mid-September, Balcarres returned

to Spanish Town to address the House of Assembly, leaving General George Walpole in command. It was Walpole who suggested a way of breaking the deadlock. 'I was Informed at Black River by a very Old Gentleman that in the last Maroon Rebellion they had a Sort of Dog which was of great Use in detecting Ambuscades,' he wrote to Balcarres on 20 September.[21] The Assembly embraced the plan, nominating one of its members to travel to Cuba, where bloodhounds were routinely used to hunt down runaway slaves, and bring back a pack of the animals. A ship belonging to Atkinson, Mure & Bogle was taken into government service – this was the *Mercury*, a copper-bottomed schooner manned by a crew of thirty-five, armed with twelve guns to fend off privateers – and on 17 October it sailed for Batabanó, on Cuba's southern coast.

George Atkinson returned to the cockpit country in November, where he observed the redcoats bombarding the Maroons with howitzers – to little effect. 'The Country they possess is so strong; so perfectly known to *them*; so much the reverse to *us*; that this will be tedious,' he commented.[22] As the seasonal rains eased off, and the island's sugar crop approached ripeness, a resolution became an urgent necessity, since most of the men serving in the militia would be required on their estates in time for the start of the harvest soon after Christmas. There was also the terrifying possibility of the cane fields being set on fire, for they would soon be so parched that a single spark might cause the destruction of dozens of plantations. 'It is equally in the power of a few Maroons, as of the whole Body of them, to burn down the Cane-Pieces,' Balcarres told Henry Dundas on 16 November. 'I have a Month still to act in, before that dry and dreaded moment arrives.'[23]

The *Mercury* returned from Cuba on 16 December, landing one hundred bloodhounds, with forty handlers, at Montego Bay. The dogs soon showed their teeth. 'A Negroe Woman having struck one of them was instantly killed by the animal. A Soldier of the 83d having teized one of them was torn very much in the arm & with difficulty saved,' wrote Balcarres in his dispatches. 'Should these Dogs have the full Effect of reducing those Rebel Maroons I shall

Two bloodhounds and their Cuban handler.

certainly endeavour to preserve the Breed.'[24] General Walpole hoped
the mere threat of unleashing the fearsome beasts would be enough
to end the conflict. On 21 December, at a meeting with the Maroon
chiefs in the woods, he gave them his solemn word that they would
not be banished from Jamaica on condition they surrendered within
ten days, and begged the king's pardon 'on their knees'.[25]

At Spanish Town, Balcarres was appalled when he heard about
Walpole's pledge – for he knew that many planters wished to be
rid of the Maroons for ever. Nonetheless, the governor returned to

the scene of the conflict, where he grudgingly ratified the treaty on 28 December. When only a handful of Maroons had handed themselves in after ten days, Walpole argued for giving them more time; but patience was not one of the governor's strong suits. On 13 January 1796, Balcarres ordered the first outing of his 'Bloody Ambassadors'.[26] Even in their muzzled state, the dogs would prove all too effective; by the end of the month, more than three-quarters of the Maroons had yielded.

A rift developed between Lord Balcarres and General Walpole over how the Maroons should be punished. Balcarres insisted the Maroons had flouted the treaty, and he therefore saw it 'absolutely as nothing'.[27] Walpole, who favoured clemency, having staked his honour upon his pledge to the Maroons, reckoned himself 'scandalously traduced' by the governor.[28] On 11 March, when martial law was finally lifted, Walpole sent Balcarres the following message, along with his resignation: 'Content yourself, my lord, with this reflection: That the island, by firmness and humanity together, has been saved, without a *single cane destroyed*; and at a time when the *slaves were set agog by Mr. Wilberforce.*'[29]

The prisoners were brought round to Port Royal in the *Mercury* and other vessels. A secret committee of the House of Assembly concurred with Balcarres' view that the Maroons' failure to respect the ten-day deadline had invalidated Walpole's promise not to deport them; only the few who had surrendered in time would be spared this fate. The cold, dark colony of Nova Scotia, two thousand miles to the north, was chosen as the place of the Maroons' exile. George assisted with the arrangements, liaising on the governor's behalf with the naval commander, Sir Hyde Parker, who offered to convey them there on board two large transport ships, the *Mary* and the *Ann*, together with a frigate, the *Dover*, as part of a sugar convoy bound for England. 'The Admiral appears most ready to forward your Lordship's wishes to the utmost of his Power,' George told Balcarres on 17 April.[30]

Late in the day, however, Lord Balcarres was beset by doubts, and decided to await instructions from London before making his final judgement on the Maroons' fate. 'Lieut. Wilson commanding the Dover has just mentioned to me that he has learned from Mr. Atkinson that it is intended for the Maroons to be continued here & remain on Board the Dover & transports a considerable time,' wrote Sir Hyde Parker, irritably, on 3 May.[31] While the ships remained at anchor off Port Royal, it was Atkinson, Mure & Bogle's responsibility to keep the soldiers guarding the Maroons provisioned with 'Vegetables and Roots of various kinds, and new baked bread', as well as rum, sugar, coffee, candles and soap.[32] (The prisoners, one can safely assume, had rougher fare.) Finally, at the end of June, Lord Balcarres received the confirmation for which he had been waiting, and 568 Maroon men, women and children departed the shores of Jamaica for ever. (They did not thrive in Nova Scotia; four years later, in 1800, they would be taken onwards to the colony of Freetown, on the Sierra Leone River in West Africa.)

The governor's uncharacteristic hesitancy had arisen after he learnt that his tactics against the Maroons were the cause of controversy back home. On 21 March, General Macleod had tabled a motion in the House of Commons denouncing in the most gory terms the use of the bloodhounds; in Cuba, he said, it was customary for the Spanish to 'feast their dogs' upon the flesh of children, 'that they might be unnaturally bloody and fierce'.[33] Although the motion was subsequently withdrawn, many MPs were dismayed by such claims. Henry Dundas had already written to Balcarres conveying the king's misgivings on this subject: 'However great the disadvantages under which Military operations must be carried on, His Majesty cannot think these, or any possible motives, sufficient to justify the mode of warfare proposed to be carried on against them by the Dogs procured from Cuba.'[34]

Balcarres angrily defended his conduct, and his reputation, in a letter published in the *Royal Gazette*. The dogs, he maintained, had been deployed as protection against ambush: 'Why do the laws and customs of war authorize a fort to fire red-hot shot and deny it to a ship of war? The reason is obvious; the one is defence, and the other aggression. It is upon that principle that I used the instrument in question in Jamaica.'[35] To the Duke of Portland, his superior, he sent a defiant response: 'I have very shortly to observe that what I have done admits of no Medium. I have either deserved the Thanks of my Country, or I merit to be branded with Infamy and separated from Society as a Monster of Cruelty and Barbarity.'[36]

ALL THIS TIME, the cost of occupying Saint Domingue, in terms of hard currency as well as human life, continued to rise to an almost overwhelming degree. Bills worth £2,232,177 would be drawn upon the Treasury in favour of George Atkinson, Agent General in Jamaica, between January 1794 and March 1796 – terrifying sums which stretched the resources of the Kingston house to such an extent that George wondered whether he and his partners had laid themselves too much 'at the Mercy of Ministers'. So when, in October 1795, he heard that John Wigglesworth had been seconded from Pitt's Committee for Auditing the Public Accounts, and would take over from Bogle at Port-au-Prince, George's reaction was profound relief – this, he felt, was the 'most fortunate Circumstance' that could have befallen Atkinson, Mure & Bogle.[37] Meanwhile, in London, Baring heard whispers that the ministry was 'disposed to abandon' Saint Domingue, or at least its 'hopes of acquiring it' from the French, and he wrote to the partners on 4 December, urging them to extricate themselves from all business there as soon as possible: 'I need not observe to you that your measures cannot be taken too quietly nor too secretly.'[38]

During 1796, the balance of power in Saint Domingue tipped decisively towards Toussaint Louverture, the black general of an army of ten thousand former slaves. A devout Catholic who had himself been born into slavery, Toussaint had three years earlier made a bold proclamation: 'Brothers and Friends, I am Toussaint Louverture, my name is perhaps known to you. I have undertaken vengeance. I want liberty and equality to reign in Saint Domingue. I work to bring them into existence.' Now that Toussaint held that sway in the mountainous north of the colony, any lingering British ambitions of completing the conquest withered away. In June 1796,

Lord Balcarres expressed the view that Saint Domingue was 'lost to Europe'.[39]

By the start of 1797, after four years of a conflict fought on multiple fronts, Britain was lurching towards insolvency. Due to the overprinting of banknotes since the start of the war, the face value of all the paper money in circulation was now twice that of the gold bullion held in the Bank of England's reserves. On 18 February, the townsfolk of Newcastle flocked to local banks to exchange their notes for gold coin, and the panic quickly spread from there. As Sir Francis Baring would observe: 'Persons of almost every description caught the alarm: tradesmen, mechanics, and particularly women and farmers (to whom I am ashamed to add many of a superior class and rank) all wanted guineas, for the sole purpose of hoarding.'[40]

Rumours of a French invasion had been rife for a while. Atrocious weather frustrated attacks on Ireland's Bantry Bay in December 1796, and on Newcastle in January 1797, but a third expedition achieved landfall. On 22 February, 1,400 French troops came ashore near Fishguard in Pembrokeshire; they surrendered two days later, following clashes with local militia. The Welsh landings brought the financial crisis to a head. On 26 February, following an emergency meeting of the Privy Council, the king declared that the Bank of England would no longer be legally required to convert paper money into gold. Through this unprecedented measure of suspending payments in coin, the nation's bullion reserves were preserved, the Treasury continued to pay its bills, and the public credit remained alive.

THE OCCUPATION OF Saint Domingue would prove a calamitous waste of life and money; it was also, due to the astronomical sums that passed through their books, the means by which the partners of Atkinson, Mure & Bogle made their fortunes. Early in 1797, Samuel Mure and George Bogle both announced their plans to retire at the end of the year. While George Atkinson, at thirty-two, did not feel ready for such a move, it was necessary that he should spend more time in England, focusing on his duties as his uncle's executor. He did not, however, relish the thought of his unreliable brother Matt running the Kingston office; and so he resolved to hand over to his youngest brother, John, who arrived at Jamaica in December 1797.

George, Susan and their three-year-old son sailed for England in June 1798. Shortly before leaving, George accounted for his departure to Lord Balcarres. 'My Constitution is so much impaired by repeated Indisposition during the last two years that I really apprehend a Return of Fever in the Autumn might be serious,' he explained. 'Under these Circumstances added to the Private Affairs in England which press for my immediate Attention, I trust you will not attribute my Determination to visit England at this Period to any other than the real Causes.'[41] But there was in fact another, secret reason for George's voyage home – he had seriously displeased Sir Francis Baring.

It was one of Baring's articles of faith that a merchant should, as much as possible, resist the distractions of public life; so he had viewed George's military and political activities with mounting concern, especially since his election to the House of Assembly. While George's attentions were diverted elsewhere, the Saint Domingue business had expanded so massively, and communications from Jamaica had become so erratic, that Baring grew alarmed at the risk posed to his own merchant house. As he later admitted in a memorandum to his partners: 'Our fortunes, & even our existence, was in real danger, in consequence of our unbounded confidence & devotion to the house at Kingston.'[42]

George wrote to Baring from Temple Sowerby on 28 August – not exactly a grovelling letter, but with a note of contrition. 'I trust my Gratitude for your unlimited Friendship will cease but with my Life,' he started, before going on to list some of the challenges he had faced over the previous five years, including seven bouts of malaria which had taken him 'to the Brink of the Grave'. He explained that motives of loyalty had led him to follow Lord Balcarres into the field during the Maroon war, but he also denied being too close to the governor: 'That I have been in his Confidence and have used private

Influence to forward his measures, is undoubtedly true; but I am safe in saying I never made an Enemy by the manner of doing it, and as to attendance upon him I am positively certain I did not during the last 18 Months of my Stay in the Island, breakfast or dine six times in the Government House.'[43]

Nathaniel Clayton offered a dispassionate view of his brother-in-law's transgressions, writing to Baring:

> The Excess of George's Misconduct may be learnt from your Displeasure, which, I know, is not easily excited. I own his military Expedition appeared to me little less than an act of Insanity, and you convince me that his parliamentary measure was nearly as absurd. His entangling himself in *new* Engagements in Jamaica was in the face of my repeated Exhortations & his own solemn Promises. I more than ever deprecate his Return to Jamaica. His Temper will not suffer itself to be controlled by a younger Brother, and he has such an unconquerable Propensity to act on the Spur of the Moment that Remonstrances from a distance are unavailing, for they come too late. It is my Consolation that you will find John the very reverse of his Brother. His Talents are not brilliant but I hope they are solid, & they are certainly accompanied with an excellent Temper & uncommon Industry.[44]

Meanwhile, the British withdrawal from Saint Domingue was well under way. Brigadier Thomas Maitland signed an armistice with Toussaint Louverture on 30 April; the evacuation from Port-au-Prince took place on 8 May, at two in the morning. Maitland wrote to Lord Balcarres on 25 June, requesting permission to evacuate the garrison at Jérémie, which he believed to be vulnerable to attack, but Balcarres refused to take responsibility for 'deciding on a point, where the consequences are so immense'.[45] In late July, following the arrival of definite orders from Henry Dundas, the Secretary of State for War, Maitland announced his intention to remove all troops from the French colony.

The British slipped out of Jérémie harbour after dark on 20 August, once 'all the Stores of every description' had been loaded on to a motley assortment of transport ships.[46] On 1 September, John Atkinson wrote to Lord Balcarres hurriedly requesting clearance to land 'from one thousand to twelve hundred Barrels of Gunpowder, the Number of Barrels could not be exactly ascertained from the Circumstance of their having been embarked in the Night'.[47] The governor did not hide his exasperation: 'I scarcely do not know in what capacity you address me – whether as Commissary for Jamaica or for St. Domingo? I have no Place to store 1000 Barrels of Gun Powder nor Artillery Stores. Fort Augusta is now entirely full.'[48]

At daybreak on 3 October the last of the British fleet, packed with troops, refugees, ordnance and other stores, sailed from the Môle Saint Nicolas, bound for Jamaica. But John was not present to supervise the landing. Four weeks earlier, a fever had suddenly struck him down, and he had died on 11 September, aged twenty-seven. His mortal remains were added with little ceremony to the overflowing churchyard at Kingston.

SEVENTEEN

Black Pioneers

NATHANIEL CLAYTON purchased the Chesters estate in 1796 – his legal practice was flourishing. Some twenty miles west of Newcastle, as the crow flies, the mansion was a rather dour stone box of a building, but it commanded delightful views across open fields down to the banks of the North Tyne. Scattered round these meadows were the remnants of Cilurnum, a Roman cavalry station which had once guarded an important river crossing. Nathaniel immediately got started on improvements to the property, first diverting the public road running through the middle of its park, then tidying up the Roman rubble. 'Large masses of ruins rising in heaps over a spacious field speak of former greatness,' wrote a visitor in 1801. 'The mutilated figure of a woman standing on the back of some animal has lately been dug up and is at present put in a wall enclosing a plantation; I should think it deserved a better situation.'[1]

Nathaniel soon proved himself a capable farmer. New field drains, dug at considerable expense, paid swift dividends. 'My Neighbours begin to think that I am not such a Ninnyhammer as they first took me for,' he told his youngest sister-in-law, Jane. 'I am greatly bent on making two Blades of Grass grow where one only grew before.'[2] Across the country, a disastrous harvest in the summer of 1799 caused many poor families to go hungry the following winter; in Newcastle, a large soup kitchen was erected in the Poultry Market to feed those who were 'ready to perish'.[3] Even that most basic of staples, peas, were hard to come by. 'I imagine they must be very scarce,' wrote Jane, who was staying with the Claytons at Westgate Street, 'for at the Soup Kitchen they substitute Potatoes, which at present bear a very high price in proportion with every other kind of grain.'[4] With vegetables at such a premium, Nathaniel felt justifiably proud of his yield at Chesters. 'My farming Skill has become notorious,' he told his mother-in-law in February 1800, 'for I had the best Crop of Turnips within 20 Miles of me, and Turnips were this year but another Name for Gold.'[5]

Ever since 1786, when he was hired by the Atkinson family to protect their inheritance, Nathaniel had worked tirelessly to promote the interests of his wife's relatives. To give one minor example: in the spring of 1798, after reading in the *Gentleman's Magazine* that a second cousin of the Atkinsons, a Miss Addison (daughter of Joseph Addison, the celebrated essayist and founder of the *Spectator*), had died intestate, Nathaniel made it his business to find out the value of her estate. 'If I find the play worth the Candle,' he told Jane, 'I see a reasonable Ground to hope that I shall prove our Brother Michael entitled to the Property.'[6] But Nathaniel's efforts to establish his brother-in-law's claim as the old lady's 'laughing heir' must have come to naught, for the subject was soon dropped.

The Clayton children often stayed with their grandmother and unmarried aunts at Temple Sowerby, and saw it as a second home; during the light summer months, it was possible to ride across the moors from Chesters in a single day. When they were seven, the boys were each in turn sent to board at the Rev. John Fisher's school at Kirkoswald, ten miles from Temple Sowerby; having acquired groundings in Greek and Latin, as well as 'broad Cumberland' accents, they would go on to public schools in the south.[7]

Nat, the eldest, went to Harrow, and his letters to Bridget show him to have been a clever, amusing boy. During the Easter holidays of 1799, when he was eleven, he visited Parkinson's Museum, which was housed in a rotunda on the south side of the Thames by Black-friars Bridge. He reported back to his grandmother:

Among other curious things, we saw a piece of beef, which had gone round the world with Commodore Anson; also a great many Indian clubs, and a goat of Angora stuffed, all kinds of Butterflies and insects, and what amused Nurse most of all, a pair of Chinese woman's shoes. In the second Gallery we saw a Chinese Pheasant, a blue bellied creeper, a Parrot, a swallow's nest which was built in the wing of an owl, a bat, and a stuffed shark. As I know that you like long letters, and as I have nothing else to write about, I will proceed. I saw also a sea Hawk, a stuffed lap dog, a Tyger, a lion, a Buck, a Toucan, a scarlet humming Bird, a blue humming bird, a green humming bird, a Pelican, also silver and Iron ore, a stuffed ostrich, and a Cougar, a common hen and chickens with which Nurse was remarkably well pleased, a large collection of Shells, which she thought were Superior even to yours, the only specimen of the bread Fruit, which Captain Cook brought with him from the Island of Otaheite, a stuffed Cormorant, and a Crane.[8]

Little Bridget and John Clayton, aged nine and seven, spent the autumn months of 1799 at Temple Sowerby. They were engaging children, and their grandmother relished having them nearby as she knitted heroic quantities of woollen stockings for them and their siblings. 'I am very glad that Mr. Clayton and you consent to Bridget and John's staying a Little Longer with me who at present are in perfect good Health and are growing Stout and Strong for which I have to thank John Ching it has made such an alteration for the better,' Bridget wrote to Dorothy on 27 October. ('John Ching' was a proprietary brand of worm lozenges – its principal ingredient being mercury.) 'Bridget is fond of Patching and sits close by me and John plays at Cards by himself with the greatest good hummor and Dummy and he never disagrees.'[9]

FOLLOWING HIS RETURN to England, George Atkinson had spent a good deal of the autumn of 1798 on turnpikes, shuttling between family in the north and various 'intricate unpleasant' concerns demanding his attention down south.[10] The winding up of the house of Atkinson, Mure & Bogle was his first priority, with funds of almost £250,000 to be shared out between the three Kingston partners, as well as Sir Francis Baring, who had financed their business from London. Inevitably, some frank exchanges of opinion ensued. The Jamaican contingent argued that they deserved the lion's share, since their possession of the Agent General's office, through which the vast majority of the spoils had flowed, predated Baring's formal connection with their business. Baring, on the other hand, reminded them that the Island Secretary was placed by virtue of his position in 'so important, confidential a situation with the Governor' that it almost always led to his appointment as Agent General – which was why, following the Mures' bankruptcy, he had gone to the great trouble of renegotiating the lease on the Island Secretary's office with its aristocratic owner, Charles Wyndham.[11]

George was unusually subdued during these discussions, perhaps on account of the dressing-down he had received from his patron that summer; certainly Baring noticed that he seemed 'disposed to acquiesce with any terms we should propose'.[12] Once the Kingston partners had conceded the point over the Island Secretary's office, Baring was generous in his settlement, accepting a lump sum of £70,000. His primary motive, he reminded his own partners, had always been to 'reestablish & thereby serve the Atkinson family'.[13] Both sides signed the letter of agreement on 1 December 1798; and thus the books of the house of Atkinson, Mure & Bogle were closed.

The news of John's death in Jamaica reached his mother and sisters at Temple Sowerby in late November. Although it must have caused them great anguish, their letters are entirely silent on the subject. Maybe the family gathered to mark John's passing; George certainly travelled up to Westmorland in early December. As was the custom of the time, Bridget would wear black for the first year after her son's death, moving on to muted colours for the second year. (On the first anniversary of Dick's death, back in May 1794, Dorothy had written from Newcastle to tell Bridget that she had just dispatched a 'french Grey callico gown for you of a sort much in use here for second mourning – also a very dark purple one for visiting the Hotbeds &c'.[14] I love the thought of Bridget pottering about the kitchen garden at Temple Sowerby, honouring her son's memory as she tended her melon pit.)

Later that winter, in February 1799, George returned to London to make preparations for what he anticipated would be a 'Hot Campaign' at the Court of Chancery, where various of the Mures' creditors were lining up to 'commence Hostilities' against his uncle's estate.[15] 'Their Claims are immoderate and very extraordinary,' George wrote to Lord Balcarres. 'Upon the whole I apprehend I shall have very ample Employment in the Liquidation of these Concerns for many months. I have abandoned all Hopes of returning to Jamaica this Season.'[16]

WITHIN DAYS OF his brother John's death, Matt Atkinson was sworn in as Island Secretary of Jamaica; the family's affairs in the colony now rested on the shoulders of its laziest member. Shortly after Christmas, Matt slipped away from Kingston to inspect the estates at the west end of the island. 'The Bogue is coming round fast I expect 200 Hhds this Crop,' he told Baring on 10 February 1799. 'There wants a great deal to be done at Deans Valley, both as to establishing Guinea Grass, draining Land, and putting on Negroes, before the Estate can be brought to what it ought to make, which is 280 to 300 Hhds.'[17] Following years of underinvestment, parts of Dean's Valley were on the point of collapse, with urgent repairs needed to the sugar works, overseer's house and other buildings – a local surveyor estimated that 'it would require 40,000 Shingles and 10,000 feet of Boards to do what is Absolutely necessary'.[18] On both estates, the workforces were 'much upon the decline'.[19] Over three years – from the beginning of 1797 to the end of 1799 – the enslaved population at the Bogue would fall by fifteen, to 215 (seven births, minus twenty-two deaths), while at Dean's Valley it would fall by thirteen, to 208 (twelve births, minus twenty-five deaths).[20]

In London, George set up a new merchant house, to be known as G. & M. Atkinson. He would look after its interests in England, while three partners – brother Matt, John Hanbury and Hugh Cath-cart – would manage its operations in Jamaica. 'I think it is time that we should begin a private correspondence,' Baring wrote to Matt on 12 August – by which he meant a frank correspondence, transcending the platitudes of the monthly letters between the two houses. Baring had been speaking to John Wigglesworth, the former commissary in Saint Domingue, who had told him that Matt could not decide whether to focus on the sugar plantations or on the mercantile branch of the business. Baring strongly urged Matt in the latter direction: 'In my opinion there can be no doubt under the present circumstances, for you cannot make your Counting house too strong whilst such various & important commercial objects are passing before you.'[21]

During the autumn of 1799, a transaction took place concern-ing the ownership of the two Jamaican estates; insignificant though it might seem, it would subsequently cause a great rupture in the Atkinson family. Now that he was rich in his own right, George agreed to buy out the interests in the Bogue and Dean's Valley estates which Nathaniel had some years earlier acquired from Paul Benfield and Captain Laird. On 6 December, Nathaniel and George visited Baring at his mansion near Lewisham. 'I have the Satisfaction to tell thee that we yesterday closed our accounts; visiting Sir Francis at Lee for that Purpose,' Nathaniel later wrote to Dorothy. 'They met with his entire approbation & after they were examined & closed he turned to George & thus expressed himself (forgive, my dear Girl, my Vanity) "George I want Power to express how much the Atkinson family & you in particular, are indebted to Mr. Clayton: It is impossible that they or you can ever forget it." This as thou wilt readily believe was very grateful to thine ever, N.C.'[22]

SUCH WAS THE mortality rate that military service in the West Indies was seen as more or less a death sentence for white rank and file; and yet, whenever the British authorities proposed draft-ing enslaved Africans, the planters made clear their aversion to the idea of 'slaves in red coats'. But the mobilization of a large black army in Saint Domingue had increased pressure to boost the sugar islands' defences; which is why, in 1795, Henry Dundas ordered the formation of eight regiments made up of Africans discreetly purchased by the government. (The discretion being necessary to avoid embarrassing ministers who publicly backed abolition.) The First West India Regiment, which assembled in the Windward Islands, acquitted itself with great credit; but when Lord Balcarres attempted to raise a West India Regiment to serve in Jamaica, the House of Assembly blocked him from doing so.

If the idea of placing weapons in the hands of black men made these powerful white men shudder, they unquestioningly accepted the use of black 'pioneers'. These were the labourers who performed the drudgework of military life; armed with pickaxes, saws and shovels, they built fortifications, dug trenches, hauled ordnance and provisions, and generally carried out the most backbreaking tasks. Two pioneers were attached to each of the fifty-six companies garrisoned in Jamaica, although Balcarres hoped to increase this number to six. For the past fifteen years, the island's pioneers had been largely composed of free blacks who had emigrated from Georgia following the American revolution; but most of them were now either exhausted or dead. To fill the gaps, the army had been hiring enslaved men for up to 5s each per day, saddling the island with an annual bill of more than £20,000 currency. In November 1797, the House of Assembly passed a resolution approving the governor's proposal to place the pioneers on a cheaper footing.

Lord Balcarres' plan involved putting the contract to supply pioneers out to public tender. The government would offer to pay £15 currency for the annual hire of each enslaved pioneer, plus an annual clothing allowance of 46s, and a day rate of 8½d – such terms, Balcarres assured the Duke of Portland, would not only prove less expensive for the island, but would furnish a 'very good Return indeed to any Contractor who may chuse to speculate' – and yet, a year after the Assembly passed its resolution, not one merchant in Jamaica had expressed interest in taking on the business.[23] Baffled by the failure of his scheme, Balcarres consulted 'some of the first

Merchants in Kingston', who told him they believed that military service would make enslaved men unfit for other forms of work.[24] At last, though, a willing merchant was found. On 24 August 1799, the contract with Balcarres, who was acting 'on behalf of the British government' – at least, that is how the official paperwork defines his role in the transaction – was signed by Matt Atkinson. The house of G. & M. Atkinson would supply 'so many able negro men as Pioneers for the several white Regiments of Cavalry or Infantry' stationed on the island, 'at the rate of 6 Pioneers per Troop or Company'; a year's notice was needed to terminate the agreement, following which such pioneers 'as shall not be dead or runaway' would be returned to the contractors in Kingston.[25]

This was a corrupt, self-serving business, and not just for the obvious reasons – for, secretly, in collusion with Matt Atkinson's firm, Balcarres had taken a one-third stake in the pioneer deal, which made him a party to both sides of the negotiations. At the beginning of 1801, eighteen months into the contract, the Kingston house (and their silent partner) would have 357 pioneers on hire to the British army.

From the very start of my investigations into my ancestors, I knew that I was bound to unearth some unpalatable details of their slave-owning activities, and as the grim revelations piled up, my sorrow and regret about this aspect of their lives increased. By the time I came upon the pioneer contract, in the archive of the National Army Museum, I was quite far along with my research, and thought I had seen it all. But this discovery exposed a new dimension to my ancestors' participation in slavery, one I hadn't anticipated. Not only had they possessed hundreds of enslaved Africans on their estates; they had also acted, to a perhaps unique extent, as suppliers of slave labour to the British armed forces.

IN JULY 1798, the United States suspended trade with France and its colonies in retaliation for privateer attacks on American merchant shipping; the embargo caused great hardship in Saint Domingue, which relied on the mainland for much of its food. However, both

General Toussaint Louverture.

Britain and the US wished to maintain a friendly dialogue with the black general Toussaint Louverture, so as to deter the 'dissemination of dangerous principles among the slaves of their respective countries'.[26] In May 1799, Brigadier Thomas Maitland, who had overseen the British withdrawal from Saint Domingue the previous year, returned there with a mandate to make a treaty with Toussaint on behalf of both nations; the ports of Port-au-Prince and Cap-Français, it was agreed, would be opened up to trade. Subsequently, Lord Balcarres prevailed on Hugh Cathcart and Charles Douglas 'of Mr. Atkinson's Office' to act as resident agents in the two towns.[27]

Toussaint had hoped to keep the treaty a secret, but his arch-rival, the 'mulatto' general André Rigaud, soon came to hear of it. The feud between the men had been simmering for a while, but Toussaint's Anglo-American convention provided Rigaud with the *casus belli* for the vicious power struggle that would become known as the War of Knives. 'Rigaud is already in motion, and has put to death a very considerable number of the White Inhabitants both at Jeremie and aux Cayes,' Maitland briefed Balcarres on 20 June. 'I find Toussaint is in very great want indeed of Provisions so much so that his Troops are at a stand for want of them.'[28] Matt Atkinson duly arranged for 'two thousand Barrels of Flour, fifty Barrels of Salt Fish, two hundred Barrels of herrings, one hundred Barrels of salt Beef, fifty Barrels of salt Pork, three hundred Barrels of Biscuit' and 'ten Hogsheads of Tobacco', along with arms, ammunition and gunpowder, to be loaded on to three ships that sailed to Port-au-Prince three weeks later.[29]

Meanwhile the French Republic's agent on Saint Domingue, Philippe Roume, was working on a plan to undermine its British neighbour. The merchants Isaac Sasportas and Barthélémy Dubuisson arrived in Jamaica in early November 1799, with orders to spy on the island's defences and incite rebellion among the enslaved population; General Toussaint's army would then mount an invasion during the Christmas holidays. But Sasportas and Dubuisson were arrested soon after reaching Kingston – and their betrayer was none other than Toussaint, who had detected in Roume's plot the motive of driving a wedge between him and his British backers. Shortly afterwards, Lord Balcarres received a shopping list of armaments urgently required by Toussaint, which included 6,000 muskets, 2,000 pairs of pistols, 30,000 pounds of lead and 100,000 pounds of gunpowder. The British agent in Port-au-Prince, Hugh Cathcart – a partner of the house of G. & M. Atkinson – was summoned for regular meetings with Toussaint about these supplies. 'I have been with him almost daily for these last three weeks (& have become an immense favourite),' Cathcart wrote on 26 November. 'He has pressed me very hard, lately, to buy him a Frigate, and seemed rather dissatisfied, at my not complying with his request – altho' I assured him that it was totally out of my power. He then asked me, if that I thought Lord Balcarres, would procure him one.'[30]

After the discovery of the French plot, the conspirator Dubuisson escaped the noose by confessing to everything; but Sasportas was hanged from gallows thirty feet above Kingston parade ground, wearing a label that spelled out the word 'SPY' in large letters.[31] Lord Balcarres – whose fate was to have been poisoning 'by an infusion' into his coffee on the morning of 26 December – declared martial law, and ordered 'every French male Person of Color above the age of 12' to be shipped off the island.[32] The house of G. & M. Atkinson made the necessary arrangements for the deportation of nearly one thousand men to Martinique and Trinidad.

Toussaint's relations with the British cooled in December 1799, however, when four of his armed ships were seized mistakenly by the Royal Navy and condemned as prizes by the Court of Admiralty. Despite warnings that Toussaint would become a 'most implacable enemy', Sir Hyde Parker, the naval commander in Jamaica, stood firm in his opposition to the vessels' return.[33] Following the theft of his ships, Toussaint was in no hurry to honour debts to British merchants, and so Cathcart – who had sold supplies to the general on credit, and invested £80,000 of his partners' silver in coffee and other produce on Saint Domingue – was forced to linger at Port-au-Prince, pressing for payment and praying that the partnership's goods would not be impounded. Finally, after an impasse lasting several tense months, Cathcart could return to Kingston with good news. 'I feel well pleased to have it in my power to be able to say to you that I have received full payment from the Black General,' he wrote to George Atkinson on 12 June. 'We are now fairly out of the scrape and I trust we shall never again get ourselves into such another. Every thing is brought off excepting about Forty Bales of Cotton, for which I could not find freight, but I look for them in a Vessel that is daily expected.'[34]

SAINT DOMINGUE HAD ENTERED the 1790s as the richest colony in the West Indies, but its productivity plummeted as it was engulfed by conflict. In marked contrast, this was a buoyant decade for Jamaica. The wholesale price of sugar almost doubled on the back of Saint Domingue's misfortunes, and the proprietors of estates returned to cultivation land previously given up as exhausted. During this decade, most Jamaican planters abandoned the old 'Creole' sugar cane, brought to Hispaniola by Columbus in 1493, in favour of the 'Otaheite' variety, introduced from the South Seas by Captain Bligh in 1793. This succulent newcomer was taller than its predecessor, tolerated poor soil, and yielded up to a third more sugar. Jamaican sugar, long regarded as overpriced, enjoyed strong demand in continental Europe.

But it all came to a juddering halt in 1799. The collapse started in the German port of Hamburg, home to more than three hundred sugar refineries, the highest concentration in Europe. The Jamaican merchant fleet arrived there later than usual that spring and was unable to offload its cargo; an American fleet carrying Cuban sugar had docked first and flooded the market. 'The total Stagnation in the sale of West India produce has occasioned such distress as cannot be described,' Baring wrote to the Kingston partners on 5 October 1799. 'Above forty houses, some of these considerable, have failed at Hamburg & we expect to hear of more on the arrival of every mail; about Ten houses have failed here.'[35] By the end of the year, the warehouses along the River Thames were clogged up with tens of thousands of unsold hogsheads of muscovado.

During the boom years of the 1790s, the Jamaican planters' hunger for fresh supplies of slave labour had reached frenzied levels, building to a peak at the end of the century. In 1800, more than 22,000 African men, women and children would land at Jamaica on board sixty-five slave ships – this would be the second highest year of arrivals on the island. The house of G. & M. Atkinson handled the sale of six of these human cargoes, comprising 2,350 people; so while it might be observed that the Kingston partners were late-comers to this line of trade, they nevertheless embraced it fully.

Usually, a slave shipowner made arrangements with a Jamaican merchant house for the sale of its human cargo at the start of a tri-angular voyage; but sometimes the ship's captain would complete the middle passage, then assign the business on the spot. Either way, the Kingston merchant handled the money side of the sale, advancing bills drawn on its corresponding London merchant house (Barings, in the case of G. & M. Atkinson) to pay the shipowner for the cargo, extending credit to planters buying the enslaved Africans, and securing guarantees from those planters to sell their produce through the London house. This despicable business was replete with financial hazard from beginning to end – especially so for the London merchant house, which depended upon the planters sending back produce of sufficient value to pay for the slaves they had recently purchased. At a time when the price of sugar was in freefall, the speculations of G. & M. Atkinson placed Barings in a dangerously exposed position.

The Kingston partners were preparing to sell off their first cargo – 275 Africans who had arrived on board the *Mary* – when they received Sir Francis Baring's gloomy letter about the collapse of the sugar market.[36] Clearly it didn't faze them too much. 'We have been induced to take up another Guineaman called the Will with 405 Eboe Negroes, the sales of which we have effected without even the expence of advertising, at an average of £75 Stg principally to people of this Town,' wrote John Hanbury, the partner driving the business, on 23 March 1800.[37] Baring's reply, warning that planters who purchased Africans on long credit might not be able to pay for them, given the current 'low prices of produce', crossed with Hanbury's subsequent letter, which notified him that G. & M. Atkinson had taken up ships called the *Sarah* and the *Young William*, and also, by prior agreement, guaranteed two cargoes from the Liverpool slave traders J. & H. Clarke.[38]

In his next letter to Jamaica, dated 8 August, Baring made plain his displeasure: 'If you carry on every branch of your business on a presumption that I am able to answer such boundless demands I must inform you very distinctly that my capacity nor my disposition are not equal to your expectations.'[39] George Atkinson further warned his partners: 'On your Guinea Concerns I have only to repeat my former Caution, that you carefully avoid any Connection which can involve you deeply with the Soil of the Island. Credits to Planters are at all Times dangerous; but just now most eminently so – for be assured a Storm hangs over our Island, the bursting of which we must guard against by every possible Precaution.'[40]

So great was Baring's alarm that he urgently called George down from Newcastle for a meeting with himself and George Bogle, who had held on to a stake in the Kingston house since retiring.

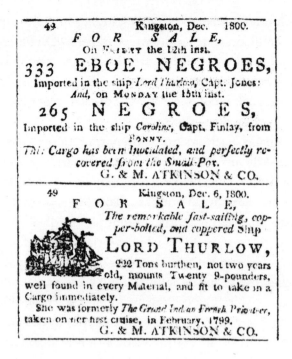

G. & M. Atkinson's advertisement for two human cargoes,
placed in the Jamaica Gazette of December 1800.

Despite his poor health (three years earlier, a lead ball had lodged
in his thigh during a naval engagement off Martinique, causing him
constant pain), Bogle agreed to go out to Jamaica to apply some
discipline to the operation. He wrote to Baring on 2 January 1801,
four days after landing at Kingston; although he was not yet able to
judge the conduct of the individual partners, it seemed that 'from an
apprehension of the War not lasting long', they had thrown themselves headlong into the slave factorage business, 'tempted by the
appearance of great profit but without recollecting that they were
thereby leading you into tremendous advances'. So as to disguise the
real reason for his 'sudden appearance' in Jamaica, he had ordered a
notice to be placed in the local newspapers, announcing the firm's
name 'being changed to Atkinsons Hanbury & Co'.[41]

 Three weeks later, Bogle was ready to offer a fuller analysis.
It seemed that the late John Atkinson, during his brief stint at the

helm, had 'constantly resisted' more hazardous lines of business. The problems had started after his death, with the establishment of G. & M. Atkinson. Instead of setting up a system by which each partner took responsibility for a branch of the business, everything had fallen upon the most experienced partner, John Hanbury – and thus, while it would be fair to say that Matt Atkinson had 'cordially acquiesced' in these speculations, Hanbury had been the 'principal mover' behind them.[42] Matt wrote privately to Baring on 28 January, expressing his 'astonishment and shagrin' at what had gone on; he had been quite genuinely under the impression that all was going swimmingly.[43]

LORD BALCARRES' devil-may-care style of governance earned him the gratitude of the island plantocracy – 'perhaps the assembly of Jamaica never agreed more perfectly and uniformly with any governor than it did with the Earl of Balcarras', a contemporary would write – but he was viewed by his ministerial superiors as a maverick and a liability.[44] In the autumn of 1800, General John Knox was appointed to replace him as governor, but drowned during a hurricane on his way out to Jamaica.

When Balcarres learnt that he was about to be recalled, he set aside his public duties and focused on putting his personal affairs in order. During the six years of his governorship he had made plenty of money – much of it through negotiating government bills for the subsistence of émigrés from Saint Domingue – and had ploughed it into coffee estates in the parishes of St George and St Elizabeth that were said to be worth 'not less than £60 or £70,000'.[45] As the time of his departure neared, Balcarres' neglect of his official workload increased. 'Our Governor is a strange Man,' George Bogle wrote on 20 June 1801. 'He has been living secluded at his Mountain in St. Georges for a Month past and although the Packet has been arrived these three weeks, he only returned to the Kings House yesterday to open his Letters.'[46]

Before Bogle returned to England, he composed a memorandum assigning clear duties to each of the Kingston partners:

The Business of the Agent General, and Settlement of
accounts with the Governor, to be under the immediate
management of Mr. Hanbury, also the correspondence with
the House in London . . . Mr. Atkinson will conduct the Island
Correspondence, with that concerning the Consignments
from Ireland &c. – also the Correspondence with Head
Quarters . . . Mr. Atkinson will likewise take upon himself
the superintendance of the Sales of produce; and I particularly
recommend to him to peruse in the Day Book every morning,
the Transactions that have taken place in the preceding day.
The Partners should be in the Office from Eight in the
morning until Four in the afternoon. Indeed in this climate
going out of Doors should as much as possible be avoided,
for a person cannot again that day set down to business in
a collected manner.[47]

On 23 July, Bogle boarded the *Lowestoffe*; strong currents, however, drove the ship aground soon afterwards in the Caicos Passage.
Bogle returned to Jamaica, and there he would remain for the rest of
the year, until the risk from hurricanes had abated.

The arrival at Port Royal on 29 July of the new governor of
Jamaica, General George Nugent, was marked with gunfire 'so
stunning' that his wife hid in her cabin on board the *Ambuscade*,
holding a pillow over her ears.[48] Maria Nugent would cut a glamor-
ous figure in Jamaica, for ladies of rank were a rarity out there – and
Mrs Nugent was a small, neat woman, with a reputation as an
'amazing dresser' who never appeared 'twice in the same gown'.[49]
More significantly, she was a sharp-eyed diarist, who left behind
easily the most vivid account of life on the island during the first
decade of the nineteenth century.

Some of her first observations relate to the filthy state in which
she found the King's House, and the poor personal hygiene of the
outgoing governor. 'I wish Lord B. would wash his hands, and use a
nail-brush, for the black edges of his nails really make me sick,' she
wrote after breakfast on her second morning. 'He has, besides, an

extraordinary propensity to dip his fingers into every dish. Yesterday he absolutely helped himself to some fricassée with his dirty
finger and thumb.' She was grudgingly amused, however, by an
'extraordinary pet' that patrolled the dining room – a 'little black
pig, that goes grunting about to every one for a tit-bit'.[50]

Before Lord Balcarres' departure from the island, in November,
he signed the power of attorney that passed responsibility for his
estates to Matt Atkinson. Martin's Hill, Balcarres' coffee estate and
cattle ranch in St Elizabeth Parish, became a favourite staging post
for Matt during his journeys to the west of the island. 'I have built a
room off the North end of the House at Martins Hill and have sent
a Bed there for myself,' he would tell Balcarres.[51] Matt particularly
appreciated the hospitality laid on by Robert White, the estate's
overseer: 'I had as good corned Pork, and poultry, as any man would
wish, and he has now got into a stock of good Old Rum. I call this
very excellent plantation fare.'[52]

Lord Balcarres had gone out to Jamaica with a view to replenish-
ing his family's coffers, and his governorship had certainly served
the purpose – even if most of his newly acquired fortune was tied up
in West Indian property. The Countess of Balcarres, who had not
seen her husband in nearly seven years, wrote to him from Edinburgh on 4 January 1802, ahead of his ship's return: 'I hope this will
greet you on your arrival in perfect health & spirits, after all the toils
& dangers you have so long encountered. No man can shew his face
to the world with a better grace, or a sounder mind, than you can,
& I am much prouder to congratulate you on *that*, with the very
moderate sum you bring home – than what you *might* have made,
with the smallest reflection on your conduct.'[53]

EIGHTEEN

The Nabob's Return

THE LAST TIME we met Lady Anne Lindsay, in June 1790, she had been boxed into the 'miserable compromise' with Richard Atkinson's executors that was supposed, at least, to protect the £700 a year left to her and her sister Margaret – but the estate had been plagued by difficulties ever since, and their annuities had not once been paid. Later that same summer, Anne had purchased 21 Berkeley Square, paying £2,600 for the house in (then, as now) one of London's most expensive neighbourhoods. Shortly afterwards, she had broken off her romance with the vacillating politician William Windham – known as the 'Weathercock' – once it became apparent that he had no plans to marry.

Finally, in October 1793, Anne had wedded Andrew Barnard, the son of the Bishop of Limerick, at St George's, Hanover Square. Fashionable folk sneered, because she was forty-two, while he was a penniless army officer twelve years her junior – but she had always held out for a love match, and the marriage would bring them both great happiness.

The Mures' bankruptcy had dealt a further blow to the Lindsay sisters' hopes of gaining anything more from the Atkinson estate. 'I now see it probable that knavery or confusion may still trick us out of our property,' Margaret wrote in January 1794, before reminding Anne about a dream she had had nearly four years earlier, the night after she signed the 'compromise' papers:

You dreamt that Atkinson opened your curtains, and with a
grave but benign countenance told you that he had liberty
to give you, as the person he loved best on earth, *one advice*,
which was to marry the first kind-hearted man who proposed
to you, as you would never get *one shilling* of what he had
destined for you. I think in the literal sense you have complied
with this, for Barnard was the first man who after the date of
this dream made direct proposals, such as required a positive
Yes or No.[1]

It was through the patronage of Anne's old friend Henry Dundas
that Andrew Barnard was in 1797 posted to the Cape Colony, after its
capture from the Dutch, as First Secretary under Lord Macartney.
The Barnards sailed out to Africa together, a fairly unconventional
arrangement for the time. Every so often, a passing British fleet
would drop off a 'parcell of delightfull letters' at Paradise, the
thatched cottage at the foot of Table Mountain where they made
their home, and Anne would momentarily immerse herself in the
latest news and gossip from London. Margaret attempted to keep
her abreast of the Atkinson business, but every advance in the Court
of Chancery seemed to be matched by a setback. In one letter, she
congratulated Anne that the drawn-out 'Cause of the Omnium', concerning the government loan stock to which the Mures had latterly
staked their claim, had gone in their favour; in her next letter she
reported, 'having been misinformed', that it had gone against them.
As Anne confided to her diary: 'For, against, it makes little difference to me, as I know that I shall never receive any advantage from
my share of West Indian property unfairly administered as it is, and
wilfully as well as accidentally intangled.'[2]

Wilfully entangled or otherwise, the Atkinson estate was certainly a mess, for which much of the blame lay with the deceased.
From the moment of Richard's death, his two sugar plantations had
proved unequal to the task of generating the income needed to cover
his legacies. 'His talents & imagination are so rapid that they always
run away with judgment,' Baring had once observed of his friend

The Torrid Zone. Yellow fever, depicted as a flame-snorting demon, reigns in hell. Above the ground (represented by a scythe blade), white Jamaicans go about their daily business; looking down, a bilious angel swigs from a bottle marked 'opium'.

A sugar boiling house. The cane juice was reduced in a tapering sequence of copper pans; it was then transferred to cool in a shallow container before being cured in hogshead barrels. This was a dangerous environment, where enslaved workers often suffered disfiguring burns.

Three of Bridget Atkinson's five sons. Dick, above, succumbed to fever soon after arriving in Jamaica. George, below left, made a fortune by financing the British occupation of St Domingue during the 1790s. Matt, below right, left debts and illegitimate children in his wake.

Mount Mascal, near Bexley in Kent. Michael Atkinson purchased the estate in 1808 but signally failed to 'disgavel' it in his will – much to the glee of the vengeful Claytons. The house fell derelict after the Second World War, and was demolished in 1959.

The Tyne Iron Company's works at Lemington, near Newcastle. Nathaniel Clayton and his brothers-in-law George and Matt Atkinson were partners in the enterprise; by the mid-1830s, when this engraving was made, the next generation had taken over.

George Atkinson, above, the disreputable head of the Kingston merchant house from 1825 to 1846; and my great-great-grandfather Dick Atkinson, right, who was the last of the family resident in Jamaica, returning to live at Temple Sowerby in 1856.

Montego Bay in the 1820s, from James Hakewill's *A Picturesque Tour of the Island of Jamaica*. The uncultivated islands dotting the bay belonged to the Bogue estate. This engraving was probably coloured by someone who had never seen the dazzling azure waters of the Caribbean.

Kingston in the early nineteenth century. Above, the
intersection of Harbour Street and King Street, a block
back from the wharves. Below, the view from the parish
church, overlooking the parade ground – the gravestone
of John Atkinson, who died in 1798, is likely among
those shown. Nowadays the parade is a public park,
while the churchyard is a parking lot.

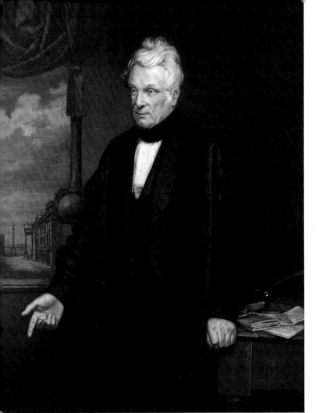

John Clayton in 1862. His black clothes, and documents tied with pink ribbon, indicate his legal profession. The backdrop of Grey Street alludes to the transformation of Newcastle while he was town clerk. The photograph of the garden front of Chesters, below, dates from around this time.

The hall at Chesters, following its makeover by Norman Shaw, photographed for *Country Life* in 1912. The portraits on either side of the fireplace show Nathaniel and Dorothy Clayton – I wish I knew where they are now.

My great-grandparents Jock and Connie Atkinson on leave from India in 1896. By this time their three children – George, Jack and Biddy – were at boarding schools in England, and saw little of their parents.

My grandfather Jack Atkinson, right, with his second cousin Dick Atkinson at Bamburgh, Northumberland, in about 1912. Dick would many years later send Jack the cardboard box full of old family letters that kick-started my research for this book.

The King's House in Spanish Town, Jamaica. This grand building was gutted by fire in 1925; its brick façade and portico are all that is left.

The remains of Richard 'Rum' Atkinson's sugar estates. The Bogue, right, is now an affluent suburb of Montego Bay, with clipped bushes and manicured lawns. The sugar works at Dean's Valley, below, has been much plundered for its dressed stone, and is fast being overtaken by bush; a cast-iron boiler nestles in the rampant vegetation.

– and nothing would expose this delusional side of Richard's character more starkly than the terms of his will.[3]

And so the lawsuits rumbled on. George Atkinson and Nathaniel Clayton went down to London together in April 1801, taking rooms at a hotel just off the Haymarket. Nathaniel was occupied by Newcastle-related parliamentary bills, while George attended to Jamaican business, but they also found time to meet some claimants to the Atkinson estate. (Though they did not see two of the main legatees – Lady Anne Barnard was in Africa, while a dinner with John Robinson at Sion Hill was repeatedly postponed.) In early June, the brothers-in-law headed north again. 'I was very much surprised to learn this Morning, that Mr. Atkinson and Mr. Clayton had left London,' William Duncan, the lawyer representing the Mures' creditors, told Robinson. 'I am told that they have for several years past (*when in London*) made professions of wishing for an Amicable Adjustment of these Concerns, but, have always gone off, as they have now done without coming to any decision.'[4]

'I am very sorry that you have not considered my letters of the 8th July & 26th October sufficiently explicit of my sentiments,' George would write to Robinson in January 1802, as he yet again defended his and the Atkinson family's position. The Mures' claim that their late partner had deliberately deprived them of the government loan stock to which they were entitled, and had instead shared it out among his friends, was particularly offensive, given its innuendo of fraud; while their attempts to claw back losses sustained by their own Jamaican plantations in the sixteen years since Richard's death were quite intolerable. 'Let the account between my uncle and his surviving Partners be divested of those charges which have been created long subsequent to the Period when his interest in the Business terminated,' George insisted. 'Unless that is done, however painful to my feelings, I own I cannot see a Probability of the Affairs being settled elsewhere than in the Court of Chancery.'[5] The Atkinsons' strategy was to play for time; whereas for John Robinson, time was running out. He would die at his constituency of Harwich on 23 December 1802, aged seventy-five.

IN JAMAICA, the first weeks of General Nugent's governorship were marked by parades and parties in his honour. Before dawn on 2 October 1801, the Nugents rose and dressed by candlelight; the fireflies covered the walls of their chamber at the King's House with 'gold spangles'. At 4 a.m. they set out for Kingston, where Maria Nugent alighted at Matt Atkinson's house on North Street; here she would spend an awkward couple of hours while her husband reviewed the 69th Regiment. 'Mr. A. made grand efforts to amuse me,' she told her diary. 'The mountain wind, the sea breeze, slaves, plantations, and the prices of different articles, were the edifying topics, till a little after 7, when breakfast made its appearance, and Mr. A.'s spirits were relieved by the appearance of Mrs. Pye, who came to offer her services, hearing that I was in Kingston. Poor man, he seemed very happy, so was I.' That evening, Matt hosted a reception attended by 'half Kingston and Port Royal' – aside from the eye-catching Mrs Nugent, no ladies were present.[6]

William Pitt had resigned as prime minister in March 1801 after seventeen years in office. Henry Addington's ministry made peace with France its first priority, and signed a preliminary treaty on 1 October. Napoleon Bonaparte decided to take this opportunity to reassert control over the wayward colony of Saint Domingue, notifying the British of his intention to send out a large army commanded by his brother-in-law, General Charles Leclerc. In defiance of Napoleon's orders, Toussaint Louverture had recently invaded the neighbouring Spanish colony of Santo Domingo and drawn up a constitution that guaranteed equal treatment for all races. In Jamaica, where the 'Black General' had once provoked derision, he now commanded a good deal of respect. On 21 October, the Nugents attended a dinner for Edward Corbet, the British agent in Saint Domingue, at which Matt Atkinson was also a guest. Toussaint was the subject of much conversation around the table. 'He must be a wonderful man,' Maria Nugent wrote afterwards, 'and I really do believe intended for very good purposes.'[7]

Following the peace treaty with France, General Nugent received instructions to behave with strict neutrality towards Saint

Domingue. 'Toussaint's Black Empire is one, amongst many evils, that has grown out of the War, and it is by no means our Interest to prevent its Annihilation,' wrote Lord Hobart, the Secretary of State for War and the Colonies.[8] French troops began landing in Saint Domingue in January 1802; soon General Leclerc had gained control of the south of the colony. On 6 May, Toussaint rode into the northern port of Cap-Français, where he negotiated an amnesty. What he did not know, however, was that Leclerc had secret orders to deport all black officers from Saint Domingue.

Within weeks, Toussaint had been tricked into arrest, and exiled to a fortress in the remote Jura mountains of eastern France. Toussaint's inglorious fate unleashed a fresh wave of violent resistance against the French by the black rebels – but mosquitoes would prove a still deadlier enemy. 'The French troops are dying very fast,' Matt Atkinson wrote on 28 June. 'It is supposed they have not more than 5,000 Men fit for service at this time.'[9]

General Leclerc now fixed upon a strategy of genocide. 'We must destroy all of the blacks in the mountains – men and women – and spare only the children under 12 years of age,' he wrote to Napoleon on 7 October. 'We must destroy half of those in the plains and must not leave a single coloured person in the colony who has worn an épaulette.'[10] But Leclerc would not see through this murderous plan, as he died from yellow fever three weeks later. Napoleon continued to send reinforcements to Saint Domingue until May 1803, by which time France and Britain were once again at war. The French army finally capitulated to the rebels six months later, and on 1 January 1804, General Jean-Jacques Dessalines proclaimed Saint Domingue the independent Republic of Haiti. One of the new president's first acts was to order the extermination of all remaining Frenchmen and women. His death squads went from house to house, killing entire families with knives and bayonets. 'Dessalines arrived here on Friday afternoon last and turned loose 400 to 500 blood thirsty villains on the poor defenceless Inhabitants,' wrote one Englishman in Port-au-Prince. 'I had five in my house & it gives me great pain to think I was not able to save a single one of them.'[11]

The bloodshed in Saint Domingue would have momentous consequences for the United States. In 1802, in a secret treaty with Spain, Napoleon had acquired the Louisiana Territory, a vast tract stretching from New Orleans into present-day Canada – approximately 827,000 square miles. But as the French army lost its sway in Saint Domingue, Napoleon realized that this American landholding might prove a liability during a future war with Britain – so instead he decided to sell it to the US for $15 million, or three cents per acre. The deal was concluded on 30 April 1803; at a stroke, the US had doubled in size.

To finance the transaction, the US Treasury turned to Barings, their banking agents in London; and Sir Francis Baring enlisted the assistance of Hope & Co. of Amsterdam. It was these businessmen who would actually purchase the Louisiana Territory from Napoleon; they would then transfer the land to the US in return for bonds, to be repaid over fifteen years. 'We *all* tremble about the magnitude of the American account,' Baring wrote to one of his sons-in-law, a partner at Hope & Co.[12] Henry Addington subsequently asked Baring to desist from 'being party to any remittances to France' on account of the Louisiana Purchase; but it seems the prime minister's plea was in vain, for the French government would receive its final tranche of gold coin, as scheduled, in April 1804.[13]

MATT ATKINSON, who would be thirty-five in 1804, was a reluctant pen-pusher. 'My Health thank God is very good, but I have at present a good deal of extra work on hand which will occupy me during every spare hour I have till the end of the Year, this consists in examining three large transcribed deed Books with the Mutilated Records from the Secretary's Office,' he wrote to brother George on 11 March. 'I assure you while I do not care for labour I have been pretty well used to it for some years past.'[14] The *Jamaica Almanac* for 1802 lists nine public offices under Matt's name – Island Secretary, Agent General, Commissary General, Notary Public, Clerk of the Council, Clerk of the Court of Ordinary, Assistant Judge for Hanover, Magistrate for Surrey and Collector of Customs at

Kingston – and they kept him disagreeably desk-bound. Although Matt remained Governor Nugent's Agent General, there was no warmth between the two men. The value of the government business, while still substantial, had fallen off since the turbulent 1790s; the largest contract was to provision the troops stationed on the island, which steadily turned over around £100,000 a year for the Kingston house.

Since the establishment of the West India Regiments in 1795, the British government had come to rely upon slave labour for the defence of the sugar islands to such an extent that it had become the largest single buyer of Africans; more than thirteen thousand enslaved men would be drafted over twelve years, often straight off slave ships. Many of these dealings were carried out by the governor of Jamaica through his Agent General – to give one example, in order to finance the purchase of 180 men for the 5th West India Regiment at £90 and £95 per capita in January 1804, the Kingston house was obliged to draw 'very largely' on Barings in London.[15]

Matt's disenchantment with his life as a colonial bureaucrat was deepened by the unnerving conduct of his partners. The main mercantile priority of the Kingston house had shifted to the collection of debts, and Hugh Cathcart's favoured approach was to pursue everything through the courts. 'There are several debts which I am sure he is making worse, but I cannot help myself,' Matt wrote to George. 'I am sorry to trouble you on this but if you could by any means prevail on him to go home, it would be of service to us all, if it cannot be accomplished I will do the best I can, but my nerves are not so strong as they once were, to enable me to meet his arguments, which God knows are curious.'[16] Matt would soon conclude that Cathcart was 'not perfect in his upper storey', after his partner ordered the senior clerk of the house to concentrate on transcribing articles about the execution of the French spy, Isaac Sasportas, even though the Barings accounts were three months overdue. 'If there was any good to be attained by what he is doing I am sure I would support it with all my power,' wrote Matt, 'but what he has done and is doing is not of the value of an old Newspaper.'[17]

In February 1804, Matt was suddenly called to the Dean's Valley estate after the death of its overseer by poisoning. While their partner was busy in Westmoreland, John Hanbury and Hugh Cathcart quietly purchased a cargo of two hundred enslaved Africans and had them shipped onwards to South Carolina. 'I rather think they will burn their fingers,' Matt wrote to George when he heard about this venture. 'They took care not to write me on this subject, or indeed any other when I was absent which was three weeks.'[18] When George received Matt's letter, in Newcastle, seven weeks later, he immediately forwarded it to Sir Francis Baring. 'It appears,' he wrote in his covering note, 'that the Spirit of Speculation is reviving.'[19]

MICHAEL ATKINSON, the eldest of Bridget's three living sons, would sail back to England in the spring of 1804, after twenty-two years in Bengal. Nabobs, as returning East India Company servants were labelled, were expected to bring back tidy fortunes with them, and Michael would prove no exception. Even so, his homecoming would turn out to be a sad business – a world away from the joyful reunion of which his 71-year-old mother had dreamed.

Towards the end of May, Bridget spotted a newspaper announcement that the *Earl Howe* Indiaman had docked in London with a 'Mr. and Mrs. Atkinson' on board – this was the first she had heard not only of Michael's return, but also of his having a wife.[20] She immediately wrote, warmly welcoming him home – and heard not a word in reply. Meanwhile, rumours of Michael's domestic arrangements soon reached Temple Sowerby. Mary Hasell of nearby Dalemain had heard that Michael had a 'Large Family of Black Children' – news which 'very much shocked' his mother. ('I told her if it was so I hoped he would leave them all in the country and provide for them there.') Another neighbour, Edward Lamb, an East India Company captain, revealed that Michael had a longstanding white consort, Sophia Mackereth, who was thought originally to have gone out to India 'as a Mistress to Lord Cornwallis'.[21]

The reason for Michael's bizarre behaviour soon came to light. It seemed that some opportunistic lawyer – no doubt anticipating years of litigation ahead – had managed to persuade him that brother George had stolen the Jamaican estates which Michael believed, as his uncle Richard's eldest nephew and heir-at-law, to be rightfully his. 'Now nothing can be further from the truth but he is gone to Law with George about your Uncle's effects,' Bridget wrote to Matt in Jamaica. 'However he has not taken the smallest notice of any of our Letters and to think how many sleepless nights his Long absence has caused me it is almost too hard to bear.' Most hurtful of all, for Bridget, was the discovery that she had a fifteen-year-old granddaughter who for the past five years had been resident at an establishment for young ladies near London: 'If Michael had thought proper to have acquainted me with his sending over a Daughter I really would have seen after her but I knew nothing about her till this year.'[22]

Dorothy Clayton travelled down to London in June, hopeful of making her brother see sense, but was repeatedly refused entry to his residence in Welbeck Street. Following the failure of Dorothy's mission, Bridget decided to make a rare visit to the capital. 'I will see the worthless woman if I can will see his unfortunate Daughter for what must she be brought up under such a Mother,' she told Matt. 'I will endeavour to purchase his Estate at Temple Sowerby and get him to change his name and go out to India again. In short he has disappointed all my hopes and made me very unhappy.'[23] But Bridget's intervention also miscarried – for Michael had given his servants strict instructions to turn his elderly mother away from the door.

Michael was not the only one of Bridget's sons with a shadowy private life. Around this time, in Jamaica, Matt received a letter from youngest sister Jane about a secret matter concerning the precious memory of their brother John. 'George gave me a piece of Intelligence,' she wrote, 'that poor John had left a Child in Jamaica to whom he requested one Thousand Pounds might be given; will you my dear Matt inform me what became of the Child.'[24] She asked Matt not to address his reply to Temple Sowerby, but instead to the house of their sister Bridget, who had lately married Henry Tulip, a 'very rich' Northumberland squire whose Fallowfield estate ran alongside Nathaniel Clayton's at Chesters.[25] Such intrigue was necessary since letters from Jamaica were considered family property and passed widely around – which perhaps explains why so relatively few of them have survived.

Matt was able to confirm the existence of a child – a boy – who had been born on 8 April 1799, seven months after John's death, and christened in the parish church at Kingston. His mother was a free woman of colour called Emilie Peychiera, identified on the child's baptism records as a 'mestee' – but where she came from, and whether she was even alive by this stage, is an enigma.[26] Her name suggests that she may have been an émigrée from Saint Domingue.

What Matt did not care to reveal – and one assumes his mother and sisters never found out – was that he had several children of his own scattered around Jamaica. There was Sarah Atkinson, the daughter of Charlotte Wright, who was four when she was baptized at Kingston on 19 December 1802.[27] Matt had already released Charlotte from slavery three years earlier, along with 'her two female Quadroon Children named Betsey and Sally'; he must have been fond of them, for it cost rather more to free an enslaved person than it did to purchase one.[28] (Under Jamaican law, a former slave received an annual allowance of £5 currency, paid out by the authorities on behalf of the former owner; so it was only once Matt had deposited £300 currency with the Kingston churchwardens that the manumission of Charlotte, Betsey and Sally was complete.) Then there was William Atkinson, a 'Mulatto child' born to an unnamed enslaved woman, and christened at Kingston on 12 March 1801.[29] But Matt's most enduring relationship in Jamaica was with Janet Bogle, a freeborn 'quadroon' woman who lived with him in Kingston.[30] Janet turned sixteen a few weeks before the birth of their first child, Bridget Atkinson, on 2 October 1800.[31] (One can only wonder what the child's grandmother would have made of her namesake.) A second daughter, Janet, was born on 18 March 1803.[32] Although it is impossible to verify – some parish records do not display the names of white fathers alongside those of black mothers, while it is also probable that these offspring would never have been baptized – it seems likely that Matt had still more children on estates in the west of the island.

Reprehensible though it may sound, Matt's conduct was quite ordinary on an island where white men viewed enslaved women as sexual prey, and openly kept free women of colour as mistresses. 'Almost every householder, for few of them are married, keeps his *miss*, without being at all thought guilty of any breach of morality or decorum,' wrote an observer of Jamaican life. These 'housekeepers', as they were euphemistically known, were expected to perform 'all the duties of a wife, except that of presiding at table'.[33] The colony's richest planter, Simon Taylor, never married, but was reputed to have large families on each of his various estates. Maria Nugent described a visit to the Taylor residence at Liguanea where, as was often the case, she found herself the only woman at dinner. 'When I left the gentlemen,' she wrote, 'I took tea in my own room, surrounded by the black, brown and yellow ladies of the house, and heard a great deal of its private history.'[34]

The Anglican church abetted such racial prejudice through the precision with which it logged the heritage of non-white mothers. The status of a black or mixed-race child born in Jamaica, whether free or enslaved, was inherited from its mother, which explains why the labels 'mulatto', 'quadroon' and 'mestee' are littered throughout the island's baptismal records. The word 'mulatto' was used to describe the child of a white man and a woman of pure African blood; 'quadroon' the child of a white man and a 'mulatto' woman; 'mestee' the child of a white man and a 'quadroon' woman. Beyond this point lay what the historian Bryan Edwards, writing in 1793, described as the 'boundary which the Law has drawn between the perfect white and the Man of Colour'.[35] The child of a white man and a 'mestee' woman, separated by three generations from the pure African blood of his or her maternal great-great-grandmother, was deemed 'competent' to enjoy the full range of civic privileges.[36] Since Emilie Peychiera was a 'mestee', this meant that her son – John Atkinson's son – was, legally speaking, white.

MICHAEL'S HOSTILITY towards the rest of the Atkinson family only grew during the months following his return from India. He began especially to fixate on his brother-in-law Nathaniel Clayton's role in the 'theft' of his late uncle's Jamaican property, nicknaming him 'Murphy', after a crooked lawyer in Henry Fielding's novel *Amelia* who was hanged for the forgery of a will.

In September 1804, Matt received not one, but *three* copies of a seemingly deranged letter from his eldest brother; it had been sent to Jamaica in triplicate to ensure that no mishap would prevent its arrival. Michael had written:

> I shall not at present enter into a most disgusting, but true
> detail to deprive me of the fair course of the service in India,
> and to prevent me from ever having it in my power to return
> to England. I shall not state this to you, but I do purge myself
> for ever from the family, and I might lay before you, a train of
> circumstances, fully proving the wish of my nearest relations
> for my death, which, horrible as the reflection is, it is
> nevertheless true. My great bane has been the connection with
> that unparalleled villain, Murphy the Newcastle Attorney. This
> detestable miscreant has long ago placed himself at the head of
> my family; and, literally, converted my father's house into a den
> of thieves. Now, Matthew, I put you to the test: I admit of no
> medium between you and this miscreant attorney, whose name
> is infamy, and whose touch is pollution. You must either adhere
> to him, or to me; I leave you to chuse; and, unless I hear from
> you by the first opportunity after receiving this, I shall consider
> you as Murphy's man.[37]

Mild-mannered Matt answered the letter in neutral language; he also forwarded a copy to his hot-tempered brother George.

By now, Matt was preparing to return to England. Bridget wrote to him at Christmas – she was on remarkably cheerful form, given that Michael had recently threatened to sue her for a larger share of his father's estate than he had already received. Bridget's letters

tend to flit between topics, which makes them somewhat hard to
edit, but here's an extract:

> I am exceeding anxious about you if you come home the
> dangers of the seas and the desire of seeing you will make me
> equally uneasy. I beg you will if you can Let me know how
> much you have made to come home with I wish to know and
> if you do I will not say a word about your affairs to any one.
> I have settled my own so far as that none of you can be plagued
> with Michael I also beg you will send me his Letter to you or
> a coppy of it. You must if you come away consider poor Black
> Thomas Leave him as happy as you possibly can. I disire you
> will my Dear Matthew Look over John's papers and Letters
> and see if there be any Letters from Michael or any coppies of
> Letters from John: to him he hinges a great deal of his Mallice
> on a Letter John wrote him from Jamaica. If John ever did write
> any such Letter it is Strainge but I hope it is only an excuse
> in Michael to cover with some degree of plausibility his
> wonderfull behaviour to us all. It certainly was not John who
> has influenced his mind to this excessive degree no it was some
> Serpent in England that has wrote to him who it is most Likely
> I shall never know but you may & whoever it may be mark
> them as Long as you Live, however it has not had a very bad
> effect on me for I have had the best Health I have had for some
> years past.[38]

Bridget's reference to 'poor Black Thomas' is particularly tantalizing, since there are so few mentions of enslaved individuals in the
family correspondence – but who Thomas was, and what became of
him, must remain a mystery. Her letter would have reached Matt
only just before he left Jamaica, for he arrived at Temple Sowerby on
30 April 1805, suffering from a chill after three days and two nights
spent in the mail coach from Falmouth.

We know that another, much younger member of the Atkinson
family made the same voyage from the West Indies to Westmorland

that spring, for within Bridget's household accounts is listed a payment of £1 16s 4d, made to a Miss Monkhouse for 'bringing the Boy'.[39] John Atkinson's six-year-old son would be raised by his grandmother and aunt at Temple Sowerby. Although the child's baptismal name was John, the family always called him James.

MICHAEL ATKINSON had for so long believed himself to be the chief beneficiary of his rich uncle's bounty that he could only assume skulduggery when he found this not to be the case. However, he failed to follow through his threats to have his uncle's will exposed as the forgery of 'Murphy the Newcastle Attorney', muttering darkly that he was unable to find a lawyer who was prepared to act against another member of the profession.[40] After a year of putting up with this nonsense, Nathaniel would tolerate his brother-in-law's slurs no more, and he sued for libel, basing his lawsuit on Michael's infamous letter to Matt.

The case of *Clayton v Atkinson* came before the Lord Chief Justice, Lord Ellenborough, at Guildhall on 6 March 1806; each brother-in-law was represented by one of the most famous silks of the day. Nathaniel's barrister, William Garrow, opened by stating that his client had been forced with great reluctance to bring the action, because by neglecting to do so he would have surrendered his character for life. 'A more malignant diabolical composition the arch-fiend of hell could never have prepared,' he observed of Michael's letter. 'I charge on the Defendant, black, poisonous, destructive malice. The libel now complained of was not uttered in the heat of conversation; it was gravely prepared in the form of a letter, and not the irritation of a moment.' Matt was present in court, and he confirmed the letter to be in his eldest brother's handwriting. Sir Francis Baring next took the stand, and gave warm testimony of Nathaniel's 'great propriety as a lawyer', and of the affection he had shown towards the Atkinson family.[41]

Robert Dallas, defending Michael, conceded that the letter had been defamatory, but described it as the natural expression of his client's disappointment on finding the estates of his uncle, from which he had expected to derive a 'princely fortune', so tied up in litigation. Dallas ridiculed Nathaniel for having brought this family argument before a court of law, and chastised Matt for having circulated what ought to have remained a private communication: 'He should either have committed the letter itself to the flames, or should have concealed it for ever from observation.' But Lord Ellenborough dismissed Dallas's suggestion that Michael's conduct had been a 'sort of temporary insanity'; he judged that a libel had taken place, and instructed the men of the jury, in assessing the damages, to weigh up the 'insult' and 'vexation' suffered by the plaintiff.[42] In a very public blow to Michael's standing, they ordered him to pay the considerable sum of £1,000.

MATT HAD BEEN ENGAGED to Ann Littledale for the whole of the twelve years that he had spent in Jamaica. 'Marry in haste, repent at leisure' was not a proverb that would apply to this particular couple. Poor Ann – with every year that Matt failed to return from the West Indies, her fear of abandonment increased. During the summer of 1804, when Ann was thirty-two years old, she and her mother Mary had chosen, in what appears to have been a desperate attempt to forge a stronger alliance between their families, to visit the Derbyshire spa town of Buxton while they knew that Bridget and Jane Atkinson would also be there. At the time, Jane had written with characteristic bluntness to Matt:

> I must say that I think Ann is too expecting. Every Assurance
> has been given to her that the moment you come to this
> Country & make her your Wife that every kind of respect shall
> be shown her, in the mean while it is uncomfortable to all
> parties, we cannot acknowledge the engagement & Ann does
> not seem satisfied with my Mother treating her as kindly as she
> would any other young Lady. But my Mother cannot consider
> her as one of the family till your return, the rest is all Romance
> & making difficulties where none exist, you need not be under
> any apprehension of loosing the Lady, there is no probability

of her having any offer at all equal to Yourself. Therefore treat
the Matter coolly, it will make you of far more Consequence
& the Lady less expecting.[43]

But before he could make good on his pledge to marry Ann, Matt
would have to draw his Jamaican affairs to a conclusion. The winding
up of Atkinsons, Hanbury & Co., which followed his departure from
the island in the spring of 1805, was marred by disputes between
the partners. George eventually agreed to buy out his younger
brother's share of the Kingston house for £20,000, for Matt had
left behind large personal debts, and had no intention of returning
there. Shortly afterwards, George entered into a new partnership
with George Bogle. They would advance the capital for a merchant
house – to be called Atkinson, Bogle & Co. – while Robert Robertson and Edward Adams, two clerks of the former house, would run
the office in Kingston.

Bridget had always cherished hopes that Matt would settle down
at Temple Sowerby, but instead he chose to move to Newcastle,
where family business connections meant his prospects were considerably brighter. One day in November 1806, he set out from the
Claytons' townhouse for the Cumberland coast, with the purpose of
fulfilling a promise 'too long delayed'.[44] On 1 December, he and Ann
were married at the church of St Nicholas in Whitehaven.

A brief postscript – and it may seem churlish to mention this,
so soon after the happy nuptials – but Robert Robertson wrote
to Matt from Jamaica a few weeks later with news of his former
'housekeeper'. Following Matt's departure from the island, Janet
Bogle had given birth to another girl, whom she called Bridget –
one can only assume that her firstborn Bridget had died in infancy.[45]
Now Robertson informed Matt that Janet had 'lost another of her
little ones' – which one, he did not say – and that he had recently
stopped her allowance, on account of her having gone 'to live with
Dr. Crosbie'. Janet had since returned various items of furniture
and plate to the Atkinson residence in Kingston's North Street, and
Robertson had decided 'upon maturer consideration' not to give her

money to buy replacements. 'I now think that you have done already quite enough for her,' he told Matt, 'and shall therefore not say a word more on the subject.'[46]

DURING THE 1790s, while the British sugar islands prospered and Saint Domingue was torn apart by racial violence, the movement to abolish the slave trade had lost impetus; even to many sympathizers, the introduction of a measure that would risk the safety of these fruitful imperial possessions seemed ill-advised. Since the turn of the century, however, with the price of sugar in free fall, the campaigners had felt the argument shift again in their favour; for the planters' strategy of maximum cane production enabled by bottomless imports of enslaved Africans no longer made commercial sense.

William Pitt returned to Downing Street in May 1804 after three years out of office. A Wilberforce-sponsored bill for the abolition of the slave trade sailed through the Commons the following month, but arrived at the upper house too late in the parliamentary session to complete its legislative passage. Unfortunately, when Wilberforce brought back the same bill in February 1805, the pro-slavery lobby was this time fully primed, and it failed to pass even the lower house.

Pitt's second ministry would be short-lived, for he died on 23 January 1806, aged forty-six, probably from a stomach ulcer aggravated by his fondness for port. His cousin Lord Grenville, a determined abolitionist, immediately formed the government that would be known as the 'Ministry of All the Talents', which embraced figures from across the political spectrum. Wilberforce's brother-in-law, the lawyer James Stephen, came up with an ingenious new plan for the abolition campaign. Stephen, who had lived in Barbados, knew that French planters in the West Indies relied almost exclusively on British slave ships for their labour supply, such was the national domination of the trade. His scheme was to introduce legislation that would prevent British subjects from trafficking slaves to the colonies of France and its allies. Dressed up as a patriotic blow against the interests of a detested enemy, the bill proved uncontentious. On 23 May 1806 it passed into law, at a stroke criminalizing more than half the British slave trade.

Now it was time to finish the job. At the start of the next parliamentary session, Grenville decided to invert the usual procedure by placing Wilberforce's bill first before the House of Lords, where it passed easily; next it went before the Commons. The bill came up for its second reading on 23 February 1807. After ten hours of debate, the House divided; it passed by 283 votes against sixteen. Wilberforce received a rare standing ovation, but was too overwhelmed to take it all in. Four weeks later, Grenville wrapped up the committee stage of the bill by congratulating his colleagues on the completion of 'one of the most glorious acts' ever performed by 'any assembly of any nation in the world'.[47]

The Abolition of the Slave Trade Act, which came into force on 1 January 1808, would outlaw the transatlantic trade, but not slavery itself. No slave would be set free as a result of the legislation; around 750,000 men, women and children would remain enslaved in the British West Indies, more than 300,000 of them in Jamaica alone. Even so, the planters saw themselves as wronged parties, and resigned themselves to ruin. 'I do now consider that all property is now annihilated in the Islands and that every person who has lent his Money or Creditt to them must look upon it to be lost,' wrote Simon Taylor, as news of the bill arrived in Jamaica. 'For my part after this Year I never mean to plant a Cane.'[48]

NINETEEN

End of an Era

NEWCASTLE'S PRE-EMINENCE as a coal town dated back hundreds of years, for the exposed seams of the combustible rock that were found along the River Tyne could be extracted and shipped with far greater ease than deposits deeper inland. The local abundance of coal in turn caused manufactories, foundries, breweries and refineries to proliferate along the lower reaches of the river. The works of the Tyne Iron Company was situated on its north bank, four miles upstream from Newcastle; Nathaniel Clayton and George Atkinson had between them purchased nine of the company's twenty shares in 1803, following a bank failure that ruined its founding proprietors, and they had since ploughed much capital into developing the 'very extensive' eleven-acre site.[1] But George soon bemoaned his investment, blaming Nathaniel for some alarmingly large outgoings. 'The very heavy Debt of Obligation which I must ever owe to Mr. Clayton, will I trust plead my Apology for engaging therein at his Suggestion and Request,' he told Sir Francis Baring in February 1805.[2]

To the company's broad quays at Lemington, the ebb and flow of each tide brought fresh supplies of ironstone, arriving by sloop from nearby coastal beds, and carried away the 'ships anchors, chains, spades, shovels, nails, steel, edge tools, files, and all kinds of domestic utensils' produced at the ironworks.[3] The coal came by waggon from Wylam Colliery, five miles away, dragged by horses along

Coal is loaded into ships on the banks of the Tyne.

iron rails – but these four-legged beasts would soon be usurped by locomotives, for 'Puffing Billy', the world's first commercial steam engine to move along 'simply by its friction against the rail road', would be built in 1813 specifically for the purpose of hauling coal from Wylam to the docks at Lemington.[4]

The Tyne Iron Company's two blast furnaces, blown by vast bellows coupled to Boulton & Watt Double Power 32 Horse steam engines, disgorged around sixty tons of red-hot pig iron each week, ready for moulding and beating into shape. The buildings at the works also included a casting house; a forge with seven puddling furnaces and a relentless engine-driven hammer and anvil; a rolling mill for making plate iron, bars and rods; a boring and turning mill for the manufacture of cannon and cylinders; joiners' and smiths' shops; twenty-eight ovens for baking coke; eleven kilns for roasting ironstone; a manager's residence and forty-three workers' dwellings. The ironworks presented an infernal sight at night, when the 'curling flames' that darted upwards from the 'numerous furnaces' were said to give the 'appearance of a city on fire'.[5]

Matt Atkinson had returned from the West Indies with insufficient wealth to slip into the leisured mode of existence that would no doubt have suited him best; and so it was decided (primarily by his brother George and brother-in-law Nathaniel) that he would run

the head office of the Tyne Iron Company on Newcastle's Quayside. Thus Matt and Ann settled down to their new life in the town,
lodging with the Claytons for the time being. 'It is a great Satisfaction to me, if I have any way contributed to your Son Matthew's
Happiness,' Nathaniel would tell Bridget on 6 January 1807. 'I derive
also much Satisfaction from the strong hope I entertain that he has
married a sensible, well informed & well disposed woman.'[6] Later
that spring, Matt agreed to buy three of his brothers' shares in the
company for £18,000, a bargain which, while consuming nearly his
entire capital, put his holding on an equal footing to theirs. So sincere were Matt's feelings of gratitude towards both men that when
Ann gave birth to a first child at Westgate Street, in April 1808, they
named him George Clayton Atkinson.

SOON AFTER HIS public humiliation in the law courts at the
hands of his brother-in-law, Michael Atkinson had taken the lease on
67 Portland Place, an imposing townhouse in Marylebone. Michael
was also looking to buy a fine country residence; a newspaper
advertisement for the Mount Mascal estate near Bexley, thirteen
miles south-east of London, caught his eye in April 1808. The property comprised a 'capital' Jacobean mansion 'suitable for a family of
the first distinction', positioned on a 'bold but gentle ascent' within
a landscaped park of fifty acres, surrounded by nearly five hundred
acres of woods, meadow, pasture and arable.[7] With fifteen bedrooms,
the house was perhaps slightly larger than necessary – any smaller,
however, and it might not have been able to accommodate Michael's
bruised dignity.

Various members of the family had reason to gravitate towards
London during the spring of 1809. Nathaniel, who was called there
on legal business – 'a ship cause of considerable Importance' – went
down with Dorothy, who renewed old friendships and fulfilled shopping commissions while he attended court.[8] Jane's trip to the capital
was precipitated by a love affair – not one of her own, it should
be said, but involving her nineteen-year-old niece Sophia, Michael's
daughter, who had passed much of the previous winter at Temple

Sowerby. Sophia was a beautiful, nervous young woman, and viewed by her close relatives with a good deal of pity. ('The tempers of both her Parents were so remarkably bad & Mrs. A never by any accident a day sober,' Jane later recalled, 'that any human being would have felt for a Girl so situated.')[9] The details are obscure, but it seems that while she was up north, Sophia formed an intense attachment to an unidentified suitor. Her father, however, flatly prohibited the match. Jane came south with Sophia in March, hoping to promote her niece's cause. Three months later she returned to Temple Sowerby, her hopes frustrated; Michael remained as 'bitterly averse' to his daughter's marriage as ever.[10]

George continued to make frequent visits to London, where the Mures and their creditors still held the Atkinson estate under siege; as one of his late uncle's executors, he was often needed at the Inns of Court. The Lords of the Treasury, meanwhile, having belatedly discovered the degree to which the merchant house of Atkinson, Mure & Bogle had enriched itself through the occupation of Haiti in the 1790s, were intent on clawing back the 'double Commission' which had arisen from the army's expenses first passing through George Bogle's books in Port-au-Prince, then George Atkinson's in Kingston, before being settled with Sir Francis Baring in London.[11] When the West India Commissioners investigated, they found insufficient grounds to support the Treasury's case, but their Lordships would not let the matter rest.

Baring was by now an old man, and very deaf, but his mind remained perfectly agile. He had officially retired from business in 1803, leaving the great merchant house which he had built from scratch in the hands of his sons Thomas, Alexander and Henry. Baring's favourite recreation during his dotage was making improvements to Stratton, the Hampshire estate he had purchased from the Duke of Bedford in 1801, and filling the mansion with old master paintings. His standards were high and his pockets deep; only the works of Rembrandt, Rubens and Van Dyck tempted him, he would tell his son-in-law, 'and the first must not be too dark, nor the second indecent'.[12] He rarely passed up the opportunity to acquire local landed property. As one wit remarked: 'Sir Francis Baring is extending his purchases so largely in Hampshire, that he soon expects to be able to inclose the county within his own park paling.'[13]

When business brought him to town, Baring lived at the Manor House at Lee, near Lewisham, and it was here that he died, in September 1810, aged seventy. 'Few men understood the real interests of trade better,' wrote his obituarist in the *Gentleman's Magazine*. 'He was unquestionably the first merchant in Europe; first in knowledge and talents, and first in character and opulence.'[14] Sir Thomas Baring, who inherited the Lee residence, rented it out following his father's death. George and Susan Atkinson, who had been searching for a house close to the capital, were the first tenants; their ninth child, Harriet, was born there in February 1811.

AFTER TWO YEARS living at Westgate Street, Matt and Ann finally bought a home of their own in 1809. Carr Hill House, built in the 1760s, had originally operated as an asylum 'for the reception of *lunaticks*, in easy, genteel or opulent circumstances'; it was located two miles south of Newcastle, on the edge of Gateshead Fell, a dark, wild moor pockmarked with pits and quarries, and notorious for its highwaymen, cutpurses and ruffians.[15] Carr Hill village, on a breezy summit nearly five hundred feet above sea level, commanded views in all directions. The area was studded with windmills, including one in Matt and Ann's fifteen-acre grounds. They shared a love of the outdoors, and their large garden would prove a 'great source of amusement to them both'.[16]

This was an unpretentious district; the Atkinsons' new neighbours included corn millers, nurserymen, quarrymen, earthenware manufacturers, a flint glass maker and a fire brick maker. Matt would forge an especially close friendship with John Hodgson, the vicar of the next village, who was primarily a writer – indeed, some years earlier he had turned down a job at the Tyne Iron Company since he wished 'to pursue a literary, rather than a mercantile life'.[17] On 29 April 1811, shortly after the publisher of the popular 'Beauties of England and Wales' series commissioned Hodgson to compile the volume devoted to the county of Westmorland, he and Matt set out from Carr Hill on a brisk, sodden tramp across the Pennines for the purposes of researching the book. Two days later, groping at times through 'thick dark mist', they reached the top of Dun Fell, where they rewarded themselves with their first glimpse of Westmorland and a late breakfast. 'In a miner's shop we had our beef and bread and some excellent rum and water – rum made in Jamaica by Mr. A. nine years since,' wrote Hodgson.[18]

That afternoon they strode into Temple Sowerby, where they found spring several weeks ahead of the east side of the Pennines, and Bridget's garden in a flourishing state: 'Mrs. Atkinson has apricots against a common stone wall as large as pigeon eggs, and the foliage of the trees is nearly in perfection, except on the oaks and ashes.' Hodgson greatly admired Bridget's library, her collections of Roman and Saxon coins, and her shells gathered from around the globe. He was equally impressed by her continuing stamina. 'Mrs. Atkinson, although 78 years old, is up every morning at six o'clock, a practice that she and her children have always pursued, as recommended as the very best preservative of health,' he told his wife. 'Never, she says, let any person, on any consideration whatever, take a second sleep.'[19]

Now that she was in her late seventies, Bridget might have put her feet up and passed the day-to-day running of the house over to Jane, but she remained cheerfully hands-on. The book of 'receipts' which she had started compiling for Dorothy in January 1806 suggests that her knowledge of cookery was based upon a lifetime of practical experience; it also demonstrates her attachment to her eldest daughter, and the love of good food they shared. Bridget and Dorothy often exchanged parcels of provisions – in February 1809, for example, a crate of honey and rose water from Temple Sowerby made the return journey filled with oranges purchased in Newcastle – but neither mother nor daughter was ever quite as diligent a correspondent as the other wished her to be. Dorothy, in particular, expressed displeasure at her mother's shortcomings in this area. 'My Dear Dorothy,' Bridget wrote on 28 June 1812, 'I find by your writing to Jane that you were quite angry and thought I ought to have wrote to you at the time I wrote to Bridget' – this was Bridget's middle daughter, Bridget Tulip – 'but realy I was so busy with the Stairs Carpet I could not affoard time for any one else so do not impute it to slight or neglesence for it was neighter and when I am done you will see what a punctual correspondent I will be. I Long to see you here and then you will Judge what I have been doing but I am afraid you will give Jane all the credit.'[20]

While not engaged in carpet-cleaning or other domestic chores, much of Bridget's time must have been absorbed by her antiquarian hobbies. Here in front of me, on my desk, is Bridget's handwritten copy of the annals of the Clifford family, contained within two leatherbound volumes. They consist of an account of the sea voyages of the Earl of Cumberland, an Elizabethan courtier, and the diaries of his daughter Lady Anne Clifford, who spent forty years in litigation before winning the right to inherit her father's estates, which included Pendragon, Brough, Appleby and Brougham castles in Westmorland. It seems most likely that Bridget took her copy from a version held at Dalemain – the mansion had once been owned by Sir Edward Hasell, Lady Anne Clifford's steward. The cyclical appearance of Bridget's handwriting – each session starting neatly, deteriorating as she tires – hints at how long it must have taken her to transcribe this work.

Bridget's collections were well known in the neighbourhood, and her coins, shells and books a draw for passing enthusiasts. They had certainly made a strong impression on Matt's friend, John Hodgson, who was now working with the Newcastle bookseller John Bell towards the launch of an organization dedicated to the history of the northern counties – the first provincial counterpart to the Society of Antiquaries of London. The inaugural meeting of the Antiquarian Society of Newcastle upon Tyne took place on 6 February 1813, at Loftus's Long Room on Newgate Street, with the election of twenty-nine founder members, including Matt Atkinson and Nathaniel Clayton. The Duke of Northumberland graciously accepted the 'honourable Situation of Patron' – but the most striking

*Bridget in old age, an engraving taken from
a miniature now lost.*

mark of distinction to be conferred that day was the first honorary membership, upon 'Mrs. Atkinson' of Temple Sowerby.[21]

Among the original artefacts to enter the society's collection were a 'Celtic Hammer of very hard granular stone, found near Kirkoswald Castle, in Cumberland; a silver Penny of Henry the Second, found with a great quantity of the same kind of coin, at Cutherston, near Bowes, in Yorkshire, about the year 1782; a Silver Penny of Edward the First, coined at London; a Silver Penny of Edward the Second, coined at Canterbury' and a 'Swedish Copper Dollar, of Charles the Twelfth, dated 1716' – all donated by Bridget.[22] She, in turn, received a diploma, printed on parchment, enclosed in a neat wooden box. In coming years, great men would have honorary membership of the society bestowed upon them – Sir Joseph Banks, Sir Humphry Davy, Sir Walter Scott – but no other woman would be permitted to join its ranks until the 1870s.

GEORGE ATKINSON had been bracing himself for the forfeiture of much of his fortune, but finally, after pondering the subject for five years, the Treasury Board gave way on the matter of the 'double

Commission'. On 26 February 1813, the Law Officers declared that while George had not, strictly speaking, been entitled as Agent General of Jamaica to charge an additional 5 per cent on the bills drawn upon him by his partner in Port-au-Prince, he would have been permitted to apply the same charge – which they acknowledged as the 'proper and usual Commission' – had he been acting in his capacity as a private merchant.[23]

The decision must have been a tremendous relief for George, coming at a time when he was weighed down by ill health and an excessive workload; too much of his energy was still being absorbed by the lawsuits which were gradually devouring his late uncle's estate, and he felt increasingly aggrieved that his siblings expected him to shoulder the burden. As he complained to brother Matt: 'Altogether my Executorship has been a ruinous Concern as well as attended with incalculable Vexation, and has been an obstruction instead of an aid in my commercial Pursuits.'[24] It was about time, he resolved, that the wider family carried some responsibility – most pressingly, in making a decision about the Bogue estate.

Back in 1791, when Nathaniel Clayton and Sir Francis Baring bought out Paul Benfield's interest in the Bogue, they had declared by deed of trust that any profits from the estate's future sale would be 'divided Share & Share alike' among Bridget's children.[25] George had acquired Nathaniel's (but not Baring's) interest in the property eight years later, following his return from Jamaica. Two decades of under-investment had since taken their toll on the Bogue, and recently the crop had fallen badly short. In 1812 the plantation had consigned a mere forty hogsheads of sugar to Barings in London, which was scarcely enough to pay the overseer's salary, let alone the interest on huge debts of more than £40,000.

Nathaniel laid out the problem in a lengthy memorandum, dated 28 June 1813, which he circulated around the family (to everyone, that is, apart from Michael, with whom he could 'hold no correspondence'). While expressing hope that they would all profit from the future sale of their late uncle's property, Nathaniel pointed out that they might also lose money on it – and here lay the crux of the matter. Surely it was unfair that any of this risk should fall upon the estate of Sir Francis Baring, who had 'acted merely for the Benefit of Mr. Atkinson's Family'? Which invited the next question – if not Baring's heirs, who would be prepared to assume the risk? On this point Nathaniel asked each family member to 'judge for themselves'; they could either buy further into 'this Adventure', or opt out from it entirely.[26] The eventual gains, or losses, would be shared out accordingly.

Matt, indecisive as ever, declared himself 'perplexed' by the question. He told Nathaniel:

> You both know perfectly well how I am situated as to income. At the same time you will recollect I owe you nearly £500, and my Mill will run me in debt £200 more which must take me some time to Liquidate, and if you deem this undertaking hazardous, I really think I ought in prudence to relinquish all hopes of advantage rather than run much risk of involving myself further – but however I shall in this be entirely governed by whatever you & my Brother George agree I should do.[27]

NATHANIEL AND DOROTHY would be blessed with eleven children, with just sixteen years separating them, every one of whom reached adulthood. As they grew up and left home to fulfil their various callings, each Clayton family gathering became an increasingly rare and precious moment. 'The Children are all well & happy & I was a proud Man indeed, when I saw them all assembled at the Table on the first Day of this year,' Nathaniel had written to Bridget on one such occasion. 'God only knows whether this joyful Circumstance will again happen to us.'[28] The boys, of course, needed careers, and their father earmarked Nat, John and Michael for the legal profession; Nat would practise at Lincoln's Inn in London, while John and Michael were articled to the family firm in Newcastle. George Clayton came second in the brotherly pecking order, between Nat and John, but was insufficiently studious to pursue a legal career. In December 1813, after graduating from Oriel College, Oxford with a third-class degree, he sailed for Jamaica to join his uncle's merchant house – the first of the next generation of the family to do so.

Another of Bridget's grandsons, James Atkinson – John's orphan son – turned fourteen in 1813. Since his arrival at Temple Sowerby from Jamaica, eight years earlier, his grandmother and Aunt Jane had discreetly raised the boy – so discreetly, in fact, that family letters contain scant clues about his upbringing. Bridget's household accounts, however, reveal that several bills were paid to a 'Mr. Robinson' between 1807 and 1811. This John Robinson, not to be confused with the late Secretary to the Treasury, was headmaster of the grammar school at Ravenstonedale, about twenty miles south of Temple Sowerby; the fees for 1808 came to just over £30.[29] More evidence of James's education can be found on the shelf beside me; within a copy of *Corderius's Colloquies*, a textbook 'designed for the Use of Beginners in the Latin Tongue', can be found both his neat signature and the date, 24 February 1808, inscribed on its front endpaper.

I had hoped to learn so much more about James's life; but the trail seemed to peter out after 1811, and I started worrying that I would never find out what happened to him. One day, however, while leafing through John Hodgson's papers at the Northumberland Archives, and trying not to be too diverted by his fascinating, but for my purposes entirely tangential correspondence with Sir Humphry Davy about ways of 'preventing explosions from fire damp' – ninety-two men and boys having perished in a blast at Felling Colliery, a mile down the road from Carr Hill, in May 1812 – I was surprised to come across a document in a familiar hand.[30] This was one of Bridget's chatty letters, addressed to Matt at the Tyne Iron Company; and it enclosed the formula for a 'Thorn-Apple Burn Ointment which is by far the best I ever saw'.[31] It also offered an ending, of sorts, to the story of James Atkinson.

Bridget was writing to Matt on 25 October 1813, the day after James had sailed for . . . she does not give his final destination, but

I would guess it to be Jamaica. The week before, Jane and James had apparently hurried to Whitehaven in the post-chaise, not stopping 'on the road to eat or drink', but they discovered when they arrived that the ship for which they were rushing had already left. They then headed without delay to Liverpool in hopes of catching a vessel to take James to Cork, where the West India merchant fleet was gathering in readiness for a naval convoy. At Liverpool, Jane had called on Thomas Littledale – Ann's brother, a cotton broker – who had offered 'every assistance and got James every thing he wanted as a Mattrass Blanket Blue woolling trousers &c', and had also helped find him a passage to Cork. 'Never one could behave better than James did – but I will tell you all when you come over and you shall shoot me a Little game for Mr. Littledale.'[32] *I will tell you all when you come over* – rarely have the confines of the written word been more teasingly articulated. Beyond this point, I have no idea how James's life panned out – for his name never crops up again in a family letter.

BRIDGET HAD LONG SUFFERED from rheumatism and poor circulation, and she spent part of the autumn of 1813 at the resort of Allonby, on the Solway coast, where she derived a 'great deal of Bennifitt' from warm indoor baths. ('I thought I had lost the use of my Fingers in writing,' she told Matt, 'but I hope I shall recover all again.')[33] The following winter would prove exceptionally harsh. In January 1814, blizzards swept the land, depositing a blanket of snow several feet deep. In the capital, for a few dreamlike days in February, the ice between Blackfriars and London bridges was thick enough to support crowds of revellers, roasting oxen and even an elephant – this would be the last Frost Fair ever to be held on the River Thames. Up north, the Tyne and Solway Firth both froze hard.

By the beginning of March, Bridget was dangerously ill. Dorothy went over to Temple Sowerby to help Jane nurse their mother, while Nathaniel consulted the family physician, William Ingham, about her condition. 'He thinks it probable that there may be some Disease about the Vessels of the Heart, but that all the Symptoms detailed to him might proceed from Debility alone,' reported Nathaniel on 13 March. 'The only Remedy is sustaining the Patient and recruiting her Strength. To this End all your united Endeavours should be directed, and he thinks that as the Strength is recruited, the Quantity of Laudanum administered may be abated.'[34] While Bridget lay in bed, the family was filled with foreboding; they would not have long to wait, though, for she died on 28 March.

Bridget left her house, land and money to her youngest daughter Jane – all her property apart from Skygarth, the tiny farm acquired through the enclosures forty years earlier, which she left to Michael. Ten years earlier, at the height of the family row, Bridget had rewritten her will with the express purpose of disinheriting him: 'I declare it to be my intention totally to Exclude my eldest son Michael Atkinson from any share or interest in any of my Estates or effects real or personal.'[35] It is not clear what caused her change of heart, but in April 1811 she had written him back into her will. However, Bridget's bequest came with a condition; if he caused Jane, her executrix, 'any trouble molestation or disturbance' by demanding more than had been left to him, then the property would be forfeit.[36] Michael was apoplectic when he discovered this stipulation, perceiving it to be Nathaniel Clayton's work. 'I am sure there is *something* in the business which will not bear the light,' he fulminated, 'and to that *something* I ascribe the Disgusting Clause in my Mother's Will.'[37]

Six weeks after Bridget's death, on 11 May, George died suddenly at Lee, aged forty-nine, leaving behind a widow and nine children. It was a great shock to the entire family; although they knew that George's years in Jamaica had 'decayed' his constitution, they had not suspected him to be in mortal danger.[38] Michael attended the reading of his brother's will. 'I am as much in the Dark as possible as to what he possessed of property, for he *specified nothing*,' he told cousin Matthew Atkinson. 'The Will appeared to me a Complete Attorney's Puzzle.' George's executors were named as the Nathaniel Claytons, father and son; 'Matt the Blacksmith' (Michael's jeering name for his brother at Carr Hill); and nineteen-year-old George Atkinson, who had inherited his father's share of the merchant house in Kingston.[39]

Matt told Lord Balcarres that he believed his brother's family would 'be reasonably well provided for', once his partnerships had been wound up.[40] This would prove an understatement. George's estate was valued for probate at £140,000, which placed him among the ten richest men to die in Great Britain that year.[41]

TWENTY

Settling Scores

FOR THIRTY YEARS, Richard Atkinson's executors had ridden roughshod over the claims of Lady Anne Barnard; so when the last of them, Robert Mure, died in January 1815, her lawyers saw a chance to step into the breach. Michael Atkinson, motivated by his deep sense of grievance against Nathaniel Clayton, decided to join Anne's cause, and together this unlikely pair filed a petition for the Letters of Administration that would grant them control of the estate's assets.

But they had not reckoned on the opposition of Richard's nine nieces. Like Anne, these middle-aged women had been left annuities of which they had not received a penny; more significantly, though, they were the 'residuary legatees' of their uncle's estate. While planning his will, Richard had been so wildly optimistic in his financial projections that he had envisaged the profits from his Jamaican plantations accumulating into a fund from which all the annuity payments would be paid, and from the *residue* of which his nieces would each receive a lump sum of £4,000. This placed them next in line to take over the administration of the estate; Jane volunteered to represent her sisters and cousins in court, and Nathaniel dealt with the necessary paperwork.

When Michael learnt that his female relatives had shown the temerity to place their own interests ahead of his, he fired off a letter to Jane – '*short* and *very very tart*' – conveying his ill feelings. She was in Newcastle at the time, and she instantly warned cousin Matthew Atkinson, who lived across the village from her at Temple Sowerby, about some petty ways in which her brother's displeasure might soon make itself manifest: 'I expect Michael will be writing to you probably to take immediate possession of the Moss field.' (This was part of the small farm left him by their mother.) 'There is a large Compost Heap which at all events I would be obliged by your telling Isaac to remove immediately & any thing that you may observe that might be claimed.'[1]

The Prerogative Court of Canterbury sat in June 1815 to weigh up the rival petitions for the administration of the Atkinson estate. As Jane predicted, the 'spirit to pursue Mr. Clayton' gripped Michael in the courtroom, and his evidence spewed forth as a litany of bitter accusations.[2] Whether Michael's animosity influenced the judgement is not clear, but Sir John Nicholl brushed aside both Lady Anne Barnard's claim as an annuitant and Michael's as a legatee. 'It is objected that Mrs. Jane Atkinson resides at a distance, and is a spinster: but really these objections are ludicrous,' he pronounced.[3] As a residuary legatee – even when there was no prospect of inheriting any residue – the youngest sister's claim took legal precedence over that of the eldest brother.

BY ANY STANDARDS, Lady Anne Barnard had lived an eventful life – from mixing with royalty and statesmen to clambering up Table Mountain – but these days she barely left her house in Berkeley Square. Her late husband, who had remained in the Cape Colony after she returned to England in 1802, had posthumously sprung a surprise upon her – for no sooner had she received word of his death out there in 1807, than another letter arrived informing her that he had fathered a daughter by an enslaved woman. Anne saw it as her duty, a 'debt of honour' even, to care for the child, as the 'accident of an unguarded moment' after she had left her 'poor husband a lonely widower'.[4] Christina Douglas, this 'dear little girl of colour', went to live with her adoptive mother in London during the summer of 1809, when she was six.[5]

The other great love of Anne's life, her sister Margaret, died in December 1814. Following Alexander Fordyce's death in 1789, when she was thirty-six, Margaret had lived on and off with Anne in Berkeley Square, before ultimately enjoying two blissful years of marriage to Sir James Burges, a longstanding admirer. Anne had spent much of 1815 mourning the loss of her sister; but the first day of the following year found her in resolute frame of mind, as she sat down to draft an eighteen-page memorandum addressed to her heirs: 'A Hasty Sketch of Particulars respecting my Acquaintance with Richard Atkinson Esq. and his management of my affairs – For the Information of those who may one day have an Interest in them'. She meant by this a *financial* interest – for she was considering how best to pass her claims on the Atkinson estate down to the next generation, having accepted that she was 'too old' to pursue further litigation.[6] 'With a nest of young Attorneys, Claytons & Atkinsons on the Estates, living like princes, war is better than peace, at least to the Clayton folks,' she observed to her brother, Lord Balcarres, on 24 March 1816.[7]

By now, Anne was immersed in a major literary project – she was writing her autobiography. For several years she would labour away on this magnum opus in her forty-foot drawing room at Berkeley Square, under the watchful eyes of her beloved sister, as portrayed by Thomas Gainsborough, surrounded by ghosts and papers from her past. Inevitably, what she had once envisaged as a 'sketch' of her life expanded into a sprawling narrative.[8] As her health and her handwriting deteriorated, she increasingly relied upon Christina, her 'young amanuensis', whose careful script would end up filling the pages of six volumes.[9]

Anne's lively, candid memoirs caused a good deal of disquiet within the Lindsay family. Her siblings – particularly the decorous Countess of Hardwicke – feared she would unburden herself of secrets that would bring discredit upon them all. Anne calmed their nerves by giving 'feigned names' to her 'real characters', including herself, and thus the manuscript acquired the title *The History of the Family of St Aubin and the Memoirs of Louisa Melford*. (Richard

Atkinson became 'Robert Williamson'.)[10] She also decreed that the work could never, ever be published: 'I utterly debar it.'[11]

FOLLOWING THE ABDICATION of Napoleon Bonaparte from the French imperial throne in April 1814, the triumphant allies – Britain, Austria, Prussia and Russia – assembled in Paris to negotiate a treaty to restore peace to the ravaged continent. Ever since Admiral Nelson's victory off Cape Trafalgar in October 1805, which had secured Britain's maritime supremacy, the Royal Navy had kept French trade in check; but now, at the peace talks, it was suggested that France might be allowed a five-year revival of the slave trade, so its planters could put their West Indian possessions back in order. There was no mistaking the reaction of the British public to this regressive proposal. Thomas Clarkson, the veteran activist and chairman of the African Institution, called for petitions to be fired at Westminster from every corner of the country; by the time parliament rose for the summer recess, on 30 July 1814, more than eight hundred petitions had already been delivered.

In the British West Indies, as abolitionists had always predicted, the enslaved workforce dwindled without regular cargoes from Africa. In March 1810, two years after the Abolition of the Slave Trade Act came into force, the Kingston house of Atkinson, Bogle & Co. had told Lord Balcarres that they were finding it 'exceedingly difficult to obtain singly, prime Negroes of either Sex', and the supply had shrunk further since then.[12] 'The Sum of my Inclination as to my Jamaica Properties is this,' Balcarres had written to the house, in clear frustration, three years later: 'I do not want Money – I want Negroes.'[13] But a proportion of the slave trade still carried on underground, and it was to smother this business that William Wilberforce tabled a parliamentary motion, in June 1815, to make the registration of slaves compulsory. Not only would the name, age and sex of every enslaved person be recorded; any changes to their status due to their sale, escape, manumission, or death, would also be logged. By keeping much stricter tabs on the numbers and movements of the enslaved population, it would be far harder for slave owners to conceal instances of illegal trafficking.

So outraged were West Indian planters at this attempt by Wilberforce's 'party of fanatical bigots' to meddle in their internal affairs, however, that the Westminster bill was withdrawn; instead the separate island assemblies were persuaded to enact the legislation at a local level.[14] The House of Assembly in Jamaica would pass its registration bill in December 1816. Prior to registration, most anti-slavery campaigners had known little about the people in whose welfare they took such interest; but the new law meant that slave owners could no longer treat their human property as an abstract mass. From now on, the enslaved population would be composed of counted, named individuals.

During this time the Kingston house was in a state of flux. After George Atkinson's death, Edward Adams and Robert Robertson had returned to England to wind up their late partner's affairs, bringing (it was said) some £300,000 with them. Subsequently, in an alliance which raised eyebrows within the wider family – certainly it was 'not impeded by any antediluvian Notions of Coyness & Reserve', remarked Nathaniel Clayton – Robertson, who was thirty-eight, had married Bridget Atkinson, George's sixteen-year-old daughter.[15] Meanwhile out in Jamaica, George Clayton, second son of Dorothy and Nathaniel, had died of a fever in April 1816 at the age of twenty-six.

It was the responsibility of the Kingston house, as Lord Balcarres' attorneys on the island, to file his first slave return. But there was a catch – for the registration process threatened to expose, after eighteen years' concealment, the corruption that lay at the heart of the pioneer contract, whereby the former governor had secretly signed up for a one-third share of the business of supplying 'black pioneers' to the army. 'I do not perceive any Means of omitting your Lordship's name in the Return,' warned Edward Adams in February 1817.[16]

Adams wrote to Balcarres again in August, this time to tell him about a letter written by a junior minister which suggested that the pioneer contract should be ended immediately: 'It also mentions

Lord Balcarres' Interest, and insinuates the Contract to have been a *Job*.'[17] The degree to which Balcarres was spooked by this message is plain from the many scrawled sheets of foolscap, scarred with crossings-out, in which he fabricated a story that would clear him of wrongdoing. 'I think I have made out a strong case,' he told Adams. 'I deny the Job & deny that I am the holder of the share.'[18] Adams counselled Balcarres to keep quiet. 'The Paragraph I quoted to your Lordship is information collected quite privately,' he wrote. 'We could give no reason for imputing to ministers, therefore, a suspicion of the Contract being underhanded. Consequently, an attempt to justify it would appear like being betrayed by a guilty conscience.'[19] This was sound advice, for neither was the pioneer contract terminated, and nor did any investigation come about. By November, moreover, Adams was able to pass Balcarres some 'satisfactory Intelligence' from Jamaica.[20] The pioneers had been registered by the commanding officers of the regiments they served, and not by the Kingston house; and thus his Lordship's good name remained unsullied.

THE ANTI-SLAVERY MOVEMENT had deep roots within Nonconformist Christianity; the majority of the founder members of the Committee for the Abolition of the Slave Trade had been Quakers. Meanwhile some of the most vocal abolitionists, notably William Wilberforce, were evangelical Anglicans who worshipped at Holy Trinity Church on Clapham Common; they came to be known as the 'Clapham Sect' or, not entirely respectfully, the 'Saints'.

In the West Indies, the planter class had long tried to keep the enslaved population as ignorant of Christianity as possible. Recently, however, a battle for their souls had broken out in Jamaica, stirred up by Wesleyan missionaries preaching the creed that all men were equal in the eyes of God. The House of Assembly, observing how the 'dark and dangerous fanaticism' of the Methodists seemed to resonate among the black population, resolved to spread 'genuine Christianity' among them.[21] The Rev. George Wilson Bridges came to Jamaica in 1816, at the invitation of the governor, and was installed as rector of St Mark's Church in Mandeville, the capital of the newly formed parish of Manchester. Bridges was almost certainly the most active of the Anglican clergymen who were recruited by the authorities to tend to the spiritual needs of the enslaved population; he would later claim to have baptized 9,413 slaves.[22] These ceremonies involved the candidates gathering 'either at the churches, or on the estates, sometimes from fifty to a hundred or more'. No religious instruction was given beforehand; they were merely asked what their Christian names and surnames were to be, and then 'baptized *en masse*, the rector receiving half a crown currency for each person'.[23]

Two estates belonging to Lord Balcarres – Martin's Hill and Marshall's Pen – were in the parish of Manchester, and Bridges baptized 220 of the enslaved population there in December 1818 and January 1819. Further west, in Westmoreland Parish, the Rev. James Dawn baptized 121 'Negroes belonging to Dean's Valley Dry Works', as the church records describe them, on 17 November 1820. One-third of the inhabitants of this estate took one of two surnames – of course, we will never know to what extent these were their own choice, or foisted upon them. Two Amelias, Eliza, Elizabeth, George, James, Mary Ann, Robert, Thomas and William – they would be known as Clayton. Alexander, Amelia, Andrew, Catherine, Diana, Eleanor, Eliza, Elizabeth, George, Henry, three Jameses, Jannett, John, Lucea, Margaret, Mary, Mary Ann, Matthew, Rebecca, Richard, Robert, Romeo, two Susans, Thomas and three Williams – they were all now Atkinsons.[24]

By this time, the long-term decline of the enslaved population at Dean's Valley had reduced the estate to near paralysis. Back in 1797, there had been 221 slaves on the property; now just 134 were left. 'Unless the strength is increased,' wrote the Kingston house, 'we contemplate not a falling off in the Crop but the utter impossibility of carrying on.'[25] As the debts on both the Bogue and Dean's Valley estates escalated, and the value of sugar plantations slumped, the Claytons attempted to clear the legal path to their sale. Michael Clayton – Nathaniel and Dorothy's fourth son – managed

Alphabetical List and valuation of Negroes on the "Bogue" Estate, with their age, occupation, & condition September 26th 1818. —

No.	Names	Males above 12 years	Females above 12 years	Males under 12 years	Females under 12 years	Males under 6 years	Females under 6 years	Total of Males	Total of Females	Grand total	Condition	Occupation	Valuation
	Adam	1	..	..	..	..	1	..	1	Able	Field	160
	Assa	1	..	..	..	1	..	..	1	Weakly	Watchman	130
	Adam	1	..	..	..	..	1	..	1	Ditto	Ditto	20
	Anthony	1	..	..	..	..	1	..	1	Able	Att.g Stock	150
5.	Apollo	..	..	..	1	..	1	..	1	Healthy	under age	40
	Affie	..	1	..	..	..	1	1		Able	Field	140
	Abigail	..	1	..	..	..	1	1		Ditto	Ditto	120
	Ann	..	..	..	1	..	1	1		Healthy	House	130
	Amelia	..	..	..	..	1	..	1	1	ditto	under age	30
10.	Belinda	..	1	..	..	..	1	1		Weakly	Field	
	Bella	..	1	..	..	..	1	1		able	Ditto	140
	Belly	1	..	..	..	1	..	1		ditto	Ditto	140
	Bogady	1	..	..	..	1	..	1		Weakly	Carpenter	160
	Bottle Rum	1	..	..	..	1	..	1		Able	Att.g Stock	140
15.	Betsy	..	..	..	1	..	1	1		Healthy	Under age	20
	Butus	1	..	..	..	1	..	1		Able	Watchman	40
	Bacchus	1	..	..	..	1	..	1		Weakly	Cook	80
	Belinda	..	1	..	..	..	1	1		ditto	Att. Nancy Steward	
	Betsy	..	1	..	..	..	1	1		Able	Field	160
20.	Bacchus	1	..	..	..	1	..	1		Old & Weak	Invalid	
	Chelsea	1	..	..	..	1	..	1		Weakly	Att.g Sheep	
	Charles	1	..	..	..	1	..	1		Sickly	In Hot house the last 12 months	
	Charles	1	..	..	..	1	..	1		Able	Field	140
	Cuthbert	1	..	..	..	1	..	1		Weakly	Watchman	50
25.	Chloe	..	1	..	..	..	1	1		Able	Field	120
	Cumba	..	1	..	..	..	1	1		ditto	ditto	80
	Chloe	..	1	..	..	..	1	1		ditto	ditto	50
	Chrishie	..	1	..	..	..	1	1		Old & weak	Invalid	
	Celinda	..	1	..	..	..	1	1		Able	Field	170
30.	Chance	..	1	..	..	..	1	1		Yaws	Ditto	150
	Clarinda	..	1	..	..	..	1	1		Old & weak	Invalid	
	Diamond	1	..	..	..	1	..	1		Able	Field	200
	Daniel	1	..	..	..	1	..	1		ditto	Carpenter	200
	Damsel	..	1	..	..	..	1	1		ditto	Field	170
35.	Doll	..	1	..	..	..	1	1		Weakly	ditto	
		16	15	..	1	1	2	17	18	35		£3130

A valuation of the enslaved population on the Bogue estate in September 1818.

the business from the London chambers of the family firm at 6 New Square, Lincoln's Inn.

But Michael Atkinson's refusal to go along with his relatives' wishes presented an obstacle to the properties' disposal, causing Nathaniel to file two chancery bills against his brother-in-law. Michael wrote to Lord Balcarres in October 1818, complaining of not having received 'one Shilling' from the estates while they were managed by those who would now sell them 'in Liquidation of Debts due to themselves', and seeking to form an alliance against the lawsuits.[26] But Balcarres brushed him off: 'Your Uncle Richard Atkinson left his affairs in that State of Confusion & perplexity as to convince me that I could be of no manner of use.'[27]

One day around this time, while he was poring over his uncle's will at Doctors' Commons, Michael noticed that it no longer bore its original seal; and so, in January 1819, he filed a 'voluminous' bill to have the document set aside as defective.[28] Although Lady Anne Barnard felt a degree of sympathy for Michael, she realized he was entirely the puppet of lawyers who saw a 'good suit for *them* out of it', and declined his invitation to join the legal action.[29] It would prove a wise decision.

The case finally came before the Lord Chief Justice, Sir Charles Abbott, on 1 August 1821. The Solicitor General started by informing the jury that it was their duty to decide upon the legitimacy of a will which had been 'in operation' for more than thirty years; the seal it had once borne had 'by time or accident' been lost, and now the testator's nephew had chosen 'for the first time' to suggest that his late uncle had deliberately torn it off 'as a mode of cancelment'. Two employees of the Prerogative Office suggested that the damage might easily have taken place at Doctors' Commons, given that the 'practice was to carry the will into the great room, where as many as 200 persons were frequently collected at the same time, and where, of course, to attend to the conduct of every one was impracticable'.[30] Michael could offer no evidence to support his argument – and thus, unsurprisingly, the jury pronounced Richard Atkinson's will to be completely valid.

SINCE HIS RETURN from India some seventeen years earlier, Michael had expended much of his remaining energy on pointlessly feuding with his relations over their Jamaican inheritance; but this would be the final lawsuit to go against him, for he died six weeks later at his Portland Place residence. Michael's daughter Sophia had five years earlier married Bertie Cator, a good-natured naval captain, and the Cators now stood to inherit a considerable fortune. But Michael's obstinacy had exacted a heavy toll on the rest of the family, and the Claytons, being lawyers, now came up with a legalistic way to settle the score.

The inheritance of landed property in Kent had, since Anglo-Saxon times, followed the laws of tenure known as 'gavelkind', which determined that in cases of intestacy without legitimate issue, it should be divided among male next of kin – all land in the county was included, unless specifically 'disgavelled'. Michael had made his will in 1807, naming his daughter Sophia as his lawful heir. He had purchased the Mount Mascal estate the following year, but had failed to update his will in order to disgavel the property. And, furthermore, the family had always strongly suspected that Michael had never married his 'wife'.

Nat Clayton spelled out the potential implications in a letter to his uncle Matt at Carr Hill. 'Supposing the Illegitimacy of Mrs. Cator,' he explained, 'it would follow, that you as surviving Brother take one half of the Mount Mascal Estate and that the five sons of your deceased Brother George take the other half amongst them in equal Shares.'[31] Nat made some enquiries, and found three highly respectable gentlemen – a director of the East India Company, an East Indiaman captain and an army general – who were prepared to swear affidavits. 'We have been hitherto very fortunate in obtaining Information relative to Michael Atkinson's Affairs; & a curious History it will turn out,' Nat told his mother, Dorothy, on 21 November 1821. 'In the course of our Inquiries one thing has led to another in an extraordinary Manner; & we have met with ample Information in Quarters where we had the least reason to expect it. The Begum's Life in point of singularity & variety looks more like a novel than a reality.'[32]

The word 'begum' was a term of respect on the Indian sub-continent. Nat was using it ironically, of course – for it appeared that Michael's 'wife' had lived a dissolute youth, to say the least. The story of Miss Sophia Mackereth had begun in London during the 1780s, where as a 'girl of the Town' she had been entangled with John Manship, an East India Company director; he had 'got rid of her by sending her off to Madras'. As soon as she landed in India, in July 1785, she had apparently 'made a great outcry' that a trunk containing her jewels and letters of recommendation had been stolen. 'The whole story was a fabrication,' recalled Joseph Dorin, captain of the *Duke of Montrose*. 'The people of Madras were imposed upon by it & treated her with great kindness.' Soon afterwards she took up with a Mr Woolley, with whom she stayed for a few months before they fell out; he later died in a duel. She then sailed up the coast to Calcutta, where she was invited 'from motives of compassion' to live in the residence of the governor, Sir John Macpherson; finally, in May 1786, she had run off with Michael Atkinson. General Mackenzie, commanding the 78th Highlanders, remembered spending several days with Michael at Jangipur in 1797: 'He had at that time a Lady living with him who took his name. In the course of conversation I asked him if he was married to her to which he replied without hesitation *that he was not.*'[33]

Although Matt stood to benefit most, the rest of the family deliberately excluded him from these discussions. 'Brother Matt must not be trusted with any one thing,' Jane reminded Dorothy, 'for the Weakest of Creatures may impose upon him.' Both sides showed a readiness to fight their corner; Sophia Cator declared herself prepared 'to go through fire & water' to prove her legitimacy.[34] 'My Father would tell you that the Begum or rather Capt. Cator is determined not to give up Mount Mascall without a hard struggle,' Michael Clayton told his mother on 13 July 1822. 'I met the Captain a few days ago accidentally and what will surprize you the introduction on his side was attended with the most cordial & hearty shake of the hand notwithstanding the exertions he knows I am making against his Interests. The subject was only slightly adverted to and Capt. Cator said it gave him of course great pain but he knew that we were only doing our duty – there is no difference of opinion as to *his* worth.'[35]

By this point, the parties were hammering out a compromise. Bertie Cator ultimately agreed to pay £14,500 – which was how much the Claytons calculated that Michael's refusal to agree to the sale of the Jamaican estates 'when implored to do so' had cost the rest of the family – to his late father-in-law's male next of kin.[36] Matt received a memorandum relating to his half-share of the proceeds, in his nephew John Clayton's handwriting: 'By the agreement now executed, Mr. Matthew Atkinson agrees to relinquish all claim to the Mount Mascall Estate on having the sum of £7250 secured to him upon it to be paid on the 5th day of August 1834 unless Mrs. Michael Atkinson shall die before that time in which case the principal money is to be paid within 12 months after her decease.'[37]

The episode must have been excruciating for Sophia Cator, the Begum's daughter, but soon afterwards she appears to have written in conciliatory language to her uncle Matt. This letter has not survived, although Matt's reply hints at his great relief that the matter was closed:

I know very few things that would have added so much to the very satisfactory & amiable compromise that has recently been made, as the receipt of your affectionate letter today. I think you know me well enough, my dear Sophia, to doubt a moment of my embracing in the most lively manner the kind & friendly terms proposed & burying all that has past in oblivion, you little know how anxiously I have always hoped some fortuitous circumstance might restore the lost affection of my deceased brother, but Providence ordered it otherwise.[38]

IN MAY 1823, aged seventy-two, Lady Anne Barnard composed a letter to her brother Lord Balcarres, to be opened after her death: 'You will not receive these few lines till I am no more – they are only to bid you adieu in the anxious hope of meeting you again in a world of everlasting Happiness and love. I wish my funds were as ample as they *ought to be*, but I will still hope that something may be gained to your family by my means.'[39] Anne was in a leave-taking frame of mind, putting her papers in order and making them fit for the prying eyes of the next generation. Much of her correspondence ended up on the drawing room fire; happily, she spared a bundle of Richard Atkinson's old letters. 'Most interesting & noble man', Anne pencilled at the top of the letter in which he had proposed marriage to her.[40] 'A strong & solemn testimony of the motives which governed the conduct of this Excellent man', she wrote on the letter he had sent her alongside the final draft of his will.[41] 'May we not call him the prince of English merchants?'[42]

Meanwhile, with Michael no longer around to block the business, the Atkinson estate was crawling towards a final settlement. By the close of 1822, terms had been agreed for the sale of Dean's Valley – the land, buildings, enslaved workers and livestock fetching just over £16,000 – and a prospective buyer had also been found for the Bogue. ('I hope we shall soon be able to submit to the Trustees for Sale a proposal for getting rid of this disastrous Property,' Michael Clayton told Lord Balcarres on 18 November 1823.)[43] Meanwhile, Richard Atkinson's heirs had mostly learnt to manage their expectations. 'I quite despair of Receiving a Shilling from our uncle's Effects,' wrote Joseph Taylor, the son of Richard's sister Margaret, on 10 March 1824. 'Indeed I dismiss the Subject from my Mind, and almost wish that no Part of my Family or myself had been mentioned in the Will.'[44]

The Master in Chancery finally made his report on the Atkinson estate at the beginning of 1825. A notice in *The Times* called on the Mures' remaining creditors to gather on 29 March at the Court of Commissioners of Bankrupts in the City of London, 'to assent to or dissent from a compromise of all matters depending between the estate of Richard Atkinson, and the estate of the said Hutchison, Robert and William Mure'.[45] Here the terms of the settlement were agreed 'to the satisfaction of all parties'.[46] Richard's estate was in the end valued at £88,000. (Forty years earlier, it had been reckoned worth £300,000.) More than three-quarters of this sum went to the heirs of George Atkinson and Sir Francis Baring, to pay off their loans to the two Jamaican estates, leaving about £20,000 to be shared out among the extended family. As for Lady Anne Barnard's inheritance – had there been anything for her, it would have been too late, for she died on 6 May 1825.

TWENTY-ONE

Human Relics

THE CLASSIC NARRATIVE ARC of a family's fortune spans three generations – the enterprising first generation amasses it, the complacent second generation sits on it, the feckless third generation squanders it. (Although my family doesn't entirely fit this template – not least because, for some truly world-class fecklessness, it would have to wait till the sixth generation.) At this point in the saga, as the second generation withers and the third generation emerges, the family splinters into branches of cousins, too numerous to follow individually.

A little confusingly, two George Atkinsons inhabit this next part of the story. (As I've already mentioned, my forebears were unimaginative where first names were concerned.) The more prominent of these Georges is George and Susan's eldest son, a Kingston merchant; I'll sometimes refer to him as cousin George. The other George is Matt and Ann's eldest son, a Newcastle naturalist; he's either George or, more formally, George Clayton Atkinson. In case you're wondering, I'm descended from his youngest brother, Dick – and it's down this branch of the family that I will be increasingly drawn. (At this point, you may be forgiven for sneaking a glance at the family tree near the front of the book.)

It's somewhat hard to reconcile Matt the careless progenitor of many illegitimate children in Jamaica with Matt the devoted paterfamilias at Carr Hill; but it would appear that he and Ann enjoyed a tranquil domestic life. George Clayton Atkinson, in a halcyon recollection of childhood, described mornings starting with his father – who was always first to rise – sneezing twice 'with much vigour' as he went downstairs, tapping the barometer as he passed through the hall, and heading outdoors with one or more children in tow. 'How delicious the remembrance of walking about the garden with him, now is,' wrote George. 'He was six feet high, & stooped a little in later years; he used moreover to roll rather in his walk; & I can just fancy him walking along the front walk with his pruning knife in one hand, & Jane or Dick holding the other: stopping now & then to trim a straggling carnation, or stepping over the border to eradicate an unsightly shoot from the far extending root of one of the peach trees.'[1]

Matt and Ann were unshowy people, and their home was simply furnished – as George remembered it, there was just one oil painting in the house, a smoky scene of Tynemouth Castle, which hung over the chimneypiece in the school room. The five children – George, Isaac, Mary Ann, Dick and Jane – were an unruly gaggle with only seven years between them, and it fell to Ann to keep their 'more fervid schemes' in check, for Matt was an indulgent parent. 'My poor father, he certainly had the kindest heart, best temper I ever knew,' recalled George. 'Nothing went wrong with him, everything pleased him: whatever happened it was all right, & he gives me in recollection, a finer personification of entire contentment than I remember to have met with.' On dark winter evenings, Matt would read aloud to the family beside the fire, with a 'very favourite grey cat' on his knee, while Ann stitched and the young ones quietly amused themselves.[2] The girls were educated at home by a governess, while the boys went off to board at St Bees School near Whitehaven, and then, to tame their 'Northern Manners & Dialect', at the Charterhouse School in London.[3]

If there was one trait that pervaded Matt's working life, it was an unfortunate allergy to paperwork – this would trigger a short but painful dispute with his brother-in-law Nathaniel, conducted via half a dozen letters in March 1816. A fraud had been uncovered at the Tyne Iron Company; the loss to the firm was nearly £100. The partners, believing Matt to be in daily attendance, were shocked to find that he had not once, during the nine years he had managed its head office, bothered to bestow 'five minutes on the cashing up of a single page of the Cash Book of the Concern'. Nathaniel was furious, and berated him for his neglect: 'Your Attendance at the Office, applied as it must have been, was at once a Snare to your Partners, and a Temptation to the unhappy Man, who is now expiating his Crimes.'[4] In reply, Matt complained of having been 'led into the concern' in the first place, and of his capital having been 'locked up so long without any return'.[5] But it was Nathaniel's suggestion that Ann was partly to blame for his inattention, by insisting that he left the office at midday to be back at Carr Hill in time for dinner, which wounded Matt most of all. 'It was no arrangement of my Wife's that obliged me to it,' he wrote, 'but my own taste for early hours as I can with Truth affirm that she has devoted herself entirely to my wishes since we married, and I may add her utmost pride has been in doing so, you may easily imagine how much we were both hurt at the insinuation of her not entering into the interest of her husband.'[6] Nathaniel terminated the exchange with a wish to 'bury the Subject in oblivion'.[7]

Matt was most in his element when out rambling with his friend John Hodgson, the local parson. Hodgson took a close interest in the Roman wall; indeed, through the study of inscriptions on excavated rocks, he would reach what was, for the time, the unorthodox conclusion that the emperor Hadrian had been its builder. During one of their long walks, Matt had been delighted to show Hodgson the words PETRA FLAVI CARANTINI – 'the rock of Flavius Carantinus' – carved on to a ridge of hard sandstone on his brother-in-law Henry Tulip's Fallowfield estate.

The two men set out on another trip to Westmorland in May 1817. This was a period of great geological discovery – William Smith's first map of England and Wales, delineating their different rock strata, had been published two years earlier – and Hodgson, the son of a Shap stonemason, had always been fascinated by the

The view across Ullswater.

diverse geology of his native county. Over several days, they would together examine the 'limestone, schist, and sandstone' in the bed of the River Lowther near Askham, the 'thin laminae and lumps of fibrous white gypsum' by the River Eden at Winderwath, and a 'bed of peat-coal' by the River Eamont.[8]

This time, incidentally, Matt and Hodgson did not sleep at Temple Sowerby; instead they put up twelve miles away, beside Ullswater, as the guests of Matt's sister-in-law Elizabeth Littledale and her husband Captain John Wordsworth, a cousin of the celebrated poet. The Wordsworths' residence, Eusemere, had been built by the great abolitionist Thomas Clarkson, after repeated setbacks had driven him to seek peace in the Lake District during the late 1790s. The house was built of rough stone and roofed in local slate; its casement windows framed magnificent views. William and Dorothy Wordsworth had often visited the Clarksons there; it was while they were walking along the lake shore, on their way home to Dove Cottage, that they had observed the 'long belt' of daffodils, 'about the breadth of a country turnpike road', which had inspired Wordsworth to write his most famous verse.[9]

Matt and Ann would pass on their great love of nature to their children; while he issued them with 'grave injunctions' not to touch birds' nests during the breeding season, she encouraged them to press wildflowers between the pages of books.[10] During the summer holidays of 1825, while thirteen-year-old Dick was staying with Aunt Jane at Temple Sowerby, he came across the nest and eggs of a bird that he did not recognize. Back home at Carr Hill, he consulted the well-thumbed family copy of Thomas Bewick's *Birds* and identified them as belonging to a pied flycatcher, although he did notice that the author seemed unclear about certain aspects of the species.

Bewick was one of the Atkinsons' neighbours, and something of a Tyneside celebrity. He had stayed with Matt and Ann at Carr Hill in August 1812, while recovering from pleurisy, and afterwards moved to a house at Gateshead, on the road into Newcastle. During his long career as a wood engraver, Bewick had illustrated many subjects; but rural scenes were his forte, often including minuscule details that revealed a wicked sense of humour. His enduring masterpiece, however, would be his two-volume *History of British Birds*, which first appeared in 1797. (Fifty years later, Charlotte Brontë would start *Jane Eyre* with her beleaguered heroine finding refuge within its pages: 'With Bewick on my knee, I was then happy: happy at least in my way.')[11] Bewick's artistic medium was dense boxwood, which accounted for the fine detail of his cuts; indeed, 'so incredulous' had George III been that 'such beautiful impressions could be procured from wooden blocks' that he had commanded his bookseller to call in the blocks for royal inspection.[12]

Dick and his eldest brother George decided to call on the old man to 'give him the benefit of Dick's observations' on the pied flycatcher.[13] Bewick expressed himself delighted to see them and questioned the boy closely on the habits of the bird, 'taking memoranda on the margin' of a copy of his book that he used for gathering corrections.[14] Seventeen-year-old George subsequently struck up a firm friendship with Bewick, and would go and sit with him two or three times a week. During one memorable discussion, the old man

Thomas Bewick's engraving of the pied flycatcher.

claimed that if George threw some eels into the pond opposite Carr Hill House, they would soon multiply to ten thousand. 'I took the hint,' wrote George, 'and shortly afterwards, put in two or three buckets full, none of which I have since had the pleasure of seeing.'[15] Another day, Bewick asked: 'Are you a collector of relics, Mr. Atkinson?' Barely knowing how to answer such a strange question, George replied in the affirmative, to which the old man responded: 'Should you like to possess one of me?'[16] He then fumbled in his desk drawer, before handing George a tiny packet. On the paper wrapping was written the following: 'I departed from the Place – from the place I held in the Service of Thomas Bewick after being there upwards of 74 Years, on the 20 of November 1827.' Folded within, George found a tooth.[17]

THE SUDDEN DEATH of uncle George Atkinson in May 1814 had led to the winding up of the Jamaican merchant house of Atkinson & Bogle; the partnership which had replaced it disbanded in December 1824, following Edward Adams' retirement, to be succeeded by Robertson, Brother & Co. The new firm took over the wharves and warehouses in Little Port Royal Street, the butchery where the beef for provisioning the navy was prepared, the running of several absentee proprietors' estates, the contract to supply enslaved pioneers to the army, and sundry other concerns on the island. The Kingston office would be run by Robert Robertson's 29-year-old brother-in-law, George Atkinson, who had inherited his late father's share of the firm. Cousin George, who was the only one of his siblings to have been born in Jamaica, and who had been educated at Harrow, was by all accounts an unpleasant individual, with a 'very great idea of his own importance' as well as a 'great lack of common sense & discretion'.[18]

Soon George's next brother, nineteen-year-old Frank, came out to join him on the island. Frank did not care much for Jamaica – a 'Dog hole', he called it – and was particularly struck by the locals' lack of enterprise, writing home:

> It would astonish you to know how science is neglected here, and to see the indolence of the people, whites & all, on that score. There is no doubt that we could obtain the finest vegetable oils in the world, not only from cocoa nuts but from mango and innumerable plants here. And in the streets of Kingston & Spanish Town the Gamboge Thistle grows in abundance, one of the strongest narcotics known, and from which many maintain opium is made and not from the poppy; this is put to no use, commercial or otherwise, and all oil is imported. Bees of various species abound. Notwithstanding the excellent market for wax in the Catholic countries round us, only one man during the last 30 years ever kept them as a source of profit, near Kingston, and he has not had any since the Storm of 1815 which blew them all away.[19]

Frank had anticipated returning to England many years later, with 'spectacles, a stomach, and the gout', but he quarrelled badly with George and left the island after just a year.[20] Another brother, William, came and went under similar circumstances; and when Matt Atkinson, in 1827, wrote to his abrasive nephew enquiring whether a clerical position might be available for his seventeen-year-old son Isaac, the reply was a decided negative. Robert Robertson found George's treatment of his younger siblings unfathomable, and wondered whether it arose from some kind of unfounded terror that they would bring ruin upon him. 'He certainly makes out his own situation as one of *great destitution*; and if we were to give full credence to his case, as he has described it, you would suppose him to be on the high road to the *Poor House*,' Robertson remarked to Matt. 'But having been one of his father's Executors, you will as far as his father's Estate is concerned, know, that in the distribution which was lately made, he received *his due proportion*: and for his situation in the house, you would hardly believe, after all he has said, that he cannot for his share be deriving much less than £4000 a year – he may try many parts of the world before he will find the means of doing better.'[21]

IT WAS ESPECIALLY HARD on Nathaniel Clayton, as an un-flagging writer of letters, that the use of his right hand would be badly hampered in his later years by gout. Nathaniel's poor health was a constant source of anxiety to Dorothy; but it was she who would die first, on 3 August 1827, after a combination of medicine and leeches failed to ease a bowel complaint from which she had been suffering.

I found myself moved quite unexpectedly by Dorothy's death. Early on during my family research, I went up to Northumberland to explore the Atkinson–Clayton correspondence in the county archives; over three exhilarating days, I read my way through six boxes filled with hundreds of letters, and met many family members for the first time. On the afternoon of my last day at the archives, as closing time approached, I had almost finished going through the final box. Right at the bottom, I found a small roll of paper, the size of a cigar, on which I noticed that Nathaniel had inscribed, in the shaky handwriting of his old age, these words: 'A lock of my beloved wife's hair.'[22] I unrolled it, taking care to disturb the contents as little as possible. The hair was mousy brown, very fine, with just a glint of silver. I fought to hold back the tears when I realized what was happening. I was reaching across five generations and touching – yes, actually *touching* – my great-great-great-great-aunt.

Dorothy's death was the first of a run of family bereavements over the next few years. I feel bad that Ann hasn't been a more conspicuous presence in these pages, especially given that she is my direct ancestor, but this is due to none of her letters having survived. One morning in October 1828 she was pacing up and down the breakfast room at Carr Hill, talking with her son George, when suddenly she grabbed the chimneypiece, murmuring, 'I feel very queer almost as if I was tipsy.'[23] Matt was called in from the garden, and he took her up to her room. She had suffered a massive stroke; soon she was unable to speak, and paralysed down her left side. Aunt Wordsworth rushed across country from Cheshire and found her sister 'still living tho' totally insensible to every thing'.[24] Within three days, Ann was dead.

At the time the younger Atkinson boys, Isaac and Dick, were in Liverpool, where they were apprenticed to the merchant house of J. & A. Gilfillan (an arrangement made through their well-connected Littledale uncles). George, in the meantime, was being groomed for a managing role at the Tyne Iron Company, while also acquiring a local reputation as an upstanding young man. On 24 January 1829, the *Newcastle Courant* ran the story of a boy who was skating on the pond at Carr Hill late one afternoon when he fell through the ice; he would have drowned but for George, who 'threw himself in, and by great personal exertion, and at the greatest risk of his own life, succeeded in rescuing his friend'.[25] In the summer of that year, aged twenty-one, George was elected to the committee of the newly founded Natural History Society of Northumberland, his first gift to its collection a 'very beautiful specimen of the Stormy Petrel' which he had shot over the Tyne.[26] As the society's curator for ornithology, George was responsible for soliciting donations from far and wide. The celebrated naturalist John James Audubon contributed the 'Skins of thirty Birds' in August 1830; he had visited Thomas Bewick at Gateshead three years earlier, while raising money for his own magnum opus, *The Birds of America*.[27]

Following Ann's death, Matt cut a shadowy, shambling figure, and his failing eyesight meant that he could barely read or write;

he died on 24 December 1830. I couldn't locate a copy of his will in the usual public archives, and it took me a while to track one down to Durham University Library.[28] I was curious to find out whether Matt had in the slightest way acknowledged his 'other' family – but this would prove wishful thinking on my part. Whatever happened in Jamaica, stayed there.

'WHO KNOWS BUT that emancipation, like a beautiful plant, may, in its due season, rise out of the ashes of the abolition of the Slave-trade,' Thomas Clarkson had written in 1808, the year the landmark act came into force.[29] His optimism had not been entirely misplaced, for the institution of slavery showed signs of crumbling; in the early 1820s, though, its collapse still seemed some way off. The inaugural meeting of the Society for the Mitigation and Gradual Abolition of Slavery took place on 31 January 1823; abolitionists now set out to present themselves as pragmatists, not seeking immediate emancipation, instead hoping to 'improve, gradually' the lives of the enslaved population by giving them greater protection under the law, and conferring upon them 'one civil privilege after another', until one day they would rise 'insensibly to the rank of free peasantry'.[30] William Wilberforce, who was too infirm to lead the parliamentary campaign, passed the baton to Thomas Fowell Buxton, the MP for Weymouth.

On 15 May, in the House of Commons, Buxton moved a resolution that slavery was 'repugnant' to both the British constitution and the Christian religion, and 'ought to be gradually abolished'.[31] Alexander Baring – Sir Francis' second son – warned that should abolition take place, the sugar islands would be of no further value to Britain. He also insisted that the hardships endured by the enslaved population had been much exaggerated: 'The name of slave is a harsh one; but their real condition is undoubtedly, in many respects, superior to that of most of the peasantry of Europe.'[32]

This mischievous argument – that the enslaved people of the West Indies were 'as well, or perhaps even better' off than European labourers – was one to which pro-slavery lobbyists resorted with such frequency that Thomas Clarkson set out to debunk it in a polemic using adverts drawn from the *Jamaica Gazette*.[33] The first example he gave was as follows: 'Kingston, June 14th, 1823. For Sale: Darliston-Pen, in Westmoreland (Parish), with 112 *prime Negroes*, and 448 *head of stock*.' (Darliston was a cattle ranch owned by the Kingston house – thirty-eight of its enslaved population had taken the surname Atkinson when they were baptized three years earlier.)[34] 'I stop now to make a few remarks,' Clarkson wrote. 'First, it appears that the slaves in the British colonies *can be sold*. Can any *man, woman*, or *child* be sold in *Britain*? It appears, secondly, that these slaves are considered in no other light than *as cattle*, or as *inanimate property*. Now, do *we think or speak of our British labourers or servants in the same way*?'[35]

Over the next few years, the government attempted to straddle two diametrically opposed viewpoints through the policy known as 'amelioration', by which the enslaved population would be gradually prepared for their liberty. The Colonial Secretary Lord Bathurst, in consultation with the Society of West India Planters and Merchants,

The lot of 'the happy free labourers of England' is contrasted with that of 'the wretched slaves in the West Indies'.

drew up a programme of measures that the legislative bodies on the individual islands were then pressed to adopt. Religious instruction would be given to enslaved people, and marriages between them would be encouraged; families could not be separated by sale; enslaved women could no longer be punished by flogging; enslaved men could receive no more than twenty-five lashes.

Cousin George Atkinson was elected to the Jamaican House of Assembly in 1826 as one of Kingston's three representatives. The members for the town were seen as radicals: 'They are strenuous opponents to the Saints and Lord Bathurst, and all attempts at *legislating* for the Island.'[36] The Assembly saw Bathurst's 'ameliorative' measures as outrageously meddlesome, of course, but nodded them through nonetheless; believing emancipation to be inevitable, they were now focusing their energies on capitulating to the will of Westminster under the best possible financial terms. 'Compensation' had become the planters' watchword.

By the start of the 1830s, however, many abolitionists had lost patience with the government's softly-softly approach to their cause. On 15 May 1830, at a rowdy meeting of more than two thousand activists at the Freemasons' Hall in London, a resolution passed to demand that parliament set a date after which all newborn babies would automatically be free. 'They ought to aim at the extinction of slavery, by taking off the supply of children,' declared Thomas Fowell Buxton.[37]

But first, before it was ready to liberate the enslaved population of the colonies, parliament would need to put its own house in order. The system by which the British electorate picked their representatives was indefensibly archaic, with most of the swelling middle classes still excluded from the franchise. The constituency map portrayed a bygone age, where tiny rotten and pocket boroughs such as Old Sarum and New Romney continued to return two MPs, while the booming northern industrial city of Manchester – an abolitionist heartland – lacked even one representative.

The summer of 1830 saw the eruption of the 'Swing riots', as disaffected agricultural labourers rallied under the battle cry 'Bread or Blood' and set about torching haystacks, barns and farms. The unrest soon spread from Kent, where it had started, across much of England. Many among the ruling class accepted that electoral reform was overdue. 'The state of England is truly grievous but there is no remedy except by the aristocracy holding together to preserve the Peace,' Bertie Cator, who was close to the action at Mount Mascal, wrote to Jane Atkinson at Temple Sowerby. 'Tho I speak of Aristocracy holding together I don't mean we ought not to yield to public opinion. I am anxious for Reform because it appears requisite. I mean that people who enjoy wealth should exert themselves to preserve Peace and good order.'[38] (In spite of all the unpleasantness which had gone before, cordial relations now existed between the Cators and the rest of the family.)

On 22 November, following the defeat of the hidebound Duke of Wellington in a motion of no confidence, Earl Grey pledged his new Whig ministry to pushing through the necessary legislation. Three months later, Lord John Russell placed a reform bill before the House of Commons; it scraped through its second reading by one vote, but was sabotaged by a wrecking amendment during the committee stage. Grey immediately took the risk of forcing another general election, and in July 1831 he won the thumping landslide that would pave the way for change.

JAMES LINDSAY, the seventh Earl of Balcarres, viewed the management of his recently inherited Jamaican plantations with considerable distrust. Following his father's death in 1825, he had gone through the old estate accounts, as submitted by the Kingston house, and was shocked to find that they had barely turned a profit in seven years. It was true that the coffee estate in St George Parish, plagued as it was by frequent landslides and a 'turbulent' workforce, had been failing for a long time; but the poor performance of the adjoining Martin's Hill and Marshall's Pen properties, in Manchester Parish, was harder to swallow.[39] For here, under George Atkinson's direction, and at vast cost, 140 acres of woodland had been felled and planted with coffee; a works had been built, a pulper installed and extensive patios laid on which to dry the beans; and three hundred acres of guinea grass pasture had been added, enclosed by three miles of dry-stone walls.

The new Lord Balcarres was far from reassured by a private letter from Edward Adams, who, as a former partner of the Kingston house, knew the estates well. With startling candour, Adams warned that he had never known West India properties to be 'ultimately profitable' to absentee proprietors. 'Subject to Hurricanes, Rebellion, Emancipation, Contagion among Slaves, at best their returns are precarious,' he wrote. 'You always are at the mercy of your local Agent, and each of them in turn, speciously and with glittering anticipations may undo the act of his Predecessor by an idle Expense of Thousands. You cannot sell it but on credit, and to recover the amount, you must wade thro' Chancery; and on selling, if you get the value of the Slaves and Cattle, your Land and Works you are well contented to sacrifice!!'[40]

George's letters to Lord Balcarres brimmed with his high hopes for the estates, but less rosy reports reached their owner by other channels. The overseer at Martin's Hill disclosed that the Kingston house, which held the contract to supply the navy's beef, regularly used the pasture there to fatten up 'their own Cattle'.[41] On one occasion, only a small proportion of a cattle shipment from Puerto Rico had been safely delivered to Martin's Hill; and George's explanation that the rest had died in transit had failed to satisfy their purchaser. 'The whole transaction about these Spanish Cattle is most disgraceful, & almost dishonest,' wrote Balcarres. 'I have no doubt he has made a pretty penny of the transaction, & pandered upon me what is not worth any thing like the value charged.'[42]

Jamaican attorneys were notorious for their chicanery, and it is not hard to reach the conclusion that George was plotting to seize these estates for himself, by saddling them with so much debt that their owner would consider it almost an act of mercy to be relieved of them. Lord Balcarres certainly believed this to be the case, but he faced a 'very delicate' predicament – for were he to appoint a new attorney to manage the estates, George would no doubt do his damnedest to cut him out of his one-third stake in the lucrative pioneer business.[43]

On 1 January 1830, cousin George wrote to inform Lord Balcarres that his partner Robert Robertson would soon be retiring. He would continue to run the house in Jamaica, while James Hosier, who had previously managed the dry goods branch of the business, would now represent its interests in England; and he trusted that his Lordship would show the partnership of Atkinson & Hosier the same 'confidence' that he and his father had been pleased to confer upon its predecessors.[44] At this point, Balcarres contemplated cutting loose, but Edward Adams offered one clear nugget of advice – on no account should the earl jeopardize his interest in the pioneer business. 'Consider the immense returns on the amount of their Investment that they *regularly* yield,' Adams wrote. 'What would you get for them, if sold? Depend on it, not a Fraction more than the intrinsic worth of the men, and nothing in consideration of the productiveness of the Contract.'[45]

And so, for the time being, Lord Balcarres' estates languished under the management of the Kingston house. 'They hope that I shall be satisfied with the improved state of Martins Pen, having 95 head of Cattle more than the last year, but they here omit to state, that most of these Cattle have been purchased and a debt incurred,' Balcarres observed to his London agent on 6 February 1831. 'It is like congratulating me that my servants have not robbed my house a second time.'[46] But on 16 May, his mind made up, Balcarres wrote to George Atkinson: 'It is now upwards of six years since I succeeded to my West India property. It is unnecessary for me to state how much I have been disappointed in the expectations held out to me.' Having read some recent comments by George about the 'dreadful state of Jamaica property', he explained, he no longer believed his own plantations could prosper under the care of an attorney who so evidently thought they 'must shortly and inevitably be reduced to actual Ruin'; and thus, 'as Drowning Men will catch at straws', he had recently dispatched a new power of attorney to a gentleman living close by the Manchester estates.[47]

George reacted with predictable fury to his discharge, firing off a letter listing the great strides taken at Martin's Hill and Marshall's Pen under his command: 'The unprofitable drudgery of getting the property into condition to be profitable has been performed by us, and your new Attorney only reaps the fruit of our exertions.'[48] Afterwards he submitted the estates' final accounts, of which Balcarres would observe: 'A more Rascally set of Closing Accounts were never delivered in.'[49]

Meanwhile, the two parties were locked in a bitter dispute over the pioneers. In March 1830, Lord Balcarres had demanded that an 'absolute conveyance be made out in *my own name* without loss of time, of my undivided third of the contract, & of the whole of the Pioneers, each Pioneer to be named therein'.[50] But George refused to comply, arguing that since Atkinson & Hosier held the majority stake in the business, they needed shielding against anyone representing the minority interest who might choose to withdraw a proportion of the pioneers, or even terminate the contract: 'Our object is merely to protect from all possibility of prejudice our own larger interest.'[51] Edward Adams, when shown George's letter, dismissed these grounds as 'utter sophistry'.[52]

POLITICAL TENSIONS had long been simmering in Jamaica, where the planter class continued to cling on to every scrap of power; although free people of colour now outnumbered whites by two to one, they were still disbarred from voting in elections or giving evidence in criminal cases, and disqualified from serving in the House of Assembly or holding a commission in the island militia. But finally, in December 1830, the Assembly passed an act declaring that 'all the free brown and black population' would be 'entitled to have and enjoy all the rights, privileges, immunities and advantages whatsoever to which they would have been entitled if born of and descended from white ancestors' – a milestone in the social and political evolution of the colony.[53]

The island elite had always tried to shield their enslaved workforce from news of outside events. 'So completely has all intercourse with Hayti been heretofore guarded against,' wrote one planter in the 1820s, 'that the slaves of Jamaica know no more of the events which have been passing there for the last thirty years than the inhabitants of China.'[54] But it was impossible to prevent whispers of abolition from circulating round the island. In late 1831, the rumour arose that parliament had voted to end slavery, and that the king had sent papers ordering the liberation of the slaves – but that the masters were conspiring to keep them in chains.

As the story spread, Samuel Sharpe, an enslaved man who was also the charismatic deacon of a Baptist chapel at Montego Bay, convinced his brethren to mount a show of resistance; they would refuse to cut the ripe sugar cane on their estates unless granted their liberty and paid for their labour. Local white missionaries soon heard about the planned strike. 'I learn that some wicked persons have persuaded you that the king has made you free,' preached the Baptist minister William Knibb in his sermon on 27 December. 'What you have been told is false – false as hell can make it.'[55] Kensington Pen in St James Parish was the first of dozens of estates to be set on fire that night, turning the dark sky a sinister shade of orange. The insurrection quickly gathered pace, with perhaps sixty thousand enslaved men and women coming out in support.

By the time the armed forces had restored peace, two weeks later, nearly three hundred properties in the west of the island had been put to the torch. (Not that they belonged to the Atkinson family any more, but both the Bogue and Dean's Valley estates were damaged.) At least two hundred blacks and fourteen whites died in the conflict, which would become known as the Baptist War. In the reprisals that followed, more than three hundred men were executed in the main square at Montego Bay. 'Generally four, seldom less than three, were hung at once,' recalled the Wesleyan missionary Henry Bleby. 'The bodies remained, stiffening in the breeze, till the court martial had provided another batch of victims.'[56] Meanwhile, vigilante groups adhering to the Colonial Church Union, an organization set up by the pro-slavery Anglican clergyman George Wilson Bridges, destroyed fifteen Nonconformist chapels. Samuel Sharpe was the last of the rebels to be executed, on 23 May 1832. 'I would rather die upon yonder gallows than live in slavery,' he told Bleby shortly before his end.[57]

THE REJECTION of a second reform bill by the House of Lords sparked serious disturbances across England during the autumn of 1831; and fears that the violence would continue for as long as the political establishment resisted change were only stoked by the shocking news from Jamaica.

At the start of the next session of parliament, in December 1831, Grey's ministry tabled yet another reform bill; it easily cleared the Commons in March 1832. However, the recalcitrance of the upper house left the government with little choice but to propose the creation of enough new Whig peers to outvote the reactionaries – a measure which William IV would not consent to. As a result, Grey resigned on 9 May. The monarch invited Wellington to form a new ministry; but the duke failed to build sufficient parliamentary support, and Grey took office again on 15 May. The Representation of the People Act – commonly known as the Reform Act – passed into law on 7 June. It swept away those swamps of vested interest, the rotten boroughs, in their place creating 130 new seats; and it almost doubled the size of the electorate, extending the franchise to small landowners, tenant farmers, shopkeepers and householders paying annual rent of £10 or more.

The general election that followed, under the new franchise, brought in a fresh generation of free-thinking MPs – some representing previously ignored manufacturing towns – who were impervious to the blandishments of the West India lobby. From the start, Grey's new ministry faced sustained pressure to abolish slavery, with dozens of petitions arriving at Westminster every day. In the House of Commons, on 14 May 1833, the Colonial Secretary Edward Stanley unveiled the principles upon which the government planned to base its abolition bill – but not before Thomas Fowell Buxton and three other MPs had manhandled a 'huge feather-bed of a petition' on to the table of the chamber.[58]

Stanley's proposals fully satisfied no one. To the abolitionists, the suggestion that former slaves should undergo a twelve-year period of 'apprenticeship', when they would be obliged to give their former owners three-quarters of their labour in return for food and shelter, smacked of slavery in all but name. To the West India interest, the £15 million loan that would assist the planters' recovery from this hammer blow seemed derisory. But the House did agree to Stanley's first resolution, which was that immediate measures should be taken 'for the entire abolition of slavery throughout the colonies'.[59]

Behind the scenes, the West Indians lobbied strenuously. On 10 June, Stanley informed the House that he believed the proposed £15 million loan was too hard on slave owners. The government now planned to offer them £20 million in outright compensation for the loss of their human property; he had received assurances that this figure would be sufficient to secure 'their full concurrence and co-operation'.[60] Twenty million pounds was such a vast sum – about 40 per cent of the annual national budget – that it exceeded the comprehension of most MPs, even those accustomed to dealing with enormous amounts of money. 'The magnitude of the sum almost passes the powers of conception,' Alexander Baring commented. 'In the present distressed state of the country, and in the still greater state of distress to which it will be reduced by the failure of this experiment, you might as well talk of £200,000,000.'[61]

By 25 June, the abolition bill was ready to receive its first reading. The debates that followed were largely passionless, and focused on practicalities; at times it seemed that MPs had forgotten who the bill was intended to benefit. 'I cannot help observing, that, in discussing this question, we do not enough bear in mind that there are such persons as a large black population,' the veteran reformer Sir Francis Burdett scolded his fellow members. 'Everybody seems to think that either the commerce of this country, or the property, as it is called, of the West India proprietors, is the only matter of importance.'[62]

The abolitionists' final objections to the bill concerned the number of years for which the so-called 'apprentices' would be expected to continue working for their former masters. They had already accepted that 'praedial' slaves – those who were connected to the cultivation of the land – would have to endure longer apprenticeships than 'non-praedial' slaves. During the bill's committee stage, Stanley proposed fixing these terms at six and four years respectively, which was enough of a concession to satisfy the abolitionists. William Wilberforce, who had recently said that he felt 'like a clock which is almost run down', heard the news of the breakthrough three days before his death on 29 July 1833.[63] The bill passed the House of Commons on 7 August. Three weeks later, and despite the Duke of Wellington's last-ditch efforts to hobble it with amendments, the Slavery Abolition Act was signed into law.

TWENTY-TWO

A Spice of the Devil

NATHANIEL CLAYTON died in March 1832, aged seventy-five, leaving the Chesters estate to his three eldest surviving sons, Nat, John and Michael, and sizeable lump sums to the rest of his children – largesse that he could well afford. He had already secured his legacy in the corporation of Newcastle, having seamlessly handed over the town clerk's office to John in December 1822.

Nat's story would be one of potential unfulfilled. As a schoolboy, he had shown vast promise, coming top of the Harrow sixth form exam above Robert Peel, the future prime minister, and Lord Byron, the future literary titan. (Byron later recalled: 'Clayton was another school-monster of learning, and talent, and hope; but what has become of him I do not know. He was certainly a genius.')[1] Nat had gone on to practise law in London, where he was appointed a Commissioner in Bankruptcy under the patronage of his father's childhood friend, Lord Chancellor Eldon. But during his thirties he had been afflicted by a nervous disorder, with symptoms that included involuntary laughter and a difficulty swallowing; and after his recovery, he found that he had no further appetite for business. He would justify his retirement to Northumberland, aged forty-three, in a melancholy letter to his disapproving father:

> I should have retired from a lucrative Practice most unwillingly,
> & certainly not without a struggle. But recollecting that

previous to my Illness my professional Prospects frequently
induced a Despondency that was very difficult to combat, I felt
afterwards that I had neither Health nor Spirits to play what is
called the whole game of the Law; & after so long an Interval,
I was willing to spare myself the mortification, not to say
Humiliation, of pursuing it otherwise.[2]

John, on the other hand, would prove a worthy heir to the
Clayton dynasty. After the passing of the Reform Act, it was local
government's turn to face scrutiny, and when royal commissioners
turned up to investigate Newcastle in October 1833, John was the
first man called to give evidence. George Clayton Atkinson would
write admiringly of his cousin's performance: 'He seemed to know
everything connected with the corporation – understand all the
little complicated byelaws, & remembered every circumstance in
such an extraordinary way, that he completely astonished the Commissioners, & has done himself immense credit.'[3]

The bustling metropolis of Newcastle, as viewed from Gateshead.

The Municipal Corporations Act of 1835, which came out of the royal commission, overhauled the local government of 178 towns and cities in England and Wales – and John Clayton emerged unscathed from the upheaval. In 1836, an anonymous Newcastle journalist described him as follows:

> Has all the craft and subtlety of the devil. Great talents, indefatigable industry, immense wealth, and wonderful tact and facility in conducting business, give him an influence in society rarely possessed by one individual. Was unanimously re-elected Town Clerk, because the Clique had not a man equal to supply his place. Can do things with impunity that would damn an ordinary man. A good voice, speaks well, and never wastes a word.[4]

Everywhere, the spirit of reform was in the ascendant, and the patronage from which the aristocracy derived so much of its wealth and influence was under attack. William Cobbett was a particular adversary of this 'old corruption' through the pages of his news-paper, the *Weekly Register*. 'These blades are brothers, I believe, of the Earl of Egremont,' Cobbett had written about Charles and Percy Wyndham, who reportedly received £11,000 a year between them for an assortment of Jamaican offices. 'They have had these places since 1763. So that they have received *Six hundred and forty-nine thousand pounds*, principal money from these places, without, I believe, ever having even *seen* poor Jamaica.'[5] In the wake of the Reform Act, an investigation into West Indian sinecures was launched; and it was perhaps a tad ironic, given the late Sir Francis Baring's dealings with Charles Wyndham on behalf of the Atkinson family, that the committee was chaired by one of his grandsons, another Francis Baring, who was an unyielding critic of the patent offices.

CARR HILL NO LONGER felt much like a family home after Matt and Ann's deaths, and over the next few years their five children would scatter round the globe. But first, in May 1831, two of the boys – George and Dick – embarked on a tour of the western isles of Scotland. George was the driving force, being keen to visit some of the 'great breeding places of the sea fowl' and gather specimens for Newcastle's new natural history museum – a mission into which he threw himself with energy, on one occasion stripping off and swimming out to a rocky island in the middle of a loch on the isle of Harris, dragging behind him with his teeth a 'water proof bag' designed for conveying eggs to shore.[6] (Dick, meanwhile, 'insinuated himself into the good graces' of the villagers. 'The old crones,' recalled George, 'used to clap him on the back and in their lack of more appropriate English, call him *pretty boy*.')[7]

The Atkinson brothers' final destination was the remote archipelago of St Kilda. To make the sixty-mile crossing from Harris they hired an eighteen-foot yawl crewed by three local men, containing a sack of oatmeal, a peat fire in an iron pot, and half a dozen bottles of whisky. Their first impression of the St Kildans who hauled the boat on to the wide beach was of good health; they had the 'most beautiful teeth imaginable'.[8] The islanders, the brothers discovered, depended upon birds for their every need: 'Except from the rocks, fishing is not pursued, for they have only one very clumsy boat, and manage it miserably; so in fact, fowling is their only occupation.'[9] Dick's terrier, Crab, soon became expert at extracting puffins from their burrows, 'for he is so small, that the larger holes easily admitted him, and the bites he at first received only made him more determined'.[10] On their third and last morning at St Kilda, some boys presented them with a pair of young peregrine falcons that they had plucked from a nest on a precipitous cliff; George took the hawks back to Carr Hill, hoping to observe 'their progressive changes of plumage' as they grew into maturity.[11] But it was not to be, for both birds would fly off.

Mary Ann was the first of Matt and Ann's children to be married, to John Dobson, a Gateshead solicitor. Not long afterwards, in 1833, the couple emigrated to Van Diemen's Land, in the far-off penal colony of New South Wales. (The territory would be renamed Tasmania in 1856.) By the time of their departure, there was no love lost between John Dobson and his Atkinson brothers-in-law, who were furious that he had drained all the ready money from their late father's estate, and grief-stricken at the permanent loss of their beloved sister.

Isaac, the middle Atkinson boy, had left for Jamaica in late 1831 – cousin George having agreed to employ him at the Kingston house – but illness forced his return after barely a year away. Soon he was placed under the supervision of a physician at Kirkby Lonsdale in Westmorland, within visiting distance of Aunt Jane from Temple Sowerby. Dick, meanwhile, sailed out to Jamaica to fill Isaac's shoes. On 10 December 1833, George would write to Dick with news of their brother's declining health: 'Poor Isaac – your forbodings that you should never see him again – I fear are too true.'[12] On 24 January 1834, in a feverish state of mind, and haunted by past sins, imaginary or otherwise, Isaac started writing what he clearly knew would be his last letter to Dick in Jamaica: 'I was as you well know sunk in Every kind of wickedness & set my God at defiance, & mocked him Continually, yet his goodness never tires & when hell was gaping for me he stretched out his arm to me, & has by prayer thro' Christ so opened my Eyes to a sense of my own insufficiency.'[13] He died on 11 May, aged twenty-four, and was laid to rest in the churchyard at Temple Sowerby.

DURING THE TWILIGHT days of slavery, the Kingston house was one of the few active participants in the market for slave labour in Jamaica; in a sense it was bound to be, for it remained subject to a £10,000 bond that guaranteed its performance of the pioneer contract. In November 1832, cousin George Atkinson agreed to supply forty-eight pioneers to the 37th Regiment; as a result, he would purchase forty-one men over the following twelve months. As it happens, the last pioneer he bought, for £45 currency on 23 October 1833, was an individual called Richard; this was during the slender gap between the passing of the Westminster abolition act, on 28 August, and the corresponding local law, on 3 December.[14] The House of Assembly in Jamaica was the first colonial legislature to ratify its own abolition act; to stall would merely have delayed the distribution of the £20 million compensation money, a process that could not commence until all nineteen slave colonies had enacted legislation deemed adequate by Westminster.

One of the first deeds of the Slave Compensation Commissioners, operating out of Whitehall, was to order a full census and valuation of the enslaved population throughout the empire; the governor of each colony appointed men to manage the process locally. George Atkinson was named one of Jamaica's eight assistant commissioners in February 1834, but he did not hold the post for long. That same month, the local Court of Chancery awarded him the receivership of Norwich estate in Portland Parish, prising the property out of the hands of James Colthirst, its indebted owner. Colthirst, who had served as a clerk at the Kingston house for fifteen years, soon took revenge by revealing to the partner of a competing merchant house that George had knowingly embezzled $5,000 which had been mistakenly overpaid while settling a transaction back in 1819. The rival merchant sued for the return of the funds, the case coming to trial in July 1834. In the face of some damning evidence, the judgement went against George, and although this was only a civil case, not a criminal one, it left a stain on his character. George was discreetly advised to retire from the compensation board, and took the hint. 'I have just received from him a tender of his resignation on the grounds of ill health,' the governor, the Marquess of Sligo, wrote to Thomas Spring Rice, the Colonial Secretary. 'I have accepted, and trust that you will approve of my adopting this mild course in preference to one more painful to his feelings.'[15]

The start of the 'apprenticeship' – the period during which it was envisaged that former slaves would learn to live freely – passed without incident on 1 August 1834, which surprised many whites who had prophesied bloodshed. 'I for one certainly expected a much more serious difficulty to have followed on a change so entire & so sudden,' wrote George. 'I augur well for the Colony even after the Apprenticeship ceases. The embarrassed Mortgagor must go and the overforced cultivation of sugar must decline but another & in my opinion a healthier state of cultivation will ensue.'[16]

The enmity between Lord Balcarres and the Kingston house would erupt again during the compensation process. According to rules published in the *London Gazette*, all claims for a slice of the £20 million compensation money needed to be filed within three months of the start of the 'apprenticeship'. By this date, 31 October 1834, cousin George had submitted nine claim forms for the pioneers – encompassing 255 men based in seven parishes – under his own name as 'joint owner with James Hosier'. Balcarres' one-third interest was not mentioned on the paperwork, since the rules specified that claims should be made by those whose names had appeared on the 'latest returns made in the office of the Registrar of Slaves' – and the earl's share of the pioneers remained unregistered.[17]

Since his dismissal by Lord Balcarres three years earlier, George had made a point of providing the earl with only vague accounts of the pioneer business, of withholding his income for as long as possible, and of using his properties without permission as places of retirement for old and infirm pioneers. 'With respect to the House of Atkinson I really do not know what is to be done with them,' Balcarres wrote to his London agent. 'Their undoubted intention is to cheat us in the winding up of the Pioneers if they can, & of course our policy is to prevent them if we can, & it is clear that they will furnish no information unless they are forced to it by Law.'[18]

Although George had shown himself to be devious, it may be that Lord Balcarres was here being unnecessarily suspicious. While it was perfectly true that George and his partner James Hosier had refused to place Balcarres' name alongside theirs on the slave register, they had never disputed his one-third share in the pioneers. Indeed, they had admitted it 'unequivocally', and in countless letters; they had also offered him a letter from Barings, their agent in London, guaranteeing his share of any compensation money.[19] Nonetheless, Balcarres chose to file a counterclaim against each of George's nine claims, a hostile act he defended on grounds of Hosier's insolent tone towards him: 'The few letters that he addressed to me personally, were of a description & language, that in this Country no Gentleman makes use of to another.'[20]

In August 1835, the Treasury awarded the contract to supply the majority of the compensation money to a syndicate led by the financier N.M. Rothschild. Meanwhile, in London, the commissioners began the process of adjudicating – colony by colony, and in Jamaica's case parish by parish – the 46,000 claims they had received to compensate for the loss of 668,000 slaves. By Christmas, the first payments had been made; over the ensuing months, snaking queues of former slave owners and their agents, waiting to pick up cheques from the National Debt Office at 19 Old Jewry, would become a familiar sight in the City of London.

Shortly after his first payment for the pioneers came through, Lord Balcarres wrote to George Atkinson: 'Perhaps this may be a proper opportunity for me to assure you that it has been a subject of great regret to me, that there has been a considerable degree of irritation in our Correspondence for some time past, and which I submit during the very short time that our connection will now subsist had better be discontinued.'[21] The final cheque for the pioneers was released in April 1836, bringing the total payout for 255 men to £6,577, or £25 per capita.

I spent the best part of a week trawling through Lord Balcarres' correspondence about the pioneers at the National Library of Scotland. He had kept every letter on the subject, later annotating some with pithy comments. 'From the House of Atkinson respecting the Compensation Claim for the Pioneers – a Bullying Letter which I answered in his own style,' he had written on the back of one of George's notes.[22] 'A most intemperate ungentlemanlike letter,' he had scrawled on another.[23] Not for the first time during my investigations, I felt bruised by the ugliness of what I was finding. Lord Balcarres' distrust of the 'House of Atkinson' was completely understandable, but even so I disliked his haughty tone and his assumption of the moral high ground, for neither party had emerged covered in glory. Following this research trip, I wrote to the current earl, who had allowed me access to these papers, mentioning my disappointment that our families should have ended up at loggerheads. I was grateful for the kindness of his reply. 'My experience of family archives,' he said, 'is that each family invariably regard their correspondents as rogues and themselves as innocent gentlemen.'

On top of his portion of the pioneer money, George Atkinson shared in payments for a further 511 enslaved men and women, most of whom were based on three properties where he was acting as receiver – Norwich and Whydah estates in the parish of Portland, and Stanmore Hill in the parish of St Elizabeth. Incidentally, claimants were not required to give the *names* of their former slaves on the official paperwork, except under exceptional circumstances; the only individual named by George, on account of his having been 'born in Gt. Britain' – which meant that compensation could not be paid out for him – was a certain William Robertson.[24]

So who *was* this William Robertson? Yet again, when it came to matters of mixed blood, the family letters offered minimal clues. All I could find was this: in the 1817 slave register for Kingston, William was identified as the eighteen-year-old 'mulatto' son of Flora, a forty-year-old 'negro' woman attached to George's household.[25] So William was born in about 1799, and had a white father. But who might this parent have been? Was it George's brother-in-law and former business partner, Robert Robertson? Or could it have been George's own father, George, who had returned to England in 1798, perhaps taking Flora with him as a servant? In this scenario, George and William would be half-brothers – which may sound quite unlikely, but I really wouldn't be surprised. Having spent so much time poking around in my family's past, it now takes a great deal to surprise me.

IN APRIL 1835, when Dick Atkinson had been in Jamaica about eighteen months, a violent strain of yellow fever swept the island. George, who was lodging with his young cousin while his own house was being renovated, had the presence of mind to send for a doctor as soon as Dick's symptoms surfaced. Mercifully, Dick managed to throw off the fever on the third day, after being 'severely bled & blistered', a swift recovery that George attributed to his 'prudent sober manner of living'.[26]

His careful temperament may, perhaps, have saved his life; but Dick was too diffident to flourish as a merchant. 'All he wants is confidence in himself, & activity – what in the world is termed a Spice of the Devil,' George (who possessed Spice of the Devil aplenty) told Aunt Jane.[27] 'His only chance of getting on is to become a clever salesman & good man of business which with the opportunities he has got depends entirely on himself. In temper & steadiness he is all I can wish.'[28]

George and Dick were regular correspondents with their aunt at Temple Sowerby. Jane continued to add to her mother's collection of shells and other natural wonders, and they were always on the lookout for specimens. 'My dear Aunt,' wrote George on 11 July 1836:

> I heard from Richard that you were desirous of getting an
> Alligator and having been fortunate enough to procure one
> about 5 feet long I have had it stuffed and send it to you by
> Capt. Hughes of the *Laidmans*. It is in excellent preservation
> & I hope will reach you so. In the same package I have sent a
> small Box containing 37 Jamaica Land Shells many of which
> I believe are unknown in England & all of which may be new
> in your Cabinet as I understand that the collecting of them has
> commenced within very few years past. Another Box contains
> a snake skin of a large size. This was the fruit of Richard's skill
> & prowess & he would have it sent. I doubt whether it will
> shew well by that hanging on the little Parlour.[29]

Dick's fascination with nature had stayed with him since childhood, and he was sometimes assisted in his explorations by a 'faithful & good servant' called William. 'I have collected a pretty good lot of Insects chiefly Butterflies which will be forwarded by the *Laidmans* next trip,' Dick wrote to Aunt Jane on another occasion. 'It was William's proposition to collect them & send them as he was very anxious to make some humble return for your great kindness to him after poor Isaac's death.'[30] To return to an earlier line of speculation, I wondered whether this 'William' to whom Jane had shown such kindness was the same 'William Robertson' who was named on George's compensation form?

FROM HOBART TOWN in Van Diemen's Land, John Dobson sat down to write to Dick, his brother-in-law, on 30 March 1837. His letter opened with the joyful news that Mary Ann had just given birth to their fourth child: 'They are both doing well, & I suppose we have a good chance of having at *least* a dozen, the more the merrier say I, especially in a land where they are wanted. I trust you are rapidly making your fortune, if not, pray come here, & turn Wool Grower, instead of a Sugar Planter.'

Here John paused, picking up his pen again three days later: 'I had written thus far, the happiest of men, & now alas I am the most miserable.' That morning, John had visited Mary Ann in her bedroom before going down for breakfast; moments later he heard a loud thump on the floor above. Mary Ann had climbed out of bed, the footstool on to which she stepped had slipped, and she had banged her head, dying instantly. 'I don't know what to think or what to say,' John continued. 'Who now can ever bring up our dear children with the same gentleness & affection as their sainted Mother, surrounded too by convict Servants I cannot bear to think of it. I write in a hurry dearest Richard to save the next ship, the last for some weeks. I must write – yet I feel stupefied with horror, & with amazement, & with Grief – I wish I was dead too.'[31]

John's letter reached Dick in Jamaica, via England, six months after the sad event it describes. A letter from Aunt Jane arrived by the same ship. Dick's reply to her reveals his distress. Not only had he been extremely close to his sister Mary Ann, but his brother George recently seemed to have forgotten about his existence: 'It is two years since I have received a line from him, & during that time I have written him repeatedly; however I suppose the Balls and gaities of Newcastle entirely drive from him the recollection of a Brother so far removed from him. My Dear Aunt if this rambling letter appear to be written peevishly or in an illnatured strain you must excuse it as my spirits are not of the most buoyant description.'[32]

WITH FLAWED OPTIMISM, the British government had imagined the 'apprenticeship' as a time when former slaves might acquire the industrious habits of free citizens, and former slave owners might adapt their businesses to the demands of a wage economy. But many planters – perceiving this to be their last chance to exploit their former human property – refused to let apprentices take days off to which they were entitled, withdrew their supplies of food and medicine, and packed wayward individuals off to 'dance' the treadmill at the local house of correction.

Cousin George Atkinson had been the sponsor of the legislation to introduce the treadmill, also known as the 'everlasting staircase', which the Jamaican House of Assembly in 1827 approved for use 'in lieu of imprisonment in the workhouse, committal to hard labour, or flagellation'.[33] A treadmill might keep 'upwards of 20 prisoners' occupied in the 'grinding of Corn, pumping of Water, or any other purpose where power is required'; it comprised a large, horizontal wooden cylinder attached to an iron frame, with shallow steps and a handrail to which wrists were strapped.[34] Stepping on to the cylinder caused it to rotate; as it gained momentum, the prisoners were forced to 'dance' ever more nimbly, while an overseer lashed them

The treadmill, or everlasting staircase.

from behind. The ground below the treadmill was invariably sodden with blood.

Eighteen months into the 'apprenticeship', a parliamentary committee was set up to look into allegations of the excessive use of corporal punishment by the Jamaican magistracy. Towards the end of 1836, the Quaker philanthropist Joseph Sturge embarked with three colleagues on a tour of the West Indies. In Jamaica, they came across a boy who had recently suffered seven continuous days on the treadmill at Half Way Tree workhouse. 'His clothes had been flogged to pieces there. His chest was sore from rubbing against the mill, and he is still scarcely able to walk from the effects of an injury in the knee, inflicted by the revolving wheel, when he lost the step,' Sturge wrote in his bestselling account of the expedition.[35] The first-hand testimony of James Williams, a young man brought back by Sturge from Jamaica, would also generate a great deal of publicity. Williams' description of the brutalities to which he and his fellow apprentices had been subjected was another reminder that the task of abolition was not yet completed.

The committee was to prove a toothless body; but soon the government could no longer ignore the clamour of the British public against the 'apprenticeship'. On 11 April 1838, less than four months before the first, 'non-praedial' category of former slaves was due to be emancipated, parliament passed a bill to amend the Slavery Abolition Act of 1833. Henceforth, the travel time to and from the apprentices' places of work would be included within the forty hours and thirty minutes of free labour they were compelled to give their former owners each week; the punishment of female apprentices through the treadmill, flogging, or 'cutting off her Hair', was prohibited; and apprentices who were cruelly treated could be freed early.[36] But ultimately it was a ruling by the Law Officers that brought the matter to a head. They directed that apprentices employed as mechanics on estates should be reclassified as 'non-praedial', even if they performed occasional field labour; this would qualify them for liberty two years earlier than their 'praedial' co-workers. Without these skilled men, the manufacture of sugar would

Beneficent Britannia bestows liberty upon an African family.

be practically impossible. Left with little choice, the Jamaican House of Assembly voted to end the 'apprenticeship' in its entirety from 1 August 1838.

On 31 July, as midnight approached, many men, women and children climbed to the hilltops in anticipation of the most richly symbolic sunrise of their lives. The following morning, on the steps under the portico of the King's House in Spanish Town, the governor Sir Lionel Smith declared the end of slavery to a rapturous crowd. All those who had grimly predicted rivers of blood were yet again proved wrong; the day passed peacefully, marked by services of thanksgiving and scenes of joyous feasting.

TWENTY-THREE

Farewell to Jamaica

AT THIS POINT, I hope you won't mind briefly visiting Temple Sowerby with me, in order to tie up an important loose end. Cousin Matthew Atkinson, whose father Matthew had died in 1789, has played a peripheral role in this saga; for while they were beneficiaries of their uncle Richard's will, he and his younger brothers wisely stayed away from Jamaica, and kept out of the feud which divided their aunt Bridget's branch of the family. Even so, I owe Matthew a debt of gratitude, since it was through him that I stumbled upon this story in the first place – for it was a cardboard box of *his* letters that my sister and I inherited, and which I spent many weeks deciphering, all the while believing them to be addressed to my direct ancestor Matt.

Although these first cousins shared a name, and enjoyed fishing together, they were cut from very different cloth. Industrious Matthew (as opposed to indolent Matt) had followed his father into the business of banking; he was a stalwart of the local magistrates' bench, three times Mayor of Appleby, and High Sheriff of Westmorland. The fortunes of Matthew's Penrith Bank had started to sink following the stock market crash of 1825, when optimistic speculation in the wake of the Napoleonic Wars peaked, then collapsed; and in February 1826 he was forced to go cap in hand to Lord Lonsdale, the local grandee, who agreed to guarantee him 'to the extent of £10,000'.[1]

By 1837, after a turbulent decade during which he was never far from the abyss, Matthew had decided to retire. 'I rejoice to hear that you have determined to wind up your Banking concerns,' John Clayton wrote to his older cousin. 'I always thought that you carried them on more for the Benefit of others, than of Yourself.'[2] But all Matthew's efforts over the next few years to merge his business with another more stable operation would come to nothing; more than thirty privately owned banks toppled during the 'dark and heavy period' which began in mid-1840, and the Penrith Bank was one of the first to fall.[3] Matthew was declared bankrupt on 15 September. 'Death would be more welcome to me a thousand times than a forfeiture of honor & Integrity,' he had once written, and in those days there were few things more discreditable than financial ruin.[4]

On 25 March 1841, Matthew's Temple Sowerby residence – The Grange – and his farms were sold by auction at the Crown Hotel in Penrith, raising £26,200 towards his debts.[5] (Cousin George Atkinson, with a view to retiring there from Jamaica, made an unsuccessful bid on the house.) Matthew was meanwhile in France, evading arrest; his accomplice in planning his escape had been his cousin Jane Atkinson. She was now in her mid-sixties, her eyesight was poor, and she rarely left the village; during that winter, however, she started sending her coach out regularly, so that it became a familiar sight around the neighbourhood. Then, one night, Matthew took flight in it. Jane also arranged for his private papers to be taken to her house for safe keeping – which is how they came, circuitously, to be in my possession.

VARIOUS FACTORS WOULD conspire to drive the planters of Jamaica to the brink of collapse during the 1840s, the most obvious being the rupture to the labour supply that occurred at the stroke of midnight on 1 August 1838. Sugar cane was a demanding crop, requiring a large, disciplined workforce, and most newly liberated men and women chose no longer to toil in the fields of their former masters. Many planters tried to hold on to their workforce by imposing coercive contracts that linked the continued occupation of huts and provision grounds to compulsory labour, and when their former slaves refused to submit to such terms, some landowners responded by demolishing settlements, slaughtering livestock and chopping down breadfruit trees. These clashes caused an exodus from estates throughout the island.

Many evicted families squatted on vacant land, of which there was plenty; the more enterprising saved money to purchase small-holdings, often from debt-ridden planters selling off plots for as little as £2 per acre. Within a few years of abolition, however, the standard charge of a day's wages as weekly rent for housing, and the same for the use of provision grounds, had been established around the island. The principle that no planter could force his tenants to work for him was also widely accepted; they were free to work for whomsoever they wished.

Cousin George Atkinson sailed back to Jamaica in January 1840 after spending nearly a year in England, much of it with Aunt Jane at Temple Sowerby, recovering from an accident that would cause him to 'hobble sadly' for the rest of his life.[6] On his return, he was relieved to find March's Pen, his property near Spanish Town, in good order. 'My Farm here has suffered some what by my absence though not more perhaps than from so great a change as the Emancipation might be expected,' he told Jane. 'I found my house here as if I had been absent only for one of my usual three weeks planter rounds – and that not one of my people had left me for Freedom or any other cause which is very gratifying. In fact I must say I doubt whether any body of people would on the whole have behaved themselves so well under such a change as my dingy Country folks have done.'[7]

A visitor to Jamaica, the Quaker minister Joseph John Gurney, attended a dinner hosted by George in March 1840, and observed the optimism of his fellow guests: 'These men of business take a hopeful view of the improved condition of affairs within the last few months, and appear to look forward, on substantial grounds, to the future prosperity of the colony.'[8] Many planters embraced agricultural machinery for the first time, having previously shown little interest in it. (The enslaved workers who were needed in large numbers to process the cane during the intensive crop period had always been relatively under-employed during the quieter months, when planting and weeding took place; the plough and harrow would only have made them even less busy.) The planters also looked to new fertilizers to revitalize their exhausted cane fields. 'You should try the Guano on your light Temple Sowerby soil,' George advised Aunt Jane. 'I am satisfied you would find it answer.'[9]

In the end, it was not the labour shortage, but a radical change of economic policy, that sounded the death knell for the Jamaican plantation system. The old imperial model of trade dating back to the Navigation Acts of the 1650s, which through preferential tariffs protected British goods and produce against foreign imports, and restricted the traffic between the mother country and her colonies to British-owned ships, now felt insular and outmoded; meanwhile British consumers were fed up with the prohibitively high prices that arose from stifled competition. For many manufacturers, merchants and shipowners, the adoption of free trade had become a burning cause.

In their shared opposition to the principles of free trade being applied to sugar, the West Indian and anti-slavery lobbies enjoyed the strange sensation of being on the same side, for perhaps the first and last time. Certainly, Joseph John Gurney shuddered at the thought of cutting import duties on foreign sugar. He told his brother-in-law, the abolitionist Thomas Fowell Buxton:

> A market of immense magnitude would immediately be
> opened for the produce of the slave labor of the Brazils, Cuba,
> and Porto Rico. The consequence would be, that ruin would
> soon overtake the planters of our West Indian colonies, and
> our free negroes would be deprived of their principal means
> of obtaining an honorable and comfortable livelihood; but far
> more extensive, far more deplorable, would be the effect of such
> a change, on the millions of Africa. A vast new impulse would
> be given to slave labor, and therefore to the slave trade.[10]

Dick Atkinson became a partner in the Kingston house from 1 January 1844, despite his older cousin's reservations about his temperament. 'I do wish he had more activity of mind and really would give himself more to Business,' George wrote to Aunt Jane. 'I know he thinks me very savage in my attacks on him but my only motive has been to rouse him and to prevent his falling into that apathy and careless fashion which in my Uncle Matthew caused such serious injury to my Father's House.'[11] While advocates of free trade made political headway at Westminster, commercial confidence ebbed away in the West Indies. 'Business is extremely dull here and I think if War was declared, it would do us good, at all events in these dull times we should have something to talk about,' Dick wrote home in October 1844.[12]

During the early 1840s, the Conservative prime minister Sir Robert Peel would abolish or cut more than a thousand tariffs, including those on cotton, linen and wool, replacing lost revenues with a new 3 per cent income tax. 'There hardly remains any raw material imported from other countries, on which the duty has not been reduced,' he declared in January 1846.[13] Peel made an exception for sugar, though, arguing that it should be 'wholly exempt' from the principle of free trade, since to give slave-grown sugar unfettered access to the British marketplace would mean 'tarnishing for ever' the national achievement in abolishing slavery.[14] He also wavered about grain. The Corn Laws had been passed in 1815, to prevent cheap continental grain from undercutting the homegrown product; but they also propped up the landed gentry at the expense of both the urban poor, who endured the high cost of bread, and industrial magnates, who needed the rural peasantry to be freed from the fields to provide labour for their factories and mills. Peel had repeatedly voted against repealing the Corn Laws, but the poor harvest of 1845 and the devastating famine in Ireland made him change his mind. In June 1846, Peel won the repeal of the statutes in the teeth of fierce opposition from protectionists within his own party. They would punish him for this victory, however, by instantly forcing his resignation.

Lord John Russell, a Liberal, followed Peel into office; by August 1846, he had carried the Sugar Duties Act through parliament. The duty on all foreign sugar would drop with immediate effect to 21s per hundredweight and fall incrementally each year for the following five years, until all sugar entering British ports was taxed equally. The effect of this legislation upon the Jamaican economy was cataclysmic. West India merchants in London suddenly stopped offering credit, to the distress of their clients who purchased estate necessaries every autumn with money advanced against the forthcoming sugar crop. A programme to ease the labour deficit in Jamaica by bringing indentured 'hill coolies' from India – the first ship had arrived from Calcutta in May 1845 – was instantly suspended. The planters saw the Sugar Duties Act as a profound betrayal, an act of heedless vandalism.

GEORGE ATKINSON RETIRED from the Kingston house at the end of 1846 – he was fifty-one – leaving Dick and another partner, Charles MacGregor, to take over the business. After twelve years under the thumb of his domineering cousin, Dick found the new set-up infinitely more congenial. As he told Aunt Jane, in a sentence that speaks volumes about his opinion of George: 'Let times be ever so bad, and our work ever so laborious, I have the satisfaction of being joined in Copartnership with an honest, good man, and who places the same confidence in me, as I should always do in him, allowing us, altho' not making money as former Firms did, to enjoy happiness, free from all suspicion of one another, and living on good terms with all our neighbours.'[15]

After the Sugar Duties Act passed into law, mercantile business more or less dried up in Jamaica. Atkinson & MacGregor's most flourishing concern was their flour mill and bakery, which produced 'excellent Bread' and hard, dry 'Sea Biscuits' for the navy – '100 puncheons of 346 lbs. each, per week' – but this barely kept one of the partners busy, let alone both of them.[16] With estates everywhere being sold off cheap, often for one-twentieth of the price they might once have commanded, Dick turned to property speculation. John

Clayton's law firm handled his purchase of the Lloyds, Coldstream and Mount Sinai estates in the parish of St David, subdividing the properties so that they might be sold off as small 'parcels of Land'.[17]

A bumper sugar crop in 1847 caused an oversupply that wiped more than a third off the London wholesale price of sugar, and bankrupted thirteen merchant houses dealing with the West Indies. Not only was British free-grown sugar more expensive to produce than the foreign slave-grown variety; it also cost twice as much to carry it across the Atlantic, on account of the Navigation Acts. Dick wrote to brother George on 7 September:

> The Colonies have been, and continue to be most unjustly treated. Why did not they grant the same free trade to us, as the Slave colony of Cuba enjoys. Why not let us get an American, German, Prussian, or Sardinian vessel to take our Produce to market at the rate of 2s. to 2s. 6d. per ½ ton – instead of paying a British vessel 5s. & 6s. per ½ ton – if the Tories have been unable to stop the very sweeping free Trade views of the Rads, they should fully & fairly for better or worse carry out the meaning of free trade – attack the navigation laws, and let us, and all the British Possessions look to the cheapest market they can find for their shipping.[18]

The Navigation Acts would finally be repealed in 1849, opening up the imperial trade to the vessels of any country.

The plunging price of sugar soon finished off many plantations. 'A great number of Estates are entirely abandoned – and others are following from the necessary supplies of money being stopped,' Dick wrote in November 1847. 'I am continuing the cultivation of Lloyds & Mt Sinai in the hopes of better times – but I must say I often think I am wrong in so doing.'[19]

Dick would hold his nerve a few more years; in October 1849 he paid £800 for the 1,400-acre Norris estate, located a few miles from his other properties in St David Parish.[20] Often, when he wished to escape the suffocating heat of Kingston, he would ride out to his 'pretty little House' at Mount Sinai in the 'certainty of enjoying a cool Bed'; the cottage nestled on the banks of the mighty Yallahs River, with views across to the Judgement Cliff, the site of a massive landslide during the fabled earthquake of 1692. 'A few days there, bathing regularly, set me up wonderfully,' Dick wrote.[21]

These days, in contrast to its past reputation as a tropical grave-yard, Jamaica was considered a salubrious place to visit. Dick's younger sister, Jane, spent the winter of 1848 on the island; he had urged her to come out for the benefit of her delicate constitution. The physician Robert Scoresby-Jackson – an expert on the effects of climate upon health – stayed with Dick around this time, and was much struck by the range in temperatures to be found in Jamaica:

> In the middle of May I left the hospitable mansion of Mr.
> Atkinson at 6 a.m., after a restless and feverish night on the
> plain of Liguanea, and at noon, under the guidance of a kind
> friend, reached Pleasant Hill, part of the journey having been
> performed in a carriage, and the remainder on mules, over
> narrow mountain roads, down steep declivities, across the rapid
> Yallahs River, and amid grand, picturesque, and ever varying
> scenery. The change of climate was delicious, the air cool,
> fragrant with the white and red rose, and perfumed with the
> orange blossom. On the Liguanea Plain, during the previous
> night, the lightest covering had been scarcely bearable, yet at
> Pleasant Hill a couple of blankets were agreeable.[22]

Dick must have made this trip countless times, for Pleasant Hill, in the Port Royal Mountains, was a property he managed. But I'm not sure he would have described it quite so evocatively – by his own admission, he was notorious for 'writing stupid letters'.[23]

ABOUT DICK'S COURTSHIP of Elizabeth Pitter, I know noth-ing – on matters of the heart his letters are silent – but they married in May 1849, when he was thirty-six and she was twenty-one. It is possible that they met through Dick's planter friend William

Georges, who was married to Eliza's older sister Julia. The Pitter sisters were sixth-generation Jamaicans, descended through their paternal grandmother from Richard James, an officer on the buccaneering Penn and Venables expedition which had seized the colony from the Spanish in 1655; their three-times great-grandfather was said to have been the first white man born of English parentage on the island.

In July 1851, Dick, Eliza and their two infant children boarded the *Medway*, one of the speedy new Royal Mail steam vessels which had cut the passage time between England and the West Indies to just three weeks. Its captain, William Symons, was Dick's brother-in-law. Jane Atkinson had married Symons within months of her return from overwintering in Jamaica three years earlier – I imagine she must have met her husband on board his ship.

The *Medway* arrived at Southampton on 20 August; Jane and her baby son were waiting to greet the party. Before heading north, Dick and Eliza were delayed a week while they recruited a new nurse-maid. 'I brought one from Jamaica, a colored Woman, but she will not do for this Country, I must send her back,' Dick told Aunt Jane. On their way through London, he and Eliza visited that triumphalist celebration of global free trade, the Great Exhibition in Hyde Park. Out of thousands of goods representing every permutation of human ingenuity – from the electric telegraph and an unpickable lock to papier-mâché furniture and a bust of Queen Victoria carved from soap – Jamaica had offered one meagre contribution, a display of artificial flowers made from the fibre of the yucca plant.

Dick planned to spend a year in England, but was not yet sure where to base his family: 'This is a puzzle that often perplexes me, I do not like Newcastle or the neighbourhood, the Lake district, or the vicinity of Liverpool might suit me, the former I am so fond of, and in the latter there are so many Friends.'[24] At his aunt Wordsworth's house near Liverpool, Dick met up with brother George and their cousin Bolton Littledale, and the three men immediately set out on a fishing expedition. Surrounded by close relatives, with a rod in his hand, Dick was reminded of all that he had missed during nearly twenty years' absence from England; next time he brought the family home, he resolved, it would be for good. 'The recollection of the few unhappy years, of constant craving after wealth, that both my cousin George & Mr. Hozier exhibited – is quite sufficient reason for me to drop Business – while I yet have constitution & strength of mind to do so,' he told Aunt Jane. 'Neither the Wife or self have extravagant tastes, and as to the children we must just bring them up to suit my *Fortune*.'[25]

When Dick and Eliza returned to Jamaica, at the end of 1852, it felt more like a backwater than ever. Everywhere, bush scrambled across the neglected fields of once-flourishing plantations – a total of 316 properties, or nearly half the island's sugar estates, would be abandoned between 1834 and 1854.[26] Kingston was in large parts a slum, with 'lean, mangy hogs' and 'half-starved dogs' scavenging its unpaved, rubbish-strewn streets.[27] 'Jamaica, the oldest colony of the British crown, presents the most extraordinary spectacle of desolation and decay the world ever witnessed,' commented one former resident. 'It now lies helpless and ruined by the policy of the mother-country, that should have fostered its resources, and smoothed its difficulties, during a transition of no ordinary nature.'[28]

Kingston in the 1850s, looking up King Street towards the parish church.

Meanwhile, the island's northern neighbour continued to welcome slave ships into its ports: 'Cuba is prosperous, and red with the blood of the African, she has splendid cities, quays, and wharfs, long lines of railroads, an unexceptionable opera, costly equipages, and every luxury worthy of the first capitals in Europe, and instead of borrowing money from the mother country she sends home a princely revenue.'[29]

It was Aunt Jane's death in March 1855, a week after she turned eighty, that ultimately prompted Dick's decision to quit Jamaica. In her will, Jane divided her possessions unequally among her nieces and nephews. To Dick, for example, she left £1,000; to her brother George's children, whom she considered quite wealthy enough, she gave nineteen guineas apiece. To Sarah and Anne Clayton, she left her furniture, plate, linen, china, books, prints, pictures and wine, and to Sarah alone she gave her shells and coins. Temple Sowerby House, her farms and portfolio of property in the village passed to her executor, John Clayton; the gossip on the Atkinson side of the family was that Aunt Jane had borrowed so much money from her rich nephew that it would all have gone in his direction, whether she had bequeathed it to him or not.

To cut a long story short, John Clayton agreed to let Temple Sowerby House to Dick for the cousinly rate of £45 a year. On 27 April 1856, as heavy rains turned the streets of Kingston into 'formidable rivers', Dick, Eliza and their three young children climbed aboard the *Parana*, and waved farewell to Jamaica for the very last time.[30]

DICK AND ELIZA moved into the ancestral home in July 1856. They found it emptier than it had been in Aunt Jane's day; only the largest, shabbiest pieces of furniture remained, unclaimed by the Clayton sisters to whom they had been left. My great-grandfather John Nathaniel (known as Jock) was born in May 1857, and four more babies would follow, bringing the final tally of children to eight; with a governess and six servants also living under the same roof, it was a busy household.

Although he was just forty-three when he returned to England, Dick would trouble himself no further with business; henceforth the family would live off the income from his investments, mostly in American railroad stocks floated by Barings. He cut the last of his financial ties to Jamaica in 1861, with the sale of the Norris estate to his brother-in-law William Georges for just £500. Apart from Lizzy, their eldest daughter, none of Dick and Eliza's offspring grew up with memories of the colony; it must have seemed a fabled place, represented by their mother's lilting accent, and the wooden cases of crystallized tropical fruits their parents sometimes had shipped over as a treat.

From now on, the flow of family correspondence declines to a trickle, which means that I must rely upon the pocket diaries in which Dick diligently recorded the events of his uneventful rural existence. Nineteen of these slim volumes, one accounting for each of his remaining years, are stacked up on the desk before me. Snow-drops in January, pruning fruit trees in February, potting geraniums in March, the first cuckoo in April, swarming bees in May, hay-making in July, the first snow settling on Cross Fell in October, the slaughter of the pig in November – the seasons beat the same rhythm every year. Most days, except Sundays, Dick devoted at least an hour or two to field sports; he kept a note of his bag, and if you were to tot up all the hares, rabbits, grouse, partridges, pheasants, pigeons, snipe, woodcock, chub, salmon and trout that perished at his hands, the number would run into tens of thousands. Apart from twice-yearly fishing and shooting expeditions to Loch Awe in the Scottish Highlands, where cousin Bolton Littledale owned a hunting lodge, Dick and Eliza rarely strayed from hearth and home; dinner with neighbours at Acorn Bank or Newbiggin Hall, barely a mile away, was almost as far as their social lives took them.

AFTER THREE DECADES as town clerk, John Clayton remained the most powerful man in Newcastle – 'like the Sphynx in the desert,' wrote a journalist, 'while the sands of time sweep round his feet.'[31] Under his watch, the town had been transformed

Grey's Monument, at the heart of Newcastle's magnificent new town centre.

from an old-fashioned place, criss-crossed by winding alleys and tightly enclosed within medieval walls, into a modern metropolis, the clanking heart of the industrial revolution. On a twelve-acre greenfield site, formerly the grounds of an ancient manor house, an elegant new town centre had been built from scratch, masterminded by the developer Richard Grainger; its principal thoroughfares were named Clayton Street, Grainger Street and (in honour of the great Northumbrian architect of parliamentary reform) Grey Street.

But for John Clayton's support, the scheme might easily have collapsed. Grainger was a visionary, but he was also an incorrigible speculator, who financed his developments through a complex web of mortgages and remortgages. John's involvement undoubtedly calmed investors' nerves; he not only acted as Grainger's solicitor, but also lent him large sums of money. Clayton Street would be the most 'chastely ornamented' of the three main roads, in keeping with the sombre dignity of the legal gentleman for whom it was named; it was left to Grey Street, with its descending curve and Corinthian façades, to project the town's swaggering confidence.[32] (John would later claim that the bend in Grey Street had been his idea, inspired by Oxford's High Street.) By 1840, six years after the building works began, nine new streets had been completed, boasting amenities that included a new market, a grand theatre, a music hall, a lecture room, a dispensary, two chapels, two auction markets, ten inns, twelve public houses, 325 combined shops and residences, and forty private houses. 'You walk into what has been long termed the *Coal Hole of the North*, and find yourself at once in a city of palaces; a fairyland of newness, brightness, and modern elegance,' wrote one visitor, a touch breathlessly.[33]

John's vast personal wealth, in part generated through his fees as solicitor not only to Richard Grainger, but also to the Corporation of Newcastle and the Newcastle & Carlisle Railway Company – a pile-up of interests that would be unthinkable today – did not go unnoticed by his fellow citizens. An anonymous observer wrote in 1855:

A pendulum of sovereigns – steady, round, and bright – appears
always to regulate the internal machinery of the Town Clerk.
It is difficult to discover more diligent success in acquiring
money over a space of thirty years by the humblest, and
meekest, and most common-place drudgery. Mr. John Clayton
never speculated. He never threw dice. He never sunk a pit.
He never founded a bank. Slow, sure, regular, and passionless
– like a Laplander trudging and toiling over a waste of snow

– Mr. John Clayton has pursued the even tenor of his way;
but instead of his feet being clogged, like the Laplander's with
snow, they are clogged with yellow dust, unalloyed gold, of
sure and most indubitable accumulation.[34]

During the week, John shared the old Clayton mansion on Westgate Street with his younger brother Matthew, his partner in the
family firm, which had grown into the largest legal practice in the
north of England. Both men were bachelors; indeed, only three
of Nathaniel and Dorothy Clayton's eleven children would marry,
and just one, their youngest son Richard, would perpetuate the
family name. Beyond his official and professional duties, John's main
recreation was the preservation of the Roman wall that stretched
between the Solway Firth and the River Tyne. Locals had freely
plundered the wall for its 'well-shaped, handy-sized stones' for as
long as anyone could remember, and a passing antiquarian had been
dismayed in 1801 to find John's uncle, Henry Tulip, in the process of
dismantling ninety-five yards in order to 'erect a farm-house with
the materials'.[35] John purchased his first section of the wall in 1834;

Hadrian's Wall to the west of Housesteads, prior to its
restoration by John Clayton.

he would end up owning eighteen miles, from Carvoran in the west to Planetrees in the east.

John started restoring the wall in 1848, and the project would continue for more than twenty-five years. The techniques adopted by the labourers working under his supervision – he set aside Mondays for site visits – were surprisingly sensitive for the times. First they cleared the loose rubble along the sides of the wall; next they used these stones, without mortar, to build a protective skin around the exposed Roman masonry, thus preserving the original core; and finally they capped it off with turf. John also ordered the demolition of a number of farm buildings that were encroaching on the wall, and he put an end to arable farming along its path, instead introducing hardy breeds of cattle and sheep to complement the upland scenery. When people think of Hadrian's Wall these days, they are most likely to picture the rugged scenery to the west of Housesteads, where the sturdy structure hugs the craggy Whin Sill – this is the section known to cognoscenti as the 'Clayton Wall'.

DICK BEGAN CASTING around for occupations for his sons as they approached manhood; his pocket diary for 1872 contains several pages of closely written notes about the admissions criteria for 'Indian Civil Engineering College', and the salary, in rupees, that its graduates might earn. It seems likely that Dick mentioned this as a possible career for fifteen-year-old Jock when cousin Annie Clayton came to stay at Temple Sowerby in April 1873, as a few weeks later her sister Sarah, the boy's godmother, sent a cheque for £100 to cover the cost of tutoring him for the fiercely competitive public exam to enter the Indian Civil Service.

Dick's health began to fail shortly after his sixtieth birthday. On 5 April 1875 he went fishing, pulled two trout from the river, walked home 'not feeling very well', sent for the doctor, and took to his bed. His diary is almost blank from then on – a break that feels shockingly abrupt after nineteen years of assiduous record-keeping – and the few remaining examples of his handwriting are visibly feeble. During the autumn, after a moment when the family believed him to be gaining strength, Dick went into a steep decline. 'We had him downstairs in the fishing room for an hour or two on Thursday, but he did not recognise the room and kept talking about leaving this house and going home,' reported 21-year-old Jane on 4 December.[36] A week later Jock, who had been cramming for the India exam in London, arrived at Temple Sowerby for Christmas. 'It is a great comfort to have him,' wrote Jane. 'Daddy recognised him as he does everybody at first sight, but the remembrance of people passes from him directly the first flush of recognition is over.'[37] Dick died, nine months after the onset of his illness, on 18 January 1876.

JOHN CLAYTON RETIRED from the Newcastle town clerk's office in 1867, when he was seventy-five – he and his father having served eighty-two years between them – and subsequently devoted himself to his Roman studies. As the objects unearthed by his excavations along the wall grew into a large collection, finding space for them became an increasing challenge. A stone colonnade was built along the front of Chesters mansion to provide shelter for some of the bigger sculptural and inscribed pieces; a wooden summerhouse in the garden was also pressed into service.

John would remain active into his nineties; under his direction, a significant hoard of sculptures and altars dedicated to the war-god Mars Thincsus was found at Housesteads fort in 1883. He kept open house at Chesters, and archaeological enthusiasts often dropped by. Treadwell Walden, a visitor from Boston, called in 1886:

> The servant who answered our ring took our cards and
> ushered us into the library – a large room, filled with
> books, and whose walls were covered with paintings. When
> Mr. Clayton was ready to receive us we found him reclining
> on a couch in the middle of the great room. He at once greeted
> us with cordial courtesy, and remarked smilingly that he had
> been troubled with an old enemy, the gout, and that 'he was
> somewhat older than was convenient,' but it would give him
> great pleasure to show us the Roman remains on his grounds,

as well as those collected in the house. He then conducted us out into the broad hall, and took us from one to another of the fine figures in bas-relief that stood there, repeating to us in full the somewhat illegible and frequently missing parts of the inscriptions. We were shown, also, the smaller articles in another room. Of these there was the richest variety. There were coins, literally by the peck, enclosed in many bags, heaped upon a box.[38]

These must have been the spoils of the famous dig at Carrawburgh, ten years earlier, when John's men had discovered the remains of a chapel dedicated to the goddess Coventina, and found a large, square well containing twenty-four altars and at least 16,000 copper coins, as well as 'sculptures, pottery, glass, bones, rings, fibulae, dice, beads, sand, gravel, stones, wood, deers' horns, iron implements, shoe-soles, and a due proportion of mud'.[39]

But mortality caught up with John Clayton in the end; he died on 14 July 1890, aged ninety-eight, and was buried on a stormy day in the churchyard at Warden, alongside his parents and siblings. Apart from some minor legacies – including money for the upkeep of a terrier, Marcus Aurelius – John's fortune passed to his nephew, Nathaniel George Clayton, the eldest son of his youngest brother Richard, who inherited personal estate valued at £728,746, more than 26,000 acres in Northumberland, and twenty-two properties at Temple Sowerby, including the Atkinson house occupied by Dick's widow Eliza and her unmarried daughter Katie.

MY GREAT-GRANDFATHER JOCK married Constance Banks in a whitewashed church in the Indian coastal town of Cocanada on 8 July 1885; at twenty-eight, he was assistant collector of Kistna district in the Madras Presidency. They had met out there, for Connie, the fifth daughter of the vicar of Doncaster, was one of those spirited young women of gentle birth – known collectively as the 'fishing fleet' – who had travelled to the subcontinent with the intention of catching a husband.

Connie brought their three children back to England in April 1893, settling seven-year-old George and five-year-old Jack into boarding school before taking two-year-old Biddy back to India. The following spring, in May 1894, Jock, Connie and Biddy came home again for a short vacation; the passage from Bombay, via the Suez Canal, took seventeen days. (A century earlier, the same voyage by sailing ship, round the Cape, would have lasted the best part of six months.) The whole family spent an idyllic month at Temple Sowerby. One beautiful day, Jock initiated the boys into the art of minnow fishing; by teatime Jack had cast his line all the way across the stream, a feat which earned him half a crown. Another day, Jock took the train over to Northumberland to see a second cousin, John Ridley, who lived at Walwick Hall, half a mile from Chesters; the two men strolled out to view the recent changes to the Clayton property. Since Jock's last visit to Chesters, its new owner had commissioned the architect Norman Shaw to add wings to either side of the Georgian house, more than doubling its size. This was pure *folie de grandeur*, for Nathaniel and Isabel Clayton surely had no need for forty bedroooms. 'Enormous & very ugly,' wrote Jock in his diary. 'Family all away.'

While old John Clayton was alive, Eliza Atkinson had enquired through his land agent whether he might sell her Temple Sowerby House; but word had come back that 'Mr. Clayton regarded that property as the apple of his eye & wouldn't part with it'.[40] Now Eliza and her daughter Katie found themselves in the awkward position of being poor relations to a landlord they barely knew. This must have been preying on their minds, for while Jock was passing through London, he called on Nathaniel Clayton at home in Belgrave Square in order to ascertain the status of their tenancy. The conversation lasted barely three minutes – he arrived just as his second cousin was about to go out – but the outcome was satisfactory enough. 'N.G. Clayton assured me that he would not let the T.S. property pass from himself & the Atkinson family to outsiders,' Jock noted.

This time, when Jock and Connie returned to India, they left all three children behind under the care of their maternal aunts.

George, Jack and Biddy waved their parents goodbye at the railway station on 20 July. 'Fortunately,' recorded Jock, 'their thoughts were distracted at the time: & they seemed hardly to realise it.' The couple's reasoning may have been sound enough – India was reckoned a dangerously unhealthy place to raise a family – but it meant they would barely know their children. In due course, the boys would follow Jock to his alma mater, Marlborough College, while Biddy attended Hendon Hall, a girls' boarding school just north of London.

Jack, my grandfather, was called to the bar after graduating from Cambridge; but he never practised law, instead falling in with a set of rich, spoilt young men. Jack was an engaging and decorative fellow, but he lacked the funds to make a proper career of loafing around, and his father's threats to cut off his allowance eventually took effect. In May 1914, aged twenty-six, he emigrated to Halifax, Nova Scotia, where he found work as a stockbroker.

Three months after Jack's departure, his parents came home to England, settling near Alton in Hampshire. Jock's loyal service to the empire had ultimately been rewarded with a knighthood. The *Madras Times* marked his retirement with a lengthy tribute that was lavish in its faint praise: 'You naturally look back upon the landmarks of Sir John's service when the time comes for parting with him, and you don't find any. And this means that he has been content with simply doing his duty. He has worked well with his equals, his superiors, and his subordinates. And this, after all is said and done, is the highest achievement possible to an Indian Civil Servant.'[41]

The Great War offered Jock and Connie a chance to rekindle their relationship with their younger son. Jack enlisted in the Canadian Expeditionary Force in December 1915; six months later, his parents bade him farewell at Folkestone as he departed for the front with the 13th Battalion Royal Highlanders of Canada. Within days, the battalion had been posted to Sanctuary Wood, a hellhole of waterlogged ditches, tree stumps and barbed wire, where it would experience the horrors of intense bombardment for the first time. Jack had the good fortune to contract trench fever in August 1916;

while he was recuperating at army hospitals in Saint-Omer and Boulogne, and then with his parents in Hampshire, hundreds of his fellow men from the 13th Battalion would lose their lives in the Battle of the Somme.

Nor was Jack to be found in the main assault on Vimy Ridge in April 1917 – an action noteworthy as the first time that all four divisions of the Canadian Corps fought together. Instead, it was his responsibility to deal with the corpses. 'Lieut. J.L. Atkinson is detailed to supervise the clearing of the battlefield,' ordered the adjutant prior to the offensive. 'He will report at Battalion Head-quarters before dawn and will work in conjunction with, and under the orders of, the Divisional Burial Officer.'[42] The capture of the ridge came at enormous cost, with 3,598 dead out of 10,602 Canad-ian casualties. No medals for gallantry would be pinned to Jack's chest, but the mere fact that he survived the war more than suf-fices for me. He would remain in France until February 1919. On the afternoon of 5 April, as the 13th Battalion was in the process of being disbanded, Jack walked up the hill behind his parents' house and fired off the last rounds of his automatic pistol, thus concluding his military career. Four months later, he sailed back to Canada.

DURING HIS RETIREMENT YEARS in the 1920s, Jock would be struck down by what he described as a 'violent attack of pedigree mania' – a seemingly hereditary condition, only treatable by visits to the Public Record Office and the British Museum's Reading Room.[43] Genealogical research became Jock's obsession, and he poured his findings into a short 'history of Temple Sowerby and of the Atkin-son family' in which, surprisingly, he did not once mention Jamaica – the family's activities there being a subject about which he was curiously ignorant. ('Have you among your papers got any infor-mation about Matthew?' he would ask a cousin about their common ancestor, Matthew Atkinson, who had died in 1756. 'I wonder did he ever go to Jamaica? His son Richard made a large fortune there, & at least one of his nephews went out.')[44] At Jock's request, Isabel Clayton, his second cousin's widow, trawled the library at Chesters, hunting for heraldic clues in volumes which had once been shelved at Temple Sowerby: 'The schoolmaster who dusts the books for me at present was here yesterday evening & we had a good search for a Crest, or arms, in a book plate of Bridget Atkinson – a great Number of books with Bridget Atkinson written at the beginning but never a sign of there ever having been a Crest.'[45]

Isabel Clayton died in April 1928, and the Chesters estate skipped a generation, passing to her 26-year-old grandson. Jack Clayton had been raised at Newmarket, where his late father kept racehorses, and he mixed with a fast, careless crowd; he soon resolved, having run up vast gambling debts, to liquidate his entire inheritance. First to go under the hammer, in a lively auction held at Newcastle's Assembly Rooms in June 1929, were 20,000 acres of agricultural land, broken up into 112 lots, including 'many capital hill farms' straddling Hadrian's Wall.[46] Housesteads Farm was one of the few lots that failed to reach its reserve; potential buyers were put off by the burden of maintaining the Roman fort that came with it. The eminent historian George Trevelyan, whose family owned nearby Wallington Hall, shortly afterwards agreed to purchase the farm minus the fort, on condition that Jack donated this, plus a stretch of adjoining Roman wall, to the National Trust. *The Times* reported 'Mr. J.M. Clayton's Gift' of Housesteads Fort in glowing terms – but the evidence suggests that Jack was a reluctant donor, and was more or less shamed into this act of philanthropy.[47]

The disposal of the mansion at Chesters was immediately followed by the dispersal of its contents – 'one of the great displenishing sales that has been held on the Borders in living memory', said the *Hexham Courant*.[48] The auction began on 6 January 1930; the eighth and final day saw the clearance of the library and the scattering of more than six thousand books, among them Moxon's *English House-wifery* (1764), Johnson's *Journey to the Western Islands of Scotland* (1775), Gibbon's *Decline and Fall of the Roman Empire* (1781), Cook's *Voyages* (1784), Dixon's *North-West Coast of America* (1789), Bligh's *Voyage to the South Sea* (1792), Edwards' *Survey of Saint Domingo* (1801) and Perry's *Conchology, or the Natural History of Shells* (1811).

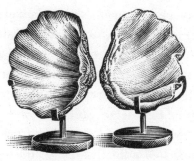

*A giant clam shell, all that remains of Bridget's shell collection,
now in the museum attached to the Roman fort at Chesters.*

These titles are so redolent of the life and times of Bridget Atkinson that I can only imagine they must once have belonged to her. I wonder where they are now.

THE LAST DECADE of Jock's life was blighted by problems with his heart, and chest pains often followed the most trivial exertion, as per this diary entry: 'Chastised dog for getting on drawing room sofa, & in consequence suffered much discomfort for a short time.'[49] He died at home in Hampshire in March 1931, aged seventy-three. Jock's unmarried youngest sister, Katie, died ten months later; she had lived at Temple Sowerby all her life. Following her funeral, Katie's executors spent two days sorting through heaps of old papers, many of which ended up on a bonfire in the garden.

The ancestral house was sold by auction at the Tufton Arms in Appleby on 27 August 1932. Everyone had expected it to leave the family for ever, but one of Dick and Eliza's grandsons – Kenneth Kay, the son of their daughter Jane – bought the property in anticipation of his retirement from the textiles business in Madras. The proceeds of the sale, of course, lined the pockets of Jack Clayton, whose 'bold betting' had recently been generating what the *Sunday Times* described as a 'good deal of animation in the rings'.[50]

Meanwhile my grandfather, Jack Atkinson, was working as a journalist on the *Montreal Star*. He married my Canadian grandmother, Evelyn Hay de Castañeda, in Quebec on 30 April 1930.

(A musical, cosmopolitan woman, she had already been widowed twice; her second husband was Secretary of the Spanish Legation in Tangier.) Jack's inheritance prospects improved markedly after the sudden death of his elder brother George, a railway engineer in India, in September 1932. He returned with Evelyn to England the following year and they set up home in London; John, their only child, was born in March 1934. When Jack's mother Connie died, in June 1947, he inherited a life interest in the small farm that his father had purchased at Temple Sowerby. At the invitation of Kenneth Kay's widow, Dorothy, who was living alone in the old house, Jack, Evelyn and John moved up to Westmorland that same year. When Dorothy died, in April 1955, she left the property to Jack.

In January 1957, Jack took delivery of a parcel from a second cousin, Dick Atkinson, containing bundles of papers spared the bonfire by Aunt Katie's executors twenty-five years earlier. 'I had hoped that I might have brought them over to you, but the petrol position forbids doing this,' Dick wrote from his home near Newcastle. (Fuel rationing was then in place, following the Suez Crisis.) 'I don't envy you your job of going over all these letters, I have looked through some of them & I wonder why they were preserved, there are very few that are of much interest.'[51]

This was the box full of old correspondence that my sister and I would inherit nearly twenty years later, and which would remain untouched for a further thirty years, until I was ready to embark on my long journey into the past.

TWENTY-FOUR

———————

Distant Cousins

THE BUNDLES OF LETTERS tied up in pink ribbon may have seemed worthless to cousin Dick – but they were gold dust to me, for they introduced me to my eighteenth-century family at a time when I was grieving for the family I would never have. Over the next few years, not only would I enjoy getting to know a whole host of dead relatives, but also, to my delight, many living ones. Phillipa was the first of the long-lost cousins I would meet, and I felt a special kinship with her from the off. (It was her grandfather, Dick, who had seen so little value in the old family papers.) I often stayed at Phillipa's house during my research trips to Cumbria, and came to see it as a kind of northern home from home.

About a year after my stay at Temple Sowerby House, when I had been in pursuit of Bridget's 'receipt book', Julie Evans emailed me out of the blue. Another guest claiming Atkinson ancestry had recently visited the hotel – would I mind if she put them in touch? This was how I found out about the Scandinavian branch of the family. Renira Müller, its matriarch, would have been my dad's second cousin, which made her my closest living Atkinson relative, apart from my sister and her children. Shortly afterwards I called Renira and said I hoped we might meet; she warned me not to 'dilly-dally', for she would soon be ninety. A few weeks later, one freezing day in December 2011, I stood on the threshold of her apartment in the Norwegian port city of Haugesund.

The moment Renira welcomed me into her cosy home, full of books and mementoes from an evidently full life, we started a conversation that would last the best part of three days. Although her eyesight was no longer what it had once been – a source of obvious frustration – her powers of recall remained undimmed. She had never met my father, but she did have a clear memory of staying with his grandparents, her great-uncle Jock and great-aunt Connie, when she was about four, and of being harassed by their small, yappy dog – this must have been the same pet that Jock would not tolerate jumping up on the sofa. Renira's father, Geoffrey Atkinson – one of Dick and Eliza's grandsons – had worked in the oil business in Morocco, and she had lived there as a child until the outbreak of the Second World War. Back in Britain, she had served as a wireless telegraphist in the WRNS, listening out for enemy Morse code signals; meanwhile she had married a Norwegian resistance fighter who was stationed in London. Their children were brought up in Norway but instilled with a strong sense of their English heritage; it was one of Renira's daughters who had lately been a guest at Temple Sowerby House.

Fast-forward five years, to April 2017, and I was still grappling with the first draft of my manuscript when an email arrived from Renira's son, Jon Müller. Not unreasonably, he was wondering whether I'd finished writing yet: 'My mother will be 95 years in May, and I would like to give her the book for a birthday present if it is done.' (No pressure, then.) Jon, who is a retired optician, added that he had started looking into his own ancestry, and had recently taken a DNA test; an American woman whose father was born in Westmoreland Parish, Jamaica, had since been in touch, identifying herself as a DNA match, and wondering how they might be related. Did I have any thoughts?

To be perfectly honest, I'm not sure why it hadn't occurred to me until that moment to have my own DNA tested, for I suddenly realized – and I feel slightly ashamed to confess that it took me so long to work this out – that the process might reveal hidden branches of the family tree. It might even lead me to descendants of Betsey, Bridget, Janet, Sally, William and any other children who my male ancestors might have left behind in Jamaica. It was too tantalizing a prospect to ignore.

Even so, I had mixed feelings about sending off my DNA for analysis – because the implications of this technology for one's privacy are quite mind-bending. (Not to mention all those stories one hears about people finding out that their parents aren't actually their parents . . .) The test involves taking genetic material, provided in the form of saliva or a mouth swab, converting it into machine-readable code, then comparing it with other samples captured on a massive database. Each of the companies offering this service has a slightly different sales pitch; which one (or ones) you choose will depend on whether you wish to build a family tree, discover where in the world your ancestors lived thousands of years ago, or find out whether you carry certain genes that might affect your health. I signed up with Ancestry DNA; with a customer database into the tens of millions, it seemed best positioned for tracking down long-lost relatives. A few days later, a small cardboard box containing a clear plastic tube dropped through my letterbox; I spat into the tube, then posted it off to a laboratory in Utah.

Our connection to our closest relatives – parents, siblings, first cousins – is always manifest through the sheer abundance of DNA we have in common with them. With distant relatives, however, we might share too little DNA to register a match, or such a small amount that it could just as easily be a mismatch, a snippet of genetic code shared by chance with an unrelated stranger. I was staggered to find, when my results came through, that Ancestry had conjured nearly 30,000 potential cousins from its database. (I say 'potential', because Ancestry's confidence in these matches ranged from 'extremely high' to 'moderate'; it expressed 'extremely high' or 'high' confidence in my connection to seventeen individuals, and 'good' confidence for 550 more, but only 'moderate' confidence that I was related to the remaining 29,000.) Anyhow – now that I had enough matches (or mismatches) to fill a football stadium, my next challenge was finding out which ones were related to me through the Atkinson line. The only way of doing this, I realized, would be to triangulate my results against those of members of other branches of the family, and see who we had in common. Luckily for me, Renira Müller and David Atkinson both gamely agreed to send their saliva off for analysis.

I felt such a strong family bond with David; not only had he encouraged my research into our ancestors, he had also entrusted me with many of their letters. Still, I wasn't too surprised when his DNA sample didn't match mine – I had read enough to know that there is only about a two-thirds probability of detecting a relationship with a fourth cousin. (If you think of two identical decks of cards, each time they are shuffled, the number and length of sequences they have in common will be reduced. This is also true with DNA, where with each 'shuffle' of the generations, the number and length of common sequences is diminished.)

Renira's test results, on the other hand, revealed that we shared 77 centimorgans of DNA across six segments. I set about compiling a list of our mutual relatives from the matches in which Ancestry had expressed 'extremely high', 'high' or 'good' confidence; this added up to about six hundred people for each of us. Within this data set, Renira and I had seven people in common, including one young woman whose surname was Pitter, the maiden name of our ancestor Eliza, who was born in Jamaica in 1829. The most startling revelation? All seven of these distant cousins of ours were of West African ancestry.

At this point I felt torn. I could easily have reached out to my new-found relatives right then – for Ancestry enables you to contact matches through its message board – and part of me yearned to do precisely that. But a more cautious part of me resisted the urge, from fear of treading where I was not wanted or welcome. I understood that for many descendants of enslaved Africans, their genealogical research was motivated by the desire to reunite families ruptured through slavery; so it was quite possible that the very last person they would wish to hear from was me, the direct male descendant of a white slave owner. I pondered this dilemma for several months

– it really weighed on me – before finally deciding not to act on it, though still unsure that this was the right choice.

MY FIRST GLIMPSE of Jamaica is from the plane; I spy the Blue Mountains swaddled in cloud, and tiny cars beetling along the coast road. BA2263 is a boisterous flight, an airborne party, and cheering erupts when the wheels hit the tarmac. We left London that morning wrapped up against the icy grip of winter; ten hours later, we have reached Kingston in the warm glow of late afternoon. By the time I emerge from the airport terminal, having shown my passport and shed several layers of clothes, darkness has fallen. Next morning, on a verandah high up in the hills, I breakfast on saltfish and ackee, locally grown coffee, and a fruit salad known as 'matrimony' – a combination of orange, grapefruit and star apple, spiced with nutmeg and sweetened with condensed milk. Nearby, a lizard basks on a banana leaf, while hummingbirds flit between brightly coloured flowers.

Idyllic this scene may be, but I am here with a purpose – for I have come to visit some of my ancestors' old haunts, not that they would recognize them today. A great fire in 1882, then an earthquake in 1907, reduced much of Kingston's historic business and warehouse district to rubble. Later, during the politically turbulent 1970s, the *rat-tat-tat-tat* sound of gunfire became familiar as gang warfare engulfed parts of the city, hastening the exodus of the middle class to the suburbs. These days only fairly adventurous tourists are drawn to downtown Kingston, as the crucible of the music for which Jamaica has become world-famous. Although the city is largely safe, and Jamaicans can be some of the most easy-going people you'll meet, its violent reputation lingers.

The streets around the Parade – a park since the 1870s – form the commercial heart of downtown. Here under shady colonnades, against a backing track of dancehall music blaring out from tinny speakers, market traders offer a wide range of wares, from goldfish to gold hotpants. Kingston Parish Church faces the Parade, on the corner with King Street, and it's here that I hope to locate the burial place of John Atkinson, my four-times great-uncle who died in 1798. But I soon realize that my guide, *Monumental Inscriptions of the British West Indies*, which was published in 1875, is hopelessly out of date – for the old graveyard now serves as the church's parking lot.[1] Only a few tombstones remain, embedded in the concrete surface and smeared with engine oil – and John's monument is not among them.

Another day I drive out to Spanish Town, the seat of colonial government until 1872. It ought to be a tourist mecca, given the fine collection of Georgian buildings clustered around its centre, but visitors are a rare species – I think I may have spotted a pair of backpackers roaming in the distance, but I couldn't swear to it. I stand on the broad, wooden verandah of the former House of Assembly, the present-day headquarters of St Catherine Parish Council, looking down on the main square, and try to picture the air thick with the cigar smoke of the slave-owning plantocracy. This requires a certain leap of imagination, since the verandah is now a dumping ground for old filing cabinets and other bureaucratic detritus.

The exquisite marble statue of Admiral Rodney, who in 1782 prevented Jamaica from being invaded by the French, still dominates the north side of the square under its octagonal cupola. The Island Secretary's Office, once the lucrative domain of the Atkinson family, remains an administrative building, although it hardly seems busy; its faded green hurricane shutters are tightly closed despite the stormy season ending two months ago. The King's House, occupying the west side of the square, was gutted by fire in 1925; only its brick façade is left. Likewise the old court house on the south side, which burnt down in 1986.

It is hardly surprising that the prevailing attitude of Jamaicans towards their built heritage is one of fatalistic neglect, especially given how little money can be spared for conservation works. It's not as though the British cared greatly about these structures in the first place, since they saw Jamaica as a colony to be exploited in the short term, not settled for the long term; for that reason they tended to build meanly, prioritizing utility over beauty. So it seems certain that Spanish Town, and countless great houses and sugar factories dotted around the island, will continue to decay – many of them discreetly, hidden beneath vegetation, others in plain view. And why, you might wonder, should modern Jamaicans give a damn about these relics of a time when their ancestors were transported there in chains, deprived of their human dignity and subjected to conditions of almost unthinkable cruelty? Why would any of this be worthy of preservation?

UNFAMILIAR AS I AM with the byways of rural Jamaica, and unversed in the local *patois*, I would be hard pressed to track down the remains of my ancestors' sugar estates without a guide; so I'm lucky that Peter Espeut has agreed to accompany me on a short road trip into the island's interior. Peter is well known for his weekly column in *The Gleaner* newspaper, has a distinct Father Christmas-meets-Fidel Castro look about him, and is recognized wherever he goes. He is also a clergyman, environmentalist and sociologist, as well as the author of a historical gazetteer of the island's estates – in short, I couldn't wish for a more ideal travel companion.

We set out from Kingston, breaking our drive to the west end of the island at Marshall's Pen, near Mandeville. This coffee and cattle estate in Manchester Parish once belonged to the Earls of Balcarres, and was managed by the Atkinsons until the falling-out of the 1830s. The great house, built for the overseer in about 1817, lies at the end of a bumpy track edged with dry-stone walls – were it not for the lushness of the vegetation, one might almost be in the Cotswolds. Its current owner, Ann Sutton, shows us round; the property was purchased by her late husband's family in 1939, and its wood-panelled rooms, chintz furnishings and mildewed pictures evoke an English country house of that period.

Ann manages the Marshall's Pen estate as a private nature reserve – the glossy brown cattle that graze its rolling pastures are part of a breed conservation programme – and also, as one of Jamaica's leading ornithologists, conducts birding expeditions all over the island. Her expertise in this field offers me an opportunity that is too good to resist. On the screen of my laptop, I show her photos of the colourful stuffed birds that used to be in the gallery at Temple Sowerby House, and are now in my sitting room in London. I assume they were my great-great-grandfather Dick's handiwork, dating from his time on the island, but it turns out that I am wrong. Ann tells me that these species are unknown in Jamaica, and probably native to Central and South America – regions which, so far as I am aware, none of my ancestors ever visited.

The following day Peter and I are in Hanover Parish, hunting for traces of Saxham estate, the property of Richard 'Rum' Atkinson's partner, Hutchison Mure. Peter has worked out its rough location from James Robertson's 1804 map of Jamaica, where a dot marked 'H. Mure's' can be found at the end of a road – although this road doesn't seem to match one that exists today. We turn off the coastal highway at Green Island and head into the hills; after several false leads, we reach the bottom of a steep track.

A farmer, Albert Miller, soon appears and offers to show us some ruins which, he says, are at the top. Ordinarily I might resist letting a machete-wielding stranger into my car, but he seems friendly enough, and we invite him to climb in. We follow the track for a mile or so, rising all the way; scrubby vegetation eventually gives way to open grass, and I park under a shady tree. We scramble under a barbed-wire fence, then tramp through undergrowth to a place near the crest of the hill. Albert points towards the ground with his blade; ankle-height stones trace the outline of an old building. Peter and I have been expecting to find Saxham's sugar works – but this lofty spot, with its panoramic view of hills and sea, seems more likely to have been the site of a great house. One of Bridget Atkinson's sons, Dick, died at Saxham in 1793, and Peter speculates that he may have been interred on the property, given the distance from the nearest church – but we see no signs of a burial place.

It is about an hour's drive to our next destination, Montego Bay, via the coast road, passing through what used to be rich sugar terrain; only the conical towers of a few windmills remain to bear witness to that era. Leaving the parish of Hanover and entering

St James, we cross a police checkpoint – in a drive to reduce the number of murders and other gang-related crimes around Montego Bay, a state of emergency is currently in place. The Bogue estate, which once upon a time belonged to Richard 'Rum' Atkinson, is these days a suburb of Jamaica's second city. During the 1960s, a land reclamation scheme merged some of the bay's mangrove islands, formerly uncultivated areas of the Bogue, into a cruise terminal and duty-free shopping area; a gleaming white ship is currently in port. We turn off the dual carriageway that cuts through what used to be cane fields into Bogue Heights, a neighbourhood of upscale villas shielded behind electric gates. Apart from a few breadfruit and ackee trees, which often hint at the past site of a slave village, there are no obvious signs of the sugar plantation that once occupied this land.

Much of the following morning is spent fixing a puncture, and it is almost midday by the time we reach Whithorn village, which lies within the boundary of what used to be the Dean's Valley Dry Works estate. We pause outside the small stone Methodist church to admire the view before dropping down to the flood plain below. Despite our best efforts at map reading, we still end up going round in circles, and I start to despair of ever locating the remains of this particular property. Then we turn on to a stony track, drive round a corner, and there, ahead of us, we see a crumbling pillar of cut limestone emerging from a backdrop of rampant vegetation, over-shadowed by a towering African tulip tree with bright red flowers. Unmistakably the ruins of an old sugar works.

We pull over. A man emerges from a nearby house, curious to know our business, and we in turn ask him questions. His name is Rawle Davis; he tells us that his family has lived here for more than thirty years, and offers to show us round. We tread carefully through dense foliage growing out of uneven heaps of rubble. It seems there are three ruined buildings – presumably a boiling house, curing house and distillery – although it's hard to discern them as separate units. In a few places, thick stone walls more than twice our height rear up out of the bush; elsewhere an enormous cylindrical cast-iron boiler languishes in the undergrowth.

I feel almost overwhelmed to find myself in this place where hundreds of enslaved Africans were once forced to manufacture sugar; and appalled to think that these people had been the *lawful property* of my family. I can't help but wonder, did my ancestors ever pause to reflect how posterity might judge them?

BEFORE I FLY HOME, the Jamaican Historical Society has invited me to give a lecture about my project. Writing a family memoir is not an undertaking to be entered into lightly; so far it has taken me eight years, but this will be the first time I have spoken about it in public. On a rainy evening, about twenty-five people turn up to hear my talk at a school in the Kingston suburb of Papine; they are a sympathetic crowd, and it feels surprisingly liberating to tell them what I've been up to all this time.

Afterwards, refreshments are served – spicy beef patties and slices of watermelon. A woman approaches me, smiling genially; she introduces herself as Suzanne Francis-Brown, before delivering the quite startling news that she has two ancestors called Richard Atkinson, a great-grandfather and a great-great-grandfather, on different sides of her maternal line. Suzanne goes on to tell me that her mother's family, the Atkinsons, were a tall, light-skinned clan from Catadupa in St James Parish, about twelve miles from both the Bogue and Dean's Valley estates. Her late uncle, a keen family historian, had always said that three Atkinson brothers came to Jamaica from the north of England in the late eighteenth century . . .

Clearly, the resonances between Suzanne's family story and mine are too great to be discounted. We meet the following day at the museum she curates on the University of the West Indies campus at Mona, and spend a couple of highly enjoyable hours indulging in wild speculation about whether we might be related – and if so, how. But there's only one way to find out for sure. Suzanne has already had her DNA tested through 23andMe, not a company I've used, and I volunteer to do the same. It's a long shot, of course – for even if we *are* distant cousins, the odds are stacked against her DNA matching mine.

Back in London, I post my saliva sample to the laboratory. Three weeks later the results come through; they connect me to more than one thousand 'DNA Relatives'. I scan the list of names, but Suzanne's isn't among them. I email to say how disappointed I am, and she comes right back with a message that is typically Jamaican in its warmth. 'Hush,' she writes, 'we'll be honorary cousins.'

APPENDIX I

———————

Richard Atkinson wrote this 'heart-breaking letter' to Anne Lindsay one evening during the summer of 1781, mindful that his future happiness depended on it.[1]

Sunday 7 o'Clock.

I was not disappointed in my expectation of seeing so far yesterday into the business I mentioned, as to satisfy my Mind of the propriety & safety of trusting to a *general* View of the present State of Affairs, without waiting for that more particular one which can only result from considerable time employed in Settlements which various intervening accidents may delay. The Night & the forenoon have afforded an opportunity of making this general Review, and I firmly believe that the anxiety of my Heart has not imposed upon my Judgement, nor prematurely broke loose from the Restraint so long imposed upon it, in flying as it does to the *Counsel* of that gentle Friend who has condescendingly promised advice, on a subject where she is *eminently* qualified to give it. The important question it wishes to submit is, whether under the circumstances to be described, its hopes are too presumptuous to be encouraged, or whether they ought to be submitted to the Object of them. To enable *my kind Counsellor* to judge of this, it becomes necessary to lay every part of the subject, & of my History as far as it relates thereto, before her without disguise, which shall be done in the very simplicity of Truth.

Introduced into Life a mere Schoolboy without fortune & without connections in this part of the Country my very early Years were unavoidably spent in the pursuit of an establishment in Life, which was not attained till the year 1766 when I entered into Partnership

with Mr. Mure upon that footing of Inferiority in point of share
which was not under such beginnings unjust or oppressive. Those
dispositions which have ever predominated in my mind, had in the
mean time at the age of twenty led to an attachment, very sincere at
the time on my part, to a Lady who (perhaps from our being almost
the only humanized Minds that were within the reach of each others
Conversation) was not insensible to it. The Family proved in a high
degree adverse. Her obedience carried her to break off a forbidden
Correspondence, and when at the end of about five years I found
myself in a situation by means of my connection with Mr. Mure to
expect better Treatment from her Friends, I found that she had not
possessed the Stability of Character I had supposed, and that my
renewed overtures were received with warm professions of Esteem
& Friendship, but *nothing more*; and there ended our Intercourse.
Whether some new attachment or what other Bizarrerie of the
human character had led to this change, whilst nothing like blame
was imputed to *me*, I could not at the time discover, and I will confess
that a spice of Indignation helped me soon to give up the least desire
to enquire farther about it.

A few Years after this disappointment, other Connections led me
into an Acquaintance with *one* whose Attractions I will not attempt
to describe because my *gentle* Counsellor shall not accuse me of a
prolixity which would be very extensive could I do Justice to my
own Conceptions of the subject, but it shall for the present suffice
to observe that if they were not in my Eye superior to those of all
the rest of the world, the asking the Advice I do would be an act of
worthless Folly. Whilst I was taking measures for securing a larger
Share in our Partnership, which would have been essential to the
success of my Hopes as it would have been vain to indulge them till
such addition was secured, the Horrors of the Year 1772 at once swept
away the whole foundation & fruit of my labours, and threw the mild
Firmness of her Virtues so forcibly on my Mind as to be absolutely
irresistible. From that Moment a tender regard for her Welfare
took the lead of every other Sentiment, and if I could think I had
pretensions to the praise of Heroism for any Act of my Life, I would

other Connections led me into an Acquaintance with
one whose Attractions I will not attempt to describe
because my gentle Counsellor shall not accuse
me of a prolixity which would be very extensive
coud I do Justice to my own Conceptions of the subject
but it shall for the present suffice to observe that if
they were not in my Eye superior to those of
all the rest of the world, the asking the Advice I do
woud be an Act of worthless Folly. Whilst I
was taking measures for securing a larger Share
in our Partnership, which woud have been essential
to the success of my Hopes as it woud have been vain
to indulge them till such addition was secured,
the Horrors of the Year 1772 at once swept away
the whole foundation & fruit of my Labours, and
threw the mild Firmness of her Virtues so forcibly
on my Mind as to be absolutely irresistible.
From that Moment a tender regard for her Welfare
took the lead of every other Sentiment, and if I
coud think I had pretensions to the praise of
Heroism for any Act of my Life, I woud ground
my Claim upon having controuled the strong
Impulse of my Soul in neglecting to improve
Moments when Compassion & Friendship left
openings to try to bring them to a softer Appellation, and upon having stood out even the apparent
Risque of losing her for ever, whilst I often shunn'd

Page three (of fifteen).

421

ground my Claim upon having controuled the strong Impulse of my Soul in neglecting to improve moments when Compassion & Friendship left openings to try to bring them to a softer appellation, and upon having stood out even the apparent Risque of losing her for ever, whilst I often shunned an Intercourse attended with Effects too powerful for my peace, rather than hazard the entangling her in Scenes of Distress which for many Years appeared hopeless.

Useful as the School of Adversity is to the Heart, its long continuance however wastes the powers of the body. And whilst like the Traveller upon the Alps, straining over one Hill, I have till lately still found a higher one behind it, altho' I have persevered from the Consciousness of right Intentions, and have overcome successive difficulties which would have appalled me had they made their appearance all at once, yet the Conflict has impaired the best powers of Life, and my nervous System has never recovered the Shock it received from the consequences of Mr. Wedderburn's conduct in the Rum business. At that moment I stood in a situation to have made *such* Use of a decision as would have enabled me to have entered upon an immediate explanation of my affairs similar to the present, and the delay which ensued with all its Train of consequences, envelopped *all* in new Obscurity and gave an adverse Turn to everything. I say this without Resentment, because he knew not what he was doing, but the consequences have been all that I describe. I confess that my Mind sunk under them, and that till very lately my Hopes were narrowed (even in contemplating a happy Event of my Engagements) to a *solitary* endeavour to pass worthily through the Administration of what providence had placed in my hands, but without almost an expectation of enjoyment to myself from any thing but trying (by means not easy soon to bring to bear) to be permitted to *take care* of a very humble part of the concerns of *one*, whose *highest* I had aspired to be united with.

But insensible Circumstances have led to a Revival of Hope. The Clouds which threatened the want of Tranquility in the Enjoyment of a Fortune in my Judgement more than sufficient, have in a wonderful way, within a very short time cleared up; indeed to such a degree as to render it perhaps a criminal Distrust any longer to stand in fear of the Event.

I cannot learn that the various applications to which I have been obliged to leave the Object of my Affection exposed, have led to any deep Impression upon her Heart, else be assured, *my best Counsellor,* I would not disturb her Peace by any explanation of my deep attachment; for it *is not* profession, but reality, *that I prefer her Happiness to my own.* Thus circumstanced I have been led to ask myself, is it *impossible* that at the age of just 42, a Nervous System debilitated by too long and too anxious an attention, might be restored in the Enjoyment of *that Union,* the eager pursuit of which has exhausted it? Should this even fail, which cannot beforehand be known, *may* it not happen that there are *unknown to herself,* in the Friendship which she undoubtedly bears me, the Seeds of a mutual affection which would lead her to more happiness with me even under the worst of my fears than in any other Connection? And *should* this be the case, am I not at once unfaithful to her Happiness and my own if I do not seize the first moment in which I can to the satisfaction of my own Conscience say that my Solicitation is not likely to draw her into Scenes of difficulty?

To enable *My Friend,* to judge how far an able Architect may with the materials before us erect the Castle of Reason, of Affection & Honour, it seems proper not only to state as I *have* done the deep rooted Attachment on one side, which if it can excite reciprocal Sentiments, would perhaps be sufficient to cement *any* Materials, but also to enter into some Detail of what may affect domestick Life, and my way of thinking upon many particulars.

My Fortune, engaged as it is, cannot be estimated within a few thousand Pounds more or less, but according to my best Judgement it is as follows – I have the half of two Estates in Jamaica, my own separate Property out of Trade which my Partners have no Concern with. The one is called *the Bogue* of which Mr. Benfield has half, the other is called *Dean's Valley* of which Capt. Laird has half. My half of the Bogue has cost me £18,000 Sterling which is by agreement to accumulate upon the Estate for three Crops after the present one, and

I am confident that the Produce afterwards may safely be relied upon to keep up at least from £3500 to 4000 Sterling a Year, which will give from £1750 to £2000 Sterling a Year for my half. In good Years it *must* bring *more* but I have not a Conception of its *ever* bringing less.

My half of Dean's Valley is nearer a state of perfect Cultivation than the Bogue and will come a Year or two sooner into its greatest produce, but will hardly ever produce so much as the Bogue. I think however it may justly be depended upon as far as £1200 to 1500 a Year for my half, so that the two together may be relied upon to produce from £3000 to 3500 a Year free of all deductions, which is a greater Sum of *Spendable Money* than most landed Estates in England of a nominal £5000 a Year would produce.

Besides these Estates, my Capital in Trade, after taking out all bad Debts that I know of, cannot, upon the Close of the existing Engagements in my opinion stand at *less* than fifty thousand Pounds. I think a prosperous ending of what is now in hand would raise it *considerably* above sixty, and the future Profits of the House upon its present Establishment, whether we have War or Peace, cannot but be very considerable over and above the Interest of the Capital invested in it. It is therefore I think clear, that in point of Property we have Elbow Room enough for every rational purpose as well in possession as in prospect, and in the confidence which becomes this Intercourse I may be allowed without the Imputation of boasting to add, that I am not conscious of possessing a single Shilling that upon my Death bed I would wish I had not acquired.

I am of opinion that a Settlement for a Lady's Life to her separate Use independent of her Husband is exceedingly proper where it can (as here) be done without crippling the Capital that might often be more profitably employed. Not that I think they should have *separate Interests*, but that Independency cannot be too securely guarded. If I become the happy Object of Approbation in other respects I know I shall not be distrusted in *this*, and I should certainly embrace any explanation of her Wishes on this head. What I should myself make a point of her permitting me to do, would be to settle upon her my half of the Bogue together with *all* her *own present Property* which

I would wish to leave at her disposal in any way and at any time she pleases, not only as to this last in point of the annual Interest but of the *Principal.*

I say nothing of Dean's Valley in this View, because it is no way unlikely that it may hereafter appear proper to part with it and try to get Benfield's half of the Bogue, which, unless Circumstances vary greatly, I should wish to add to the Settlement so as to give her the whole Produce of that Estate for Life. To talk beforehand of what destination it might further be right to make of Property by Will, would be absurd. The Event of having a Family or not, and many other Circumstances ought to render it dependent on future Events, but the Principle of *bare Justice* in my opinion is, that a Widow should be enabled to maintain the same way of Life as in her Husband's Life time. How much farther her power should be extended must depend on Circumstances. Abhorring as I do all Attempts at judging for others after we are dead, I should reprobate the Idea of restraining a second marriage. But whilst I strongly approve of a Settlement on a Wife, I greatly object to extending it to Children, as tending to weaken the Parental Authority provided by God & Nature for their Guidance in Youth, and which I hold to be of much more Importance to them than property.

With respect to Modes of Life, I have no settled Plans or opinions, but conceive they must arise out of a few simple Principles applied to Connections and circumstances as they occur. Those Principles appear to me to be solid, but like everything else dependent on Judgement, they would be liable to alteration from the effect of that intimate Communication of every Thought & every Wish which I aspire to. I hold that the true Spring of all human Happiness rests upon an humble Reliance on Providence, upon conscious Rectitude of Intention, and a constant endeavour as far as human Frailty admits to do what appears right under every Circumstance. That where two Minds unite in this disposition and in an unbounded Confidence, they deserve infinite Support & Strength from each other; that every ignoble Passion, every false Shame, and every trifling Vanity, flies before them. That if a certain degree of knowledge of the World has unmasked the warm expectations formed in early Youth of a degree of felicity not compatible with the State of Humanity, no Inequalities of Temper, no unkind Sentiments will in *such* Minds arise from disappointment to such a Height as to sour or estrange them from each other, but that mutual Love will make them abundantly indulgent to each others failings and watchful to prevent Inroads from any turbulent Passion upon their Felicity.

I conceive that *such* a Pair enjoying the Power, will endeavour to pursue what is really agreeable to themselves, rather than merely what is fashionable, and will not affect an over ostentatious Parade. In short they will *use* their fortune in the amplest Sense of the Word, but will not disgrace themselves by abusing it, nor sacrifice their time and attention (beyond what a common Compliance with the Habits of the World they live among renders necessary) to the frivolous, but rather bend their attention to cultivate the Society of the amiable the cheerful & the worthy in a domestick way, which they can never do too much.

I conceive that their *mutual* Honour in the World can only be supported by the respect in which the Husband is held in the Line in which he moves, and consequently that their Way of Life in many respects will be governed by his Avocations. The Mercantile Line is by no means divested of either Power or Distinction without affecting to mix in Politicks which together with the characters of nearly all the Ministers I have ever known, are by no means Objects of my Admiration. I have no wish to be in Parliament, but rather the contrary (unless I am doomed by the failure of my Hopes to seek Amusement instead of Happiness) because the Evening attendance would interfere with the domestick Enjoyments my Soul thirsts after. To dispose of my Avocations so as to have ample time for this purpose, cannot in the nature of things be done on the Instant, but I think that in a few Weeks I can bring up every thing that is in arrear, and that afterwards, even during the War (getting into the Habit of Hours moderately early) I can very rarely have occasion to do any business taking up much time after dinner; and in time of Peace the business of a West India Merchant of all others requires the least personal attention. If his affairs are well regulated, he may with facility spend two or three days in the Week in the Country or make any excursions he pleases.

I am conscious that from the Scene I have been confined to, I am grown quite a Rustick, and that in the presence of that Person before whom alone I am anxious to cut the best figure I uniformly cut the worst. But these appearances against me will soon wear off; my disposition to social Life is as warm as ever. I love some of the nearest Friends of the Object of my Pursuit not only for *her* sake but their own & flatter myself that I stand well in their esteem. In short I am not aware of a single Circumstance except the fear of Health &ca as above stated, that should lead me to doubt my power of doing Justice to the Partiality I seek to excite. But I love her too sincerely to hazard from false Delicacy or any other Motive the Concealment of anything that could have the remotest Tendency to mislead her Judgement.

And now, by what *tenderest* Epithet, shall I adjure *My Counsellor* to tell me whether my Desires ought to be laid at my fair Friend's Feet or not! I tremble from the fear of diminishing the Share I at present hold in her Esteem, but the Knowledge I have of the Generosity of her Heart supports me in the Hope that she will not put an unkind Construction upon any part of my Conduct. And altho' I suspect her in one particular to be *an Economist* yet I am sure she is *no Niggard*, but that her Heart will feel the *inestimable* Value of a frank Avowal – and that if *your happy* Counsel at eleven tomorrow (if not forbid) is to embolden me to submit my Passion – *she* will with *one* Look of Kindness at our *first* Interview extend to me the Golden Sceptre and tranquilize my Spirits by *that* assurance that there exists no absolute & insurmountable Bar to my Happiness; beyond which meaning I will not attempt to interpret her Goodness till she gives me leave. How many Blessings does my Heart wish to pour upon her!

APPENDIX II

Richard Atkinson's will was the mechanism by which he hoped to spread his wealth among his family and closest friends; this is how he envisioned it would work.[1]

An Abstract of the Will of Richard Atkinson, Esq., of Fenchurch Street in the City of London, made on 23 December 1782.

The remainder of the purchase money for the Bogue & Dean's Valley Estate to be paid out of the Personal Estate. The said Estates given to Trustees for the following purposes, vizt.

1st. To carry on the Cultivation & Improvement thereof.

2nd. To pay the following Annuities, vizt.
£700 per annum to Lady Anne Lindsay – To commence at my decease
£700 per annum to Lady Margaret Fordyce – ditto
with £300 continued after her death to Mr. Fordyce – ditto
£700 per annum to John Robinson – ditto
£50 per annum to Thomas Hogg – ditto
£1,800 per annum to nine Nieces – To commence as they come of age
£200 per annum to Geo. Fordyce's 2 Daughters – ditto

And for the five first years during which the Estates may hardly come to their full yielding, the Personal Estate to make good all deficiencies.

3rd & 4th & 5th. To raise a fund out of the overplus of the produce of the Real Estates, which is to stand as a security against accidents to the Estates and to make good all such, and to accumulate till the year 1803 when my youngest nephew will come of age. And at that time if the Fund does not amount to £15,000, it is to be continued till it does.

If it amounts to more, then £15,000 is to be reserved for the purpose herein after mentioned, and the overplus to be added to the balance of the Personal Estate, and if both shall be sufficient to give £4,000 a piece or more to each of my nieces & each of Lady Anne Lindsay's Daughters (after paying the Legacies of £3,000 a piece to my nephews out of such balance) then the whole is to be so divided; but if the Fund is not sufficient it is to be continued till it becomes sufficient.

6th. If the Savings & Personal Estate added together shall have raised the Fund of £15,000 and paid the Nephews & Nieces as in the last article, before the annuities are reduced to £2,500 per annum the further savings till such Reduction happens to be added to the £15,000.

7th & 8th. When the annuities shall be so reduced to £2,500 per annum, to pay Lady Anne Lindsay £5,000, and all the savings above £15,000, or in case of her death as she shall by Will appoint, and to convey my half of the Bogue Estate to my Brother George's Male Heirs.

9th. Thence forward to pay the annuities out of Dean's Valley and the £10,000 remaining in the Fund, & pay the future Savings to my Brother Matthew's Male Heirs.

10th. When the annuities are reduced to £2,000 per annum, to pay Lady Anne Lindsay out of the Fund £5,000 more.

11th. When reduced to £1,500 per annum, to pay her the remaining £5,000.

And lastly, when all the annuities cease, to convey Dean's Valley Estate to my Brother Matthew's Male Heirs.

All Estates the property of the Partnership of which the legal Title may happen to be vested in me given to the Partnership.

The Sums of £4,500 lent to Lord Wentworth & £15,653 to the Bentinck Estate declared to be Lady Anne Lindsay's property, and all accounts settled with her to the time of my death.

All Sums advanced to Mr. Nevill given to John Robinson.

All Sums due by Mr. Fordyce given to Lord Balcarres.

House in Fenchurch Street and all loose scattered Effects left to the Partnership and the Balance directed to be settled at £75,000.

Out of the Personal Estate the future payments for the purchase money of the Bogue and Dean's Valley to be made.

Also £10,000 to be laid out on those Estates.

And £5,000 set apart for Lady Margaret Fordyce.

And to pay £200 per annum annuity to my Brother Matthew & his wife

    £200 per annum to Mr. & Mrs. Taylor

    £200 per annum to my Brother George's widow

    £200 per annum to Wm. Bentinck till his mother dies

And to pay £3,000 a piece to my nephews as they come of age. And at the Division of the Personal Estate in the year 1803 as above mentioned to pay them £3,000 a piece more and then divide the remainder as before mentioned.

A NOTE ON LANGUAGE

When quoting from letters, newspapers and other sources I've kept original capitalizations and spellings, except where they obscure the meaning. In addition to pruning some long-winded passages, I've taken a few liberties with punctuation; to Bridget Atkinson's letters, in particular, I have added a sprinkling of full stops.

Slavery was a condition imposed upon millions of Africans against their will, and its terminology was devised to strip them of their dignity. Much of this language is today considered derogatory or offensive. Where possible, I have referred to 'enslaved' men and women, rather than 'slaves', to highlight their humanity and not simply the cruel status that was forced upon them.

A NOTE ON TYPE

The text is set in Bell, a typeface commissioned by the publisher John Bell, and created by the engraver Richard Austin in 1788.

A NOTE ON MONEY AND MEASUREMENTS

Under the old, pre-decimal system of pounds, shillings and pence, £1 consisted of 240 pence (denoted by the letter 'd' for the Latin *denarius*), with 12 pence making a shilling, and 20 shillings ('s' for *solidus*) making a pound. A guinea was worth 21 shillings, or £1 1s.

During the period covered by this book, Jamaican currency was worth less than its counterpart in Britain – £1 8s currency equalled £1 sterling. Monetary figures in the text are in pounds sterling, except where I have specified 'currency'.

It is impossible to estimate the modern value of historic sums with even the slightest accuracy, for the relative values of what money might buy – commodities, food, labour, manufactured goods, property – have fluctuated too greatly in the interim. Moreover, it depends on which yardstick you use – retail prices, say, or average earnings. MeasuringWorth.com, a useful resource on this subject, estimates the 2018 value of £1 from the years given below:

	using retail price index	using average earnings
1750	£155	£1,925
1775	£125	£1,650
1800	£79	£1,147
1825	£81	£841
1850	£105	£796

The gulf between these figures rather suggests the limitations of the exercise. When George Atkinson died in 1814, his fortune was valued at £140,000; according to these criteria, it would today either be worth £9.6 million, or £107 million.

Some container sizes, mostly taken from Johnson's *Dictionary*:

Barrel: 36 gallons
Bushel: 8 gallons
Cask: a barrel of any size, smaller than a hogshead
Chaldron: a measure of coals, 2000 lb in weight
Firkin: ¼ barrel, 9 gallons
Hogshead (Hhd): 60 gallons
Pipe: 2 hogsheads
Puncheon: 102 gallons
Quarter: 8 bushels

BIBLIOGRAPHY

ABBREVIATIONS

AF	Atkinson Family
AP	Abergavenny Papers, Eridge Park
BA	Baring Archive, London
BC	Boston College, Chestnut Hill
BL	British Library, London
BLO	Bodleian Library, Oxford
CAE	Cambridgeshire Archives, Ely
CAK	Cumbria Archives, Kendal
CL	Caird Library, National Maritime Museum, Greenwich
CUL	Cambridge University Library, Cambridge
DM	Devonshire Manuscripts, Chatsworth
DUL	Durham University Library, Durham
EUL	Edinburgh University Library, Edinburgh
GM	*Gentleman's Magazine*
HA	Hertfordshire Archives, Hertford
HL	Huntington Library, San Marino
HRO	Hampshire Record Office, Winchester
ICWS	Institute of Commonwealth Studies, London
JA	Jamaica Archives, Spanish Town
KA	Kent Archives, Maidstone
KCUP	Kislak Center, University of Pennsylvania, Philadelphia
LSF	Library of the Society of Friends, London

NA	National Archives, Kew
NAM	National Army Museum, London
NAW	Northumberland Archives, Woodhorn
NHSN	Natural History Society of Northumbria, Newcastle
NJHS	New Jersey Historical Society, Newark
NJSA	New Jersey State Archives, Trenton
NLS	National Library of Scotland, Edinburgh
NLW	National Library of Wales, Aberystwyth
NRS	National Records of Scotland, Edinburgh
NYHS	New-York Historical Society, New York
RGDJ	Registrar-General's Department, Jamaica
RM	Ringwood Manor, New Jersey
SA	Staffordshire Archives, Stafford
SRO	Suffolk Record Office, Lowestoft
SV	Slave Voyages (see Digital Resources)
TWA	Tyne & Wear Archives, Newcastle
UNA	University of Nottingham Archives, Nottingham
WL	Wellcome Library, London
YUL	Yale University Library, New Haven

DIGITAL RESOURCES

The Burney Collection
(https://www.bl.uk/collection-guides/burney-collection)
The vast newspaper collection of the Rev. Charles Burney, now digitized and searchable online. A tip for researchers: bear in mind that during the eighteenth century a letter resembling 'f' was used for an 's' at the start or in the middle of a word, so a word search for 'Atkinfon' (for example) will yield many more results than one for 'Atkinson'.

Founders Online (http://founders.archives.gov)
The correspondence and other writings of six founding fathers of the United States – George Washington, Benjamin Franklin, John Adams, Thomas Jefferson, Alexander Hamilton and James Madison – searchable by date, author and recipient.

Legacies of British Slave-ownership (https://www.ucl.ac.uk/lbs/)
A centre for the study of colonial slavery and its legacy in
modern-day Britain. Its database identifies all the slave owners
in the British West Indies, the Cape and Mauritius who claimed
compensation following the abolition of slavery in 1833; it also
includes the ownership histories of thousands of estates.

National Library of Scotland: Maps of Jamaica
(https://maps.nls.uk/jamaica/)
James Robertson's map of Jamaica, published in 1804, is the most
detailed survey of the island at the height of its prosperity, showing
the location of more than eight hundred sugar plantations. Now
georeferenced, it can be viewed as a zoomable overlay on a modern
Google map – an invaluable resource for those tracking down
old estates.

The Papers of George Washington: Digital Edition
(https://rotunda.upress.virginia.edu)
The letters and diaries of the first President of the United States,
searchable within the text as well as by date, author and recipient.

Slave Voyages (https://www.slavevoyages.org)
A comprehensive database of the transatlantic slave trade, drawing
on British, Dutch, French, Portuguese and Spanish-language
archives around the Atlantic world. It shines light on more than
36,000 slave-trading voyages, giving details of itineraries, dates,
nationalities, names of ships, captains and shipowners, embarkation
numbers and mortality rates.

PRIMARY SOURCES

Acts of the Council and General Assembly of the State of New-Jersey
    (1784)
Almon, John: *Anecdotes of the Life of the Right Hon. William Pitt,
    Earl of Chatham*, Vol. 3 (1797 edition)
Almon, John: *The Parliamentary Register*, printed for J. Almon,
    opposite Burlington-House, in Piccadilly, Vols. 9–11 (1778–9)

Annesley, George (Earl of Mountmorris): *Voyages and Travels to India, Ceylon, the Red Sea, Abyssinia, and Egypt* (1811)

Archaeologia Aeliana, or, Miscellaneous Tracts Relating to Antiquity, published by the Society of Antiquaries of Newcastle upon Tyne, Vol. 1 (1822)

Aspinall, A., ed.: *The Correspondence of George, Prince of Wales,* Vol. 1, 1770–1789 (1963)

Atkinson, George Clayton: *Sketch of the Life and Works of the late Thomas Bewick* (1830)

Atkinson, John Nathaniel: 'Notes on the history of Temple Sowerby and of the Atkinson family' (AF: unpublished MS)

The Bankers' Magazine, and Statistical Register, Vol. 4 (1850)

Baring, Alexander: *Mr. Alexander Baring's Speech in the House of Commons on the 15th Day of May, 1823, on Mr. Buxton's Motion for a Resolution Declaratory of Slavery in the British Colonies Being Contrary to the English Constitution and to Christianity* (1823)

Baring, Francis: *Observations on the Establishment of the Bank of England, and on the Paper Circulation of the Country* (1797)

Barnard, Lady Anne: *Memoirs,* Vols. 1–6 (NLS: Crawford Papers: Acc 9769 27/4/14)

Barrett, Charlotte, ed.: *Diary & Letters of Madame D'Arblay* (1842)

Beche, H.T. de la: *Notes on the Present Condition of the Negroes in Jamaica* (1825)

Beckford, William: *A Descriptive Account of the Island of Jamaica* (1790)

Bewick, Thomas: *A History of British Birds* (1804)

Bigelow, John: *Jamaica in 1850: or, the Effects of Sixteen Years of Freedom on a Slave Colony* (1851)

Bleby, Henry: *Death Struggles of Slavery* (1853)

Boswell, James: *Boswell's London Journal, 1762–1763* (1951)

Bridges, G.W.: *The Annals of Jamaica* (1828)

Bridges, G.W.: *A Voice from Jamaica; in Reply to William Wilberforce, Esq.* (1823)

Brontë, Charlotte: *Jane Eyre* (1850)

Bruce, Gainsford: *The Life and Letters of John Collingwood Bruce* (1905)

Bruce, John Collingwood: *The Roman Wall* (1851)

Budge, E.A.W.: *An Account of the Roman Antiquities Preserved in the Museum at Chesters, Northumberland* (1907)

Camden Miscellany, Volume XXIII, Fourth Series, Vol. 7 (1969)

Catterall, H.T.: *Judicial Cases Concerning American Slavery and the Negro*, Vol. 1 (1926)

Christie, Octavius F., ed.: *The Diary of the Revd. William Jones, 1777–1821* (1929)

Clarkson, Thomas: 'Negro Slavery. Argument, That the colonial slaves are better off than the British peasantry. Answered, from the Royal Jamaica Gazette' (1824)

Clarkson, Thomas: *The History of the Rise, Progress, and Accomplishment of the Abolition of the African Slave Trade by the British Parliament* (1808)

Clerk, John: *An Essay on Naval Tactics, Systematical and Historical, with Explanatory Plates* (1827 edition)

Collections of the Massachusetts Historical Society, For the Year 1792, Vol. 1 (1859 edition)

The Corporation Annual; or, Recollections (not Random) of the First Reformed Town Council, of the Borough of Newcastle upon Tyne. Dedicated (without Permission) to T.E.H., Esq. Leader of the Clique (1836)

Cox, Francis A.: *History of the Baptist Missionary Society, from 1792 to 1842* (1842)

Cumberland, Richard: *Memoirs of Richard Cumberland* (1807)

Dallas, Robert: *The History of the Maroons* (1803)

The Debates in Parliament – Session 1833 – on the Resolutions and Bill for the Abolition of Slavery in the British Colonies (1834)

Defoe, Daniel: *A Tour Thro' the Whole Island of Great Britain: Divided into Circuits or Journeys* (1748 edition)

A Description of Brighthelmstone and the Adjacent Country, or, The New Guide for Ladies and Gentlemen resorting to that Place of Health and Amusement (1784)

Douglas, Sylvester (Lord Glenbervie): *Reports of Cases Argued and Determined in the Court of King's Bench, in the Twenty-Second, Twenty-Third, Twenty-Fourth, and Twenty-Fifth Years of the Reign of George III* (1831)

Edwards, Bryan: *The History, Civil and Commercial, of the British Colonies in the West Indies* (1793)

Elwin, Malcolm: *The Noels and the Milbankes: Their Letters for Twenty-five Years, 1767–1792* (1967)

Evans, Henry B.: *Our West Indian Colonies. Jamaica, A Source of National Wealth and Honour* (1855)

Falconbridge, Alexander: *An Account of the Slave Trade on the Coast of Africa* (1788)

The Festival of Wit; Or, Small Talker, being a Collection of Bon Mots, Anecdotes, &c. of the Most Exalted Character (1793 edition)

Foote, Samuel: *The Patron: A Comedy in Three Acts* (1764)

Fortescue, John, ed.: *The Correspondence of King George III, from 1760 to December, 1783* (1927–8)

Fox, William: *An Address to the People of Great Britain, on the Propriety of Abstaining from West India Sugar and Rum* (1792)

Franklin, Benjamin: *The Interest of Great Britain Considered with Regard to Her Colonies and the Acquisitions of Canada and Guadaloupe* (1760)

Fremantle, Anne, ed.: *The Wynne Diaries*, Vol. 3 (1940)

French, Gilbert J.: *The Life and Times of Samuel Crompton* (1859)

Gardner, William: *A History of Jamaica from its Discovery by Christopher Columbus to the Present Time* (1873)

Glasse, Hannah: *The Art of Cookery Made Plain and Easy* (1805 edition)

Greig, J.Y.T., ed.: *The Letters of David Hume*, Vol. 2: 1766–1776 (1932)

Grenville, Richard (Duke of Buckingham): *Memoirs of the Court and Cabinets of George the Third* (1853)

Grosley, Pierre Jean: *A Tour to London, or New Observations on England and its Inhabitants* (1765)

Gurney, Joseph John: *A Winter in the West Indies, described in Familiar Letters to Henry Clay, of Kentucky* (1841)

Hakewill, James: *A Picturesque Tour of the Island of Jamaica from Drawings made in the Years 1820 and 1821* (1825)

Hansard, T.C.: *The Parliamentary Debates from the Year 1803 to the Present Time*, published under the superintendence of T.C. Hansard, Old Series, Vol. 9 (1812)

Hansard, T.C.: *The Parliamentary Debates: Forming a Continuation of the Work entitled 'The Parliamentary History of England, from the Earliest Period to the Year 1803'*, published under the superintendence of T.C. Hansard. New Series, commencing with the Accession of George IV, Vol. 9 (1824)

Hansard, T.C.: *The Parliamentary History of England, from the Earliest Period to the Year 1803*, printed by T.C. Hansard, Peterborough-Court, Fleet-Street, Vols. 16–32 (1813–18)

Hardcastle, Daniel: *Banks and Bankers* (1842)

Harford, John S.: *Recollections of William Wilberforce during nearly Thirty Years* (1865)

Hawkesworth, John ed.: *An Account of the Voyages Undertaken by the Order of his Present Majesty for Making Discoveries in the Southern Hemisphere* (1773)

Hoare, Prince: *The Memoirs of Granville Sharp* (1820)

Hodgson, John: *A Topographical and Historical Description of Westmorland* (1810)

Hodgson, John et al.: *The Beauties of England and Wales: or, Original Delineations, Topographical, Historical, and Descriptive, of each County*, Vol. 15, Part 2 (1814)

Holroyd, John (Lord Sheffield): *Observations on the Commerce of the American States* (1784)

Howitt, William: *Visits to Remarkable Places* (1842)

Hutchinson, William: *An Excursion to the Lakes in Westmoreland and Cumberland; With a Tour Through Part of the Northern Counties, In the Years 1773 and 1774* (1776)

Hutton, William: *The History of the Roman Wall, which Crosses the Island of Britain, from the German Ocean to the Irish Sea* (1801)

An Impartial History of the Town and County of Newcastle upon Tyne and its Vicinity (1801)

Jackson, Donald, ed.: *The Diaries of George Washington*, Vol. 1 (1976)

Jackson, Robert: *A Treatise on the Fevers of Jamaica* (1791)

Johnson, Samuel: *A Dictionary of the English Language* (1805 edition)

Johnson, Samuel: *Taxation no Tyranny: An Answer to the Resolutions and Address of the American Congress* (1775)

Journals of the House of Commons, from 10 January 1765 to 16 September 1766, Vol. 30 (1803)

Journals of the House of Commons, from 26 November 1772 to 15 September 1774, Vol. 34 (1804)

Journals of the House of Commons, from 29 November 1774 to 15 October 1776, Vol. 35 (1803)

Journals of the House of Commons, from 31 October 1780 to 10 October 1782, Vol. 38 (1803)

Knight, William, ed.: *Letters of the Wordsworth Family from 1787 to 1855* (1969)

Knox, William: *Extra Official State Papers, Addressed to the Right Hon. Lord Rawdon, and the Other Members of the Two Houses of Parliament* (1789)

Laprade, William T.: *Parliamentary Papers of John Robinson, 1774–1784* (1922)

Lawrence-Archer, James: *Monumental Inscriptions of the British West Indies* (1875)

Lenta, Margaret and Le Cordeur, Basil, eds: *The Cape Diaries of Lady Anne Barnard, 1799–1800* (1999)

A Letter to a Merchant of Bristol; concerning a Petition of S. T. Esq. (S. Touchet) to the King, for an Exclusive Grant to the Trade of the River Senegal. By a Merchant of London (1762)

Lewis, Matthew G.: *Journal of a West-India Proprietor, 1815–17* (1929)

Lindsay, Alexander (Earl of Crawford): *Lives of the Lindsays* (1849)

A List of the Liverymen of London, who voted for Mr. Alderman Sawbridge, and Richard Atkinson Esq., at the late election for Members of Parliament for the City of London, Carefully Corrected from the Sheriff's Attested Copies of the Poll (1784)

Long, Edward: *The History of Jamaica: or, General Survey of the Antient and Modern State of that Island* (1774)

Lustig, I.S. and Pottle, F.A., eds: *Boswell: The English Experiment, 1785–1789* (1986)

Mackenzie, Eneas, ed.: *An Historical, Topographical, and Descriptive View of the County of Northumberland* (1825)

Madden, Richard: *A Twelvemonth's Residence in the West Indies, during the Transition from Slavery to Apprenticeship* (1835)

Manuscripts of Captain Howard Vicente Knox: Report on Manuscripts in Various Collections, Vol. 6 (1909)

Martin, R.M.: *The British Colonies, Vol. 4: Africa and the West Indies* (1853)

Moore, Thomas: *Works of Lord Byron: With His Letters and Journals, and His Life* (1832)

Moorman, Mary, ed.: *Journals of Dorothy Wordsworth: The Alfoxden Journal 1798, The Grasmere Journals 1800–1803* (1971)

Moreton, J.B.: *West India Customs and Manners* (1793)

Nicolson, Joseph and Burn, Richard: *The History and Antiquities of the Counties of Westmorland and Cumberland, in Two Volumes* (1777)

Papers presented to the House of Commons on the 7th May 1804, Respecting the Slave-Trade; &c. &c. (1804)

Peach, W.B. and Thomas, D.O., eds: *The Correspondence of Richard Price* (1983–94)

Peel, Robert: *Six Speeches: The Tamworth Election* (1841)

Phillimore, J., ed.: *Reports of Cases Argued and Determined in the Ecclesiastical Courts at Doctors' Commons*, Vol. 2 (1812–18)

Phillippo, James: *Jamaica: Its Past and Present State* (1843)

The Picture of Newcastle upon Tyne, containing a Guide to the Town and Neighbourhood, an Account of the Roman Wall, and a Description of the Coal Mines, etc (1807)

The Poll for Knights of the Shire, To represent the County of Westmorland, Taken at Appleby, On Thursday, Friday, Saturday, Monday, and Tuesday, the 13th, 14th, 15th, 17th and 18th Days of October, 1774 (1774)

Postlethwayt, Malachy: *The African Trade the Great Pillar & Support of the British Plantation Trade in America* (1745)

Postlethwayt, Malachy: *The Universal Dictionary of Trade and Commerce* (1774 edition)

The Proceedings of the Governor and Assembly of Jamaica, in Regard to the Maroon Negroes (1796)

Proceedings of the Society of Antiquaries of Newcastle-upon-Tyne, Vol. 3 (1889)

Quine, David A., ed.: *Expeditions to the Hebrides by George Clayton Atkinson in 1831 and 1833* (2001)

Raine, James: *A Memoir of the Rev. John Hodgson* (1857)

Register of Ships, Lloyd's (1764)

The Remarkable Case of Peter Hasenclever, Merchant: formerly one of the proprietors of the iron works, pot-ash manufactory, &c. established, and successfully carried on under his direction, in the provinces of New York, and New Jersey, in North America, 'till November 1766 (1773)

Renny, Robert: *An History of Jamaica* (1807)

Reports from Committees of the House of Commons, Vol. XI, Miscellaneous Subjects: 1782–1799 (1803)

Rochefoucauld, François: *A Frenchman's Year in Suffolk: French Impressions of Suffolk Life in 1784* (1988)

Russell, Richard: *A Dissertation on the Use of Sea-Water in the Diseases of the Glands; particularly the Scurvy, Jaundice, King's-Evil, Leprosy, and the Glandular Consumption* (1752)

Sainsbury, W.N. and Fortescue, J.W., eds: *Calendar of State Papers, Colonial Series, Vol. 10, America and West Indies, 1677–80* (1896)

Scoresby-Jackson, Robert E.: *Medical Climatology: or, A Topographical and Meteorological Description of the Localities Resorted to in Winter and Summer by Invalids of Various Classes, Both at Home and Abroad* (1862)

Seaton, A.V., ed.: *Journal of an Expedition to the Feroe and Westman Islands and Iceland, 1833, by George Clayton Atkinson* (1989)

Second Series of Recollections (not Random) of the Reformed Town Council of Newcastle-upon-Tyne (1855)

Sheridan, Richard Brinsley: *Clio's Protest* (1819)

Sheridan, Thomas: *A Course of Lectures on Elocution* (1762)

Sketches of Public Men of the North (1855)

Skinner, John: *Hadrian's Wall in 1801: Observations on the Roman Wall* (1978)

Smith, Adam: *An Inquiry into the Nature and Causes of the Wealth of Nations* (1776)

Stanhope, Philip: *Life of the Right Honourable William Pitt* (1861)

The State of the Nation, with Respect to its Public Funded Debt, Revenue, and Disbursement; comprised in the Reports of the Select Committee on Finance, Vol. 2 (1798)

The Statutes of the United Kingdom of Great Britain and Ireland, 1 & 2 Victoria (1838)

Stephen, George: *Anti-Slavery Recollections: In a Series of Letters addressed to Mrs. Beecher Stowe, written by Sir George Stephen, at Her Request* (1854)

Stewart, J.: *An Account of Jamaica and its Inhabitants* (1808)

Stewart, J.: *A View of the Past and Present State of the Island of Jamaica* (1823)

Stockdale, John: *The Parliamentary Register . . . in Seventeen Volumes*, reprinted for John Stockdale, Piccadilly, Vol. 2 (1802)

Sturge, Joseph and Harvey, Thomas: *The West Indies in 1837: Being the Journal of a Visit to Antigua, Montserrat, Dominica, St. Lucia, Barbados, and Jamaica* (1838)

Terrill, Anne E.: *Memorials of a Family in England and Virginia, 1771–1851* (1887)

Thomson, Thomas: *Annals of Philosophy: or, Magazine of Chemistry, Mineralogy, Mechanics, Natural History, Agriculture, and the Arts*, Vol. 4 (1814)

Tooke, John Horne: *Facts Addressed to the Landholders* (1780)

Toynbee, Mrs Paget: *The Letters of Horace Walpole, Fourth Earl of Orford* (1903–5)

The Transactions of the Jamaica Society of Arts, Vol. 1 (1855)

Transactions of the Natural History Society, of Northumberland, Durham, and Newcastle upon Tyne, Vol. 1 (1831)

Transactions of the Natural History Society, of Northumberland, Durham, and Newcastle upon Tyne, Vol. 2 (1838)

Walpole, Horace: *Memoirs of the Reign of King George III* (1845)

Walpole, Horace: *The Last Journals of Horace Walpole during the Reign of George III, from 1771–1783* (1910)

Welford, Richard: *Men of Mark 'twixt Tyne and Tweed* (1895)

Wilberforce, R. and Wilberforce, S.: *The Life of William Wilberforce* (1838)

Wraxall, Nathaniel: *Historical Memoirs of His Own Time* (1836)

Wraxall, Nathaniel: *Posthumous Memoirs of His Own Time* (1836)

Wright, Philip, ed.: *Lady Nugent's Journal of her Residence in Jamaica from 1801 to 1805* (1966)

Young, Arthur: *Annals of Agriculture, and Other Useful Arts* (1784–1815)

SECONDARY SOURCES

Ashton, T.S.: *An Economic History of England: The Eighteenth Century* (London, 1964)

Ashton, T.S.: *The Industrial Revolution, 1760–1830* (Oxford, 1948)

Ashton, T.S.: *Iron and Steel in the Industrial Revolution* (Manchester, 1951)

Austin, Peter E.: *Baring Brothers and the Birth of Modern Finance* (London, 2015)

Baker, Norman: *Government and Contractors: The British Treasury and War Supplies, 1775–1783* (London, 1971)

Baker, Norman: 'The Treasury and Open Contracting, 1778–1782', *The Historical Journal*, Vol. 15, No. 3, pp. 433–54 (1972)

Black, Jeremy: *A Brief History of Slavery* (London, 2011)

Black, Jeremy: *Eighteenth-century Britain, 1688–1783* (Basingstoke, 2008)

Bouch, C.M.L. and Jones, G.P.: *A Short Economic and Social History of the Lake Counties, 1500–1830* (Manchester, 1961)

Bowler, R. Arthur: *Logistics and the Failure of the British Army in America, 1775–1783* (Princeton, 1975)

Brathwaite, Edward: *The Development of Creole Society in Jamaica, 1770–1820* (Oxford, 1971)

Brewer, John: *The Sinews of Power: War, Money and the English State, 1688–1783* (London, 1989)

Buckley, Roger N.: *Slaves in Red Coats: The British West India Regiments, 1795–1815* (New Haven, 1979)

Buel, R.: *Dear Liberty: Connecticut's Mobilization for the Revolutionary War* (Middletown, 1980)

Burn, William L.: *Emancipation and Apprenticeship in the British West Indies* (London, 1937)

Burns, Alan: *History of the British West Indies* (London, 1954)

Cannon, John: *The Fox-North Coalition* (Cambridge, 1969)

Carrington, Selwyn H.H.: *The Sugar Industry and the Abolition of the Slave Trade, 1775–1810* (Gainesville, 2002)

Christie, Ian R.: *Crisis of Empire: Great Britain and the American Colonies, 1754–1783* (London, 1966)

Christie, Ian R.: *The End of North's Ministry, 1780–1782* (London, 1958)

Christie, Ian R.: 'The political allegiance of John Robinson, 1770–1784', *Historical Research*, Vol. 29, Issue 79, pp. 108–22 (1956)

Clapham, J.H.: *The Bank of England: A History* (Cambridge, 1958)

Colley, Linda: *Britons: Forging the Nation, 1707–1837* (New Haven, 1992)

Collins, Rob and McIntosh, Frances, eds: *Life in the Limes: Studies of the People and Objects of the Roman Frontiers* (Oxford, 2014)

Cundall, Frank: *Historic Jamaica* (London, 1915)

Derry, John W.: *Politics in the Age of Fox, Pitt and Liverpool* (Basingstoke, 1990)

Dickerson, Oliver M.: *The Navigation Acts and the American Revolution* (Philadelphia, 1951)

Donoughue, Bernard: *British Politics and the American Revolution: The Path to War 1773–1775* (New York, 1964)

Draper, Nicholas: *The Price of Emancipation: Slave-ownership, Compensation and British Society at the End of Slavery* (Cambridge, 2010)

Drescher, Seymour: *Abolition: A History of Slavery and Antislavery* (Cambridge, 2009)

Duffy, Michael: *Soldiers, Sugar, and Seapower: The British Expeditions to the West Indies and the War against Revolutionary France* (Oxford, 1987)

Ehrman, John: *The Younger Pitt: The Years of Acclaim* (London, 1969)

Eisner, Gisela: *Jamaica, 1830–1930: A Study in Economic Growth* (Manchester, 1961)

Fell, Alfred: *The Early Iron Industry of Furness and District, 1726–1800* (Ulverston, 1908)

Ferguson, Niall: *Empire: How Britain Made the Modern World* (London, 2004)

Fetherstonhaugh, Robert C.: *The 13th Battalion Royal Highlanders of Canada, 1914–1919* (Montreal, 1925)

Furber, Holden: 'The East India Directors in 1784', *The Journal of Modern History*, Vol. 5, No. 4, pp. 479–95 (1933)

Geggus, David: 'Jamaica and the Saint Domingue Slave Revolt, 1791–1793', *The Americas*, Vol. 38, No. 2, pp. 219–33 (1981)

Geggus, David: *Slavery, War and Revolution: The British Occupation of Saint Domingue 1793–1798* (Oxford, 1982)

George, M.D.: *Catalogue of Political and Personal Satires Preserved in the Department of Prints and Drawings in the British Museum* (London, 1952)

George, M.D.: *London Life in the Eighteenth Century* (London, 1996)

Gerzina, Gretchen: *Black England: Life before Emancipation* (London, 1995)

Green, William A.: *British Slave Emancipation: The Sugar Colonies and the Great Experiment, 1830–1865* (Oxford, 1976)

Hague, William: *William Pitt the Younger* (London, 2004)

Hall, C., Draper, N. and McClelland, K.: *Emancipation and the Remaking of the British Imperial World* (Manchester, 2014)

Hall, Catherine et al.: *Legacies of British Slave-ownership: Colonial Slavery and the Formation of Victorian Britain* (Cambridge, 2016)

Hall, Douglas: *A Brief History of the West India Committee* (Barbados, 1971)

Hall, Douglas: *In Miserable Slavery: Thomas Thistlewood in Jamaica, 1750–1786* (London, 1989)

Heusser, Albert H.: *George Washington's Map Maker: A Biography of Robert Erskine* (New Brunswick, 1966)

Hibbert, Christopher: *Redcoats and Rebels: The War for America 1770–1781* (London, 1990)

Higman, B.W.: *Jamaica Surveyed: Plantation Maps and Plans of the Eighteenth and Nineteenth Centuries* (Jamaica, 1988)

Higman, B.W.: *Plantation Jamaica 1750–1850: Capital and Control in a Colonial Economy* (Jamaica, 2005)

Higman, B.W.: *Slave Population and Economy in Jamaica, 1807–1834* (Cambridge, 1976)

Hochschild, Adam: *Bury the Chains: The British Struggle to Abolish Slavery* (London, 2005)

Holmes, Richard: *Redcoat: The British Soldier in the Age of Horse and Musket* (London, 2001)

Howard, D.S.: *Chinese Armorial Porcelain*, Vol. 2 (Chippenham, 2003)

Hudleston, C. Roy: 'The Dalstons of Acornbank', *Transactions of the Cumberland & Westmorland Antiquarian & Archaeological Society*, Series 2, Vol. 58, pp. 140–79 (1958)

Ingram, Kenneth E.: *Sources of Jamaican History, 1655–1838: A Bibliographical Survey with Particular Reference to Manuscript Sources* (London, 1976)

Inikori, Joseph E.: 'Slavery and the Revolution in Cotton Textile Production in England', *Social Science History*, Vol. 13, No. 4, pp. 343–79 (1989)

James, C.L.R.: *The Black Jacobins: Toussaint L'Ouverture and the San Domingo Revolution* (London, 1980)

Johnson, Carol, ed.: 'Robert Erskine's letters of 1770 about the British iron and steel industry', *Historical Metallurgy*, Vol. 43, pp. 75–97 (2009)

Kup, A.P.: 'Alexander Lindsay, 6th Earl of Balcarres, Lieutenant Governor of Jamaica 1794–1801', *Bulletin of the John Rylands Library*, Vol. 57, Issue 2, pp. 327–65 (1975)

Leach, Stephen and Whitworth, Alan: *Saving the Wall: The Conservation of Hadrian's Wall, 1746–1987* (Stroud, 2011)

Logan, Rayford W.: *Haiti and the Dominican Republic* (Oxford, 1968)

Mackesy, Piers: *The War for America, 1775–1783* (London, 1964)

Mintz, Sidney W.: *Sweetness and Power: The Place of Sugar in Modern History* (London, 1985)

Monteith, Kathleen E.A. and Richards, Glen: *Jamaica in Slavery and Freedom* (Barbados, 2002)

Namier, Lewis: *England in the Age of the American Revolution* (London, 1930)

Namier, Lewis: *The House of Commons, 1754–1790* (London, 1964)

Nelson, Louis P.: *Architecture and Empire in Jamaica* (New Haven, 2016)

O'Shaughnessy, Andrew J.: 'The Formation of a Commercial Lobby: The West India Interest, British Colonial Policy and the American Revolution', *The Historical Journal*, Vol. 40, No. 1, pp. 71–95 (1997)

O'Shaughnessy, Andrew J.: *An Empire Divided: The American Revolution and the British Caribbean* (Philadelphia, 2000)

O'Shaughnessy, Andrew J.: *The Men Who Lost America: British Command during the Revolutionary War and the Preservation of the Empire* (London, 2013)

Pares, Richard: *King George III and the Politicians* (London, 1967)

Pares, Richard: *War and Trade in the West Indies, 1739–1763* (Oxford, 1936)

Parker, Matthew: *The Sugar Barons* (London, 2011)

Penson, Lillian M.: 'The London West India Interest in the Eighteenth Century', *The English Historical Review*, Vol. 36, No. 143, pp. 373–92 (1921)

Perry, Keith: *British Politics and the American Revolution* (Basingstoke, 1990)

Petley, Christer: *Slaveholders in Jamaica: Colonial Society and Culture during the Era of Abolition* (London, 2015)

Philips, C.H.: *The East India Company, 1784–1834* (Manchester, 1961)

Phillips, Maberly: *A History of Banks, Bankers, and Banking in Northumberland, Durham, and North Yorkshire* (London, 1894)

Picard, Liza: *Dr Johnson's London* (London, 2000)

Porter, Roy: *English Society in the Eighteenth Century* (London, 1982)

Pressnell, Leslie S.: *Country Banking in the Industrial Revolution* (Oxford, 1956)

Ragatz, Lowell J.: *The Fall of the Planter Class in the British Caribbean, 1763–1833* (London, 1928)

Robertson, James: *Gone is the Ancient Glory: Spanish Town, Jamaica 1534–2000* (Jamaica, 2005)

Roebuck, Peter: *Cattle Droving through Cumbria, 1600–1900* (Carlisle, 2016)

Rubinstein, W.D.: *Who Were the Rich?: A Biographical Dictionary of British Wealth-holders* (London, 2009)

Ryden, David B.: *West Indian Slavery and British Abolition, 1783–1807* (Cambridge, 2009)

Sheridan, Richard B.: 'The British Credit Crisis of 1772 and the American Colonies', *The Journal of Economic History*, Vol. 20, No. 2, pp. 161–86 (1960)

Sheridan, Richard B.: 'The Wealth of Jamaica in the Eighteenth Century', *The Economic History Review*, New Series, Vol. 18, No. 2, pp. 292–311 (1965)

Sheridan, Richard B.: *Sugar and Slavery: An Economic History of the British West Indies, 1623–1775* (Baltimore, 1974)

Sutherland, Lucy S.: *The East India Company in Eighteenth-century Politics* (Oxford, 1962)

Sutherland, Lucy S.: *Politics and Finance in the Eighteenth Century* (London, 1984)

Sutton, Jean: *Lords of the East: The East India Company and its Ships* (London, 1981)

Syrett, David: *Shipping and the American War, 1775–83* (London, 1970)

Tattersfield, Nigel: *Bookplates by Beilby & Bewick, 1760–1849* (London, 1999)

Taylor, Stephen: *Defiance: The Life and Choices of Lady Anne Barnard* (London, 2016)

Thomas, Hugh: *The Slave Trade: The History of the Atlantic Slave Trade, 1440–1870* (London, 1997)

Thomas, Peter D.G.: *British Politics and the Stamp Act Crisis* (Oxford, 1975)

Thomas, Peter D.G.: *Lord North* (London, 1976)

Thompson, A.S. & Frentzos, C.G., ed.: *The Routledge Handbook of American Military and Diplomatic History: The Colonial Period to 1877* (New York, 2015)

Thomson, Ian: *The Dead Yard: Tales of Modern Jamaica* (London, 2009)

Tyson, Blake: 'Oak for the Navy: A Case Study, 1700–1703', *Transactions of the Cumberland & Westmorland Antiquarian & Archaeological Society*, Series 2, Vol. 87, pp. 117–26 (1987)

Tyson, Blake: 'Two Appleby Houses in the 18th Century: A Documentary Study', *Transactions of the Cumberland & Westmorland Antiquarian & Archaeological Society*, Series 2, Vol. 85, pp. 193–218 (1985)

Uglow, Jenny: *In These Times: Living in Britain through Napoleon's Wars, 1793–1815* (London, 2014)

Uglow, Jenny: *Nature's Engraver: A Life of Thomas Bewick* (London, 2006)

Wadsworth, Alfred P.: *The Cotton Trade and Industrial Lancashire, 1600–1780* (Manchester, 1931)

Wake, Thomas: 'The Society's Fifteenth Century Fede-ring Brooch', *Proceedings of the Society of Antiquaries of Newcastle upon Tyne*, Fourth Series, Vol. 6, pp. 172–4 (1935)

Walvin, James: *England, Slaves and Freedom, 1776–1838* (Basingstoke, 1986)

Walvin, James: *A Short History of Slavery* (London, 2007)

White, Jerry: *London in the Eighteenth Century: A Great and Monstrous Thing* (London, 2012)

Wilkes, Lyall and Dodds, Gordon: *Tyneside Classical: The Newcastle of Grainger, Dobson and Clayton* (London, 1964)

Williams, Eric: *Capitalism and Slavery* (London, 1964)

Woodside, Robert and Crow, James: *Hadrian's Wall: An Historic Landscape* (London, 1999)

Ziegler, Philip: *The Sixth Great Power: Barings 1762–1929* (London, 1988)

NOTES

1 A Tangled Inheritance

1 AF: JLA to JREA, 29 Jul 1968

2 The Tanner's Wife

1 Nicolson & Burn, Vol. 1, p. 8
2 CAK: WDX 82
3 Hudleston, p. 160
4 AF: WA's will, 17 May 1645
5 Defoe, Vol. 3, p. 258
6 NA: E 179/195/73
7 AF: JA's will, 18 Oct 1680
8 Hodgson, *A Topographical and Historical Description*, p. 106
9 Tyson, 'Oak for the Navy', p. 120
10 Tyson, 'Two Appleby Houses', p. 198
11 CAK: WPR 81
12 Nicolson & Burn, Vol. 1, p. 10
13 CAK: WDX 82
14 NA: IR 1/20
15 *Public Advertiser*, 22 Apr 1756
16 NAW: ZAL 95/7/2: BM to GA, 7 Jul 1756
17 NAW: ZAL 95/7/3: JT to BM, 29 Jul 1756
18 NAW: ZAL 96/2/6: BS to BM, 5 Sep 1756
19 NRS: CS96/2154
20 NAW: ZAL 96/2/7: GA to JM, 4 Mar 1757

21 NAW: ZAL 95/7/5: BA to JM, 13 Jan 1758
22 NAW: ZAL 95/7/6: BT to DM, BA to DM, 13 Jan 1758
23 *GM*: Vol. 28, p. 46
24 NAW: ZAL 95/7/7: BA to GA, 13 Jul 1758
25 NAW: ZAL 96/2/9: BA to JM, 12 Jan 1759
26 NAW: ZAL 95/7/8: BA to JM, 28 Jan 1759
27 NAW: ZAL 95/7/9: GA to JM, 3 Mar 1761
28 NAW: ZAL 95/3/7: MT to JA, nd

3 Atlantic Empire

1 Grosley, Vol. 1, p. 37
2 Ibid., Vol. 1, p. 35
3 French, p. 254
4 Postlethwayt, *The African Trade*, p. 2
5 NA: T 70/1523: Thomas Melvil to Committee, 10 Aug 1754
6 Falconbridge, p. 34
7 SV: Voyages 77616, 77617, 90647
8 SV: Voyage 90839
9 Postlethwayt, *Universal Dictionary*, Vol. 2, 'Privateers and Prizes'
10 NA: HCA 26/6, fo. 68

11 Sheridan, T., p. 30
12 Ibid., p. 24
13 *London Chronicle*, 26 Feb 1761
14 BL: Add MS 32923, fo. 282: JW to Newcastle, 28 May 1761
15 HRO: 92M95/NP3/1/8: EB to FB, 31 Mar 1766
16 BA: HC 5.3.4/18: Nathaniel Clayton to Alexander Baring, 4 Dec 1822
17 Foote, pp. 5, 6, 13
18 SV: Voyages 75031, 75095, 75781, 75975, 77099, 77771, 77773, 77817
19 Greig, p. 52: DH to Richard Davenport, Jun 1766
20 Almon, *Anecdotes*, p. 222
21 Franklin, pp. 14–15
22 Hibbert, *Redcoats and Rebels*, p. xvii
23 *Collections of the Massachusetts Historical Society*, p. 83
24 *Providence Gazette*, 27 Oct 1764
25 BL: Add MS 38202, fo. 368: RA to CJ, 29 Jun 1764
26 Hansard, *Parliamentary History*, Vol. 16, cols. 37–8
27 *Halifax Gazette*, 13 Feb 1766
28 BL: Add MS 33030, fo. 166
29 *Camden Miscellany*, p. 318
30 *Journals of the House of Commons*, Vol. 30, p. 790
31 CAE: R 55/7/122(0)4: RA to JT, 13 Jul 1767
32 CAE: R 55/7/122(0)4: MSA to JT, 15 Nov 1767
33 *GM*: Vol. 34, p. 493
34 Sainsbury & Fortescue, p. 120
35 Catterall, p. 9
36 Ibid., pp. 12, 13
37 Hoare, p. 35

4 Four Dice

1 *Founders Online*: BF to William Brownrigg, 7 Nov 1773
2 NJHS: MG 199: 'An Account of some of the Uses of the Patent Centrifugal Hydraulic Engine'
3 NYHS: American Iron Co. MSS: Trustees to Messrs R&Y, 30 Jan 1770
4 NJSA: RE to RA, 16 Sep 1770
5 RM: Erskine Papers: RE to RA, 18 Oct 1770; NJSA: PHEUS001: RE to RA, 20 Oct 1770
6 NJSA: PHEUS001: RE to RA, 27 Oct 1770
7 NJHS: MG 199: RE to RA, nd
8 *Scots Magazine*, Vol. 34, p. 421
9 *Middlesex Journal*, 13 Jun 1772
10 NLS: MS.4944: RA to Baron Mure, 2 Apr 1768
11 Young, A., Vol. 18 (1792), pp. 164–8
12 Sheridan, R.B., *Clio's Protest*, pp. 17–18
13 Lindsay, Vol. 2, p. 332
14 Knight, Vol. 3, p. 25: WW to Alexander Dyce, 4 Dec 1833
15 Barnard, Vol. 2, pp. 2–3
16 Ibid., Vol. 2, pp. 5–6
17 Ibid., Vol. 2, pp. 2–4
18 Ibid., Vol. 2, pp. 3–4
19 Ibid., Vol. 1, pp. 162–3
20 Ibid., Vol. 2, pp. 5–10
21 Ibid., Vol. 2, pp. 56–7
22 Ibid., Vol. 2, pp. 50–1
23 NA: B 3/3675
24 Barnard, Vol. 2, pp. 50–1
25 Ibid., Vol. 2, pp. 53–4
26 *Scots Magazine*, Vol. 34, p. 311
27 Smith, Vol. 1, p. 388
28 Barnard, Vol. 2, pp. 81–3

29 *GM*: Vol. 42, p. 293

30 Toynbee, Vol. 8, Letter 1413,
    p. 178: HW to Sir Horace Mann,
    1 Jul 1772

31 Greig, p. 463: DH to AS,
    27 Jun 1772

32 Barnard, Vol. 2, pp. 91–2

33 Ibid., Vol. 2, pp. 92–4

34 Ibid., Vol. 2, pp. 95–6

35 Ibid., Vol. 2, pp. 97–9

36 *Public Ledger*, 22 Aug 1772

37 *London Evening Post*, 15 Sep 1772

38 *Morning Chronicle*, 14 Sep 1772

39 *London Chronicle*, 15 Sep 1772

40 *The Festival of Wit*, p. 144

41 Holroyd, p. 201

42 NYHS: American Iron Co.
    MSS: Trustees to Messrs R&Y,
    2 Dec 1772

5 All the Tea in Boston

1 *Evening Post*, 22 Sep 1772

2 *Boston Evening-Post*, 20 Dec 1773

3 DM: CS4/1134: Sir Anthony
   Abdy to Devonshire, 3 Jun 1759

4 UNA: Pw F 3269: WD to
   Portland, 24 Feb 1769

5 Walpole, *Memoirs*, Vol. 4, p. 78

6 BL: Add MS 38206, fo. 285:
   JR to Charles Jenkinson, 26 Sep
   1770

7 *Journals of the House of Commons*,
   Vol. 34, p. 345

8 *GM*: Vol. 44, pp. 40–1

9 Hansard, *Parliamentary History*,
   Vol. 17, col. 1165

10 Ibid., Vol. 17, col. 1169

11 NJHS: MG 199 (K26.31 &
    K26.32): RE to RA, 2 Nov 1773

12 NJHS: MG 199 (K26.31 &
    K26.32): RE to RA, 1 Jun 1774

13 *GM*: Vol. 44, pp. 40–1

14 NA: T 1/500, fo. 56

15 NA: T 1/500, fo. 48

16 Fell, pp. 339–40

17 *The Poll for Knights of the Shire*,
    p. 2

18 NJHS: MG 199 (K26.31 &
    K26.32): RE to RA, 5 Oct 1774

19 *Evening Post*, 19 Jan 1775

20 ICWS: M915: West India
    Committee, Mar 1775

21 Hawkesworth, Vol. 2, pp. 80–1

22 NA: CO 5/92, fo. 123: TG to
    Dartmouth, 28 Mar 1775

23 NJHS: MG 199 (K26.31 &
    K26.32): RE to Trustees, 3 May
    1775

24 Stockdale, *Parliamentary Register*,
    Vol. 2, p. 89; NA: CO 5/92, fo.
    187: TG to Dartmouth, 25 Jun
    1775

25 Almon, *Parliamentary Register*,
    Vol. 9, Appendix No. 1: TG to
    Grey Cooper, 19 May 1775

26 Fortescue, Vol. 3, Letter 1682,
    p. 234: North to King, 26 Jul
    1775

27 Almon, *Parliamentary Register*,
    Vol. 9: Report from the Select
    Committee, p. 12

28 NA: T 1/513, fo. 140: MSA to
    William Howe, 25 Sep 1775

29 BL: Add MS 38206, fo. 179:
    JR to CJ, 19 Sep 1775

30 NA: T 1/513, fos. 140–5: RA to
    WH, 25 Sep 1775

31 Ibid.

32 BL: Add MS 37833, fo. 18: JR to
    King, 2 Nov 1775

33 *Evening Advertiser*, 5 Oct 1775

34 NJHS: MG 199 (K26.31 &
    K26.32): RE to RA, 10 Oct 1775

35 NJHS: MG 199 (K26.31 & K26.32): RE to RA, 23 May 1775
36 NJHS: MG 199 (K26.31 & K26.32): RE to RA, 6 Dec 1775
37 NA: T 64/108, fo. 34: WH to JR, 31 Dec 1775
38 NA: T 64/108, fo. 38
39 NA: CO 5/93, fo. 172

6 The Rum Contracts

1 Bowler, p. 3
2 NA: T 29/45, fo. 27: 22 Feb 1776
3 Ibid.
4 NA: CO 5/147, fo. 226: RA to JR, 10 Apr 1776
5 CAK: WD/Ho, Plan 25
6 Hutchinson, Vol. 2, p. 43
7 NAW: ZAL 95/27/2: BA to DA, 26 May 1776
8 NAW: ZAL 96/2/11: William Borradaile to BA, 18 Jul 1776
9 *Bibliotheca Nautica*, Part III, No. 585, Maggs Bros, 1933: GD to George Atkinson, 24 Nov 1776
10 AF: BA pocket journal, 1776
11 WL: MS.5231, fo. 2: 1 Dec 1772
12 NAW: ZAL 95/7/11: BA to GA, nd
13 Hansard, *Parliamentary History*, Vol. 18, cols. 1365–6
14 Library of Congress, United States & Continental Congress Broadside Collection
15 Johnson, S., *Taxation no Tyranny*, p. 89
16 NJSA: PHEUS001
17 Almon, *Parliamentary Register*, Vol. 11, p. 361: WH to Lord George Germain, 30 Nov 1776
18 Library of Congress, *George Washington Papers, Series 4,*

General Correspondence, 1697–1799: GW to John Augustine Washington, 18 Dec 1776
19 NA: CO 5/93, fo. 228: WH to Lord George Germain, 6 Aug 1776
20 NA: T 64/106, fo. 62: RA to William Howe, 14 Sep 1776
21 BL: Add MS 21687, fo. 304: RA to GC, 20 Sep 1776
22 BL: Add MS 37833, fo. 32: King to JR, 16 Sep 1776
23 Hansard, *Parliamentary History*, Vol. 19, col. 56
24 Ibid., Vol. 19, col. 266
25 *Morning Post*, 20 May 1777
26 NA: T 1/537, fo. 24: RA to WH, 14 Jan 1777
27 SA: Dartmouth MSS 1732: RA to JL, 14 Jan 1777
28 NA: T 38/269, fos. 1–11
29 NA: T 64/108, fo. 105: WH to JR, 5 Apr 1777
30 NA: T 1/535, fo. 368: Agreement, 1 Apr 1777
31 NA: T 29/46, fo. 90: 18 Jun 1777
32 NA: T 1/538, fo. 199: RA to JR, 12 Aug 1777
33 SA: Dartmouth MSS 1772: RA to Treasury, 23 Jul 1777
34 NA: T 1/534, fo. 179: RA to Treasury, 15 Aug 1777
35 *Founders Online*: GW to the Congress Committee to Inquire into the State of the Army, 19 Jul 1777
36 *The Papers of George Washington Digital Edition*: Robert Erskine to George Washington, 1 Aug 1777
37 *Acts of the Council*, p. 271
38 BL: Add MS 37833, fo. 200: King to JR, 24 May 1777

39 AP: Abergavenny MSS 147: North to Mr Forth, 25 Sep 1777

40 NA: SP 78/305, fo. 186: Stormont to Weymouth, 10 Dec 1777

41 NA: T 64/108, fo. 154: WH to John Robinson, 30 Nov 1777

42 NA: T 1/546, fo. 379: RA to John Robinson, 12 Jan 1778

43 SA: Dartmouth MSS 1828: RA to Treasury, 22 Jan 1778

44 SA: Dartmouth MSS 1830: RA to Treasury, 24 Jan 1778

45 *Morning Post*, 13 Feb 1778; *Gazetteer*, 14 Feb 1778

46 *Evening Post*, 5 Mar 1778

47 Hansard, *Parliamentary History*, Vol. 19, cols. 901–8

48 Johnson, S., *Dictionary*, Vol. 2, 'Job'

49 Hansard, *Parliamentary History*, Vol. 19, cols. 972–80

50 NA: T 1/548, fo. 31: HH to JR, 27 Jan 1779

51 HRO: 75M91/A25/7: RA to Contractors, 13 Jun 1778

52 KA: U1350 O86/5: WK to Amherst, 18 Jun 1778

53 KA: U1350 O86/9: WK to Amherst, 23 Jun 1778

54 *Evening Post*, 23 Jul 1778

55 BL: Add MS 38343, fo. 75

7 Jamaica Imperilled

1 NA: T 1/540, fo. 165: TS to RA, 14 Jul 1778

2 NA: T 29/47, fo. 143: 29 Jul 1778

3 NA: T 1/546, fo. 404: RA to JR, 13 Oct 1778

4 BL: Add MS 37834, fo. 39: King to JR, 6 Nov 1778

5 NA: CO 5/97, fo. 28: HC to Germain, 15 Dec 1778

6 NA: CO 5/151, fo. 122: RA to JR, 25 Feb 1779

7 NA: T 27/32, fos. 360–1: JR to RA, 13 Nov 1778

8 NA: T 29/48, fo. 141: 27 May 1779

9 NA: T 29/48, fo. 185: 20 Jul 1779

10 NA: T 1/552, fo. 128: RA to Treasury, 21 Jul 1779

11 Fortescue, Vol. 4, Letter 2241, p. 73: North to King, 23 Mar 1778

12 Ibid., Vol. 4, Letter 2657, p. 356: King to North, 15 Jun 1779

13 Wraxall, *Historical Memoirs*, Vol. 1, p. 318

14 BL: Add MS 38212, fos. 248–53: JR to CJ, 28 Nov 1779

15 Fortescue, Vol. 4, Letter 2773, p. 433: King to Sandwich, 13 Sep 1779

16 *London Chronicle*, 3 Dec 1778

17 Christie, O.F., p. 61

18 BC: Fuller Letterbook, p. 109: Stephen Fuller to Germain, 23/24 Dec 1778

19 *Morning Post*, 18 Oct 1779

20 *Manuscripts of Captain Howard Vicente Knox*, p. 163: RA to WK, 28 Oct 1779

21 *Evening Post*, 11 Nov 1779

22 NA: WO 34/122, fo. 26: Germain to SF, 13 Dec 1779

23 BL: Add MS 37835, fo. 77: King to JR, 15 Dec 1779

24 KA: U1350 O76/19: Memorandum

25 Hansard, *Parliamentary History*, Vol. 20, cols. 1383–9

26 BC: Fuller Letterbook, p. 169: Minutes, 17 Dec 1779

27 *Whitehall Evening Post*, 10 Feb 1780; *GM*: Vol. 50, p. 352

28 Toynbee, Vol. 11, Letter 2137, p. 368: HW to Lady Ossory, 14 Jan 1781

29 Hansard, *Parliamentary History*, Vol. 21, col. 72

30 *London Courant*, 30 Mar 1780

31 *Morning Chronicle*, 5 Jun 1780

32 NA: CO 5/152, fo. 238: RA to WK, 4 Jul 1780

33 NA: CO 5/152, fo. 234: RA to WK, 12 Sep 1780

34 NA: T 29/49, fo. 190: 20 Sep 1780

35 BL: Loan MS 72/29, fo. 75: JR to CJ, 3 Oct 1780

36 Knox, pp. 15–16

37 *Journals of the House of Commons*, Vol. 38, pp. 827–8

38 Ibid., Vol. 35, p. 611

39 Buel, p. 349

40 *Founders Online*: GW to John Cadwalader, 5 Oct 1780

41 NA: T 29/49, fo. 256: 21 Dec 1780

42 AF: Ledger, pp. 19, 62

43 Hansard, *Parliamentary History*, Vol. 22, col. 1345

44 *London Chronicle*, 7 Mar 1782

8 A Heartbreaking Letter

1 Barnard, Vol. 2, pp. 119–21

2 Ibid., Vol. 2, pp. 157–8

3 Ibid., Vol. 2, pp. 209–10

4 *Whitehall Evening Post*, 22 Jan 1782

5 Barrett, Vol. 2, p. 149

6 Barnard, Vol. 2, pp. 206–7

7 Ibid., Vol. 2, pp. 206–7

8 Ibid., Vol. 2, pp. 218–19

9 Ibid., Vol. 2, pp. 244–5

10 Ibid., Vol. 3, pp. 101–2

11 NA: C 104/76: HM to PB & RA, 31 Dec 1780

12 SRO: 741/HA12/B1/5/92: HM to RM & RA, 20–21 Apr 1781

13 Hansard, *Parliamentary History*, Vol. 21, cols. 1342–9; *London Chronicle*, 8 Mar 1781

14 Ibid., Vol. 21, cols. 1342–9

15 Ibid., Vol. 21, cols. 1349–62

16 Barnard, Vol. 3, pp. 1–2

17 Ibid., Vol. 3, pp. 3–5

18 Ibid., Vol. 3, pp. 4–6

19 NLS: Acc 9769 27/2/3: AL to RA, nd

20 *Gazetteer*, 26 Mar 1781

21 *Gazetteer*, 27 Mar 1781

22 Hansard, *Parliamentary History*, Vol. 22, col. 11

23 Barnard, Vol. 3, pp. 5–6

24 Ibid., Vol. 3, pp. 18–19

25 NA: T 1/569, fo. 63

26 *Journals of the House of Commons*, Vol. 38, p. 828

27 Barnard, Vol. 3, pp. 21–2

28 Ibid., Vol. 3, pp. 23–4

29 Ibid., Vol. 3, pp. 23–4

30 NLS: Acc 9769 27/2/3: RA to AL, nd

31 Barnard, Vol. 3, pp. 30–2

32 NLS: Acc 9769 27/2/3–4: AL to RA, nd

33 Barnard, Vol. 3, pp. 35–6

34 NLS: Acc 9769 27/2/7: RA to AL, nd

35 NLS: Acc 9769 27/2/5: RA to AL, nd

9 Mortal Thoughts

1 NLS: Acc 9769 27/2/11: RA to AL, 22 Aug 1781

2 Barnard, Vol. 3, pp. 42–3

3 Ibid., Vol. 3, pp. 22–3

4 Reprinted in *Penrith Observer*, 12 Jan 1926

5 NLS: Acc 9769 27/2/10: RA to AL, 13 Aug 1781

6 Wraxall, *Historical Memoirs*, Vol. 2, p. 435

7 *Public Advertiser*, 24 Sep 1781

8 NA: PRO 30/20/17

9 Wraxall, *Historical Memoirs*, Vol. 2, p. 468

10 *General Advertiser*, 22 Feb 1782

11 NLS: Acc 9769 27/2/13: RA to AL, 23 Feb 1782

12 Barnard, Vol. 3, pp. 65–6

13 *Morning Chronicle*, 5 Mar 1782

14 Toynbee, Vol. 12, Letter 2283, p. 190: Horace Walpole to Sir Horace Mann, 11 Mar 1782

15 *London Courant*, 11 Mar 1782

16 Fortescue, Vol. 5, Letter 3560 (enc), p. 389: JR to Charles Jenkinson, 16 Mar 1782

17 Wraxall, *Historical Memoirs*, Vol. 2, p. 607

18 Barnard, Vol. 3, pp. 67–8

19 Fortescue, Vol. 5, Letter 3584, p. 415: North to King, 26 Mar 1782

20 Ibid., Vol. 5, Letter 3594, p. 421: King to North, 27 Mar 1782

21 Ibid., Vol. 5, Letter 3593, p. 421: King to North, 27 Mar 1782

22 Hansard, *Parliamentary History*, Vol. 22, cols. 1346–7

23 *London Courant*, 3 Jan 1782

24 Clerk, pp. xxxvi–xxxvii

25 Cumberland, Vol. 1, p. 407

26 *The United Service Journal*, 1829, Part 2, pp. 562–74

27 BL: IOR B/95, p. 637: Court of Directors, 10 Apr 1780

28 Barnard, Vol. 3, pp. 67–8

29 Lindsay, Vol. 2, p. 343

30 HA: DE/HCC/27730: Settlement, 12 Jul 1782

31 *Morning Herald*, 31 Jul 1782

32 Barnard, Vol. 3, pp. 70–3

33 Elwin, p. 204: Wentworth to Judith Milbanke, 20 Aug 1782

34 NLS: Acc 9769 27/2/162: 'Leon' to AL, 9 Jan 1783

35 NLS: Acc 9769 27/2/162: RA to 'Leon', 16 Jan 1783

36 *Morning Herald*, 5 Feb 1783

37 Barnard, Vol. 3, pp. 89–90

38 Ibid., Vol. 3, pp. 81–2

39 NLS: Acc 9769 27/2/21: RA to AL, 22 Dec 1782

10 A Royal Coup

1 BL: IOR/L/MAR/B/259A–B: Bessborough Journal, 26 Dec 1776 to 31 Oct 1781

2 YUL: MS 58: RA to JB, 15 Feb 1782

3 Howard, D.S., p. 512

4 CL: HMN/142

5 CL: HMN/143

6 BL: IOR/L/AG/14/5/18: East India Company Stock Ledger A–K, 1769–1774

7 NA: C 104/76

8 BL: Add MS 29154, fo. 134: JM to WH, 22 Apr 1782

9 Thompson & Frentzos, p. 117

10 AP: Abergavenny MSS 493: JR to North (draft), 1 Feb 1783

11 AP: Abergavenny MSS 494: RA to JR, 6 Feb 1783

12 Hansard, *Parliamentary History*, Vol. 22, col. 1106

13 Toynbee, Vol. 11, Letter 2176, p. 449: Horace Walpole to Sir Horace Mann, 17 May 1781

14 Fortescue, Vol. 6, Letter 3871, p. 97: King to John Robinson, 7 Aug 1782

15 NA: PRO 30/8/12, fos. 201–2: WP to Lady Chatham, Nov 1780

16 Fortescue, Vol. 6, Letter 4133, p. 249: King to Thurlow, 24 Feb 1783

17 NA: PRO 30/8/12, fos. 286–7: WP to Lady Chatham, 25 Feb 1783

18 BL: Loan MS 72/29, fo. 130: JR to Charles Jenkinson, 14 Mar 1783

19 Barnard, Vol. 3, pp. 87–8

20 BL: Loan MS 72/29, fo. 130: JR to CJ, 14 Mar 1783

21 Ibid.

22 NA: PRO 30/8/103, fo. 1: King to WP, 20 Mar 1783

23 BL: Add MS 37835, fo. 202: RA to JR, 21 Mar 1783

24 AP: Abergavenny MSS 506: RA to JR, 25 Mar 1783

25 Aspinall, p. 104: King to Prince of Wales (draft), nd

26 BL: Add MS 38567, fo. 145: JR to Charles Jenkinson, 1 Apr 1783

27 Barnard, Vol. 3, pp. 99–100

28 BL: Add MS 34523, fos. 371–3: King to Shelburne, 2 Apr 1783

29 Hansard, *Parliamentary History*, Vol. 23, col. 1200

30 Stanhope, Vol. 1, pp. 140–1: William Pitt to Rutland, 22 Nov 1783

31 Hansard, *Parliamentary History*, Vol. 23, col. 1224

32 Ibid., Vol. 23, col. 1247

33 Ibid., Vol. 23, cols. 1263, 1272

34 Ibid., Vol. 23, col. 1280

35 *English Chronicle*, 27 Nov 1783

36 BL: Add MS 88906/1/1, fo. 106: FB to Shelburne, 30 Nov 1783

37 *London Chronicle*, 6 Dec 1783

38 Grenville, Vol. 1, pp. 288–9

39 AP: Abergavenny MSS 520: RA to JR, 3 Dec 1783

40 BL: Add MS 38567, fo. 167: JR to CJ, 7 Dec 1783

41 Laprade, pp. 66–105

42 AP: Abergavenny MSS 525: RA to JR, 8 Dec 1783

43 BL: Add MS 38567, fos. 169–70: JR to Charles Jenkinson, 9 Dec 1783

44 AP: Abergavenny MSS 526: RA to JR, 12 Dec 1783

45 AP: Abergavenny MSS 530: RA to JR, 15 Dec 1783

46 AP: Abergavenny MSS, Box 2 A/5, Part One

47 AP: Abergavenny MSS 535: RA to JR, 17 Dec 1783

48 AP: Abergavenny MSS 541: RA to JR, 18 Dec 1783

49 Fortescue, Vol. 6, Letter 4546, p. 476: King to North, 18 Dec 1783

11 Secret Influence

1 Barnard, Vol. 3, pp. 100–1

2 Laprade, p. xx

3 BL: Add MS 47570, fo. 156: CJF to Elizabeth Armistead, nd

4 Wraxall, *Historical Memoirs*, Vol. 4, p. 664

5 *Morning Chronicle*, 3 Jan 1784

6 *Public Advertiser*, 29 Dec 1783

7 *Public Advertiser*, 30 Dec 1783

8 AP: Abergavenny MSS 551: RA to JR, 31 Dec 1783

9 *Morning Chronicle*, 13 Jan 1784

10 NLS: Acc 9769 23/2/13: RA to Balcarres, 12 Jan 1784

11 Hansard, *Parliamentary History*, Vol. 24, col. 318

12 AP: Abergavenny MSS 568: North to JR, 27 Jan 1784

13 NLS: Acc 9769 23/2/14: RA to Balcarres, 27 Jan 1784

14 *GM*: Vol. 54, Part 1, p. 70

15 NLS: Acc 9769 27/1/340

16 Barnard, Vol. 3, pp. 102–3

17 NAW: ZAL 95/3/6: DA to BA, 2 Mar 1784

18 AP: Abergavenny MSS Box 2 A/5, Part One (see also Laprade, pp. 114–18, 124–9)

19 Hansard, *Parliamentary History*, Vol. 24, cols. 734–5

20 Barnard, Vol. 3, pp. 100–1

21 *Gazetteer*, 30 Mar 1784

22 AP: Abergavenny MSS 599: RA to JR, 29 Mar 1784

23 *London Chronicle*, 30 Mar 1784

24 *Gazetteer*, 30 Mar 1784

25 AP: Abergavenny MSS 600: RA to JR, 31 Mar 1784

26 *Morning Chronicle*, 2 Apr 1784

27 *St James's Chronicle*, 1 Apr 1784

28 Wraxall, *Posthumous Memoirs*, Vol. 1, pp. 117–21

29 *Morning Herald*, 7 Apr 1784

30 *Morning Post*, 20 Apr 1784

31 NA: PRO 30/8/355, fo. 271: RA to Henry Dundas, nd; BL: Add MS 88906/1/1, fo. 122: Francis Baring to Shelburne, 26 Apr 1784

32 AP: Abergavenny MSS 602: RA to JR, 15 Apr 1784

33 BLO: Ms. Eng. hist. b.190, fos. 32–7: LS to Richard Sulivan, 20 Nov 1784

34 *Evening Post*, 24 Apr 1784

35 *St James's Chronicle*, 24 Apr 1784

36 *Evening Post*, 1 May 1784

37 *Morning Herald*, 6 May 1784

38 BL: Add MS 88906/1/1, fo. 127: FB to Shelburne, 18 May 1784

39 Walpole, *Last Journals*, Vol. 2, p. 280

40 NA: PRO 30/8/129, fo. 127: ED to WP, 24 Sep 1794

41 *Morning Herald*, 11 May 1784

12 A Dose of Vitriol

1 *Morning Herald*, 18 Jun 1784

2 NA: PRO 30/8/355: Report, 31 May 1784

3 *Public Advertiser*, 25 Jun 1784; *Evening Post*, 24 Jun 1784

4 NA: PRO 30/8/356, fos. 10–18: Report (margins numbered by RA); NA: PRO 30/8/355, fos. 216–39: RA's rebuttal

5 AP: Abergavenny MSS 613: RA to JR, 1 Jul 1784

6 Barnard, Vol. 3, pp. 97–8

7 Ibid., Vol. 3, pp. 106–7

8 NLS: Acc 9769 27/2/23: RA to AL, 2 Jul 1784

9 Barnard, Vol. 3, pp. 109–12

10 *Morning Chronicle*, 15 Jul 1784

11 NA: PRO 30/8/283, fo. 148

12 *Reports from Committees*, p. 284

13 NA: PRO 30/8/294, fos. 171, 182, 186, 220

14 *St James's Chronicle*, 21 Sep 1784

15 NLS: Acc 9769 27/2/22: RA to AL, 21 Jul 1784

16 NA: PRO 30/8/103, fo. 119: King to WP, 29 Jul 1784

17 *Morning Chronicle*, 31 Jul 1784

18 AP: Abergavenny MSS 615: RA to JR, 30 Jul 1784

19 NLS: Acc 9769 27/2/24: RA to AL, 3 Aug 1784

20 NLS: Acc 9769 27/2/26: RA to AL, 17 Aug 1784

21 AP: Abergavenny MSS 616: RA to JR, 16 Aug 1784

22 Glasse, p. 227

23 BL: Add MS 29166, fo. 368: John Scott to Warren Hastings, 30 Oct 1784

24 BL: Add MS 12567, fo. 104: 6 Oct 1784

25 AP: Abergavenny MSS 622: RA to John Robinson, 29 Sep 1784

26 *Morning Post*, 6 Oct 1784

27 NLS: Acc 9769 27/2/28: RA to AL, 12 Oct 1784

28 NA: PRO 30/8/181, fo. 218: Sydney to WP, 24 Sep 1784

29 NLS: Acc 9769 23/2/17: RA to Balcarres, 29 Oct 1784

30 *Gazetteer*, 17 Nov 1784

31 AP: Abergavenny MSS 626: RA to JR, 2 Dec 1784

32 KCUP: Ms. Coll. 888: RA to HD, 31 Jan 1785

33 *Gazetteer*, 19 Feb 1785

34 BL: Add MS 29168, fo. 79: John Scott to Warren Hastings, 18 Feb 1785

35 Ibid.

36 *Gazetteer*, 19 Feb 1785

37 *Gazetteer*, 5 Mar 1785

38 Hansard, *Parliamentary History*, Vol. 25, cols. 174, 180

39 Ibid., Vol. 25, col. 251

40 Ibid., Vol. 25, cols. 249–50

41 Wraxall, *Posthumous Memoirs*, Vol. 1, p. 261

42 Barnard, Vol. 3, pp. 189–91

43 Ibid., Vol. 3, pp. 189–91

44 Ibid., Vol. 4, pp. 6–7

45 NAW: ZAL 95/7/14: BA to DA, 19 Apr 1785

46 NA: PRO 30/8/353, fos. 76–7: 22 Apr 1785

47 NLS: Acc 9769 27/1/282: Elizabeth Yorke to Anne Lindsay & Margaret Fordyce, 30–31 May 1785

13 The Newcastle Attorney

1 Wraxall, *Posthumous Memoirs*, Vol. 1, p. 120

2 NLS: Acc 9769 27/1/282: EY to AL & MF, 30–31 May 1785

3 Barnard, Vol. 4, pp. 14–17

4 RGDJ: LOS Deeds 337, fo. 27: 1 May 1785

5 NLS: Acc 9769 27/2/21: RA to AL, 22 Dec 1782

6 Peach & Thomas, Vol. 2, p. 281: RP to Lansdowne, 2 Jun 1785

7 *Morning Chronicle*, 9 Jun 1785

8 *Public Advertiser*, 23 Jun 1785

9 NLS: Acc 9769 27/1/282: EY to AL & MF, 30–31 May 1785

10 NLS: Acc 9769 27/1/102: Balcarres to AL, 20 Jun 1785

11 *Public Advertiser*, 14 Jun 1785

12 NLS: Acc 9769 27/1/339

13 NLS: Acc 9769 27/1/340

14 Barnard, Vol. 4, pp. 7–8

15 Rochefoucauld, p. 103

16 NLS: Acc 9769 23/9/379: RM to Balcarres, 3 Jun 1785

17 NLS: Acc 9769 23/9/385: RM to Balcarres, 20 Aug 1785

18 AF: 1 Nov 1783

19 Barnard, Vol. 4, pp. 16–17

20 NAW: ZAL 95/7/15: DA to BA, 31 Mar 1786

21 NAW: ZAL 95/7/16: DA to BA, nd

22 *Morning Herald*, 22 Apr 1786; 10 May 1786
23 Barnard, Vol. 4, pp. 32–3
24 Ibid., Vol. 4, pp. 34–5
25 AF: Victoria Atkinson notes
26 NAW: ZAL 95/7/17: NC to DA, nd
27 NAW: ZAL 95/7/18: NC to DA, nd
28 NAW: ZAL 95/7/20: NC to DA, nd
29 NAW: ZAL 95/3/3: DA to BA, nd
30 NAW: ZAL 95/7/21: BA to DA, 29 Oct 1786
31 NAW: ZAL 95/27/4: NC to DA, 17 Nov 1786
32 NAW: ZAL 95/3/5: Dorothy Clayton to Bridget Atkinson, nd
33 NAW: ZAL 95/27/5: DC to BA, nd
34 NAW: ZAL 96/1/3: DC to BA, 8 Jan 1787
35 NAW: ZAL 95/6/2: NC to DC, 30 Jun 1787
36 NAW: ZAL 96/1/4: NC to BA, 17 Aug 1787
37 NAW: ZAL 95/1/12: Nathaniel Clayton to Bridget Atkinson, nd
38 NAW: ZAL 95/1/1: Nathaniel Clayton to Bridget Atkinson, 11 May 1788
39 NAW: ZAL 95/1/12: NC to BA, nd
40 Lustig & Pottle, p. 203
41 YUL: Gen MSS. M 190: 1 May 1788
42 Barnard, Vol. 3, pp. 81–2
43 Ibid., Vol. 4, pp. 36–7
44 NLS: Acc 9769 30/1/485: RL to AL, 27 Dec 1789
45 AP: Abergavenny B14 bundle: 'Plan of Arrangement', nd
46 NLS: Acc 9769 27/1/340
47 Barnard, Vol. 4, pp. 117–18

14 Taking Possession

1 *Morning Chronicle*, 18 Mar 1783
2 SV: Voyage 84106
3 Douglas, Vol. 3, p. 232
4 Hoare, p. 241
5 Harford, p. 139
6 Clarkson, *History of the Rise*, Vol. 1, pp. 286–7
7 Ibid., Vol. 1, p. 418
8 NA: CO 137/87, fo. 260: SF to Sydney, 25 Jun 1788
9 Clarkson, *History of the Rise*, Vol. 2, pp. 24–5
10 NA: PRO 30/8/349, fo. 135: SF to Hawkesbury, 16 Apr 1788
11 BL: Add MS 38416, fo. 73: Rodney to Hawkesbury, Mar 1788
12 Clarkson, *History of the Rise*, Vol. 2, p. 48
13 SV: Voyage 80666
14 Hansard, *Parliamentary History*, Vol. 28, col. 42
15 Ibid., Vol. 28, col. 76
16 Sotheby's, Catalogue, 9 Dec 1981, p. 58
17 NAW: ZAL 95/7/22: RA to BA, 6 Sep 1789
18 AF: Victoria Atkinson notes
19 NAW: ZAL 96/2/14: Bridget Atkinson to Nathaniel Clayton, 29 Oct 1789
20 Ibid.
21 BL: Eur C307/4: Nathaniel Wraxall to Paul Benfield, 27 Oct 1789
22 BL: Eur C307/4: NW to PB, 3 Dec 1789

23 BL: Eur C307/4: Nathaniel Wraxall to Paul Benfield, 8 Apr 1790

24 BA: NP1.A15.2: Agreement, 28 May 1791

25 Hansard, *Parliamentary History*, Vol. 29, col. 278

26 Elwin, p. 230: Wentworth to Judith Milbanke, 21 Feb 1784; Hansard, *Parliamentary History*, Vol. 29, col. 281

27 Hansard, *Parliamentary History*, Vol. 29, col. 343

28 Toynbee, Vol. 14, Letter 2793, p. 418: HW to Mary Berry, 23 Apr 1791

29 NLW: Slebech Papers, MS. 8386: Thomas Barritt to Nathaniel Phillips, 8 Dec 1791

30 Fox, pp. 4–5

31 LSF: Wilkinson MSS 114/3: TC to Thomas Wilkinson, 1 Mar 1792

32 Hansard, *Parliamentary History*, Vol. 29, cols. 1105, 1110

33 Moreton, p. 81

34 Beckford, Vol. 1, p. 14

35 Ibid., Vol. 2, p. 1

36 Ibid., Vol. 2, p. 120

37 Renny, p. 128

38 AF: GA to FB, 13 Feb 1792

39 Beckford, Vol. 1, p. 20

40 Moreton, p. 34

41 AF: GA to FB, 11 Jun 1792

42 AF: GA to Nathaniel Clayton, 11 Jun 1792

15 Fevered Isle

1 *Evening Post*, 26 Feb 1793

2 NAW: ZAL 96/1/9: DC to BA, 20 Mar 1793

3 NAW: ZAL 96/1/10: DC to BA, nd

4 NAW: ZAL 96/3/17: DC to BA, 5 May 1793

5 BA: HCOS 126/5–7/126: NC to Francis Baring, 15 Jul 1792

6 AF: DC to Matt Atkinson, 26 Dec 1820

7 Edwards, Vol. 2 (1801 edition), p. 586

8 AF: NC to GA, 1 Apr 1793

9 AF: GA to NC, nd

10 NAW: ZAL 96/3/19: NC to BA, 5 Jun 1793

11 Jackson, D., p. 281: 19 May 1760

12 Renny, p. 198

13 Jackson, R., p. 261

14 Annesley, p. 51

15 NAW: ZAL 95/21/48: JA to Matt Atkinson, 9 Apr 1791

16 NAW: ZAL 96/3/24: JA to BA, nd

17 NAW: ZAL 95/21/49: JA to Jane Atkinson, nd

18 CUL: Add. 8908/2: CW to Christopher Crackanthorp, 12 May 1793

19 NAW: ZAL 96/3/21: JA to BA, 29 Jul 1793

20 NAW: ZAL 96/1/15: NC to BA, 14 Oct 1793

21 NAW: ZAL 96/1/16: NC to BA, 15 Oct 1793

22 NAW: ZAL 96/1/17: NC to BA, 20 Oct 1793

23 NA: CO 137/91, fo. 327: Adam Williamson to Henry Dundas, 18 Oct 1793

24 NA: CO 137/92, fos. 49–50: George Bogle to Adam Williamson, 18 Nov 1793

25 BA: HCOS 126/1/118: WM to HD, 14 Sep 1793

26 BA: HCOS 126/1/119: HD to FB, 19 Sep 1793

27 BA: HCOS 126/2–4/9: GA to Francis Baring, 20 Jan 1794

28 BA: HCOS 126/1/116: NC to FB, 3 Jan 1794

29 NAW: ZAL 95/2/1: NC to BA, 3 Jan 1794

30 *Morning Chronicle*, 21 Feb 1794

31 NAW: ZAL 95/2/6: NC to BA, 25 Mar 1794

32 *GM*: Vol. 64, Part 2, p. 771

33 BA: HCOS 126/12–14/291: Memorandum, Dec 1798

34 www.baringarchive.org.uk

35 EUL: Laing Collection: La.II/481: Agreement, 22 Mar 1781

36 Long, Vol. 1, p. 82

37 Stewart, *An Account of Jamaica*, p. 35

38 NAW: ZAL 95/2/23: NC to Bridget Atkinson, nd

39 BL: Loan 57/107: HD to Richmond, 8 Jul 1793

40 BA: HCOS 126/2–4/12: GA to FB, 8 Feb 1794

41 NAW: ZAL 95/2/6: NC to BA, 25 Mar 1794

42 NA: CO 318/13, fo. 203

43 BA: HCOS 126/2–4/14: GA to Francis Baring, 4 Apr 1794

44 NA: CO 318/13, fo. 283: Charles Grey to Evan Nepean, 23 Apr 1794

45 BA: HCOS 126/2–4/18: GA to FB, 29 Apr 1794

16 Maroon War

1 BA: HCOS 126/2–4/20: GA to FB, 17 May 1794

2 BA: HCOS 126/2–4/24: GA to FB, 15 Jun 1794

3 BA: DEP41: Francis Baring Atkinson to F.H. Atkinson (transcript), 28 Jan 1863

4 NAW: ZAL 95/2/20: NC to BA, 18 Nov 1794

5 NAW: ZAL 95/2/24: JA to Jane Atkinson, nd

6 Edwards, Vol. 3 (1807 edition), p. 174

7 BA: HCOS 126/2–4/35: GA to FB, 17 Nov 1794

8 NA: T 1/740, fos. 8–9

9 *The State of the Nation*, p. 311

10 Ibid., p. 300

11 BA: HCOS 126/2–4/56: GA to FB, 5 Jul 1795

12 BA: HCOS 126/2–4/48: Francis Baring to AMB & Co, 6 May 1795

13 NAW: ZAL 95/4/1: JA to BA, nd

14 BA: HCOS 126/2–4/42: GA to FB, 4 Feb 1795

15 NA: CO 137/95, fo. 51: Balcarres to Portland, 30 May 1795

16 Lindsay, Vol. 3, p. 35: Magistrates to Balcarres, 18 Jul 1795

17 Ibid., Vol. 3, p. 48

18 Terrill, p. 88: Mary Yates to John Yates, 31 Dec 1795

19 NA: CO 137/95, fo. 107

20 NA: WO 1/92, fo. 58: Balcarres to Henry Dundas (in George Atkinson's hand), 24 Aug 1795

21 NLS: Acc 9769 23/11/103: GW to Balcarres, 20 Sep 1795

22 BA: HCOS 126/2–4/67: GA to Francis Baring, 29 Nov 1795

23 NA: WO 1/92, fo. 149: Balcarres to HD, 16 Nov 1795

24 NA: CO 137/96, fo. 58: Balcarres to Portland, 29 Dec 1795

25 *The Proceedings . . . in Regard to the Maroon Negroes*, p. 12: GW to Balcarres, 22 Dec 1795

26 NLS: Acc 9769 23/1/332: Balcarres to Elizabeth Lindsay, 13 Jan 1796

27 NA: CO 137/96, fo. 112: Balcarres to Portland, nd

28 *The Proceedings . . . in Regard to the Maroon Negroes*, p. 78: GW to Balcarres, 5 Mar 1796

29 Ibid., p. 82: GW to Balcarres, 11 Mar 1796

30 NLS: Acc 9769 23/11/3: GA to Balcarres, 17 Apr 1796

31 NLS: Acc 9769 23/10/595: HP to Balcarres, 3 May 1796

32 JA: IB/5/1/42, fo. 143: House of Assembly Journals, Nov 1796–Nov 1797

33 Hansard, *Parliamentary History*, Vol. 32, col. 924

34 NA: WO 1/92, fo. 273: HD to Balcarres, 21 Feb 1796

35 NLS: Acc 9769 23/11/155: Balcarres to Charles Yorke, 2 May 1796; NA: CO 137/96, fo. 262: *Royal Gazette*, 7 May 1796

36 NA: CO 137/96, fo. 270: Balcarres to Portland, 9 May 1796

37 BA: HCOS 126/2–4/64: GA to Francis Baring, 27 Oct 1795

38 BA: HCOS 126/5–7/92: FB to AMB, 4 Dec 1795

39 BL: Add MS 35916, fo. 202: Balcarres to Hardwicke, 6 Jun 1796

40 Baring, F., pp. 53–4

41 NLS: Acc 9769 23/10/26: GA to Balcarres, 3 Jun 1798

42 BA: HCOS 126/12–14/291: Memorandum, Dec 1798

43 BA: HCOS 126/5–7/160–2: GA to FB, 28 Aug 1798

44 BA: HCOS 126/5–7/158: NC to FB, 31 Jul 1798

45 NA: WO 1/70, fo. 20: Balcarres to TM, 6 Jul 1798

46 NA: WO 1/70, fo. 85: Thomas Maitland to Henry Dundas, 28 Aug 1798

47 NLS: Acc 9769 23/10/37: JA to Balcarres, 1 Sep 1798

48 NLS: Acc 9769 23/10/853: Balcarres to JA, 1 Sep 1798

17 Black Pioneers

1 Skinner, p. 35

2 NAW: ZAL 95/5/2: NC to JA, 6 Apr 1798

3 *An Impartial History*, p. 123

4 NAW: ZAL 96/1/28: JA to Bridget Atkinson, 22 Jan 1800

5 NAW: ZAL 96/1/29: NC to BA, 1 Feb 1800

6 NAW: ZAL 95/5/2: NC to JA, 6 Apr 1798

7 Budge, pp. 15–16: John Clayton to W. Campbell, 24 Jul 1889

8 NAW: ZAL 95/27/6: NC to BA, 29 Mar 1799

9 NAW: ZAL 96/2/16: BA to DC, 27 Oct 1799

10 NLS: Acc 9769 23/10/27: GA to Balcarres, 4 Nov 1798

11 BA: HCOS 126/8–11/177: FB to George Bogle, 17 Nov 1798

12 BA: HCOS 126/8–11/181: Memorandum, 1 Dec 1798

13 BA: HCOS 126/12–14/291: Memorandum, Dec 1798

14 NAW: ZAL 95/2/8: DC to BA, 29 May 1794

15 NLS: Acc 9769 23/10/27: GA to Balcarres, 4 Nov 1798

16 NLS: Acc 9769 23/8/3: GA to Balcarres, 3 Feb 1799

17 BA: HCOS 126/5–7/167: MA to FB, 10 Feb 1799

18 NLS: Acc 9769 23/8/189: James Mackintosh to MA, 24 Sep 1799

19 BA: HCOS 126/5–7/167: MA to FB, 10 Feb 1799

20 *Papers presented to the House of Commons on the 7th May 1804*: G. pp. 26, 37

21 BA: HCOS 126/8–11/184: FB to MA, 12 Aug 1799

22 NAW: ZAL 96/1/27: NC to DC, 7 Dec 1799

23 NA: CO 137/98, fo. 150: Balcarres to Portland, 28 Jan 1797

24 NLS: Acc 9769 23/10/1167: Balcarres to War Office, 13 Sep 1800 (not sent)

25 NAM: 6807-183-1, fo. 163; NLS: Acc 9769 23/10/1770

26 NA: WO 1/71, fo. 255: Maitland memorandum, 20 Apr 1799

27 NA: WO 1/72, fo. 27: Grant to Thomas Maitland, 14 Jul 1799

28 NA: WO 1/71, fo. 440: TM to Balcarres, 20 Jun 1799

29 NA: WO 1/71, fo. 438: Thomas Maitland to Balcarres, 17 Jun 1799

30 NA: WO 1/71, fo. 493: HC to Grant, 26 Nov 1799

31 NA: CO 137/103, fo. 204

32 NLS: Acc 9769 23/1/380: Balcarres to Lady Balcarres, 6 Jan 1800

33 NA: WO 1/74, fo. 77: John Wigglesworth to John King, 20 Dec 1799

34 BA: HCOS 126/8–11/216: HC to GA, 12 Jun 1800

35 BA: HCOS 126/8–11/187: FB to GMA, 5 Oct 1799

36 SV: Voyage 82553

37 BA: HCOS 126/8–11/199: JH to FB, 23 Mar 1800; SV: Voyage 84028

38 BA: HCOS 126/8–11/204: FB to JH, 9 May 1800; SV: Voyages 83515, 84102, 80741, 82374

39 BA: HCOS 126/8–11/211: FB to JH, 8 Aug 1800

40 BA: HCOS 126/12–14/317: GA to MA, JH & HC, Aug 1800

41 BA: HCOS 126/8–11/223: GB to FB, 2 Jan 1801

42 BA: HCOS 126/8–11/225: GB to FB, 27 Jan 1801

43 BA: HCOS 126/8–11/245: MA to FB, 28 Jan 1801

44 Stewart, *An Account of Jamaica*, p. 58

45 BA: HCOS 126/8–11/268: George Bogle to Francis Baring, 1 Nov 1801

46 BA: HCOS 126/8–11/254: GB to George Atkinson, 20 Jun 1801

47 BA: HCOS 126/8–11/261–3: Memorandum, 17 Jul 1801

48 Wright, p. 10: 29 Jul 1801

49 Fremantle, p. 26

50 Wright, pp. 11–12: 31 Jul 1801

51 NLS: Acc 9769 23/8/20: MA to Balcarres, 18 Nov 1802

52 NLS: Acc 9769 23/8/33: MA to Balcarres, 7 Oct 1804

53 NLS: Acc 9769 23/1/62: Lady Balcarres to Balcarres, 4 Jan 1802

18 The Nabob's Return

1 Barnard, Vol. 5, pp. 67–8
2 Lenta & Le Cordeur, Vol. 1, pp. 19–20: 15 Jan 1799
3 BL: Add MS 88906/1/1, fo. 106: FB to Shelburne, 30 Nov 1783
4 AP: Abergavenny B14 bundle: WD to JR, 15 Jun 1801
5 AP: Abergavenny B14 bundle: GA to JR, 13 Jan 1802
6 Wright, pp. 29–30: 2 Oct 1801
7 Ibid., p. 33: 21 Oct 1801
8 Ibid., p. xx
9 NLS: Acc 9769 23/8/19: MA to Balcarres, 28 Jun 1802
10 *Lettres du Général Leclerc*, 256, no. 145: Leclerc to Napoleon Bonaparte, 7 Oct 1802
11 NA: CO 137/111, fo. 353: 24 Mar 1804 (unnamed)
12 BA: NP1.A4.4: FB to P.C. Labouchère, 15 Feb 1803
13 BA: NP1.A4.28: HA to FB, 16 Dec 1803
14 BA: HCOS 126/12–14/297: MA to GA, 11 Mar 1804
15 BA: HCOS 126/12–14/297: Matt Atkinson to George Atkinson, 15 Jan 1804
16 Ibid.
17 BA: HCOS 126/12–14/297: MA to GA, 11 Mar 1804
18 Ibid.
19 BA: HCOS 126/12–14/298: GA to FB, 30 Apr 1804
20 *Morning Post*, 23 May 1804
21 AF: Bridget Atkinson to Matt Atkinson, 2 Jul 1804
22 Ibid.
23 Ibid.
24 AF: JA to MA, 2 Jul 1804
25 AF: Bridget Atkinson to Matthew Atkinson, 30 Dec 1804
26 RGDJ: Kingston, Register of Baptisms, Vol. 2, 1793–1825, p. 86
27 RGDJ: Kingston, Register of Baptisms, Vol. 2, 1793–1825, p. 128
28 JA: IB/11/6/25, fo. 220
29 RGDJ: Kingston, Register of Baptisms, Vol. 2, 1793–1825, p. 105
30 RGDJ: Kingston, Register of Baptisms, Vol. 1, 1722–92, p. 348
31 RGDJ: Kingston, Register of Baptisms, Vol. 2, 1793–1825, p. 105
32 RGDJ: Kingston, Register of Baptisms, Vol. 2, 1793–1825, p. 136
33 Renny, p. 324
34 Wright, p. 65: 5 Mar 1802
35 NA: CO 137/91, fo. 146: BE to Henry Dundas, 16 May 1793
36 Stewart, *An Account of Jamaica*, p. 296
37 *The Times*, 7 Mar 1806: MA to MA, 29 Jul 1804
38 AF: BA to MA, 30 Dec 1804
39 CUL: MS Add. 9723: Bridget Atkinson waste book
40 *The Times*, 7 Mar 1806
41 Ibid.
42 Ibid.
43 AF: JA to MA, 2 Jul 1804
44 BA: HCOS 126/12–14/322: Nathaniel Clayton to George Atkinson, 19 Nov 1806
45 RGDJ: Kingston, Register of Baptisms, Vol. 2, 1793–1825, p. 158
46 AF: RR to MA, 24 Apr 1807
47 Hansard, *Parliamentary Debates*, Old Series, Vol. 9, col. 170
48 ICWS: ICS 120, 1/I/24: ST to George Hibbert, 22 Apr 1807

19 End of an Era

1 *The Picture of Newcastle upon Tyne*, pp. 100–1

2 BA: HCOS 126/12–14/301: GA to FB, 7 Feb 1805

3 *The Picture of Newcastle upon Tyne*, p. 98

4 Thomson, T., p. 232

5 Mackenzie, p. 382

6 NAW: ZAL 95/5/4: NC to BA, 6 Jan 1807

7 *The Times*, 20 Apr 1808

8 NAW: ZAL 96/1/40: Dorothy Clayton to Bridget Atkinson, 18 May 1809

9 NAW: ZAL 95/5/5: JA to Dorothy Clayton, 17 Jan 1822

10 NAW: ZAL 96/1/40: Dorothy Clayton to Bridget Atkinson, 18 May 1809

11 NA: TS 25/3, fos. 421–2: 22 Nov 1809; NA: TS 25/5, fos. 424–38: 17 Jun 1812

12 BA: NP1.A4.67: FB to P.C. Labouchère, 9 Oct 1804

13 *The Bankers' Magazine*, p. 882

14 *GM*: Vol. 80, Part 2, p. 293

15 *Evening Post*, 22 Mar 1770

16 NAW: ZAL 96/1/36: Dorothy Clayton to Bridget Atkinson, 15 Mar 1809

17 Raine, Vol. 1, p. 17

18 Ibid., Vol. 1, pp. 80–1: JH to Jane Hodgson, 2 May 1811

19 Ibid.

20 AF: BA to DC, 28 Jun 1812

21 NAW: SANT/ADM/4/1/1/12

22 *Archaeologia Aeliana*: Donations, p. 3

23 NA: TS 25/5, fos. 424–38: 26 Feb 1813

24 AF: GA to MA, 24 May 1813

25 Ibid.

26 AF: NC to Henry Tulip, 28 Jun 1813

27 AF: MA to NC, 5 Jul 1813

28 NAW: ZAL 95/27/8: NC to BA, 7 Jan 1805

29 CUL: MS Add. 9723: Bridget Atkinson waste book

30 NAW: SANT/BEQ/18/11/13

31 NAW: SANT/BEQ/18/11/3/66–8: BA to MA, 25 Oct 1813

32 Ibid.

33 Ibid.

34 NAW: ZAL 95/21/3: NC to DC, 13 Mar 1814

35 AF: Scrapbook

36 NA: PROB 11/1620/355

37 AF: MA to (cousin) Matthew Atkinson, 29 Jun 1814

38 NLS: Acc 9769 23/8/73: Matt Atkinson to Balcarres, 16 Aug 1814

39 AF: MA to MA, 29 Jun 1814

40 NLS: Acc 9769 23/8/73: MA to Balcarres, 16 Aug 1814

41 Rubinstein, p. 87

20 Settling Scores

1 AF: JA to MA, 14 Mar 1815

2 AF: JA to (cousin) Matthew Atkinson, 14 Mar 1815

3 Phillimore, pp. 316–20

4 Barnard, Vol. 6, p. 114

5 NLS: Acc 9769 27/2/318: AB to B.W. van Rijneveld, 27 Aug 1809

6 NLS: Acc 9769 27/1/340

7 NLS: Acc 9769 23/1/21: AB to Balcarres, 24 Mar 1816

8 Lenta & Le Cordeur, Vol. 2, p. 112: 22 Apr 1800

9 Barnard, Vol. 1, p. 2

10 Ibid., Vol. 1, p. 2

11 Ibid., Vol. 1, p. 10

12 NLS: Acc 9769 23/8/61: AB & Co to Balcarres, 6 Oct 1810

13 NLS: Acc 9769 23/8/246: Balcarres to George Atkinson, 4 Jan 1813

14 *The Jamaica Almanack*, 1821

15 NAW: ZAL 95/20/2: NC to Sarah Clayton, 2 Feb 1816

16 NLS: Acc 9769 23/8/87: EA to Balcarres, 25 Feb 1817

17 NLS: Acc 9769 23/8/91: EA to Balcarres, 1 Aug 1817

18 NLS: Acc 9769 23/8/256: Balcarres to EA, nd

19 NLS: Acc 9769 23/8/93: EA to Balcarres, 17 Aug 1817

20 NLS: Acc 9769 23/8/96: EA to Balcarres, 1 Nov 1817

21 *The Colonial Journal*, Vol. 1, Jan–Jul 1816, p. 246

22 Bridges, *A Voice from Jamaica*, p. 27

23 Beche, p. 27

24 RGDJ: Westmoreland Parish, Baptisms, Marriages, Burials 1739–1825, Vol. 1, pp. 350–3

25 NLS: Acc 9769 23/9/608: AR & Co to Barings, 7 Oct 1820

26 NLS: Acc 9769 23/9/38: MA to Balcarres, 16 Oct 1818

27 NLS: Acc 9769 23/9/519: Balcarres to MA, 30 Oct 1818

28 CUL: MS Add. 9723: Michael Clayton to (cousin) Matthew Atkinson, 19 Jan 1819

29 NLS: Acc 9769 23/1/25: AB to Balcarres, 26 Jan 1819

30 *The Times*, 2 Aug 1821

31 AF: NC to MA, 6 Nov 1821

32 NAW: ZAL 96/1/50: NC to DC, 21 Nov 1821

33 AF: Affidavits, nd

34 NAW: ZAL 95/5/5: Jane Atkinson to Dorothy Clayton, 17 Jan 1822

35 NAW: ZAL 96/1/51: MC to DC, 13 Jul 1822

36 CUL: MS Add. 9723: Michael Clayton to (cousin) Matthew Atkinson, 24 Jan 1823

37 AF: Memorandum, nd

38 AF: Victoria Atkinson transcript: MA to SC, nd

39 NLS: Acc 9769 23/1/26: AB to Balcarres, 18 May 1823

40 NLS: Acc 9769 27/2/3

41 NLS: Acc 9769 27/2/21

42 NLS: Acc 9769 27/2/6

43 NLS: Acc 9769 23/9/198: MC to Balcarres, 18 Nov 1823

44 AF: JT to (cousin) Matthew Atkinson, 10 Mar 1824

45 *The Times*, 26 Mar 1825

46 AF: Robert Robertson to George Atkinson, 4 May 1825

21 Human Relics

1 AF: GCA, childhood description

2 Ibid.

3 AF: Victoria Atkinson transcript: Matthew Atkinson to Sophia Cator, nd

4 AF: NC to MA, 5 Mar 1816

5 AF: MA to NC, 7 Mar 1816

6 AF: MA to NC, 11 Mar 1816

7 AF: NC to MA, 13 Mar 1816

8 Raine, Vol. 2, p. 214

9 Moorman, p. 109: 15 Apr 1802

10 AF: GCA, childhood description

11 Brontë, Vol. 1, p. 4

12 Atkinson, G.C., p. 16

13 NHSN: NEWHM: 2006.H3.1: *British Land Birds*, Thomas

Bewick, Vol. 1 (inc. draft memoir by GCA)

14 Atkinson, G.C., p. 18

15 NHSN: NEWHM: 2006.H3.1: *British Land Birds,* Thomas Bewick, Vol. 1 (inc. draft memoir by GCA)

16 Atkinson, G.C., p. 24

17 NHSN: NEWHM:1994–H6 (tooth and wrapping)

18 NAW: ZAL 96/4/1/32: Michael Clayton to Nathaniel Clayton, 12 Jul 1826

19 AF: FBA to (cousin) Matthew Atkinson, 19 Dec 1825

20 Ibid.

21 AF: RR to MA, 28 Sep 1827

22 NAW: ZAL 96/1/61

23 AF: GCA to Isaac & Richard Atkinson, 7 Oct 1828

24 AF: EW to Thomas Littledale, 9 Oct 1828

25 *Newcastle Courant,* 24 Jan 1829

26 *Newcastle Courant,* 3 Oct 1829

27 *Transactions of the Natural History Society,* Vol. 1, Presents and Purchases, p. 13

28 DUL: DPRI/1/1831/A16/1–6

29 Clarkson, *History of the Rise,* Vol. 2, p. 464

30 HL: Thomas Clarkson Papers: CN 73

31 Hansard, *Parliamentary Debates,* New Series, Vol. 9, cols. 274–5

32 Baring, A., p. 6

33 Bridges, *A Voice from Jamaica,* p. 36

34 RGDJ: Westmoreland Parish, Baptisms, Marriages, Burials 1739–1825, Vol. 1, pp. 347–50

35 Clarkson, 'Negro Slavery', p. 1

36 AF: Francis Baring Atkinson to (cousin) Matthew Atkinson, 2 Jan 1826

37 *Morning Chronicle,* 17 May 1830

38 NAW: ZAL 95/21/7: BC to JA, 10 Nov 1830

39 NLS: Acc 9769 25/11/523: Balcarres to Robertson, Brother & Co, 31 Dec 1826

40 NLS: Acc 9769 25/11/8: EA to Balcarres, 20 Aug 1825

41 NLS: Acc 9769 25/11/74: Thomas Fowlis to Balcarres, 4 Oct 1828

42 NLS: Acc 9769 25/11/570: Balcarres to Thomas Fowlis, 4 Jan 1832

43 NLS: Acc 9769 25/11/76: Thomas Fowlis to Balcarres, 9 Dec 1828

44 NLS: Acc 9769 25/11/27: GA to Balcarres, 1 Jan 1830

45 NLS: Acc 9769 25/11/28: EA to Balcarres, 22 Feb 1830

46 NLS: Acc 9769 25/11/32: Balcarres to Thomas Fowlis, 6 Feb 1831

47 NLS: Acc 9769 25/11/533: Balcarres to Atkinson & Hosier, 16 May 1831

48 NLS: Acc 9769 25/11/34: GA to Balcarres, 24 Oct 1831

49 NLS: Acc 9769 25/11/649: Balcarres, nd

50 NLS: Acc 9769 25/11/530: Balcarres to GA, 4 Mar 1830

51 NLS: Acc 9769 25/11/29: GA to Balcarres, 14 Jun 1830

52 NLS: Acc 9769 25/11/30: EA to Balcarres, 7 Aug 1830

53 *Accounts and Papers, Eighteen Volumes,* Session 6, December 1831–16 August 1832, Vol. 31, p. 284

54 Stewart, *A View of the Past and Present State,* p. 352

55 Cox, Vol. 2, p. 83

56 Bleby, p. 26

57 Ibid., p. 116

58 Stephen, p. 197

59 *The Debates in Parliament – Session 1833*, p. 81

60 Ibid., p. 462

61 Ibid., p. 501

62 Ibid., p. 657

63 Wilberforce, Vol. 5, p. 368

22 A Spice of the Devil

1 Moore, Vol. 1, p. 63

2 NAW: ZAL 95/12/5: NC to NC, 2 Oct 1831

3 AF: GCA to Richard Atkinson, 10 Dec 1833

4 *The Corporation Annual*, p. 71

5 *Cobbett's Weekly Register*, Vol. 43, No. 1, cols. 21–2, 6 Jul 1822

6 Quine, pp. 3, 37

7 Ibid., p. 36

8 Ibid., p. 42

9 *Transactions of the Natural History Society*, Vol. 2, pp. 215–25

10 Quine, p. 50

11 Ibid., p. 58

12 AF: GCA to RA, 10 Dec 1833

13 AF: IA to RA, 24 Jan 1834

14 NLS: Acc 9769 25/11/651

15 NA: CO 137/193, fo. 304: Sligo to TSR, 18 Nov 1834

16 AF: GA to (cousin) Matthew Atkinson, 29 Dec 1834

17 *London Gazette*, 18 Apr 1834

18 NLS: Acc 9769 25/11/583: Balcarres to Thomas Fowlis, 13 Jan 1835

19 NLS: Acc 9769 25/11/38: George Atkinson to Balcarres, 11 May 1833

20 NLS: Acc 9769 25/11/549: Balcarres to GA, 22 Jul 1835

21 NLS: Acc 9769 25/11/555: Balcarres to GA, 8 Jan 1836

22 NLS: Acc 9769 25/11/43: GA to Balcarres, 8 Aug 1835

23 NLS: Acc 9769 25/11/46: GA to Balcarres, 28 Sep 1835

24 NA: T 71/703, claim 694

25 NA: T 71/74, fo. 188

26 NAW: ZAL 95/21/10: GA to Jane Atkinson, 20 Jun 1835

27 NAW: ZAL 95/21/21: GA to JA, 1 Feb 1840

28 NAW: ZAL 95/21/15: GA to JA, 11 Jul 1836

29 NAW: ZAL 95/21/15: GA to JA, 11 Jul 1836

30 NAW: ZAL 95/21/18: RA to JA, 27 Sep 1837

31 AF: JD to RA, 30 Mar–2 Apr 1837

32 NAW: ZAL 95/21/18: RA to JA, 27 Sep 1837

33 NA: CO 140/115: p. 100

34 NA: CO 137/192, fo. 273: *Jamaica Despatch*, 24 May 1834

35 Sturge & Harvey, p. 176

36 *The Statutes of the United Kingdom*, p. 76

23 Farewell to Jamaica

1 AF: Charles Mills to Lonsdale, 3 Mar 1826

2 CUL: MS Add. 9723: JC to MA, 6 May 1837

3 Hardcastle, p. 258

4 AF: John Clayton to MA (draft reply), 4 Jan 1832

5 CAK: WDX 82

6 NAW: ZAL 95/21/23: GA to Jane Atkinson, 17 Apr 1841

7 NAW: ZAL 95/21/21: GA to JA, 1 Feb 1840

8 Gurney, p. 104

9 NAW: ZAL 95/21/25: GA to JA, 29 May 1843

10 Gurney, p. xiv

11 NAW: ZAL 95/21/25: GA to JA, 29 May 1843

12 AF: RA to George Clayton Atkinson, 9 Oct 1844

13 *GM*: New Series, Vol. 25, Part 1, p. 413

14 Peel, p. 6

15 NAW: ZAL 95/21/29: RA to JA, 7 Jun 1847

16 *The Transactions of the Jamaica Society of Arts*, p. 46

17 TWA: D/CG 39/17: Clayton & Dunn to RA, 30 Jun 1846

18 AF: RA to GCA, 7 Sep 1847

19 AF: RA to George Atkinson, 8 Nov 1847

20 RGDJ: LOS 895, fo. 181

21 AF: RA to George Atkinson, 22 Nov 1847

22 Scoresby-Jackson, p. 499

23 NAW: ZAL 95/21/28: RA to Jane Atkinson, 7 Feb 1846

24 NAW: ZAL 95/21/34: RA to Jane Atkinson, 27 Aug 1851

25 NAW: ZAL 95/21/35: RA to Jane Atkinson, 4 Sep 1851

26 NA: CO 137/330: Report of Richard Hill (1856)

27 Martin, p. 77

28 Evans, p. 7

29 Ibid., p. 11

30 *Daily News*, 19 May 1856

31 *Second Series of Recollections*, p. iii

32 *Newcastle Journal*, 31 May 1834

33 Howitt, p. 310

34 *Sketches of Public Men*, pp. 75–85

35 Budge, p. 6; Hutton, p. 202

36 AF: JA to Elisabeth Atkinson (GCA's second wife), 4 Dec 1875

37 AF: JA to Elisabeth Atkinson (GCA's second wife), 13 Dec 1875

38 *Proceedings of the Society of Antiquaries*, p. 28

39 Bruce, G., pp. 163–4

40 AF: Victoria Atkinson notes

41 *Madras Times*, 7 Jul 1914

42 Fetherstonhaugh, p. 167

43 AF: JNA to G.A. Atkinson, 21 Oct 1923

44 AF: JNA to G.A. Atkinson, 30 May 1928

45 AF: IC to JNA, 1 Nov 1923

46 Hampton & Sons, 18 Jun 1929

47 *The Times*, 3 Jan 1930

48 *Hexham Courant*, 13 Jan 1930

49 AF: JNA's diary, 6 Aug 1922

50 *Sunday Times*, 31 Jul 1932

51 AF: RLA to JLA, 15 Jan 1957

24 Distant Cousins

1 Lawrence-Archer, p. 106

Appendix I

1 NLS: Acc 9769 27/2/3: Richard Atkinson to Lady Anne Lindsay, nd

Appendix II

1 NLS: Acc 9769 27/1/330

PICTURE CREDITS

ACKNOWLEDGEMENTS

It has somehow taken me nearly a decade to write this book, and I wouldn't have managed it without the help of a great many people along the way. First, before singling out individuals, I'd like to express my gratitude to the multitude – family, friends, colleagues, complete strangers – who have been kind enough to show even a flicker of interest in my project. I really can't begin to articulate how much I have appreciated your support.

I've been fortunate to be able to draw on an astonishing range of primary sources for my research. Most of all, I'd like to thank the Earl of Crawford and Balcarres for allowing me access to his voluminous family papers; and Kenneth Dunn, who smoothed the way for my visits to the National Library of Scotland. I'd also like to thank the Marquess of Abergavenny for letting me see his ancestor John Robinson's correspondence; and Pat Stallwood and Arland Kingston, who made my outings to Eridge Park so enjoyable. I would often marvel, during my trips to the British Library and the National Archives, at the speed with which obscure documents were summoned up from the depths, and it would occur to me how lucky I am to live in a country where so much history is at hand. The curators and librarians at all the public and private archives I visited were unfailingly helpful; in particular, I'd like to thank Clara Harrow at the Baring Archive, June Holmes at the Natural History Society of Northumbria and Doug Oxenhorn at New Jersey Historical Society.

Julie Evans, Georgina Plowright, Andrew Connell, Irene Dunn and Andrea Stuart offered invaluable encouragement right at the beginning; while Frances McIntosh, Peter Roebuck, Ian Thomson,

Margaret Gowling, Frances Wilkins and the late Iain Bain gave generously of their knowledge further down the line. Ivan Day, amazingly, led me to another of Bridget's cookbooks. Bill Swainson was kind enough to show me some revealing family papers of his own. My former employers at Bloomsbury were extraordinary for keeping faith in me for so long; Alexandra Pringle and Natalie Bellos, especially, proved the warmest and most constant of colleagues. Valerian Freyberg accompanied me on a life-changing visit to Temple Sowerby. Bill and Karen Chaytor kept me wonderfully well fed and watered during my frequent research trips up north. Tom Gilkes and David Kellie-Smith helped decipher my family's old business ledger. In Jamaica, Peter Espeut, Audene Brooks, Dianne Frankson, Ann Sutton and James Robertson unlocked treasures, archival and archaeological, while Suzanne Francis-Brown gifted me the book's ending. Jonnie Cook and Whitney Mortimer were delightful travelling companions on the island. Chris Lloyd provided good cheer and wise counsel at times when I was struggling with my task. Stephen Taylor – Lady Anne Lindsay's biographer – was a most congenial fellow time traveller. Pascal Cariss hacked his way through my dense first draft with great fortitude, and inspired me to make my second draft a lot better. Jenny Uglow, Nicholas Draper, Jeremy Black, John Watherston, Gavin Hasselgren and Jasper Gerard-Sharp were also generous enough to read early versions of the manuscript, and the book would be the less without their perceptive comments.

It is no exaggeration to say that *Mr Atkinson's Rum Contract* wouldn't exist had not Claire Paterson Conrad hounded me to write the proposal, for which I must remain in her everlasting debt. My agent Rebecca Carter offered kind words of encouragement throughout the writing process, and saw the manuscript at a stage when it really shouldn't have been seen by anyone. By bizarre coincidence, it turned out that my editor Louise Haines had stayed the night at Temple Sowerby House before she even knew about my connection to the place. I could not be more grateful for the quiet persistence with which she has coaxed me to turn in my best work; and for the forbearance she has shown towards an author who delivered his manuscript *five years late*. I would also like to give special thanks to Steve Gove, for the extra polish he lent the manuscript; Sarah Thickett, for handling the editorial process (and my endless tweaks) with great poise; Rachel Smyth, for her elegant page layout; Julian Humphries, for his excellent cover design; Anne Rieley, for meticulous proofreading; Mark Wells, for methodical indexing; and Michelle Kane, for putting the word about. Many thanks, too, to Andrew Davidson for his beautiful woodcuts; David Atkinson (no relation, as far as I am aware) for his evocative maps; and Adrian Gibbs, Lucy Grange, Felicity Page, Peter Dawson, Alice Kennedy-Owen and Matt Livey for their help wrangling the pictures.

While writing this book I discovered a fair few cousins I had not realized I had, and getting to know them has been a joy. I will never forget the warmth with which Phillipa and her daughter Laura welcomed me into their lives. David Atkinson not only entrusted me with a mass of family papers, but offered unflagging support from the start. The Scandinavian branch of the family – Renira Müller, Karen and Tomas Tunemyr, Jon and Grete Müller, and Sigrun Müller-Steen – showed me great hospitality, involving memorable crayfish feasts. Closer to home, Anthea Guthrie, Ridley Scott, Hilary Vidnes, Caroline Garrett, Jenny Tyler and George Atkinson-Clark shared the contents of family scrapbooks and shoeboxes.

My final thanks, however, are saved for the three most important people in my life: my beloved mother Jane, whose difficult decision to sell Temple Sowerby House liberated me from a painful choice; my dearest sister Harriet, who is co-heir to the 'tangled inheritance' at the heart of this story; and my darling wife Sue, whose belief in me never wavered and who (together with T&T) has been my steadfast companion during this most exhilarating, and at times daunting, adventure of my life.

Richard Atkinson
London, January 2020

INDEX